MONSTERS

MONS

TERS

BOOK THREE

ILSA J. BICK

EGMONT
USA
NEW YORK

EGMONT

We bring stories to life

First published by Egmont USA, 2013
This paperback edition published by Egmont USA, 2014
443 Park Avenue South, Suite 806
New York, NY 10016

1 3 5 7 9 8 6 4 2

www.egmontusa.com
www.ilsajbick.com

THE LIBRARY OF CONGRESS HAS CATALOGED
THE HARDCOVER EDITION AS FOLLOWS:

Library of Congress Cataloging-in-Publication Data

Bick Ilsa J.
Monsters / Ilsa J. Bick
pages cm — (The Ashes trilogy ; book 3)
Summary: Alex and Tom's future is uncertain as they continue the struggle
to survive in a post-apocalyptic world, and their lives are threatened
by the Changed and other human survivors.
ISBN 978-1-60684-117-8 (hardcover) -- ISBN 978-1-60684-444-1 (ebook)
[1. Science fiction. 2. Survival—Fiction. 3. Zombies—Fiction.] I. Title.
PZ7.B47234Mon 2013
[Fic]--dc23
2012045750

Trade Paperback ISBN 978-1-60684-544-8

Printed in the United States of America

FOR THE SURVIVORS

I hold a beast, an angel,
and a madman in me.

—D<small>YLAN</small> T<small>HOMAS</small>

ALEX HAD FALLEN LIKE THIS ONLY ONCE IN HER LIFE. THAT happened when she was nine and took a wild leap from Blackrocks Cliff off Presque Isle into the deep sapphire-blue of Lake Superior. She remembered that the air was laced with the scent of wild lilacs and early honeysuckle. Although hot sun splashed her shoulders, her bare arms and legs were sandpapery with gooseflesh because the wind skimming Superior was, even in June, still very cold—and she was also, frankly, freaked out. Standing at the cliff's edge, her monkey-thin toes gripping rough basalt, she looked down past her new emerald green bathing suit, felt her stomach drop, and thought, *Seriously?* That cove looked pretty puny. Her dad, who'd gone first with a whoop and a leap, was only a dot.

"Come on, you can do this, honey!" She could see the white flash of his grin—a tanned, muscular, bluff, and confident man, who carried her on his shoulders and boomed out songs. "Jump to me, sweetheart! Just remember, feet first and you'll be fine!"

"Oh-oh-oh . . ." She meant to say *okay*, but her teeth chattered. Heights scared her something stupid. Stephanie's birthday party last month? The indoor climbing wall? *Mistaaake.* Not only was she the *only one* to freeze and then slip; she came *this close* to wetting her pants. And now her dad was daring her to jump from way up here? For *fun?*

Can't do this, I can't . . . Every muscle locked in a sudden, whole-body freeze, except for her head, which swelled and ballooned. *I'm going to faint.* Her brain seemed surprised. *This is what it's like to—*

There was a whirring sensation, like the blast of a jet engine gushing through her skull, blowing her sky-high. All of a sudden, she wasn't in her body at all but floating *waaay* up there, looking down at this teeny-tiny girl in a deep green bathing suit, an emerald smudge with hair as red as blood. Far below, so small he was nothing more than a mote in a very blue and watery eye, was her dad.

"Alex?" Her dad's voice was the size of a gnat. "Come on, sweetheart, jump to me."

"If she doesn't want to . . ." Her mom, the worrier, on a faraway crescent of gravel, hand to her eyes as the wind whipped her hair. "She doesn't have to prove—"

But yes, I do. Her mom's words—her doubt that Alex had the guts—cut the string of the strange kite to which her brain was yoked. That weird distance collapsed, and Alex plunged back into her skin, faster than a comet, to flood the space behind her eyes.

Then she was out over open water, with no memory of launching herself from the cliff—probably a good thing, because she'd have spazzed, *I'll slip, I'll slip, I'll bust a leg or break my face,* and only scared herself more. Long red hair streaming like a failed parachute, she sliced through air in a high whistle of wind.

Slapping the water, still icy at that time of year, was a shock. She punched through with her hip, a hard smack that jolted a mouthful of air past the corkscrew of her lips. Silvery, shimmering bubbles boiled from her mouth and all around her. Water gushed up her nose, the pain of the brain freeze scaring her even more than losing what was probably no more than a sip of air. She could hear herself, too: a choked little underwater raspberry, a *bwwwuhh*, not quite a scream but close enough. The water wasn't blue at all but murky and a really weird, brassy green. She couldn't see more than a few feet—and was she still sinking? *I'm going to drown!* She could feel a panic-rat skittering in her skull, nipping her eyeballs as she whirled, her hair fanning like seaweed. *I'm going to drown!* Wild with fear, she looked for her dad but didn't, *couldn't* see legs or feet or hands or *anything*. She wasn't sure where the surface was. Craning, she saw how the water yellowed with diffuse sun. *Go, that's up, go, go, swim!* Thrashing, she bulleted up and then crashed through, her breath jetting in a thin shriek: *"Ahh!"*

"Attagirl!" Her father was instantly there, laughing, his wet hair dark and slick as seal skin. "That's my Alex! Wasn't that *fun?*"

"Uh," she grunted. Still booming a delighted laugh, her dad wrapped her up and boosted her—shrieking deliriously now—way up high, nearly out of the water, before bringing her back down to earth and to him, because he was *that* strong.

Then, together, they stroked for the gravel beach, her father pulling a slow sidestroke, staying with her the whole way as she churned for shore, and home.

That was where the memory ended. She couldn't recall if she and her dad climbed the cliff again. Knowing her dad—how much she adored and wanted to please, be *his* girl and dare anything—they probably had. Knowing her dad, he'd treated her to a waffle cone of chocolate custard topped with Mounds and Almond Joy chunks because, sometimes, you just feel like a nut. Her dad probably stole from her cone so she could dip into his, right backatcha. She bet her dad told her mom, *Relax, honey, she's wash and wear*, as Alex crunched almonds and chewy, juicy coconut and licked sweet chocolate runnels, molten in the afternoon heat, from her wrist and forearm and the knob of her elbow. Her father was that kind of man.

More than likely, she'd been underwater less than ten seconds. She got herself out of it, too, and all because her dad dared her to try. After that leap, she really believed she might dare anything, because no matter what, if she jumped, her father would be waiting to swim by her side, stroke for stroke, into forever.

Of course, she was nine and her dad was immortal.

And nothing lasts forever.

Years later, after her parents were dead, her doctors said she'd had an out-of-body experience. Commonplace, no voodoo. For example, certain epileptics had similar experiences all the time. Hoping to walk the stars and know the gods, mystics and shamans drank potions. It was all funky brain chemistry, the doctors said, the mind's switches already primed, requiring only that you tickle the brain in the right spot, goose it just so. Easy-peasy. Figure out how to bottle it, and we'd all be rich.

In fact, her last doctor thought what happened at Blackrocks— that shove from the shell of her mind—might've been the monster, just beginning to wake. That her sleep going to hell and the smell of phantom smoke weren't her first symptoms after all. That her little baby monster was hatching, chip-chip-chipping a peephole to peer with one yellow baby-monster eye—*why, hello there*—way back then.

And she had been falling, falling, falling ever since . . .

Into now.

PART ONE:
INTO THE DARK

1

Alex fell, fast, into the dark, in a hail of splintered wood, a shower of stone as the mine came down around her ears and water stormed up the throat of her escape tunnel. She could smell the end, rushing to meet her, the water so icy and metallic, a scent of snow and steel laced with that queer, gassy fizz of rotten eggs. High above, so far away, she saw the stars wink out. The exit where Tom had been only minutes before now swarmed with viscous, oily shadows as the earth folded and fell in on itself.

She'd taken physics. Terminal velocity was . . . well, they didn't call it *terminal* for nothing. Fall far enough and even an ant will shatter. After a certain height, coming to a sudden stop, even in water, would be like slamming a car into a brick wall. Sure, the car crumpled, but everything else—passengers, seats, anything movable—had its own momentum. People hurtled into one another or the seat or windshield, and then the brain, the heart, the lungs smashed against bone. So, fall far enough onto *anything* and the impact wouldn't just break her; it would obliterate her.

She thought she was screaming but couldn't hear herself over the combined thunder of falling rock and churning water. Something hard smacked the back of her head, not a rock but Leopard's Uzi still slung over her shoulders, the carry strap slicing her right armpit. Leopard's Glock 19 was a fist digging into the small of her back. For the first time in her life, she wished all Glocks had safeties. She didn't think the weapon would discharge and blow a hole through her spine or into her butt, but there was a first time for everything, like the end of the world. Like falling to your death. On the other hand, a nice, quick, lethal bullet—

And then, suddenly, that was it. In that very last second, she closed her mouth, held her breath, thought about just maybe saving herself for . . . well, for something. Someone. For Tom, maybe. No, no *maybe* about him at all. She hadn't wanted Tom to leave, but she couldn't let him die in this place either—not for her. It was the last good thing she could do. She so desperately wanted him to live that it hurt—

Then, no more seconds. No more thoughts or memories. No wishes or dreams or regrets. Nothing. End of the line.

She hit.

2

It wasn't gentle.

Alex clobbered the water like a sledgehammer. A jag of agony spiked her right ankle; the impact blasted into her hips. A cannonball of pain roared up her spine to detonate in her head. Her vision blacked from the spinal shock. For a second, maybe two, she was out cold, helpless as a puppet cut loose from its strings.

Ironically, the water that had just tried to kill her slapped her awake for round two. Her mind came back in a scream as icy water jetted up her nose, gushed into her mouth, tried to flood her lungs. Having clamped down to keep her from drowning, her throat was a knot. She couldn't manage a single breath. Muscling through with sheer will, she gulped one shrieking inhale before the water wrapped steely fingers around her ankles and calves to pull her down, down, down below the surface.

No! A fist of red, burning panic punched her chest. Completely underwater and totally in the dark, she thrashed with no sense of where the surface was. Caught in a whirlpool created by competing currents, she was spinning, whirling, tumbling. Her right shoulder slammed stone, a stunning blow that sent electric tingles down to her wrist and numbed her fingers. She tried swimming—*where's up, where's up?*—but her movements were spastic, feeble. Her back was a single, long shrill of pain. She wasn't sure her legs were even working.

Nearly out of air. Got to do something. Her throat bunched and clenched, trying to force open her mouth for air that wasn't there. A solid steel band cinched down tighter and tighter around her chest, squeezing, *squeezing*. Desperate for oxygen, her heart pounded fast and then faster and faster and faster, a fist frantically banging her caging ribs: *Let me out, let me OUT, LET ME OUT!*

A sudden lurch. Something had snagged. She felt a jolt between her shoulder blades, and then a vicious cut as the Uzi's strap sawed her throat. Lifted by the current, her legs went nearly vertical. She was still underwater—on the brink of drowning—but she wasn't spinning anymore, at least for the moment.

I'm caught. The Uzi. The metal plate barrel must've jammed into the rocks. If that was true, and the Uzi was locked tight and didn't move . . . *If I can get myself turned around, I'll have something to hang on to, get my head out of the water.* Straining against the current, she hooked her left hand around the Uzi's strap, still cutting into her neck, and reached back with her right. All she grabbed was water. She tried kicking herself closer. *Come on, come on, come on.* Her chest was one bright blister. Her throat was doing that *urk-urk-urk*, battling with her to give it up already, stop fighting, let go. *Please, God, help me.*

Her fingers scraped rock, and then there was the Uzi, jammed in a V-shaped cleft of stone above her head, not by an inch or two but at least two feet. No way to get her head above water, not while she was tangled up in the carry strap and on her back. She would have to flip completely over. In order to do *that*, she would have to release the death grip she had on that carry strap and trust that she was strong enough to counter the pull of the current. That she could hang on with only her right hand for those few seconds. Otherwise, she would drown.

She tried to let go of the carry strap; she really did. But her left hand, frozen in a rictus of panic, refused to obey. She couldn't do this. No way. She wasn't strong enough. The water was going to get her. One last second of blind fear and then she would have to breathe. Her mouth would snap open and her life would be over.

Then there came a voice, a phantom of memory, so small and distant, barely audible over her terror: *Come on, honey, let go of the gun or you'll die. Jump, Alex, jump—*

But then, all at once, it was too late. It was over, and even her father, as strong and sure as he was, couldn't save her.

What was left of her air boiled from her lips, drawing with it the thin, fiery ribbon of a final scream. Her mind shimmied, and she bled from her body, her consciousness detaching, letting go, hurtling up and away until she saw herself as if from a great height and through the wrong end of a pirate's spyglass: faraway, helpless in the chop and churn, red hair streaming like bloody seaweed. With no conscious thought at all, no planning whatsoever, her left hand slipped off the Uzi. The greedy current instantly snatched her ankles. If not for the hump of her right shoulder, she'd have been torn free of the strap to swirl away and drown. But it held, and then, somehow, she was twisting, flipping herself around. Her right hand was locked tight, and the Uzi held; her left hand found the weapon, and the Uzi held; and then she was surging up with a mighty kick, the sudden shear in her ankle only a twinkle against the greater agony in her chest, because she had no air, she was out of air and time; but the weapon still held—

She shattered through, breaching the surface like a clumsy whale. She managed a single, wheezy, strangled *aaahhhh*, and that was all. No match for the pounding current, her elbows unhinged, and she instantly submerged, her head going completely under.

Hang on, hang on, hang on! A drill bit of fear cored straight into her heart. As far as she could tell, the Uzi was locked tight. With every shudder of the earth, however, the gun bucked like a bronco, and it was so far below the surface, she had to work for every breath.

Another kick, another gulping razor of air, and then down she went again. The burn in her chest was less, which was to say that her lungs weren't on fire and her mind was clearing, slewing back into place. But she couldn't do this forever. Although it felt like a century, she probably hadn't been in the water more than two minutes. Her waterlogged clothes and boots were so heavy she might as well have been wearing chains. She was tiring, her muscles going as shivery as Jell-O, the icy water burning her skin, leaching heat and the last of her will. Another kick. A sobbing breath. There was an almost continual stream of stone: small rocks that bit her arms and nipped her scalp and drew blood, which the water washed away as soon as she submerged. Much larger chunks rained down, too, some so close she heard the *whir* and *sploosh.*

Maybe try to rest somehow, wait this out until things calm down. Which was almost funny, in a bizarre way. Calm *down?* She'd be a Popsicle long before then. If she hadn't needed the air, she might've laughed. Kicking for the surface, she opened her mouth for a breath—

And that was when she realized, as she sucked in not air but water, that the tunnel was still filling, the water level rising—and fast.

3

No. Flailing, she fell back with a splash. Her left hand slipped from the gun, and she was nearly swept away. Kicking, she fought, got her left hand around the Uzi, and surged up for a breath. She only just made it. The water was now so high, she had to tip her head and still, water slopped over her chin to lick at her lower lip.

Got to get out. But how? She dropped beneath the surface again. From far below came a strange heaving, as if the earth was a shell that a giant was trying to crack. An instant later, there was a dull *boosh* as another boulder bulleted into the water just off her right shoulder. God, what if this tunnel broke up, or a wall collapsed? That might happen, too, and then it would be like the *Titanic.* It was that damn physics again, water displacing air. The sudden rush of water *out* of this tunnel and into an adjacent, dry cavern would be too much. She'd never hang on then but be swept away to spin and drown in the dark.

She held her breath as long as she could before struggling up for another precious sip of air. She tried to think of what she could do to save herself, and came up empty. Her only tools were the Uzi to which her hands were locked tight, the Glock 19 at the small of her back, and Leopard's tanto strapped around her leg. While great for dirt or even chopping handholds in ice, the tanto was useless here. The Glock was an option, but only if she wanted to go out with a bullet. Could she risk butting the Uzi free, reseating it higher? Submerging again, she forced her eyes open. The cold was a blowtorch against her corneas. Couldn't see a thing, not even her hands resting on the weapon. Working blind, going by feel alone with numb, icy fingers—that was a nonstarter.

No tools, then. Just numb hands and clumsy feet. Resurfacing, she eked in a meager snuffle of air. High above, the tunnel seemed to have closed down, gone black. *Moon must've set.* But the space also felt dense and . . . crowded. Something jammed up there, probably rocks sealing the tunnel's mouth to cork her in like a genie in a bottle. And that was it, wasn't it? Up was a dead end. Probably just as well. She truly *did* suck at climbing.

But life is precious and the body is stubborn, and so was she.

Dad is right. You have to try. Surfacing again, the peak of her nose just barely clearing, she pulled in another panicky breath. Maybe two more and that was it. Her mind kept doing that swimmy slip, a mental sleight of hand that gave her brief, bird's-eye views of herself, *waaay* the hell down there. *Jump, Alex, jump. Climb, and do it now before you lose your nerve.*

Eyes shut tight, she let herself fall back. Water closed over her head. Then, gritting her teeth, she scissored her legs hard at the same moment that she pulled with her arms. Shifting her hands as fast as she could, the right first and then the left, she went from an underhand grip to overhand. Her elbows locked, and then she was swinging her left boot up so fast and hard and high, her hip joint shrieked. She jammed rock, felt the jolt in her knee and then metal under her foot, and thought, *Push.* She hung on, driving up, locking her left leg as she straightened. Her head broke the surface, followed by her chest and now her torso. Panting, she hugged stone, balanced a quick second, then bent her right knee and repeated the process. There was a white blink of pain in her ankle before the sturdy toe of her boot stubbed rock. She managed an awkward, sidelong shuffle, gradually easing onto her right foot, testing the joint, her knee. *Easy, easy, go slow, don't push your luck.* She gradually relaxed, let her legs take her weight from her shrieking hands. Her ankle held, and her knee, too. And so did the Uzi.

"Oh God." For the first time since the ladder disintegrated, she let herself enjoy a tiny squeak of triumph. There was no relief, not yet; if she was right, there was a lot of distance to cover and, oh yes, all that rock jammed in the mouth of the tunnel besides. Pain sparkled in her ankle, and her temples throbbed, a rapid *puhpum-puhpum-puhpum* in time with her pulse. Water streamed from her hair and clothes. Air stroked her cheeks, her neck, and she was starting to really shiver. But she was standing, clutching razor-thin rock, precariously balanced on a thin ridge of metal as the tunnel shook and water bulled and sucked and eddied around her knees. The shuddering was much stronger than before, the rock sawing at her fingers. Between the water pounding and surging into minute crevices and cracks, and the continual shifting of the earth itself, the rock had to fatigue sooner or later. She didn't think she had much longer.

"Okay, come on, Alex," she whispered. "Get going, honey. You can't stay here." But, oh God, she was so scared. A fit of trembling grabbed her. Her eyes pooled, the first tear swelling, then trickling down her right cheek. *Don't cry, come on, stop—*

A sudden swoon swept her brain. In her skull, the monster shimmied and twisted and stretched. Beneath her hands, the rock seemed to evaporate as a black void opened in her mind.

No, not now. Her knees were unhinging with the faint. *Not when I've made it this far . . .*

And then a hand spidered onto her shoulder.

4

That touch snapped her back as crisp and sharp as a slap. Shrieking, Alex flinched. Her left leg shot off slick metal, like a cartoon character skating on a banana. Her full weight dropped onto her battered right ankle. She screamed again, this time with pain. Her vision purpled. Off-balance, she scrambled for purchase, fingernails frantically scratching stone. Just as she was about to peel away, the hand on her shoulder grabbed a fistful of her parka and yanked her back. She righted, blundering onto the precarious ledge of that Uzi.

"No," she gasped, horrified, her heart a hard knot in her chest— because now the pieces fell into place. Everything fit: the slip-slides of her mind; the monster, so suddenly awakened; that sensation of a crowd and swarming shadows above her head.

And there's the smell. She hadn't noticed before; been a little busy trying to save her ass, thanks. But now, it was close: rot and roadkill.

And shadows. Cool mist. A darkness more profound than a starless sky.

"Oh my God," she said. "Wolf."

5

A bolt of bright yellow light sprang from the dark. Nearly blinded by the glare, Alex squinted and would have put a hand up if she hadn't needed both to hang on. Belatedly, she realized that the light must be for her. The Changed saw very well in the dark. She saw Wolf, his legs braced against rock, dangling from some kind of crude rope harness looped around both thighs.

Sniffed me out, just like I caught his scent earlier this morning. Came to get me. Had he tracked them all along? Possibly. The Changed followed a route, kept to a pattern. So maybe Wolf had bided his time, waiting to see if she was still alive, then planned a way to get her out. Before the Zap, when Wolf was Simon Yeager and not a monster, maybe he and his friends had done a *lot* of rock climbing, exploring all the ins and outs of the Rule mine.

Then she remembered: *Tom.* Her heart stuttered. Tom had been up there. He'd called to her, and then she'd heard shots. "Did you kill him?" She was so afraid for Tom she thought her chest would break. Was Tom lying dead in the snow because of her? "If you killed him, if you hurt him . . ."

Wolf said nothing. He couldn't. But now that he was so close, she smelled something else in all that mist and shadow: a scent sweet and . . . *gentle*, a light perfume of lilacs and honeysuckle. Her dad's face suddenly flickered in a quick flashbulb of memory: *Jump to me, sweetheart.*

"Safe." The word slipped off her tongue. For an instant, where she was, what was happening, ceased to matter. It was as if she and Wolf had slipped into a private, silent, well-lit room built only for them. *And not only safe* . . . "Home," she whispered. "Family?"

The scent deepened. His face smoothed, and for a second, there was the ghost of Chris—the lips she had kissed, the angles and planes of a face her fingers knew—and she felt her monster suddenly reach; was aware of an ache and a fiery burn that was need and desire flowing like lava through her veins.

The monster knows Wolf. This was new, as was the hard throb in her neck and the claw of something so close to raw, red yearning that she felt the rake of it across her chest. What the hell was going on? The times her mind had sidestepped from her to end up behind the eyes of the Changed—Spider, Leopard, Wolf—had been few, and mainly in response to *their* intense emotion, not hers. Long ago, Kincaid wondered if her tumor was reorganizing, the monster becoming something separate and distinct from her. *God, and now it has. The monster wants Wolf.*

"No, *I'm* in control," she ground out, no longer sure whether she spoke to the monster or Wolf. She clung to the rock. "I'm Alex. I'm not a mon—"

CRACK!

A yelp bulleted from her mouth. The sound, somewhere to her left, had been enormous. At first, Alex thought she saw more water, a wide stream running a jagged dark course over stone. But then there were more snaps and cracks, the crisp sounds like thick ice over a deep lake in the dead of winter, because ice is restless, never still, always in flux, the stress building and building to the breaking point. Before her eyes, that jagged seam became a black lightning bolt, growing wider and darker and *longer*. . . Water still swirled around her waist, but now she also detected an insidious tug, much stronger than before.

From above came a hard *bang* and a *thunk* as rocks ricocheted and rebounded before slamming down in a stony fusillade. *Crack!* The rock wall squealed, singing with the strain. Crack-*CRACK!*

And that was when the Uzi actually *moved*.

Terror blazed through her veins. Almost without thinking, she sprang, her right hand splayed in a grab. If her ankle shrieked, she didn't feel it. All she saw were Wolf's hands, the one knotted in her parka and the other, gloved, clinging to the taut snake of rope that would have to be strong enough to hold them both. She felt his wrist sock into her palm, and then she was swinging a half-assed trapeze move as Wolf whipped her, hard and fast, like a stone in a bolo, trying to fold her against his chest. He might have done it, too. He had the strength she lacked, and he was solidly anchored besides. But then the Uzi shifted again, a sharp jolt down that knocked the breath from her chest.

She missed, dropping as the rock crumbled beneath her feet. Skating away, the Uzi was swept in a sudden tidal surge into this new and ever-expanding fissure, one that had grown so wide it was a sideways grin and then a toothless leer and then a black *scream* that matched her own.

In the next instant, the wall shattered and split and opened with a roar.

6

"Wee-wee-wee." Aidan's right arm blurred. There was a whickering sound and then a mucky *whop* as a whippy car antennae connected with bloody mush that had once been the sole of a right foot. *"Wee-wee-wee,* little piggy!"

"Don't hit me anymore, please, *don't* . . . AAAHHH!" The guy, Dale Privet, let go of another shriek as Aidan whapped his left foot while Mick Jagger shouted about how pleased he was to meet you.

God, Greg *so* wished that wheezy old cassette recorder would just die already. He had another monster of a migraine that was keeping time with Charlie Watts. But Aidan loved the Stones: *The pros, like, blast it 24/7.* How this little rat-creep even knew *anything* about guys who were professionals at torturing other guys scared him shitless. This whole nightmare was like the time Greg was six and his older brother—really, an asshole, so Aidan would've *loved* him—took Greg to the old Mexican place, a rotting husk hunkered at the end of a one-way country lane. What Greg remembered most was when a couple of giggly guys in these glow-in-the-dark *Scream* masks plunged his hand into squelchy cold goo they called monster guts. It was only spaghetti, but Greg was so freaked he peed himself.

Another quicksilver flash, a whicker—and *whop!* Dale gave a violent lurch. Aidan's soul mates, Lucian and Sam, bore down to keep the whole mess—a barn door to which they'd fixed seat belts and ropes—from skittering off its sawhorses and crashing to the floor.

Aidan liked the sawhorses. If or when he got around to waterboard-
ing, all they had to do was slide a couple two-by-fours under the
sawhorse at Dale's feet. (Aidan said it was all about the angle; you had
to get it just so or the water wouldn't flood the guy's nose and throat.)
Each time Dale jumped, the barn door jumped with him.

"AAAHHH, *stop!*" Dale babbled. "*Stopstopstop*, please, *stop!*"

"Then tell us, little piggy." Aidan's tongue eeled over his lower lip
and a glistening splotch of Dale's blood. Aidan was just that type: a
psychopath in training, lean and rat-faced, with slanted gray eyes and
draggled hair so grungy and soot-slimed he probably sucked out the
lice for a midmorning snack. A double trail of jailhouse tears trickled over his narrow cheeks. When a prisoner broke, Lucian—a whiz
with needles, nails, hammers—added a tat. Give it another month
and Aidan would weep nothing but ink. "How many in your camp?"

"I *told* you!" Dale wheezed. From the wattles of loose flesh hanging from the old guy's arms, Greg thought Dale once had been pretty
big and probably strong. Now, he was just one more old geezer in
grimy boxers, reeking of urine, oily sweat, fresh blood. Greg didn't
like looking at the sparse gray hairs corkscrewing from Dale's chest.
It was like they were beating up on his grandpa. Which, in a way, he
guessed they were.

Not that any of this was doing them a damn bit of good.

It was the third week in February of the worst winter of his life.
Having overreached, Rule was nearly out of food, ammo, medicine.
The village was collapsing in on itself like the fevered firestorm of a
disease that had coursed through its host, burning too hot, too bright,
until there was nothing in its wake but bones. Without enough manpower to protect them, the farms had been ravaged, their remaining
herds either stolen or dead of starvation. Having butchered most for
the meat, they were down to twenty horses, and about two dozen
dogs. People old and young were dropping from illness, starvation.

For all his skill and his weird potions filched from arcane books on herbal medicines, mushrooms, and folk magic, there wasn't a damn thing Kincaid could do.

The talk was that the ambush had been the start of it all, the beginning of the end: the day almost six weeks ago, when Peter was murdered in an ambush the Council said Chris set up. Greg's first thought when he heard that? Those people didn't know shit. Chris was Greg's friend, and a good person, and *brave*. A stunt like that would never cross Chris's radar. Chris and Peter were a team; they were tight, like brothers.

But look, people argued, Chris ran when the going got tough. So that was proof, right? Mark 13:12: *Brother will betray brother to death, and a father his child,* was what Reverend Yeager said. Hell, Matthew liked that so much, he slotted in the same shit, chapter ten, verse twenty-one. Now, the very *next* verse also mentioned that kids would rebel against their parents and put them to death and the good guys had to stand firm to the very end and blah, blah. Greg just didn't know what *that* was supposed to mean. These days, he was having a hard time telling who the good guys were, or what that boy in the mirror was thinking.

On the other hand, Greg had no better ideas. He was exhausted, half-starved, appalled by what the situation was compelling him to do—to *consider*—and so afraid of the blackness welling in his chest that he was six all over again and only just realizing that he'd blundered into a house of horrors. Most of the time, he felt like bursting into tears. But he had to be strong. They were in big trouble here, life or death, and no Peter or Chris to tell him what was right.

Considering how things were going, there were moments when Greg truly believed: *Show your face in Rule, Chris, and I'll put a bullet through your eye.*

Which only proved how far gone *he* was, too.

* * *

"There *is* no one else." Dale's mouth pulled into a desperate, fearful rictus. "It's the *truth!*"

"Oh, bullshit." Sam's voice was lazy, almost bored. But Greg knew better. If Dale didn't cough up the information, those boxers were going to go next. Then Sam, armed with his collection of hardware—pliers and wire cutters and handsaws—would go to work. Greg's stomach somersaulted. Because Aidan's crew really *were* sick little freaks. Having sussed out Lucian and Sam as like-minded brothers, Aidan now provided Rule with its version of gangbangers: punks heavy on the blood and torture, light on the graffiti. Greg imagined it was the reason Peter tagged Aidan for the job in the first place. It was also why Greg didn't have the guts to stop them, even though *he* was the one who was supposed to be calling the shots now.

In charge, my ass. For about the billionth time, he wondered what the hell Yeager was smoking. Greg wasn't Peter or Chris. He'd only just turned fifteen. He was having a hard enough time being *him*— whoever that was.

"No, no, I'm telling the truth! It was me, it was just me—*Aaahhhh!*" Dale shrieked as Aidan's antenna razored meat right down to bone. "*Jesus Jesus Je*—"

And that was when Greg felt the earth move.

7

As one wall of the tunnel cracked apart and the rock gave way, Alex screamed. Her right shoulder was a fireball of red, liquid pain, the tendons and muscles stretching until she thought her skin would rip, the arm simply pop from its socket. Clutching Wolf's forearm in a death grip, she could feel his muscles quivering from the effort. She had visions of the rope to which Wolf clung, fraying, unraveling, breaking, and the two of them being swept away. She had no idea if the Changed above were trying to pull them up. They probably couldn't, because of the current. She was barely holding on, and the pain was building, her shoulder trying to come apart. If only the drag would let up!

Unless it doesn't. The water had dropped to just below her knees but no further. *Must be filling almost as fast from somewhere else.* The rope had swayed left, and there it stayed, drawn to the doomed course that the water charted, their weight fixed to the end of a gigantic pendulum. If the rope snapped, or Wolf couldn't hang on—

I should let go. An insane thought, but one that, under the circumstances, had all the bald certainty of an irrefutable logic. *I'm too much for him. I'll get us both killed.*

A jolt. She felt the quiver down her arm and into her teeth. Above, she saw Wolf's head jerk and then his left foot slide up the rock wall. Another jolt, and now she could see, quite distinctly, that crude harness tighten as he managed another half step, jamming his right boot against a lip of protruding rock that she could've *sworn* had been a good four inches above him only a second before. She looked down at her legs. Was it her imagination, or had the water fallen, just a little? *They're trying to pull him up.* But if this was the best they could do, it wouldn't be nearly enough. Could she move her legs, drag one out? Anything would help. *Come on, come on.* Her thighs tensed, battling the clutch of all that water. As if sensing what she meant to do, Wolf tightened his grip around her wrist and *pulled*, working to lift her just a little higher—

The earth suddenly *heaved*. She could feel the pressure of it. In the next moment, there was a crack and then a *BOOM*, like thunder. Debris skittered over the rocks; to her right, jagged seams suddenly splayed. Someone screamed, and then a boy, arms and legs spread in a star, hurtled past in a sudden hail of stone. He hit the water not twenty feet away, although she couldn't hear the splash over the roar. The boy bobbed to the surface, and then one hand appeared to claw at air. His jaw unhinged, maybe to scream, but whatever sound might have emerged was lost as a gush of water flooded down the boy's throat. The claw-hand tightened to an agonized fist. His bulging eyes rolled back to the whites. A moment later, the boy was jerked under and away.

There was a sudden lurch. The tension in her screaming shoulder eased a smidge, and she thought, *Oh hell.* She looked back up, then gasped. Wolf's face was a mask of blood. *Must've been hit by a rock.* She saw him give his head a groggy shake. His arms were shuddering now, uncontrollably, his muscles nearing their breaking point.

He's going to lose it. Instead of the panic she expected, the realization brought a certain calm. Monster or not, he was risking his neck to save her. So the math was simple, the equation neat. If she wanted to live, there really was only one way.

Help him. Do something.

Grimly, she put everything she had into getting her boots out of the water. Her knees bunched; she felt the cramp and quiver of her thighs . . . and her feet inched up. Not much. A little, but enough.

Yes. "Come on, come on," she chanted. Her teeth clamped together; she felt her belly tighten, her neck muscles cord with the effort. You really didn't appreciate how *thick*, how *powerful* water was until you had to fight it. To Alex, it felt like gigantic hands were cupping each heavy heel, but either she was winning or the water level *was* dropping. Same diff. "Come on, come—"

Both boots popped free so quickly her burning thighs tried to relax, send her legs pistoning down. Gasping, aware that she was truly swaying now and free of the water, she caught herself just in time. For a moment, she simply dangled, her shoulder coming apart in Wolf's grasp, the water surging only inches away and ready to grab her again, take her down for good.

Then Wolf tensed, his fingers so tight it felt as if her wristbones were being ground to dust. She began to move by minute degrees, see-sawing back and forth: first a few inches and then a few more as he tried swinging her closer to the rock wall so she could make a grab. The arc of her travel lengthened, her body nothing more than a sodden little yo-yo depending from a very short string. Toward the juddering wall, then back, then closer—those crags first ten and then only five feet away, but still too far for even a very determined, very desperate person to have a hope in hell—then back, and now one more time . . .

Now! her brain screamed. *Do it now, do it now, do it now now now!*

Her left hand made a grab. Rock chewed her fingers. She clawed, wildly, but then physics—that *bitch*—took over. Her swing's momentum reversed, carrying her away.

"*Shit! Shit*, god—" A lurch and the words dried up on her tongue as Wolf's fingers slipped, his muscles shivered, and that greedy water drew closer—so close. *No, no, don't lose it, Wolf! Don't lose it now, just a few more seconds* . . . And then she was sailing back, and she could tell from the frantic twist of Wolf's fingers—slick with blood and water and sweat—that he wouldn't be able to hold on for another go. This was it. She felt the air whisking through her hair, whiffling past her ears. The rock wall suddenly loomed, but she'd picked her spot: at her ten o'clock, a slight curve of shadow, an inverted grin of stone. At the last second, just before she butted the wall, her hand shot out, fingers hooked. She grabbed that stone lip, felt a ridge of rock slot beneath her knuckles—

Wolf must've felt the moment she connected, because his elbow suddenly kinked and then he was leaning in, shifting his weight, trying not to let go or pull her off. Anyone looking would've sworn she and Wolf were engaged in a weird variation of arm wrestling. Yet, at that moment, on the rock, they were a single unit, a team bent to one purpose. Jamming her knees against sharp stone, Alex clung to the rock with both legs and her left hand like a three-legged fly.

"Get them to pull us up, Wolf," she croaked, not knowing if he would understand speech, and beyond caring. The earth was groaning, fatiguing fast in a swoon that might still take them all down, and she knew: they weren't close to being safe yet. *"Hurry."*

8

What? Startled, Greg aimed a look at the rough brick floor. He could've sworn the bricks moved. *Unless I'm going crazy.* The stable was so cold their breaths plumed, but Greg still felt sudden anxious sweat on his upper lip. Another flashing stab of light skewered his eyes as his sledgehammer of a headache pounded. *Please, God, please. I can't be losing it. Not now.*

What convinced him that he was still semi-sane was when he saw Daisy, his golden retriever, scramble to her feet and give a sharp yap of alarm. So, he knew she'd felt it. There was also something else—a sound, something that was not Mick Jagger or a bluesy guitar or Dale's dribbling sobs: a faint, faraway, hollow *whump.*

That was real. I heard that. What the— Greg tossed a glance up to Pru, who stood at his right elbow, a wrinkle of worry between his eyebrows. At seventeen, Pru was two years older and one of the biggest kids Greg had ever seen: six foot six, square-jawed, and broad, the kind of bullnecked hulk a high school football coach would sell his grandmother's soul for. Pru was also the only boy Greg considered close to a friend these days, now that Peter and Chris were gone. *Pru heard that, too. Could it be thunder?* Greg shot a quick glance out the stable windows. No lightning; only the diffuse, muddy green glow of the setting moon. Unless it was snowing near Lake Superior; that might explain it. Thundersnow happened around the Great Lakes all the time. *But the lake's more than a hundred miles away. Even if it's thundering up there, we shouldn't be able to hear it.*

The floor shivered again in a bizarre undulation, the grimy, blood-spattered brick heaving as if a gigantic underground monster had rolled over in its sleep. The vibration, much stronger than before, went straight up Greg's calves and into his thighs.

"Holy shit," he said. "Did you guys feel that?"

9

They were ten feet from the edge, then five. At the lip, still clutching Wolf's left wrist, she managed a last stumbling lurch, felt the rock beneath her boots skate and shift. A red rocket of pain raced into her right ankle. Pushing through it, she planted her boots and heaved herself away from the ledge—

And into a nightmare.

The world was coming apart at the seams. The roar of the earth was huge, a grating bellow counterpointed with the sharp pops and squeals of overstressed rock. Jagged fissures scored the snow; a clutch of trees to her left weren't swaying but *jolting* back and forth. The crowns of several trees had snapped, leaving trunks that were little more than ruined splinters. There'd been fresh snow the night before, but the brutal cold had solidified the layers beneath. With every shudder of the earth, this more rigid, hard-packed ice layer was cracking and shifting into unstable slabs.

God, isn't this how avalanches start? She watched a jagged chunk, this one as large as a kiddie sled, jitter down the rise. *Got to get off the hill before it collapses.*

A brief, sweeping glance. The moon was going down, the light no longer neon green but murky and so bad that the others—six Changed in all, including Wolf—were only slate-gray, boy-shaped silhouettes: parka hoods cinched down tight, their faces ghostly ovals. The five who'd pulled them up were jittering like cold butter hissing on a hot skillet. Their fear was a red fizz in her nose. Wolf was having as hard a time keeping to his feet as she, and he'd dropped her wrist to fumble with the rope harness. The other boys were staggering, working at the hopeless task of gathering up rope, trying to corral their gear. One Changed, though, snagged her attention because he smelled . . . familiar. Who *was* that? She lifted her nose, pulled in air. There, floundering toward them from the end of the conga line that had hauled her and Wolf to safety: a tall, slope-shouldered kid, his features now pulling together out of the gloom.

And she thought, *No, no, it can't be.*

She'd waffled over this all the way up the tunnel: whether to make a break for it if she managed to reach the top, or stay. Her ankle was messed up, but she was managing. From Kincaid and all her hiking experience, she knew how to splint it, if needed. But the fact that she was soaking wet was a much bigger problem. Her sodden pants were already stiffening, and she was trembling, getting hypothermic. What she needed was to get warm, which meant a fire, a change of clothes, something hot to drink. Wet, with no supplies and nothing to keep her alive except Leopard's knife and the Glock 19, she might as well have let go of that rope and saved Wolf the trouble of rescuing her from the tunnel. She would probably die if she ran now.

On the other hand, Wolf had come back. He wanted her. Or maybe . . . *needed* her? So, go with him? Bide her time? God, it would be Rule all over again, and probably just as stupid, but she'd nearly talked herself into it.

Until now, this moment, because heading toward them was a boy she recognized by sight and scent: Ben Stiemke.

Acne. He'd been part of Wolf's original gang, before Spider and Leopard took over. The fact that Acne was here, on the surface, actually frightened her just as much as this nightmare. But there was no mistake. Acne had made it out of the mine. Had he left before the attack, the explosions? Maybe slipped out when everyone else was in the chow line because he'd smelled Wolf earlier in the day, just as she and Spider and Leopard had? She would never know. The important thing was that Acne was with Wolf now. That meant some of the others—Spider, Slash—might have gotten out, too.

That decided her. She was not going through this again.

Her eyes clicked to the quivering snow. To her left, maybe fifty feet away, she spotted a scatter of cross-country skis and poles—and rifles. One, lying near a pair of skis staked in the snow, caught her eye: scoped, a bolt-action with a carry strap. She darted left, digging in with her aching right ankle and launching herself toward the weapon. She saw Wolf start; saw the others trying to get at her; spotted a kid with very long dreads, the tallest of the six, suddenly reaching for her; felt his fingers whisk her hair. . . .

"No!" she gasped, twisting, dancing out of the way. The sudden twist sent a spike of red pain from her ankle to her kneecap, bad enough that tears started. She clamped back on the shriek that tried bubbling past her teeth. *Keep going, come on, it's not that far.* Snowy slabs slipped and rocked beneath her boots like dinner plates on ice; a sudden skid to the right and she nearly lost her footing, her right boot kicking free. Her left jammed down hard, driving into snow that grabbed at her calf, but then she was hopping free, nearly there, thirty feet, twenty-five . . . *shuck a round into the chamber* . . . no more than fifteen feet now . . . *throw the bolt, swing up on an arc, because they're moving, they're behind you.* This was something she'd practiced with her dad, hitting a moving target with the Glock: *Lead, honey, and mount the gun. Don't duck down.*

The earth shivered. She could see the skis waggling back and forth. The rifle began to scoot and skip. But she was close now; it was almost over; she could do this. The rifle was to her left, two feet away. And if Wolf got to a weapon or pulled a pistol? Could she shoot him? After all this? It would be like sticking a gun into

Chris's face. She didn't want to have to make that decision.

She slid the last foot—and then felt the snow tremble. There was a monstrous jolt, a stunning *whack* as something very big—another cave, maybe—collapsed underground. The sensation was nearly indescribable, but it was as if she were a glass on a white tablecloth that a magician had tried to snatch away, only he'd muffed the trick. The impact cut her legs out from under; she felt her knees buckle and her feet leave the snow. With a yelp, she came down hard on her butt. A white sunburst of pain lit up her spine. For a second, her consciousness dropped out in a stunned blank. She couldn't move. Her chest wouldn't work. Electric shocks danced over her skin, tingled down to her toes and fingers. Gagging, she finally managed a gulp of air and then another. Rolling to her stomach, she dragged in air, shook the spots from her vision.

All the boys were down. Most were crabbed on their stomachs, digging in, hanging on, riding the earth like rodeo cowboys on bucking broncos. That kid with the dreads was lower than the rest, his fall taking him closer to the edge of the rise and far away from her. A lucky break. She watched him trying to clamber his way straight up. For her? That was stupid, a mistake. He should move out of the fall line and *then* up before the snow collapsed.

But that was when it dawned on her: the kid with the dreads wasn't coming for *her*. Wrong angle. Her eyes swept up again—and then she saw where he was going.

Wolf was maybe fifty feet away, close to where they'd popped out of the mine, and to her right. He was still flat on his back—but not moving. God, was he unconscious? He'd lost a lot of blood. Maybe it wasn't the fall. Maybe he'd fainted. She almost shouted to him but snatched that back before it could spring off her tongue. *Doesn't matter. Let old Bob Marley there worry.* And, grimly: *At least this way, I don't have to decide whether to shoot him.*

But she couldn't set her feet. The earth was heaving, trying to shake her off its skin. Panting, she pulled her left knee to her stomach, got her hands planted, pushed up. The skis had toppled to the snow, and the rifle—where was it? Her gaze snagged on a gray-green glint of moonlight, just beyond a ski pole, reflected from the rifle's scope. *Yes.* On hands and knees, she spidered for the weapon, fighting the quaking earth, working her way around the skis. Stretching for the rifle, she felt her fingertips brush the cold black steel of the barrel . . .

From somewhere behind her came a loud, lowing moan.

Her first thought: *Wolf?* No, this wasn't a natural sound at all. It was too *deep*, as if something that lived only in the center of the earth were coming awake. The sound was *big*.

That was the ground. That was rock, breaking open. She was afraid to look back. The rifle was right in front of her. Another inch, she'd have it and make a run for it, just keep going: traverse the hill, get out of the fall line and out of danger, but get *away*.

But Wolf's unconscious. The whole rise is collapsing.

And so what? It was her here-and-now brain, a voice firmly planted in a world where there were blacks and whites, rights and wrongs. *Are you* insane? *Forget him. He's a monster, for God's sake. Grab the rifle and get out, get out now!*

"Oh, shut up," she said. As far as she was concerned, the world to which that voice belonged had vanished after the Zap. Nothing was black-and-white anymore. So she risked a look back—and felt a scream gather in her throat.

Whatever it had been, the opening through which they'd popped only minutes before wasn't simply a hole anymore. The gap was widening by the second as the guts of the rise—and the entire mine—fell away. What lay behind her was a sore, a black and insidious blight. It was the mouth of a monster eating the earth, chewing its way to Wolf.

"Wake up! Wolf!" Twisting back toward the rifle, her hand shot out—and grabbed a ski instead. Turning, she lunged back toward the crater. "Wolf, wake up, *wake up!*"

She swam for him, eeling over the snow, panic giving her strength as she fought the trembling earth. Beyond Wolf, maybe thirty feet away, the hill was dissolving, the snow buckling and folding. The air was misty with pulverized rock and ice that pecked her cheeks.

Meanwhile, that voice, the one that lived in the black-and-white world, was babbling: *What are you doing, are you crazy, are you nuts? Let his guys worry about him. Get off the rise, grab the gun, get off, get off, get off!*

"Wolf!" This time, she thought she saw his head move. She was ten feet away now, no more. *Far enough.* Still on her stomach, she jammed the toes of her boots into the snow and thrust the ski toward him, stretching as far as she could. If she could get Wolf up, get him to grab the ski, the principle ought to be the same as pulling someone off thin ice. All she had to do was back up, pull him away from the hole, give him a fighting chance.

And then I'm done; we're even. "Wolf, come on!" she shouted over the clatter of rock and the boom of the earth. "Get up, wake *up!*"

What she got was a rumble—not in front of her but behind, where she'd been. *What?* She shot a quick glance over her shoulder just in time to see the snow beneath the rifle shudder. In the next instant, the weapon skated away, riding the swell before sailing over the lip of the rise to disappear. If she'd been there, she'd have gone with it. She still might anyway.

She felt the ski jerk and looked back. Wolf was awake, on his belly, and clinging to the ski. So strange, but she didn't know how she truly felt about the fact that she was trying to save his life—only that this was what she *had* to do. It was illogical, but it was also right. "Come on, Wolf, damn it! Move your ass!"

He began crabbing away from the hole, scuttling toward her, using the ski as a guide and an anchor as she slithered back five feet, then ten. *Just a few more feet, enough to give you a chance.* The entire rise was quaking now; she felt the snow slipping and sliding in front of her, the earth bucking against her stomach. *Then I let go, and I'm done, I'm—*

In the next instant, the skin of the earth rose in an enormous inhale. She felt it happen and thought, *Oh shit*. Against all reason, she looked down the length of the ski, toward Wolf, this boy with Chris's face who had brought her to one hell, saved her from another. Their gazes locked, and she saw her terror mirrored in his eyes, reflected in his blood-caked face. "Wolf—" she began.

The earth suddenly collapsed. The giant exhaled, and she hurtled down. The force, so hard and fast, was a fist that punched a gasping scream from her chest. The snow just broke apart, shattering into shards like thick, white glass. A second later, she felt herself beginning to slide sideways as the icy slab on which she sprawled followed the lie of the land.

She began to move and pick up speed, the layer of snow to which she clung shearing away. She lost the ski and then she was whirling, the slab spinning like a top. A scream ripped from her mouth as the slab hurtled for the edge of the rise. The snowfield was now only a dim blur; behind, above, the hill was breaking up. She had no idea where the others were, what had happened to Wolf; she just had time to think, *No!*

The side of the rise fell away with a thunderous roar, in a shuddering avalanche of snow and ice and rock.

And she went with it.

10

"That's twice." It was Kincaid from his place along a far wall between two mumbly denture-suckers who served as the prison house guards. The old doctor turned his seamed face first left and then right, searching the dark corners of the old stable, lifting his chin like a bloodhound straining to catch a scent. "I felt it," he said, looking back at the two old guards. "What about you?"

Neither answered. Now, if Greg or Pru or Aidan and his minions hadn't been around, they might have said something. But maybe not. Having decided that a doctor was too valuable to Ban or execute, the Council had made Kincaid into a ghost, an untouchable to be avoided unless absolutely necessary.

"Shut up, you old douche bag," Lucian said, the silver fob of a tongue stud ticking against his teeth. Scabs beetled Lucian's patchy, moth-eaten scalp. Greg wondered if maybe one of these days, the kid's hand would slip while he shaved his head and instead slice open a carotid or jugular and do them all a favor. "I didn't feel anything," Lucian said. "I didn't *hear* anything neither. Probably just this guy bouncing around, or the music."

"No, I don't think so." Kincaid transferred his eyes to Greg. Well . . . *eye*. The left. The right was gone. A bit of Aidan's handiwork. Greg thought Kincaid didn't wear a patch on purpose. Like he was *daring* Greg to take a nice, long look at what they'd done. The worst had been the first week or so after, when the socket was raw and wept blood. "Sound came from the south." The baby-pink flesh of Kincaid's socket twitched. "Might want to check with—"

"You deaf, old man? We're busy, and you're not here. Unless"—Aidan favored Kincaid with a snaky grin—"there's something wrong with that other eye? Want me to scoop it out, too, take a look?"

"Well now," Kincaid said, mildly, "you do that and then get yourself shot, Aidan, I just might have to operate by *feel*. I wouldn't lay odds on that turning out so go—"

A fast whicker, something cutting air. A *snap* that made Greg jump and Pru straighten out of his slouch as Kincaid doubled over, grunting with pain and surprise, as the too-red lips of a slash opened beneath his remaining eye.

"Duuuude!" Sam crowed as Lucian cracked up. The two mumbly guards jostled out of the way like startled sheep, putting distance between them and a man they'd probably once called a friend.

"Aidan, are you *nuts?*" Pushing aside the ache in his head, Greg started forward but stopped when Pru clapped a huge paw around his wrist, tipped his head toward Aidan, and gave a warning shake of his head. His meaning was clear enough, but Aidan slicing and dicing their only doctor into ribbons did no one any good. Greg pulled free of Pru's grip. "Doc, you okay?"

"Of course he's *okay*." Aidan's lips skinned from a ruin of yellowing teeth. Whatever else Aidan had cared about before the world went bust, good oral hygiene hadn't been at the top of his list. "If I'd wanted it any other way, I'd have done worse."

"Yeah. Old asshole's lucky I ain't clipped off his tongue with a wire cutter and fed it to the dogs," Sam drawled.

"I don't know." Uncoiling his own very long, very pink muscular rope, Lucian flicked his tongue at Kincaid like a serpent tasting the air. His stud gleamed. "My dad used to boil up this big old cow's tongue every winter, eat it with this sauce of raisins and wine and shit? Some Jew thing, but it was pretty good."

"Yeah, but you need a cow first," Sam said.

"Or a Jew," Aidan said, and the three boys sniggered.

Greg ignored them. "Doc?"

"I-I'm all right, Greg. Th-thank you, son." Fumbling open his bag, Kincaid ripped open a gauze pack with shaking hands. Whimpering, Daisy left her corner to nuzzle Kincaid's elbow. "Yes, girl, thank you, it's okay," Kincaid said, gently shoving the dog back as it tried licking the blood sheeting over his fingers. "Greg, she's all upset. You want to call her off, please?"

"Daisy, *down*," Greg snapped, ashamed, the heat crawling up his neck. He should go to Kincaid. "Go on, now, *sit*."

"Leave the old bastard," Aidan said. "He's fine."

"No, he's *not*," Greg shot back. "You do that again—"

"And *what*?" Aidan tossed the blood-smeared aerial aside. The thin whip ticked to the grimy brick and then rolled into a purple puddle of Dale's blood. Aidan unzipped his parka, revealing a baggy, red-checked flannel and white thermals so grimy the collar was the color of ash. "You want to fight, Greg? You want to take a shot? Go on." Squaring his bony shoulders, he slipped to his falsetto again. "Or is poor widdle Greggie-weggie too *scaaared*?"

Aidan's minions howled. "Hey, hey, knock it off, A," Pru said, his eyes pinging from the Three Musketeers to Greg and back again. "Greg, man, let it go."

"Screw that." Heat crawled up Greg's neck, and before he stopped to think, he was shucking his parka. "Stay out of this, Pru."

"Greg, listen to him. Don't do it." Kincaid struggled to his feet. His hand was still clapped to his cheek, the gauze pad going crimson and drippy. "I'm fine. Just calm down."

"Stay *out* of this, Doc!" Greg roared, thinking, *I don't want to calm down. I haven't been calm in months. Why start now?* His heart was drumming so hard he could feel the knocking all the way in his teeth. His brain was bleeding, the migraine stabbing like knives. No one was supposed to get on top of him, no one! He was *in charge* and Peter was dead and Chris had run away; he'd *run* and left Greg to pick up the pieces, and *goddamn* Chris, what kind of *friend* did that? And Aidan was there, grinning, and probably had a shiv for sure or just a good sharp knife, or one of his crew did, and they'd stick Greg in the gut or the heart and say it was self-defense and get off, scot-free, because the Spared were Spared and special and got away with murder; and there was Mick Jagger, wailing, *Please, Doctor, I'm damaged.*

"All of you, back off!" A hot, rose-red bloom of rage expanded in Greg's chest. "Just back off, *back off!*"

"*No,* Greg!" Kincaid and Pru shouted at the same moment—but it was, of all people, poor Dale Privet who probably saved Greg's life.

"My God," Dale said, with a touch of wonder in his wheezy old man's voice, "what is wrong with you people? What are you boys doing to each other?"

11

Alex had no idea what she should do or how to save herself. A tumble down a regular vanilla mountain, no sweat: roll onto your stomach, dig in, protect your head, do a self-arrest. Oh, and don't panic.

But one thing her dad never taught her was what the hell to do in an avalanche.

The snow was her world. It was like being carried in the crush of an enormous wave, only instead of riding it like a surfer, the snow had scooped her up and swallowed her whole in its mad, churning thunder. She was tumbling, somersaulting, slamming sideways, then crashing onto her back. The snow was a boot planted between her shoulder blades, and it ground down, as inexorable and unforgiving as gravity. She'd lost the night, wasn't even sure which way was up. She kept trying to dig in with her boots and hands, attempting to stop her slide the way she might if she'd stumbled into a chute. But the snow kept pillowing over her head, cresting then curling and breaking. Snow jammed into her mouth and up her nose. Spluttering, she coughed it out, started sweeping her arms in front of her face, desperately shoveling away the white, punching out an air pocket.

Snow is like water. The snow was still screaming down the rise and she knew she must be going very fast. She kept swimming, aiming for what she hoped was up, scooping away snow, pushing for space—for air. *If I can just get to the surface . . .*

Something *whacked* her left hip. Maybe a tree or a rock; she didn't know. A blaze of pain raced across her pelvis, and she opened her mouth to scream. A fist of snow instantly jammed into her mouth, forcing its way down her throat—and now she was choking, flailing, no air at all. Another *wham!* The impact slammed her shoulder blades. The plug of snow in her throat popped onto her tongue and then she was spitting, scraping her hands in the white space before her mouth and nose, dragging in a lungful of air and then another—

She was slowing down. The drag of the snow was decreasing, no longer rushing past in a roar. *Getting near the bottom.* She kept clawing snow from her face, pulling in what air she could. *The rise can't be that high. Has to stop—*

All at once, the snow and she stopped moving. It was as if someone had thrown the switch, killing the power. Stunned, she could only lie there a moment. Where there had been a roaring, there was now nothing but a profound, dead silence. It was completely dark. She knew her eyes were open, but there was nothing to see. At all.

I'm under the snow. Horror erupted in her chest. *Got to dig myself out. I'll run out of air, I'll suffocate, I've got to . . .* Her left arm was bent at the elbow, close to her face. Her right had worked its way over her head, and was starting to hurt. She needed both hands to dig her way out, and something rigid: Leopard's knife or even the butt of the Glock, except . . . no hard knuckle of plastic in her spine. *Lost the Glock; must've gotten ripped out.* But the knife was secured to a leg sheath, and she thought it was still there. Hard to tell with all this snow, but if she could get at it . . . She felt her right biceps flex.

But her arm wouldn't budge. For a crazy, wild, terrible moment, she thought, *I broke my back. I'm paralyzed, that's what it is.* Then she sent a silent command to her toes, felt them wiggle in her boots. After three more seconds, however, she discovered her *legs* wouldn't move at all, no matter how much muscle she put into it. She felt the fingers of her left hand feather her cheek, but that arm wouldn't move either.

Then she knew the truth. She wasn't paralyzed. Oh, she *could* move, but only a little because of all that snow, compressed around her body, molded to her like concrete. The snow had her and wasn't about to let go.

She was buried alive.

12

"Shut up!" Quick as a snake, before the thought streaked from a glimmer to a certainty, Greg whipped Dale a fast one across the jaw. The blow was hard, a *crack* like the shout of a walnut bursting under pressure. The punch jerked a gasp from Dale at the same moment that it exploded in Greg's hand, a bright ball that mushroomed to a burn he felt all the way to his elbow. "Shut the fuck *up!*" he screamed.

"Attaboy!" Aidan crowed as Lucian and Sam whooped their approval. But Pru only groaned, "Greg, man, what are you doing?"

Kincaid—his friend, a nice man, someone Greg really *liked*—held out his hands. They were saturated with blood. "Greg," he said, that one eye shining and so bright it hurt to look. "Stop, son. You're better than this. Don't you see what's happening? Peter and Chris would never—"

"BUT THEY'RE! NOT! *HERE!*" Greg bellowed. He could feel the cords knotting in his neck. One more second, and the top of his head would blow like a grenade. "They're *gone,* and it's all on *me,* and you're a fucking *ghost*, you're *nothing!*"

But he thought of his mom and dad at the same moment: how ashamed they would be. His mom never cursed, and the one time his dad really let go, he'd smashed his thumb with a hammer, so that was understandable. Neither ever raised a hand to him or his jerky older brother, never.

Yeah, yeah, but you guys aren't here either. Things aren't so easy any-more, so give me a break.

"And you," he said to Dale Privet, "you're one to talk about us. You're a thief. You came to steal. You're no better than the rest of us."

"But you don't understand. I was just so *hungry*," Dale whispered, tears leaking from his eyes to trickle down his temples. The purple imprint of Greg's fist was stenciled on the old man's cheek, and there was a smear of fresh blood on Dale's chin. The rest of his face was the color of salt. "You don't know what it's like, now that there's nothing coming in. Peter and your boys used to bring food, but now we got nothing. No deer either, no raccoons—all the game's run off or dead. There's nothing out there anymore, and I got no ammo to speak of even if there was. What am I supposed to do, eat bark? Eat dirt? And my granddaughter, she's just a baby, she—" Dale's mouth suddenly clamped shut.

"Granddaughter?" Greg was breathing hard, and *God*, his head *hurt* from the thump of that migraine, a molten throbbing that pushed behind his eyes and might just dribble out of his ears. But his heart—he felt that clench and go hard as stone. "You said you were alone."

"I—" Dale's eyes were so huge with terror and dread, the irises were nothing but pinpricks. "Please. They haven't done anything. It was me. You have the power to save them. Do whatever you want with me, but—"

At that moment, Greg's radio, which was clipped to his hip, let out a rapid series of clicks: *break-break-break.*

"Well, look at that, Dale," Greg said, with absolutely no humor. "Saved by the goddamned bell."

Backing away, Greg acknowledged by keying the unit with a quick double-click. One of a half dozen World War II relics Rule had scrounged and then doled out to key personnel, the radio was always kept to a single dedicated channel. To save on batteries and boost transmission distance, no one used anything but coded clicks and Morse. Greg listened to the comeback, responded, then seated the radio on his hip again. "Come on," he said to Pru. "Lookout says something's up."

"That's what I'm telling you." Kincaid finished taping gauze to his cheek. His blood was already drying to a rusty bib on his parka. He favored them all with his one-eyed stare. "I felt it, and this isn't earthquake country. It's the beginning of something else, something . . . *bad.*"

"Uh-huh." Aidan snorted. "Next thing you know, he'll be spouting Bible shit like Jess."

"Leave him alone, A." Although Greg had to admit, what was going on with Jess *was* strange. Kincaid kept her apart from everyone else, fed her strange potions, even slept in her room at the hospice. The rumors were she was bat-shit crazy, spouting gibberish half the time or completely in la-la land and totally zoned. Greg was so curious that when he'd delivered a prisoner to the hospice, he'd waited until Kincaid was busy, then sidled to her room for a peek. Except for a rumpled cot and night table filled with books, the room was nothing special. But then, of course, there was Jess.

She doesn't even look real. Like plastic. Jess was like a body laid out for a viewing, only propped on her left side with a pillow wedged against her back to keep her from rolling and another tucked under her right arm. Her mane of steel-gray hair was scraped back into a long, neat braid from skin as white as the bandage over half her forehead. Her face was off-kilter, the dome of her forehead sunken over her left eyebrow from where the shotgun's butt had cratered bone.

But then he noticed Jess's eyes roaming their sockets beneath her closed lids. *Dreaming?* He hadn't expected that. The effect was bizarre and more than a little creepy because the rest of her was so disturbingly slack. Then, all of a sudden, her lips twitched as she pulled in a gasping inhale and breathed, "Leavethemboytheyareblind . . ."

The hair rose on the back of his neck. Boy? Was she talking about him, *to* him? *That's nuts, that's crazy.* The words were only air. They held no meaning. They were so incredibly spooky, he did a one-eighty and beat feet and you could not *pay* him to go back.

Now, ignoring Aidan's aggrieved sputter, Greg turned to Sam and Lucian. "After Kincaid patches him up, I want you guys to put Dale in a cell, all right? No more working him over right now. Just give him a chance to think about things."

"Sure, anything you say, *boss*," Sam said, his tone dripping with sarcasm.

"Yeah, *boss*. You want we should use the chains, hang him up by his arms?" Lucian asked. "It'd make things go faster."

Kincaid shook his head. "That poor man's so worn out, there's no way he can support his weight. You let those boys string him up, Greg, and I guarantee he'll suffocate by morning."

"Yeah?" Greg said. "Ask me if I care."

13

Nothing and no one could have prepared Alex for this.

She lost it. "Help, *help!*" Spitting and blowing, she tried turning her head but couldn't move more than a few inches right or left. The snow's weight was terrible, wouldn't let up, and then she was wailing incoherently, a shriek that wanted to go on and on . . .

Stop stop stop! She muscled back her fear. *Don't move, stop screaming. You'll run out of air and only kill yourself faster.*

But so what? She was alone. She couldn't reach her whistle. *No one to hear it anyway.* Her heart boomed; tears streamed over her cheeks. *I'm going to die in here.* Pulling in air was getting very hard, like sucking up the last dregs of lemonade through a slowly collapsing straw. Her lungs were starting to ache, and she was already gasping. Three seconds later, she realized that her eyelids had shut without her realizing it.

No, no! She fluttered them open in another spasm of panic. *Not ready to die yet. Not . . .* But her lids slipped again, and so did her mind. Below, so far away, it was so dark . . .

. . . not . . . ready . . .

14

"You ready?"

Boy. A voice. Not his. Whose? Chris didn't know. His mind felt as if it were teetering on the brink, like the smallest tap or tiniest misstep would tip him hurtling over the edge and into oblivion and maybe, this time, for good.

"*Pull,*" the boy said.

A second later, a blowtorch went off in his back and scorched its way from his pelvis through his chest. The pain was enormous, like an atom bomb. Before that moment, he hadn't realized he'd even been gone, but now he slammed back, hard and fast and all at once on a heaving red tide of agony. "*Aaahhh,*" he moaned.

"Is that him?" The boy sounded astonished.

"Yeah, wait!" A girl's voice, young, and very close, almost at his ear. "Wait, stop! I think he's awake! Hello? Are you there?"

There . . . yes . . . He lost the thread. Had he even spoken? Blacked out, maybe. He just couldn't tell.

"Probably just reflex." The boy, again. "Eli, let's try—"

"Wait." A second girl, older, her voice deeper, gently insistent. "Are his eyes open? Did they move?"

The boy: "What does that matter?"

The older girl: "If he's conscious . . ."

"No, his eyes are still closed." The younger girl, again, and now he realized that she was *very* close. He could feel the warm whisper of

5 1

her breath. "But when you guys moved the door, his face twitched. Maybe we're hurting him more?"

Door . . . what . . . where . . . He couldn't hold the thought. He faded in and out, his consciousness like the bob of a lost balloon high above the distant lights of a faraway carnival. He thought he might be on his stomach. What was the last thing he remembered?

"I don't know if we got a choice. Unless you guys have a better idea of how to get him out from under there?" When there was no response, the older boy said, "Okay, then let's do this. You ready in there?"

"Just a sec," the little girl called. Her voice dropped. "You need to go, girl. Go on."

He sensed movement; heard the shuffle of something over snow, a crinkle, and then a strange chuffing. *Dog?* A moment later, the weight on his back rocked. His middle cramped against another grab of pain, and he heard the *uhhh* drop from his mouth.

"Sorry," the little girl whispered. "Sorry, sorry, but I have to do this, I'm so sorry . . ."

"You ready?" the boy called.

"Yeah. He moaned again." The little girl sounded shaky.

"Don't get freaked, honey," the older girl said. "He's probably out."

No . . . here . . . I'm . . .

"I'm okay." Pause. "Got my feet up."

"All right, on three," the boy said. "You push, I'll pull."

That snagged his attention in a way nothing else could. *No, wait . . . hurt, don't hurt me again.* Marshaling his strength, Chris put everything he had into the simple act of opening his eyes. But there was a strange pressure around his forehead and over his eyes, and he just couldn't.

A second later, there came another fiery jolt. *No, no.* A grinding shudder rocked his hips, and he moaned. *Door.* That must be it.

They're trying to lift . . . His mind skipped, tried tripping off that cliff of what passed for consciousness again. *"Nuhhh . . ."*

"Stop, stop!" The little girl, her voice hitching up a notch. "We're hurting him!"

"Can't help that." The boy again, not angry but impatient and unhappy, almost annoyed: the voice of someone who'd rather be anywhere else. "It's going to hurt no matter what—"

"Wait, let's think this through," the older girl said. "If we can give him a few seconds and let him wake up, he might be able to help *us* help *him*."

"How's he going to do that if his back's broken?" the boy said.

Broken. The word was a razor that sliced through Chris's pain. *Broken?*

"I can't assess him until he's fully conscious. Even if he can't move his legs, he could brace himself with his arms," the older girl said.

"I don't know," the boy said. "You saw his hand."

Hand. What were they talking about? Chris didn't feel anything. God, maybe that meant his hand was—

"Maybe we can bandage it. I don't know. But if he *can* help, enough for us to slide something solid underneath, get him off the snow . . ."

Snow. As soon as she said it, he could feel the wet against his right cheek and beneath his chest where his body warmth had melted the snow. *I'm on the snow.* No, that wasn't quite right. He was *in* it. That had to be it. He was *down* in the snow. Yet he wasn't freezing. The air felt warm and carried a scent that was strange and wet, not snowmelt or regular water but like a rusted fender.

"Hannah's right." Not the older boy but one closer to the little girl's age: the kid called *Eli.* "I bet I could get in there with the bolt cutters. Then all I got to do is cut the spikes and we lift the door right off. Bet it wouldn't hurt him as much. It might even be faster."

Bolt cutters? Spikes?

"It would be better than taking a chance of ripping them out,

Jayden," Hannah said. "He's already bleeding pretty badly."

Blood. What he smelled—that wet rust stink—and lay in was his own blood. *Hurt. Bleeding . . . what . . .* But his back couldn't be broken, it couldn't, it—

"I thought you said he's bleeding out," Jayden said.

"I said maybe, and there's no point in making this worse. The more I think about it, the more I worry that if a spike's compressing an artery and we pull it out—"

Oh Jesus. The girl, Hannah, was still talking, but her voice receded to a buzz as the memory suddenly crashed into his mind as if the dam holding it back had burst: Nathan, the brittle snap of his neck as that gigantic log swept back to knock him from his horse. Then *he'd* started forward—stupid, a mistake—and there had been a monstrous sound of something *crashing* through trees, but not from the side. From above. Something dark, *huge*, rushing for his face. For a moment, he hadn't been able to move, not only from surprise but because his feet . . . *No, snowshoes, they were stuck, jammed into the snow.* . . He'd spied a bottle-green glint of glass, the bristle of iron spikes, and then he'd understood: the thing was a tiger-trap made out of a huge barn door, barreling straight down from the trees, heading right for him.

Pushed off, tried getting out of the way. But he hadn't been fast enough. He remembered the weight driving him down, that ripping in his legs, his flesh tearing. The unbelievable pain of those spikes. The sudden pulse of blood. *Can't let them move the door.* He had visions of the spikes that might be both threatening and saving him being suddenly withdrawn, popping free like corks, and then his life surging in hot red rivers onto the snow.

Come on. Chris put everything he had into it; felt the twitch of small muscles. The pressure against his eyelids was huge. *Or I'm really this weak, and if I am, I will die.*

"Hey!" the younger girl called. "Hey, guys, he's opening his eyes, he's—"

"Uhhh." His lids cranked back by degrees, a superhuman effort that brought out the sweat along his upper lip and on his neck. But he just couldn't manage to open his eyes all the way. "Huhh . . ."

"Oh gosh," the girl said, and then he felt her fingers tugging, the pressure suddenly easing as she pushed his watch cap onto his forehead. "No wonder. Is that better?"

Yes. His lids creaked open, and there she was, less than six inches from his face. He couldn't tell much. Not only had the effort drained him, the light was dim, and his eyes didn't want to focus. "Uhhh," he said again.

"Hey, he's awake! His eyes are open!" The little girl beamed. "Hi."

"Huh," he grunted, then raked his swollen tongue over numb, dry lips.

"Are you thirsty? Do you want a drink of water?"

"Mmm." He thought her eyes were light blue, and she looked about eight, maybe nine years old. How had she found him? Nathan was dead. Then who? *Someone else* . . . Then he had the name, saw her face floating like a gauzy cloud across his vision: *Lena.* They were on their way to Oren, had taken the long way because . . . *Rule, chasing us, Weller* . . .

"Hey, he's thirsty!" she called. Beyond the girl, he now saw a wide funnel trenched out of snow where she must've dug her way in. "He wants a drink!"

"Scoot on out, honey," Hannah said. "Let me take a look at him."

"Okay." To him: "Don't worry. There's plenty of time before dark. We'll get you out. We found you, me and Eli. I shook out my emergency blanket to make you a tent, and then me and my dog crawled in to keep you warm until Eli could get back with help. But it's going to be okay now. We got you. What's your name?"

55

"Cuh . . ." His parched throat made a clicking sound. "Cuh-Chrisss." The word sounded like a balloon with all the air rushing out. "*Chrisss . . .*"

"Chris?" she said, brightening as he managed a nod. Sudden tears pricked the backs of his eyes because, oh God, hearing his name never had seemed quite so wonderful.

"Well, hi," the little girl said. "My name's Ellie."

15

Ellie? That warm bloom of relief suddenly shriveled in his gut. He remembered the argument, Alex pleading with him to search for the little girl. There just couldn't be that many Ellies in this general area. *She's the right age. This has to be her.*

"Chris, are you okay?" A wrinkle of worry creased the space above Ellie's nose. "Are you feeling sick? Does it hurt more?"

"I . . ." His tongue balked. With fresh terror, he thought, *Can't tell. Mustn't.* They might leave him here to die. They might kill him. "Y-yes, it . . . it h-hurts," he managed, and this was no lie.

"Ellie?" It was Hannah. "Is he—"

"I think you better get in here. He doesn't look so good." Scooting sideways, Ellie batted away one crinkly corner of that emergency blanket. A spoke of light speared the gloom. Chris could clearly see how the barn door had driven him a good foot into the snowpack before lodging itself tight. He also had a much better view of the blood.

No. A fresh spasm of horror twisted in his chest. When he exhaled, his breath showed in small red ripples. *That's too much, I've lost too much—*

Beyond the limits of his prison of snow and spikes and blood, he heard a dog's welcoming *huff* and then Ellie say, "What?" Pause; a murmur from the older girl. "Yeah," Ellie said, "there's a lot, and I can feel it still coming. It's not spreading, but—" Evidently, someone up there understood this might not be great for him to hear, because that emergency blanket dropped back into place, shuttering out the light.

Talking about the blood. He swallowed back a scream. *Not spreading, because it's melting into the snow under me.*

A moment later, he heard a rustle, saw the gloom peel back and then a gloved hand appear, followed by an arm, a shoulder, and finally a girl, on her back, slipping down the chute.

"Hi." Stopping short of the blood lake in which he lay, she brushed a thick, buckwheat-brown braid from her shoulder and hitched onto her side to face him. "I'm Han—" She stopped dead, a look of disbelief spreading over her face.

"Oh my God." Her voice was small and shocked. She raised a gloved hand to her mouth as if to somehow stopper what came next. "Simon?"

16

"What?" His own voice was faraway, foggy with pain. "Who?"

"I—" she began, and then he saw her eyes, which were the color of soft ash, flit to his throat. Her eyebrows tented in a frown. "What did you say your name was?"

"Cuh-Chris." His dry throat gnarled. "Prentiss."

"Oh. I see." She gave him another close look, then seemed to recover herself. Stripping off her gloves, she laid two fingers on his neck at the angle of his jaw. "Sorry. I'm Hannah. I'm here to help you. Let me check your pulse."

"H-how . . ." His throat clicked when he swallowed. "How b-bad . . ."

"Shh." Her lips moved as she silently counted the seconds on her wristwatch. "How's your breathing?"

"H-hurts. Hard to . . ."

"To breathe? Like you can't pull in enough air?" Her gray gaze studied his face. "What about pain?"

"Like nuh-nuh-knives." He grimaced against another inhalation. "Get . . . getting . . ."

"Harder to breathe?" When he moved his head in an incremental nod, she continued, "Is the pain worse on one side?"

"R-right." He closed his eyes a moment to gather himself. "How b-bad?"

"Very." Her fingers traced the hump of his Adam's apple, and then her gray eyes clouded. "Where else does it hurt?"

"St-stomach." His tongue was so huge he was afraid he might choke. "B-b-back."

"The back, I'd expected. That door's very heavy. Can you move your toes?"

It hadn't occurred to him to try. Had he before he passed out? He focused, sent the command down to his feet. After a few anxious seconds, he felt the bunching of wool, but the sensation was very distant, as if the signal were being relayed on a very long and sluggish cable. "Yes."

"Okay," she said, although Chris thought her expression didn't match the word at all. "Listen, I'm going to slide my hand under and press on your stomach a little. I'll try to be as gentle as I can, but I have to check, okay?"

He steeled himself as her fingers wormed beneath his sopping parka and began working their way along his right side. When she pressed, he winced. "That hurts?" she asked, those eyes never leaving his face. "How about . . . ?" She abruptly pushed in, then let go.

"Ugh!" A bolt of nausea streaked up his throat, and he could feel sudden tears oiling down his cheeks. "D-don . . . don't . . ."

"Okay, okay." She touched a hand to his cheek. "Try to relax."

"Jus . . ." He was shuddering, and that only made the pain much worse. Not moving was best. "Puh-please, get m-me out, g-get me . . ."

"We will," she said. He wasn't sure if it was his panic, but it seemed to him that her smile didn't make it to her eyes. "I'm going to get you some water, all right? Are you thirsty?"

"Y-yes, but d-don't leave . . . don't leave m-me here." He heard how freaked he sounded, and didn't care. The fear and a sudden sensation of doom draped him in a dense, airless mantle. "Puh-*please*."

"Of course not. Try not to panic, Chris. Just let me . . ." Turning away, she rolled, pushed back a corner of the emergency blanket, and called, "I need my water bottle, please."

"Which one?" It was the older boy, Jayden.

"Left saddlebag."

A pause. "Okay," Jayden said, at the same moment that Ellie said, "What? Wait—"

Hannah cut her off. "Eli, I think you and Ellie should make sure we're in the clear."

"In the *clear*," Ellie began.

"Okay," the younger boy, Eli, said. "Come on, Ellie."

"No, *don't*," Ellie said. Her tone was sharp and—through the filter of Chris's fear—angry, verging on horrified. "You know it's—" Whatever else she was going to say was lost in the crunch of snow as someone, probably Eli, took her aside.

Upset. Why? He watched as Hannah took a Nalgene bottle that was passed through, tugged out a long drinking tube, and slid the mouthpiece to his lips. "Here," she said.

Both the water's scent, warm yet somehow sweet and earthy, and the scream of his need were so overpowering his fear and apprehension vanished. Yet he was so horribly weak that when he pulled at the mouthpiece, only a thin trickle spilled over his parched tongue before dribbling from the corner of his mouth.

"Oh." She made a small sympathetic sound. "Wait a second." Moving closer, she unwound her scarf before slipping a gentle hand beneath his cheek. "Let's raise you up a bit," she said, supporting his head and balling the scarf into a makeshift pillow. She was so close, he could smell her skin, an aroma of milk and warm oatmeal. Cradling his head in the crook of her arm, she offered him the mouthpiece again. "Try now," she said.

He sucked, the first precious drops slithering over his tongue to course down his tortured throat. The sweetness of the water was balanced against a yeasty aroma that reminded him of fresh-baked bread. He let slip a low moan.

"Take it easy," he heard her say, and realized that his eyes had slid shut. The water was so good, *so good*. "There's no rush," she said. "I won't leave you. They won't do anything else until I say it's okay."

He felt his body relax against her, and for a few blissful seconds, he did nothing but drink. As the water trailed a warm finger down the middle of his chest and into his stomach, his fear vanished. He forgot to be embarrassed about the fact that a strange girl was holding him as close as a baby. With every swallow, he felt his heart, racing before with fear and pain, begin to slow.

After another minute, she touched his cheek. "That's enough for now," she said. He opened his eyes to find her gray ones intent on his face. She had very high cheekbones, but her face was square, her mouth wide, her nose a little too big. "Wouldn't want you to bring that back up. Let's wait a little, see how it goes."

"Thank you." The rustiness in his voice was gone. He skimmed a lazy tongue over his lips. "Sweet."

"That's the honey." Her tone was very calm yet somehow familiar, like the tune of a favorite song he only half-remembered. "We keep our own hives. Let me . . ." She slid back, carefully withdrawing her arm. "Chris, what were you doing out here? Where are you from?"

"Trying . . ." He was feeling better, almost peaceful. "Trying to . . . to get to O-Oren. F-find . . ." He licked his lips again. "Settlement."

"A settlement in Oren." Her tone betrayed nothing. "Why?"

"Mmm." A strange but not unwelcome sensation of drowsiness swept through him. He could feel his muscles beginning to relax. "C-came from R-Rule . . ."

"Rule." The word sounded flat and hard. "Why? And why come this way? It's not the fastest, or even a straight shot."

"R-running."

"You were running away?" When he nodded, she continued, "Were you followed?"

"D-don't think so. Been on the trail . . . long time."

"I see." She offered him the mouthpiece again. "Drink."

The water, still so wonderfully wet, was nevertheless a touch *off* this time. Just beneath the honey and that yeasty tang, he detected something weird, a brackish aftertaste.

"Have you been to Oren before?" she asked.

"Mmm." He had to work at breathing, timing his words so he had enough air. His chest was heavy again. "T-took kids."

"Yes, everyone knows Rule does that."

"N-not what you think," he said. "Sick kids."

A pause. "That was you? You're that boy?" He registered the note of surprise in her voice. Another pause. "Tell me how you found them."

Was this a test? "The . . . the designs, on the barns." His lips tingled as if he'd eaten too many jalapeño poppers. "That's how . . . that's how . . ." He fumbled for the thought, lost it.

"Yes, that's right," she said, as if confirming something to herself. "What are you doing here, Chris? You've never come this way before."

"Running. Came to f-find . . ." Who? Maybe it was the light, but her face was going out of focus. *Tired.* How strange that time felt as if it was unwinding like a spring at the end of its useful life. The tick of his heart was slowing. His lids kept wanting to slip shut. *I want to sleep.* "Hunter."

The corners of her mouth tightened. "Why do you want to see Isaac?"

Isaac. "You . . . you know him?"

"Why do you want to see him?" she repeated.

"N-need . . ." His thoughts were beginning to fuzz. He couldn't remember what he was there to do. He was growing cold again, the sunny feeling in his chest beginning to dissipate even as the trembling that had seized him earlier was nearly gone. "Need him to . . ."

"Need Isaac for what?" She tapped his cheek. "Chris?"

He barely registered her fingers. He had the feeling her gray eyes were watching, very closely, but his own gaze was wavering, his grip on consciousness beginning to slip. His mind was drifting again, the string tying the tiny, bobbing balloon of his mind to the here and now loosening. He couldn't think, didn't remember. In his chest, there was a blackness, a blight, that was first a fist and now a slow and insidious palm with sinuous fingers unfurling, worming their way through his lungs, following the course of his blood: a cold, dark hand reaching into his brain, cupping his mind and smothering his thoughts, who he was and where.

Ellie. A tiny spark flickered in his mind. Ellie had been upset, and then she'd been hustled away. *When Hannah asked for the bottle of—*

And then he understood.

They weren't saving him.

They were killing him.

17

"Wuh?" Chris didn't know if he meant *what* or *why*, and it really didn't matter. His eyes skidded, as slippery as oiled ball bearings in his sockets. If he could just hold on . . . *Dark, so dark, like my chest . . . not right.* "Ha . . . uhh," he grunted. Had she left him? Was she gone? Why was it so dark? *"What—"*

But whatever he meant to say next simply fizzed to nothing on his tongue as he realized: it was dark because he was completely blind.

Can't see . . . and he was drifting now, the world dissolving, his mind—that buoyant balloon—sailing into air that was too thin . . . *can't breathe, can't—*

"Hannah." He felt a surge of sudden strength born of panic. "Hannah, *b-blind . . .*"

"I know. I'm sorry." Her voice, as transparent and fragile as a soap bubble: "Let go, Chris. Stop fighting it. Let it go."

"N-no." The cold was a boot on his back, a fist on his chest, a hand draped over his eyes. *Can't see, can't move, can't . . .* "Wuh . . . why . . ."

"Shh," she said. "I'm sorry, Chris, but there's nothing we can do for you. You're hurt too badly. This is better, Chris. Trust me. It'll go easier if you stop fighting."

But what if he *wanted* to fight? *I don't want to die, I'm not ready, I'm not . . .* "Nooo," he moaned. *"Don't."*

"Shh," she said again, but now her voice was no more than a sliver, a waning crescent of sound. "Don't fight it, Chris. Accept this and let go. I'll stay with you until the end. You won't be alone."

No. But he couldn't stop this. His mind was drifting away, higher and higher, the margins of his world closing down like an iris. *No . . . don't let go, Chris . . . don't . . . let . . .*

18

She woke in agony.

Gasping—no, not gasping; croaking, *straining* for air, the sound a ragged *awk-awk*, an invisible fist crushing her throat. She swam up from the dark of nothing and into the blackness that was her now. The pain in her lungs was awful, more than a burn; every breath was like sucking down broken glass. Her brain was pulsing so hard it felt like her heart had crawled into her skull. Or maybe that was the monster, straining to get out, beating its fists against bone.

From just above her left eye came a dim, sulfurous glow. *White light?* Was this how it was supposed to go? First, the light as her brain, starved for oxygen, gave up the ghost, and then that tunnel, and at the end . . .

No, not a glow. Tiny pinpricks. Not breaks in the snow either. She worked at bringing the light into focus and understood: Ellie's Mickey Mouse watch. She hadn't taken it off since the night before that terrible morning that Harlan shot Tom and took Ellie. Mickey said it was—she forced her vision to firm—five after seven.

Past dawn. Been here for . . . She couldn't do the math. The glow from Ellie's watch was fading, the lights winking out and pulling apart even as her mind shimmied and seemed to swell beyond the limits of her skull. For a brief moment, she actually thought she was standing above, on the snow, as her gaze swept over splintered trees, rocks fractured to rubble, and . . . a ski pole? She couldn't tell, had no time to parse it out. The vision faded and what was left was something blinding and too white, like the eye of a full moon before the world died.

This must be that last tunnel. There was the light. That was where she had to go, because Tom had been there, high above and unreachable, and if only she could float far enough, fast enough . . . *Tom . . . wait . . . wait for me . . .*

All of a sudden, her mind shifted with a hard, panicky clench, a flutter, the sudden bunch and twist of the monster sensing that she really was on her way out. That this was it, end of the line—and it was fighting like hell to work its way free.

Despite everything, she wanted to laugh. Might have, if she'd had the air. The monster had become something more, the way Kincaid thought it would, but it was still trapped inside her head, and *she* was buried alive.

Got you . . . I g-got you . . . Her thoughts were slurring. *Hurts, this hurts.* So hard to focus. Words slipping through her fingers, dropping out of her mind. Everything going away, except for the pain. *Hurts. No air. Chest . . . hurt, hurt. Dark. No . . . air . . . n-no, can't let go.*

She fought to suck in one more breath.

Can't . . . l-let . . .

19

Outside the torture house, the horses were restless, nickering and tossing their heads. Matching him step for step, Greg's golden retriever, Daisy, alternated between anxious pants and high whimpers.

"Man, you see that?" Pru asked in a low voice.

"Yeah. All the animals are spooked." He looked up at the older boy. "You felt it, too. I know you did."

"Felt what?" With his fun nixed, Aidan had attached himself to Greg and Pru. For Aidan, an alert over the radio? Excellent. Go where the trouble was, because you just never knew when the next opportunity for a little mayhem might present itself. "I didn't feel nothing."

"Well, I did. Ground shook, just like Kincaid said. Like a . . . a rumble, something vibrating. You know? When a semi goes by? Or a big lightning strike, real close?" Pru lifted his nose and sniffed.

"What are you doing?" Aidan said.

"Sniffing for the ozone," Pru said. "You know. The way air smells after lightning."

"Shut up." Aidan snorted. "Lightning's electricity. It ain't got a smell."

"Yeah, it does," Greg said. "Like car exhaust in summer."

"Ozone," Pru repeated, then shook his head. "I don't smell anything but the snow."

"Well, I *can't* smell because it's so damn cold," Aidan said. "My nose froze five minutes ago. You guys are just being pussies, letting Kincaid psych you out."

"Oh yeah?" Pru pointed to the left of the stable's slider. "Look at the snow, A."

Greg saw what Pru meant at once. They'd had fresh snow the night before, but instead of only a new layer icing the hard pack piled atop the entry ramp, there were discrete hummocks, like miniature mountains of sifted confectioners' sugar. Digging out his flashlight, Greg scrutinized the roof. The stable had no gutters, so whatever melt there'd been showed in a glittering bristle of long icicles, as sharp and pointed as bloodied fangs. Several had snapped, however, and now protruded, like silver stilettos, from the hard pack.

"So?" Flipping up his snorkel hood, Aidan jammed his gloved hands into his parka pockets and hunched his shoulders against a sudden snatch of wind. "Snow slid off," he said, his voice so muffled and far back it reminded Greg of second grade: tin cans on string.

"Yeah, no shit, Sherlock." Pru said. "But why'd the snow slip? It hasn't been warm enough for a melt, and the snow's not soft. Those icicles are snapped clean."

"Slabs got shaken so much they slid right off." Greg skimmed the light over the roof and saw naked shingles where snow had caromed down the incline. "Same as an avalanche."

"Come on." But Aidan sounded uncertain now. "What could do that? Like . . . an earthquake? That's crazy. This is Michigan. Stuff like that doesn't happen here."

"Until now," Greg said.

PART TWO:
WHERE THE BODIES ARE

20

It was another foot this time—the left, and a guy's. Those tufts of hair sprouting from the toes? Dead giveaway. The owner was a pig. Terminal case of corns, two huge bunions, calluses so rough you could use them for sandpaper, and toe rot. Since the person had been old—they were all old—the skin was mottled, papery, wormy with bulging blue veins. The crumbling nails were so long they actually curled into snot colored talons. Peter couldn't imagine how the old geezer had walked.

"You've got to kill the guards," Simon hissed.

"I know," Peter said, over the *bong-bong-bonging*. Damn bells had started up eight days ago, right after the Rule mine blew, and just wouldn't quit. Naked as a jay, he sat cross-legged on the chilled concrete of his corner cell, trying very hard not to look around for Simon. No point. That little bugger—

—*hallucination*—

was *fast*. And Peter *certainly* didn't want to linger over the others, who watched from the remaining nine cells: glittery-eyed Changed, their faces pressed to the bars like monkeys in a zoo. The only thing they didn't do was hoot. Peter thought there had to be at least sixty kids. Knowing Finn, there were probably a lot more Changed stashed in other cages throughout the camp.

The thing that got to Peter? Well, besides Simon and the *bong-bong-bong* of the bells and being naked and stewing in his own shit? Some of *these* Changed had names. He knew these kids, and that freaked Peter out, big-time. For example, in the cage directly opposite, that honking big kid with the Neanderthal brow? Lee Travers: Forest Road, third house on the right. His squirrelly grandma spent all day whacking furrows with this wicked-sharp Warren hoe, whether that garden needed to be dug up or not.

And what about this very pretty, doe-eyed brunette in the cell to his left? That girl who made him hungry in ways he couldn't hide well without clothes? He was pretty sure that was Kate Landry: sixteen, liked cats, and oh my God, those lips, those *breasts*. Peter got these *flashes*, the two of them, naked, thrashing in the snow . . .

Stop it. Peter's breathing had sped up, his mouth gone dry with desire. *Get control. Think. Why is Finn snapping up these particular kids? Their friends?*

"You know, instead of thinking about sex," Simon said, "you should be figuring a way out."

"I understand that, Simon," Peter muttered, averting his eyes from the very luscious Kate, those lips, her breasts. At times, another idea floated into his brain, something right out of *Rise of the Planet of the Apes*: kill the guards, open the cages, and they'd surge out to conquer the world. Or *The Wizard of Oz*: *Fly, my pretties! Fly, fly!* But first: sex. Lots and lots of sex, in the snow, on concrete, anywhere; take Kate, bend her back, and take her and take her and take—

"Don't you wish," Simon said. "Be lucky she doesn't bite it off for a snack."

"Jesus, Simon, shut the hell up." Christ, he couldn't have even a good fantasy in peace.

"Make me. You've got way more important things to worry about, like me and Penny, not to mention *Finn* and why he's rounding up Changed, kids from Rule, the *mine*, and all you can think about is hooking up with some *girl*? We *need* you!"

"Yes, I *know*. Stop, Simon, *please*." Moaning, he rolled onto his

belly, away from Kate's eyes, her hunger, his thoughts. Simon was a
spike in Peter's right ear, like those needles they used on frogs back in
. . . God . . . junior bio.

And look who's the frog now.

Stunning but true.

The Rule mine had blown eight days ago, and when Peter wasn't
screaming or raving like a crazy person because of the bells, those
damn bells in his head, those *bong-bong-BONGs* . . . when he wasn't
doing that, Peter was either awake and dreaming awful nightmares
that clung like burrs—*water and a dark fan of sea grass and the boat and
eyes in stone*—or he was awake and not dreaming but thinking, hard,
the thoughts bubbling in the pressure cooker of his skull: *Get out of
here, Peter, get out, get out, got to get out!* If he didn't find a way out, his
mind would go *ka-BOOM*. Nothing left but a drippy red socket.

Because there was something *in* there.

Yeah. For *real*. In his skull. This red . . . *scuttling* behind his eyeballs,
spidering over the soft pink cheese of his brain. He thought maybe it
had crawled in through an ear. Or boogered up his nose. He wasn't
sure. But he felt it all right. Sucker was growing.

He tried getting rid of it. Once, he used his shirt. He remembered
only snatches: slowly strangling from his own weight; the raw pain of
it; that wild, frantic moment when his vision blacked as he ran out of
air and his lungs imploded; the knot so taut the noose sawed his skin
like a length of fine piano wire. Another ten, fifteen seconds, he'd
have cut through his carotids.

So, they took his clothes. Nowadays, he wallowed, naked as a
baby, in his own filth, because they took his crap bucket, too. His
fault, but taking the shot was worth it. The raw, primal satisfaction of
drenching Lang—that *traitor*—with rank piss and runny shit . . . Oh
Jesus, that was good.

But those bells were killing him. They were so damned *loud*.

When he *could* think about it, Peter suspected the water. Good delivery system. When those first few muted clangs started up, Peter tried rationing himself. Just a swallow here and there, until his tongue was so thick it clung to the roof of his mouth and breathing got too hard. Eventually, Peter drank because he had to, and then the bells just *bellowed*. Shrieking at Finn—JESUS, GOD, WOULD YOU TURN THESE DAMN THINGS OFF?—only earned him cryptic mumbo jumbo: *Don't you find it fascinating, boy-o, that the people who call on God the most believe in God the least?*

In quieter, more rational moments, Peter understood how tempting it was to see Finn as a crazy, broken-down old Vietnam vet turned militia leader: a creepily intelligent and sadistic son of a bitch with a bug up his ass about Rule; a guy who'd arranged an ambush seven weeks ago so he could take out his frustrations on Peter first. If that were the only truth, then Finn's conclusions, his methods and experiments, would be much easier to dismiss.

But Peter had gone to college. Hadn't graduated for . . . reasons, ones that had to do with *eyes in stone and orange water*. And Penny. And Simon. And that damn boat. He didn't talk about any of that, not about college or the accident. Not even Chris knew. No point. But Peter had studied genetic rescue and evolution and endangered species. Once upon a time, he'd had big ideas and grand dreams, too. He was going to save the world. So, sometimes, Peter really understood where Finn was coming from. There was a ruthless logic to Finn's madness that a true Darwinian might find very appealing.

Then, again: *bong-bong-BONG.*

Peter wasn't exactly sane.

"So, when?" Simon pestered. "You're just sitting on your ass."

This was the literal truth. "It's a little more complicated than that," Peter said, still trying to hold it together, keep it down. "Just give it a rest, Simon. Okay?"

"Who the hell's he talking to?" That was the new guard, a jowly oldster with a hound-dog face and jug handles for ears in a standard, olive-drab uniform. Sidearm on his right hip, expandable baton in a cross-draw, slide side-break scabbard on the left. Jug Ears and the other duty guard were behind a plain wooden desk squared before a deep hearth in which a fire crackled, all the way down at the other end of the prison house.

A voice Peter recognized: "Beats the hell out of me." The second guard, Lang—*Traitor*, Simon hissed, *tear out his throat, pop his eyes, eat 'em like grapes*—yawned hugely, stretched. "He's always going on like that."

Now, those guards had to be fifty, sixty feet away, and yet Peter heard all this, loud and clear, and despite the bells. He'd become like this bat, see, picking up *sounds*: the *sssss* as the residual water on a fresh log hissed and evaporated, the *CREE-cree* of Lang's leather belt as he walked, even the squeak of boots over snow outside the prison house. Sometimes, he thought he actually heard other, *very* tiny voices inside his head. Nothing distinct but more of a hubbub like being in a crowded train station with a very high ceiling.

"Well, Jesus, the way he talks to himself," Jug Ears said, "it's kind of spooky."

Spooky. BWAHAHAHA. They didn't know spooky. The *bong-bong-BONGs* were spooky. Not sleeping, at *all*, was spooky. An old nightmare you saw while you were awake—*orange blood in murky water and the boat and eyes that were holes in stone*—that was spooky. Something growing electric red wings in your brain was spooky.

He watched as Lang's hand crawled into an oily gray helmet of thinning hair and dug in for a good *scritch-scritch*. "Boss says they're hallucinations," Lang said as dandruff salted his shoulders. "They're supposed to go away. He gets too loud, go ahead, give him a couple whacks. That'll shut him up."

"I'm not a hallucination," Simon whispered. His voice always came from Peter's blind spot on the right. Hoping to catch him out, Peter sometimes whipped around, but Simon danced away in a quick-silver sparkle.

"I know that," Peter said, although a very small, still sane part of his mind also whispered, *Oh, riiiight.*

"Where is the boss, anyway?" Jug Ears asked. "He's been gone over a week."

"You *know* I'm real," Simon said.

"Shh," Peter whispered. "Simon, please, be *quiet.* I need—"

"Last I heard, boss took a bunch of Chuckies. Wants to see how they do," Lang said. "Said they learn faster when they go out in teams, especially once they got enough in them."

"Uh-oh," Simon said.

That got Peter's attention. *Enough* in *them? Of what?* Lang and Jug Ears weren't talking only about his fellow inmates. So who? Finn had *different* Changed? Different how? He thought about the bells. Thought about how well he heard things and the constant scrim of the old dream. Thought about the scudder in his skull. *And Simon; I hear someone I know can't be here. So what if—*

"Well, Jesus, them and us together . . . that makes my skin crawl. And what happens with that stuff? To their *eyes?* Like what's going on with *him?*" Jug Ears hooked a thumb at Peter's cell. "Scares the bejesus out of me. Like something out of a movie."

Wait. What's going on with me? His fingers traced the bone of his sockets and dragged over the soft hummocks of his closed lids. His eyes were so raw they might be weeping blood. *Eyes, eyes in the dark, holes in stone. But I have real eyes. Unless I'm Changing, too, into something else. Unless Finn is—*

"Yeah, but you'll be glad when the time comes. Whole lot *more* of them. Better a Chucky eats a bullet than me," Lang said.

"Maybe." Jug Ears sounded doubtful. "But I'm telling you, the first time one of them looks at me crosswise? Blow its fucking head off. And what about these Chuckies here and the other holding areas? You got any idea what the boss wants with them?"

"Well, some he takes," Lang said. "The ones he thinks are smarter, I guess. But what we're going to do with all the rest . . . hell if I know."

Finn has more Changed, and not just here. He's divided them into groups: the ones he leaves alone, and then the ones he . . . drugs? Peter could see it. How stupid was it for him to believe Finn when the old bastard said they could handle only ten Changed at a time? It had been almost five months since things went to hell. Finn's militia was in place long before. Finn was ready for things to fall apart. *So he's working with the Changed, on them somehow, not only taming a couple as pets. He wants only the smartest, the fastest, the best.*

What Finn might want with these *others*, though, the ones in here with him, Peter couldn't imagine. They weren't food—well, not for the Changed, anyway, who killed but never fed on one another. So what was Finn up to with all these kids, a ton of whom were from Rule?

Another thought: *He has me. He knows all about me.* So did Finn know about Simon? About Penny? What if Finn was looking for them, too?

Relax, he won't find them. No one knows where Penny—

"I don't know," Simon said. "Finn got you. What makes you think he can't figure it out? You have to do something, Peter."

"I've done what I can. I've kept you alive." Peter's overstressed brain felt as if someone had crammed it into a blender. "I've lost *everything* for you."

"No," Simon said—and damn if he didn't sound like Finn. "You were lost when you decided the Zone was a good idea. You were lost the second you lied to the police, didn't tell the truth about the accident and the boat and Penny."

"Don't you think I know that?" A shout boiled in his chest. *Don't, don't, don't, can't scream.* He bit the soft flesh of his cheek, really ground down. The pain was bright but not nearly enough, no sir. *Screaming doesn't help. You scream, they hurt you, Lang kicks you, he beats you. But they won't kill you. So this isn't going to end until you—*

"Then do something, Peter," Simon said. "Stop Finn. Make a move. Do *something*."

"Shut *up*!" Snarling, Peter flung that left foot across his cell. "Shut up, Simon, just shut up!"

"Hey, hey!" Lang said.

"Please, *God*." Groaning, Peter struggled upright, hooked his fingers around the iron bars snugged against the wall, and hung on, fists working the metal against another wave of pain. "No no no, Peter, don't scream, Peter, don't scream."

Not for the first time, Peter wondered how long and hard he'd have to whack his head for his skull to crack and his brain to squish out like runny yolk. Or he could let himself drift close to the bars where the Changed waited. Thread his hands through and pull Kate close, let her sink her teeth into his throat, give her the first taste. It would be over before the guards could beat her and her cellmates back. But he was a coward; he couldn't let himself die. He wasn't ready, and there were Penny and Simon to think about. There was Chris.

Count; he should count. Counting was good. *Ten cells, there are ten. . . .* His feverish gaze touched on one after another. *Five to a side, one two three four five . . .* "This little piggy went to market, this little piggy stayed home, this little piggy had roast beef . . . help me, help me, help . . . bong, bong, bong . . ."

"Okay, that's pretty crazy," Jug Ears said.

"No, no, no, nononono," Peter chanted, knuckling his temples, shaking his head back and forth. "Eight . . . eight eight eight eight days since the bells, but ten cells ten ten ten, ten little piggies, wee, wee, wee . . ." He heard his voice rising to a cracking falsetto. "Wee, wee, wee, weeweewee . . . no, stop! Stop, *stop*!" He wasn't aware he was punctuating the word with a punch to his jaw until his knuckles barked with pain.

"Shouldn't we do something?" Jug Ears asked.

"If he starts digging out his eyes or something," said Lang.

"He ever done that?"

"Only once."

"Stop," Peter panted, but he was no longer sure to whom he spoke. He had to let go of this, get control. He punched his jaw again and again, harder, *harder!* This time, the soft inner flesh of his cheek ripped against his teeth. His mouth flooded with the tang of metal and swamp water—*the boat, deep in the dark*—a taste he now knew very well. *But this is me, this is good.* He drank himself back. *This is my blood; it's not anyone I had to eat*—

"No." He straightened abruptly as if a hidden spring had suddenly released at his waist. "I'm not going to think about *that* either. I'm going to think about something else. I'm going to think think think." He began to pace the limits of his cage, past the eyes of the Changed but well away from their grasping hands and Kate, Kate, *Kate*, around and around and around. *Count, do something, do anything, but get a grip.* "Get a grip, get a grip, I'm Peter, I'm in a cell, I'm in a camp . . ."

"You're Peter, you're in a cell, you're in a camp." Simon was an echo, a ghost from the graveyard of Peter's memories. "You're in a cell, this is hell, and I'm Simon, and it's ten little piggies and they went wee wee wee . . ."

"I'm not listening to you."

"You're talking to me."

"I'm not *hearing* you!" Peter shouted, over the *bong-bong-BONG.* "Jesus, please, let me go!" The top of his head hurt so much it felt like someone had cratered his skull with a brick. *Please, God, please. Why won't you let me die?*

"Because it's not your time," Simon said.

"But I can't take this anymore." Peter ran his tongue over his upper lip, skimming a rank and now very familiar lace of dried copper and old salt. "Please, Simon—"

"Simon?" said Jug Ears.

"Old rev's grandson," Lang said, bored. "Kid he was real close to."

"Grandson? I thought Chris Prentiss was Yeager's grandson."

"Him, too—which is weird, 'cause the old guy had only one kid."

"So how's that work?" asked Jug Ears.

"Beats shit out of me," said Lang.

"You're not allowed to die yet, Peter," Simon said. "Penny and I need you."

"Don't you think I *know* that?" Raging, he whirled, trying for a grab, coming up empty as Simon danced away, always out of reach. "*You* need me, *Penny* needs me. But I can't help you right now—don't you get that? I can't even help myself!"

"Who's Penny?" Jug Ears said.

"His sister. Guys from Rule said she was a real looker. Just"—Lang cupped his hands in front of his chest—"*fine.*"

"Shut up!" Peter whipped his head so fast bloody spit flew. But in his heart, he was also glad because it gave him someone else to hate other than himself. "Don't you say my sister's name! Don't you even *think* it!"

"Gone by the time I got there. Heard she maybe went native." Lang kept talking as if Peter wasn't there—and this was so true, in so many ways. Lang skimmed the pale pink eel of his tongue over teeth stained black with decay and ancient nicotine. "Damn shame. Be real sweet to show all those girls what a *man* can . . ."

"Shut *up!*" Fisting the bars in both hands, Peter cranked his elbows like a chimp. "Shut up, Lang! I'll fucking *kill* you if you don't shut up shut up *shut up!*"

"Yeah, *yeah?*" Scraping back his chair, Lang reached for his scabbard. A whip of his wrist, and twenty-six inches of black chromed steel snapped into place. Lang advanced half the distance to Peter's cell, smacking iron with sharp, clanging *bang-bang-bangs* that somehow synchronized to the *bong-bong-bongs*. In the other cells, the Changed cringed back. "You getting tough, boy, huh? You going to *kill* me? Like to see you try."

Yes! Go ahead, split my skull, pulp my brain, kill me kill me kill me! "Bring it, *bring* it!" Peter howled. "Come on, you prick, *come* on! You're brave out there; you can talk about showing girls what kind of *man* you are, so come on!"

Lang's cheeks flooded scarlet. "Don't think I won't—"

"Lang!" Jug Ears was on his feet. "I don't think this is a real good—"

"Shut up!" Advancing, Lang cut iron with a vicious *BAP*. "You little pissant—"

"Peter." It was Simon—and then it wasn't. Calm and small, this voice was nonetheless powerful, a kick in the gut that knocked the wind right out of him. "Peter, don't."

Like that, Peter felt the fight drain away, leaving him boneless, water-weak. He looked to his right, where Simon always hovered out of sight, then gasped as the air suddenly split—and Chris, shimmery and bright, slid into being.

"Peter." Chris's face was a white blare. "Stop. You can't beat them like this."

"Chris," Peter breathed. His knees tried to buckle. The sight rocked him back so hard that if he hadn't been clinging to the bars, he'd have crumpled to the filthy concrete. Chris couldn't be here; he knew that. The fact that Chris *was* . . . *What if he's dead? No, please, God.* Peter's throat knotted with grief. His vision clouded, and he squeezed his eyes tight. "Chris, you can't be here. I can't be seeing you. I'm *not*."

"Yeah?" Lang barked. When he whapped the bars again, the sound was much weaker and didn't hurt Peter's ears as much. Why was that? "Look at me when I'm talking!"

"Open your eyes, Peter," Chris said. "Look at me. Let me help you."

"No." He was trembling and cold, so cold. "If I do . . . if I can see you, it means you're dead, or Changed and . . ."

"See me," Chris said. "Hear me."

He couldn't help himself. His lids crept open, and then he cried out. Chris's face was chalk-white, his eyes not black but a stunning, glistering violet. He shouldn't look. He ought to cover his eyes. Keep this up, he'd go blind. But he was also afraid that if he took his gaze elsewhere—if he looked for Simon or doe-eyed Kate or Lang or even Finn—the sight would destroy him completely. The dark was its own terrible light.

"I see you." This was a hallucination, a vision conjured by a fevered mind because he had nothing else, no hope. *I'll never wake up from this, because I never sleep.* "Chris . . . God . . . *help* me."

"*I'll* help you." Lang whapped the bars again.

"I will." Always the calm one, Chris's voice was a cool cloth on a hot brow, water in the desert. "But you have to listen. You have to trust me and do what I say."

Chris wasn't here any more than Simon was real. They were hallucinations. They were symptoms of the past and his choices and eyes like holes in stone and black water as deep and still as the grave. This was a conscience divided against itself. Yet if Chris was the voice of sanity, a piece of real estate in Peter's mind no larger than a dime trying to talk itself down and help him survive . . . *Listen to this voice, listen hard.* "What?" Peter said. "What do you want me to do?"

"Step away from the bars, Peter," Chris said. "Don't let them hurt you anymore. You're not strong enough yet."

"I'm not *anything* anymore." A slow, hot trickle leaked down his cheeks. "I'm not strong. Simon's right. I'm nothing."

"*Now* you're learning," Lang said.

"You can be strong again," Chris said. "You will. But you must be brave enough to let go of this fight for now."

"But I'll fall," Peter said.

"Only to the floor," Chris said. "Trust me, Peter."

"Oooohhhh," Peter moaned. He retreated four blundering steps before his joints completely unlimbered, and he sank to his knees.

"See?" Lang broke down his baton. "Can't let the little shit get on top of you."

They're already on top of me. Bowing his head, Peter screwed his fists to his eyes like a weary child, and then he was choking, his pent-up grief and guilt a terrible sound that still, somehow, seemed to quiet those damn *bonging* bells, just a little. Or maybe Lang was right, and whatever Finn had done would pass into something much worse, if that was even possible. He thought it might be, and he was afraid. Maybe it was good he couldn't sleep, because when he woke, what would he be then? *I'm sorry, Chris, I'm so sorry, I'm so—*

"It's okay," Chris said, as if soothing a little kid who'd scraped a knee. "Shh, it's fine. You did the best you could. You can't give up."

"But what I've *done.*" Peter covered his face with his hands. *God, you'll never forgive me.*

"You have to forgive yourself first," Chris said, and hallucination or not, this is what Peter needed to hear. Much later, in fact, Peter wondered just who had answered.

"Help me," Peter whispered.

"Help yourself." It was Chris's voice, and it wasn't. It was a little of Simon, and it was not. It was small, the calm at the center of the storm, the eye of a hurricane where the air is still as glass, a bubble out of time. "Control yourself. Find a space to hide."

"Space to hide?"

"Yes, a special place only you know about. Put Peter there and I'll find you again. Wait for the right moment." A pause. "Now, eat, Peter. Forgive yourself, and live."

"Okay." The word was salty and his voice faraway. Knuckling away tears, he shuffled on hands and knees over dried urine and desiccated feces to the foot, which lay on its side like a forgotten shoe.

"Go on," the small voice said. "Do what you have to."

"Okay," Peter said again. The stump above the ankle was edged with clot, scanty shreds of raw muscle, and ratty gray tendon. Clamping his front teeth on a flap of loose skin, Peter gave a careful, experimental tug. There were an initial, slight resistance. He used his hands to help, stripping foot meat like barbecue from a rib. The skin gave with a soft *riiippp*, a sound that reminded him of his mother tearing his old cotton underpants into dust rags—and then Peter began to chew.

The taste was indescribably vile, like rotting liver left to turn green. That taste was his life.

"Now *that*," said Jug Ears, "is so fucking gross, I cannot tell you."

21

"I have something to tell you, honey. About that phone call?" Her dad slowly retracts his line, the reel going *click-click-click* as he jerks the rod up and down, up and down. Crappies love a jumping jig. "The one last night?"

"Uh-huh?" Ellie's not really listening. A light breeze, still chilly in early June, whispers through the down on her arms. The water's so glassy there's a whole other sky trapped underwater. She should be focused on her float, but her attention is on a male loon drifting along the far shore. When it tilts its head, she can see the red flash of its eyes. Lifting its neck, the loon wails, a spooky call—the sound of Minnesota's Boundary Waters and fishing with her dad—that always sends fingers creeping down Ellie's spine.

"Cold?" Her dad slips an arm around her shoulders. "Want my sweatshirt?"

"No." She snuggles. He smells of Dove soap and scorched sand, because Iraq never washes off. After his first deployment, he climbed into Grandpa Jack's shower with all his clothes and gear on as she perched on the tub and Grandpa leaned, unsmiling, against the jamb. *I washed everything before I left,* her dad said, cranking the shower full blast. *But watch this.* The water gushed out clear and drained out muddy gray, which surprised her because Grandpa Jack did a newspaper story on the troops and her dad sent video of a sandstorm. The color of Iraq then was this really funky neon orange, not dead ash-gray. *Two minutes after you take a shower, you're dirty again*, her daddy said, through spray. *Stuff never comes out.* (Grandpa Jack was pissed for days after, though: *All that damn sand clogging my drains.* But she caught him carefully scraping crusts of leftover sand into a small jar, like a souvenir.)

"Just watching the loons," she adds. She wishes her dad wouldn't talk. This is the time she likes best: before a fish strikes. Once the bait's taken, it's as if something breaks, because what happens next is a matter of life and death. That fish's life is over, just like that, and all because Ellie danced a jumping jig with a juicy waxworm on that particular morning when a crappie swam by and decided, *Saaay, that looks pretty interesting.*

"Oh." Her dad pauses. "Anyway, that phone call."

"Yeah?" From the brush on shore, the mom loon suddenly emerges, with two brown-black fluff balls. Ellie feels a jolt of excitement. The morning's so still, the wind's sigh so light, she can hear the chicks' peeps and the mom's soft hoots. "Look," she whispers. "Babies!"

"Uh-huh." He squeezes her arm. "Honey, I need to tell you something important."

"Sure." Her eyes are glued to the peeping chicks. The dad glides over as the mother slips into the water and the babies follow: *plop-plop!* "What?"

"I have to leave again," he says.

For a second, the words just don't sink in. Across the lake, the loon family is dodging around lily pads. Somewhere close she hears the *plunk* of a fish shattering the surface to snatch a bug. But inside everything has gone as dead and ashy as Iraqi sand.

"What?" she says, sitting up fast, as if she's the waxworm on the jig now. The adult loons jerk their heads, too, as if they're just as startled by the news. "You just got back!"

"Six months ago," he says, his eyes on the water, jumping that jig as if his life depends on it. Her dad keeps his hair military-short, and a red flush creeps into the fish-belly skin behind his ears and at the base of his neck. "It was supposed to be a year, but they need me. One of the other handlers and his dog were . . . they're out of commission." The way he says it, she knows it means *dead*, but that's a taboo subject, what her daddy calls bad juju. KIA is a jinx; say *dead*, it's like stepping on a crack. Men and dogs don't die; they're *out of commission*. "Mina's with another handler, but he's rotating out, and I know her, so . . ."

It's not a she. I'm *a she*. That's what Ellie wants to say. *It's a dumb dog.* It is as if her dad and Grandpa Jack have decided she's like this Mina: must be time to rotate Ellie to another handler.

"When?" That's not what she wants to say either, but fighting won't help. She bounces her gaze from him to his water-twin. "Never mind. Doesn't matter."

"Two weeks." In the water, the twin dad turns her a look. "Got to square some things away, but we can . . ." His voice trails off. She can't even imagine what he thought he could say to make things better.

She doesn't say *okay*. Or *I hate you*. Or *every time you go, it's like you die and I'm so scared I die, too*. Besides, one is a fib. She has no interest in the loons now. Instead, she stares down at the little water-girl, trapped next to her water-dad, who says—

". . . much longer?"

"Huh?" Ellie blinked away from the memory of that June morning and into the here and now of March. Stuffed with high clouds, the afternoon sky was the color of boiled egg white. As she looked up from the blue-black eye of her ice-fishing hole, she had to raise a hand against the glare. "What did you say?"

"I said, how much longer?" Eli's long eyelashes were feathered with frost. Flecks of ice clung to his scarf and dangled from a fraying watch cap, like Christmas ornaments. His cheeks were cranberry red.

Cradling his rifle, he stamped his feet with an exaggerated shudder. "I'm *freezing*. How can you *do* that?" He chinned the rod in her naked right hand. "My fingers would fall off."

"That's because you're not moving around," she said, returning her attention to the rod and gently playing it, up and down, up and down, jumping that jig. To be honest, her hand *was* turning icy, the nails bluing with cold. The few times she and Grandpa Jack ice-fished, he'd always started a fire on shore so she could warm up with hot cocoa and charred brats and blackened hot dogs. Her mouth watered at the memory. She would *kill* for a hot dog. With mustard and relish. Grilled onions.

"You okay?" Eli's eyebrows, honey-colored and delicate, pinched together.

"Yeah." She worked to stopper the sigh. Something her grandpa said drifted through: *If wishes were fishes.* . . . No good wishing for anything these days. You just ended up depressed or in tears, or both, and she'd be darned if she bawled in front of Eli. He was cute, and despite the fact that he was twelve, they hung together. (Jayden called them the *Killer Es*, which Ellie just didn't get.) But Eli could also be kind of a goof. Like, sometimes she thought she ought to be guarding *him*. She tilted her head at two nearby holes where she'd lowered stringers. "Could you take those back? I have to break down the tip-ups, and since I've got, like, fifteen of *those* . . ."

"Me?" Eli wasn't fond of fish slime, and Ellie had had a very good afternoon: fourteen black crappies, all ten-inchers. "Well," Eli said, twisting to look toward shore and their patient horses waiting beneath drooping boughs of tall hemlock. Nearby, a clutch of crows hopped over the snow, probably hoping for a nice steaming mound of fish guts, while a stern-looking, solitary gull perched on a thumb of icy rock. "I guess I *can* wait. You'll need help with the auger."

Right, so then I carry all *the fish* and *the tackle.* On the other hand, she knew what Eli really wanted to avoid was *storing* the tackle. Well, avoiding the place that was *near* where they stored tackle. Even the horses hated that part of the woods. She wasn't wild about it either, but at least she wasn't such a *girl*.

"Well," she said, withdrawing her rod and reaching, with studied casualness, to an inside parka pocket. Pulling out a plastic container, she popped the lid. In a bed of sawdust, warmed by her body heat, were thick white maggots, each about as long as the tip of her pinky. She delicately tweezed one fat boy from the wriggling mass. "Oh-*kaaay*," she said, stabbing the maggot with the jig's hook. It was really a waste; she'd already hooked one. But Eli needed a fire lit under his butt. "If you want to *waaait* and help me with the *taaackle . . .*"

"God!" Eli's lips, bright as cherries and almost too delicate for a boy, corkscrewed. "I *hate* it when you do that."

"Nom, nom." Plucking out another waxworm, Ellie smacked her lips. "*Taastee—*"

"Gah." Eli did a mock heave, but he was also grinning. *Sunny* was what Grandpa Jack would've said. "Fine, you win. Just *stop*." Eli reeled up a steel chain stringer and eight dripping black-spotted crappies, attached via snap hooks through their gills, from an ice hole. "Gah," he said again, holding the flapping fish at arm's length as Roc, a gray bullet of a mutt, bounded up with Mina on his heels. "My gloves always smell like fish," Eli complained as the dogs pranced excited circles. "Roc always smells like fish. My *saddle* smells like sardines."

She bit back a snark about killer farts, although even *she* was tired of smoked crappie and bluegill. But a *hot dog . . .* "At least everyone's eating."

"And you always smell like fish, too." Eli dragged up the second stringer. "How much longer are you going to be, so I know when it's time to get worried that you've been eaten?"

"Oh, ha-ha. Maybe another hour, hour and a half." It was just something to say. Since Alex had Mickey Mouse, Ellie hadn't the foggiest what time it was. "Not too long. It's still plenty light."

"You're sure you're okay with the tackle?"

"Of course I'm okay. I'm always okay," she muttered under her breath, but she called Mina to heel and tipped a cheery wave. The crows perked up as Eli neared shore, but when he passed to his horse without stopping, they lifted in a black cloud to scold him on his way.

Only two tip-ups had anything: seven-inchers that she released. With Mina trotting alongside, she hooked a handle of an old plastic primer bucket she used for her tackle and headed over the ice to holes she'd drilled this morning *waaay* out there.

This lake, which was very deep, was fed by a spring located somewhere off the western shore. That meant the water nearest the spring was much warmer and the lake never entirely froze. Instead, the ice sheet petered out in a ragged scallop of slushy ice from which she always kept a healthy distance. As she neared the far tip-up, she saw the orange flag standing upright and felt a burst of elation.

"All *right*," she said to the dog. "We got something." Jogging the last little way, she dropped to her knees and worked at unhooking her line. As soon as she felt it—how light the line was—her excitement died. "Well, shoot." Something had grabbed the bait and split. But then she saw how the monofilament line curled and realized there was no sinker at the end, no weight at all. The dripping line had snapped in two. She'd used monofilament on purpose; it had a lot more give and cushioned the set of the hook so the fish's mouth wouldn't tear.

"Wow, that was one strong fish." And big. Walleye liked deep water. So did pike. Lots of meat on those fish. "So maybe I should use braided line," she said to Mina, who only licked water from her fingers. "And auger the holes a little wider if we're going for the big boys."

Unclipping her knife, a stainless steel Leek, from a pants pocket, she deployed the blade with a practiced flick of her thumb. In a very small, dark closet of her mind, she wished she could show Tom and Alex what she knew how to do now. But she always wished that.

You have to stop this. She used the Leek's sharp point to pick out the knot of ruined line, then dumped the tip-up into her primer pail. For the past week, ever since Chris, she'd been thinking way too often about Tom and Alex, much more than was good for her.

This is your home now, so just deal. She should think about things she could actually do something about, like how to catch more and bigger fish dreaming their slow winter dreams in deeper water under the thinner, weaker ice of the shelf. More holes meant more time keeping them clear with her axe, though. Crunching back toward shore, she worried the problem. Grandpa Jack used rubber mats from his old pickup for fish-hole covers. But finding a car might be tough. Isaac and Hannah and a bunch of other kids were once Amish and still kind of big into God. All the places they stayed were Amish, and Amish didn't use cars. But maybe regular carpet or cut-up rug?

"I should ask Jayden," she said to Mina. "He's like Tom. You know . . . a fixer-upperer? Like, remember that old truck Tom and I . . ."

Stop. Clamping down on that memory, she thumbed away a fast, stinging tear. She had to cut it out, this dumb looping back to Tom and Alex, or her dad and Grandpa Jack. Her hand snuck to her neck and found a length of leather cord from which dangled a small wooden pendant. Hannah said the charm, some weird Amish or German magic thing, would protect her from evil or sad thoughts. *Ha.* It was just an upside-down peace sign. Dumb. Like it did any good for all the memories that kept slipping out of that dark closet. The ones of Tom always led to Alex and vice versa. Each came to the same end: with Tom, his face twisted in agony as the snow bloomed a violent rose-red under his leg; and Alex, her hands painted with his blood, screaming, *You bastards, you* bastards!

Good-luck charms? *Ha.* Her fingers fell from the leather cord. *She was total bad-luck juju.* It was her fault Tom got shot. *Tom said he was only trying to take care of his people and Alex saved me from the mountain and now look, because of me, probably they're both—*

"Nooo." She caught the moan with a cupped hand. Another fast tear chased down her cheek. Now she wished she'd kept Alex's whistle. Dumb to give that away. A whistle was actually something you could *use*, not a stupid piece of wood with a dumb German doohickey. The whistle was Alex, too. *Just like the letter from her mom.* Placing a palm over her heart, Ellie felt the envelope crinkle in its Ziploc, folded in an inner pocket. She hadn't been able to stop Harlan from stealing Alex's parents. *But I got your mom's letter, Alex. I saved her for you.*

As, perhaps, Alex and Tom might save her? Not that Hannah or Jayden or Eli were so horrible, but Ellie just couldn't shake the idea that things would never be right again until they were all back together. Which had led to the whistle. Giving Alex's whistle to Tobe had been partly impulse, partly design. Tobe was so sick and scared about being left behind. She'd hoped the whistle—that *Alex*, she guessed—would cheer him up, make him strong the same way it made her feel both better and really sad at the same time. *You'll give it back when you get well*, she'd said.

But in the back of her mind, a place she didn't visit often because it hurt too much, she'd also nursed another idea. The night before Harlan and Marjorie and Brett, Tom and Alex had talked about Rule. She remembered the rustle of maps and Tom's voice. *She'd* tried going there after Harlan, only she'd gotten *so* lost. It was just luck that Jayden found her. So, maybe, when the boy from Rule came and took Tobe to get better, someone would find the whistle and then show Alex. (Why anyone *would*, she didn't know. It was stupid. But it was something, like a message in a bottle.) Then Alex would know where to find her, and *she'd* tell Tom—because, of course, Alex would've saved him—and they would come for *her* . . . just like that.

If Tom was really okay, too. If he was still alive. If he wasn't like poor Chris, the boy from Rule who had only tried to help.

Until Hannah had gone and done what she'd done and couldn't take it back.

From the sky came more hard, mournful cries as a trio of crows arrowed left to right, west to east, followed by six more. Even higher, she spotted the telltale glide of several seagulls. Frowning now, she craned a look behind her, toward shore. That gull was still there, but the crows had vanished. Even deeper in the trees, something flickered—a flash of light green—and then a cedar swayed with a sudden shake and shiver, spilling a fine curtain of snow.

"Well, that's weird," Ellie said. Crows *loved* fish guts or just about *anything* dead or dying. (Well, except the people-eaters.) This was something Jayden said, too: if you want to know where that deer you clipped had got to, don't follow the blood. Look for the crows.

But they're all gone now. She jumped her eyes over low-hanging branches and snow-laden evergreens. That still-billowing cloud of fine snow. Where there'd been plenty of birds before, now there was only that one gull. Which was a little strange.

Shouldering the auger over her left and a .22 on the right, she grabbed up her primer bucket again and resumed her slow trudge toward shore. The gun, a Savage, was what Jayden called a *plinker*, meaning it didn't do squat and only added weight, but it made her feel better. While her hand auger wasn't a thirty-pounder like Grandpa Jack's, it was long and unwieldy—essentially a spear tipped with two incredibly sharp, stainless-steel blades.

Ahead, she could see Mina squirting after that one gull. With an alarmed cry, the gull lifted from its perch, circled, and let go of a long, drippy streamer. Mina skidded at the last second but not fast enough. A stringer of green-white goo splashed her muzzle, and then the gull was winging higher, shrieking gull-laughs: *Ah-hah-hah-hah!*

"Serves you right," she said, while Mina only snorted and groveled in the snow. As they passed into the woods, she saw the gull, back on its rock, and could swear it was still laughing.

This particular farm was huge, once probably two farms or even three, with a gazillion acres and lots of outbuildings. Eli had gone left, following a wooded path back to the farmhouse. She peeled off right on her horse, a poky, muddy brown mare named Bella, down a meandering trail through oaks and tall tamaracks. Ahead, in a crescent-shaped clearing, the trail elbowed right and left. One look at that fork and Bella spooked, prancing and shaking her head in a clatter of metal and leather.

"Okay, okay, you big baby." Dismounting, she looped the reins around a stout oak. None of the horses liked this part of the woods. Nothing good lay down that right-hand trail.

"So totally *lame*," she muttered, darkly. Trotting by her side, Mina turned her a look, and Ellie said to the dog, "Bet if it'd been you and me, they wouldn't have given up so fast." Yeah, but when Jayden and Hannah found her and Mina, they hadn't been hurt like Chris. *Mortally wounded* was what Hannah said about Chris, which was a fancy way of saying *hurt so bad I can't fix it*. But there *might* have been a chance. Chris could be really strong, or Hannah might be wrong. Not *trying* wasn't fair. Tom and Alex always tried. *They* would've fought . . .

"You know, Ellie, it really doesn't do you any good to think about this. You'll just get to feeling sorry for yourself and all." She let out an exasperated sigh. Why *was* she remembering Tom and Alex and her dad and Grandpa Jack so much today? It couldn't be the fishing. She fished all the time. "Yeah, but I miss them all the time," she said, mad that her nose was starting to itch again. Soon she'd be bawling like a little kid. Focus on the positive: that's what Grandpa Jack always said—and Hannah and Jayden and Isaac *were* nice.

"But they're not Alex." She veered for the left fork. "They're not T—"

By her side, Mina suddenly alerted with a soft but distinct *huff.*

Uh-oh. Caught in mid-stride, one boot above the snow, Ellie went absolutely still. In her chest, her heart slapped a fast fish-flop of alarm. Mina was looking not left but down the *right* fork. Not growling—a good sign—but her dog's ears were up, her body stiff. So that was not good. Not *bad.* Growling was bad because growling meant either unfamiliar adults, for whom she had no use, or people-eaters, for whom she had even less. *Wrong time of day for them anyway.* But something was spooking the dog. What?

From the sky came another harsh bray, and that was when she finally heard what it was that Mina had picked up. Heck, for all she knew, her horse had probably spooked early because Bella could hear what she hadn't. But now Ellie did: a sound like . . . *voices?* Lots of them, too, like a crowded school yard at recess, coming from somewhere down that right fork. She watched Mina listening. The dog was still alert but not growling. So . . . not dangerous? Probably no adults, anyway; no people. Not alive, anyway.

Then it dawned on her. "Oh boy," she said, and almost—*doh!*—smacked her forehead like Homer Simpson. The birds. The *crows.* That was why there were so many. Crows were scavengers, drawn to death. It was just like Jayden said: if you wanted to know where that poor wounded deer was, look for the crows. Made perfect sense.

Yeah, but do I want to go down there? Because now it was a choice, wasn't it? Someone would have to check this out. It would take her a good hour to dump her gear, slog back to her horse, then hoof it back to the farmhouse. She was here now. Someone had to put that poor deer out of its misery, and she should grow up already. Tom would do it. So would Alex.

Carefully squaring the auger across the mouth of her pail, she unlimbered her rifle and threw the bolt. At the sound, Mina's tail whisked in approval.

"Yeah, better safe than sorry. So, come on." Ellie gave her dog a pat. "Let's make it quick."

The walk wasn't terrible, although this wasn't Ellie's favorite trail or place in the universe. Within ten minutes, the chattering swelled and consolidated into caws and squawks. The racket was enormous, like on the mountain in the Waucamaw when Grandpa Jack died and her head seemed to explode. This time, though, instead of blackening the sky, glossy crows seethed and roiled in the trees.

Wow, something's got their attention. A cold finger ticked down the knobs of her spine. Something told her that this had to be more than birds waiting for something to die. But what could it be? She dropped her eyes to the snow. The last time she, Jayden, Hannah, and Eli had been down this trail was a week ago. In between, there'd been snow, and she saw where their tracks had filled.

And she also saw fresh tracks. People tracks.

Oh boy. One set was small. Not much bigger than hers, actually. *A kid?* Her hands tightened around her rifle. *A kid, a hurt kid?*

Or this might be the kind of kid she really didn't want to meet. *No, it can't be a people-eater. Mina would know; she always knows.* She checked the dog, who was still on alert but keeping pace. Again, not *alarmed* but definitely telling her that something wasn't quite right. The dog's attention was fixed straight ahead, and now Ellie looked that way, too—and heard herself pull in a hard gasp.

The clearing was small and dominated by a gray limestone building with a slate roof. Two windows were set on other side of a wood slider. A ramp ran down from the slider in a broad tongue.

The hex signs painted on the stone were kind of weird. Just below the eaves were five-pointed, bone-white stars that ran around the entire building, and that Hannah said were supposed to represent heaven. Above the double slider was a single high arch, outlined in black paint and filled in with purple. Within the arch were three evenly spaced blue triangles. The arch was supposed to be a false door—a *Devil's door*, Hannah said—designed to trick Satan into bumping his head.

There were other hexes, too: painted half-arches, done in the same design, above and below each window so if a witch tried to climb in, it would trip over what Isaac called a *witch's foot*.

With all those hex signs, at first glance you'd think *barn*. But that made no sense, because this building was *all* stone and really far out, way off by its lonesome in the woods and well away from fields and pasture. Neither Jayden nor Hannah had a clue as to the building's original purpose. When they first came across it, the structure had been totally empty.

To Ellie, though, those windows always looked like empty sockets with funky purple and blue eyelids. If she let her own eyes defocus a little, she could see the skull.

Which was kind of apt, considering what was inside.

Something, it seemed, had reached out and grabbed those crows, too, because there were hundreds. Birds lined the slate roof, clung to shingles, clutched the eaves. More crows swarmed over the snow or strutted up the ramp like soldiers. They oiled over the building in a heaving mass of bright eyes, gleaming feathers, and black beaks.

Crows knew where death lived, all right.

Because that gray skull building was where the bodies were.

22

Eight days after the mine went, at the very beginning of March, the crows came in big black thunderclouds. Tom knew what they meant. Hang around a war zone and you learned. Want to figure out where the bodies are? Look up.

A fact: the colder it is, the slower things decompose. But it's also true that a mine's deepest levels are very warm, even so hot that they're impossible to work without fans and ventilation. Evidently, the old Rule mine was just warm enough for people to start rotting, fill with gas, and bob to the surface of that new lake like so many human-skinned balloons.

The question was when to go. Cindi came every morning, so that was out. Afternoons were safest, but there were the lookouts to consider. He didn't want anyone, especially Cindi or Luke, to figure out what he was doing. They would try to stop him or insist on coming along, and he needed to be alone for this. So that left late afternoons. Time it just right, and he could ski it pretty fast, skirting the path that would put him in the lookouts' sights, and still have daylight to spare, although it would be well past dark when he got back.

When. Really, wasn't it more a question of *if* he came back? Ever? Or *never*? Because, in some ways, Tom was already gone, finished, used up. He had never been like this before either—not after Afghanistan, not after Jim. Not after he'd been shot and Harlan had taken Ellie. Not after Jed and Grace, when he'd thought, *Yes, kill all the enemy; no sweat*. Despite what he'd said to Luke, choosing life with no hope of seeing Alex again was only going through the motions. Putting one foot in front of the other until you couldn't walk anymore.

Regardless, one thing was crystal-clear. It stood to reason that she was up there, at that lake, with all the other dead.

And there was absolutely no way in hell Tom would let the crows have her.

He had taken the Long Walk before. In Afghanistan, the bomb suit was always a last resort, when robots wouldn't work or, as in his case, there were choices to be made in no-win scenarios. So he had walked, alone, toward death many times. Yet, somehow, this was even worse, the longest and loneliest walk of his life.

The lake was surreal: a logjam of partially decomposed bodies mired in ice and black with crows. From the looks of it, the Chuckies had believed in stocking up on rations for a rainy day. Or maybe it was just that there had been a lot of hungry little Chuckies in that chow line, and it was easier to take a quick trip down to the corral whenever you needed to rustle up a little grub. There were plenty of dead Chuckies, too, which were easy to distinguish from the other dead. Not only were the Chuckies all young, nothing—not even a crow—touched them.

Through binoculars, he glassed the lake, skipping his careful gaze from face to face. Paying him no mind, the birds jabbed at empty sockets, jackhammered bone, jumped from one hideously distended body to the next, as if playing a complicated game of hopscotch. One crow skidded to a landing on the icy bloat of a man's belly before working its way to a safer perch on the nub of the old guy's nose. The bird stabbed down and pried loose a flap of cheek with its beak. The frozen, greenish flesh came away with a tinkle that reminded Tom of crinkly cellophane.

Tom watched the crow work the meat into its mouth and down

its gullet. If that had been Alex, he'd have drawn down so fast with Jed's Bravo, that crow would've been a cloud of blasted feathers and red mist and in hell before it knew it was dead. *Or maybe I only wound the thing. Then grab it, rip it apart.* He could see that, too. As detailed as any flashback, the movie spun out in his mind: the bird struggling as Tom squeezed harder and harder until he felt the thready kick of its heart against his palms and now the crunch of bone. . . .

Only then, somehow, the movie shifted in his mind. Instead of a crow, now Tom had a boy by the neck and the boy was bucking and fighting, but Tom was riding him, strangling him, watching the boy's face turn purple, *killing* Chris Prentiss for what he'd done. This vision was so real, Tom could feel the frantic scratch and cut of Chris's nails over his hands.

You can't get away, Chris; I won't let you go. I'm strong and I will kill you, I will crush you, I will make you pay for what you did to her . . .

A deep moan worked its way from Tom's chest. God, killing Chris would feel *good*, it would feel *so good*, and, Jesus, he *wanted* that. This *need* to kill something was the claw of something new, scraping the cage of Tom's ribs, raging to be born.

But I can't let you out. Untangling his mind from the vision made the sweat pop on his upper lip. *Got to hang on.* Pressing a trembling hand to his chest, Tom felt for the two tags hanging from a beaded chain around his neck. One tag was Jed's from Vietnam; the other had belonged to his son, Michael, who'd died in Iraq. Tom gripped the dog tags the way his grandmother used to clutch a rosary. *Got to stop this. Can't let myself get* lost *in this thing.*

His tongue ached from where his teeth had sawed through flesh. He spat a coin of blood, watched it melt into snow stenciled in irregular stars from the birds. A lot of animals up this way, actually. His eyes drifted to some elongated, five-fingered splays that had to be raccoons, and then to a single deep trough scalloped from snow. Wolves, probably. They'd be heavy enough, and most packs went single file.

Crows, wolves, raccoons scavenging a meal. He swallowed against the rusty tang of his blood, then spat again. A lot of animals. His gaze skated over a smaller set of prints that looked almost like a dog's. *Foxes have been busy, too.* No wonder. All these bodies, the lake was practically a . . .

"A buffet," he whispered, and at that, his thoughts stuttered to a halt because he'd suddenly realized what kind of prints *weren't* there.

Wait a minute. Blowing the mine was like kicking over an anthill. While a whole lot of Chuckies had died, the rest had dispersed, presumably heading north toward Rule. There'd been no activity at the mine since. But he'd been in a war zone. Survivors always came back to salvage what they could. Yet *his* were the only human prints around the lake—which made no sense. All this free food and nothing to stop new Chuckies from moving in, or the old ones from drifting back. Except no one had.

So where the hell are they?

Hoisting himself onto a flat-topped boulder, he glassed the shore right and left. No human prints at all, that he could see. He turned his gaze directly west. The sun was already midway to the horizon, its thin light beginning to curdle to the color of a fresh blood clot. His eyes touched first the debris-littered flat before shifting to the ruined trees. The night the mine blew, Chuckies had come from that direction. In his mind, he replayed what he'd seen as the mine deteriorated beneath their feet: those boys, black as ants, lurching across the snowpack. Five came on foot, but two had been on skis. Eventually, the Chuckies had opened fire and driven him, Luke, and Weller from the rise. But what Tom hadn't given a lot of thought to was *why* those boys were headed this way in the first place. Why run *toward* a disaster? More to the point, what was up *here* that was nowhere else?

"Alex?" This was right; he could taste the tingle, feel the thrill work through his veins. "Jesus. You weren't interested in *us*. You came for *Alex*." That had to be it. Hundreds of tasty meals to choose from, but they came for Alex and *only* her. But how did they know? The whistle was *his* first clue, but he'd heard it *after* spotting the Chuckies, so it could only be . . .

"Smell?" The word came on a breath cloud. "You *smelled* her? Oh my God." Glassing the flat, he jumped his gaze over the snow, sweeping left to right, following the natural lie of the land and that flood of rubble. "You were on skis. You came up the rise. You came *right* for her; you didn't deviate, you didn't hesitate. So if you made it, if you were in time, if you were *prepared* because you *knew* where she was . . ." He was shaking, his thoughts tumbling like those numbered balls they used for a Powerball jackpot. "You go down, you get her, and then you book, fast as you can. Just point your skis, get yourself in the fall line, and bomb down—"

The words evaporated on his tongue as his gaze snagged on something spindly jutting from a small mountain of debris. A branch? No. Too straight. What *was* that?

"Oh God, oh God, oh please, please," he sang as he slowly feathered the focus. "Please, please, puh . . ." Something inarticulate, breathless, not quite a shout, jumped from his mouth. His heart gave a sudden hard knock he felt in his teeth. "Jesus," he gasped. "Oh Jesus."

Because there, fixed in the binocular's sights, was the black handle and wrist strap of a ski pole.

23

In winter, when someone died, there were three choices. You could bury the body, burn it, or store it. Burial was preferred; it was some religious thing for Hannah and Isaac. For Ellie, it was like, okay, whatever. But without backhoes, there was no way to dig deep enough for a proper grave until spring. A shallow grave was like an invitation to scavengers and—no one would say it, but they all thought it—maybe even the people-eaters, if they got desperate. Or if the people-eaters were like crows and would eat anything.

Cremation was a no-go. Isaac just wouldn't allow it. That religion thing again, or maybe it was his and Hannah's hex-y magic stuff . . . Ellie didn't know. The only bodies they ever burned were the people-eaters. But they hadn't crisped a single one since before Christmas because it was just too cold and Jayden thought the people-eaters had all gone south where the pickings were better.

Which left storage: a place where, in the deep freeze of the Upper Peninsula, bodies couldn't, wouldn't rot. No decay, no smell, no scavengers.

Yet now, at the death house, there were crows.

But I don't understand. Stunned, Ellie turned a cautious circle, sweeping her gaze from the ranks of crows on the death house's roof to the canopy overhead. The majority of trees here were hardwoods and barren of leaves, their bare branches lacing together in skeletal fingers. Some branches now were so weighed down with birds they bowed. *Where did they all come from? Why?* The sound those crows made was almost mechanical, like thousands of scissors snapping open and shut. Yet the birds didn't seem dangerous. Mina would've growled or barked or something. But Mina wasn't worried. She was only . . . interested.

"Well, I'm not," she said to the dog. This was way spooky. "We should go back. We should tell Jayden . . ." What? Gee, there were all these crows at the death house, and *she'd* been too pee-in-her-pants freaked out to take a look?

Alex wouldn't wuss out. She tightened her grip on her Savage. *Tom would go.*

"All right, come on, Mina. We can do this." Heart thumping, she eased down the path as her dog matched her step for step. Ahead, the birds milled, ebbing and flowing around the building like the waves of a ceaseless black sea. At the edge, where the snow effectively ran out and the crows began, she paused, then slid a boot forward six inches. The crows swirled away. She took another slow, sliding step and then another, as the birds first parted, then closed ranks after she and Mina passed. The effect was eerie, like skating through a pool of black mercury.

At the sliders, she paused. The doors weren't locked. Isaac and Hannah always said the hex signs were protection enough. But to get in meant that Ellie would have to use both hands, and she wasn't wild about letting go of her rifle.

"Don't let anything bad happen, girl," she said to Mina. Hooking the Savage's strap over her right shoulder, Ellie wrapped her hands around the wrought iron handle and heaved. The door let out a grudging squall, its iron wheels grating against metal; the death house exhaled icy air that smelled of burlap and pine tar. Nose crinkling against the strong odor of resin, Ellie glanced up to check the birds. In return, the crows cocked their heads, turning the black pearls of their eyes to Ellie as if for a better look. Suddenly afraid to stare at them for too long, she quickly dropped her gaze and stepped from the ramp into the building before she remembered, too late, that all the birds had to do now was surge in after her. But they didn't. Clacking and cawing, the crows rustled and bunched right up to the threshold. Yet not a single bird took wing or hopped to catch up and follow her in. Still, she slid the door closed, just to be on the safe side.

She waited a moment as her eyes adjusted to the sudden gloom. The interior was huge, almost a cave with those stone walls soaring to a ceiling of exposed beams of the same dark wood as the slider. Directly ahead and in the center were wooden pallets, stacked three deep and three high, the kind farmers normally used for hay.

Except now, they held bodies.

Ellie knew the routine. After a corpse was washed and rubbed with spice-scented oil, it was wrapped in a clean white sheet. Hannah always placed a small spell bag on the chest before sewing the body into burlap, on which she also painted a purple, five-pointed star. The corpse was then laid so the head, supported by a small pillow, faced east. The direction was important—some blah-blah about heaven and resurrection—but Ellie had tuned out. *Her* dad died *waaay* east of here and came home in the equivalent of a really tiny shoebox. She sure didn't see him coming back to life and walking through the door anytime soon. Okay, it was snarky. Still.

After the ruckus outside, the death house was so quiet Ellie heard her own liquid swallow. Far as she knew, nothing wrong here. Well, if you didn't count the bodies. Of the dead kids there, two were mauled by people-eaters. But that left five who'd been fed poison because they'd begun to turn. The next-to-last body was the old man with Chris, the one whose neck had been broken by that swinging mace.

"So, now what?" she whispered, because it didn't seem right to talk any louder. At the sound of her voice, Mina anxiously shifted her weight and then took a few hesitant steps toward the pallets. Her nails ticked on stone. Ellie thought maybe she should call Mina back but then thought, *Wait. See what she does.*

She expected her dog to snuffle each bag. But Mina didn't. Instead, the dog went to the foot of the last pallet—and the body there, all by its lonesome—before turning a look back at Ellie. *Well?* the dog's amber eyes seemed to ask. *Aren't you coming?*

Ellie wasn't aware that she *was* moving or had even *thought* about it until she felt the icy palm of stone on her knees as she knelt next to Mina. The dog wasn't really staring at the body so much as . . . well, *watching* it really, really carefully. *But looking for what?* Ellie let her eyes drift over the bulge of the head, then sweep down to that shelf of feet and toes. Nothing really to see. Her gaze crawled back to the slight tent of that purple star over the body's chest. She had no idea what the hex sign meant, or what Hannah put in those spell bags—

In the next second, her thoughts whited out as Ellie finally *did* see something that shouldn't, couldn't be.

When the star over the chest . . . moved.

24

Tom had no true memory of moving. But he must have, and very fast, switching from skis to snowshoes and scuffing down in long, sweeping strides to wallow through snow, over rocks, and around broken trees, because there was a jump in time, a bizarre stutter step like the hitch of a damaged DVD, and then he was on his knees, at the ski pole. His daypack and Jed's Bravo were now on the snow, and he was chopping icy rubble with his KA-BAR. His breath came in harsh, sobbing pants as he stabbed, working his blade to expose a silvered fiberglass spear speckled with a stencil of cheery white snowflakes. When he'd sliced enough away, he slipped his knife back into his leg sheath, then wrapped both hands around the plastic grip and gave a quick yank. The pole popped free. The touring basket was gone, but the hard metal tip was still intact. From the length, he thought it must've been used by a boy, or a tall girl.

It has to be one of theirs. Sweat lathered his cheeks and trickled down his chest. Craning a look over his shoulder, he eyed the swell of land behind. He was in the fall line, and so was the pole. That meant one of three things. In the worst-case scenario, the pole was swept down here while its owner had still been on the rise. In the best case, the owner made his skis and outran the avalanche but lost the pole somewhere along the way.

And then there's the somewhere-in-between. He swept his eyes over the flats, hunting for the telltale jut of a broken ski, maybe even another pole. *He's bombing down on his skis, surfing over snow, but then the avalanche trips him up—*

That thought skipped to a halt as his brain registered something protruding from the snow perhaps six feet and change to his right: a small brown hump, easy to miss because it looked so much like a pebble.

Except it wasn't. The sun was low enough now that the light on the sparkling snow was ruddy, the color of new blood. He knew, exactly, what that brown lump was.

A boot. Tom's breath gnarled in his chest. *It's the toe of a boot, that's a boot, it's . . .*

"No, no! Alex, *Alex!*" Tearing off his gloves, he jammed his fingers through a thin layer of crackling ice even as his mind screamed that this couldn't be her; that was insane. But here was the pole, and now there was a boot, and they came for her, and so this *could* be her, *might* be, and he had to get her out, get her out get her out *get her out!* Frantic, he clawed at the snow. In a few moments, the laces appeared, and then a thin rime of blue wool sock. The cup of her heel was solidly wedged in the deep cleft of two large boulders, and he could tell that she'd come to rest at an angle, her head lower than her boots.

Unless it wasn't Alex. Wasn't that boot too big? And the ankle . . . *Thick, too large, but maybe that's only the sock and the angle and . . .*

"No, it's you, it's you, it has to be you, I know it. Oh God, Alex, Alex," he said, driving his hands into the snow up to the elbows. His fingers closed around something stiff, wooden. A leg, and it was her right; he knew that from the boot. There was a body here, and it was Alex; she was down there; he knew it.

Unless . . . A great black swell of horror churned in his chest. Unless this leg was *all* he would find. Anything powerful enough to crater a rise and drive a monstrous sweep of snow and rock and trees would have no trouble leaving a person in pieces, snapping bones as easily as brittle twigs, strewing a leg here, an arm there.

Straddling where he thought her body must be, he began to pis-
ton his fists through the snow, driving them like jackhammers. He
didn't dare use the KA-BAR. What if he hurt her, cut her? The snow
broke apart in chunks, compacted not only by pressure built up by
the avalanche's momentum but its own weight. There were rocks
here, too, that he wrenched free and heaved aside. He couldn't stop,
he wouldn't, but oh God, he wanted to stop. He knew he should.

*I have to know, I don't want to know . . . This can't be her, because if it
is, there'll be nothing left for me after this.*

But he *had* to see, he had to *know.* He dug, heaving out blocks of
snow, unearthing this tomb hewn of ice and rock. The curve of her
hips, just the barest suggestion, appeared, and then the outline of a
torso encased in a frozen balloon: a moss-green parka, swollen with
snow, rucked up her sides. He gave this a cursory swipe and kept
going. Later, yes, later, he would free her completely, but now he had
to see her, find her face, her face, her face. . . . He plowed through
snow, smashing and breaking and scratching his way up to the humps
of her shoulders and then her neck, shouting like a crazy person:
"Alex Alex Alex Alex *Alex?*"

At last—it seemed like an age; it went by in a minute—all that
separated them was a thin veil of snow and ice. And that was when
he paused.

I don't want to see this. A deep, hard shudder worked through his
bones. Tiny red pinpricks from his torn hands dotted the snow like
candy sprinkles. He'd seen buddies like this, cocooned in yards of
bandages into rough, anonymous mummies. Trying to find their
faces was always the worst. Sometimes the location of the blood
helped, huge blotchy patches of rust leaking over gauze to mark
where something wasn't. But the very, very worst moments came
when what he stared at was a blank: no peak of a nose, no broad
expanse of a forehead, or even valleys where the eyes might be. The
worst was when there was nothing at all.

This was like that, as if Tom were poised over a satin-lined casket, looking down at a body so brutalized, so utterly destroyed, that the undertaker had draped gauzy linen over the face as a final kindness, an act of mercy.

Please, God, it can't be her. I need it to be, but I won't be able to stand it if it is.

"Oh, Alex," he said, and used the side of his hand, as gently as he possibly could, to sweep the last of that ice-shroud from her face.

Five stunned seconds later, he began to scream.

25

"Aahh!" Screaming, Ellie flung her arms like Wile E. Coyote just figuring out that he's run off the cliff. Her Savage clattered against stone. Mina yipped as Ellie tumbled from her knees to her butt. Frantic, she crabbed back. She could feel her mouth hanging open, her eyes bugging from their sockets, the next scream boiling its way up from her stomach.

That was it; she was getting out of here. The crows, this creepy room full of dead people, a bag that *moved* . . . Probably a mouse or a rat or something in there, eating the body's eyes or tongue or—

But there are no mouse turds, a small voice from somewhere in the more reasonable part of her mind said. *There are no holes in the burlap.*

"So it's a s-s-small h-hole," she said.

It's cold, the voice said, patiently. *The bodies are frozen, remember? They can't rot. They don't smell.*

"Yeah, but then why are the crows here?" This was stupid; she was arguing with herself. But hearing her own voice made her feel better, too, more in control. "Because they must *not* be frozen, right?"

That could be. Unless crows also mean something else, the voice suggested.

"What?" Ellie frowned. How could crows be anything more than what they were? She was about to ask the voice what the heck it was talking about when she thought, *You dummy, you're talking to you. So what do you think you mean?* She had absolutely no idea, and the voice sure wasn't saying. From her place by the pallet, Mina was looking at her with a perplexed expression, as if wondering what all the fuss was about.

The star moved, didn't it? Could she be wrong? Ellie squeezed her eyes tight enough to see fireflies flitting across the dark. *Maybe it was a cloud or something.* The fact that there was no blue sky and no possibility of a cloud was . . . well, that didn't matter.

Oh, come on, you big baby. Opening her eyes again, Ellie gave her head an angry shake. *You walked through crows. You opened the stupid door. So why bother if you're going to be a little girl about it?*

She retrieved her rifle, her hands shaking very badly. She balled them tight, squeezing out the fear. Her legs felt wobbly, like overdone noodles, so she hitched over to the pallet on hands and knees, thinking over and over again, a little like a prayer, *Tom could do this; Alex would do this; Tom could do this; Alex would* . . . But she kept her eyes on the floor the whole way, not daring to look at the body, that burlap bag—not just yet. Instead, she let her head butt Mina's shoulder just ever so slightly, the way Mina sometimes nuzzled her palm when she wanted a pat. Her dog snuffled at her neck, then dragged a warm, reassuring tongue over her cheek as if to say, *Hey, it's okay, Ellie; we're all entitled to a freak-out every now and then.*

"Yeah." Burying her face in Mina's shoulder, she slid her arms around the dog's neck. Then she blew out and turned her eyes back to the pallet. The purple star was still. So was the burlap bag. No big, bad boogeyman. Just a dead person in there, a people-sicle.

The little voice was suddenly back: *Yes, but what about the birds, and Mina—*

"Oh, be quiet." It had been a shadow. Her imagination. For a second, she felt an absurd disappointment, as if her panic had been just a beginning emotion, something you had to get out of the way first before getting down to the real feelings. Like when your Grandpa Jack took you home and didn't tell you about your daddy, who you thought was in Iraq and not due back for two months. But then you opened the door and there was your dad, and Grandpa's yelling, *Surprise!* But you, you're so *stunned* that you have to reach to touch your daddy's cheek—

"To make sure you're not dreaming. To make sure he's real." Her voice was thick. She was crying again, and how stupid was that? *Why can't anything good ever happen?* Still weeping and without understanding why, she laid her hand over the star and the tiny bulge of the spell bag just beneath. The body was still, but . . .

No. Blinking, her tears suddenly drying up, she took her hand back and turned it over to inspect her palm like a fortune-teller studying a lifeline. *No, that can't be right.*

Well, the little mind-voice said, *you could* check *one of the others. Then compare, right?*

"This is dumb." But her right knee crick-crackled in the hush as she rose and sidestepped to another body in the row just above: Travis, dead—well, *put out of his misery,* as Hannah liked to say—only a month ago. Ellie feathered her palm over that tent of burlap and the spell bag beneath. The hex star's purple paint was riddled with thin fissures, like a dried-up creek bed. Travis was still. But Travis was also very, very cold. Cold as the stone, as the snow. As ice. So was Rudy, one body over, and Mrs. Rehymeyer two rows up.

They're all cold. Returning to the last and freshest body, she eased her hand over the star. *They're ice cubes. But* this one is—

"Warm." A lance of shock stabbed her chest. "You're *warm.*" Not *blazing* hot or feverish, or even normal-warm like her. But the difference between this body and the others . . . *This is real.* She watched her fingers walk the hills and ridges of ribs, reading the chest like a blind person. Lower down, just below that last rib, she traced the bit of wound wood—a piece of an ash tree prepared in some weird Amish magic way—that Hannah had placed over the rip where that killing spike had driven through. *I really feel this.*

Her hand drifted back to the star. Now that she was allowing herself to linger, to concentrate, she detected a very light but very distinct flutter, like the flip of a goldfish in a too-large bowl. Hannah said that when you took a pulse, you had to be careful not to mistake your heartbeat for the other person's. So Ellie pressed her hand just a little more firmly against the body's chest. The fish-flutter nudged her palm again, but stronger now, as if the spell bag was a heart struggling to fill with blood.

"Oh!" Gasping, Ellie jerked away again and saw that it was . . . the star was . . . "Moving," she whispered. "You're really *moving.*" The words came out sounding too ordinary, but there was no mistake. The hex sign *heaved* and *rolled*: not the up-and-down, in-with-the-good, out-with-the-bad of a breath but the slow roll of a wave, like there was something eeling along under there. *Animal.* She could feel her mind snatch at the idea. A mouse or even a snake, and no, don't bother her with little details like snakes didn't come out when it was *freezing.* There had to be an animal in there. It was the only explanation that made sense.

But the body's warm, Ellie, the little voice said. *It's not frozen or ice-cold, it's—*

Ellie lost track of what the closet-voice said next.

Because from that burlap shroud came a low moan.

26

It wasn't Alex.

A boy stared up at Tom. Stared *through* him and beyond, into the red socket of that dying sky. If a look had a sound, this boy's was silence. The kid's eyes were vacant, their color as flat and murky as stones in deep water, and so still. Nearly bleached of color, the boy's face was frozen in a death mask, a bloodless, gaping scream. Or maybe he'd only been choking to death on that ball of ice, jammed in his mouth like an apple in a roast pig, or suffocating because of the snow plugging both nostrils.

"*Nooooo,*" Tom groaned. A weird palsy shook him to the bone. In a saner moment, he might have been glad it wasn't Alex. Every second he didn't find her—entombed in ice, torn apart under the snow, broken to bits among the rocks—was one more moment when she still might be alive. Those Chuckies had had the time. They'd reached her, stolen her from him, spirited her away. But for him, this was the rise all over again, the feeling of the earth swelling and heaving and breaking, and then he was gasping, shuddering, staring down through streaming eyes at that dead boy, the bright flare in his chest exploding in a scream: "God, *why*? What are you doing, what are you doing, what are you *doing*?"

His vision purpled. He didn't remember picking up the rock, which, he saw later, was jagged and long as an ax head, completely right for the job. But time shrieked to a halt, stuttered . . .

And when he came back, it was to sounds, raw and crisp and glassy: the boy's frozen flesh breaking, the face and skull shattering and splintering to bits. Or maybe that was only Tom's mind finally blasting apart; the black thing inside cracking him wide, wide open to be birthed on a bellow of agony and grief.

"No, God, no, no, *no!*" On his knees, rearing up, his arms hurtling down, the rock-hatchet cleaving air with a whistle, as he smashed and hit and *hit* and *destroyed*: "Fuck you, fuck you, *fuck you!*"

Why did he stop? Hell if he knew. But that burst of manic energy suddenly drained away; all his muscles went wobbly and weak, and he couldn't hold on anymore. The rock tumbled from his fingers, and then he was falling back, his lungs working, the sweat running in rivers down his face and neck and over his chest. God, he was burning up. Pawing at his parka, he finally managed to drag down the zipper and flop his way free of that tangled embrace.

Of course it wasn't Alex. *You* knew *it was a boy's boot; look at the ankle, look at the size, you idiot—how could you miss that?* "Because," he choked, pulling in icy air that slashed his lungs, "you want it to be her, Tom; you don't want it to be her, but you want it, you need it, you need her, and oh God, oh God . . ."

His maddened eyes skated over the rest; saw now the hips that were much too narrow. *And the hands, look at the hands, the* hands! He'd skimmed right over the large knuckles. Snugged on the right hip, just below where the parka had ridden up, was a holster with a real cannon he'd recognize anywhere: Desert Eagle .50AE, a huge weapon for a Chucky with big hands.

"I am losing my mind." Groaning, he rolled to his belly and grabbed the snow, the white blushing to pink as he dragged himself from the wreck he'd made of that boy's head. When he just couldn't keep on, he stopped, let himself sink. His head was pulsing, the pressure pushing at the limits of his skull. Clamping his bruised, bloodied fingers to his temples, he *squeezed*. Under his belly, he could feel the earth opening, as welcoming as a grave; the snow melting, bleeding to water, stealing his heat. Above, the fickle wind streamed down from the lake, licking sweat from his neck, his shoulder blades, and wicking the wet from his hair and scalp so that he shivered. His breath came in sobs, and the taste of snow on his tongue was bitter, like gunmetal.

Just lie here and let go. Lie here long enough so you fall asleep, pass out, freeze to death. Or take the damn shot, you coward. One shot, and then you can just let go of all this. Not with the Bravo, though; it wouldn't be right to use Jed's weapon for that. The dead Chucky had that Eagle, though—a real monster. Yes, but the gun had been buried under snow. *Mechanism's probably frozen. With my luck, it'll explode in my hand.*

So, not the Eagle either—and not here. Someone from camp would eventually wonder and come looking, sooner rather than later. Cindi, most likely, and she'd bring Luke. Even with the crows and other scavengers, it would take time to pick him down to bone. He couldn't do that to any kid. It wouldn't be right. Moaning, he craned up from the snow as the wind sighed past his right cheek. He was turned halfway around and was now facing northwest, the dead Chucky at his two o'clock, the blighted woods at nine. Bolts of light, laser-bright, burned tears, and he winced, instinctively raising a hand. *I don't even know what living feels like any—*

He blinked.

Maybe it was the angle and the fact that he was low on the snow and facing a different direction. Or maybe he'd been so focused on that ski pole and then the boot, and seen only what he wanted instead of what had been in front of his nose all along.

Another gun.

No. He didn't believe it. *Can't be. It's a trick. I'm seeing things.* He armed his streaming eyes. That portion of the snowfield was incredibly chewed up, pocked with stones and potholes. When he really stopped to consider, the snow was also piled very strangely in a few places, as if someone had dug down into the snow. As if someone had been searching for something.

But the shape remained, crisp and unmistakable. What his vision sharpened on was a gun, jammed bore-first into the snow.

That was surprise enough. But he got the shock of his life after staggering over, his boots stubbing on hidden rocks and debris that kept trying to trip him up. Enough of the weapon was visible for him to know the make well before he dropped to his knees and parsed out the words *Austria* and *19* stenciled on the barrel.

It was a Glock.

27

Ellie didn't stop to think. When she looked back at it later, she didn't remember how the knife even got into her hand. But in the next second there was a wink of steel, the *snick* as the Leek's blade socked home, and then she'd grabbed burlap and begun working the point of the knife through the tight weave, sawing as fast as she could. *Careful, careful.* She made a hole just big enough for her hands, then put aside the knife, hooked her fingers on either side, and pulled. There was a loud *riiip* as the burlap tore in two.

Spiced air spilled out. Seated over the chest, the red spell bag, no bigger than her fist, quivered like a heart trying to remember how to beat. The body was completely cocooned in that white sheet . . . except the material wasn't strictly white anymore. Tiny ruby spiders were spreading their legs over the fabric swathing the thighs and chest, that right side.

Fresh blood. Bleeding . . . She stared, spellbound, her horror slipping into a kind of awe. *How can there be bleeding?*

And then the chest . . . *rose.*

"Ah!" She let out a mousy squeak. The body was starting to rock and shiver as it fought against the sheet like a butterfly too weak to battle its way out of its cocoon. *I have to help, I have to do something!*

But wait, did she? It . . . *he* was alive or coming back to life . . . and that was *nuts.* She'd never seen any of the *Mummy* movies, but isn't this how bad things went down? Stupid person stumbles into a cave or tomb or something, and finds a stone coffin and thinks, *Whoa, I think we'll just open this puppy and see what's what.*

"And then the stupid person gets killed," she whispered. Or the mummy ate his tongue and ripped out his eyes or something. For a split second, she thought, *Run, run fast, just go!* Leave and roll the slider back into place and shut up the death house and stick her fingers in her ears—*la-la-la-la, I can't hear you*—and pretend she hadn't seen a darned thing. No one would ever know. Of course, when they came back at the spring thaw to bury the bodies, they'd notice that the burlap was all torn up. They'd see the blood. But *she* didn't have to fess up. Because here was the thing: how did *she* know that *this* wasn't what happened to some kids when they became people-eaters? Not everyone was done turning, or turned in the same way. So what if? What if the *second* she ripped open that sheet, that person—who might not be a person anymore—*grabbed* her and . . .

By her side, Mina pawed at her shoulder and let out an anxious whimper.

Listen to Mina, the little voice from deep in the closet of her mind said. *She would know if this is trouble. Come on, you've got to do something, Ellie, and you've got to do it quick, or he'll die.*

"But he's already dead," she said, only meekly, the way you offered an answer in class you weren't quite sure of. *Unless he really isn't. It could've been a mistake. Hannah doesn't know everything.* And that calmed her down, enough to stop her thoughts from skittering out of control like boots on slick ice. *Mina knows it's okay. She wants me to help. Mina always knows.*

The heck with it. Swallowing back her heart, she patted her hands over the dome of his head. Of all the places she could cut, this was probably the best way not to hurt him. *Not* hurt *him?* She tented up a handful of sheet, stabbed with her knife, worked a horizontal slit. *He's dead, or he was dead . . .*

She could hear him now: a low, muffled groaning that went on and on. Through the slit she'd made, Ellie could see black hair and now the broad plain of his forehead. Slipping in her fingers, she jerked the cotton sheet hard, grunting as the fabric first resisted then gave. His face appeared. His skin was very white, almost like a grub's. Bluish-gray smudges brushed the hollow beneath his eyes, which were still closed. His lips were dusky blue, like dead worms after a bad rain. His mouth was open, and he was gasping, his chest heaving against the sheet, the wiry cords standing in his neck.

"Chris! Chris!" She was crying again, ripping the sheet apart and crying, screaming his name. He was naked—as in no clothes at all, a fact her mind only dimly registered, like the flicker of something you passed on the road in a really fast car. His chest strained to suck in air. She could see the way the skin actually bowed between his ribs.

But what really riveted her to the spot, made her actually start back with a little shriek, was the blood: scarlet roses unfurling where Hannah had placed the wound wood after blessing it.

That can't work. She saw that the wounds weren't raw or ragged anymore either but dimpled with half-formed scar tissue. *It's just a charm, it's only wood.*

Chris was shuddering, all over, as if he'd stuck his finger into an electrical socket. She battled the sheet away from his hips and then his jittering legs. Chris had many injuries: nicks and smaller rips, a gash on each palm, punctures in his thighs. The killing blow, the real monster rip that sealed the deal, drove straight down, a through-and-through that had shredded first his diaphragm, which Hannah said helped you breathe, and then his liver, which was nothing more than a big bloody sac, easily torn by a broken rib. Or, in Chris's case, obliterated by the weight of the door and that iron spike. No way to stop the bleeding either, not from something this bad. Chris had lasted as long as he had only because he was young and strong.

But now there's blood. That terrible wound glistened like the red eye of a loon in high summer—and yet there was also a rim of very pink flesh, like the new skin of a baby. *It's all just voodoo; there's no such thing as magic, there's no such thing.*

"Chris!" Ellie grabbed his face and realized with a shock that as he got more air, his skin was growing even warmer, his cheeks going hectic with fresh color. "Chris, can you hear me? Are you—"

All at once, his eyes flew open. At the same instant, Chris's hands shot out, fanning a thin spray of new blood, and hooked her shoulders. It happened so fast her shriek was only halfway to her mouth when he spoke.

"*Help.*" The word rode on a ferocious gasp. Chris's eyes, the centers black and huge, bored into hers—and for Ellie, it was like staring into the mouth of nothing and everything at once.

"P-please," he gasped again. "*H-help* me."

28

Tom might have been a couple cans shy of a six-pack right about then, but he knew the gun wasn't hers. No cross-trigger safety, for one thing, and Alex's had been a Glock 22, standard police issue with a fifteen-round mag. Besides, Alex had been a prisoner. No way the Chuckies would let her keep her father's weapon.

This gun was smaller, a Glock 19, but with an extended magazine. He eyeballed it as nineteen rounds altogether. Yet he had no way of checking for sure, or even jacking back the slide to shuck a chambered round. A thin scrim of ice coated the weapon, like the petrified sugar glaze over a stale doughnut.

It got wet. His own battered hands were stiff with cold, and he was starting to shiver all over. Wincing, he clamped his right hand under his left arm to warm it as he lurched back to the dead Chucky. Bracing his butt against boulders, he shrugged back into his parka, but his torn hands were shaking so badly he couldn't work the zipper and finally gave up. Had to warm his hands first. Fumbling up his gloves, he studied the rise directly east. No question about it: that Glock was in the fall line, either carried here all by itself or stripped from its owner as the avalanche roared downslope. So . . . this Glock had belonged to a Chucky? That stood to reason. There had been seven plowing up the rise, and he'd already found one. The Chuckies had only just breached the hillside when Luke and Weller forced him to leave. So, prepared or not, unless you were a real monkey or a trained Army Ranger like Weller and knew your way around ropes and rocks, reaching Alex would have taken precious time the Chuckies might not have had to spare. So wasn't it much more likely that *none* had survived, and other dead waited, entombed under his feet? Of course. He'd found a ski pole. That dead kid had an Eagle and now here was a Glock. Probably rifles under the snow and skis and all sorts of goodies. Only time and the spring melt would tell, unless he came back with a shovel and excavated the entire flat. A futile effort. He knew that. Didn't mean he wouldn't do it, but . . .

The ice. He slid a thumb over the Glock's grip, felt the smooth glide of his glove. Spied a tiny frozen teardrop hanging from the trigger's tip. *The ice is wrong.*

Squatting over the Chucky, he laboriously worked the Eagle from its hip holster. To his utter lack of surprise, the massive gun was locked up tight; he couldn't budge even the safety. "But there's no ice *on it*," he muttered, hefting the Eagle, a heavy sucker, in his left hand. So the gun probably hadn't gotten sopping wet. "What the hell does that mean?"

Before the avalanche, the water had been belowground, *in* the mine, and rising. There was plenty of ice now, not only a skin of it over the new lake itself but also frozen into beards over the rocks along the shore. But the only ice down *here* was a brittle surface crust, and what you'd expect from snow exposed to sun and wind.

Laying the Eagle on the dead boy's stomach but still clutching the Glock, he pushed up on his thighs. No ice on the Eagle meant no water, nothing to explain how the Glock got wet. *Unless Alex got her hands on a weapon.* The thought was a golden blaze, and crazy, too, just another loony-tunes item in a long afternoon of insanity, but he couldn't help it. *That would explain it, because that would mean . . .*

"Oh Jesus." He felt a knot loosening in his chest. His eyes sprang hot. *Hold it together. Don't get ahead of yourself.* But it *might* have been hers, right? Alex had been in that tunnel, working her way to the surface. If anyone could've found a way to get a weapon, it would be Alex, and what if, what if . . .

"Alex." Closing his eyes, he folded his hands, pressing the weapon to the hard thrum of his heart. "Alex, oh God, did you make it? Did you get out?" *Or did they take you? Is that how you lost the gun?* He hated that thought because then, more likely than not, she really *was* here, now, beneath the snow, waiting for him to find her.

The only answers he got were virtually none at all: only that wind, laced with decay, sighing down from the lake.

And then, a minute grate of stone at his back. Just a *tick*, to his left. Say . . . eight o'clock. A tiny *tock* as rock butted rock, a sound that did not belong but that he heard even past the pulse and pound of his rampaging blood because, after all this time, he was still a soldier. So he knew.

Something was storming over the snow, and coming fast.

29

She had to get him out of here, and fast. But how? Thrusting her bare hands under her armpits, Ellie winced against the sting. Now that her initial burst of shock had dribbled away, she was starting to feel the cold. Shucking out of her coat, she'd draped that over his chest, then stripped burlap from all the other bodies and piled the shrouds over Chris to keep him as warm as she could. On the pallet and under his burlap blankets, Chris was quiet now, eyes closed again, but he was panting, his breath chuffing in wavering gray clouds.

There were really only two things she could do: leave Chris and ride for help, or take him back herself. The first was easiest. Leave Mina to guard him, race back to Bella, and gallop all the way to the farmhouse. Maybe an hour, and maybe a lot less if she got poky old Bella to really book.

But there was also the issue of time, and her reluctance to let him out of her sight. She cast an anxious eye at the windows. She could tell from the gray cast of the sky that what had been early afternoon was now slipping well into late. They might be lucky enough to make it here before dark, but they'd be working their way back at night. It was also true that they'd spotted no people-eaters in weeks this far north. Chris and that old guy he'd been with, the one clobbered by the mace, had tripped booby traps that hadn't seen action in a good two months.

So I need to take him. Ellie chewed the inside of her cheek. She realized that her eyes had fixed on his chest, noting every struggling breath, holding her own until the burlap rose again. She knew she expected every breath to be his last, like in the movies. A final dramatic gasp and then bye-bye. *Got to get him onto my horse somehow.* But Chris was too heavy to lift. Her eyes roamed the deepening shadows of the bare rafters. Even if she could find a rope and tie it around his chest or something *and* figure out a way of slinging the rope over a beam, she wasn't strong enough to hoist him two inches. Could she drag him? That might work. Just roll him off the pallets, watch that his head didn't go *bump-thump* on the stone, then drag him the way you hauled a little kid up the hill on a sled. Chris would be much heavier, of course, but she'd only have to manage twenty, thirty feet. She was much stronger now than back in October when all the bad stuff started. She rode horses, she walked for miles, she hauled augers and tackle, and she handled her Savage without too much trouble. So she could do this. But getting him onto her horse was a different problem.

And what about the birds? *Will they let him leave?* Cocking her head, she listened and then picked up their mechanical chatter. Still out there. They hadn't bothered her, but maybe that was as far as this went. The birds might be—she didn't know—a sign or something, like the way Alex once said you could tell if a storm was coming when the animals got really quiet.

"I can't do nothing," she said to Mina, who leaned against her leg. Her chilled fingers buried themselves in the fur behind the dog's ears. "I have to keep him warm *and* get him out."

What if she stayed? The others would come looking, and probably soon. They would know where to go. Bella was tethered at the fork. So she could stay put, keep Chris warm. But she might also be waiting a long time. No one would worry for another hour, maybe even an hour and a half. She could hear Eli now: *Oh, you know how Ellie is once she gets fishing; she can sit out there forever.*

Beneath the burlap, Chris let out another long moan. She was across the room in an instant, dropping to her knees to study his face. Through the crescent moons of his lids, she could see his eyes roaming. Chris was dreaming, and pretty badly, too. Deep, dark lines of fear and pain cut alongside his nose and across his forehead. Maybe a nightmare. Or maybe he was dreaming about being dead, which was probably just as bad.

She stood and patted the pallet. "Mina, come." The dog obediently jumped up, careful not to step on Chris. Mina turned an expectant look, but Ellie shook her head, placed a hand on the dog's neck, and maneuvered the animal as close to Chris as she could manage. "Just you," she said, applying a bit of pressure to get her meaning across. "Down, girl, lie down. I need you to keep him warm." *And protect him until I get back.* Mina wasn't as big as a shepherd, but lying at full length her body heat ought to help. "Stay," Ellie said, and put her hand up like a traffic cop. With a soft whine, Mina stretched her neck and nosed Ellie's fingers.

"Love you, too, girl," Ellie said, and planted a big kiss between Mina's ears. She turned to go, then hesitated. Reeling out a length of leather cord, she ran a finger over the lines of that upside-down peace sign. *For protection,* Hannah said. Kneeling, Ellie gently slipped the cord over Chris's head. He was a boy, almost a man, and his neck was bigger, so the cord was snugger, the charm only reaching to the pulsing hollow of his throat.

And then—don't ask her why—she kissed him, too. Just a touch of her lips to his forehead, the way her daddy used to: *Love you, kiddo.*

"For luck," she said.

30

Dumb luck, that's what it was. With the *tick* of that rock, Tom's training snapped into place, his reaction as instinctual as breathing: a quick shift of his weight, a backhanded swipe with his left as he spun, the Glock slashing up and around on a steep trajectory because he was aiming for a chin, a cheek.

He missed. Hell, he couldn't even see what he was trying to hit. The Chucky had put itself in a direct line with the setting sun and was coming for him at his blind spot to boot. All Tom made out was a gray-white blur and two dark coins as the Chucky read his move and dropped below the arc of his swing. Tom went into a staggering spin, his momentum pulling him off-balance as the Glock whirred through empty air. In the next second, the Chucky drove in low and hard, plowing into Tom's back, wrapping him up, pushing him into a blundering swan dive.

"Ugh!" Tom felt the air gun out of his throat. His arms shot out to break his fall, and he thought, *Roll; plant your fist and roll, get on your side!* If he hit face-first, it would be over, fast. He could see his end: the Chucky straddling his back, riding him, grinding his face into the deadening snow, holding him there until he suffocated. Or maybe the Chucky planned to simply dump him on his ass. One good slam of a fist to stun him and then Tom would spend his last thirty seconds on earth with his hands wrapped around the spurting rip in his throat as his blood pulsed hot and wet, and the Chucky watched and waited for Tom's veins to run dry. *Roll, go to roll, ro—*

He tried; he really did. But two things happened in quick succession, like a one-two punch. The first was the jolt of his right boot on a hidden rock. Tom stumbled, his right leg crimping at the knee. The Chucky had him so low around the waist that the little stutter should've been enough for it to set its feet and drive Tom's chest the rest of the way down. But Tom *was* trying to roll, and while this Chucky was good—and it was *very* good; it knew how to anticipate, how to fight—Tom still clutched the Glock in his left hand.

The gun, *her* gun, saved his life, not because he could shoot or use it as a club but because his hand was fisted in a death grip, and a rigid fist is stronger than an open, empty hand.

Tom's left arm speared the snow. His fist held; his elbow didn't crumple and his wrist didn't break. It hurt like hell; electric jags of pain jittered through bone. Grunting, Tom willed his arms to remain ramrod straight, rigid as pipes. For one split second, Tom was holding both himself and the Chucky on his shuddering arms, his heaving chest hanging a foot from the snow.

Then the moment slipped past and Tom was gathering himself, thinking, *I've got one shot.*

Jackknifing his left knee to his chest, he twisted, cranked his left hip, then drove his leg back as hard and fast as he could, putting all his strength into a single, vicious kick. He felt when his boot made contact, the jar of it in his hip; understood from the give that he'd struck the Chucky's left thigh, high above the knee.

It was a perfect, incredibly lucky shot. Howling, the Chucky crumpled left. Shifting his weight, Tom squirted right, pushing off with his stronger, left leg, fighting against the suck of deep snow as he spun free.

And he still had the Glock. In another time and place, he might have pitched it. The weapon was useless as anything other than a club, while fingers could clutch and claw and gouge eyes. But if the gun got away from him—say, the Chucky made a grab—with enough pressure on that frozen trigger, the weapon might just fire. Tom couldn't take the chance. On the other hand, if he threw it away, the Chucky might go after it. In a way, letting the Chucky try would be smart, a way of diverting its attention so Tom had time to strike with his KA-BAR. After all, a knife didn't run out of bullets.

But he couldn't do it, couldn't make himself let go of the Glock. That gun had just saved his life. It was an omen, a sign, as if Alex was fighting by his side. He could feel her in the tang of adrenaline on his tongue, the blood that roared through his veins. So he hung on to that weapon—and her—as he tugged his knife from its sheath.

All right, come on. His gaze strafed the rubble-choked flat. For a disorienting moment, he thought the Chucky was gone. It was possible. A peroneal strike, one that caught the nerve above the knee, could incapacitate an enemy anywhere from half a minute to five. Maybe it knew it didn't stand a chance, or spooked easily. But God, if it *was* gone and got help, brought friends—worse, if that Chucky's buddies were already *here*—he might as well slit his own throat and save them the trouble. He probably could take two or three, but without a decent weapon . . .

Wait, the Bravo. But it was behind him, by his pack and that ski pole, and he just didn't want to risk a peek. Besides, he simply didn't believe the Chucky could've moved *that* fast. *So where is it?* Frantic, the panic starting to climb his spine, he jumped his gaze west, toward the woods. There was still a good hour before it was full dark and plenty of ruby light left, but long shadows now blued the snow. Still . . . at the edge of those cantilevered trees, he was certain something moved. *Someone else out there?*

A shushing sound, to his right, and then a small squeal, the sound of icy snow squeezed by pressure. As he wheeled around, he realized just how lucky he was to still be alive.

The Chucky had been there on the snow, recovering, silently

gathering itself, all along. Now it was clawing to its feet, but in his fear and disorientation, it looked to Tom as if the snow itself had assumed human form. The Chucky's camo over-whites were the best he'd ever seen. Even the boots were sheathed in white. Somewhere along the way, though, the Chucky had lost its white balaclava. So instead of only the dark coins of its eyes—which were *strange*—he saw its lips skin back in a snarl, and that brown snake of a braid.

Because *it* was a *she*: about the same age as Alex, but much taller and more muscular. He still outweighed this girl, but his height advantage was gone, and she was fast, a good fighter.

And yes, he had a knife.

But the Chucky had two.

31

Well, the crows didn't come at her. Instead, they oiled out of Ellie's way as they had before. Once she was out and down the ramp, she waded through birds, walking alongside the ramp all the way back to where it joined up with the death house's front wall and sliders. She knew nothing about geometry, but the point where the ramp was married to the entrance was over her head. At her last physical, the pediatrician said she was of average height: *Four feet, plenty of room to grow into your shoes.* Whatever *that* meant. But she thought that what she had in mind really might work.

Running all the way back to her horse cut fifteen minutes down to five, although it gave her a stitch in her side. Even with the exercise, she was also very cold, shivering as the sweat between her shoulder blades and over her face immediately began to wick away.

"Oh-k-kay," she said to the mare. Her fingers were shaking as she wrapped up its reins. Her face was so frigid her lips was numb. "C-come on, girl." But Bella was having none of it. Balking, the horse huffed an enormous snort and dug in its hooves. *"Please,"* Ellie panted. Hooking the bridle, she tried dropping her weight. Skinning its lips from yellow peg-teeth, the animal twisted, trying to angle for a bite while pivoting and aiming a back hoof for a swift, decisive kick. Gasping, Ellie snatched her hand back as the horse's teeth clacked on air and dodged a hoof that whizzed past her head to plow into her primer pail with a solid *chuck.* The pail went airborne, sailing for the trees and spilling a trail of tip-ups in its wake. The heavier auger whipped around in a complete circle, like one of those spinners on a game board.

"Easy, easy," she said. Screwing up her courage, she darted forward and grabbed the auger's handle, dragging it back before Bella could slice a leg. "Calm down. I'm sorry, okay?"

This was bad. Without Bella, she would have to either wait or walk, and both were out. *Too long; we're wasting time.* Fuming, impatience spiking her skin so badly she wanted to peel right out of it, she forced herself to wait while Bella stomped and blew. She had to fix this. Her teeth sawed at her cheek. How did you calm down a horse? *Reins are brakes. You stop a runaway by taking away the head.* But she had to be *on* the horse for that, and besides, the mare wasn't running anywhere. Her problem was that the silly thing didn't want to *go* anywhere. *Must be a way to take its head, though.* She thought back over what she knew about spooked horses. Precious little. But there was a book . . . *Flicka?* No, *Black Beauty.* The fire. *James ties a scarf around Black Beauty's eyes.*

Her hand crept to her neck. Chris had her coat, but she'd kept her fleece and wool scarf. Carefully, slowly, she unwrapped the loops of wool, then bunched the scarf into a fleece pocket.

"Okay, girl," she said, moving much more slowly than she wanted. The mare was quivering; she could see its hide twitching. When her hand found Bella's bridle again, Ellie resisted the urge to pull or do anything but stroke the animal's neck. "Easy," she said as the horse tossed and blew a loud and long horsey raspberry. Ellie kept stroking, telling the horse, *It's fine, that's good, it's okay.* When the horse was only breathing and no longer stamping, Ellie inched out the scarf, thought for just a second—*you watch; this only works in books*—then reached up and draped the scarf over Bella's eyes.

To her astonishment, the mare didn't toss or even move. Ellie could actually see the tension rippling and then running out of the horse's powerful shoulders. Still talking nonsense, she tied the scarf, lightly knotting it behind the horse's jaw.

"All right, let's go," she said, cautiously gathering up the reins, bracing herself for the bolt Bella would surely try. The horse *did* tug but only once.

It was, Ellie decided, a good omen.

In five minutes, the mechanical rasp and clack of the crows swelled through the trees. Bella's ears pricked, angling toward the sound like radar dishes homing in on an alien signal.

Don't bolt, please don't shy. Ellie held her breath but then thought that if *she* didn't get spooked, the horse probably wouldn't either. The milling crows parted as they had before, like waves retreating from a beach. Ellie led the horse all the way to the point where the ramp met the slider and felt a burst of elation. Her saddle was just even with the ramp at its highest point.

This is gonna work. Throwing the reins over the horse's head so they draped over the horn, she scurried up the ramp. The slider complained, and that made Bella turn her head, but Ellie was already wheeling inside to where Mina, tail thumping, patiently waited. *This has to.*

She spared a few seconds to press her ear to Chris's chest. His heart balled with a dull *thump . . .* pause *. . . thump . . .* pause *. . . . thump . . .* Boy, that was *really* slow. She wished she knew if that was good or bad, then decided anything was better than zip. His eyes still roamed, but his breathing was better, no gasps now, and his skin was pinker.

Drag him. That was what she'd decided. Grabbing up pillows from the other bodies, she eyed Chris, the distance he would fall, then arranged the pillows into a landing zone. Shaking out two of the burlap sacks, she spread these over the pillows, then clambered back up to Chris, braced herself on her knees, hooked her hands under his arms, and levered him into a slouch against her lap. His arms were heavy but floppy, his limp hands dangling, the fingers like the legs of dead spiders. Chris's head slewed then lolled, and she could see the steady but slow throb of his pulse in his neck. The smudges under his eyes were bluer now, not as gray.

"Okay," she said. She hitched toward the edge in fits and starts, scooting him what seemed an inch at a time, feeling with her feet for the moment when her boot tipped over the pallet's lip and into air. Chris was much heavier than she'd expected, and she was sweating, her breath coming in harsh pants. Tail swishing encouragement, Mina watched as Ellie worked her butt toward the edge with another gigantic heave—

Her right foot shot into thin air. Gasping, she felt herself tilt as Chris's weight shifted against her chest; her left knee, still bent to support him, fired with a sudden tearing pain as she tumbled sideways off the pallet. She came down hard on the pillows, on her back, and in an awkward splay, like a ballerina doing a really bad split. The impact slapped the air from her lungs, and pain roared all the way into her groin. Chris was so much dead weight on her chest, and he'd jack-knifed, although he was now mostly off the pallet, his legs loosely flexed at the knees. Squirming out from under, she got her boots planted and pushed to a stand. Her left knee yelled, but she could gimp on it just fine and that was all that mattered.

All right, hurry up, hurry up. Pulling his legs off the rest of the way, she got Chris arranged on the burlap sled, tucked all the remaining sacks and her coat around his body. Then she went to his head, fisted up tongues of burlap, and *pulled*, really put her weight into it. He moved—not by a lot, but the burlap let out a *shush* as it skidded over stone, and suddenly, his head was six inches closer to the slider than it had been only a second before. Huffing, grunting, her boots clapping stone and Mina keeping pace, she hauled him all the way to the slider, which she'd left open this time around. The crows were bunched up at the edge but backed away in that black eddy as she slid the burlap onto the snow. Here, the going got even easier. As she dragged Chris to the left and toward Bella, she eyed the saddle. *Okay, slide him as close as you can, then roll him onto his tummy, and you'll have to push, get his chest over the saddle—*

As if someone somewhere flicked a switch, the crows went completely still and silent. Just a dead stop, like a soundtrack suddenly cutting out. *What?* For a second, Ellie actually thought there was something wrong with her ears. But then she heard Mina's pants and her own harsh breaths, and the hard drum of her heart. *Uh-oh.* All the fine hairs bristled on her neck. She was still in her crouch, but now she let go of the burlap and straightened. Beneath her boots, the snow spoke in tiny, alarmed squeals. In his burlap cocoon, Chris sighed a low moan.

As one, the crows lifted in a huge, silent storm, exploding from the snow and the death house to rocket away in a swirling cloud. It was so much like the day everything died that Ellie threw her arms over her head and screamed, "No, no, not again!" She couldn't help it. But there was no detonation of pain in her head. *So it's not that.* Eyes wide, she threw her head back, watching the crows silently spin away. *Then what? What could—*

By her side, Mina began to growl, deep in her chest, a sound that swelled to a snarl.

Oh . . . Her mind couldn't squeak out the *no.* Heart slamming her ribs, Ellie swept her eyes from the sky and those silent birds and down to the snow and the woods. *Oh boy, I'm in so much trouble.*

Because there, in the clearing and at the mouth of the trail that would take her and Chris from the death house to safety, was a girl.

32

Those knives were real trouble. The Glock in his hand wouldn't fire. Neither would the Eagle. His Bravo was out of easy reach. Tom thought about that silver glint in the trees and wondered just how many other Chuckies were out there, knives at the ready, and what they were waiting for, unless this was simply the way they did things. Send in an attacker, one right after the other, to tire him out before swarming in for the kill, like wolves.

For the first time, it occurred to him to wonder just how long this girl had waited, watched. He'd been on the snow, exposed, for . . . what? A half hour? At least that—and a good portion of that time, he'd been out of it, so consumed with visions and flashbacks and the manic jitter of something close to insanity that it would've been smarter and easier to take him then.

But she wants to fight. The Chucky was on her feet now, and God, she recovered fast. Fear iced his throat. She didn't want to just *kill* him. She had knives and she'd plowed right into him. He should already be dead. Come to think of it, she could probably handle a rifle or pistol just fine. But this girl wanted the rush, the fun of the kill. The blood.

And there's something wrong with her, different. Given she was a Chucky, this was an understatement. *It's her eyes, something about them; the color . . . too dark.* But she was so far away he wasn't certain, and that was just fine, thanks.

Forget her face. Concentrate: don't lose track of the knives. Tom watched as she began to circle, very low, moving carefully left to right—and Jesus, she wasn't sinking much. Shuffling, he turned, keeping her in sight, feeling the shift of uneven stone beneath his boots, dismally aware that she was compensating for his longer reach by forcing his knife hand further away and off-target. He didn't know what kind of knives she had, but they were wicked: silvered steel, long and thin, single-edged, with only the suggestion of a curve. Hers were real fighting knives, made for cutting and slicing. Her blades were already in motion, scything back and forth, sparking in the setting sun, and he had trouble keeping track of both. As the light got worse, that would also get harder, assuming he lasted that long. He thought this might be over pretty quick. She didn't need to get in a killing thrust. All she had to do was cut him a couple of times and then stand back and wait for him to weaken, or bleed to death.

Any soldier knew hand-to-hand combatives, how to grapple and kill, and part of basic training was the rifle-bayonet course. The reality was a lot simpler: the guy who survived was the one who held off an attacker until his buddies arrived with guns. Unlike Special Forces and Black Ops guys, all of whom were big into close-quarters combat, Tom knew only the basics of what to do with a knife: *cover the middle, defend the face and neck, deflect with the left hand and forearm, stab hard and fast, put your weight into it.* If he could get close and behind her knives, he might slash her face. Better yet, cut her forehead, let all that blood spill into her eyes and blind her. But he knew he wasn't good enough for anything fancy. Rush her, and he'd probably end up impaling himself on her knives and doing the job for her.

One thing was certain, though. He had absolutely no reason to hang on to the Glock now. He needed his hands free. But instead of dropping the weapon to the snow—the smart move—Tom did something incredibly dumb. Angling his body, keeping the tip of his knife pointed at her head, he swept his left hand around and under his open parka to shove the weapon into the small of his back—

And that was all it took, that little move. He wasn't centered and she knew it. He saw her dart forward, low, a white blur, stepping in. His reaction was clumsy, an awkward stumble as he tried backpedaling fast. Her right hand, which was closest, swept in a high cut. Gasping, he struggled to whip his left arm back into line to fend off the strike. Too late, he read the cock of her elbow, registered the feint.

Suddenly, she was there, twisting beneath his right arm, ducking under his knife. Her blade flickered, its silver tongue licking side to side—one-two-three, *zip-zip-zip.* He couldn't follow it, didn't really see the knife at all, but on the third pass, he felt a lick of cold as his clothing ripped and then a snaky burn, a line of fire across his exposed belly. Biting back a shout, he arched, pulling himself out of reach, but she was already withdrawing, backing up. The setting sun bathed her skin as richly red as the blood welling from the gash across his stomach. He could feel the oozy drizzle, warm and thick.

She could've killed me right then. Cold sweat oiled his face as she began to circle again, a balletic move, her knives sketching their slow, mesmeric back-and-forth. *She had me, dead to rights.* A single thrust, a twist, and she could have watched him bleed out. *Playing. She wants this to go slow.* Grunting, he clamped his left forearm across his middle. A slow slither of blood was beginning to worm over his thighs and drip to the snow. This wasn't going to kill him, but if he got cut too many more times or she decided to slash just a little deeper, unzip him so his guts spilled out, he'd never keep his feet. *Got to do something . . .*

Moving again, lightly despite the snow, she came in fast, jabbing with her right. Acting purely on instinct, he tried countering with his own knife, which meant that he had to twist to his left. As she pulled the thrust in a perfectly timed feint, he realized much too late that not only was his right side exposed, but he'd taken his eyes from the knife in her *left* hand. *Shit!* He tried to correct, to turn, but she was so damn fast! The knife ripped in a backhanded slice from his right hip all the way up to his chest.

This time, a shout of pain leapt from his mouth. Doubling over, he tried to protect his torso—stupid, stupid, *stupid*; that brought his face into her strike zone—and she was right there, the knife whickering for his face.

What happened next was all reflex. Uncoiling, he whipped up with his left arm to defend himself . . . and damn if he didn't still have that Glock.

She saw it coming, tried going with the blow, but she was a fraction of a second too late. The hard butt clipped her nose. It was so fast, he didn't know he'd connected until her neck snapped back. A bright red bib spumed down her chin and over her chest, and then she was blowing, off-balance, shaking her head like a wounded dog, her blood flying in ropy spatters.

Come on, come on, move, move! She was less than twenty feet away when he charged because, he figured, what the hell. He was outmatched, and she was going to kill him if he kept letting her dictate the fight. So he had to move; he had to step into this; he had to muscle past his fear and own this one.

Bellowing, he closed the distance in three big strides. Snarling, her face cramped with fury, she thrust to deflect with her left and jab with her right, but his reach was longer and for once he did exactly the right move at exactly the right moment.

Dropping to his left knee, he swept his left arm up, knocking her blade out of line, and then he thrust his KA-BAR into her middle with all his might. He felt the blade jam through thick down and clothing. For one terrible second, he thought that either she had on too many layers or maybe even a Kevlar vest. But then he felt her jump, heard her scream, felt the give of flesh and muscle. Dropping his right elbow, he twisted the knife, tearing both cloth and something much denser and wetter. Still screeching, she arched back, trying to get away. His knife jumped in his palm as the serrated edge snagged on cloth and, more likely, guts. So, two choices now, and only two:

Go with her, press the advantage; get her on her back in the snow. Suffocate her, choke her to death, beat in her skull with the Glock, maybe even get his hands on one of her knives.

Or drop the Glock and go for the Bravo.

He flung the Glock aside. Didn't follow its arc. Either he'd find it later, or he'd be dead. Fisting her parka, he yanked her as close as a lover, then put some muscle behind it and drove his knife into her as fast as he could, as far as it would go.

She screeched again. Her own knives flashed, and he ducked, tur-tling his head and neck. One knife missed. The second didn't. First, the parka and then the flesh of his left forearm parted in a fiery red shriek. Roaring with pain, he pushed up, still holding her close, his KA-BAR so deep she could've been a chunk of beef skewered for a kabob. He could smell their blood mingling now, the rank iron stink of it. His stomach was slick; his chest and left arm were dripping. Before she could slash up, he gave her a mighty shove. She flew a good ten feet to collapse in a loose-limbed bundle. Her own knives fell from her hands to glimmer darkly against snow that was begin-ning to pink and then grow bright red as a bloody puddle overflowed the cup of her belly and spilled down her sides.

For anyone or anything else, that would've been the end. The bad guy pulling a knife out of his stomach to use against you? Only happened in movies. In real life, that little trick never went well, and not just because it hurt like a bitch. Extracting a knife or any stab-bing weapon was, in fact, an excellent way to hasten death. A knife might slice into an artery, but it might also be a cork. Pull it out, and stand back as the blood flowed. When the knife was serrated, like his KA-BAR, it was worse. Those barbs hooked. That was the point. So in addition to bleeding like stink, which was its own special kind of agony when it came to abdominal wounds, you might also pull out a sausage string of guts at the same time. His squad medic once told him to imagine someone peeling your face from your skull, and then multiply that by about a billion. Clawing out your eyes would hurt less than ripping out your own intestines. Pain like that, you wished it *could* kill you.

But this . . . *thing*? It didn't seem to feel pain, not for long. Look how fast it had recovered from that kick. Now, dumbstruck, he watched as she wrapped her hands around the KA-BAR's grip. Even that tiny jostle of the blade hurt; he could see it in the flare of her blood-soaked nostrils, the tight grimace, the strain in her neck, the arch of her back.

My God. What was this thing? This couldn't be a feral Chucky, unless there was a difference between new Chuckies, ones turning now versus those who had turned right away. Ferals weren't organized; they were crazy, they couldn't plan. Not even Jim, his friend, had been anything other than a rabid animal. So this girl was something new and different: nearly immune to pain, crazy-fearless. Smart. A killing machine. *And I've seen this before, too—but where?*

She pulled—

And then, to Tom's horror . . . the KA-BAR *moved*.

33

Ellie couldn't move. Her insides jellied, and her knees began to quiver. When she swallowed, she could hear the sharp click in her throat. *My rifle, where is it?* She didn't dare take her eyes from the girl to look, but she didn't think she'd remembered to take the Savage when she went for Bella. *That means it's behind me, still in the death house.*

The girl only watched, which was good because that gave Ellie a little breathing room. *Unless there are others and they're circling around.* Mina's growl had swelled to an open-mouth snarl, and Ellie risked slipping her eyes down for a quick peek. Mina's attention was fixed on the girl. So either there was only this one people-eater, or many others far enough back that Mina couldn't smell or see them. She also saw Bella's nostrils flare and that quick flick of the mare's head as the horse got wind of the people-eater. *No, no, no, please don't bolt, you stupid horse; just wait, wait.*

The *girl* was sure waiting for something. Ellie felt the truth of that without understanding why. Her gaze ran over the grimy snarl of the girl's hair, which was frozen solid where it dangled below a watch cap that was once cream-colored but now a filthy gray. Ellie couldn't tell what color that grubby parka might have been, but the snake of a scarf dragged from the people-eater's neck in a limp, lime-green coil.

That scarf . . . Ellie thought back to the moment on the lake when all the crows had left. *That snow, the cedar swaying, and a flash of lime green that I thought was just pine . . .* The girl had been there? Watching all along and following, and keeping downwind so Mina couldn't smell her? *Smart.* But why show up now? Why not wait a little longer?

Maybe because she knows she won't get another chance. The girl's narrow face was all angles and shadows, the cheeks hollowed into valleys, the eyes far back in their sockets. *She's starving, so hungry she just couldn't wait one more second.*

But the girl wasn't acting right. People-eaters came at you with guns and knives, bare teeth, hands. Claws. They did it all: set up ambushes, stormed out of the woods. Maybe they'd show themselves after they surrounded you—that had happened to Eli and his sister—but this girl was alone and only *watching.*

On the snow, by her feet, Chris moaned.

I have to get out of here. What am I standing around for? She was panting, part of her brain going in a swirly-whirly scream: *Run run run to the death house, shut the door so she can't get in!* She could do that, grab Mina—*what about Bella, what about Bella, will she be all right?*—get inside, get to her gun, and then wait wait wait, like a bunny in its hole, for Eli and Jayden to find her. But Chris, what about Chris? *She'll kill him, she'll eat him and . . .*

You can't let that happen. It was the little closet-voice. *Think, Ellie, think think think. She's watching, she's not moving.*

"Because she's waiting for the others." Her voice was squeezy-wheezy small, riding the up-coaster to hysteria. Once she hit the top, there'd be no stopping the zoom into crazy-scared. Across the clearing, the girl's head perked, cocking a little at the sound of her voice the way Mina did when she was puzzled. "She knows she can't get past Mina alone."

Stop breathing so fast. Listen to what you said. If that's true, you still have time.

"And what if it's not?"

Mina will protect you. The closet-voice was very patient, like Grandpa Jack when he said, yes, life wasn't fair, but no, being hateful wouldn't help. *She's got teeth, you know.*

"Is that a joke?" she squeaked, then thought, *Oh, is that dumb or what?* But the closet-voice did have a point. Should she get the gun?

Don't leave Chris. She wasn't sure who that was, the closet-voice or her, but knew that was right. Just had to keep her head, stay calm like Alex and Tom. It took every scrap of self-control to turn her back, but she couldn't both roll Chris onto his tummy and then pull him onto the saddle *and* watch the girl. "Don't let her get me, Mina," she said in that squeaky-scared voice. Bending, Ellie planted her hands against Chris's side and pushed, a pitiful little shove as her strength tried to flee with her voice. Chris was *big*, and she was such a runt. *Come on, don't be such a girl.* But she had to try twice more before Chris flopped onto his tummy. The burlap bags slid, revealing white thigh and part of his bottom.

"Ohhh-kaaay," she sang, thinking she'd never seen so much of a boy *this way.* She tucked the bags back into place as best she could. "Oh Alex, oh Alex, oh T-Tom . . ." Planting her boots, she fisted burlap and jerked Chris all the way to the ramp's edge, so close that his hands dangled. Jumping down, bracing herself for the *shush-shush-shush* of snow as the girl charged, she swung onto Bella. Then she hooked her left foot into the stirrup but dug her right heel into the ramp. Grumbling, the horse tried to sidestep away.

"No, no, no, come on." Ellie hauled on the right rein to turn the mare's head. Then she reached over, grabbed Chris's arms above the elbows, and *heaved.* "Daddy, help," she said, as Chris's head cleared the saddle. "Oh, Daddy Daddy Daddy." She kept pulling, using her boot to steady the horse as she yanked Chris onto the saddle, awkwardly walking her hands up Chris's sides until he folded at his waist to drape over Bella's withers and shoulders like a too-long blanket.

This would have to do. For a brief moment, she considered the

Savage, still inside the death house, and wondered if she should close the slider. Hannah would be really pissed if this girl and any friends went inside to snack. *Heck with that. I'm getting Chris out of here.* Pulling in a big breath, she coaxed Bella into a turn. On the saddle, Chris's body shifted but didn't slide. The girl was exactly where she'd been, too: no closer, no further.

"Mina, get ready, girl." Ellie's fingers trembled as she untied but didn't remove Bella's scarf. Bunching the reins in her left hand, Ellie leaned over and across Chris, planting her elbows against his right side to bracket his body and hold him in place. Then, with a fast flick of her wrist, she snapped off the scarf.

"Mina!" At the same instant, she gave the horse, already starting to rear, a sharp giddyap kick. "Mina, off! *Release!*"

Snarling, the dog surged down the ramp at the same instant that Bella came down with a spine-jarring crash, and bolted. Ellie's breath jammed out of her throat, and she landed in her saddle with a thump. Chris's body jounced and he started to slide. *No no no!* She dug her elbows in hard enough to feel the birdcage of his ribs. *Hang on hang on hang on!*

Ahead, she could see the girl's face suddenly snap up, the glaze of hunger quickly shading to astonishment and then fear. The girl leapt aside in a swirl of dirty hair and lime-green scarf as Bella flashed past, and then they were speeding away, Bella kicking snow, Mina racing after, the trees slipping into a blur as they crashed down the trail.

Craning, Ellie snatched only a single glance back. The people-eater wasn't running after them or charging onto the trail with her pals. Instead, she only stood there, and to Ellie, she didn't look remotely dangerous. All Ellie saw was a forlorn, lonely, tattered scarecrow of a girl in a green scarf, and for an instant, Ellie wondered if, maybe, this girl was somehow different. But then Bella swerved right and the girl was gone.

Safe, we're safe. That was when it hit Ellie, like the full heat of the sun suddenly blasting through clouds. *I did it. Me and Mina and Bella, we really did it.* And all by themselves, too—no Eli, no Jayden, no nobody but her and Mina and her horse—and she wanted to tell her daddy and Grandpa Jack all about it. She wanted to tell Alex and Tom. She wanted that so bad she could taste the story in her mouth, every word, each syllable.

I miss you guys. Her eyes stung, and a second later, she felt the dash of a tear. Or maybe it was only the blade of that icy wind. Whatever. For once, it was all right. This was a good cry.

Yeah, the closet-voice said, *just as long as you don't fall off.*

"Oh, be quiet." Her laugh was shaky and a little watery, too, as she hugged Chris even closer. "Hang on, Chris. It'll be okay, I've got you." And then Ellie began to chant, her heart leaping with every surge of Bella's hooves: "I got you, Chris. I got you, I got you, I got you."

34

She's going to get me. Tom's horror solidified into grim certainty as the girl tugged and his knife, smeary with the Chucky's blood, appeared inch by gory inch. *She'll have that out in five seconds.*

He had to get to the Bravo, the last weapon he had, the only one that might work. If she got close again, he didn't think he could stop her. Rocking back onto his right foot, he turned and churned in an awkward stagger through snow and debris. His pack seemed impossibly far away, the Bravo another mile beyond that, receding as if by some tricky camerawork. He thought he was moving fast, but his vision was starting to go fuzzy with every step, his head beginning to balloon. He was still losing too much blood. His chest was smeary and wet. Cooling gore slicked his thighs. *Keep moving, don't pass out, don't faint.*

Ahead, the boulders that marked the foot of the boy Chucky's tomb loomed, filling his sight. Staggering to the rocks, he nearly fell but braced himself with his right hand. Swaying, he could see his pack now and, beyond that, the Bravo. As he lurched past the open trench, his boot banged that rock-hatchet he'd used to smash that frozen Chucky to bits, and he stumbled. Now, wildly off-balance, he actually turned in a half circle, struggling to keep to his feet. But he didn't, couldn't, and knew he was going down.

And there she was, coming for him, blistering over the snow, hurling herself in a tackle. The blow was a sledgehammer to his sternum, a vicious blast he felt straight through to his spine. His breath jolted from his mouth. He was aware that he was falling straight back, pole-axed, his lungs on fire and the electric shock working into his brain. Out of the gray fog that passed for his vision, he saw the girl loom; felt the drip of her blood on his cheeks and the hard pressure of her knees as she tacked his shoulders. The ruin he'd made of that dead Chucky was to his left, and he saw her head flick that way as the Eagle glinted in the setting sun.

For a crazy second, he wanted to scream, *Pick up the Eagle, pick it up, pick it up, take a shot, take it!* It was a suicidal thought, it was insane, but she was on top of him, and he was desperate, out of options. The Eagle shouldn't work; it ought to come apart in her hands. Not kill her—that only happened in movies, too—but if she *did* try it and the weapon gave out in a burst of shrapnel and bullets, that might buy him just a little more time. Because he had nothing else: no air, no weapons, very little strength, no options.

Unfortunately, a gun either wasn't her style or the end for him that she had in mind. Snarling, she jammed her left hand under his chin. His neck muscles instinctively tightened, fighting the relentless pressure. He tried bucking her off, but despite the rocks, the deep snow gave him no leverage. He'd sunk down so far that his hips and legs were above him. He was fighting for his life from the equivalent of a bathtub. Hoist someone by his ankles, and he has no way of keeping his head above water. Hold him long enough, he drowns. So she had a choice: push him far down into the snow and wait for him to suffocate, or take out his throat. He couldn't fight her forever, and she was riding him, her center of gravity directly over his chest, and if he let go . . .

If I let go. Not exactly a thought. More like a last gasp. All at once, he stopped pushing and let his shoulders sag, his neck stretch. He felt her knees stutter as she began to slide, her center of gravity shifting. Off-balance, she rocked forward.

"AAHH!!" He shrieked it, unaware that the scream was even in his mouth until it wasn't, and then he was surging up, his right arm suddenly free, the hand hooking into her parka. He yanked her down as quickly and viciously as he could. At the same time, he whipped his head up. There was a loud *kunk* as the dense bone of his forehead smashed into the delicate ridge just above her left eye. He knew the hit was good the instant he felt her socket cave, the second her whole body unlimbered from the shock.

The Chucky didn't wail or scream. She had no time, or breath, for it. Stunned, she pitched right, and he went with her, using her weight as a fulcrum. Even then—bloody, a wound in her belly, blind in one eye, and probably in ferocious pain—she sensed what he meant to do. Somehow, she got her hands up, fingers clawed, and flailed, wildly, trying to snag something: his parka, an arm, anything. Yet, to his relief, she had no knife, and the advantage was his now.

They spooned, her back against his chest. In a novel, he'd have broken her neck. A quick snap, the crackle, done deal. But that kind of move, what they showed on TV or in a movie like it was no big deal . . . it's make-believe. The neck is much stronger than you think.

Instead, he hooked his right arm under her chin. Ramming his left hand against the back of her head, he grabbed his left arm with his right hand, the better to hang on to the blood choke—

And felt something that did not belong.

In a classic figure-four choke hold, eight to ten seconds of pressure on the carotids—thirteen at the max—and an opponent, even that burly, double-wide guy with the neck of an ox, slides into unconscious.

Unless that guy is smart enough to protect his neck somehow.

Which, apparently, this Chucky was—because what circled her neck was a leather collar with a metal D-ring. *Jesus, a dog collar?* Frantic, Tom tried shifting his grip, working his arm higher to hook directly under her ears, but they were wallowing in snow and he was already tiring, his grip starting to weaken. Then his arm slipped.

Her reaction was instantaneous. Bucking, she threw her left arm up and back, her fingers aiming for his eyes. He jerked his head right, a reflex he knew, too late, was a mistake and exactly what she was counting on. Cocking her right elbow, she thrust back, fast, jamming the bony point into his ribs. Pain sheeted his vision and he gagged. Dimly, he felt her twisting, knew he no longer had the advantage. *Get up, get out from under, get to the Bravo!* Going for the weapon was another mistake, because it meant turning his back on her, but he simply didn't see any other option. She was strong, and he couldn't hang on forever. That she'd even thought to wear something to protect her neck was a whole other level of crazy, and he couldn't wait and hope she might bleed to death, because a gut wound takes time, more than he had. Shoving her to the left, he let go, rolled right, spun onto his hands and knees.

That was as far as he got. She kicked him, high, at the small of his back. A red tidal wave of agony roared up his spine, and he let out a choking *UNGH!* The next thing he knew, he was on his belly, writhing, coughing against the snow, trying to worm away. Every nerve sputtered; his muscles sizzled. He felt as boneless as a jellyfish from the spinal shock. Blinking through sudden tears of pain, he made out his pack, the Bravo, but it was so far away! Then he spied something else, much closer, less than twelve inches from his nose . . .

There was a crunch of snow, the chatter of rock. The sun was behind him and he saw her shadow, black and inky, leaking over the snow, seeping onto his flesh as she came for him.

With a wild cry, he lunged, got his hand around the ski pole only a foot away, and then he was whipping onto his back, the pole whistling through the air; and now she wasn't a black shadow but a white and red missile launching itself—

Just in time, he got his arms tucked. She saw what he was doing, tried twisting in midair, but she wasn't a cat, just a crazy-ass and very smart Chucky, and she failed.

Shrieking, she slammed down, the metal tip of the ski pole punching through just beneath her breastbone. The force was so great his arms nearly buckled. By some miracle, the fiberglass pole didn't snap in two but held as her arms and legs splayed in a weird star.

Yes! Still hanging on, he shoved, knocking her to one side, but he wouldn't let go. This was one weapon he would not lose. How he got to his feet, he didn't know, but then he was crouched, his thighs bunching, and she was still skewered, feet planted, her own hands wrapped around the pole to brace herself, as if they'd decided to play a strange game of tug-of-war. They stayed like that for a second that seemed a century.

In that moment, he finally saw what was wrong, how very strange her eyes were: not only fevered with a killing frenzy but jittery, the pupils so wide the irises were reduced to thin dark rims.

And there were no whites. At all. The whites of her eyes weren't bloodshot; they were crimson, as if her eyeballs had been cored with a grapefruit spoon to leave mucky, blood-filled sockets.

My God. The sight chilled him to the bone. *Where did you come from? What are you?*

As if in answer, her lips skinned back in an orange grin.

"Jesus," he said. "Just die." Heaving with all his might, he flipped her to the snow the way a fisherman might jam a speared fish into sand, and then dropped his weight in a single, killing thrust.

And then it was done.

Almost.

Spent, the adrenaline that had fueled him for just long enough now seeping out with his blood, Tom could feel his joints trying to buckle. Trembling, he staggered back until he felt a knob of stone at his back. He was going cold, all over, in an insidious black creep as fatigue and blood loss stole his strength. Propping his hands on his thighs, he struggled to stay upright and sucked air, trying to clear away the cobwebs, waiting for his mind to firm.

Got to get out of here, back to camp. He didn't have a med kit, and it would be dark soon. With his blood perfuming the air, who knew when the next Chuckies would show? *Strip out of as much of my stuff as I can and take hers. Those over-whites have her blood on them. So maybe they won't smell me. But I have to be careful. Can't lead Chuckies back to camp; got to protect the kids.*

This was all so strange. A ton of dead people up at the lake, plenty to eat, but absolutely no Chuckies snacking on anyone. Lots of juicy kids at camp—an abandoned farmstead, out in the open, plenty of pasture—and no Chuckies there either, as if the camp existed under a dome, an invisible force field. Which he had always wondered about.

He stared down at the dead girl. He'd seen plenty of corpses. There was *dead*, something you knew just by looking, because death steals, especially from the eyes. Something evaporates. The eyes of the dead are the empty windows in a deserted house. But then there was battlefield *juju*, those few moments when a prickly spider walked the back of your neck; when the dread ate its way into your throat, crowding out fear. At those moments, you just couldn't believe that the dead wouldn't rise.

This Chucky was like that. Even in death, the Chucky's vermillion stare, still so crazy and manic, was what stayed with you after a nightmare.

And I've seen your kind before. But where? What are you? A violent shiver made him gasp. Grabbing his arms, he hugged himself tight, now truly afraid. *Where did you come from?*

Then, jumping to the front of his mind in an involuntary tic: *Who made you?*

"You're losing it, Tom." His voice sounded strange but felt good. He needed to hear himself. "That's crazy. Who could make Chuckies worse than they are? Why would anyone do that?" *That* made him laugh, a hacking sound harsh and far back in his throat, like the distant saw of those crows. "Jesus, listen to yourself. You were in the Army. Who doesn't want a better killing machine, a soldier who doesn't even know how to quit?"

And who, he wondered, wouldn't train it?

The woods. That black blur. That glint. He dragged his binoculars from his parka, thankful that he hadn't hung them around his neck. Good way to end up strangled.

"You don't have time for this," he said, glassing the trees. "You got ten seconds, Tom, and then you really need to get—"

But it didn't take him ten seconds, or even seven.

All it took were three.

35

This was *so* bad. Cindi had *known* Tom was up to no good. *Her gut talking* is what her mom would've said: this really queasy sense that Tom would try something dumb.

Since that second day after the mine, Cindi went to see Tom early mornings before hoofing to her lookout post. (Which had been *borrring* before it turned terrible. Nothing to look at now but a gouged-out hill and that big blue-white eye of the lake for the longest time until the crows showed up, and then . . . well . . . she was twelve, but she wasn't *stupid*.) Sometimes, Luke came with, but he was fourteen, the next oldest after Tom, and didn't have tons of time. So, mostly, she went alone and brought food because Tom wasn't eating enough to keep a tick alive. His eyes had dropped so far back into his skull it was like staring into deep, dark caves. You could get lost down there. She never pushed him and they didn't talk much, but she wasn't sure that was even important. *Just be with him.* That's what her mom would've said. *Remind him you're still there, waiting for him to come back.*

On the fourth day, tired of *let's give Tom space*—Mellie's go-to for the whole awful mess—Mellie decided, *Hey, mind if I tag along?* What could Cindi say? *No, butt out, you old witch?* Boy, if it was freezing in that tower before, the temperature went *waaay* below zero the second Tom's eyes clicked to Mellie corkscrewing through that trapdoor.

Everything human in Tom shriveled until there was only a husk that just happened to wear Tom's face.

To Mellie's credit, she did try. She did *nice*; she tried *you can tell me*; she touched on a tough *buck up, soldier* (but only Weller was any good at that). In desperation, Mellie even trotted out a whiny *but we need you*.

To which Tom said about four syllables, all of them chipped from ice: *Leave me alone*.

Twenty minutes later, Mellie clumped back down the way she'd come. But when Tom turned Cindi a look, she could tell: for the first time in days, the veil was gone, and he was seeing her, recognizing who she *was*.

"It wasn't my idea," she said. "She invited herself."

"I know that." Tom paused. "You don't have to go, Cindi. I'd like it if you didn't."

"Sure." A lump pushed into her throat. Tom hadn't smiled. There wasn't this choir of angels or anything. There was only Tom and his monster, the black fist around his heart that, sometimes, she worried might squeeze so hard it would crush him altogether. But hearing him say that he'd *like* her to stay, that was a beginning. It was a place to start.

But now . . . *this*.

"And you're absolutely sure he never mentioned going to the mine?" Mellie gave her and then Luke, seated beside Cindi at a rough-hewn kitchen table, the stink-eye. They'd made their camp in a long-abandoned farmstead: a motley collection that included an old two-story farmhouse, hog barn, cow barn, silo, and a clutch of tumbledown outbuildings hemmed on all sides by wide pastures and distant knolls where they mounted a few lookouts. Only Weller and Mellie slept in the house, along with anyone who was ill or hurt. At the moment—*bad news, bad, bad, bad*—that was Tom, tucked in Weller's first-floor back bedroom. "No warning at all?"

"No," Cindi fibbed, her right leg jumping and jiggling and making the table rock, a really bad habit that used to drive her mom crazy: *Cindi, you make coffee nervous.* Considering that her mom had been a child psychiatrist, that was saying something. "Is he going to be all right?"

"I'm sure he'll be fine and . . . please." Mellie laid a hand on Cindi's wrist. The other was wrapped around a steaming mug. "Coffee's not so easy to come by these days that I want to waste a drop."

"Sorry." Cindi clamped her hands between her thighs. "There was a whole lot of blood. He was pretty cut up."

"Not all the blood's Tom's. It probably looks worse than it is."

"Well, I hope so." Luke was so pale his eyes looked smudged on with blue finger paint. "Because any worse and he should be dead. Did Tom say how many he saw? Are we going after them? Or maybe we ought to, you know, *move?*"

"Let's not get ahead of ourselves, all right?" Mellie was very good at sliding around questions. "I think the most important thing we can do now to help Tom is—" She looked around at the sound of heavy footsteps. "Well?"

"We're doing okay," Weller said, but his tone was brusque, preoccupied. Always a little grumpy, the thick grizzle of gray stubble over Weller's cheeks and chin only made him look meaner, like an old bear with a toothache. Cindi thought Weller would be a lot nicer once the mine was gone, but the longer Tom hung out in the tower, the blacker Weller looked. On the other hand, considering the rusty-looking bandage plastered over the right side of Weller's neck and that shoulder . . . well, she'd be an übergrouch, too, if some Chucky snacked on her.

"Okay, as in . . . ?" Mellie prompted.

"As in we'll see." Heading for a counter where a Coleman hissed,

Weller rooted through a cardboard box. "You kids, go back to your racks. Best thing for Tom is we let him rest."

From the look on his face, Cindi thought Luke would argue, but he only nodded and scraped back his chair. "Just tell him we were here, okay?" he said to Weller.

"Can we come tomorrow morning?" Cindi asked.

"Let's see what tomorrow looks like," Mellie said, and gave Cindi's arm a little pat-pat the way you'd pet a puppy to encourage it to make wee-wee. "All right?"

"Does that feel all right to you?" Cindi glanced at Luke, but his expression was lost in the dark. She turned her attention back to following the yellow cone of their flashlight as they crunched over snow. The moon wouldn't rise for hours yet, which suited her just fine. Every time she looked, she couldn't help but think of some bug-eyed green cyclops and the night sky as an eyelid taking a whole month to slowly open and close.

"No," Luke said. "But I can't figure what freaks me out more—that there are Chuckies close by and they haven't found us yet, or Tom almost got killed."

"And why we aren't doing something about them."

"Beyond posting a couple more kids who can't hold rifles as guards? Yeah. It's almost like . . ."

Cindi waited, then said, "Like Mellie's not worried enough."

"Uh-huh." Pause. "Maybe she doesn't want us to panic. My dad was like that. He always worried we couldn't hack it, so he'd say things were fine, or think of something to distract us stupid little kids."

"Is that the only thing bothering you?"

"No," Luke said, and sighed. "They're not saying it, but Tom just got lucky. He *really* should be dead."

A screw of fear. "But he's not. He made it back."

"Believe me, Cindi, I'm just as happy about that. I don't think I could stand it if . . . But if Tom got killed, then what? It'd be just you and me and Chad, with thirty other kids, all of them younger."

"Weller would still be here. So would Mellie." She wasn't thrilled with either, but they were better than nothing.

"Come on. Weller joined up with us when Tom did. Before the mine went, Mellie would disappear."

"To get other kids. She was never gone for long."

"But long enough." He stopped walking and looked down at her. "You may not have wondered what would happen if she didn't show up again, but I did. I worried the whole time. Like, what would we eat? Where would we go? And this whole Rule thing? It's crazy to think that we're going to go marching anywhere. I mean, think about it. There's me and Tom, Weller and Mellie, about two, three other guys I can think of who are decent enough shots, but that's all we got. Tom never came right out with it, but I could tell he thought us going against Rule was a bad idea. The only reason he helped us at all was because of her. Because of Alex."

"You don't have to tell me that." Her teeth made a grab for her lower lip in time to stifle the sob. She gave her stinging eyes an impatient scrub with a fist. Only babies cried. "Are you saying he won't help us now?"

"No. If he comes back to stay, he will. He'll put the brakes on kids like Jasper. Like, what Jasper did to that bucket the other day? I mean, yeah, there are manuals and that old chemistry book we dug up— which, you know, I only sort of understand—but there really wasn't anything in what we read that said thermite might make plastic catch on fire."

"Thermite?" Jasper was a spazzy, twitchy-smart ten-year-old, and a complete pyro with a fixation on pipe bombs, water impulse charges, and anything that made a bang.

"Take a while to explain." Luke blew out in a white plume. "The thing is, Mellie's encouraging Jasper to just go on ahead. She's got other kids experimenting with napalm and Molotov cocktails."

"But won't we need to learn how to do that anyway? To protect ourselves?"

"Do we? Don't you think there's something just a little crazy about us maybe blowing our heads off? That stuff Mellie's so hot for . . . it's *dangerous*. That's why Tom never let us watch him work, much less taught us what to do. Mellie doesn't seem to care."

"But . . ." Cindi slicked her lips. "She's a grown-up."

"So? Remember what Tom said, about the monster inside and killing because it feels good? I watched Weller do that, kill this one Chucky really slow. Suffocated him in the snow and *smiled*. It was spooky. It wasn't only killing. What Weller did was *murder*. And now Mellie wants thermite, flamethrowers, claymores. But how does that help us? We blow up a bunch of people, rescue those other kids—and then what?"

"Well," she began, and stopped. "I don't know. I never stopped to think."

"Right. The *adults* do all the thinking. But what if we want something different?"

"So what are you saying?"

"I'm wondering," Luke said, "if the Chuckies and Rule are our only enemies."

36

"So?" Mellie glowered. "*Is* he as bad as he looks?"

"Worse." Reaching for two enameled mugs, Weller winced against the sudden grab in his right shoulder. Damn thing got stiff if he didn't remember to keep moving the joint.

"I thought you said you could handle the cuts."

"Oh yeah." Weller wasn't anywhere close to a medic, but any soldier, even an old, broken-down wreck like him, knew battlefield medicine. "Tom's strong, he's young. He ought to heal. Damn lucky they weren't bites."

"He's *lucky* he's alive." Mellie wasn't a tall woman or even especially beefy, but solid as a brick and pugnacious, with a fondness for big guns like that chromed .44 Mag cannon riding high in a crossdraw on her left hip. "What the *hell* was he thinking? Was he *trying* to get himself killed?"

"I don't think he understands what he was after, Mellie." One look at Tom in those blood-soaked camo over-whites—one good long gander at those wicked slashes—and *his* first impulse had been to knock some sense into the boy's skull. "We just need to give Tom time and some space to get through this."

"*Space*? He's been in that tower for over a week."

"Cut the boy a little slack, Mellie, all right?" Weller shook a packet down before ripping it open and dumping the contents into a mug. "I know what I'm doing."

"Do you?" In the Coleman's flat light, her gray eyes were stones and her lips were purple. "Because I'm starting to wonder, Weller. No one is indispensable, not even Tom."

"Jesus Christ on a crutch, I hope you're listening to yourself." Exasperated, he turned, propping his butt against the kitchen counter. "Tom is actually the *one* person in this camp who is. Think about Luke and Cindi, what they're willing to do for him. I guarantee not one kid would take a bullet for you or me."

"Tom is only useful so long as he remains an asset, Weller, not a liability. The last thing we need is for him to decide that this girl is alive and it's his mission to track her down."

Weller had to work to keep the chagrin from making its way to his face. This was precisely what Tom thought and wanted: *There was the ski pole, Weller. There's the Glock. Tell me how I can ignore that. If those Chuckies got her out, if there's even a chance she's alive . . .*

"Why don't you focus on the fact that he's out of that damn tower, and he came *back*." Although *that*, Weller thought, was more a matter of luck than anything else. If that Chucky hadn't shown her face, he wasn't sure Tom would've returned. He could picture the boy taking off, looking for some sign of where those Chuckies had taken Alex—which, he thought, wasn't necessarily as crazy as it sounded. What Tom said about that entire fiasco on the ridge the night they blew the mine and the way those Chuckies just kept coming . . . made a lot of sense, damn it. "Right now, he wants to talk, so I'll listen."

"Yeah, and I bet you're just so very understanding." Her eyes suddenly slitted. "Did you promise to help him look for her?"

It was a little disconcerting that she'd jumped to that conclusion so easily. "Not exactly."

"Oh, for God—" She huffed. "What did you say?"

"That when we're done with Rule, *if* there's some sign, a direction . . . I'll help him."

Mellie's mouth unhinged. "She's *dead*, Weller. He's basing this on a ski pole and a gun that's not even *hers*."

"Look, Mellie, he's not so far gone he doesn't see it's nuts, a long shot at best. But you weren't up on that rise. You're not carrying what he is. The last thing he needs is us rubbing his nose in it, or you interfering, lecturing . . ."

"I will do whatever I think—"

"Shut the hell up," he rapped. "Mellie, I need you to listen good and hard. Tom is a soldier. He's smart, he's strong. He's braver and more loyal than almost anyone I've ever known—"

"And *insane* to go up there alone—"

"Because he still has a heart to *break*," Weller grated. "For God's sake, Mellie, think for a damned second. Tom's not eating; he's barely slept. He's *grieving*. Now, there's that Glock, and he's grabbed hold of this little bubble of hope, but it's a fragile thing, and so is his soul, and I am not going to be the one to crush either. I know he has to let go eventually. He does, too, I think. But people let go in their own way at their own time. He's not ready yet, but he will be. This fight was a good thing, all in all."

"How do you figure that?"

"Nothing like a little near-death to make you reevaluate the merits of living," Weller said, but didn't smile. "That boy nearly got his head handed to him today, and that scared the hell out of him. Now, he's talking and that's good. But it can go either way. Push him too hard and he'll bottle himself right back up. That's what Tom does: handles things on his own."

"Like going to the lake by himself."

"Yeah, yeah." She was tiring him out. "Can we get past this already? And give the kid some credit: other boys'd crawl into their bags and never come out after a fight like this."

"My God." Her eyes sharpened. "You *admire* him. What is he, the boy you always wanted to be but weren't? Or is it more? Don't tell me you *care* about him. For heaven's sake . . . he's a *tool*, Weller."

"Anyone can tell you, you got to take good care of your tools, you want them to work."

"Don't give me any of your folksy cowboy bullshit." She let go of a humorless grunt. "So when the sudden conversion?"

On the rise. When I heard her call and him answer and near about kill himself to get to her. Then I realized just what I'd done and that nothing, not even revenge, is worth this. If ever anyone needed to let go of the past . . . But he doubted it would be wise to share any of this with Mellie, who had her own allegiances and none of them to *him*. Showing her his back, Weller tore open a second packet of instant. The aroma of strong coffee hit him the way it always did, something so fine and good it hurt to think there would come a time when this simple pleasure would also vanish. No one would be importing coffee beans or manufacturing instant for years, maybe decades. "I'm only saying I understand where he's coming from. I also think it's in our best interest to get at what's bothering him about that Chucky. I'm just not sold that he's told us everything."

"Oh?" He practically heard her eyebrows arch. "What do you think he's leaving out?"

"I don't think it's conscious," he said, tipping the pack of instant so the granules came in a slow stream. "Just a hunch. I think he *knows* something but can't put his finger on it. Understand what I'm saying? Like seeing someone in a crowd you could swear you've met but you can't remember their name or even how you know them. Anyway, I figure, sit with him awhile, don't push, let him calm down . . . whatever's bothering him will find its way out." *With a little help, that is.* But Mellie didn't need to know that. "Best thing for him now is some rest; then get him back out there with the kids. They'll anchor him better than anything."

"Uh-huh." Pause. "I wonder how well you and Tom will get along once we get to Rule."

His heart skipped a beat. *Easy. Don't let her goad you.* He tried relaxing the angry jut of his jaw. "Yeah, what's the word on that anyway? How much longer we going to sit here?"

"You have a problem with that?"

He stirred, watching as the liquid quickened and grew dark. "Just asking."

Another pause. "We're supposed to wait."

He turned a look. "For what?"

She favored him with a wintery smile. "Well, let me see. You're a little banged up, Tom is a mess, and only a few of these children can actually fight. I agree that with Tom back, it's best to put his time to good use. Instead of running all over creation looking for a girl who's *dead*, a few bombs, some flamethrowers—they'd be nice."

"But that's not why we're waiting," he said. "*He* has plenty of firepower to spare. That's where we got the C4 in the first place. So what's the holdup?"

"What do you care? Frankly, I'd think you'd be relieved. Every second we delay is one more when Tom never knows just how much you've lied."

Despite himself, he felt a jab of fear. "I don't recall you being all that honest yourself."

"True, but you and Tom being blood brothers all of a sudden . . . have you ever considered that it might be better all around if Tom never makes it?"

He gave her a sharp look. "Don't you even think it."

"Someone has to." She spread her hands, which were blunt and weathered, like the rest of her. "Once Tom discovers the truth, I wouldn't be surprised if he can't decide between throwing you to the Chuckies or killing you very, very slowly."

"Why don't you let me worry about that?"

"Sure. That's your call . . . until it's not. As for when we go"—she hunched a shoulder, then let it fall—"I do what I'm told. He wants us to wait."

Wait for what? That was the question. To be honest, the idea of going back to Rule wasn't all that appealing, because Mellie was right. Weller *had* told a lot of lies to a lot of people. He'd thought that bringing down Peter, who really *was* to blame, then destroying the mine and killing all of Rule's precious little Chuckies would ease the old grief that just wouldn't let go. Or make the face of sweet dead Mandy finally fade. Yet he had done much worse, not only lying but turning in Kincaid, a *friend*, so that little pissant Aidan could do his devil's work as Kincaid screamed and *screamed*, sacrificing himself to buy Chris time to get clear. And for what? If the cold hadn't taken Chris, the Chuckies would've. Nathan, too, and the girl, Lena.

And now here's Tom, self-destructing in front of my eyes, and this is on me, too.

"So." He looked away from his thoughts to find her steady gray gaze. "Can you control him?" she said.

"Oh yeah," he said, not at all sure, and not liking that one bit either. He reached into the box to rummage for sugar. "Last thing we need is a martyr."

Because his back was turned, he missed her expression.

He would live to regret that.

37

"Look, unless you have a better idea, keeping him locked up ought to be fine. I mean, he's not a ghost or a zombie or Lazarus." Jayden ran a hand through his light brown mop. "The dogs gave him a pass, so we know he isn't turning. You need to take a breath, Hannah. This kid being alive isn't a miracle any more than Ellie's a superhero."

"She dragged a boy easily twice her body weight." Hannah sipped anise tea, rolling the steaming drink around her tongue, enjoying the light aroma of sweet licorice. The fact that the drink was still *hot*, almost a half hour after brewing, was nearly as wonderful. Equipped with its own woodstove, this second-story bedroom was toasty warm, and spacious, with its own sitting area. It was also the only room that could be locked from the outside, unusual in an Amish home. Sometimes Hannah wondered if the previous owners had been forced to keep a lunatic relative under lock and key, like Mr. Rochester squirreling away crazy Bertha.

Now, if we can keep Ellie from camping out in the hall. Reluctant to let Chris out of her sight, the little girl had argued for moving into the sickroom. Thank goodness for Eli: *Ellie, he's not a pet.*

"You know that death house," she said. "There's no way she could've gotten Chris to the ramp, much less hoisted him across the saddle. She doesn't have the strength."

"Which doesn't make it a miracle. In an emergency, more

adrenaline means increased blood flow to muscles and, therefore, more strength. You know the science as well as I do."

"Granted, but science doesn't explain it all. And what about the crows? Ravens and crows and sparrows are psychopomps." She'd lugged up books from her collection downstairs and now tapped a text from a sophomore seminar: *Encyclopedia of Myth, Magic, and Mysticism.* "Guides to help the soul reach the afterlife."

"And bring a soul to a newborn." Jayden shrugged. "I read the same entry. Angels performed the same function. You saying that *crows* brought this kid's soul back?"

Or were drawn there to take it away. She stared into her mug. "I don't know what I mean. There are just too many questions for which I have no answers."

"Which, I repeat, does not make any of this a miracle." Jayden eyed her askance. "I know you and Isaac do the hexes and charms, but you don't still *believe* all that, do you? I mean, you went to *college.*"

Oh, she could tell him a couple stories. Amish pow-wow and folk magic paled compared to the weird rituals she'd seen from some kids at school who decided they were Wiccans. "But all sympathetic magic has some basis in fact. The brain's wired to seek the mystical, so . . ."

"Just because we're hardwired to *want* to believe doesn't make it true."

She could easily point out that there must be some evolutionary advantage to belief or out-of-body experiences. Hard science was a language Jayden would understand. He demurred to Isaac and Hannah about the hex signs, the Brauche bags, and charms because he saw no harm. Besides, she was the botanist and Isaac's apprentice, with just enough physiology and biology under her belt to understand which folk remedies might actually be helpful.

"Okay. Fine. It's not magic," she said. "You got a theory?"

"I've got ideas. I think *he*"—Jayden tipped his head toward the bed and the boy under a heap of comforters—"is a combination of serendipity and really good luck. There's a logical explanation for why he survived. We just don't know what. But that doesn't mean there isn't science behind it. That's like saying thunder's Thor's hammer. A much bigger problem is what to do when he wakes up."

"If he does." While Chris's color had improved in the last hour, the blush coming back to his nails and gums, he showed no signs of waking. If he really was asleep. She honestly didn't know. In the hush, his raw, jagged breaths were very loud but normal, if you were dreaming. The rough gasps Ellie heard might not have been proper breathing at all, not in the technical sense of drawing in air. It was normal for people on the verge of death—and those teetering on the edge of a deep coma—to gasp.

Except I saw that already; I listened to this boy die, and now he's come back to life?

"If?" Jayden frowned. "But I thought you said he's dreaming."

"I think so, but he's been like this for hours. Ellie said he was in REM back at the death house." From her exam, it was clear that Chris wasn't in any coma or other state of unconsciousness described in the books at her disposal. For all intents and purposes, Chris was deep in the sleep of the dreaming dead, a state from which he couldn't or wouldn't be roused. Lord knows, she'd tried: shone her tiny penlight in his eyes, pricked him with a needle, shouted, squirted icy water into his ears. Zip. "REM sleep shouldn't last this long."

"But you said there are people who have breakthrough episodes of REM all the time."

"Those who have narcolepsy, yes. It's the closest match." She placed a hand on the topmost book in her stack, *Standard Textbook of Clinical Neurology, Tenth Edition*. The solidity of those embossed letters against her palm was reassuring. "It's not an illness or true sleeping sickness. It's a disorder, like diabetes, where people are overcome with an urge to sleep."

"But you said narcoleptics have these really vivid hallucinations."

"Hypnagogic, yeah. They're not true dreams." She bracketed a sliver of air between two fingers. "They happen in this very narrow window *between* dreams and wakefulness."

"So how do you know he's not on a really wild trip? Isn't that what the mushroom was for?" Jayden flicked a finger at a hand-stitched leather diary. "Not to kill but help you dream?"

"According to the original recipe. The encyclopedia says the Ojibwe drank the decoction in order to help the soul find its way to the Land of the Ghosts."

"By way of visions, right? Weird dreams? Like, they took a helluva trip?"

"Yes, in low doses. And in higher doses, it kills you," Hannah said, a little impatient now. What a formula using hallucinogenic mushrooms was doing in an old handwritten journal of Amish Brauche spells and pow-wow charms, she had no clue. Neither did Isaac. They both supposed the original Amish settlers had incorporated local customs. But why this decoction from this particular mushroom? While the old ways involved a fair amount of folk magic and white witchcraft—and most practitioners were Pennsylvania Dutch—as a rule, the Amish weren't into ecstatic experiences. If she were back in Houghton, she could consult the university library, the science department's database, maybe figure it out, but . . . She gave the idea an irritable mental shove. Wishing would get her nowhere. "I know all that, Jayden, but isn't the more pressing question, why isn't Chris dead?" *And what brought him back?*

"That's easy. The dose is weight-dependent and you had to guess. He was so weak already, he slipped away fast and you figured you'd given him enough."

She'd already thought of the same thing. "I accept that. But think, Jayden. It's really *cold*. Why haven't his tissues frozen? Or let's say that, by some miracle, his core temperature didn't drop far enough. That still leaves hands, fingers, toes, his ears. But he doesn't have frostbite. His wounds are half healed. How did that happen?" She didn't bother pointing out that a badly lacerated liver ought to be a death sentence all by itself. That and his collapsed lung were why she'd poisoned Chris in the first place. Letting him slip away into sleep was a final kindness.

Looks like you were wrong about that, too. Which brought up unsettling questions about the other children to whom she'd given the poison. *But you had no choice. They were turning. The dogs told you so. Once that happens, there's no coming back.* As far as they knew. Considering the people-eater's limited menu, just how would you keep someone like that alive long enough to find out?

"Doesn't it say in the encyclopedia that the old Vedic recipe used honey and that it was supposed to make you immortal?" When she only gave him a look, Jayden shrugged. "Look, you have to get past this. *I* accept there's science underneath all this. But we'll never explain it without a detailed chemical analysis and a couple dozen experiments."

"So, take this resurrection on faith?" She couldn't resist. Clinging to science was, when you got right down to it, just a god of a different flavor.

"Ha-ha. Let's hypothesize, all right? For whatever reason, his metabolic rate slowed down. There are precedents in nature. Many species of fish and insects and flies can live perfectly well in intense cold. They manufacture glycerol from fat, which lowers the freezing point of their blood. And before you tell me that he's not a fly or fish, I'll remind you that the human body also makes glycerol as a by-product of fat metabolism. So what if this particular mushroom also stimulates the production of glycerol? Then he'd be protected. His body would cool down, but his core and brain wouldn't croak." He pointed at the neurology text. "It says in there that they put coma patients on cooling blankets and used drugs to lower body temperature."

"To protect the brain," she said. "I know. But that's still a lot of *ifs*."

"A heck of a lot easier to accept than a miracle. There's also something else we're not considering. Maybe he's just, you know, *different*." Jayden tapped his temple. "Something about his brain protected him from the poison and turned it into something else. I mean, think about *us*. We ought to be people-eaters and we're not. You can say it's a miracle, but I'll bet if there were scientists, they'd eventually figure out why we're still okay."

"If we stay that way. Some of the younger kids, like Eli and Ellie and Connor—they still might turn. We all might."

"Okay, yeah, I'm not wild about the idea of waking up one morning with a hankering for a people-burger, but I can't live every day waiting for the other shoe to drop. Know what I think is *really* bugging you?" Jayden stretched across the table and gave the back of her left hand a tentative touch. "You're freaked because you think you made a mistake."

"Because I was obviously *wrong*, and I don't like mistakes. Make a mistake, people die." She screwed her gaze to his fingers, long but rougher now and calloused from long hours of swinging an ax and reining horses. "And I didn't give Chris a choice."

"He wouldn't have taken the drug. You know that," he said, gently. "Besides, how do you know that we didn't *save* him? What if the decoction was *exactly* what he needed? Think about that. This could be something really big." His hand closed over hers. "It might *help* us in the future."

She had to be careful. They made a good team. Just because Jayden wanted more didn't mean she should encourage him—especially now, with the appearance of this strange boy whose face revived a host of other memories, most of them very bad. "If we understood it. It's not an experiment I can run again until . . ." *Until one of us is injured so badly we'll die anyway.* After another moment, she eased her hand away, covering the move by picking up her mug. "What about the girl? The one Ellie saw?"

"I don't know," Jayden said, his tone as suddenly stony as his face. "Tomorrow, I'll take Connor and we'll fetch Isaac to take a look at this kid. While I'm there, I can check with the others, see if anyone turned and got away before they could be . . . you know . . . dealt with. Just be glad that girl was alone. I'm not sure Ellie would've made it past more than one."

"But what was that girl doing there? We've been so careful. We're in the middle of nowhere. The winter won't break for another month or two. There's no reason for any kid to be wandering *back* where there were no kids in the first place. *And* she was out during the day. Jayden, what if they're adapting, or changing again?" Lord knew, they already had enough problems without having to worry about people-eaters taking over their days, too.

"I don't know, Hannah. If they are, there's not much we can do about that. Let's just chalk it up as one more big booga-booga supernatural mystery, all right?" Pushing back from the table, he gave her a tight smile. "Or a God-miracle, how about *that*?"

"Don't." Her eyes dodged to her books. "Don't be angry with me."

"Angry? Oh, Hannah." There was a short silence and then the heavy tread of his boots as he headed for the door. "I wish I could be, because that would be so much easier."

38

Two hours into this, and he was still doing all the talking, telling stories from after 'Nam: ". . . laid open my leg with a saw, and I'm thinking, no way I'm going to the emergency room. So I wander over to my neighbor, this lady doc, and show her—"

"S-someone . . . someone m-made them."

Story forgotten, Weller pulled from his slouch. *Now we're cooking.* He'd settled Tom onto his cot, and Weller now saw that the boy's eyes were glazed, a little unfocused. Setting his own mug on the floor, Weller slid a finger to one of Tom's wrists, felt that slow, steady pulse. Tom was a tough nut, but not even *he* could fight two Xanax, their aluminum bite covered with strong coffee and sugar. *Better living through chemistry.* A grim thought but entirely appropriate.

"Made them." When there was no response, Weller gave the boy a little shake. "Tom?"

"Uhm." Rousing himself, Tom swallowed. "Well. More like . . ." Tom had squared his mug on his chest, but when he tried to drink, the mug nearly slipped from his slack fingers.

"Here, let me take that." Weller gently extricated the mug and set it down beside his. "Tell me what you saw."

"They're different."

They. "More than one?"

"Uh-huh." Tom gave a lethargic nod. "Boy, in the . . . the trees."

"A boy. Waiting?"

"No." Tom's head rolled left then right. "Watching." He licked his lips. "He should've come . . . come after me. I was beat up. Hurt. Had the Bravo by then, probably could've taken him down, but if there'd been more . . . don't know if I would've made it. Only the kid . . . didn't. He was . . . learning? No, s'not right. *Studying*. Maybe even . . . *connected* somehow."

"Connected?" That got his attention. *Jesus Christ, don't tell me he actually figured out how.* "How do you know that, Tom? What do you mean, *connected*? To the girl?"

"Yeah. Jusss . . . a feeling. I think there were others, too."

"More Chuckies? Back in the trees?"

Tom nodded again. His skin was paler than his bandages. "But I thought . . . I also saw *men*."

Weller felt the spit wick off his tongue. "What?"

"Men. Old. At least two, maybe three. They were—"

"Watching," Weller finished for him. His stomach went icy. "Maybe evaluating?"

"Or working together. I think so." Withdrawing his right arm from beneath a thick blanket, Tom held it, unsteadily, in front of his face before turning it to show Weller the crisscross of cuts and scrapes. "It makes no sense. That girl could've come for me earlier. I was . . ." His eyes rolled, drifted away, then gradually tacked to true. His words got mushier. "I wassen . . . wasn't paying attention. Sh-she only showed herself after . . ."

"After you cut your hands. When the wind changed and she got your scent." Which meant something Tom was *not* saying: that the girl, the boy, those other Chuckies and *men* probably came from somewhere relatively close—and *goddamn* it.

"Her . . . her *eyes*. J-jacked u-up." Tom rubbed a slow hand over his mouth. "D-drugged."

Even though he'd steeled himself for this, the word knocked him back. "Drugged. You think she was fed something?"

Tom moved his head in a slow, deliberate nod. "When you're out-side the w-wire . . . d-don't sleep. Can't."

"Because there are pills." He knew exactly where this was going now. The standard Vietnam myth was that every American soldier was some kind of crazed junkie. Total bull. Oh, he'd known his share of potheads, dopers, boys into junk or fat A-bombs, which were blunts mixed with heroin. But it wasn't as if the military didn't help things along. Weller's dad, a pilot, served during World War II, when the Army Air Force was only too tickled to dole out their little go-pills: good old-fashioned speed, which Weller used plenty of in his day, too. Ate it like candy sometimes. No other way to stay awake and alert. It could also screw you, big-time, the crash afterward so bad you thought you'd never dig yourself out of that hole.

There had been *other* pills, too, ones that did a whole lot more: not only kept you up but turned off sleep altogether. Weller knew plenty of guys who'd volunteered as guinea pigs, because, hell, he'd *worked* on them. For those soldiers, anything was better than playing the odds, when the life expectancy of a machine gunner in a hot LZ was about eight seconds.

"Or you find pills. I never . . . too scared they'd mess me up the way the Army—" Tom ground to a halt.

There we go. That's what this is about. "What about the Army, Tom? What did they do?" When Tom was silent, Weller pressed: "In 'Nam, they got volunteers. Ran experiments. Not just the LSD or sarin or BZ. I'm talking drugs to make you crazy-good at killing—"

"I think they might have tried that," Tom whispered. It came fast, as if he knew he was sinking and needed to get this out. "Because you got to stay alert. Can't let yourself sleep. You live on speed and fear, or just plain fear."

"Or you're dead."

"Or dreaming," Tom said. "Just as bad. The dreams . . . they take over, like the flashbacks, until it's like you're in this bottle, no way out, and dreams and what's real . . . they all mix together. So the shrinks . . . they have lots of pills." He let out a cawing laugh, but it was wheezy and weak. "Call it 'damage control.' Keep the guys worst off close to the front lines, let them rest and get some decent chow, but also feed them all kinds of pills. So you take what the Army shrinks dole out, and other stuff, too."

"Black market?"

"Some. Yeah. But if you take too much, or the wrong type . . ."

"You go crazy."

"Worse." The smudges under Tom's haunted eyes were livid as bruises. "You can't be stopped. You keep going in this . . . this *frenzy*. And that girl . . . her eyes. Blood eyes . . ."

"What?" Weller said sharply. "You mean, blood*shot*, right? Like a bad hangover."

"No." Tom's head wobbled, and his voice was dwindling like water spiraling down a drain. "No no no . . . no whites. Just red and black."

Oh, you crazy bastard, you really did it this time around. "I've seen that," Weller said. "In 'Nam, we called them berserkers."

"Yeah?" Tom's lips thinned in a faint grimace. His eyes drifted shut. "We didn't."

"No?" Weller waited, noting how Tom's breathing had settled. "Tom?"

Tom didn't reply. The deep lines of weariness and grief were still there, but his muscles had relaxed into sleep. That was all right. Weller now knew more than enough and understood that they all might be in real trouble. If the Chuckies *could* be manipulated, if that was possible, he knew precisely who was insane enough, *smart* enough, to do it. The world had gone to hell in a handbasket almost five months ago. Plenty of time, especially if you were well supplied, a planner and an experimenter, someone with a prepared mind. Lord knew, he'd nurtured *his* hunger for revenge long enough.

So what in hell am I going to do now? Weller skimmed a hand over his forehead and was not at all surprised that the palm came away oiled with sour sweat. This whole ugly business was out of control. It had changed to something he didn't recognize. He should have gotten clear as soon as the mine went. Just picked up and left. For God's sake, hadn't he already avenged Mandy? Peter was dead, and Rule couldn't be far behind, what with their precious little Chuckies well on their way home by now. Shouldn't that be enough for him? Because there was revenge, and then there was . . . End Times. Revelations. *And I don't even believe in that crap.*

Should he fight this? Try to do something? Did he even have to? Sure, he *could* take a chance, soldier to soldier, and tell Tom what he knew. But Mellie *was* right. Tom was on the brink, had been for a while, and there was no way to predict what the boy's reaction might be. Getting *himself* killed trying to come clean wouldn't help anyone, and he wasn't even sure, exactly, of the bigger picture here or what was going on. All he had were bits and pieces, suppositions and sus-picions. So, would it be better to get out now, while he still had the chance? Build himself a new life someplace where he wasn't known, with what time he had left?

But there are these kids, just starting out in life. There's Tom, carrying grief he shouldn't have had to bear. We got them into this. No doubt Mellie saw the kids as expendable, too. But Weller just didn't know what he should do, what was safest and which the lesser evil . . .

Tom sucked in a sudden breath as if he'd just found something in the dark of his mind and dragged it up to the light. When Weller looked back, Tom's eyes were open again but so clear that it was like looking into the clean, deep, chilling blue of Superior.

"What?" Weller asked.

"Zombies," Tom said, very clearly. "We called them zombies."

PART THREE:
BREAKING POINT

39

Ten days after the avalanche, in the first week of March, Alex staggered from the wreckage of a tumbledown cabin just off a nondescript fire road somewhere west of the mine and southwest of Rule. At least, she thought it was west-southwest. After days on the trail, she had a lot on her mind. Like finding food before she became it.

There was new blood in her mouth and a huge knot on the back of her head. She didn't need a mirror to see the swelling under her left cheek where Acne had clobbered her not so long ago. God, the kid's fist had felt like the business end of a pile driver.

She was headed toward the shed—and that weird mound she'd seen earlier—but halfway there, she either fell or tripped, she wasn't sure. Blundering through snow, her boots probably tangled. When she hit, she let herself sink, really dig in so the cold could start its work of burning her skin, scorching its way through her brain. Maybe reduce the monster to a cinder.

God, please. Please, help me. She had to fight. *Can't break. Can't give in. Got to stay me, no matter what Wolf wants or thinks.*

She began to swim, dragging herself on hands and knees, carving a snail's path through snow, heading for a dilapidated shed next to a curtain of corroded chicken wire, sucking air through a windpipe that felt as if it had been slashed by razor wire. Another few seconds with his hands around her neck and Acne would've crushed her throat.

On her knees now before that mound. Patchy with snow, the hill was about three feet high and reared on the shed's south side, where there was the most light and warmth. She stared at the mound a good ten seconds, maybe as long as thirty. A loamy aroma steamed from the rich, dark earth. The smell was a little like flat beer.

Then her eyes snagged on something small and black scuttling over a white patch.

Don't think, Alex. She eyed another tiny black scuttle. *Fight, you've got to fight. Just do it.*

Because things were bad. Really, really bad.

Ten days ago:

Her memories of what happened after the avalanche were vague, a jumpy, chaotic collage about as comprehensible as a badly edited YouTube video. What came to her first was a rhythmic swaying like the pitch of a small boat in a high swell. Her chest was very hot, the tortured lining of her lungs on fire, even as her body shuddered with cold. Mostly, everything was a swirly blur as she swayed back and forth and back and forth—and then she went away again, sinking into the dark waters of unconsciousness. She probably did that a couple times, like a periscope coming up for a peek.

Finally, fading back, she was first aware of a hand cupping the back of her head. She was falling, too, and she landed on . . . a bed? A boat? Her head was swimmy but also ballooning, expanding, the monster swelling and stretching as if it had sprouted arms and hands and fingers and was searching for something—someone—to grab. She was very relaxed, almost peaceful, which was strange if you considered the cold and the steady pressure on her chest, like the heel of a sturdy boot.

Then something skimmed her right cheek. The back of a hand— and were those fingers? Her head lolled toward a coil of scent that was black mist and something sweet, crisp . . . *Chris?* Or wait, no—the aroma was deep and rich and smoky. *Tom.* It felt like a thought and then a sigh because she tasted his name in a dreamy whisper. "Tom. Tom?"

In the next moment, she was falling even further, sinking away from herself but pulling *him* down with her, tasting him, warm, so warm, Tom's urgent mouth on hers, the sigh of his breath over her tongue, the desire a hot rose that unfurled in her chest. A strange liquid heat raced up her thighs, and she felt her back arching, her heart beginning to thump harder and harder, and then his weight on her body, her arms twining around his neck, his hands slipping into her hair, over her face, and she moaned into his mouth—*yes yes yes yes*—as Tom's fingers trailed over the sensitive skin of her throat, the ridge of her collarbone, before slipping just a little further—

And that was when she felt a very strange tug.

Tom was . . . working a zipper? Yes, that's what it was, and that was fine, it was *good*; she wanted this and him; she was so hot, burning up. And yet, she was also strangely cold, and why was that?

Suddenly, all these things—the sensations, her thoughts—slid and shifted like a slow dissolve in a movie. Now, there were other hands and a different body on hers. The aroma of wood smoke and musk gave way to shadows and sweet apples as—*Chris, that's Chris*—his mouth found hers. The moment was electric, exactly like the morning, months back in Rule, when she and Chris had kissed in the sleigh: mist and darkness and a blaze of desire as their hands twined, and their bodies, too.

Yet there was still something off. She felt the hitch, the way her mind tripped over a detail that did not belong, and then she had it. It was the smell, no longer mist and apples but something fetid and spoiled. Oozy green pus flooded into her mouth. *Wait.* Choking, she recoiled, her throat working, the muck slithering down her throat, and now she couldn't breathe, she couldn't breathe, she *couldn't* . . .

"Ugh!" Gasping, she slammed back into herself, her consciousness collapsing to a point as she pulled away from the dream, and woke.

Wolf was there, haloed against a stunning, bright blue sky. He wasn't draped over her body. His hands weren't tracing her cheeks or the angle of her jaw, and his mouth was most certainly *not* on hers. But she *was* flat on her back, not in the snow but on a sleeping bag, and his fingers *were* working at a snarl of parka trapped in the teeth of a zipper, and he *was* trying to undress her.

"*No!*" She gave a spastic little jerk. She tried punching, but her arms were lead pipes, her muscles balky and uncooperative. This was like Leopard, coming for her in the mine and . . . *Wait. Knife. I have Leopard's knife . . . Get up, get up!* She bolted to a sit. Caught off-guard, Wolf flinched back to sprawl in the snow, dangerously close to a small, crackling fire. Heart sputtering, she slapped awkward fingers along her right leg, clumsy fingers searching for the sheath.

Someone jammed a hand into her right shoulder and slammed her back. Thrashing, she got both hands up before Acne—the boy who had been Ben Stiemke—grabbed her wrists. Pinning her, he let his weight drop with a hard *thump* that drove the air from her lungs in a grunt. If she'd been thinking, she'd have twisted around for a bite or tucked her knees, but she was so panicked that she reared instead, craning her neck, teeth clashing. He jerked his face out of the way, a little too far, and that was just as good. She felt the pressure on her chest let up, read the bow of his back. Acne was off-balance and she wouldn't have another chance. Howling, she rammed the point of her knee into his groin.

Acne let out an abortive *guh!* It was like she'd hit the emergency override. Acne's eyes went round as headlamps; all the blood fled his face. She didn't think he was even breathing. Then he crumpled, slumping to one side, hands cupping his crotch, mouth hanging open to let out this weird, choked *aaawww.*

As soon as his weight left her legs, she bucked him the rest of the way. Awkward as a crab, she scurried off the sleeping bag. Her body was electric, as if all the circuit breakers had been reset, the connections sizzling back to life. Dimly, she heard the clatter of bolts being thrown, the rasp of metal, and knew the others—wherever they were; she was so wild with fear she'd lost track even of Wolf— had drawn their weapons. She didn't care. Screeching, she scrambled to her feet, Leopard's knife now in hand, and shouted through terrified tears, "Get away, get away, get *away!*"

Discounting Acne, now moaning and slobbering on the snow, and Wolf, there were three others: Marley, that lanky kid with the dreads she remembered, and two younger boys, maybe sophomores and obviously brothers. Same pug nose, same piggy little eyes. Both had hair that was either very dark brown or black, and toted Bushmaster ACRs, the business ends pointed her way. The taller brother was the nervous, twitchy type; the minty fizz of his anxiety leaked through his pores. By contrast, his brother was rounder, shorter, calmer, and she thought, *Bert and Ernie.*

Wolf had made his feet. His expression, which was Chris's in another life, was taut and intent but not drawn in the predatory snarl he wore right before zeroing in on his next Happy Meal. A second later, she also sussed out that telltale resin pop, the sparking of pine sap from a fire burning too hot, very bright. The air grew weighty as a heavy coat as the Changed did their weird, unknowable Changed-speak mumbo jumbo. Seated in her brain, the monster shifted, nosing up for a sniff as if about to butt into the conversation. Or only land her inside Wolf's head again, as had happened in the tunnel during the mine's collapse.

Oh no, you don't. Her mouth felt crawly, as if there was a busy little spider in there, bustling over her tongue. Had Wolf *kissed* her? *No, no, that was a dream.* Or, maybe, that was what Wolf *wanted*: her and him, together. She could feel a new flare of hysteria as her self-control tried to unravel. *It didn't happen. You didn't want him, you* don't. *It was the monster, it was all the monster.* Reaching out to its own kind, the way it had when she was slipping away, slowly suffocating under the snow? She remembered that bizarre moment when her mind had shimmied, stepped away, and how then she'd seen a field of snow and broken trees and rocks . . .

And a ski pole. My God, that wasn't the bright light at the end of the tunnel. I was in Wolf's head again. He was looking for me after the avalanche, trying to figure out where I was under the snow.

That was the only explanation for why she was alive. When she'd passed out for that final time, only minutes from death, the monster had slipped its noose, oiling out in black tendrils. Because like seeks like.

"What do you want from me?" Her voice quaked. Leopard's knife wobbled, and she clutched with both hands to steady it. She was hunched over, very cold now, trembling uncontrollably. Her hair hung in icy clots, although her parka was . . . dry? How could that be? Her clothes were still wet. *Wait, wait a minute.* Her breath hung in her throat. *My parka was sopping wet. How can it—*

Her gaze drifted to her right arm, and she saw, immediately, why *this* parka was dry. The color, gunmetal gray, was wrong. It was also too large, the cuff loose around her wrist. The coat puffed out from her chest, and was clearly intended for someone much bigger and more muscular. The parka actually reminded her of Tom's turtleneck, the one he'd given her in the Waucamaw after he'd carried her, bleeding, unconscious, and soaked through, back to his camp and then gotten her out of her wet clothes to keep her warm.

Her eyes shot to Wolf, who reeked of sweat and boiled raccoon guts and damp iron. Blood crusted half his face. That rock; she remembered he'd been hit. Now that she was shocked enough to notice, she saw that he wore only a bulky wool sweater over which was knotted a wolf's skin. From the streaks of amber in the fur, she knew this cowl was new, a replacement for the one Leopard had stolen when Spider took over the pack.

She understood then: Wolf had given up his parka for her. Her grimy white coat, still wet, was spread over rocks, close to the fire.

Only later would she appreciate the huge risk Wolf was taking. The day into which she'd awakened was clear. Judging from the stabs of strong light through trees, it was well into mid-morning, maybe close to noon, and yet the Changed were still awake, still moving. That fact alone—Wolf's crew pulling their version of an all-nighter—should've clued her in on just how desperate they must be, and how dangerous the current situation was. The mine was gone. A lot of Changed *and* prisoners were dead. Any Changed who'd gotten away or been somewhere in the vicinity would be hungry—and she was fresh meat. Catch her scent, might as well ring the dinner bell. Once Wolf and his crew had pulled her from that icy tomb, they *had* to make tracks or risk being overwhelmed.

But then Wolf had made them stop and build a fire. He'd stripped her sodden parka and given up his to save her from freezing to death. It was exactly what Tom had done, what Chris would do in the same situation. Wolf was doing his best to keep her alive, and warm.

"Why?" she said to him. "What do you want from me, Wolf? What do you *want?*"

She got a partial answer when the Changed got ready to move out and Wolf handed her a green canvas combat medic's pack.

She'd seen one before. Her dad once stowed something just like it in the trunk of his cruiser because, by definition, all cops were first-responders. His wasn't all that stuffed: just the barest essentials to keep a smashed-up person from tanking before the EMTs arrived.

This pack was much different, with a gazillion pockets and flaps, and loaded for bear: bandages, gauze, glucose tablets, syringes, scissors, a few dozen packets of antibiotics—even that special QuikClot gauze combat medics used to staunch bleeding PDQ. Kincaid would've given his eyeteeth for something like this.

She also knew what the pack meant and now had an inkling about why Wolf had gone to such trouble to rescue her. Wolf knew she had the basics down. After all, he'd eaten part of her shoulder and then seen her dress the wound. True, Wolf might have grown very attached to her, might *want* her . . . but for him, she was also a very valuable prisoner: a camp nurse with a skill-set that just might come in handy.

Winters were long in the U.P.; spring was a good month and a half in the future. The days were so bone-chilling that whenever Wolf and his crew weren't out hunting, they all burrowed deep into their bags and in every stitch of clothing. Alex slept with her boots clamped between her knees and a water bottle tucked against her stomach to keep everything from freezing.

More and more frequently, Wolf and his people also hunted by day, because that's when the scarce game was out and moving around. (Or maybe the Changed were Changing in other ways. If they grew to own the days . . . that was bad.) So far away from Rule, there were no more pit stops at the equivalent of a McDonald's drive-through, no regular game trail or route they followed. This meant no convenient herd to drive from one fun house to the next. So, no more getting down, getting funky, getting laid, getting wasted on a Saturday night.

This also translated into no real possibility of predictable resupply for her either. She sometimes ate when they ate, depending on whether the person they hunted down had a pack. If that poor soul did, she might score jerky or a granola bar or sardines. Once, she even gagged down a tiny foil packet of cat treats that promised to maintain good gum health and scrub away all that nasty tartar: *Crunchy outside! Soft inside!* Whatever worked.

More often than not, however, she got zip because Wolf came up empty. Then she was reduced to pebbly, desiccated rose hips, withered cattail tubers, dried-up platters of oyster mushrooms. And forget those wildly popular novels where the heroine muses on how raw pine would do in a pinch. Hah. HAH. Drinking turpentine would have been easier. Boiling the mess worked, but she wasn't prepared for what happened to the water, which turned a bright blood-red. Just oh so appropriate. On the other hand, since rose hips and pine had loads of vitamin C, she wouldn't die of scurvy.

Oh. Yay.

Something was tracking them, too, and had been for the last week. An animal, although she wasn't quite sure what. The scent was familiar and yet indescribable, one that made her think both of Ghost, her blue-eyed Weimaraner, and the road to Rule, where she'd seen the wolves and that yellow-eyed alpha male. Whatever *this* was, it wasn't a wolf, not quite. She hadn't spotted it yet, but kept a nervous eye peeled and her nose up. Any animal hungry and desperate enough would look for a chance to take down a person. Or maybe it was only after scraps? Shit out of luck, if true; Wolf's crew even cracked bones to suck out all the yummy marrow. If anything, one whiff of Wolf's cowl ought to send this animal running for the hills.

And *that* was odd, too. Because Wolf *did* have that wolf skin, yet neither he nor the others showed any awareness of this animal at all. Maybe they were too hungry to care.

Still. Freaked her out. Just one more thing to worry about.

She didn't know where they were going, or even why. But there was something stuck in Wolf's craw. It was in his smell, one that said *family*; that breathed *safe* in a sweet perfume of lilacs and honeysuckle; that was the scent of her father, ghosting from the haunted attic of her mind: *Jump, sweetheart.*

So she knew. Wherever they were headed, Wolf had been there already: hiding, healing, biding his time. Waiting for the perfect moment to come back and snatch her.

She supposed she ought to be grateful that she was off the Changed's takeout menu, and that Wolf let her forage. Given how well *they* were doing—like, *not*—his new crew could've mutinied, killed him, and then eaten her. The fact that the other kids stuck with Wolf *was* a mystery, although in tough times, desperate people gravitated to a leader who at least held out hope. From the sparse pickings, she doubted other Changed were doing any better. Tom once said Napoleon figured out that armies marched on their stomachs, and the best leaders were those who not only got right down in the trenches with their men but took care of them first.

Wolf seemed to understand that. Whenever his crew bagged a nice, juicy someone, Wolf always hung back and made sure the others ate first before helping himself to whatever scanty leavings remained. So Wolf must have known just how precarious the situation was.

Which probably explained why, as they slept, Wolf always wedged himself between her and the others, spooning against her back: a proximity that made her throat flutter and her pulse quicken when her skin wasn't trying to tear itself from her bones.

Now, ten days after pulling a Lady Lazarus, her luck had finally run out. She only had herself to blame. At the time, she was boiling a mess of white pine, daydreaming about food, and plotting murder—and so just wasn't on her game.

Their current accommodations were miserable: a sad, two-room pile of aging logs and a couple busted windows. The walls were so warped, thin drifts of snow had silted in through the chinks. From the lingering aroma of aluminum and that small mountain of crushed empties in one corner, she suspected the original owner was some guy who came out to get away from it all. A little shooting, a lot of boozing—what's not to like?

Judging from the rose light spraying an intact west window, it was late afternoon. Out of habit, Alex's eyes automatically fell to Ellie's Mickey Mouse watch, still on her wrist: 7:13. Of course, that wasn't the correct time. For Mickey, it was always thirteen past seven, the moment when the watch finally threw in the towel after all that water. Another minute or so under the snow and she figured she would have, too.

Anyway, call it . . . five o'clock? Wolf and the others should be back soon, oh goody.

God, I hope he's got something. An awful thought, but it wasn't as if getting all broody about it would help whoever Wolf hunted down. Carefully easing Leopard's knife into a dented camp pot seated over coals in the cabin's fireplace, she gave her bloodred pine bark stew a stir. She couldn't live on this stuff. It was famine food, like acorns. Of course, since she *was* starving, it was better than nothing. Hadn't she read somewhere that you could fry the bark with olive oil, add a dash of salt? Yeah, the backwoods equivalent of potato chips. At the thought, a ghostly aroma of crunchy fried potatoes, of *grease* and *salt*, made her mouth water.

Come on, cut it out. This was the problem with hunger: all you thought about was food. She had to get a grip. Having been here before, she knew she was heading into dangerous territory as her body crept ever closer, day by day, to a very desperate place. Every time she pushed to a stand now, she got dizzy. The pit of her stomach was a continual sharp, beaky gnaw. Sometimes, she thought her monster had migrated down and was trying to eat its way out of her guts.

We're all starving. She poked at the pine, moving very slowly, all too aware of Acne's glittery stare and the urgent, raw fog of his hunger and just how closely his Mossberg tracked her. The last thing she needed was for Acne to mistake a sudden move and splatter her brains over a lousy piece of boiled bark. Given how famished he was, he might do it anyway, then beg Wolf's forgiveness later: *Yeah, Boss, I know, bad call.* Acne's hunger had a real reek, too, the gassy aroma of fermenting fruit. *Wonder if I smell the same way.* She'd never stopped to think much about that. Probably, to Acne and the others, she smelled like raw steak. *Nice southwest rub, juicy and done rare so the fat melts when you take a bite* . . .

"Oh God, what I wouldn't give for a steak," she said. (To her left, Acne's response was a fresh fume of rot and starvation. No surprise.) If only Acne hadn't been in such a rush to get back indoors. Outside, she'd spotted all that chicken wire and thought, *Garden?* Somehow those crushed cans argued against it, but it was worth checking out. Man, she would kill for a wrinkly old potato or wizened carrot.

Also near the garden, against a shed, was a weird mound that smelled like a bakery. A compost pile? Could be. Stuff that hadn't rotted yet, especially with the cold: gnawed melon rinds, leathery apple cores. Half-eaten cobs. Banana peels had potassium. She would take anything she could get. Boil the hell out of it, swallow it back, and not think too hard about it. And what about that rickety shed? People left all kinds of things in drawers or tucked in knapsacks or hanging from hooks and joists, jammed in glove compartments. Petrified granola bars. Candy. Power bars. Those little boxes of raisins and bags of nuts. Just thinking about what she *might* find made the saliva pool under her tongue.

And there could be other things I might use. Sheds were excellent places to forage for weapons. Anything would do; she wasn't persnickety. Nails, an old hammer. Rope. Electrical cords. Saw blades. A gun would be best, but shotgun shells would be almost as good. Crack 'em for the powder, make bang-sticks. Something.

Yet she had to be cautious. She had more freedom this time around. Wolf let her forage and keep Leopard's knife. No way in hell she'd risk losing *that.* The knife and a flint striker were her only survival tools. Without them, she was good as dead when and if she managed to make a run for it.

When and if? Oh, dream on, honey. Honestly, some days, even she got exasperated with herself. This was like sitting through *Titanic*: *just* sink *already*. She was always under guard. And exactly where would she hide all these marvelous weapons? Get herself caught and she could kiss her little foraging forays good-bye. Then she'd completely starve. While Wolf might protect her, she didn't think he'd take kindly to her whacking him with a crowbar. If she even could. Because she already *had* a knife. That Wolf let her keep it after that first day was nothing short of miraculous. Yet had she gotten all Princess Bride and slunk around at night to slit a couple throats? To reach over as Wolf lay dreaming his happy, lusty little wolf-dreams and cut out his heart?

No. Get real. That stuff only happened in the same books where the heroine scarfed down raw white pine. This was real life.

And yet she had motive. She had opportunity. She knew exactly where the carotids were, and how deeply to hack. Do it fast and she actually might pull it off. After all, it was only five against one. So what was she waiting for?

Well, hell, I don't know. Focus on what you can do, all right? Like that garden; you ought to check it out. Sighing, she sheathed her knife. *If I get a chance . . .*

Acne exploded. No warning, no red-alerts from the monster, no change in Acne's scent at all—really, how much hungrier could the kid get?—and he did it fast, in absolute silence, launching himself like a missile she only half-registered from the corner of her eye. Gasping, she jerked her arm partway up just as his fist rocketed for her face.

The hit was blinding, a stunning white detonation in her left cheek, just below her eye. A cry tried jumping off her tongue, but then his hand muscled around her throat, clutching at her jaw. Yanking her upright, Acne began drunk-walking her across the cabin.

"Ac . . . B-B-Ben!" she wheezed as she stumbled, off-balance, her hands hooked onto his. "Ben, d-don't! St-stop, *stop!*"

But Acne, the boy who'd called himself Ben Stiemke, was an

insatiable storm, in the mood for meat. Driving her the length of the room, Acne slammed her against the wall. Her head thunked hard enough for her vision to drop out, like a jump cut in time. Her jaws snapped. Pain erupted in a red dazzle as her teeth tore her tongue. Blood flooded into her throat. Gagging, she felt Acne's hand shift and knew, instantly, what he was going to do.

Panic sheeted her brain. Try to kill her by strangulation and she still had a chance: a knee to his groin, a punch, maybe take out his eyes with her fingers. But pinch off her carotids in a blood choke, and she'd gray out in seconds, be dead in minutes, and with a lot less fuss.

Then she thought, *The tanto.* She'd sheathed the knife. Dropping her right shoulder, she twisted, fingers straining. It was a desperate move, hopeless from the start because even in a killing frenzy, Acne read the set of her body. Viper-fast, he snatched the tanto from its sheath and turned the blade until that razor tip was poised over her left eye.

Her blood slushed; she stopped fighting. She could see how this would go. A quick flash of cold steel and then she'd be screeching, eye gone, the screaming socket dripping eye jelly and blood.

They hung there, unmoving, a shuddering instant out of time. Then, Acne dragged in a harsh, preparatory breath and she had time to think, *No!*

Lips peeled in a snarl, Acne drove forward. Whirring, the knife flickered past her face to bury itself in the wall. From the green, liverish stink boiling from his skin, she knew then that, however much Acne wanted to rip out her throat and gorge himself on her meat—feel its warmth and her blood in his mouth—first, he wanted her to suffer. He had her, and he was going to enjoy this. He would enjoy *her.*

She began to thrash. Bracing her back against the wood, she kicked, aiming for Acne's groin. But this wasn't as it had been days ago in the snow. His reach was so much longer it wasn't really a contest, and he arched out of the way. Yet it did her some good, bought her just a few more seconds, because he had to shift his grip to hang on. As soon as he let up, she managed a single sip, a terrible sensation of dragging air through a rapidly collapsing straw, and then that was it—and not nearly enough. She had nothing with which to fight, and she was starting to lose it, her vision going first blurry then moth-eaten.

Deep in the dark, the monster came alive, a spider skittering in the cave of her skull, and then she was tumbling into that black whirlpool behind Acne's eyes, watching her face going the color of an eggplant, the whites showing in half-moons as her eyes rolled. The end of her life unspooled in a jumble of images: Acne choking her, but only to the point where she passed out, then allowing her to wake, driving her to the floor, letting her wake just enough to do it all over again . . . three times, maybe four . . . with the peculiar sadism of a kid pulling wings off flies before crushing them underfoot. He would wait for her to surface, regain consciousness, all the better to *feel* the instant his teeth clamped onto her throat and tore and her blood fountained to bathe his cheeks a bright, stinging red.

From . . . somewhere . . . there came a hard bang that might have been sharper and louder but for the cotton stuffing her ears. An instant later, Acne let out a sudden, sickening *ungh*, and the pressure around her neck was gone. Why, she didn't know. Something scraped her back. *Wood, the wall—I'm falling.* Hacking, she landed in a heap, limp as wet laundry. For a few seconds all she concentrated on was dragging air through a throat that felt as stable as the crushed stem of a tulip.

Through the blur that passed for her vision, she saw them: Wolf and Acne, across the room, facing off. The air in the cabin had quick-ened, popping and crackling with heat, the acrid sting of murder, the cold steel of Wolf's rage. Blood trickled from Acne's nose, and he was shaking his head like a bull. Crouching, eyes narrowed, Wolf began to circle. Acne tried to follow, but he was either still stunned from Wolf's first punch or simply weakened by lack of food, because he stumbled. Seizing his chance, Wolf ducked and charged. Dazed, Acne actually backed up and tried a sidestep, but not fast enough. Plowing into Acne, Wolf wrapped his arms around the other boy's waist and gave a mighty heave. Acne's legs flew out from under as Wolf upended and then smashed him to the floor. Acne's head rebounded against wood with a sharp *crack*. His limbs went limp, the connections between brain and body winking out as Wolf dropped like a boulder on top of him. He brought his fist down like a hammer, once, twice—

A huge *roar* shook the cabin. From her place on the floor, Alex saw Marley, long dreads still frosty from cold, swinging the Mossberg's muzzle from the ceiling and bringing it to bear on the two boys. Wolf and Acne froze in an almost comical tableau: Wolf astride Acne's chest, his bloody fist cocked for another blow. Acne's eyes were swelling and purpling in a mask of blood. Combined with all those acne scars, the boy looked as if his skin was being chewed from the inside out. His chest was a broad bib of red. With every breath, blood bubbled through his shattered nose.

To Marley's left were the brothers, Bert and Ernie. From the smell drifting out of that green duffel slung over Bert's shoulder, she knew that the woman was frail and birdy, wreathed in a fruity bouquet of starvation, with very little meat. Look at it a certain way, maybe Wolf and his crew had only done the birdy woman a favor, in the same way that sheriffs shot deer too weak to even realize they'd wandered into the middle of the road during a hard winter. If, that is, you really *could* see things from the Changed's point of view.

It scared her, a little, that she could.

Wolf didn't kill Acne, and neither did any in his crew. What they did was send Acne packing. Curled in a corner, throat aching, cheek throbbing, Alex kept still as Acne, moving very slowly and stiffly, rolled up his sleeping bag under Wolf's watchful eye and Marley's Mossberg.

Don't notice me. She hugged her knees a little closer. *Don't see me. I'm not here.* Fat chance of that. Through it all, she thought about the monster: that jump behind Acne's eyes, Wolf's sudden appearance. It was possible that Wolf was close by anyway, and banged through the door just in time. *But just as likely that the monster had something to do with this, same as when I was under the snow.* Now as then, she'd been teetering on the edge of consciousness, and the monster panicked. Wouldn't be the first time, and what the hell was she going to do about that? What *could* she do?

Got to think of something; got to keep the monster under control. Her face throbbed. She thought about her med pack. Might be something for pain. *No, stay sharp; it's when you start to lose it that the monster gets out.* She sucked blood from a tear on her lower lip. *I can take this. Besides, I really ought to save that stuff for when we need it.*

Only after another second did she truly *hear* what she'd just thought: *We?*

Stop it, Alex; you're going to drive yourself crazy. For want of anything better to do, she watched as Bert grabbed that green duffel, pulled it up, gave the nylon bag a shake. The birdy woman's body slithered out in a loose-limbed splay like a limp, white, plucked chicken. After Bert smoothed the duffel on the floor, Ernie rolled the body onto the sack, then pulled a well-used knife, with a fine and silvery edge, from a leg sheath and went to work.

Don't look, Alex. Fighting the sting of tears, she dropped her head on her knees. The air bloomed with wet iron, raw meat, fresh bone. *Hell with the monster. You're Alex. You'll always be Alex, no matter what . . .*

She felt the suck of cold air as the door closed behind Acne. A moment later, she heard hesitant footsteps coming toward her. Even before he knelt—before she felt his tentative hand in her hair—she knew who it was. For a moment, she didn't move, but not because she was afraid.

She didn't move because—God help her—she *wasn't* scared of him. At all.

Wolf's rage, that steel bite, was gone. What remained was rot and mist, gassy flesh and crisp apples, and for a second, she surrendered to a very simple, basic need. For her, at that moment, even the touch of a monster would do.

I am so scared. All at once, she was crying, silently, shoulders shuddering. Angry at herself, too. *Stop this, stop this . . . no one will rescue you but you. No one else can.* Yet here was Wolf, and she wasn't fighting this, or him. Maybe she should. But she was so worn out. She felt his hand move through her hair, very gently, quite carefully, as if he were trying not to hurt her more than she was already. *Don't touch me, don't touch me.* But she wanted this, craved it—a touch that was not a blow—and she thought that meant she was pretty far gone. She let his fingers travel over her uninjured cheek, felt his thumb skim away her tears, trace her jaw. When he lifted her chin, she didn't fight that either.

Wolf's face—Chris's face—was very still. Watchful. Trying to . . . understand, she thought. His dark eyes were riveted to hers, as if trying to see behind these windows to her mind. His scent was hard to read, but it was light and floral, the smell of *safe* and *family.* There might even be a smidgeon of pity there, or sympathy.

"Please let me go, Wolf." She winced against a stinging swallow of salt. "Don't you see? I don't belong with you. I'm not one of you."

Nothing changed in his scent. Maybe nothing could because he couldn't understand, or didn't want to. But his thumb kept stroking her cheek the way you might comfort a small child or lost kitten. Right around then, she realized she wasn't crying anymore either.

What type of monster are you, Wolf? It was a question she could've asked herself. What was *she* now? What lived in her head that could do these things: jump behind Acne's eyes, slide into Spider, slither into Leopard?

Reach for Wolf?

The monster wants him. Because she did? *No, not like that, never.* Whatever the monster was doing, its needs were its own; she had to believe that, or she might as well use the tanto on herself.

But . . . what if I *can use the monster somehow?* Her mind brushed that idea, lightly, not lingering, a touch that was as gentle as Wolf's on her cheek. *What if I can control when and how the monster jumps? Or maybe let the monster try to reach Wolf, talk to him? Just let go and get into Wolf and see myself the way he* really *sees me*—

"What?" Abruptly, she sat up. "What the hell are you thinking, Alex?" Her voice came out angry, and that *was* something Wolf understood, because she saw him flinch, felt his hand fall away from her face.

"I'm going outside." She wasn't going to run—she wasn't stupid—but she had to get out of this miserable little room with its smells of death and Changed. Walking the wall with her hands, she made her feet. For a moment, she thought Wolf would try to help. "Don't," she said, flattening herself against cold wood. "Leave me alone. I don't want—"

She stopped talking then, the words turning to dust in her mouth as she saw Bert, just beyond, coming toward her. . . .

With dinner.

The arm was spindly. It was the right. Not tons of meat. Tattered remnants of skin and ropy veins dragged over the pinkish knob of the birdy woman's funny bone; and—*oh God*—the slim steel band of a watch was still tight around that twig of a wrist.

Something seemed to snap in her head. She stared at the arm, horrified—and yet she was so *hungry* that this thought actually bubbled to the surface: *If there's no other choice; if it's life or death . . .*

"No!" Grabbing back a scream, she bullied her way past Wolf and Bert. Clawing open the cabin door, she stumbled into the bronze dazzle of a sunset. The cold was stunning, like blundering through glass, but she couldn't stay in that cabin another second. Of course, the Changed would feed; they *had* to eat. *But I do have a choice.* After a half dozen yards, her knees unlimbered—just plain gave out—and she toppled to the snow. She dug in until her face and neck and bare hands flinched with the cold. Eventually, she would feel the burn, which was fine.

Burn my eyes out, take a blowtorch to my brain, anything. She dragged her head from side to side like a dog trying to get a bad smell out of its snout. *I can't go down that road. I do that, then I might as well have eaten Jack and snacked on those kids—or let the monster out all the way.*

No matter what Wolf was thinking, what *he* wanted, *she* had to fight. *Can't give in, can't go there.* Behind, she heard the cabin's door open; felt his eyes, knew his scent. He only watched, though, and didn't follow.

I'm me. Ahead, by the shed, she saw that strange mound. *I'm me, I'm Alex.* She battled her way there, slithering through snow until the mound loomed. She knelt before it, sweeping her eyes over patchy snow—and spied a dark pinprick scurry over a patch of ice. And another pinprick, and another. And another.

Fight.

She thrust both fists into the mound, right up to her wrists. Almost at once and despite the cold, a black tide boiled to the surface and over her forearms. Withdrawing a hand, she inspected her fingers, smeary with dirt and so many ants her skin was a black, writhing mat. Many carried eggs and tiny, milky larvae clamped in their mandibles.

Do it, Alex. Just do it. Hang on to who you are. Don't let them break you.

Before her brain could really kick in and stop her, she stuck two fingers into her mouth and sucked. Ants foamed over her tongue. She tasted dirt, the coarse pop of grit and the yeasty tang of fermenting earth; felt the spidery scampering of many legs, the minute pricking of mandibles nipping at her flesh—but she bit down and killed them all and swallowed them back and went back for seconds. And thirds.

Because, yes: things were that bad.

40

"Sarah, I know things are bad. That weird earthquake spooked everyone—" Greg broke off as Tori, with Ghost in tow, bustled into the church's main office. "Everything okay?"

"Yeah, what took you so long?" Pru had parked his butt on a desk still heaped with stacks of Xeroxed announcements for October 2. Given that they were at the end of the first week of March of the following year, an Amish Friendship Bread and Whoopie Pie church bake sale scheduled for October 8 *last* year was probably moot. "Cutter and Benton'll be back in less than twenty minutes, and Greg and me have to be gone. A couple cans of refried beans only buy you so much time."

"I know. I'm sorry. Caleb's pretty sick." Tori backhanded honey-blond frizz from her forehead as Alex's gangly Weimaraner made a beeline for a muscular black German shepherd curled at Sarah's feet. "Honestly," Tori said, "if one more kid decides to chow down on play-dough, I'm going to throw it all out."

Greg made a face. "Play-Doh? That stuff stinks."

"Not the homemade stuff. The little kids made it back when we actually had flour. Looks and smells like bread dough. Really salty, though." Propping her shotgun, a Remington 870 with a carved floral design on the walnut stock, in a corner, Tori said, "Then I had to shake Becky. *She* wanted to know if I was going to see you."

"What? How'd she find out?" Greg blurted. At the dart of dismay in Tori's eyes, he wanted to kick himself. When the girls lived with Jess, he'd drunk so much tea just to be *near* Tori, he could've floated his own battleship. After Alex's escape and the ambush, the Council moved Tori and Sarah into the church's rectory. That should've made things a little easier, especially since the girls' housemother, a lumbering hag named Hammerbach, keeled over from a stroke. But he always seemed to say the wrong thing.

"Becky saw me unlock the choir door while I was sweeping the basement. She was *under* the altar, playing hide-and-seek, she said. But I think she was scoping out the pantry. A couple kids tried to break in yesterday."

"Because they're starving." A tiny girl to begin with, Sarah had shriveled. At her right hip, a holstered Sig P225 jutted like a black knucklebone. Greg wondered if she even knew how to fire the thing. She turned Greg a hollow stare. "You can only live on watered-down oatmeal, corn syrup, peanut butter, and the occasional acorn for so long. We've already lost seven kids. Another few weeks, they're going to start really dropping like the old people."

"Without their pills, those old guys were going to kick anyway," Pru said. "Nothing Kincaid can do about that either. Get pneumonia, kiss it good-bye. Going to be big trouble."

"We're already in deep trouble." Sarah spooled a listless curl around a finger. "Why do you think they moved all of us Spared to the center of town? We get a *little* more to eat than everyone else. But they might as well paint a bull's-eye on our backs."

"Sarah's right," Tori said. "Wasn't it just yesterday that old man took a shot?"

"A .30-06," Pru said. "I thought Greg was going to shit his pants."

"The guy was just scared." Greg still thought they could've talked the old man down, but Pru's Ruger Mini-14 put the period to *that* conversation. In a bedroom, they found what the old guy was protecting: a cage of three scrawny parakeets. The sight made Greg want to cry.

"But people are shooting back, and it's worse since the rationing. They're killing horses, they're shooting dogs." Sarah ruffled the shepherd's ears. "Jet and Ghost are still alive because they guard the kids, and Daisy's yours, Greg. But they'll come for them, too, eventually."

"Then people, I bet." Pru's expression darkened. "Start off with the real old guys who won't last much longer anyway."

"Eating people? Come on, get real," Greg said. "This isn't *Lord of the Flies*. The Council would never allow it."

"Oh, like they're *so* relevant." Pru gave an exaggerated eye-roll. "The only reason they've held on this long is because everyone was fed, and the village was real tight before everything went to hell. They had Peter, their miracle boy: too old to Change, not old enough to survive but Spared anyway—*and* his grandpa's on the Council. Then, here comes Chris, another Spared, and, oh, he just happens to be Yeager's grandson. A total God thing, and everyone calmed down. Peter cleared out the Changed, killed them all. People were fed; they felt safer. Remember their ceremonies on Sundays, how Yeager would bless us and spout all that crap about holy missions? Now with Peter and Chris gone and nothing coming in, it's all falling apart."

"Then we *have* to get out before we all starve, or get traded for food or something," Sarah said. "Or maybe they'll only pass us girls around as a reward. The way some stare, like Cutter—"

"Cutter?" Something flitted through Tori's eyes, but when she said nothing, Greg looked back at Sarah. "He's one of your *guards*."

"Yeah, and I sleep so much better knowing he's got *keys*. He hasn't done anything, but you can hear the wheels turning. If he could figure a way . . ."

"I'll get him moved somewhere else."

"It'll end up being the same no matter who gets posted." Tori's voice was strangely toneless. "I never used to worry. When Peter and Chris were in charge, they were like this indestructible team. But now?" She turned him a shimmery look. "Greg, we can't count on the adults anymore. We need to take care of ourselves. So, either we take over or we leave."

Greg threw up his hands. "And go where? East is out. Lot of cities, lot of people, a ton of Changed. That's why Peter and Chris didn't want us patrolling out that way. South is no good either. Once beyond the mine and closer to Iron Mountain, it starts getting real crowded."

"If there's anyone left." Tori wrinkled her nose. "I don't like south anyway. That earthquake two weeks ago? From the cave-in? That was pretty weird."

If a cave-in's all it was. A finger of unease dragged over Greg's neck. *Subsurface vibrations was what one of the real old-timers had said: You can get spontaneous combustion in a coal mine. But the Rule mine was iron first, gold second, and the rock's inert. For that mine to cave bad enough to set off an earthquake, you need high explosives, and a lot of them.*

Which begged the questions: who had access to high explosives, and why do it at all?

Aloud, he said, "So that leaves west. Wisconsin, Minnesota . . ."

"Wyoming," Pru said. "Betcha it's pretty empty."

"Or we go north, maybe even into Canada."

"Oren is north," Sarah said. "Chris and Lena went north."

There was a silence. "They went east," Greg said.

"Greg, Chris knew east was dangerous, and he's been to Oren. So if he's alive . . ."

"Big *if*," Greg said.

"Yeah, and I'll bet he'd be real glad to see us, too, seeing as how he's come back to rescue us and all," Pru added sourly.

"No matter where we go, you're talking forty kids," Greg said. "We'd need wagons, food, ammo, *horses*. All stuff we don't have."

"If we take everyone," Sarah said. "Maybe we don't."

"Oh?" Pru raised an eyebrow. "You got someone you want to kick off the island?"

"Yes. Aidan, Lucian, and Sam." Sarah leveled a look. "I don't trust them."

Pru shrugged. "I'm okay with that."

"Wait. I don't know if it should be that simple," Greg said. "We're not choosing teams for a pickup game. Sure, I don't *like* what they do, but I don't have any better ideas."

"You guys could *not* do it," Tori put in. "Just because Peter decided torture was okay doesn't mean it is. Won't a prisoner say anything so you'll stop hurting him?"

"Hey, that's not fair," Pru said. "Council had to approve, too."

"Which most of us didn't know about until Chris ran. So if torture was so okay, why hide it?" Tori's attention stayed on Greg. "What would happen if you refused?"

"I don't know." Greg didn't want to find out. It would be like telling the principal he was doing a sucky job: *Gee, thanks for your opinion, kid, and that'll be detention for the rest of your life.* Look how easily Yeager decided to throw Chris into the prison house, and Chris was his *grandson.* He stood. "We gotta go. Can we just not decide on *who* until we figure out *how*, or if we should do this now? It's still *winter*, for God's sake."

"Not for much longer. We need to decide, and soon." When Greg only bent to zip his parka, Sarah continued, "Look, if you're not with us? Fine. But stay out of our way."

"What?" Greg snapped. "Sarah, in case you haven't noticed, *I'm* not the enemy."

"She's just upset," Tori said.

I'm not? "Don't make excuses for her."

"But don't you see, Greg? It's all coming down." Sarah's eyes brimmed. "Peter's dead and Chris is gone and it's all falling apart!"

"You think I don't know that?" The red blaze of sudden anger was acid on his tongue. "Let me tell you about falling apart. Peter was my friend. The only reason I didn't die in that ambush is because I went to Oren with Chris. There isn't a day goes by I don't think about how, maybe, I could've saved Peter. And what about Chris? He *trusted* me. If Chris had asked, I'd have helped him get out. But he didn't and he's gone. Now when there are decisions the Council wants enforced, they come to me, and you know what I get to do now? Boost some old people on a *rumor* that they got a couple spare gerbils lying around. So don't tell *me* how things fall apart, Sarah." He yanked his zipper so hard the metal should've sparked. "Been there, done that, bought the goddamned T-shirt."

Tori caught up as he and Pru were halfway down the nave. "She's just upset."

"Lot of that going around," Pru said.

"Don't worry about it," Greg said, still angry. "No big deal."

"Yes, it is. Look, I . . ." Tori's eyes flickered to Pru and then back. "Can we just talk a sec?"

"Uh . . . sure." Greg looked over at Pru, who only hunched a shoulder and headed for the altar, hung a left, and ducked through an arched entry. Greg waited until he heard the clump of Pru's boots on the steps, then turned back to Tori. "Yeah?"

"I didn't mean to give you a hard time," she said, giving his arm a light squeeze. "I'm glad the Council picked you to take Chris's place and not Pru."

"Oh." His mouth dried up. Tori had never touched him before. *No* girl had. How strange was this, to be standing in a church with a girl he was majorly crushing on—and he was armed? "I don't, ah . . ." He muzzled a cough. "It's not like I had a lot of choice."

Tori's eyes were very blue, but that could've been because she was standing even closer than before. "You could've said no. But you didn't. It's easy for people to complain, like how I always got on my mom's case when she wouldn't let me stay up late?" Tori's mouth moved in a smile so sad Greg had this weird impulse to cup her cheek the way his mom used to when he had a bad fever. "Now that we have all these little kids, I understand where she was coming from."

"Most days I'd give anything for my mom to nag about homework or put away the Xbox. I don't think she'd even recognize me anymore."

"She'd recognize you. You're doing the best you can."

"But what if it isn't my best?"

"Then figure it out," she said, and before he knew what was happening, her mouth was on his.

Greg was so startled he gasped. His heart began to bang and he thought he might faint, this felt so good. He didn't know what to do with his hands, couldn't catch his breath, wasn't really thinking anymore. They came up for air at the same moment, and he said, "T-Tori—"

"Shh," she said.

So they stopped talking for a while, and that was fine. That was good.

At least, there were a couple moments where Greg didn't have to think about what a terrible person he was, heading out to kill some grandma's poor old cat.

41

An hour later:

"Go rest," Tori whispered, laying a light hand on Sarah's shoulder. "I'll sit with Caleb."

"No. It's all right." Sarah tried a smile, but her muscles felt frozen, a feeling that reminded her of when her dad repaired their driveway and she'd tested just how long you *could* stick your sneaker into wet cement. A million years from now, an archaeologist would discover a little pink sneaker and wonder where the rest of the body was.

"What's so funny?"

"Huh?" Sarah actually had to put a hand to her face. Her lips were so stiff they would've been at home on a corpse. "Nothing. I was just remembering something." By her feet, she felt Jet whimper. Normally calm, Jet had been restless ever since Greg and Pru left. "I'm sorry about earlier, with Greg. It wasn't fair."

"No, it wasn't." Tori draped a moist cloth over the little boy's forehead. "You've got to stop this self-pity crap. We all miss Peter. *I* keep expecting Chris to walk in any second."

"To rescue us?" She marveled at how easily the bitterness oozed back. When had she gotten so mean? All this moaning and woe-is-me . . . Still whining, Jet had clambered to his feet. She ruffled his ears to quiet the animal—and herself—down. "I'm sorry. That was nasty. I just can't seem to find a balance, like I'm on this emotional teeter-totter."

"You're not the only person having a hard time. Greg *is* trying, and he's got feelings to hurt. You think I'm always so cheerful and understanding? Most of the time, I'm faking it. Otherwise I'd spend half the day crying and the other half daydreaming about food I can't have. I'm going to be eighteen in two months. I should be thinking about college and driving my mom crazy and if I'll be a blimp in a prom dress." Tori squeezed out a small, bleak laugh. "Wish my mom could see me. She was always on me about my weight."

"So were you faking it before? Talking about getting away, I mean."

"No. We better do it soon. Pru's right. You can feel it in the air, how angry everyone is. The food went so fast, and so did the rest of the supplies. We've got plenty of guns but no bullets and no game left to hunt anyway. We'll be lucky the Council doesn't get lynched. Things are starting to get out of control." Tori paused. "Remember I mentioned unlocking the choir door? What I *didn't* say was . . . Cutter was waiting, right outside, hours before he was scheduled to show."

"What?" Of their two night guards, she most disliked the shaggy, thickset old man who'd wandered into Rule with Lang and Weller. Other oldsters darted a quick glance, but Cutter actually *stared*. "Why didn't you say anything?"

"Because he didn't exactly *do* anything. He pretended he needed to check the door. You know how small that landing is?"

She did. The stairs were narrow, meant for the choir to access the chancel. The landing between the basement and sanctuary was a square no larger than a couple doormats placed side by side. "Did he . . . you know . . ." She didn't want to say *touch you.*

"Pretty much. He was inside so fast he copped a pretty good feel. His face was . . . dangerous. Like I'd better not scream or fight."

"You really think he would've hurt you?"

"I honestly didn't want to find out. But there are the littler kids, and I thought, all of a sudden, well . . . better *me* than one of them. How sick is that?"

"That's not sick. You were protecting the kids." Sarah took Tori's chilled hands in hers. "Something else happened, though. I can tell. What was it?"

"He said that if I didn't want Pru or Greg to end up in trouble, I might want to be *nice*. So I . . . I let him get in a good, long, dirty little grope." When Sarah pulled in a breath, Tori said, "Don't, okay? I already feel like I've crawled through a sewer. But you know those beans Pru gave him? Cutter offered the can to me, like *payment*. He said he didn't expect something for nothing. That . . . that the kids might like more food if I would, you know, do *more*. And what's horrible?" Tori's eyes dropped to her lap. "For a second, I thought . . . okay."

"Tori." Sara could taste the acid boil from her empty stomach. "You don't *mean* that."

"I don't know." Tori gave a hopeless shrug. "Maybe I do. The kids are hungry, and what if Cutter threatens to hurt Greg? Or Pru? None of us are safe."

"Look, let's just take a step back, okay? Nothing's happened yet. We'll talk to Greg and Pru. We'll think of something. Know what? I'd like some tea. Want tea?" Sarah stood up so quickly her heart couldn't keep up, and a sweep of vertigo blacked her vision. She gulped back a shaky breath, then another. "You want chamomile or chamomile?"

"Chamomile'd be great." Tori managed a wobbly smile. "Look, I already put Daisy and Ghost with the girls. Would you drop off Jet with the boys? That dog goes crazy when you're not around."

Not as crazy as I feel right now. "Sure." She turned to go, Jet on her heels. "It'll be okay, Tori."

"It's nice," Tori said, "that you think so."

God, the thought of *Cutter* hitting on Tori . . . Sarah shuddered as she walked the breezeway connecting the school to the church. The idea made her want to take a cup of bleach to her brain and hit *rinse*. The thought of his creepy old hands on her, or his *mouth* . . .

"Gag me with a fork." Frosty air palmed her face as she pushed through double doors and into the west vestibule. Directly ahead were two sets of stairs. Bear left and you had a choice: either up three steps to a cloakroom or down twelve to the basement. Choose the right set of steps, however, and you accessed a circular stone stair coiling up to the bell tower.

She flicked on a flashlight and took the left stairs. The church was not her favorite place. The place creeped her out, day or night. Constructed entirely of off-white, native limestone, the church was a soundproofed ice cube that held onto a deep gloom and a stone-cold chill. Following her light, she descended into the midnight gloaming of the windowless basement. Grit crackled like cap guns under her shoes. The gelid air was fiery on her skin. The basement was domi-nated by the inky cave of a common room that seemed only blacker with the cold. Shivering, she hung a left for the kitchen, a long, nar-row throat of a room designed on the cheap. The cupboards were puke-yellow, vintage plywood. The floor and counters were stained Formica. The industrial-sized stainless-steel sink sported two spigots, not that she'd ever known water to run from either. All their water came from snowmelt, and they always kept an aluminum camp pot, with a plug of ice, at the ready.

It was when she fumbled out a match that she heard it: a very small but crisp crunch like sand under a heavy boot. *What?* Her heart cramped. She went completely still, unlit match in hand, then eased right to peer down the long throat of the kitchen's one aisle and toward a closed storage room where they kept their meager rations under lock and key. As her weight shifted, she caught the snap and crackle again: grit under her feet. *You heard yourself, silly.* Touching off the Coleman, she squared the pot of ice over the burner. *Just freaking yourself out.*

Shaking out her keys, she walked to the storage room, socked in a key, turned it, and heard the *thunk* as the lock didn't release . . . but engaged. *Huh?* She frowned. The door was open? That wasn't right.

Then she recalled what Tori said: *When I went to sweep out the basement* . . . Tori had used the chore as an excuse to open the side door, so Greg and Pru could slip inside. *But now there's sand.* She thought about how much colder the vestibule seemed, and her pulse ramped just a little higher. Always icy, the church had been frigid because the side door was *open?* Would she know? No, not if she didn't stop to check or feel a draft. *And the basement's freezing, which follows because if the door is open, the air has two ways to go, up into the sanctuary . . .*

Or down here, into the basement, with her.

But hold on, hold on. Tori had gone after Greg. Had she mentioned locking up once the boys left? Sarah hadn't asked. It wasn't something she'd have checked anyway, because Tori had enough common sense to realize that you *always* locked doors.

Even if she did lock it, something could *have come in earlier, and be here now.*

No, that was silly. Why hang out in a frigid basement? What was *here* that was nowhere else? Well, *food.* Duh. And that made her think of something else Tori said: when she opened the side door, Cutter had been there.

Oh God. What if Tori had jumped to the wrong conclusion? Cutter had keys. *So maybe he was really there to steal food. A spoonful of peanut butter here, a few crackers there—who's to know?* It wasn't like they counted every bean.

Maybe she should just get out of here and close off the basement. Yeah, but that meant going through that dark, spooky common room to the stairs. From there, the only way out was through the side door, or the chancel the next flight up. So, maybe best to retrace her steps, make a beeline back for the school, and then the girls could lock themselves in. If something came after them . . .

Tori has the shotgun. I've got the pistol. But she wasn't good with guns, didn't like them. *Fine, don't fight the boogeyman. Lock the doors, open a window, and scream.* If anyone heard them. It was late afternoon, slipping into early evening. Not a lot of people moved around these days if they could help it. Very little food meant very little energy—

The sound came again, and it was harsher this time, not merely a pop and crack but a scuff like a heavy boot.

That was when she knew. There wasn't something lurking in the storage room. There was something *behind* her, spiriting out of the black well of the common room.

Coming right for her.

42

"Don't." Greg wedged his boot between the door and jamb. "Don't make this tougher than it has to be."

"But you've made a mistake." From what Greg could see through the crack—one glittery bat's eye far back in the cave of her socket—Verna Landry looked as if she'd have to stand twice to throw a shadow. "I don't know who told you—"

"Well, we can talk about that," he said, trying to inject notes of both sympathy and steel. *A cat. I'm harassing this poor woman over a cat.* It was always a toss-up, trying to decide how many guys to take, and whether they should be really, really ancient or just normal old. This time he'd opted for six, with four Spared—him, Pru, Aidan, and Lucian—and two geezers: a really ancient denture-sucker with a bugle of a voice named Henry, and Jarvis, who was just plain old and knew the woman's husband, Chester. "I really need you to open the door, Mrs. Landry."

"This is my house. You have no right to come here making accusations." That single gimlet eye clicked right. "Jarvis, you took all our food seven weeks ago."

"Well, Verna, see, that's the problem." A pallid geezer, Jarvis had the kind of knobby neck Greg always associated with a turkey, but he was one tough old bird. "Chester kept going on about how he got the runs eating cat food—"

"It was a ration."

"No one's giving out cat food to people." Lucian skimmed that serpent's tongue over his lips. His silver stud winked. "Cats, maybe," Lucian drawled, "but not cat *food*." Beside him, Aidan sniggered and blocked off a nostril with his thumb, let out a juicy honk, did a quick peek, then wiped his hand on his jeans.

"That all goes to the dogs," Greg said, unsure if he only wanted to kick Lucian in the teeth or never touch anything Aidan got near again. Maybe both. "So where'd Chester get it?"

"Fine." Verna's voice ratcheted up a notch. "*Fine*, yes, we had a cat. It was Lisa's, but it ran away once she . . ." Verna petered out, then revved up again: "We still had the food."

"Then you should've turned that in last time we did a door-to-door." Pru moved a little closer and said, "Council gave orders right after the ambush."

"All right, we made a mistake. But did you find a cat *then*? No. And why pick on cats? Why not dogs and horses?"

This was why Greg had left Daisy with Tori and Sarah. All they needed was a pissed-off villager taking a potshot. "Please, ma'am, this'll go a lot easier if you just open the door."

"Not until Chester gets home. You'll just have to come back when he—"

"Do it." Greg was suddenly just so sick of the whole thing. Let them just get in, get out, get this over with, so he could go back to Tori.

"Playing our song," Aidan said. Moving in a swift sidestep around Greg, he and Lucian pistoned quick cop-style kicks. The old woman saw them coming, let out an abortive squawk, but didn't move fast enough. There was a splintering scream as both the lock plate and chain popped free of the jamb. Greg heard a sickening *thuck* and an *ugh* as the old woman's head first connected with wood, then snapped on the spindle of her neck. Lurching back, a hand clapped to her streaming nose, she began a stuffy screech: "Mah noth, mah noth!"

"Lucky it's still attached," Aidan said.

"Fucking A," Lucian said, though whether he was agreeing or commenting on his friend's prowess at breaking an old woman's nose, Greg didn't know and didn't care.

"Henry, make sure she doesn't go anywhere," Greg said, stepping over the blubbering old woman as Henry doddered up and piped on an improbably high note: "Now, Verna, I coulda tole you . . ."

Man, I hate this. Striding past an understairs closet, Greg moved down the hall, darkened now with late afternoon gloom, and toward the kitchen with Pru and Jarvis on his heels. For no particular reason, his scalp suddenly tingled, and a maddening itch dug at the back of his neck. *Whoa, something wrong here.* He had this very weird sense that the house was both empty and yet occupied. He shot a glance over his shoulder. Aidan and Lucian were sauntering, their eyes roaming over walls of photographs, tables cluttered with bric-a-brac, ready to liberate anything they took a fancy to the second Greg or Pru or Jarvis might not be looking. He watched Aidan open that under-stairs closet, peek, then move on.

Nothing really untoward. He frowned. *So why am I so spooked? Something wrong . . .*

"Bingo. Food dish." Pru chinned a cheery yellow placemat tucked into a corner of the kitchen, behind a farmhouse table and chairs. A round ceramic bowl decorated with fish skeletons and the words *Meow* and *Yum Yum* squatted next to an aluminum water bowl, which was half full. The food dish held a single kibble. "I don't see a litter box."

"Maybe they let it out," Aidan said. "Might still *be* out unless the old geezer run off."

"Hey," Greg said, uncomfortably aware of Jarvis, who fit the definition of both *old* and *geezer*. Aidan really needed to watch his mouth. "Just keep it zipped, okay?"

"What?" Aidan managed to look confused. "What'd I say?"

"Nothing, *kid*," Jarvis said, laying it on thick, then looked at Greg. "Chester wouldn't run. And that fuss Verna put up? Ten to one, that cat's still here."

"Maybe they shoved it into a closet or something." Spying a corner pantry, Greg pulled the door. The pantry was completely enclosed and pitch black. Pulling out his flashlight, Greg sprayed orange light over the pine floor. "Got a bag of dry, couple cans of wet . . ."

"What?" Aidan and Lucian both asked when Greg trailed off.

"Hang on." The wood floors of the old house were none too clean, but with so little traffic here, the pine was much lighter, and he spotted one board that looked scuffed, its seams wider than the rest. *Like it's been replaced or popped.* When he pushed, the board rocked. *Oh boy.* He was afraid to hope, but his heart drummed just a little faster. *We might have something here, we might really* . . . Flicking open his pocketknife, he worked the tip into a seam. The blade passed through easily.

"Hey," he called. As the others crowded in the doorway, he pointed. "This board's been pried. I can't get enough leverage to pop it, though."

"Here." Lucian pulled a black, carbon steel machete that probably could carve a buffalo from his waist sheath. "Try this."

Working the blade, Greg eased it a good eight inches through the gap before the steel *ticked.* Metal? "Got something."

"Sure you don't got just a joist?" Pru asked.

"It's not wood. I can feel a draft. I think this is a crawl space under the house." Another five seconds and Greg popped the board, stared, then said, "Oh, holy shit."

In the cone of orange light thrown by his flashlight into this hidey-hole, the jars sparkled like a hoard of rare gems: small, beveled glass jars of strawberry jelly, deep orange marmalade, blueberry jelly; larger pint and glittering quart mason jars packed full of pickled carrots, asparagus spears, mushrooms, potatoes, and other vegetables, as well as fruits.

"Whoa," Lucian said, and Aidan added, "Oh, fuck me."

"Jesus Christ." Jarvis said it like a prayer. Crowding in, he reached past Greg and withdrew a quart of tightly packed fruit swimming in clear syrup. In the light, the peaches looked like golden half-moons. "They've got all this *food*. They've got *food*."

Gooseberries, Greg read on another jar, the word done in delicate, precise letters, along with a date. He'd never tasted gooseberries, but they sounded deliriously good. His stomach was moaning, and there was so much saliva pooling under his tongue, he was afraid he'd start drooling. *Apricots. Cherries*. To distract himself, he counted jars. "Thirty-six. Not huge, but . . ."

"Hell with huge." Jarvis had folded that quart of peaches to his chest the way Reverend Yeager sometimes clutched his Bible during a sermon. "I should've thought of this. I've known Verna since we were kids, going on sixty years now. Her mom canned like crazy all summer and fall. We searched here six weeks ago. Bare as a bone, and I thought how strange that was. Not like Verna at all, but it'd been months since everything went to hell and I thought, okay, they ate it all." Jarvis's face suddenly darkened. "And they've still been taking rations."

"Assholes," Aidan said.

"Yeah, that isn't right; it's not, you know, *fair*," Lucian put in.

"But I don't get it." Pru was examining a jar of bright purple eggs pickled in beet juice. Greg bet if anyone had suggested eating something like that to Pru five months ago, he'd have told you to get real. "Why does that old lady look like she's starving?" Pru asked.

"Maybe this is their emergency stash," Lucian suggested.

"Or they've been eating only a little bit here and there." Aidan hefted a jar of pickled brussels sprouts. "Man, I used to hate this shit, but now? No problem. We got to tear up the rest of the house. We oughta tear up all the houses, X 'em off."

"Wait, wait, not so fast." Greg was getting dizzy. The urge to crack the seal of that jar of cherries was nearly overwhelming. "This is cool, but we came for the cat." *What am I saying?*

"Screw the cat." Lucian fished out a mason jar swimming with ruby-red plums. "Man, we could—"

"Don't even think about it." Greg replaced the cherries, although letting go took effort. "Come on, hand them over."

"Hold on." Lucian cocked his elbow, holding his jar out of reach, leaving Greg with air. "Don't we get a say?"

"No." Greg's stomach fluttered. From the knot of frustration on Pru's face, he wasn't sure this wouldn't end up being four against one. Maybe even five, if you counted doddering old Henry. "Listen, I understand, but we can't. It's not fair to everyone else."

"Fuck fair." In the gloom, Aidan's tats looked like bugs that had chewed their way out of his cheeks. "Dude, I'm hungry. We keep quiet, no one has to know."

"Old woman'll know," Lucian rumbled.

"We can do something about that," Aidan said.

"No," Greg repeated. "The only thing we're doing is turning this stuff in."

"What if I don't?" Aidan said. "You can't make me."

The words were so like a five-year-old's, Greg had to bite his cheek. *Just get one of them to hand over a jar.* "We can't go there. Come on, guys." He held out his hands to Pru, who, he thought, would relent first. "Hand it over."

After what seemed a very long second, Pru pushed the jar into Greg's hands. "Here," Pru said. "Take the damn thing before I accidentally break it on purpose."

Slotting the jar back, Greg tilted his head toward Aidan and

Lucian. "You, too. You know the rules. We share food. That's the way it has to be."

Aidan's head swiveled to Lucian, whose shark eyes ticked to Pru and then back, weighing the options. A moment later, Lucian shrugged and silently passed over his jar.

"Fuck." Aidan tossed his brussels sprouts in an underhand pitch that Greg fumbled and nearly dropped. "Asshole. Hope you fucking choke."

"Jarvis?" Heart banging, Greg looked up at the old man. "Come on."

"It's a jar of peaches." Jarvis's tongue flickered over his lips. "No one has to know."

"I'm with you, brother," Aidan put in.

"I'm seventy-fucking-five years old," Jarvis said, and then his face knotted. "Council cares more about you. Spared eat better. You'll get it *all*."

"Hey, fuck that, Jarvis," Lucian said. "I'm scraping empty."

"Yeah," Pru chimed in. "We Spared are doing *so* great."

"All I'm asking for is a lousy jar of peaches, for God's sake," Jarvis said.

"Jarvis." Greg swallowed around the stone in his throat. "We're all hungry. But you know the rules."

"Rules." Jarvis's eyes narrowed. "Real easy for you when the rules break your way. Guess that's what comes with being the Council's private pets."

"Whoa, who you calling a pet?" Aidan said. "We gave up our food, too, you know."

"Yeah, but why?" Jarvis rifled a glare at Greg. "Because the Council gives you the authority? Here we've supported them for *years*. We gave up on our grandkids. We let them get rounded up and shot without ever being given the *chance* to get better, come back to us—and now we're supposed to starve, too, to save *you*? Kids that aren't our blood, not our family? Hell with that."

"Okay, wait." Pru put his hands up, palms out. "Let's all just cool off, okay?"

"What if I don't *want* to cool off?" Jarvis's eyes hadn't left Greg. "What if I'm *done* taking orders from the Council? From *punks*?"

"Hey." Lucian's forehead furrowed so deeply the scabs on the dome of his skull bunched. "Watch the punk shit."

The pantry was, suddenly, very cramped, and much too dark, and he'd left his rifle in the kitchen. So had Jarvis, but he also carried a pistol in a paddle holster. Greg flicked a glance to the old man's waist, then wished he hadn't given himself away like that.

Jarvis read the move. "Afraid I'm going to take a shot?"

Before Greg could think of the right answer—was there one?— Pru said, "Seeing as how I'm right behind you, Jarvis, that would be a real bad idea."

"You got a Ruger, kid." Jarvis cracked a laugh. His Adam's apple wobbled in his turkey neck. "Punch right through. Blast me, you blast him."

There was the sound of metal sliding over plastic, and then Greg saw Jarvis's back stiffen. "Yeah, but this don't have bullets," Aidan said, and he must've pressed the tip of his knife just a touch more into Jarvis's neck, because the old man gasped. "I did this once in bio, to this big honking bullfrog."

"I remember that lab," Lucian said. "Kind of a rush, the way the frog spazzed?"

"No one's pithing frogs, and no one's blasting anyone. Now I'm just picking up Lucian's knife here, okay? Everyone be cool." Slowly unfolding himself from the floor, Greg raised his right palm out while he held the machete's blade in his left and prayed Lucian didn't grab it so quickly he lost a few fingers in the bargain. Beyond, he could see Pru, his Ruger Mini-14 holding steady on the back of Jarvis's head, and Aidan, whose lips were drawn into a predatory grin Greg knew all too well. Lucian only looked thoughtful, like all the gears were clicking away in there, all the angles being considered. *That* was somehow even scarier.

"Here's what we're going to do." His jaw was so tight, Greg could barely get the words past his teeth. "Screw the cat, okay? We pack up this stuff and then we all leave, *together*. We take everything to the food stores and then we don't have to worry about it anymore, all right?"

"Out of sight, out of mind?" Jarvis gave a bitter cackle, like the snap of bad ice. Didn't sound—or look—much like a gobble-gobble now. "You think it's that easy?"

"Hey." Aidan's teeth showed in a snarl. "You threatening us poor little punks?"

"Aidan, put the knife away." Greg's eyes slid to Pru. "You, too." After a long second, Pru's elbows broke, and Greg heard the click of the Ruger's safety. "Aidan," Greg said again.

"Yeah, yeah," Aidan said, but from the way Jarvis's cheek twitched, Greg thought the little rat-creep still managed a cut.

"Okay," Greg said. "We need something to carry this stuff. Pru, you and Jarvis go look for some pillowcases."

"How do we know you won't slip a jar into your pocket or saddle-bags while we're gone?" Jarvis said. "Why should we trust you?"

"Because you can. Jarvis, really, we're on the same side," Greg said.

"Yeah?" Jarvis said. "Which side is that?"

43

Move! The fine down on Sarah's neck bristled with an electric surge of terror. *Something coming, move, move!*

"No!" Gasping, she bolted like a spooked rabbit, springing for the storage room door, keys tinkling to the Formica, but no time to search for them, just enough to get away! The door crashed open with an enormous bang. As Sarah bulleted through, she felt fingers whisking through her hair. With a wild yelp, she spun on her heel and lunged for the door to clap it shut. Her flashlight jittered crazily, ripping wide gashes, cutting shelves out of the dark before she lost her grip. The light clattered to the floor, the orange spray winking out. Blind now, she swam through the dark, made a wild grab, felt the bite of wood, and then she was muscling the door home with a solid *clap.*

Safe, she was safe. Chest heaving, she leaned back, bracing the door with her body, expecting to feel the thud. But nothing happened. No bang. No battering of a fist. No kicks.

Barricade the door. Without the keys, she couldn't lock it, and this might be her only chance. She knew the storage area well enough to navigate in the dark: freestanding, largely barren metal shelves right and left. The only shelves with any food at all were on her left. So grab a shelf off to her right, haul it in front of the door. Unless she'd imagined the whole thing. She pulled in a screaming breath, held it, listened over the clamor of her heart. The air smelled, very faintly, of peanut butter, but she heard nothing. So, nerves? No, she'd felt something grab for her hair. Unless that had been a phantom terror, too.

Felt so real. Maybe only her mind playing tricks? *Because I'm stressed, starved, exhausted . . .*

What to do now was the question. She could stay here, barricade the door. But the Coleman was on. Eventually the ice would melt, boil off. Forget the waste of fuel; the flame would burn a hole through that pot and then they'd have a fire.

She listened again, pressing her ear against the keyhole. Still nothing. If she decided to leave, go back out there, she would need light. Which meant retrieving her flashlight from the floor and hoping to God that it worked. Sarah dropped to her hands and knees. Grit bit through her jeans. *Okay, which way?* She'd been spinning for the door when she lost the flashlight. From the sound the metal tube made as it struck the floor and then rolled, she thought it might be ahead, at roughly ten o'clock. Moving carefully, she swept her trembling right hand over the cold floor. She kept expecting something to skitter across her skin. A spider, maybe, but no self-respecting spider would set up shop here, and it was too cold besides. Her fingers skimmed more dirt—a lot of it, and that was so strange because Tori was such a stickler about neatness. But Cutter *had* interrupted Tori this afternoon. So she might not have swept here at all.

Sarah inched forward, her hand moving back and forth like a metal detector, for what seemed like an hour but which was likely no more than a minute before her fingers nudged a curve of cool metal that tried rolling away. The flashlight. Snatching it up, she rocked back on her knees, let out a long sigh of relief, and butted her thumb against the metal switch.

A cone of yellow light leapt away, spraying itself against the darkness to reveal bare metal, cinderblock, and—

"No!" The word jumped from Sarah's throat as huge hands shot from the dark. One battened on her jaw, clamping down on her mouth. The other jumped into her hair, fisted, and yanked as if pulling a long cord. Her head whipped back, exposing her throat, and then she was tottering, her balance gone. She crashed to the ice-cold floor, legs kinked at an excruciating angle, the impact smacking the breath from her lungs. Terrified, wild not only with fear but the need to breathe, she flailed, the flashlight she still clutched whipping around. She felt when it clubbed bone, the solid *thunk* shuddering into her hand. From the hulking dark above her came a strangled grunt, a deep and guttural *unh*. The hand in her hair jerked like a fish trying to flip from a net, then groped for her thrashing wrist, found it, ground down. An enormous bolt of pain shot up to her elbow and she relaxed her grip. The flashlight tumbled to the floor again. This time, however, the light did not wink out, which wasn't necessarily a mercy.

"Quiet!" Cutter snarled. Dropping onto her chest, he brought his face so close his spit sprayed her cheeks. Sweeping up both her arms, he grabbed her wrists in one hand and pinned them to the floor. "Be *quiet*, unless you want me to snap your little neck right now!"

She wasn't screaming; she had no breath for that. Shaking her head wildly from side to side, she strained, her tortured lungs singing, the blood booming in her temples. Breathing was like trying to butt a mountain out of the way with her chest. She managed another suck of air, her nose wrinkling against a weird perfume souring Cutter's flesh: oily onions, greasy sweat—and peanut butter.

"Guh." If she could've opened her mouth, she'd have bitten him. "Guh-get *off*."

"You gonna scream?" When she shook her head, he eased his hand away. "We need to have ourselves a little talk."

"There's n-nothing to t-talk about," she stammered. "You . . . you're st-stealing f-food from little *k-kids*."

Cutter's eyes flattened. "I'm taking my share. I'm taking what's mine."

"You g-get rations." By now, Tori must be wondering. She'd come down to check, probably with one of the dogs, too. Even if she didn't, Tori had that shotgun. If she could keep Cutter talking . . . God, where was their other guard, Benton? Unless he was in on this, too. "We're all on rations."

"But you kids get more. They save the best for you." Cutter sported a full, gnarled gray wire of beard so dense there might be things living very comfortably in there. "We take all the risks and we're supposed to be *grateful* for a cup of watered-down tomato soup?"

"Please. Just let me go. I won't say anything." For some reason, her eyes zeroed in on a glop of peanut butter clinging to a tangle at the left corner of his mouth. In the bad light, the smear looked like a rat turd. "You can have *my* rations. You can just *have* them."

"Yeah? Well, what if I want *more*?" He drew the word out, his voice in her ear again, his reeking breath hot on her neck—and yet she never had felt so cold in her life.

Her heart tried dying in her chest. "I . . . I don't have anything else. Please, just . . . I won't tell anyone, I promise."

"Who you going to tell? The Council? Your boyfriend, that Pru? What if *I* was to tell how some *kid* thinks he can buy me off with a measly can of beans? You think people might be *interested* in why those boys come to pass the time with such pretty girls? And here that Peter only seven weeks in his grave, and you already finding someone to warm you up."

"No. I . . . ." Her tongue clung to the roof of her mouth. "It's not what you think."

"Oh, I got a good imagination. So . . . you *liiike* Pru?" He drawled the word, his voice lazy even as she became aware of the increased grind of his hips. "You *liiike* what he does?"

"No. He's just . . . ." She strained against Cutter's weight. "Please, let me go, let me—"

"Here's what I want." His mouth, the lips thick and cold and moist as worms, dragged over her throat. "I want you to be as sweet to me as you've been to that Pru."

"No." She was gasping again, trying to hold back tears. "Please. I'll scream."

"You scream, and I'll tell how those boys were here, and it won't matter what you're up to, how *nice* Pru is. They'll be watched. But you don't want them anyway. You want a man, and I can be *niiice*." His hips jerked in a sudden, hard thrust, his breath suddenly clogging as he worked his knee between her legs. "I can be *sweet* to a sweet thing."

In the next moment, she felt his body lift, his free hand dropping and then fumbling at her waist. She let out a short, sharp cry. *"No! N—"* His mouth clamped on hers, and she gagged as he worked his thick tongue between her lips and licked her teeth. Bucking, she tried to bite, but he wrapped his free hand around her throat and rapped her head so hard that all the circuitry shorted.

"You like it *rough*?" His voice was ragged, his face choked with blood. "I'll show you rough; I'll show you what a *man*—"

She heard the loud bang, an explosion of wood against cinderblock. In her terror, she thought it was her mind snapping. Hadn't they talked about that in health; how the brain could let go, be elsewhere, hide? But then she felt Cutter rear in surprise, saw his eyes go wide with shock, and thought, *Tori*.

"Jesus!" Cutter started up. "N—"

Something—someone—hurtled over her head. Slamming the still-shrilling Cutter to his back, whatever this was darted its head, once, like a snake striking at prey. There was a loud tearing sound, a ripping of wet cloth—and then Cutter was only thrashing, gurgling, both hands trying to staunch sudden, pulsing red jets from a throat that was no longer there. His blood hit concrete in hard, frantic splashes. The Changed—a boy—rode him, but only for a second.

What happened next nearly splintered her mind.

Planting a hand on Cutter's forehead, the Changed plunged a clawed hand straight down into Cutter's throat. Sarah couldn't see Cutter's face, but the old man's legs stiffened, his boots jerking as if he'd been electrocuted. The boy's back tensed and there came another of those loud, wet-cloth *rips*. Cutter was still juddering in his death dance as the Changed sank his teeth into a limp red tube of steaming flesh.

On the floor, Sarah began to scream.

44

Reining in his horse at the village hall, a hulking two-story brown-stone capped with a clock tower, Greg dismounted. Tethering his mare to a wrought-iron railing, he untied a bulging navy blue pillowcase from his saddle. The contents ticked, glass against glass, as he hefted the makeshift sack over his left shoulder. It had taken them a long time to both search the rest of the house and then pack up the stash, which the stuffy-nosed, still-bleeding Verna assured them was the very last of what they'd squirreled away. Chester still hadn't shown by the time they left. Neither had the cat.

By then, Greg didn't care. His only concern was getting the jars out of his hands, out of his sight, then finding someplace quiet to lie down, and screw food. He passed a hand over his suddenly watering eyes, wincing at a needle of pain jabbing his temples. Another whopper of a migraine muttering in there, building itself up to a real roar, the kind of monster headache that made him queasy and fractured his sight with wavering lines and jagged shards of light. Kincaid said that was normal—called it *scintillating* something or other—and doled out some advice, too: *Reduce your stress, son, and you might feel better.*

Oh yeah, right. What had happened back at the Landrys was just too damned close for comfort. No matter what Tori said—and, yes, kissing her was the best thing that had happened to him in *months*—he knew it was all bullshit, too. *Maybe she believes in me, but I sure don't.* That fiasco back there only proved he wasn't Chris or Peter. No good pretending he could be either anymore, no matter what the Council said or wanted. If Aidan had rebelled, or Pru had sided with Jarvis, or Jarvis had taken a shot, what then? Kill Jarvis? Shoot anyone else who disobeyed? Or make the exception and look the other way as the guys cracked open those jars and ate the evidence? Hell, he might have joined in.

Can't even trust myself. Got to go to the Council in the morning and just quit. Tell them Pru's a better choice. He's older, and he thinks things through better than me.

And really, what could the Council do? Send him to the principal's office? *Ban* him? His lips curled in a sour smile. Not likely. He wasn't refusing to help. There were patrols to mount, places to guard, the occasional foraging expedition. He'd settle for chopping wood. Plenty to do. Besides, he was Spared, woo-hoo, and way too valuable to toss.

I'll trade valuable for normal any day. He skimmed a look toward the church. His mind drifted back to the shock of Tori's mouth, how *nice* that felt, and *warm.* For those few seconds, he'd actually felt human again. *So maybe, after we're done here, sneak back to the church? It'll be dark soon. Lob a snowball at her window and then . . .*

"What you grinning about?" It was Pru, two steps below.

"Nothing." God, he couldn't even daydream in peace. Another scintillating splinter of light skewered his left eye. He ought to see Kincaid, maybe beg some aspirin or Tylenol, if there was any left. Or maybe in all Kincaid's reading up on plants and mushrooms, tinkering with decoctions and infusions, he'd come up with something that could deal with this monster headache that just wouldn't quit.

"Come on," he said, turning, his gaze sweeping past the church, "let's—" Suddenly, he froze.

Pru let a beat slide by. "Greg?"

He didn't reply. He could feel his eyebrows bunching together in a sudden frown. Out of the corner of his eye, he could've sworn there'd been a light? *No, a flash.* But that was probably the headache . . .

"Greg?"

"I don't know," he said to Pru. "But I thought I heard something."

45

From what Sarah could see, Cutter wasn't quite done dying yet. His fingers fluttered and flapped like dying starfish. The close air in this back storage room was saturated, almost fogged with the heady stink of wet pennies. Hunched over the body, both hands full of Cutter's meat, the Changed was feeding with a single-minded ferocity that reminded Sarah of a film they'd seen in science about wolves: how a pack brought down a full-grown moose. Once the animal was on the snow, the wolves ripped open the abdomen and literally ate the moose to death.

Starving. Horrified, Sarah watched the boy's Adam's apple bob in a swallow as he simultaneously crammed in another mouthful. The boy had one of the worst cases of acne she'd ever seen. His face looked broken and bruised. With all that blood smeared over pitted skin and bulging sacs of yellow pus, the Changed looked *diseased*, something out of *The Walking Dead*.

She had to get out of here. Clawing to her feet, she lurched in a stumble-stagger that sent her crashing into the door. At the sound, the Changed twisted, seemed to see her for the first time, and began to surge up from the floor. Turning, she blundered down the narrow alley of the kitchen, banging like an errant pinball between counters. With no flashlight, she was blind, driving forward on memory and fear. As she crashed through the dark, she felt a sudden, slight change in temperature, a puff of even colder air from the common room.

Wheeling drunkenly to the right, she groped, found the corner, and then she was half falling, half sprinting up the stairs.

Her ears caught a thump behind and below. A steady, fast clump of boots. Coming for her. Not much time. Even starving, the Changed boy was faster. Sarah tore a screaming breath from the air and then another. Above, she could see the slight gray-green glow of the vestibule. Once she made it up and then out of there and into the breezeway, if she could just make it to the doors, lock him out of the school . . .

My keys. A moan fell out of her mouth. Her keys were behind her, on the floor. She doubted she was fast enough to outdistance this boy anyway. Even if she could, there might be more. Cutter was dead. There was no reason for anyone to check on them until the guards switched off. And what if someone *did* notice that the side door was open and came in to investigate? What if that someone was Pru or Greg? This Changed would be on them in a second.

Flinging herself up the last step, she staggered into the vestibule. From below, she could hear the boy's grunts, a stumble as he misjudged the distance between one stair and another. *Can't lead him back into the school.* Darting right toward the bell tower door, she fumbled for the handle. *Please don't be locked.* Mashing down on the icy iron thumb plate, she cocked her elbows, jerked back hard. The door was oak and as solid as any other in the church, but it moved, swinging open with a rusty squall. Cold air spilled and she saw a shimmery curlicue of narrow stone steps. *Bell tower must open at the top. That's why it's colder and there's light.*

A sudden gush of air sucked at her back and stoppered her ears. Someone was pushing through from the breezeway into the vestibule, following a cone of orange light that splashed her shadow onto stone. For a crazy moment, she thought the Changed had her flashlight, but he was coming from the wrong direction. Then she heard Tori call, "Sarah? Where are you going? What's hap—"

No. Darting a glance left, Sarah saw the boy storming up the last few steps. "Tori, run!" Sarah spun on her heel and waved the other girl back. "Run, *ru—*"

Surging from the dark like a demon summoned from hell, the Changed threw himself into the vestibule. Cringing, Tori raised both arms to ward him off. Her flashlight tumbled from her right hand as she unlimbered her shotgun, racked the pump, socked the butt to her shoulder—

And in that small span of time, Sarah finally remembered.

The gun. Sweating, Sarah fumbled for her pistol just as the boy ducked his shoulder, dropped below Tori's line of fire, and sprinted across the vestibule at a dead-on run. Tori let out an explosive *oomph* as the boy smacked into her middle and bore them both crashing to the stone. Somehow, Tori still had the shotgun clutched in her right hand and was trying to bring it around when the boy balled his right fist, still smeary with Cutter's blood, and smashed Tori across the jaw. A yelp jerked from her mouth, her hold on the shotgun loosened, and in one swift, practiced motion, the Changed boy swept up the weapon and jammed the muzzle under her chin.

"N-no." Tori's bloody lips were purple in the yellow glow of the flashlight. "Pl—"

"Stop!" Sarah poked the Sig out in both hands, but the gun wavered and she was shaking so badly her knees wobbled. The Changed went rigid, and she thought, *Now, shoot him, shoot!* Gritting her teeth, Sarah squeezed the trigger—and nothing happened. The trigger didn't budge.

"The safety!" Tori shrieked. "Sarah, release the—"

Too late.

46

"Heard what?" asked Pru.

"I don't know. A . . ." Greg groped for the word. A *thump*, but so muffled it was more like the sound of a heavy cardboard box on a wood floor. "Sort of a thud. I'm not sure I really heard it." Maybe migraines made you hallucinate sounds, too? He didn't remember Kincaid mentioning that.

"I didn't hear anything." Pru turned to look down at the others clustered at the bottom of the village steps. "You guys?"

In reply, Jarvis cut Pru a curt shake of his head, while Henry and Lucian only looked blank. "Man, I can barely hear you," Aidan said from the depths of his snorkel. "Can we, like, *go*? I'm freezing my ass off."

"Just a sec." *Maybe this is all the headache's doing, but . . .* Puzzled, Greg peered through the gathering twilight at the hunkered edifice of the church, the bony finger of its bell tower stabbing a sky beginning to turn cobalt. From this vantage point, he couldn't see the attached school or the rectory. He stared a long second, saw nothing, then tossed a look opposite, at the far end of the square toward a brooding row of shuttered shops and a defunct Christian combination coffeehouse and bookstore. The storefronts were dark, the black windows empty as sockets. In the center of the square, the snowy mushroom of an octagonal gazebo, probably once used for summer band concerts, huddled beneath a trio of towering oaks. "Thought I saw something, too. This *flash*."

"What? Where?" Pru twisted a look right and left and then behind, across the square. "I don't see anything."

"Me neither," the snorkel put in.

"You getting another headache?" Pru asked. "Didn't Kincaid say that might make you see flashes of light and stuff?"

"Yeah." Greg realized his hand had snuck up to pinch the bridge of his nose. "But I could've sworn—" Behind, Greg heard the scrape of a door and then a guard call: "Everything okay out here?"

"He thought he saw something," Pru said to the guard.

"I heard something, too," Greg said.

"Yeah? I didn't see anything." The guard craned a look at his companion, who shook his head, and then back. He chinned the sacks. "Whatcha got?"

"Loot," the snorkel said, "which I would really, really like to put away now, please."

"Sure. Okay," Greg said. His headache felt like it was sprouting claws and digging at the back of his left eye. "You're right. It was probably nothing."

47

The shotgun blast was enormous, a *BOOM* Sarah felt and heard crash and bang against the vestibule's stone walls. A tongue of muzzle flash, bright as lightning, spurted from the weapon's throat, sheeting the stone gray where it wasn't purpled with Tori's blood and bits of her brain and skull.

Without pause, the boy simultaneously worked the pump and pivoted as Sarah shrieked and leapt again for the bell tower steps. Hooking the wrought iron latch with her left hand, she dragged the door partly shut just in time. Another flash, a gigantic *BOOM.* Something slapped her right calf, and she stumbled as more buckshot punched through the wood, exploding in splinters that nipped her back and blew past her cheeks. She careered up the slippery steps as her calf bawled, the blood streaming in runnels down her pant leg and sock.

Shot, I'm shot. She gimped up steps before her leg suddenly gave. Pitching forward, she sprawled against stone. Her heart was yammering, not only in fear but pain. With all these gunshots, someone would hear, wouldn't they? She didn't know. All this heavy, thick stone and wood . . . Maybe no one could.

He was down there, waiting, *deciding.* She could feel him. *Have to save myself.* She still had the Sig. *Is there a round ready?* She didn't remember or know how to check. Any sound would give her away. The Changed had already seen her with the weapon. The longer he assumed she didn't know what to do—not such a stretch—the better off she might be.

Then, the glimmer of an idea . . . *Find the safety.* Her fingers walked the weapon. This time, she found the lever and thumbed it off. Grimacing, she eased onto her back, reached down, and skimmed an oozy handful of warm blood to smear her cheeks and neck. Scooping another palmful, she slathered her chest. *There, that ought to sell it. One look at me and he'll think I'm dying.*

Shuddering, she scrubbed her hand on her jeans, then pulled herself into as tight a crouch as she could manage, hissing at the pain in her calf. No expert on guns, but she knew geometry. They were in a tight tube, a circular space with narrow, essentially triangular steps that tapered to a point around the stone newel. He was a boy and much bigger, and had the long gun besides, which meant he had no choice but to hug the outer wall. But she was above him, and small. Clutching the Sig, she steadied her hands on her knees, aiming for what she thought would be the most logical spot.

"Help." She injected as much fear and pain into that little whimper of a word as she could. It wasn't such a stretch. "I'm *shot.* Please don't hurt me. I won't tell anyone you're here, I promise."

Nothing. *This isn't going to work.* She listened, straining above the thump of her heart, the buzz in her ears. She was trembling so badly her teeth stuttered. Sweat, oily and as thick as the blood seeping into her right boot, spilled over the shelf of her eyebrows to burn her eyes. "Help." She threw in a long grind of a groan for good measure. "I'm *hurt.* Please, *help* me."

A second later, from somewhere below, she heard the distinctive rasp of a boot over stone. A *clup.* Then another *clup.*

Coming up. How many steps had she managed? She couldn't remember. "Help." Her hands were cramped so tightly around the Sig's butt, the ridged grip digging into her palms. Her right index finger curled over the trigger. "I'm *hurt.*"

Another *clup*. And another.

"Please. Help me." The newel was cold on her neck. She was staring so hard into the silvery gloom, her eyes watered. "I'm bleeding, I'm—"

A dark, stiff finger slid into view. She felt her breath catch as the barrel of Tori's shotgun—just the tip—hung there a moment. She was afraid to call out again because she didn't want him to look her way. The sound of his boot on stone reached her again, just that single step. The shotgun moved. The shotgun was pointing up, away from her and at an angle. He had no choice because of the tower's geometry. It would take time to swing down for a shot.

Heart rampaging in her chest, she watched the barrel bob as he took another step and then another. First, his hands came into view—*wait, wait*—then the hump of his forehead, the jut of his nose—*wait, just another second*—and then he was only three steps below her—*wait, wait*—and she saw shoulders, his chest, how his head was swiveling, his face ballooning to a gray oval—*almost, almost*—and then she heard his quick inhale the instant he realized he was looking in the wrong place at the wrong time and the sharp rap of the shotgun's butt against stone as he tried swinging down but couldn't—because he was a tall boy with a long gun trying to turn in a too-tight space.

"*Ahh!*" The sound was more wheeze than scream. But she squeezed the trigger.

And this time, the gun went off.

48

Greg's headache still pulsed in his teeth. His vision was fuzzing around the edges, but as he shouldered open the door and stepped from the village hall's entryway and back into the cold, Greg huffed out in relief. The village hall triggered a lot of bad memories: images of refugees, all of them old and decrepit, cringing along the walls; the Council eyeing him owlishly from their raised bench in that bat cave of a courtroom the very first day he'd sought sanctuary.

Probably that post-traumatic stuff. Pulling on his gloves, he stomped his feet in a freezing-kid two-step, shuffling from right to left as he waited. The others were still inside, offloading their loot. Located belowground and through a double set of iron doors, the basement jail was where they stored what remained of their food and feed as well as stockpiles of fuel, high-grade fertilizer, and ammo.

What nagged even more was how much they *didn't* have. The jail was wide and deep, equipped with ten four-person cells, five to a row. One huge iron cage—probably once a drunk tank, from the faint, steeped-in odor of old vomit—dominated the wall at the very back. This was where they kept their fuel stores: propane tanks, red plastic cans of gasoline siphoned from stalled cars, fuel oil, premix. Of all their supplies, their fuel situation was the least dire simply because no one did any welding, went boating, fired up a chain saw, or headed out for a nice country drive anymore. All that combustible material made him nervous, too. No one had asked him, but he always worried about what might happen if someone got careless, or a spark flew. Couldn't you use premix or fuel oil and fertilizer to make ANFO?

Of the remaining cells, only three held food, and of those, one was devoted to dog food: cans of wet, twenty-pound sacks of dry kibbles. While not exactly barren, the steel shelves in the remaining cells weren't fully stocked either. What had looked so amazing in the tight, dark cubby of the Landrys' pantry hidey-hole made barely a dent. Those eight jars he'd hauled now huddled in a forlorn little knot, surrounded by a lot of empty space. As the guard had slotted in the jars, Greg had counted the cans of condensed soup on the shelf above . . . just to see.

Thirty cans. The thought sent a shiver down his neck. That would last forty hungry kids about three minutes. The guards also kept a very careful tally of every single can and jar, every sack of kibble. So just how were *they* supposed to sneak out food, much less bricks of ammo, for their great escape? *Hopeless.* He massaged his right temple with a forefinger. *We'll never find enough—*

Something *snapped*. The sound was very brief, crisp, firecracker-short. Greg stiffened, his ears suddenly tingling, aware of just the faintest echo bouncing off brownstone. *That* had been a shot. Headache forgotten, he turned in a full circle. But from where?

Behind, he heard the door scrape open. "Boy, I'm glad that's . . ." Then Pru must've gotten a look at Greg's face. "What is it?"

"Either I'm going crazy," Greg said, "or I just heard a shot."

49

Sarah wasn't aware she'd screamed or even fired until she felt the burn in her throat and the kick in her hands. The sound was monstrous, although the muzzle flash was more like the burst of a spent bulb. Yet in that brief, spastic light, she saw him drop, not straight down as if he had ducked—or, better yet, had no head left to duck *with*—but backward. Just falling? Or dead? She didn't know, couldn't hear anything. Scrambling to her feet, she turned to scurry up but pivoted much too quickly. Her right boot skidded on a slick of her own blood. Her center of gravity shifted; she could feel her balance going, and then the scream tear itself from her throat.

Sarah knew how to run with a weapon about as well as she knew how to fire it. So she was holding onto the Sig in exactly the wrong way, with her finger through the trigger guard. When she tripped and fell up the stairs, her hand hit stone, and the gun went off again. This time, she lost her grip, too. The Sig went skittering down the steps as shards of stone—blowback from where the bullet punched into the newel—nipped her face and neck and cut fresh blood.

God, oh God, please make him be dead or hurt or gone. . . . If he was still alive, he'd now have her pistol. How many bullets did that thing hold? *Doesn't matter. One will be enough.*

She scrabbled up the slippery steps. All she could hope now was that the Changed was running the opposite way. Maybe no one had heard the shotgun because the church's walls were so thick, but *someone* had to have heard those pistol shots through the open bell tower. So where *was* everyone?

All at once, she ran out of stairs and stumbled into a short, stone-lined passage slotted with rectangular openings on either side to let in light. Dead ahead, no more than ten feet away, she saw an array of trusses and ropes and handles that reminded her of a weaver's loom.

But where are the bells? She stood, panting, heart thudding, calf screaming with pain, ears still roaring. The bells must be above her somewhere. Lurching to the tangle of ropes, she saw how they looped around dowels and were tied off in hard knots. The icy ropes would be stiff, and her chilled fingers were tacky with blood. If the knots were too tight, she'd never loosen them. But all she needed was one, right? She yanked ropes, searched the knots with quaking fingers, then gasped as the tip of her right index finger slipped through a very small loop.

Yes! Tugging, she felt the rope give. She worked in another finger and then a third, and felt the knot suddenly relax as the ropes parted in her hands. *All right, come on!* Grasping a single rope, she hauled straight down as hard as she could, let her weight drop, grunting as her wounded calf screamed—and heard a hollow *bong*.

Hurry, please, hurry! She sent the thought winging after each *bong-dong, bong-dong* of the bell. *Hurry, hurry, help us, help us, help us!*

50

"Come on!" Storming down the village steps, Greg dashed to his horse and yanked his Bushmaster from its scabbard. He was already spinning away as the village hall doors popped open and Aidan spilled out, shouting over the *dong-bong* of the bell, "What the *hell*?"

Greg sprinted for the church, only a hundred yards away, with Pru hard on his heels. Now that the bell was ringing—now that he knew something was wrong—he could hear the dogs, too: very faint, but unmistakable, a rhythmic *oof-oof-oof* floating from the rear of the church. The dogs and kids must be in the school; God, he hoped so. Which meant Tori and Sarah were in the bell tower.

Or it might be only one of them. Instead of bounding up the front steps, he turned, saw Aidan, Lucian, and now Jarvis and two of the village guards running after, and shouted back: "The kids! Go make sure the kids . . . !" Then, pivoting, he blasted past the church's front entrance, dodged right, and headed around back, slipping into slate shadows painted on snow by the coming night.

"Side door?" To his left, he could hear Pru's ragged breaths. "Thought . . . Tori locked it. Where . . . the hell . . . are Cutter and Benton?"

"Don't know." He was sure Tori locked up after he'd left, too. What was in the church that anyone would want? *Food, mostly. Not a lot, but easier to get to than the jail.* Suddenly, his boots skated on something slick. He landed with a *splish* in a mucky, slithery tangle that reeked of salty metal and the fouler, rank odor of guts.

"*Guh.*" Pru sounded as if he was going to be as sick as Greg felt. "Oh, fuck me."

"God." Greg's voice was thick with sour puke. He spat. In the bad light, Greg couldn't see if he was wallowing in Cutter or Benton. Didn't much matter. From the size of the puddle and spools of chilled intestines, most of the body—or bodies—was elsewhere. He swam forward, leaving a snail's slick of gore, then got a knee under as Pru dragged him upright.

"Jesus." Pru pressed a hand to his forehead like a kid taking his fever. "A Changed?"

"Maybe more than one." The bell was still tolling. Greg could feel the dry air wicking the wet from his face and chest, leaving behind a tacky, toxic sludge of half-congealed blood and ruptured guts. "Whatever. I'm going inside."

"Are you nuts?" Pru's hand shot for Greg's arm. "What's gone down has gone down."

"Stay here if you want." Greg tore himself free. "I don't care what you do, but Tori's in there, and Sarah, and I'm *going.*"

"*No.*" Pru tried another grab but missed. "Greg, be smart. Chris or Peter wouldn't—"

"*Fuck* smart," he said. "And that just shows what you *don't* know, because *they* would, and so will I."

Turning, he dashed the last hundred feet. The door was open, not yawning but wide enough for him to scuttle through with room to spare. He held his breath as he did it, expecting the shot. None came, and he heard the air sigh from his mouth. As soon as he was inside, the bell's clanging diminished. Directly ahead and up a short but very steep flight of stairs, he made out the arched entryway into the sanctuary. Enough of the day's dying light splashed in through the open door for him to see a stack of folding chairs leaning against the wall to his right. This was bad because it meant that he could be seen if someone was on the altar platform, maybe waiting out of his line of sight.

If anyone's still in here. When the bells started, the smart thing for the Changed would be to get out, fast, just as the wiser play for Greg would have been to wait, like Pru said. He hoped the Changed were smarter than he was. He'd been here only a couple of hours before and remembered the layout: that the stairs to the basement were on his right. He peeked, saw the door was open, and thought, *Oh boy, that's bad.* With no flashlight, it would be crazy to go down—

He heard something shuffle off his left shoulder, tensed, swiveled, socked the Bushmaster in place, then felt a surge of relief. "I thought this wasn't smart."

"Yeah, so we're both stupid. Now wha—" Pru's voice died as he saw the gaping maw of the basement door. "Shit. Block it?"

The door opened out, so that should work. "I'll do it," he murmured. He didn't want to let go of his gun, but he couldn't do this with one hand. He laid the Bushmaster flat, then gently pulled one folding chair away from the other ten, the metal letting out a faint, rasping *scaw* that made him wince. Slowly padding down the steps, he levered the door closed, all his muscles trying to turn to jelly at every creak and squeak, and wedged the chair under the knob. He repeated this maneuver twice more, moving as fast as he could. Total time: maybe a minute.

"Good deal. Anything in there'll be trapped like a bug in a jar. You remember the layout?" Pru chinned toward the sanctuary. "Sundays, I try to sleep with my eyes open."

"Three steps and you're on the platform. Choir on the right, altar on the left along the wall and under the cross. Pulpit at one o'clock on the far end. Go straight through and you'll be in the organist's pit." He thought. "I'll go right, down the side aisle. Depending on what happens next, you head for the platform."

Pru nodded, and Greg took the stairs as fast as he dared. He saw the cross suddenly slip into view on his left and then the high arches of stained glass lining the sanctuary's far wall; heard a sudden creak under his boot and thought, *Shit, in the movies they hug the wall, so stairs won't—*

There was a thundering roar, a clap of lightning. Greg let out a startled gasp as the wall above his head suddenly cratered. Swaying, he stumbled back, tripped over his boots, and fell the rest of the way as another shot blasted past. Greg felt the *whir* of a slug cleave air by his left temple.

"*Shit.*" Pru's face swam into view. "You hit?"

"No." His left ear felt as if someone had crammed in a fistful of cotton, but he could hear the *tick-tick-tick* of buckshot and the lighter patter of grit and pulverized drywall. Well, at least they knew what kind of weapon the Changed had. Eyeing the hole in the drywall, Greg saw the teardrop shape and how it curved *up*. "I think he's under the altar table."

"Yeah? *And?*" Pru sounded angry. "How the *hell* are we supposed to . . . wait, Greg, why are you taking off your boots?"

Giving him something else to look at. Quickly yanking off his other boot, Greg stripped the sock, then crammed both socks into a parka pocket. Hefting the boot in his left hand, Greg glanced back at Pru. "He's got a shotgun."

"So?" Pru gave him a strange look and then Greg saw the second his friend got his meaning. A shotgun had a max effective distance of about forty yards. Plenty of stopping power, but if he could get far enough away, his rifle, or Pru's Mini-14, would be much more effective. Pru jerked a nod. "Okay," Pru said. "Just . . . run *fast*."

I hear that. Greg pulled in a breath. *Oh God, please make this work.*

Then he stopped thinking and moved. Dashing up the steps, Greg lobbed the boot in an awkward throw and then immediately dodged right. The shotgun roared at the same instant, following the trajectory of his boot. Through the ringing, he heard Pru squeeze off a shot as Greg hit the stone floor in a hard thump. The shotgun thundered to life again. This time, the pew just above his head exploded in a mushroom cloud of wood splinters. Ducking, Greg threw up a hand to protect his head and neck as he scuttled as fast as he could down the side aisle. Behind, he caught the sharp *crack-crack-crack*, the Ruger's raps growing closer and louder as Pru stormed up the steps. Wheeling to his left, still hunched over, Greg dashed the cramped length of the pew, bare feet slapping stone, the center aisle dead ahead.

At that moment, the bell cut out. *The others are in. They're safe.* He felt a sting in his throat, gulped it back. *Tori's safe.*

From the altar to his left, he heard something shrill—a shout, a *scream?*—and then he was lifting onto the balls of his feet, pivoting, thighs tensing, his Bushmaster swinging clear of the pew, thinking, *Aim up.*

But he never had a chance to take the shot.

51

In the sudden thrumming silence, Greg saw Pru looming over the writhing body of a boy. When he'd been shot—a belly wound from the way the Changed was curled in a comma—the boy had tried rolling away, because once Greg squirted past, the Changed needed to move, fast, or end up full of holes. But the kid couldn't move fast or far enough to outrun Pru's bullets, and Greg saw why.

A forked splinter of bone jutted from a juicy rip in the boy's thigh. Now that Greg was standing, he saw the trail of blood smeared over the sanctuary's floor and up the altar platform's steps. The altar carpet was purple and sodden. *Dragged himself all the way.* Turning, Greg followed the blood trail's wavering path and realized that the boy must've broken his leg outside the sanctuary. Maybe in the vestibule, or even the breezeway. But how? That kid would've had to fall pretty far.

Through the sanctuary's thick double doors, he could hear a growing gabble and maybe . . . was that a scream? Couldn't tell. Way back, he'd read that you lost some of your hearing if you shot at a range and didn't wear gear. Keep this up, he'd be deaf by the time he was twenty. His ears still buzzed so badly he couldn't tell or tease apart the muted sounds seeping through the doors. No gunshots, though, so that was good. As desperately as he wanted to burst through those doors and find Tori, he knew he ought to wait. No rush now. The girls were safe.

We did it. So why didn't he feel good about that? It was the Changed boy, the screw of his face, the way he writhed. *Dying hard,* Kincaid would say. Not right to feel good about that. He started back for Pru. "You okay?" He thought he said it too loudly.

"Yeah. Can't say the same for our buddy." Pru toed a shotgun away from the boy's spidering fingers. "Can't decide whether to finish him or let him bleed to death." He paused. "Dude's pretty messed up. Carpet's ruined. So's the altar cloth."

Greg picked out splashes of blood on the wood, even the walls just below the cross. If you didn't know better, you'd think Jesus's ghost was up there, dripping. He stared down at the boy. Seventeen, eighteen, he guessed, greasy hair down past his shoulders and a ton of yellow pus balloons and zit scars to boot. Someone had rearranged his nose, too, and recently. The boy's skin was the color of moldy cheese, and his eyes, already glazing, were sunk deep in sockets rimmed with fading yellowish bruises. This Changed was starving to death, just like them.

Stooping, he reached for the shotgun—and froze. He must also have . . . what . . . gasped? Cried out? He didn't know, but Pru said, sharply, "*What? Greg?*"

No. Maybe his heart had stopped somewhere along the way. He thought that must be it, because he felt the muscle seize in his chest and his center go cold and still and black. For a crazy instant, he thought, *This will be what it's like when I'm dead.* He watched his hand float toward the weapon; saw his fingers—small, so distant—wrap themselves around the shotgun's walnut stock, then creep over the ridges and swirls of those intricate curlicues of carved flowers and vines as a blind boy reads Braille.

"Oh Jesus," Pru said. Then: "Greg, look at me, man. This doesn't mean anything—"

But he was on his feet, backtracking a stumbling step and then another, and now he'd gotten himself turned around and had begun to run, the Changed's blood sticky against his bare feet, and then the sanctuary's double doors were suddenly swinging wide, as if in a bel-low, because now the voices all crashed through in a huge wave that the men rode, spilling into the sanctuary. The faces blurred—all black mouths, black eyes—and now hands were floating to meet him like exotic sea life on an incoming tide.

Of them all, he recognized only three people in those first few seconds: Sarah, hair wild, face smeared with blood; Yeager, somehow pathetic in a red-checked flannel he hadn't managed to button cor-rectly; and Kincaid, who crowded through, with his arms out to grab him, hold him back, spare him for one more second: "No, son. Don't look, don't look, son, don't . . ."

"Nooo! Tori? *Tori?"* Greg wailed as Kincaid wrapped him up, and then there were more hands and other men bearing him to the cold stone as Greg thrashed. *"No no no!"*

And in all of that, there was one thing more: the moment doddering old Henry stumped up the altar to stare down at the Changed boy, who was, miraculously, still alive.

"Jesus Lord," Henry piped, his high voice cutting above the gabble. "It's Ben Stiemke."

52

"What?" At first, Greg wasn't sure the voice, so dead and flat, was his. Still huddled in the circle of Kincaid's arms on cold, blood-smeared stone, Greg felt eight years old again, a little boy waiting for the adults to make everything all right, and he had never missed his father quite so much. "Stiemke? Like on the *Council*?"

"Holy shit, you've got to be kidding me," Pru said, his rifle still trained on the dying boy. "I thought all the kids from Rule were dead."

"Oh Lord," Kincaid groaned in an undertone. His face was ashen. "You sons of bitches, you did it. You really did it."

"Did what?" Greg asked as Sarah staggered toward them through the crowd. Her right pant leg was sodden, and tears had eaten tracks through the blood caked on her cheeks. "Doc, what are you talking about?"

Before Kincaid could respond, Henry said, in his clear bugle, "Yup, that's Ben, all right. Known him since he was a little guy, oh . . . yay high." Henry patted the air down around his knees. "Recognize him anywhere. on account of that bad case of the acne." Henry looked down the aisle toward the Council members, who'd worked their way through the swell of people crowding into the sanctuary. Greg saw that none of the Council wore their robes, and while Yeager was in the lead, only Ernst, broad-chested and very tall, with a still-substantial gut in spite of rationing, retained even a vestige of authority. Stiemke, a withered little man, blind in one eye, only cringed alongside

Ernst. Greg couldn't decide if Stiemke was in shock or trying to hide.

"Mr. Stiemke?" Henry called. "This is your grandson, isn't it?"

Yeager spoke for the quailing Stiemke. "Yes, that's Ben." Yeager's tone was even enough, but his skin was bleached so white his bald head looked like a cue ball. Without his robes, Yeager looked like a homeless person in mismatched socks, sagging trousers, and that red-checked flannel. Yeager's eyes, usually so bird-bright with calculation, only looked furtive and a little frightened, like those of a mouse that can't decide if running will only make the cat spring faster. "Obviously, Ben got away, a fact of which we were unaware."

"Obviously? Got away? *Unaware?*" Rifle held high, Jarvis shouldered his way past the others to stand in the center aisle. Any resemblance to a turkey was gone. Jarvis looked more like a buzzard. "You run this place for decades, make all the decisions. You tell *us*, grown *men*, to follow orders from *kids*"—Jarvis jerked his head down at Greg—"but we do it because we are loyal and God-fearing, and now you say you didn't *know* this boy had gotten *away?*"

Peter. The realization broke over Greg in a kind of icy wash. *He said they rounded up all the Changed and shot them; that no one got away.* Greg's eyes drifted to the dying boy. *So Peter would've* known *Ben wasn't dead.*

"Where I was from, before Rule? Those kids always came back," someone in the crowd said. Murmurs of assent rippled through the rest of the men, and now Greg saw more than a few women had filtered in, too, armed with baseball bats, shotguns, like a village mob from an old black-and-white monster movie. He spotted one woman—Travers?—her hair a gray fury, clutching a Warren hoe, its blade tapering to a wicked point. "Lot of 'em hunted in packs. It was one of the reasons you said we'd be safer here, 'cause all your kids were dead."

"So how that little monster's alive in the first place is what I want to know." It was Travers, the stormy woman with the hoe, which she now shook at Stiemke. "What'd you do, only kill kids like my Lee? Because we're not important enough? Did you *spare* this monster because he's *yours*?"

"Hell with that," someone else rumbled. "How many others like that one are there? Because if one kid got away—"

"Or they *let* him get away!" another person shouted.

"There got to be others." Travers brandished her hoe like a spear. "So where are they?"

"Where the hell do you think?" Jarvis aimed a look of black thunder at Stiemke. "They've been out there all this time, maybe even close by. But why? You said you were doing God's work, taking our grandkids, ending their torment. What did you do, you and that son of a bitch, Peter, and *Chris . . .*"

"My grandson knew nothing about this," Yeager said, and Greg thought from his tone that this was the truth. Yet Ernst remained silent, not a flicker of emotion on his bullish features.

But Peter knew. Greg saw Sarah study Ernst's face, then drop her eyes as the first fingers of scarlet crept up her neck. A tear splashed onto a cheek, which she knuckled away. Greg gave her free hand a small squeeze, but she didn't look up or acknowledge him in any way. *Sarah knows it now, too. Peter was in on it all along. Letting some of the Changed get away might even have been his idea.* Peter was the one who'd told each patrol where to go, and when. Because he *knew* where the Changed were most likely to be at any given time?

And Jarvis had said *maybe even close by . . .* Changed, in the Zone? *Of course.* Now that someone had finally said it, this made perfect sense.

"So did Chris find out?" Travers, the woman with the hoe, shouted. "Is that why you got rid of him, said he organized an ambush when he didn't?"

"Chris *ran*." Yeager said the words like a curse. "He betrayed us."

"Like you betrayed us?" Until the words hung in the air, Greg hadn't known they were on his tongue. He tottered to his feet. "You didn't give Chris a choice. He denied it, but you'd already decided. No matter what he said, you'd have sent him to the prison house."

"Because he *defied* me." Yeager seemed to be getting some of his old fire back. His coal-black eyes shifted to Jarvis. "You owe *Rule* your life. Don't dare to judge—"

"Shut up. Let's judge *you* for a change." Jarvis jabbed a finger into Yeager's chest, hard enough to rock the old man back a stumbling step. "You lied. I don't know how many of our grandkids you let go, but that *abomination* on the altar is a councilman's grandson. You had to know. Does that mean *our* grandchildren are still alive? *Why* would you do that?"

"So what are we going to do about it *now?*" Travers's wrinkled face was the color of a prune. She jabbed the point of her hoe at Ben. "What are we going to do with *that?*"

Uh-oh. Greg rifled a warning look to Pru. The other boy gave a small nod and took a step back from Ben Stiemke, who had gone still and watchful, his lips frothy with blood bubbles.

"Leave him be," Stiemke wheezed. His face was contorted, his blind left eye as milky as a white marble. His remaining eye, with its faded gray iris, was runny, the lower lid sagging like melted candle wax to reveal pale pink flesh. "Let the poor boy die in peace."

"Peace?" The way Travers's hands were wrapped around the hoe's wooden handle reminded Greg of the fighting sticks Naruto used in *Ultimate Ninja Storm.* "*Boy?* It's an *abomination!*" she shrieked, and darted at Stiemke. With a sudden, violent thrust, she whipped around the blunt handle of the hoe like a bat. There was a muted *thuck.* Stiemke's head snapped back so quickly it was a wonder his neck didn't break. A fan of blood unfurled as Stiemke let out a gargled *ugh* and dropped to the stone floor.

"No!" Yeager squawked, at the same moment that Kincaid bawled, "My God, what are you *doing?*"

"Doc, no!" Greg grabbed Kincaid's arm as the doctor started forward. *"Don't."*

"Listen to the kid. Stay out of this, Kincaid," Jarvis warned.

"Peace? I'll showing you fucking *peace!"* Travers aimed a kick at Stiemke, who was on his belly, moaning, trying to eel away. This time, the *crunch* and *crack* as Stiemke's nose shattered and his neck kinked too far to the right weren't muted. Blood burst over Stiemke's mouth and chin, but his neck did not roll back. It stayed exactly where it was, the ear neatly cupped over the hump of Stiemke's left shoulder. Stiemke's body went as limp and flaccid as a drowned worm.

For a moment, there was that kind of stunned, surprised, soundless hiccup Greg knew well from years of school lunches and dropped cafeteria trays, when everyone was craning a look, getting ready to burst into laughter and shouts of *duuude!*

She killed him. Greg couldn't tear his gaze from the buggy white marble of Stiemke's dead eye. He felt his legs try to turn to water. *She broke his neck, she—*

Pulling away from Greg's suddenly boneless fingers, Kincaid squatted alongside Stiemke. He put a finger under Stiemke's ear, then raised his stricken face to the woman. "Do you realize what you've done? What you're *doing*? You think *this* will make things right? Killing each other isn't the way to solve this!"

"Yeah? Well, it's a goddamned good start." Travers hawked out a rope of spit. Half splashed Kincaid's hand; the rest splatted Stiemke's glassy cheek to slither in a snot-trail onto the old man's lips.

That seemed to trigger something, as if the crowd was a coiled spring under more pressure than it could bear. In the next instant, what seemed like a solid shock wave of screaming people surged forward, some stampeding for the altar, others moving to surround Yeager and the rest of the Council. Greg felt hands plant themselves on his chest as Jarvis gave a mighty shove. "Out of my way, boy, outta my *way!"* Jarvis bellowed as Greg staggered back. "I'm *done*! You hear me? From now on, you're taking orders from me, boy, from *me!*"

Greg couldn't have answered if he wanted to. Dazed, he saw Travers and that fury of gray hair lead the charge to the altar as Pru darted left and out of the way. Mouth dropping wide in alarm, Henry crossed his hands in a warding-off gesture. "Wait, wait! I didn't do nothing, I'm on *your* side," he piped. "I'm—"

The charging mob simply plowed the little man under. On the carpet, in front of the blasted altar, Ben Stiemke managed to raise an arm so awash with blood that it seemed to be drizzling red paint. With a screech that was also a growl, a rising note feral and terrible in its rage, Travers heaved the hoe in a huge, sweeping arc. The blade whickered.

Ben wailed a single piercing shriek as the blade cut three of his fingers away, cleaving them from his hand like sausages. The hoe's point buried itself in his chest with a loud and hollow sound like an ax biting wood. Somehow, Ben managed to grab the handle before Travers could yank it free, and hung on, grimly, acne-pitted face contorted in fresh pain and new fear. Blood sheeted from his ruined hand.

"Son of a—" Unable to retrieve her hoe, Travers let out another of her monstrous ululating howls. Darting forward, Jarvis raised his rifle and pistoned his arms. The butt slammed into Ben's abdomen and then Jarvis put his weight into it, grinding down. A fountain of blood gurgled from the boy's mouth in a soundless scream. His hands went slack while Travers planted her boot and pulled the hoe free with a brisk snap of bone.

The crowd closed ranks. Gargling, choking to death on his own blood, Ben Stiemke was lost under a heaving, thrashing sea of backs and legs, rifles and fists, those bats, a rake, that hoe. In the cavernous stone church, the clamor built and fed on itself, mushrooming into an explosion of inarticulate shouts and grunts and snarls. It was like watching ants boil out of a mound to swarm a tiny, wounded animal. Somehow it did not surprise Greg at all to see Aidan and Lucian and

Sam in the thick of it. Fresh ruby tears mingled with those of blue ink spilling down Aidan's cheeks. Not to be outdone, Lucian dragged that long and obscenely pink tongue over Aidan's face, licking away the blood. Laughing, the two high-fived.

At that moment, Greg understood that this was like the morning *his* world broke apart: when his parents sat him down to say they were divorcing, and he'd spat something awful before bolting away from his father, who called after him, *Son, son, wait, please. You know I'll always love you.* And what he'd said in return, something so hateful it hurt to even think it: *Fuck you, fuck love!* After, still fuming, he'd glanced through his bedroom window—just in time to see his dad suddenly slump and their ancient riding mower mutter on, narrowly missing his mother. Not that this mattered, because she was already stone-dead. The old mower kept on, eating its way over the lawn and plowing under a bed of late mums before cratering their shed.

This was like that: a disaster in progress, unstoppable, perhaps inevitable.

There was a wild triumphant roar. On the altar platform, a tidal surge of hands and arms hoisted Ben Stiemke into the air. The boy's blood rained onto the stone steps. Ben's right socket was a blast crater of crimson eye jelly. Greg and the others cringed back as the mob rampaged down the center aisle, pausing only to scoop up Stiemke's body, too.

When the crowd was gone, the sudden silence was a sound all its own. On the altar, a huge crimson lake was overflowing down the stone steps, spreading in a blood tongue down the center aisle. Bits and pieces of Ben were scattered here and there, too; Greg spotted a thumb and a chunk of something raw and liverish.

"What are they going to do?" Sarah asked in a small voice.

"We're not sticking around to find out," Kincaid said. "Let's get you three to the hospice. Safer there. Got to work on that leg anyway, Sarah. Come on, I'll carry you."

"No," Sarah said, grimacing as she hobbled a step. "I'll be fine."

"Oh, just shut up." Pru scooped her into his arms so easily, Sarah nearly went flying over his shoulder. The big boy nodded toward the side aisle. "Greg, your boots. One of them's pretty messed up from . . . you know."

"Blood washes off," Greg said. The left boot was soupy and flecked with spongy pink flesh. Lung, maybe, or brain. No use ruining his socks. Wriggling his left foot home, he felt his face screw into a pucker as his toes squelched. "Horses are tethered by the village hall. Unless we want to go on foot, we'll have to cross the square."

"No help for it," Kincaid said. "Just so long as we get—".

"Doc?" When the old doctor didn't answer, Greg looked up from ramming his right foot home and felt his heart flip.

"Weapons. On the floor," Aidan said, from behind a shotgun and smears of gore. Lucian pointed a pair of mismatched pistols, gunslinger-style. "Now."

53

The sky had bled of color. The moon wouldn't rise for hours yet, and the stars were mica-bright. The snow sparkled, reflecting the combined light of flashlights as well as Colemans and, Greg now saw, dancing, dirty yellow flames from torches of oil-soaked rags. The air was thick and bitter with the smell of soot and engine oil.

Greg thought most of the village's remaining adults must be here, in the square. Along the way, some had indulged in a little mayhem, a bit of destruction. To his left, jagged teeth showed around gaping holes in several storefront windows. More shattered glass winked from the snowy sidewalk. The crowd yammered and milled in a restless, expectant clot at the base of a naked oak. Off to his right, Yeager and the remaining Council members stood motionless in a circle of armed men.

"What are they doing?" Greg asked, his voice as thin as piano wire. Aidan and Lucian had marched them out through the vestibule and past Tori's body. While someone had the decency to cover her with a coat, Greg might have fallen to his knees if Kincaid hadn't clamped a strong hand around his arm and practically carried him down the church steps.

"Nothing good," Kincaid muttered.

The village hall's doors banged open, disgorging four men, who staggered under bulging sacks. They were followed by Jarvis and another man who scuttled out with coils of rope. Some people fell on the sacks of food and began wildly tugging out cans and jars; other hands grabbed the coils from Jarvis's and his partner's shoulders. One man on horseback took charge of hurling rope over a stout, low-hanging oak limb that was still a good fifty feet from the snow. Eager townsfolk crowded in to grab at the free ends. There were so many that those who'd lost out grabbed hold of the waists of the people before them in a human chain. Straightening, Jarvis made large sweeping motions with one arm. An astringent odor spiked Greg's nose, and he thought, *Charcoal briquettes.* Stepping back, Jarvis said something Greg couldn't make out, and then there was another of those enormous jungle bellows as the people manning the ropes and forming those chains heaved.

Backlit by the combined glow of all those lights, Ben Stiemke and his grandfather jerked limply from the snow, dangling from nooses like ghastly, deflated parade floats. Because the old man was so much lighter, he rose much faster, his feet clearing the ground in a matter of seconds. Ben went more slowly, both because he was a heavier boy—

And because Ben was still alive.

Not by much, perhaps. Greg hoped that what he saw was the lizard part of Ben's brain sparking its last. But he didn't think so. As the noose tightened and Ben's air cut out, his one good leg fluttered and kicked; his bloody hands scratched at the rope. They were too far away to see his face, but Greg could imagine it: Ben's mouth agape, his intact eye starting while that blasted socket stared in startled amazement.

Jeering, the mob closed on the boy, swatting at his kicking leg and body with rifle butts and clubs. Then one person darted forward with a torch, and in its light, Greg recognized that gray fury. Screeching, Travers thrust the flame into Ben's gore-soaked middle.

With a sudden *whump,* Ben Stiemke erupted in a sheet of rippling blue as the lighter fluid Jarvis had used to saturate his body ignited.

Sarah screamed, a sound lost in the mob's clamoring cheers and hoots. Ben's body flailed, the one leg bicycling round and round but much more feebly now, trailing a blue streamer that was rapidly yellowing as the lighter fluid was exhausted and new fuel—Ben's clothing— ignited. His grandfather's body, now also ablaze, flared like a candle.

The crowd fell utterly silent. Aidan and Lucian were rapt, their faces dreamy. It was so quiet, so completely still, that Greg heard the spit and crackle as the flames feasted and Ben's flops became jitters and then twitches and then nothing at all.

He would think about this for days; grow queasy at the lingering taste of cooked blood and scorched hair on his tongue. And he would dream about it: these old men and women, and the very few boys, their expressions shifting and changing in this play of shadow and light, reshaped by fire into something Greg no longer recognized as human.

What came to him as well was Jess, in her unending sleep, walking her dreams, and what she'd said the one and only time he saw her: *Leave them, boy. They are blind.*

"Aw, *dude*." Lucian breathed. "This so *rocks*."

54

"Lang said he's playing possum," Jug Ears said. "I only been working here a couple days, and he's only ever been off his rocker. Screaming, talking to thin air, sometimes beating up on himself pretty bad. See around his face there? But I've never seen him like this before."

"Yeah, he does look pretty out of it. My God, he stinks, too. Like an animal, worse than these Chuckies." (*Old coot*. Peter didn't recall his name. The next thing Peter heard was the scrape of a boot over concrete, a pop of grit. But no *bong-bong-bongs* or Simon. No visions of holes in stone or orange water. No Chris either. Was that bad? *Bwahahaha*. Who knew?) "How long he been like this?" Old Coot said.

Jug Ears: "You mean the shakes or the not breathing real good?"

Old Coot: "Both."

"Uh . . ." Mutters as Jug Ears counted under his breath. "Couple hours? He was like this when I come on shift. Lang gave him a whack with his baton. Right there in the side . . . see where the bruise is coming up? Kid didn't even flinch. Ask me . . . I don't know. The way he's breathing, he's either *real* crazy or dying."

Both. Neither. Bwahahaha. Naked, eyes screwed shut, sprawled on the floor of his cell, Peter let go of another gargling, guttural groan and shuddered, his hands fluttering like dying moths. His skin was so caked in filth, huge dried chunks cracked from his flanks. *And it's showtime, folks.* Dragging in another grudging inhale, he began to jitter and flop like a dying fish, spluttering and choking, the foam bubbling to froth over his lips. From the taste, there was some blood, too. The back of his head bounced against concrete and he felt a spray of pain, but it was muted and very distant.

"Oh, shit, *shit*." He heard the tinkling chatter of metal, then a *clack* as Old Coot slotted in a key. "Son of a bitch is having a fit. Come on, before he swallows his tongue."

"I don't know." Jug Ears. "Lang said we shouldn't—"

"Screw Lang. He's not here. The boss is back, too, from that training exercise. Now, *you* want to explain how this kid choked to death on his own damn tongue while we watched it go down with our thumbs up our butts? Get something to stick between his teeth and come on!"

There was a harsh bawl of metal hinges, and then boots on concrete. A hand on his forehead now and another on his jaw. Jug Ears, on his left, shouting: "Okay, I got a ruler, I got a ruler. Come on, open his mouth, open his *mouth*!"

"Hang on," Old Coot grunted, trying to hook his fingers in the soft notches at the corners of Peter's mouth and away from his clashing teeth. Peter obliged, letting his lower jaw sag, throwing in a choking *guh guh guh* for good measure.

"Jesus, he's goddamn dying." Old Coot wrenched Peter's jaws open so far Peter heard the tendons creak. "Damn it to hell! Come on, get that thing in there, get it over his tongue, get it—"

"I got it." A rigid edge of wood sliced Peter's lower lip, and then there was a *tick-tick-tick-tick* as Jug Ears tried butting the ruler between the shelves of Peter's teeth. Jug Ears wormed his fingers over Peter's tongue. "I got it," Jug Ears sang, "I got—"

Peter snapped, hard and fast. There was an audible *crunch,* a burst of blood in his mouth, and then he was grinding his jaws from side to side, his teeth sawing through skin and stringy tendons down to the joints. The bones snapped as Jug Ears screeched and beat at Peter's face with his free fist: *"Get him off, get him off, get him—"*

Spitting out the ruin of what had been two fingers, Peter surged from the floor. His left hand was already driving for the man's throat, his right sweeping up the dropped ruler. Jug Ears got out a pained *gah* as Peter cocked his right elbow and then pistoned fast, driving the ruler into the old man's mouth. Jug Ears gave a tremendous jerk. A huge gush of blood jetted, hot and wet, splashing Peter's face and hand. Through the wood, Peter could feel the harder plate of bone at the back of the man's throat. The guard's eyes bugged; his hands flew to Peter's wrist and tried clawing the ruler free, his nails and jagged splinters of bone from his missing digits frantically scoring Peter's wrist. Rearing up, Peter flipped Jug Ears onto his back, stabbed the ruler down like a pike, and bellowed: "Eat it, eat it, *eat it!*"

There was another bony *crunch*, this one duller, muted by the boil of blood. Jug Ears flailed in a brief but violent spasm as if he'd stuck a wet finger in a live socket, the connections between brain and body suddenly severed as the ruler slammed through to skewer vertebrae and the delicate spinal cord.

All this took less than five seconds. Without pause, Peter rounded on Old Coot, who'd scuttled back only a few feet and was now fetched up against the iron bars of Peter's cage. His knobbed fingers scrabbled for his pistol, but when Peter's shadow swam over his body, the guard screamed: *"N-nuh-nuh-noooo!"* Horror bleached all the color from the guard's face, and Peter had a moment's clarity where he understood what he must look like to this old man: naked, painted with gore, a Medusa's crown of jungle hair, as inexorable as fate. He was something born from a nightmare, or hell.

"D-don't look at m-me with th-those *eyes!*" Old Coot shrieked. "I n-never . . . I never *h-hurt* you!"

"True," Peter said. "But you never helped me either."

* * *

Two minutes later, flipping the globe of Old Coot's left eyeball onto his tongue, he was at the door. He'd strapped the guard's knife to his right calf but taken nothing else. No clothes, no coat, no boots, not even gloves. He didn't need any of that.

But it's cold, Peter. It was that still-sane, dime-sized portion of his mind. *You're outnumbered. Don't you think you might want a rifle and some clothes?*

"Clothes are for the rest of you." Swallowing back eye jelly, he worried the lens between his teeth, then crunched. About the consistency of a slightly stale Tic-Tac, minus the peppermint. From the milky color, Old Coot had been on his way to a major cataract.

He felt the press of the Changed staring but didn't look back. Although, yes, he *had* considered releasing them—*Fly, my pretties, fly, fly!*—and taking the doe-eyed Kate right there on the filthy concrete in the bargain. But while he was nuts, he wasn't crazy. As strong as he was now, he doubted even he would survive a fight with so many Changed.

Instead, cocking his head, he listened with his oh-so-acute hearing for Lang or another guard. All that came was the sough of the wind. The icy air smelled of razors and cut through the sour reek steaming from his flesh.

I want to be clean. Sprinting across the threshold, he plunged face-first into a pillow of snow. His heart gave a startled jump at the shock of it, a baptism first of ice and then fire as his skin shrieked. After so long in the prison house, it was the most wonderful thing he'd ever felt in his life. Gasping, he rolled once, twice, came to rest on his back. Clots of snow clung to his hair; he could feel lumps of ice on his lashes. He let out a laugh that was another of those breathy, ecstatic moans. Snow cupped his back; he was melting into it but felt no cold. For him, cold was only a concept, nothing more than a faraway twinkle of a distant star.

I am new. He felt the winged presence, the one that had been

growing for days now, pulse and swell. Its low muttering surged. *Yes.*
He pounded his chest with a fist. *Yes, yes!* He was butt-naked and
maybe out of his mind, but this was *his* time, it was his. *No one's ever
seen anything like me before. I'm a fucking warrior, I'm—*

A very distant, very dull thud. And another. His ears tingled as
his brain translated: boots, on snow, coming this way. *Lang. Or Finn.*
Either would do. Rising, he bulleted down the wooded path toward a
bend where, if he remembered right, the hemlocks were thick—the
perfect cover because no one remembered to look up. His feet slapped
snow, a dull *puh-puh-puh-puh.* His soles should be shredded, cut by ice,
but he felt no pain at all, no fingers of cold kneading his flesh. Wind
tugged his blond hair. His heart thumped, strong and steady, fueled
by the manic exhilaration of the winged thing and freedom.

Ahead, hemlocks pulled together out of the gloom. Then he spied
a knotty red pine to the right. This was better still because its lowest
limbs were even higher, a good six feet off the ground and big around
as his thigh. Backing up, he dug in with his toes, and took off in a
diving run. He didn't even think about whether he might slip. As a
boy, he'd climbed higher, taken greater risks. The thought did flash
through his mind that, really, he wasn't a featherweight kid clambering up to his tree house to read or dream or sneak his first smoke;
that this was an awful risk; and where was he finding the strength,
the stamina?

Then he stopped thinking, and leapt. His palms slapped wood, his
fingers hooked, and then he was heaving, boosting himself from the
snow, swinging up like a gymnast. Hitching a leg up and around, he
seated himself, got a foot under and then the other, and stood. To his
right, another branch jutted at a thirty-degree angle, an easy straddle.
The path was directly between the V of his legs.

Reaching into his long blond hair, he fished out a slender spike
of bone. The bone, which he'd hidden between his butt cheeks, had

come from that left foot. Over the last week, he'd laboriously ground the bone to a needle: perfect for popping an eye or jamming through a throat. Of course, if all else failed, he still had the knife. His hands. His teeth. But he really wanted to try out the bone.

His ears prickled with the sound of a man's breaths, the squeal of snow. *Wait for it, wait* . . . In the well of his mind, the winged thing waited, too: taut, breathless. Then Lang was there, passing immediately below: a hunched, plodding old man in olive-drab.

Now. Peter dropped. There was a millisecond's free fall, the rush of air past his ears. At the last instant, Lang must've sensed something, because Peter saw a startled, silver oval flicker up and then the black holes of Lang's eyes. *Eyes, eyes in the dark, eyes in stone.* Peter's feet hammered Lang's forehead, an impact that jarred Peter's heels and shivered into his shins. A wild *ah* leapt from Lang's mouth. Peter hit the snow, rolled, set his feet, then swarmed over Lang, still turtled on his back, who was gagging and choking against blood. Lang saw him coming, tried getting his hands up, but Peter batted them away and dropped on Lang's chest. As Lang began to buck, Peter slammed Lang with a stunning blow. There was a crackle as Lang's nose caved, and more blood, a river of it.

"Ha-how?" Lang gargled. The old man was far down in the snow, with no leverage at all. He tried a weak punch that Peter blocked with his forearm. "How d-did you . . ."

"Does it matter?" Planting his knees in the knobs of the man's shoulders, Peter ground down until Lang moaned. Jamming the bone needle between the second and ring fingers of his right hand, Peter cupped his left over Lang's throat and squeezed—not a crushing grip but enough that Lang's face suddenly darkened. Peter held the quivering spike of bone just above Lang's left eye, so close that Lang's eyes crossed. "You're a traitor and I'm going to kill you. But first I'm going to blind you. You'll hear it, that little *pop*." Leering, Peter dragged his tongue over his lower lip, cleaning it of Lang's blood. "Then I'll *eat* it. I'll rip out your tongue so you can't scream. I'll take you apart a piece at a time."

"Peter." Lang's voice was nasal, stuffy, and the word came out, *Peeyuhh*. He was breathing fast, his chest heaving against Peter's thighs. "It wasn't . . . it wasn't just me. It was Weller, too, it was— *uhh!*" Lang's voice choked off as Peter squeezed.

"I don't *care*." Teeth bared, Peter rode Lang's bucking hips. Lang's face went from beet-red to purple; his bluing tongue bulged through pink foam. "All I want is for you to die, Lang. Die and know that I beat you, I beat you, I got you, I—"

Peter felt the hit, registered the impact as a solid body blow that slammed him left and off Lang. Caroming to the snow, he fell heavily on his left wrist. A rocket of pain shot into his elbow. The wrist buckled and then he was wallowing, thrashing, his face half buried in snow. Spitting, he rolled, already aware that the needle was gone. *Still have the knife.* Righting, he planted and then rose on the balls of his feet, calves bunched, ready to spring . . . and felt his heart clutch with fury.

Squared in his fighting stance, Davey—a Changed boy Peter hadn't seen in more than two weeks—only waited. He wore camo-whites. His leather control collar was a black cut across his throat, and there was something terribly wrong with his eyes. At first, Peter thought that Davey had been blinded, the eyeballs scooped out, leaving only scarlet sockets. Then he realized that the whites of Davey's eyes were a deep, dark bloodred.

Jug Ears: *What happens to them? Their eyes?*

"No." The word foamed in a snarl from Peter's lips. "No, he's *mine*. Lang's—" Uncoiling, Peter sprang. At the same instant, Davey leapt, matching Peter move for move in an eerie, silent pas de deux. They crashed together in midair, then tumbled to the snow in a thrashing tangle. Peter's fists bunched in the boy's camo-whites as Davey's hands slipped and slid over Peter's skin. Planting both feet in the boy's chest, Peter bucked him up and over in a somersault. Floundering in the deep snow, Peter got over onto his left side just in time to see Davey somehow tuck, hit, tumble—and set his feet with the nimbleness of an acrobat. In a split second, the boy was steaming over the snow. Turning, Peter swam to his hands and knees, but not fast enough to avoid Davey, who vaulted onto his back. A second later, Peter's right shoulder exploded with pain.

"*Aahh!*" Now *this* hurt. Rearing, Peter flailed, spinning a mad circle around and around. Clinging like a wolf latched onto prey, Davey readjusted his jaws and sawed his teeth deeper into muscle. Peter felt the spurt of blood down his back. Reaching around, he clawed wildly for the boy's face, then thought, *I'm heavier.* Throwing himself straight back, Peter dropped to the snow. He felt the boy's grip loosen; that maddening grind of teeth and jaws suddenly ceased. Bellowing with both pain and rage, Peter kicked up, twisted, got a fist in Davey's hair, cocked the other for a punch—

An orange-red blaze of heat detonated in his head, an immense thunderclap like a pillowing wave of napalm. Peter wailed in agony as another shock wave blasted him back. Still screaming, he toppled. The pain was molten and all-consuming. Through the clamor, he just made out a voice he knew too well: "All right, boy-o. Let's everybody cool down."

As suddenly as the pain swept through, it evaporated, as if someone had flicked a hidden switch. Wallowing in snow, Peter turned a look to where Finn stood, massive and compact, a monolith in a uniform as black as a crow's wing. A long, curved parang hung in a scabbard from his left hip. At his right rested his pearl-handled Colt. Flanking him were two Changed girls, also in camo-whites, and their eyes were like Davey's: bloodred pools.

"Ease down, boy-o," Finn said.

"No, *no!*" Peter rolled to all fours, like a seething animal. "Let me *finish!*"

"And you will, but not today or with Davey. Unless you *want* a repeat?"

It was a question that required no response. Peter spat a bullet of blood. "How did you do that?"

"Oh, it's complicated. Come on, on your feet. We're all friends here."

"I'm not your *friend.*" Blood from his torn shoulder spilled to the small of his back and leaked along his right arm to drip from the knob of his elbow and melt into the snow. The red on white was, eerily, like the girls' eyes set against the white ovals of their faces, and Davey's— and, probably, his own. "I'm not *his.* I'm not *theirs.*"

"But you *are* mine." Finn's fissured face didn't crack a grin. "I'm your world, Peter. Look at yourself. Naked as a jay but not cold, are you? Don't need to sleep?"

"No. But I dream." To his left he saw Lang, coughing, struggle to a sit. Already on his feet, Davey slid to Finn's right. Peter's blood was smeared over Davey's mouth in a drippy clown's grin. "With my eyes wide open," Peter said. "Daymares."

"Ah, yes, the flashbacks. Those'll wear off. They're a . . . glitch."

"You drugged me from the beginning, didn't you? When I was in the infirmary and after I broke down and ate . . ." He clamped off the rest. "Will it wear off?"

"Possibly, but I sincerely hope not. The withdrawal's a bitch. But you were too good a specimen to pass up. Your brain is already different. We know because you're still alive." Finn regarded him with the kind of curiosity reserved for a new and fascinating lab specimen. "Do you really *want* this to wear off, Peter? To end?"

"I—I," he began, and stopped. Weren't those two different questions? Being with Finn, yeah, he wanted out. Yet riding that electric red swoon was like nothing he'd ever felt. And really, had that been so bad? *No. I want that feeling back. I'm new, different, better than I was, but if I can hang on to part of who I was, maybe I can use this somehow.* As for the winged thing muttering its dark language . . . he could live with that.

Which perhaps proved that he really was insane and never coming back, no matter what. Maybe Simon had been right: *You were lost the moment you decided the Zone was a good idea.*

"I don't know," he said.

"Not surprised. Great high, isn't it? Betcha that shoulder isn't too happy, but you'll muscle through. And all that energy? *Maaania?*" Finn waggled his thick eyebrows, which were as white as his square-cut hair. "You're not indestructible, but you *are* different. Tell me: say you killed Lang, what was supposed to happen next? Where could you run?"

Peter realized that he hadn't thought that far ahead. Strange, too, how that electric red swoon was guttering. Already, he could feel his body yammering after it, craving the rush.

There is no going back to Rule, or even Chris. All I can do is press my face against the window. I'm an exile, an Azazel: the red heifer that bears all sins, sent to wander the desert. Considering his eyes, that was apt.

"You've come too far to turn back," Finn said, as if Peter had spoken aloud. "And do you know why? Because you chose to live. To *survive,* whatever the cost."

"Chose?" There was no choice involved. Finn had broken him. "You fed me a drug, locked me in a cage, made me fight, wouldn't give me water or f-food . . ." His tongue stumbled.

"You chose to fight, to eat. You broke yourself, Peter, because of the compromises you're willing to make and the rules you're willing to break to stay alive. And don't you see? You *are* the Changed."

"No." There had to be a way of coming out the other end of this. "What do you want? If I was an experiment, if *they* are . . ." He jerked his head at the red-eyed horrors. "What now?"

"Depends. What would you like?"

Revenge. Because what the hell? He was already lost. "I want what's coming to me." He pointed a dripping finger at Lang. "You've got me, but I want *him.*"

"In your dreams." Snuffling, Lang spat out a jellied clot.

"How about a trade?" Finn said. "I give you something, you give me something."

"What?" Startled, Lang looked up, eyes wide above a crimson bib. "Boss?"

"A trade?" Peter cawed a harsh laugh. "What's left that I could have or give?"

"A few things," Finn said. "Depends on how badly you want Lang, I guess."

"What?" Hand drifting for his pistol, Lang backed up a step. "This wasn't the *deal.*"

"Well"—Finn's black eyes flicked toward Davey—"deals meant to be broken and all."

"I don't *think* so," Lang began, as Davey stiffened like a dog catching a new scent. In the blink of an eye, both girls swiveled in an eerie, silent synchrony toward Lang.

"How are you doing that?" Peter asked, sharply—just as he realized something else. At the moment the Changed reacted to Finn, that electric red rush also thrummed through his brain, but it was much more muted now, only a tingle. His thoughts were still clear. *It's like I'm picking up only the overflow.*

"Oh, trial and error." Finn's mouth stretched in a death-head's grin. "I've been at this awhile, for decades, and well before the world did me the immense favor of giving us the Chuckies."

As if suddenly released from whatever held them in check, the girls charged. They went so fast that Lang never cleared his weapon. In a flash, the first girl head-butted the old man to the snow as the other whipped her knife to his throat.

How is he doing this? Peter watched as one of the girls confiscated Lang's pistol. "Is this . . . telepathy?"

"Not entirely," Finn said. "At least, not the way books and movies would have you believe."

"*B-B-Boss!*" Lang brayed, eyes round as moons as he craned over the girl's blade. "I've been loyal! We had a *deal.*"

"I—" Finn held up a finger as the walkie-talkie, always clipped to his hip, chirped. "Hold that thought, would you, Lang? Little busy here."

"But boss!"

"Shh." Finn shushed the other man as if chiding a two-year-old: *Now, Johnny, no candy before supper.* "Don't piss me off, Lang."

The code was Morse with something else Peter didn't understand. He caught a *t* and *w*, maybe an *r*. He watched Finn acknowledge: *break-break.*

"And where were we? Oh yes, telepathy. Well, it's nothing supernatural, boy-o. You've got the ability. We all do. Think of ecstatic experiences, how people speak in tongues or crave to let *Jeeesus*"— Finn sang it like a tent preacher—"into their hearts. People *love* that expansive, bigger-than-me feeling. It's why people have been mixing potions and using psychedelics for centuries since Og wondered about the stars. My particular favorites are those found in the writings of the Hindus: Vedas devoted to decoctions and hallucinogenic elixirs derived from a very particular, very special family of mushroom that not only allowed for communication with the divine but conferred immortality and brought the dead back to life. But read any religious text and you'll find that all the greats—Shiva, Vishnu, Moses, Ezekiel, *Jeeesus*—get high, see visions, come back from the underworld or the Land of the Dead . . . and they *all* hear that still, small voice."

Chris. Peter remembered how his friend suddenly appeared . . . and that clear, calm voice. *So what did I hear? Who?* A horrible new thought: *God, what if that was Finn?* "But hearing . . . well, *God* . . . that's not *communication*."

"Ah, boy-o, but it's a beginning." Finn tapped a finger to his temple. "All this suggests multiple modalities through which the brain can be rewired to receive and issue commands. We *know* that not only is the brain hardwired to seek the mystical, we can recreate the experience. Goose that temporal lobe with an electrode in precisely the right spot, spark it just so—and you, too, can have an out-of-body experience. The potential's there, except we've let it go fallow, using speech instead. Yet *now*, we have the Changed, who do not speak but still act together and clearly communicate with one another." Finn favored Davey with the look of a proud dad whose kid had just won the hundred in ten seconds flat. "What makes you believe that the Changed *can't* access senses and abilities you've let atrophy, and that *we*—well, *I*—can't alter the chemical mix to allow for new possibilities? You're not the only one whose brain is different, boy-o."

Or who's been fed a drug. And what did Finn mean by *not the only one*? Was Finn referring only to the Changed? Or was Finn talking about himself?

My God, is Finn different? Has he been like the Changed in this way for years now and only waiting to find people like him?

Or had Finn given himself the same drug he'd used on Peter and Davey and these girls? History was littered with examples of doctors and scientists experimenting on themselves first.

"You can't have figured all this out just now," Peter said.

"Of course not. I told you, Peter." Finn arranged his fingers in a professorial steeple. "I experiment. I have *always* experimented. And I infer, I deduce. Think of how much more *efficient* an army might be if they moved to a single purpose. If *commands* did not rely on only one sensory modality or communications channel. There are no miracles, boy-o, only things we can't explain and abilities we don't know how to exploit, switches we can't throw . . . until we can and do."

The idea—the *image* of Finn marshaling an army of Changed—stilled his blood. *And he said decades.* Finn was in Vietnam; maybe he was experimenting back then, too, the way the military did with LSD and sarin and other drugs. So if Finn had been at this awhile, he just might succeed. The Changed were his happy accident, a stroke of very good luck and serendipity. A Eureka moment.

I must be the same thing. I didn't die or Change, and I should have. All the Spared—Chris, Alex, Sarah, Greg, me—we're specimens.

"What do you want?" It finally hit him that he was completely naked, in the snow, having a conversation with a lunatic. The ache in his shoulder had dulled to a grumble, and the pain in his head was only a memory. He hugged his arms to his chest, more from habit than because he was cold. Could you fake your way to being human again? "You've taken everything else. You won't even let me die."

"*That's* not true. You wouldn't let yourself die. Oh, wait." Finn did a mock Homer Simpson slap. "*Doh.* You mean, not letting you hang yourself? You weren't in your right mind, but if you're really hot to finish the job, you've got a knife. Go ahead, slit your throat. Stab yourself in the heart. Dig out your eyes for all I care."

Choices that were no choices: Finn excelled at this. "What do you want?" he repeated.

And so Finn told him.

What bothered Peter most was he could muster only a small flower of outrage. Yet as he listened, this also answered a very important question. *Finn had to ask. He can't read my mind, but only influence it.* Peter recalled the explosion in his head, and the ecstasy of the red swoon. *He can give pain and pleasure.* Which was much less than Finn managed with Davey and the other Changed. So what did that mean?

"No," he said when Finn was done.

"Then you guarantee extermination," Finn said. "You know they return to the familiar, and the clock is ticking, boy-o. Less than two months to go, right?"

How does he know that? If Finn couldn't read Peter's mind, then the old man must've heard rumors, or maybe had spies in Rule all along. Instead of answering the question, he said, "Why would I agree?"

"Because it's a question of the lesser evil. It's a way out."

"Way out?" Now he did laugh. "How?"

"You need me to spell this out? You're a smart college boy. Michigan Tech, right? Oh, but you didn't graduate, that's right. A semester shy, as I recall, because of that little"—Finn wiggled his fingers—"*accident.* But you *studied* this phenomenon, did field research on the wolves of Isle Royale?"

"Yes." God, Finn *did* know all about him. "Genetic rescue in captive populations."

"So, think of what I offer, Peter: protection, enough diversity to keep the population humming along, food." He did Peter the favor of not smiling. "Think of me as providing genetic rescue."

"But you're not using *all* the Changed the way you have Davey and these girls. What about the ones in the prison house? I recognize a few. What are you going to do, Finn?"

"I might not have to *do* much at all. You know history, Peter. Rome wasn't built in a day, but it did fall in three. Rule's like that. With the mine gone, no supplies, and everyone so *old*, the village will eat itself alive, like a cancer, inside and out. Remember, Chuckies return to the familiar. So just think what's heading their way as we speak."

The idea of even a few Changed actually making it back to the village sent a slow shudder up his spine. He knew Finn *had* kids from Rule; he'd recognized the doe-eyed Kate Landry and burly Lee Travers. *And if Finn's gathering Changed like Kate and Lee and the rest are his new army . . .* It would be like the last emperor of Rome watching the Visigoths boil through the city's Salarian Gate to storm the Seven Hills.

"I give it"—Finn tipped his wrist to check a phantom watch—"oh, another day or two. Or the prodigals might already be there, Peter. So what do you *imagine* will happen?"

It was on the tip of his tongue to say that the Council couldn't fall and Chris would find a way. *But Chris came in a vision. Forget the drug. Something's happened to him and in Rule; I know it. Finn is too confident.* The hurt—the idea that Chris really might be dead—was a barb of grief in his heart. Yet he grabbed hold, pulled it closer, deeper, wanting the pain, wishing for the hurt. *If I know what grief is, there's a chance I might come out the other side.*

"Why do you hate Rule so much?" he asked. "Who *are* you, Finn?"

"I am what I am." Finn spread his hands. "And mine is the way, boy-o."

No, but you are the only way left. He closed his eyes not so much against Finn but the sudden icy tide that passed for his blood. In his brain, he could feel the winged thing's claws hook a little more firmly. He almost wished for the bells again. Or Simon. Then he would be only insane and have an excuse.

"All right." He opened his eyes. "But I want to be there. I need your word."

"Scout's honor. Now, whaddaya say we get you inside before you lose a foot?" Finn tipped him a wink. "Or something more *vital* that a healthy young buck like you would be sorry to see go? Oh, but wait." Finn did his mock head-slap. "We forgot Lang. You still want him?"

"Yes." Peter felt the winged thing shift. "You know what they say about revenge served cold."

"No!" Lang reached for Finn like a bawling baby. "Boss, no, I'm your man!"

"Plenty more old farts where you came from, too." There was a scrape of keen steel on leather as Finn unsheathed his parang. "Who's hungry?"

PART FOUR:
TRIALS BY FIRE, AND ICE

55

"Think you can *leave* me?" His father's voice was a roar that carried from the downstairs kitchen like a megaphone blast. There was a very loud *bang* of metal on wood, the chatter of dishes, and then a muffled shriek from Deidre, his father's girlfriend of the moment. "Think I don't got *eyes*?" his father raged.

I don't hear this. Shivering under the dark dome of his blanket, Chris screwed his eyes tight, tight! He clapped his hands over his ears. *This is just a bad dream—*

But then, somehow, he was huddled on the stairs. Below, his father loomed. Bright red spatters of blood painted his father's face and wifebeater. The hammer was clotted with a gory jam of blond hair and brain and blood.

"D-d-don't," Dee quavered—except now Chris saw that it wasn't Deidre at all but Lena. Lena's face was a pulpy, misshapen horror. The left half of her head was staved. A glistening slug of pink brain slicked her neck. *"P-please."* Lena raised her hands but not to Chris's father.

To him. Because, now, Chris wasn't eight. He wasn't in bed either, or crouched on a staircase, hugging his knees, wishing he were anywhere else. Instead, he stood in a swirl of icy wind and stinging snow, and his was the hand with the hammer now. He hefted it, felt its weight, the handle slick with Lena's blood. Gore dribbled over his face, bathed his neck. He sucked wet, warm copper from his lips, and it was the best thing he'd ever tasted, and he wanted more.

"P-please, Chris," Lena said. "H-help me."

"I can't help you." His voice was older, rougher. He liked that, too. "No one can."

"B-but . . ." Lena's eyes dripped blood instead of tears. "I d-don't want to *die*."

"You should've thought of that before you Changed. Someone has to die."

"Yes, someone must." It was another voice, a person Chris also knew well. Jess was suddenly there, silver hair lashed by wind into a Gorgon's curls, the snow spinning itself into a long white gown. "Someone will," Jess said.

"But not me!" Lena cried. "Why does it have to be—"

"You're already lost, girl." Jess's voice was wind. "But you are not, Chris. Leave this place. This is a fight you will not win here. You don't belong in the Land of the Dead."

"Hell you say," said his father, who was now grinning down at another body. This one was jittering and twitching in an enormous lake of steaming gore. Chris looked and saw that it was Peter, splayed on his back, his head as broken and misshapen as a Halloween pumpkin run over by a car. "That's my boy you're talking about," his father said to Jess, "and he belongs to me, *with* me, *my* blood."

"There's a time you must kill, Chris, but also a time to heal." Jess's eyes were black mirrors in which he saw himself doubled: Chris on the right, Chris on the left, like the twin angels of his nature—his father and Jess—but he couldn't tell which was good. Maybe neither was, entirely. "Leave the thing with a father's face," Jess said. "Go back. It's not yet your time."

"The hell it's not," he said, and then Chris was swinging—both Chrises swung, their hammers whickering—but when they connected, they collapsed into one Chris, one hammer, one desire. There was a dull *chock*, and a ripping sound as Lena's scalp tore. The hammer juddered in his hand, the metal cratering bone before passing to the softer pink cheese of her brain. Lena crumpled. When the hammer pulled free, he looked up to find that Jess had disappeared.

"That's my boy." Scraping a gob of brains from his cheek, his father stuck his fingers in his mouth. "Yum—"

And then the scene shifted in a quick jolt, as if a hand jammed itself in his back and gave him a huge push, catapulting Chris from this horror to somewhere entirely different—and Chris had one second to think, *A nightmare, it's a nightmare, this isn't real, it's not—*

Chris's chest suddenly erupted in a spray of raw agony. An electric blaze streaked through his body, all the connections sizzling to life. Now he registered that the air was warm—*inside, somewhere, not on the snow*—and was aware of the slosh and gurgle of water, the creak of a spring, the rustle of cloth. The insect-like *tick-tick-tick-tick-tick* of a clock. *Bed, bedroom, where?* He lay on his back, quivering, every nerve singing. There was a strange pressure on his chest—*hand, a man*—and the side of a thumb on his forehead tracing something, drawing down and across, sketching some symbol like a pen over blank paper. What followed was a swirl of sounds, whispers and the guttural murmurs of a dark language, like trees weighed down by murders of crows all muttering in tongues: *Durch das Blut und das Wasser seiner Seite . . .*

Where was he? He remembered cold and snow, the trap tearing through the trees—*Lena, run, run*—and then an oily blight moving through his body, smothering his mind. *Water. Something in the water . . .* There was that splashing sound again, close by, and now something wet dragging over his chest. An enormous gust of fear blasted through him. *God, no, poison, killing me, no, no!*

"No!" Chris heard himself suck in a sudden, ragged shriek. *"No!"* His eyes snapped open at the same instant that the hands on his side jumped away like startled birds. Someone cried out as he bolted upright, coming alive to a room full of shadows and too little light, and still screaming, "No! Don't touch me, don't touch me, get away from—"

"Christopher!" An old man's face swam from the gloom. "Christopher, stop! It's all—"

Get out, got to get out! Chris reacted on instinct and raw panic. Lashing out, he felt his left hand hook cloth. There was a startled squawk, and then Chris was yanking the old man close, reeling him in, his arm slipping around the man's neck, his eyes skipping to a wink of metal at the man's left hip. Chris's hand darted; in a flash, the gun was in his fist, and he was jamming the muzzle to the old man's temple: "Get away from me, get away from me, *get away!*"

"No, Chris, no, no!" A chorus of voices, boys and girls. Rasps of metal against leather, the sounds of handguns being drawn, the unmistakable clack of a rifle bolt. The voices were still jabbering, overlapping, everyone talking at the same time: "Chris, don't!" "Chris, it's all right!" "You're safe, Chris, you're safe!" One boy, louder than the rest, booming from behind the rifle: "Put the gun down, put it down, drop it, drop it!"

"*No*, Jayden!" It was the old man, his voice surprisingly strong. "Everyone, stay calm! Give him a moment to—"

"But I've got the shot," Jayden sang, "I've got the shot!"

"Jayden, no!" The girl's voice was familiar, and then Chris had it: *Hannah.* "Chris," Hannah said. "Please, put the gun down!"

"All of you just stay back!" Chris cried, except the words now came in a harsh, grinding choke. A lone candle gave off a thin, uncertain light, but it was enough for him to see that he stood in a tangle of linen and down comforter, half on, half off a bed—and that he was completely naked.

"Where am I?" *It wasn't a dream. Hurt, I was hurt, bad. I was bleeding, I felt . . .* He'd felt that black creep through his chest, squeeze his heart. *I felt myself die, I was dying, I was . . .* No, he couldn't think about that. Get out, he had to get out! He still had the old man by the neck, but his eyes jumped from face to face—Jayden, Hannah, two other boys—and then the long rectangle of this room, with its slanted ceiling and trio of windows. *Attic or second-story. Bedroom.* A closed door, the way out, was to his left, but the others were blocking his way.

There came a series of muffled barks, and then someone, at the door: "Are you all right? Is he okay? What's happening?"

"No, no, wait—" Hannah made a grab, but a little girl suddenly squirted through.

"Chris?" The girl's face was pinched with anxiety. Her blue eyes widened, and he understood what he must look like: naked, in a frenzy, a gun in one hand and an old man in a chokehold. By her side, a dog, smaller than a shepherd and with sable markings, watched him through a black mask. "Chris, it's all right," the little girl said. "Remember me?"

"Y-yes." Chris gulped against a sudden wave of vertigo. *No, can't black out again.* He fought to clear his head. "You're . . . you're Ellie."

"Right, and this is Mina, my dog." Relief flooded Ellie's face. "We kept you warm, remember? We rescued you. You're safe now."

"*Safe?*" He heard the whip of his fear. His arm tightened around the old man's neck. "I'm not safe. Leave me alone, all of you. Just stay away!"

"Christopher." The old man wasn't fighting but instead stroking the arm Chris had locked around his neck the way you might soothe a frightened animal. "Christopher, I know this is confusing. You're scared. Put down the gun before you hurt someone."

"No." But Chris felt the scrape of panic falter. He was starting to lose it, his weird strength dribbling away. "Who are you people? Where am I?"

"You're safe," Hannah said from a swirl of shadow—or that may have been his vision beginning to dim. "Chris," she said, "let us help you."

"Help?" His laugh was weak and strangled. "You tried to kill me."

I have to get out of here. He took a swaying half step. His legs were sud-denly wooden. The gun was growing unbelievably heavy, as weighty as a boulder, and he understood that in two or three seconds, he would faint. "Please," he groaned. "Let me go. I don't want to hurt anybody, I don't—"

With no warning at all, his strength fled as if he'd been unplugged. His knees buckled. From somewhere distant, Chris heard the thud as the gun hit the floor. There was nothing in his hands now, not even the old man.

"You tried to kill me, y-you t-tried . . . oh God . . ." His eyes rolled; there was no more light and nothing to see, and he was hurtling fast in a black swoon.

"Quick, catch him!" someone said. He thought it might be Ellie. "Don't let him fall—"

"Chris?" A voice from the dark. "Chris, answer me. Are you okay?"

"I . . . I don't kn-know." His tongue was bloated, his mouth numb. His chest was heavy, a huge weight pressing him down, down, down into the black.

I'm on the snow again. I'm under the trap.

"N-no." When he tried to turn his head toward the voice, his neck locked tight. "Don't k-kill me again. P-please. I don't w-want to d-die."

"Shh. Don't be afraid. I'm here now, Chris. I won't leave you." A hand, strong and sure, cupped his cheek. "Open your eyes. It's time to come back. It's time to see."

"I c-can't." He was shivering. "I d-d-don't want to *see.*"

"You have to. No more hiding in the shadows." The voice was calm but remorseless. "You're not eight anymore. Come on. Come back now."

"N-n-nuh . . ." But his lids were lifting, the darkness peeling away, a film seeming to dissolve from his eyes. At first, there was nothing but a glaring bright fog, like strong light bleeding through heavy mist. Then he saw the fog curl and eddy as Peter's face pulled together, the pieces knitting from the neck up: chin and mouth, nose and forehead.

But no eyes. Only blanks, smooth skin over bone.

"Where are y-your eyes?" A fist of horror squeezed his heart. "P-Peter, wh-*where* . . ."

"Oh, silly me." And then the skin over Peter's sockets peeled apart. "There. Better?"

Chris felt the scream boil up his throat and try to crash from his mouth. Peter's eyes were caves, not deep black mirrors like Jess's, but red and vast and filling fast. They brimmed in bloody rills that oozed down his cheeks and leaked over his lips. When Peter smiled, his lips skinned to reveal a bristle of too many teeth that were wet and orange.

"Peekaboo," Peter said. Thick scarlet teardrops trembled on his upper lip to drip directly onto Chris's face and splash into his own staring eyes. There was a *sssss* sound, the hiss of a snake, the boil of acid, and then the pain, and Chris was blind and he was screaming—

"Huh!" Chris heard the cry bolt from his mouth.

"Christopher?" Not Peter or Lena or his father, but an old man. A dry, cool palm found his forehead. "Christopher, are you back with us?"

Is this another dream? He lay absolutely still for a long moment. *A new nightmare?* He was under a thick down comforter and still mostly naked, although someone had slipped on a pair of underpants. There was also something unfamiliar around his neck. Cord?

"Christopher?"

"Y-yes," he croaked. He dragged his lids up, wincing against bright spokes of yellow-white light jabbing through two windows directly opposite the bed. He would've raised a hand to shield his eyes, but he couldn't move his arms. Sheets were noosed around his wrists, and his ankles were tethered to the bedposts.

"There you are. Welcome back." Reaching for a stoneware jug on a nightstand, the old man splashed water into a clear glass. "Thirsty?"

He was about to ask why he was tied down but then considered that if a kid had grabbed *his* gun, he'd have done the same thing. "Is it drugged?" he rasped.

"No. Here." Slipping an arm under Chris's shoulders, the old man propped him as he drank. The water was clean and odorless and cool as a balm. He felt the chilly slide of its course from his tortured throat down the middle of his chest and then the cold explosion in his empty stomach. When he'd drained the glass, the old man lowered him, then settled back into his own chair. "That should stay put. We fed you a bit of broth yesterday, so . . ."

"Yesterday?" When he ran his tongue over his still-dry lips, he tasted old blood from where the skin had cracked. "How long have I been here?"

"In *this* room?" The old man laced his fingers over his stomach. His hair, which floated around his shoulders, was as snowy white as his beard, although his upper lip was bare. But the resemblance was clear, especially the eyes, which were as bright and black and keen as an old prophet's. "Six days ago. I arrived last night just before sunset. I was here when you surfaced the first time."

He caught the emphasis. "What do you mean, in *this* room? Where was I before?"

"What do you remember?"

"Snow," he said, hoarsely. He didn't want to think about the dreams. "The trees. Spikes and green glass, and the sound of the limbs breaking, like bombs."

"That was the tiger-trap. What else?"

"Weight on my back, and I remember the cold, and it hurt . . . my chest, whenever I tried to move. I couldn't breathe, like kn-knives . . ." He was starting to shiver. "I c-couldn't . . ."

"Easy." The old man laid a calming hand on Chris's forearm. "That's in the past."

"But how far in the past?"

"Two weeks."

"I've been out for two *weeks?*" His heart skipped. "What month is it?"

"It's the end of the first week of March. Take it easy, Chris. You're safe now."

"That's what you keep saying. Was I in a coma? What happened to me?"

"You got caught in the tiger-trap. Hannah said you couldn't breathe, were in intense pain, had lost a tremendous amount of blood. Every time they tried to move you or the trap—"

"It hurt." His heaving chest was suddenly prickly with sweat. "I . . . I couldn't . . ."

"Take it easy." The old man patted his arm. "Slow down."

"I thought I was dying," he whispered. "When Hannah gave me that water . . . I thought it was poison and she was trying to kill me. I guess . . ." *It was all a bad dream, like the one about my dad and me and Lena and then Peter.* He didn't know whether to laugh or break into tears. "I dreamt that I died. I thought I was dead."

"That's because, for all intents and purposes," the old man said, "you were."

56

"What?" When he tried to start up from the bed, knots dug into his wrists and ankles. "What are you talking about? What are you *saying?*"

"Easy, Christopher," the old man said. "Calm down."

"Calm *down?*" He thought he was screaming, but he could only muster a tortured squawk. He strained against the sheets, his neck so stiff he heard the creak of bone. "You're telling me I was *dead?* That Hannah *really* poisoned me?"

"Yes. She wished to ease your suffering, to help you let go. She stayed with you until you slipped away. It didn't take long. You were quite weak already. If Ellie hadn't found you when she did and sent Eli for help, you might've been stone-dead long before Hannah and Jayden got to you."

"Ellie and her dog k-kept me alive. Th-they . . ." His throat suddenly clogged as he collapsed back onto the bed. "They kept me w-warm." Chris's eyes burned, and when he closed them, he felt a tear leak onto a temple. *Why am I crying?* Embarrassed, he rolled his face away.

"Yes, our little fisherwoman's quite resourceful," the old man said, and then Chris felt the slight pressure of a thumb wiping away the wet on his face. "It is not weakness to become emotional after a shock. You're clearly a very strong boy, Christopher."

"But how can I still be alive?" Chris whispered. He opened his eyes. "You said I was dead. I *f-felt* myself die."

"I know what I said. You were given poison that should've killed you but didn't. You should be dead, but you're not." The old man laid a gentle hand on Chris's cheek, a touch for which Chris was almost absurdly grateful. "I can't explain it."

"Maybe it wasn't as bad as Hannah thought." He could feel the tears dribbling into his hair. "She shouldn't have done that. I'm not a horse with a broken leg."

"Fair enough, but would you have drunk poison willingly? Would you have had faith in a girl you'd never met, that she was right: you were going to die and this was more merciful?"

"Well, she was *wrong*, wasn't she?"

"She may have been . . . mistaken about the extent of your injuries. Hannah's quite skillful. She'll be a fine healer someday. But no, she's not a doctor."

"Are you?"

"No. But I've been a healer for a very long time, and I know that tiger-trap."

"How did they . . ." He heard himself hyperventilating but couldn't stop it. "They couldn't get the trap off. It hurt too much. I heard them argue. Hannah was worried I would bleed even more."

"That's right." The old man's tone was dry, factual. "After you slipped away, they turned you over and pulled you off. I believe they cut a spike or two to do it."

Cut me off. The image of them flipping the door and his limp body, tacked on iron spikes like a frog pinned to a dissecting pad, stroked the small hairs along his neck. They would've bundled him up, too, before throwing his wrapped corpse onto a horse. *Or had the horse drag me if it got spooked.* He supposed he was lucky they hadn't decided to bury him under rocks.

"Nathan was hit with a mace," he said. "That big log? I heard his neck break. Did he come back from the dead, too?"

"No. His body's still in the death house."

Still. He could feel the scream trying to squeeze past his teeth. *That's where I was. They thought I was dead. They put me with Nathan. Then how—*

"We'll bury him come spring, if you like. We don't cremate remains, although we did butcher his horse for our dogs. We also have Nathan's belongings—clothing, rifle, a radio? I suppose they're yours now." The old man paused. "I know you don't agree, Christopher, but I've had ample time to examine you. From the extent of your injuries and visible wounds—well, what's left of them—Hannah did the right thing."

"Left of them?" Every time this old man opened his mouth, Chris felt his mind scrambling to keep up. "What do you mean, what's left of them?"

In reply, the old man reached and peeled the sheet from Chris's chest down to his waist. "You have half a dozen wounds, three of which are quite serious. This one"—the old man laid a dry palm over Chris's right side, just below his ribs—"was the worst: a through-and-through that collapsed your lung. Your difficulty breathing? Hannah said you had tracheal deviation." He touched a finger to his own knobby Adam's apple. "Your windpipe had shifted to one side. That happens when air collects inside your rib cage instead of the lung. And do you remember the pain in your belly? That was probably from blood pooling in your abdomen. But look now."

Chris craned to peer down at his stomach. A pink eye of taut, raw-looking scar tissue, about as big around as a half-dollar, stared up from his abdomen, just below the shelf of his ribs. *My God.* He heard his sudden intake of breath. The first time around, when he came to . . . he remembered the old man's hand on his stomach. *How can this be?*

"You have a matching exit wound to the right of your spine. From its location, I suspect you sustained a laceration of your kidney as well. Yet that, too, is almost healed. Here." Chris felt a tug at his left wrist as the old man worked the knot. "As long as you promise not to choke me again, let me . . . There. Look at your hand, Christopher."

At first, he thought there was nothing, but then his eyes picked out the half-moon of the mostly healed slash running from the web between his thumb and first finger down to his wrist. He stared, dumbfounded.

"A spike did that," the old man said, although his words were faint, nearly lost in the sudden buzz that filled Chris's ears. "As you can see, the thumb was nearly severed. But here you are, almost healed. All your wounds are in much the same condition."

"But how?" He turned his hand over, then made a fist. It didn't hurt at all. "That's not possible. How can this be happening? Why am I still alive?"

"Can't say." The old man threw up his hands. "Is it the tonic? Or a mistake, as you say? A combination of both the tonic and your physiology? Or is this only a miracle or magic?"

"There's no such thing as magic," Chris managed through numb lips. He recalled the dark guttural mutters, the strange incense that filled his nose. *And his hands, on my chest; I remember how I felt something . . . leaving.* A bolt of fresh fear burned a path through his chest. "I don't believe in miracles."

"I don't either. Although you could argue that an eight-year-old slip of a girl finding the strength to hoist a seventeen-year-old boy onto a horse to be a touch miraculous. That is, until you consider that the human body reacts to emergencies by flooding the tissues with adrenaline. This increases blood flow, gives more energy, greater strength. So Ellie was frightened; it was an emergency, and her body reacted. She even gave up her coat for you and should have been *really* cold. But she never felt it because the same physiological mechanism also kept her warm. So, see?" The old man spread his hands in a no-tricks-up-my-sleeve gesture. "No miracles. Just science."

"But that's not what you were doing when I woke up. That wasn't science."

"No, that was faith, like the *grudafoos*." The old man stroked a finger over a wooden charm hung around Chris's chest on a leather cord. "Ellie believed it would protect you. Whether it did is immaterial. It was something she could give, and in return, that gave her courage. It gave her faith. But all emotions are chemically mediated and may be manipulated. Every drunk, every lover, any ecstatic mystic knows that. There is no heart"—the old man palmed his own chest, then touched a temple—"without the head."

"So what were you doing then?"

"I was calling on God to heal you," the old man said simply. "I was also suggesting to *you* that it might be time to wake up—and you did, rather spectacularly. And don't bother objecting. I'm sure it was coincidence and no miracle. There is only what we don't understand. Of course, this"—he touched Chris's stomach—"I don't understand at all."

"I don't understand any of this," Chris said.

"Do you *remember* it at all? Because we think you were dreaming, and for quite a while, too. Days. Your . . ." The old man traced a circle in the air before his own eyes. "They were moving as they might in intense REM sleep."

"I—" His tongue tangled. *Dreams, all those dreams, they felt so real.* "I only remember a little, right before . . ."

"Yes?" the old man prompted. "Did you see something, Christopher?"

The nightmares were in pieces, daggers of glass from badly smashed mirrors—and, he thought now, just as a dangerous. *I saw Lena and Peter—and my father. . . .* He felt his heart suddenly sprinting in his chest. *Lena.* God, in all that had happened, he'd forgotten about her. She'd been with him. Where could she have gone? And didn't she know Jayden? *Yes, she said she was in a group of ten kids,* with *Jayden. So that means I've found a group,* her *group.*

"Christopher?"

"I don't want to talk about it," Chris said, hoping he didn't sound as frightened as he suddenly was. If Lena *wasn't* dead, where was she? Could she have headed back to Rule? *But Lena's no good in the woods, not alone, and she was sick, pregnant.* She'd said that Peter was the father, so that must be why *he'd* linked the two of them together in his nightmares. Her going back to Rule made no sense either, especially since Jayden *was* here. So what had happened? Had she simply freaked out and run into the woods—and become lost? She'd never survive that. Could the Changed have gotten to her? *But then why didn't they kill me?* Maybe it was as simple as they couldn't get at him. Lena was easy pickings. Yet that made no sense. The Changed wouldn't have cared if he was alive, barely alive, or dead. Meat was meat. By rights, he ought to be in pieces, or bare bones.

Regardless, saying anything about Lena now would be a mistake. His mind went through the same mental calculus as it had with Ellie and Alex. Telling about Alex wouldn't have helped the little girl, and might make things ten times worse for him. He was at a disadvantage here, and effectively a prisoner. These people were not his friends. Hannah had only proved he couldn't trust them.

So keep your mouth shut. They've already tried to kill you once. Say nothing.

"It was a pretty bad dream," he said. "That's all I remember."

"I see." That dark gaze was clear and very direct, and Chris had the uncomfortable feeling that this old man read exactly what was behind his eyes. "Was it the only one?"

"I don't know," he said, resisting the urge to sneak his gaze elsewhere.

"You sounded very frightened."

"I was scared." This was true. "I couldn't move. The dream felt very . . . *real.*"

"Ah." The old man nodded. "Probably a hypnagogic hallucination. They can be quite frightening because your body's still in the grip of a sleep paralysis. It's the brain's way of protecting you from yourself. Otherwise, we'd all act out our worst nightmares. Given how long you've been in REM sleep, how active your brain's obviously been, I'm not surprised."

"Could it be a side effect of the poison? I mean, another one, other than not ending up dead?"

"Perhaps." The old man showed a thin smile. "Intense dreams were commonly reported. That was the *point* of ingesting the mushroom to begin with. This particular genus is loaded with psychedelics, toxins, and other interesting compounds."

"Mushroom?"

"*Amanita pseudomori.* The False Death mushroom. Apt. It and a cousin, the Fly Agaric, have a very long and colorful history. You can read about it, if you wish. In any event, Jayden—quite a bright boy, a real scientist—he thinks the decoction induced a bizarre sleep-coma. That, combined with the cold, put you into a hibernative state. Slowed down your metabolic processes, somehow protected your brain. It's a decent theory. We know that coma is sometimes protective for brain-injured patients, children who've drowned in cold water."

"My brain wasn't injured. I didn't drown." *I bled out. I couldn't breathe. And what explains the scars?*

"No, you didn't. You're quite unique, Christopher, beyond the fact that you're still *you.*"

"You mean that I haven't Changed. That's our name for it. Your brother's. He's my . . ." His throat moved in another dry swallow. "My grandfather. Reverend Yeager?"

"Ah. Yes. I've been told that my brother and I have the same eyes."

Isaac Hunter's were, however, still kind. "I suppose this makes you my great-nephew."

"I guess." He didn't have a clue. "I was sent to find you."

"I assumed as much. Was it Jessica?"

"In a way." *Jess, with black mirrors for eyes, in the Land of the Dead. And Peter was there, too, and Lena.* He was suddenly exhausted, the events of everything that had happened finally catching up. "It's kind of a long story . . ." And so pointless now. Nathan was dead. Given his dream, he bet Lena was, too.

What am I thinking? I don't believe in magic or dreams. And yet he'd pulled . . . what? A Lazarus? That was crazy. He'd accept a weird coma before coming back from the Land of the Dead.

"I don't understand what there is for me to find here, or why you're so important," he said. "Yeager's my grandfather. That's not news. So, fine, you're his brother, and you're either Amish or lead some breakaway sect. But so what?"

"Well, I agree," Hunter said. "If that were the only story or all there was to discover."

"What more is there?"

"That depends."

"On what?"

"On how much you know about Simon Yeager," Hunter said, "and Penny Ernst."

57

Somewhere west of Rule and four days after the ants—two weeks after the avalanche—Wolf led them down a single, unmarked, dead-end rut along an isolated and very large lake nestled in the cup of broad, rolling, forested moraines. From the lack of houses ringing the shore and that rut, Alex thought the lake might be privately owned, a secret getaway. About two miles in, she spotted a boathouse and lone stake dock, with a single slip, perched on the water's edge down a steep hill to her right. On a high hill to her left and directly across from the lake was a rough-hewn, two-story house, with a large, chalet-style picture window on the left and a partially completed wraparound porch, still on bricks and cinderblock, running off the front door and curling around to the right. The house was surrounded on three sides by tall stands of densely packed evergreens and hardwood—

And the dusky, flayed, and gutted carcasses of four wolves, dangling like totems.

All the blood drained from her head. The last time she'd seen anything like this was just outside the Zone, guarding the way to Wolf's feeding grounds and that arena with its grisly pyramids of decaying human skulls. Purple tongue jutting in a stiff apostrophe, one wolf dangled from a thick iron hook punched through its chest. The body hung to the right of the front door, where you might put up a cheery flowered banner: *Welcome, Friends!* To the extreme left, a second wolf, its eyeless sockets wide with eternal wonder, was suspended thirty feet up a weathered spruce. Alongside, a very large, navy blue Cordura stuff sack hung from a carabiner clipped to red paraline tied off around the trunk of a smaller adjacent tree.

A bear bag. She watched as the fingers of a light westerly breeze snatched the naked wolf and gave it a playful twirl. The paraline let out a soft *squee*. Her lips were numbing, as was her brain. From the aroma of chilled people-steak, she understood that the sack was where the Changed stored their kills. The idea that she'd come all this way only to be hacked up for storage in the equivalent of a deep freeze . . . Her throat began to clench, and she'd clapped both hands to her mouth, unsure if she would vomit or scream or both.

The front door opened then. A second later, a bull-necked boy lumbered out, trailed by another Changed: honey-blonde, blue-eyed.

The shock of recognition was physical, a splash of icy water. The hair wreathing the girl's haggard features was what Alex recalled from a picture in yet another lake house. The square jaw, the nose were right. Willowy before, the girl was much thinner now. Well, mostly thin. Alex wasn't really certain until the girl turned and Alex saw her in profile.

Then everything clicked into place: that green medic's pack, the lengths to which Wolf had gone to save and protect her, his scent of lilacs and honeysuckle: *safe* and *family*. Regardless of *how* he might feel about her, she now understood *why* Wolf needed her, too. She finally *got* what was going on.

Penny Ernst—Peter's sister—was pregnant.

58

"... *correspond with images of the naked, red-eyed, wild-man god known in Vedic mythology as the Red Howler, the Raw-Eyed Beast, or Red Storm. As father of the Hindu storm gods, Rudra was clearly linked to intoxication. With his mad eyes and golden hair, this is a white-skinned god, the divine link to the Land of the Dead ..."*

"Which doesn't prove anything other than people have been getting high for thousands of years," he muttered, eyeing the stack of books Isaac had carted up: *The Ethnobotanical Encyclopedia of Psychoactive Plants. Medicinal Plants of the Great Lakes Region. Little Deaths: The Physiology of Coma and Trance States.* Not light reading, but they'd kept him isolated in this bedroom for the last two days, and Chris had plenty of time on his hands. Anything was better than stewing over what Isaac had said about Penny Ernst and Peter, Simon, his grandfather—and Jess.

"*Tempting as it may be to regard Rudra as the physical manifestation of the Fly Agaric mushroom, I believe there to be a much better candidate for this lost, mysterious, and mystical drink. Close study of Vedic poetry—with its frequent mentions of regenerative 'death sleeps,' resurrection, and divine visions—point to the much rarer and more lethal cousin, A. pseudomori. 'Death sleeps' clearly suggest comas of varying durations, during which times metabolic demands ..."*

From across the room came a timid knock. "Chris?"

"Come on in. Oh, sorry, I forgot. It's locked." Yes, it was perverse and a little nasty, but he was starting to go bat-shit stir-crazy. There were only so many sit-ups and push-ups a guy could do. Any longer in solitary and he'd be as beefy as an inmate. Now, the fact that he *was* feeling so strong after both weeks on the trail and some time in cold storage . . . he didn't want to think about that.

An uncertain pause on the other side of the door. "Do you want me to go away?"

Don't be a creep. It's not her fault. Other than Isaac, the rest were hanging back, spending as little time with him as possible. As pissed as he was, he wasn't sure he blamed them. "No," he said, and shoved back from the table. "Come on in, Ellie."

There was the thunk of a lock being thrown. The door cracked a few inches, revealing the worried eyes of that morning's guard—a strawberry blond named Eli—and then a flash of golden braids as Ellie pushed past.

"*Ellie.*" Eli made a grab that Ellie easily dodged. "Jayden said we should wait for the dogs."

"Mina knows he's okay." Ellie gave her dog an affectionate ruffle. "Don't you, girl?"

"Relax, Eli, I'm still talking," Chris said as Mina trotted over, gave Chris's hand a welcoming snuffle, then immediately flopped on her back, tail thumping. Grinning, Chris obliged with a furious belly scratch that set the dog to squirming. "You like that, girl, you like it?" he said as the dog's back legs pedaled. "That's a good girl."

"She's such a baby." Dropping to her knees, Ellie brushed aside a corn-tassel curl that had escaped her left braid to coil at her temple. "Like I *never* pay attention to her."

"It's okay," Chris said as Mina stretched both front legs and let out a blissful moan. "I like it. My dog did this all the time."

"You miss him?"

"Yup. Jet's a good dog. I bet you'd like him." Chris gave Mina's belly a firm clap, then looked up at the little girl. "Going fishing?"

"She's *always* going fishing," Eli put in.

Ellie showed Chris an exaggerated eye-roll. "I was wondering if, maybe . . . in a couple days, if they let you out . . . you want to come with me?"

"Sure," he said, then couldn't resist the dig. "But I guess it all depends on whether Isaac and Hannah think I'm going to eat you."

"God." Eli's face darkened. "Don't be such a jerk."

The hopeful shine on Ellie's face dimmed. "They don't think that, Chris. You know they have to be sure."

"Yeah, yeah." *Don't be such a turd.* "Sorry. I'm not usually an ass . . . uh, such a creep."

"It's all right. You're just upset." But her smile was more tentative than before.

"No excuse." Reaching across the dog, he tucked that corkscrew curl behind her ear and let his hand linger a moment, enjoying the flush of delighted surprise that spread over her face. Cute kid, but he could see the sadness in the slightly dusky hollows under her eyes. "The least I can do is be nice to the girl who saved my life . . . and don't start." He held up a finger. "It is *so* a big deal."

"Yeah, I guess it is." Ellie looked pleased enough to burst. "Now that you're feeling better, is it okay if I ask you a question?"

"Of course." He said it easily enough, but he felt his stomach suddenly knot with apprehension. "Shoot."

"Before I came here, I had these friends." Ellie nibbled at her lower lip. "Alex and Tom. Not my age, but older like you? Actually, I think Tom was even older. He was a soldier, like my dad, only Tom was in Afghanistan, not Iraq, and worked on bombs and stuff. Anyway, we were all together. They . . . they took care of me, but then we got separated. When Tom . . ." Her eyes shimmered, and her mouth twisted exactly the way a little girl's would if she was trying hard not to cry. "When these adults took me, Tom got shot and . . ."

He listened with growing dismay as she narrated a story he'd heard once before. Ever since that morning on the snow, when he'd swum back in such pain and fear to put two and two together, he knew this moment would come. Until this second, he wondered what he would do—and why that should be a question.

This kid risked her neck for you. The least you can do is man up.

"So, what I was wondering"—Ellie dropped her gaze to her hands as if afraid of finding the answer in his face—"was if Tom and Alex . . . if they got to Rule?" A tear broke against her fingers. Eyes still averted, Ellie knuckled her cheek. "Are they there? Are they okay?"

He was going to hate himself forever.

"I'm sorry, Ellie," he said. "But I never met them."

You are such an asshole. Through the windows, Chris watched as Isaac put a hand on the little girl's head. That loosened something, because Ellie suddenly flung her arms around the old man's waist and buried her face. Even two stories up and across a half acre, Chris could see the little girl's shoulders shudder. *She's the only one who cares, and you go and lie.*

"Yeah, well, you get fed poison, cut off from a bunch of spikes, and left for dead, see how you feel." The self-disgust on his tongue was so thick a bottle of mouthwash wouldn't cover the taste. "You think she's going to like you so much once she finds out that you got Alex killed? That you decided it was easier to pretend there was nothing the slightest bit weird going on with the Zone?" He wouldn't be surprised if Ellie wanted dibs on the firing squad, and *no*, he was not *overreacting.* These kids *put down* people.

What bothered him, too, was how quickly the lies came. He thought he was past all that, the Night of the Hammer and his father and the strange, meaty thunks and Deidre's screams. Ten years later, and he still remembered answering that detective's questions: *No, sir, I didn't hear anything. No, I was asleep. Hammer? No, sir, I haven't seen a hammer anywhere. I don't think we even have one.*

"No, Detective, I love my dad." He leaned his forehead against chilled glass. Just below the sill were stark coils of some very thick but snow-covered vine winding up a high iron trellis. "I'm only eight, and I've just listened to my dad kill someone, and no, sir, he never hurts me."

Despite the bright sun of early afternoon, the double-paned window fogged with his breath. Through the patchy haze, he watched Ellie boost herself onto the saddle of a dingy brown mare. The way to the lake wound through thick woods fringing a vast bowl of glittering snow that, from the wire and steel posts, must be the farmstead's garden plot. Chris saw the old man raise a hand as Ellie, Eli, and their dogs disappeared and then gather the reins of a dun-colored saddlebred, which he led toward a weathered, dark gray stable just off the long frozen oval of a duck pond south of the house. Switching to the south-facing window, Chris tracked Isaac's progress as the shadows of the man and his horse, long and spider-thin, dashed away toward distant, wooded countryside. Nestled a short distance to the right of the stable, a clutch of cows had gathered in a white corral around a feed station outside a red, high-pitched gable barn with a stone foundation. Like the stable, the barn was decorated with several hex signs: half-stars in fake arches over the windows that Hannah had called "Devil's doors," as well as white rosettes. With its east-to-west orientation, Chris could just make out a swirling blue and gold Wheel of Fortune beneath the peak at the gable end. As he neared the barn, Isaac waved to another boy—not tall enough to be Jayden, so maybe Connor or Rob—pushing a barrow of soiled hay.

Man, I would muck stables 24/7 if they'd just let me out of here. Sighing, Chris closed his eyes. He wasn't stupid, so why was he acting that way? Forget how this would hurt Ellie in the long run. What about the fact that he was only digging himself in deeper with lies? Once the truth got out—and it would—they'd find it that much harder to trust him.

Yeah, but look how long everyone's been lying to me.

The story was so incredible, he doubted anyone could make it up. As much as he didn't want to believe it, what Isaac said answered a lot of questions. It even explained Peter's reaction when Chris showed up in Rule. One look at Chris, and Peter probably stalked into the Council to demand an explanation. What would Yeager have admitted?

"Betcha not much," Chris said. "You really think an old asshole like that is going to fess up to getting his business partner's wife pregnant?"

Or that Chris's grandmother . . . was Jess?

All Isaac knew was that when Yeager and Jess's daughter—Chris's mom—showed up with twin baby boys, Yeager agreed to take only one, who turned out to be Simon. Chris was sent back to his dad, who probably raised a huge stink or got some money out of it. Not that his father spent a dime more on Chris than he had to. This was a man who never had two nickels to rub together; who always kept the money Chris made from summer lawn mowing jobs. *For safe keeping* was what his dad always said. *For college.* Right. When you boozed as much as his dad, you needed all the pocket change you could scrape together.

But how had Yeager decided something like that? Put him and Simon side by side and done eeny-meeny-miny-mo? Drawn straws?

Chris could count the number of times he'd actually spent more than five minutes with Yeager on one hand. But he now understood why all his meetings with Yeager only happened once a year, and always in restaurants in other towns outside of Merton and nowhere close to Rule. No way Yeager would risk anyone seeing him and asking Chris, *Hey, Simon, how's it hanging, kid?* Or risk him and Simon laying eyes on each other.

No wonder Dad always got roaring drunk afterward. Every time he saw Yeager was just one more reminder of how he'd ended up stuck with—

The knock was perfunctory, a warning more than a request. He heard a jingle of keys, the rattle of the knob, and then Hannah was hip-butting in on an aroma of stewed carrots, boiled potatoes, and rich sauce. A handgun rode just below her right hip.

"Lunch. Better late than never," she said, by way of greeting. "Got tied up with the lambing. Still have four ewes waiting to deliver."

"What, no Jayden to make sure I don't jump you?" he said.

"He and Connor are out hunting and checking traplines. They won't be back until they have something. Jayden always pushes the envelope."

"At least he gets to do something. I *could* help out around here, you know."

"No, that won't be necessary." Butting the door closed, she walked to the table where he'd laid his books. "Do you mind?"

Although the smell was driving him crazy, he didn't move a muscle. "You aren't worried I've got a sudden hankering for a chicken wing instead of beef stew?"

"No, you're still talking; it's venison; and I don't insult easily." Her gray gaze was unflinching. "I'm also much faster, younger, and quite possibly a better shot than Isaac. Now, are you going to help, or would you like me to leave this on the floor?"

Wordlessly, he swept the books into an untidy heap and dumped them on the bed. Leaning against a brass bedpost, he crossed his arms and watched her lay out his food with efficient, economical movements. It bothered him that he noticed how neatly that buckwheat mane wove into a smooth braid. Or that she still smelled like honey and oatmeal.

"Besides the stew," she said, showing him her back, "there are some peaches put up last year, and I brewed you a cup of nettle tea. It's high in iron, and good for correcting any anemia."

"Yeah? Maybe I should have a taster first."

When she turned, she did it without a lot of drama, the way a kindergarten teacher understands that screaming at the annoying lit-tle kid will only make him tantrum harder. "I've already apologized. I know I'm not perfect, but given the circumstances . . ."

"Yes, blah, blah, blah . . . if you had to do it over again, you'd still make the same choice. I know. Like you said, we've been over this."

"Then what do you want from me?"

Someone to argue with, so I don't have to think about what to do next. "How about letting me out of here for starters?"

"You know that's not my decision."

"But Isaac would listen to you."

"Probably, but I don't think this is a bad call either. While I've not seen that many kids turn, what happened to you is very different."

"Like you said, I'm still talking. I came back as me." From *where* was a question he didn't want to think about and couldn't answer anyway. He made a sweeping gesture at the books. "You're the col-lege kid. There's the science. What more do you want?"

"My advice is still the same. Take this up with Isaac. Now, if that's all"—she began to move toward the door—"I have chores that need doing, and lambs that need feeding."

"Wait." As angry as he was, he needed a break from himself. "Look, I'm sorry I'm being a jerk. I guess I'm not used to getting killed and then waking . . . Sorry." He held up a hand. "Sorry. That was the wrong thing to say. Can you stay for a little while? No one but Isaac and Ellie talk to me. You treat me like I'm some kind of leper; I can't decide if Jayden wants to dissect me or run experiments to figure out what makes me tick."

"If he had access to a lab, he'd probably do both" Hannah said, though she didn't smile.

That did not make him feel better. "Why are you guys so afraid of me?"

"You need to ask that? We can't explain you, we don't know what will happen, and, oh, you've been just a little violent."

"I was confused, okay? You try getting crushed, poisoned, and then woken up with some old guy doing a bunch of mumbo jumbo on you and see if you're not just a little freaked out."

"Has it ever crossed your mind that I *am*, Chris? I'm not exactly *thrilled* to have misread the situation." She sounded angry now.

Misread the situation? Had she just admitted to making a mistake? "So can we agree that we're all a little on edge? Please, stay awhile. I *hate* being alone all the time. All I've got is what's running around in my head. Five minutes. If I'm a jerk again, you can leave."

"I don't need your permission," she said, although he thought there might be the ghost of a smile this time. "What do you want to talk about?"

"Um . . ." Now that she was staying, everything seemed to jam behind his teeth. *You thought I was Simon. How well did you know him? Did you know Peter? Tell me more about Penny.* But all that felt too personal, too fast. "Do you want to sit?"

"Thanks." Slipping onto a straight-back, she clutched the tray to her chest like a shield. "So . . . what's on your mind?"

"Okay, here's what I don't understand." Actually, there were quite a few things he didn't get, but he decided to start with something that was not only safe but pointed out that, really, he *could* be trusted. (*Oh, riiiight,* his inner voice needled, *that* so *explains why you lied to Ellie and haven't told them about Lena.*) "You know I'm the one who's been taking *your* sickest kids back to Rule. *I'm* the one who's left food and supplies."

"Yes, and you can leave kibbles out for a stray cat," she said, with that same neutral tone, "but that doesn't mean you won't skin it for stew the minute it gets close."

"But all I did was show up at that bookmobile. I never knew you guys were there until you left that first little girl for me to find." This was only a small lie. He'd made it his business to visit Oren after Jess pointed him that way. Why she never said she'd broken from the

Amish herself or mentioned boo about Isaac was something only Jess could answer.

"Actually, no. That was another group's decision. I had no part in that, and I wouldn't have agreed if I'd been asked."

"That's pretty harsh."

"Is that a question or an observation?"

"Both. Don't you guys have rules or something? Doesn't Isaac tell you what to do?"

"Of course not. He's an . . . adviser."

"So you guys run things yourself?"

"More or less. We're free to disagree, but there's a certain consensus from group to group."

Yeah, like the one about putting down kids you don't think will make it. Yet even that must not be an absolute. He'd rescued several, very sick kids, some of whom had died once back in Rule. "Isaac's the only adult?"

"The only one left. He keeps tabs on us, moves from group to group."

"How many groups are there?"

"Is that important?"

Okay, so they weren't going there. "Fine, you're right. Not important." Not entirely; Peter had talked about carrying capacities, how alarmingly fast Rule had grown beyond its resources. "So, what about my original question? You guys made the first move, not me."

Which was not entirely true. After Jess mentioned there might be kids around the old Amish settlement, he made it his mission to rescue as many as possible. He'd visited, frequently, aware of the eyes on his back, careful to always leave some token supplies—batteries, food—at the old bookmobile where he'd found that first Spared, a very sick girl, just inside the front door. She was also the only child he hadn't had to jump through hoops to find.

"Discovering that girl wasn't a fluke," he said. "Those kids made sure I found her. After her, they left a note to clue me in on the hex signs. They obviously didn't think I was a threat."

"And as I said, it wasn't my call. Look, we could go round and round about this for days, so let me ask *you* something, Chris." She leaned forward. "If there *had* been other children who weren't sick . . . say, you stumbled on us . . . would you have taken us back to Rule? By force?"

"Probably." He could feel the heat splash his cheeks. "Yes."

"Then that makes you no better than the people who stole Ellie."

"It's not so black-and-white."

"Yes, it is. *I* never stole a child. I've never allowed anyone to use a child as a way to buy sanctuary."

"As you might say . . . that wasn't my call."

"But you enforced it."

"We've all had to make choices. All I ever wanted was to help. I did what I thought was right at the time." Coming out of his mouth, they sounded like the platitudes they were.

"And you'd still do it, all over again."

"You mean, like you deciding to kill me?" he shot back. "Yeah, I guess I would. So we're even. I'd try to find ways to keep kids alive, and you'd *trick* people into taking poison."

He could hear the echo of his shout in the sudden silence. She was rigid, the skin around her mouth tight, her cheeks high with wild color. *Idiot.* He had to stay calm, be reasonable. Push people too far and they exploded. *Sorry, Dad, sorry, it's my fault; I won't do it again.*

"I never . . ." She cleared her throat. "It's never a trick. When someone is beyond help, when there is no hope, it's a choice. When we know for certain, when the dogs warn us that a child is"—her gray eyes shuttled away—"*turning*, it's still a choice."

"A choice between what and what?"

"What do you think, Chris? If you were turning, if you knew that you'd try to kill your friends, people you loved . . . are you telling me that you'd choose to become one of *them?*"

"Between what and what?" he asked again. At that moment, he understood, completely, why Peter set up the Zone. Despite the secrets and lies, he knew Peter still loved him, would die for him. If Peter had confided in him, would he have helped?

Maybe I would. Because if Alex Changed . . . if Peter did . . . I could never pull the trigger. He bet Peter would've felt no differently. Watching his friends and people he loved Change in front of his eyes, Peter would've tried to find a way. Where there was life, there was hope. They might Change back, get better. The trick was keeping them alive long enough to give them that chance.

Yes, but how long would you run the experiment? Months? Years? Does hope have a termination date?

"Don't tell me you let *any* kid you think is Changing wander around. So what's the choice?" He realized that he really was spoiling for a fight, some way of hitting back. "What do you do, lock them up and starve them to death, or only shoot them when they go rabid?"

"Don't you judge us." Her gray eyes went flinty. "Don't you *dare*. I don't owe you answers, Chris. You think you're so superior, so right? You know nothing about us."

"You don't know me either. You're not even interested in my point of view. You've already judged me." His voice was shaky. The low simmer in his gut was near a boil. "So, fine. Let's do a little math, Hannah, because math is clean, it's pristine, it's so scientific that Jayden would approve. You can't massage numbers. There's no arguing with two plus two."

"This is pointless—"

He rode over her. "Not counting me and Nathan, there are eleven bodies in that death house. Assuming your group started with twenty people, give or take, that means you've lost seventy percent of your original population in five months."

"Some of those people were old."

"But the majority weren't, isn't that right? Some kids Changed *after* and either you killed them before they could Change all the way or once they had. But there were others, Hannah—others who were sick and you couldn't help. So they died."

"You can't always cheat death, Chris."

Yeah, but there's a time for everything, even death. Then he thought, *Get out of my head, Jess.* Aloud, he said, "Let's exclude the kids who Changed, okay? What about the others, the ones who were just plain sick? Why not accept help? Hannah, do the math. At this rate, by the end of the year, there won't be any of you left."

"Is that why you came, Chris?" Her voice was cold. "To convince us to go back with you?"

"Maybe. In the beginning."

"What about now?"

"Beats me." He threw up his hands. "I don't know. I think there's a better way than simply giving up and accepting, all right?"

"You want to fight."

"Of course I want to fight. Life may not be great, but it beats dying. I just don't know how to change things in Rule, or if I even can."

"Is that where you want to go? Back to Rule?"

"I don't know." If his grandfather had anything to say about it, he'd be dead or in the prison house before he had a chance to do anything. "This whole thing about Isaac? It was a setup. I was supposed to find out about Jess and Simon and Yeager. I was supposed to figure out about the Zone." *And Peter.* "I see it's wrong. But I also understand."

"You *understand?*"

"Yes, I really do see both sides," he said, and thought, *Chris on the right, Chris on the left. Eeny-meeny* . . . "Not everything about Rule is bad. Like, take Ellie: You seriously believe an eight-year-old girl isn't better off someplace where she can be protected? Or that she even has the ability to *make* that choice? What if she was seven? Or four? How young is too young to know better?"

"You've got a point?"

"Yes. You have a cutoff where it's no longer a kid's choice. But how did you get there, Hannah? What makes you think you're right?"

Hannah threw up her hands. "Fine. We'll never agree. You are *so* like Peter, wanting to reduce all of life and death to cutoffs and percentages, when to step in, when not to."

Of all the things she could've said, this wasn't it. "Wait a minute," he said as she stood. "What do you mean? How well did you know Peter?"

"Well enough." She was already turning away. "I really don't want to talk about this right now, Chris."

"But what if I do? What if I *need* to? Hannah." He had to snatch back the impulse to grab her wrist. "Please. Please don't go. Please . . . what are you talking about?"

He saw the warring emotions chase over her face, and the moment she made her decision. "I'm talking about the accident," she said.

"Accident?" he said. "What accident?"

"You're not going to like it, Chris. You think you've found out all there is to discover about Peter? About Simon?" She showed a brittle smile. "Believe me, those waters run deep."

"What accident?" he said again.

"The accident two years ago," she said. "When Penny killed a girl."

59

"Wait. Just . . . just hold on." Gulping air, Alex eyed a splashy tangle of guts and one tiny paw with its broken nib of bone. Squashed bunny didn't bother her. What ticked her off was that in the last two days since arriving at the lake house, this was the only rabbit she'd snared.

As the trammeled and bloody snow wavered, Alex propped her hands on her thighs and hung her head, praying both that the dizziness would pass and Darth—the nickname she'd given to her guard—wouldn't feel inspired to use the butt of his rifle, or a fist. A chronic mouth-breather, Darth was the kind of sinus-challenged kid with adenoids the size of baseballs that always had the seat behind yours for a major test. If anyone ever felt the need to make another *Star Wars*, though . . . When Wolf wasn't around, Darth enjoyed the random punch, a swift swat. She even understood. She got grumpy, too, when she was starving. Except Darth had the Mossberg.

"Just give me a minute, Darth," she said. "Okay?"

While this was only her second day at the lake house, she was fast coming to know Darth's scents and moods. From his impatient fizz, she knew it wasn't okay at all, but screw it. The kid was a brute and as noisy as a locomotive. She wouldn't put it past Darth to let her faint and then either quietly slide back into the house until she froze or put a boot on her throat. By the time Wolf got back from his hunting expedition with Ernie and Marley, she'd be bones: *Gee, Boss, I dunno; she was just here.* After the fiasco in the cabin, she doubted

Wolf would've left her alone if there hadn't been enough in that bear bag to tide over the natives until his return. But she was finding it very tough to relax while Darth toyed with guess-who's-coming-to-dinner.

Just when I thought things might finally break my way. That coil of wire she'd discovered in a cardboard box with other camping paraphernalia four days ago was the first piece of good luck she'd had. With Darth tagging after, she'd tramped far back into the woods and around the house, scoping out game trails. Plenty of tracks, lots of juicy little bunnies running around. Lay out sixteen snares and pray like hell.

Well—she studied the mess in the snow—she'd caught something, all right, only to have the rabbit snatched by an animal just as hungry as she. *Got to be whatever's following us.* Probably a wolf, too. Those tracks were right. So was the smell, although there was still that queer something that was a little off and . . .

Oh, screw it. Wolf, not-wolf, who cares? She smeared an angry tear from the corner of her right eye. Crying wouldn't help either. Only thing to do was move the snare to a different game trail and start over.

And look on the bright side, Alex. Here you were so worried about what to use for fish bait. Mounding the half-frozen guts into a rough snow bowl, she gave the mess a grim stir with her forefinger and fished out a small, roughly triangular squib of flesh. *Oooh, and what do we have here?*

"Darth, want to see another trick my dad taught me?" Popping the rabbit's heart into her mouth, she swallowed it back and licked her lips. "Yum, yum," Alex said. "*Deelish.*"

Maybe an hour later, she eyed Ellie's watch. (Habit. Mickey was still dead. But wearing the watch made her feel better.) Whenever *now* was, it was as good a time as any to search the boathouse before all those great bunny guts went to waste.

The day was brilliant, the snow dazzle bright enough to scorch purple afterimages, the sun a gold coin that made her shadow puddle at her feet. She shut her eyes against the glare, tried to imagine her cells wringing energy out of sunlight. She had to find something more to eat than bark and twigs and the occasional ant or bunny heart. The boathouse was the only place left where she might find something useful. After scrounging around the main lake house, basement, and garage, she'd come up with some nice stuff: the snare wire, a camp stove, bottles of propane fuel, a Coleman lantern, even a decent one-man tent. The stove seemed like a taunt. The wire she was using for snares was too stiff for fishing, though. Unless she decided to start pulling out her hair and braiding it together for fishing line, that left the boathouse. Because lakes had fish, right? Hack through the ice somehow, drop in a line. Offer a sacrifice to the gods, or something.

Earlier, when Alex was stewing up her oh-so-wonderful pot of white pine, she'd happened to glance over at Penny, stretched on a frayed leather couch squared before the great room's picture window. Plenty of light to see by—and damn if Alex hadn't spotted this brief but very distinct little ripple. Not a punch or a kick. More like something *rolling over* in its sleep.

She knew more about quantum physics than she did about pregnancy, and since Alex knew as much about quantum physics as she did Outer Mongolia . . . she was virtually clueless. None of the very few kids she'd hung with in high school got pregnant or knew anyone who had. All she remembered from those informational drool-fests from high school health was that how much you showed and when depended on how tiny you were. And you could feel the baby move on the inside . . . at four months? And from the outside at five to six months? Something like that.

So Penny's at least five months, and maybe more like six or seven. Alex had folded a drippy strip of boiled pine into her mouth. The stuff smelled like Christmas and tasted like stale Dentyne peeled from the underside of a school desk, right next door to a booger. *Meaning she was pregnant before the Zap.*

Which was something to think about.

So had Peter brought Penny here before or after things fell apart? Peter had to be involved, somehow. Peter and the Council set up the Zone, Peter was head of security, Peter made sure the Changed were fed. Unless Penny was already here before the Zap, Alex couldn't see how Peter managed to move her without Penny ripping off his face. Knocked her out somehow?

Or what if she knows Peter the way Wolf knows me?

Neither scenario accounted for Wolf, who'd been with Spider and the rest of his high school buddies when Alex had bumbled into the Zone. Unless she had it the wrong way around. From the lake house photograph at the Yeager place, she'd seen that Simon and Peter were tight. So maybe Simon knew about this place, and *Wolf* had wanted to take Penny someplace he thought was safe, a place he could visit every now and then to resupply and check up on her?

This begged an obvious question, too. Alex had assumed Wolf was the father. Now, she wasn't sure. Oh, Wolf cared about Penny plenty. He was always watching out for her, carrying things that were too heavy, making sure she—and then his guys—ate before he took a single morsel for himself.

But Wolf *never* touched Penny. They didn't snuggle. He didn't hug her. Never put a hand on her stomach. (Although maybe guys only did that in chick flicks; *she* didn't know.) There was nothing *intense* between Penny and Wolf, no *spark*. In high school, you always knew who the couples were, no matter how übercool and below-the-radar they were about it. Their heat was in their eyes, the glances they shared, the way the air thickened. Like how the very first time *she* got close to Tom, inhaled his smoky musk, the tug of her attraction had been immediate. When they had kissed, that one moment deepened to something vital, as elemental as air.

The only time anything like that happened with Wolf, when his scent shifted and became an aroma that was *safety* and *family* and *desire*, was around her. The only person to whom Wolf seemed truly attached and *attracted*, and for whom he would risk his life, was . . . *her*.

Which was just so frigging great.

The boathouse was an A-framed one-room cabin on stilts, but with no boats or canoes or even kayaks slotted underneath. As soon as she forced the door, she realized she was looking at a man cave: a place where a guy and his buds crashed to get away from the main house. The décor screamed *boy*, too. Two single beds, one still rumpled; a tiny four-drawer bureau; two straight-backed chairs; a bookcase crammed with puzzles, a cribbage board, two decks of cards, board games, and stacks of smeary magazines she knew better than to leaf through. A curling *Star Wars* poster, Luke battling Vader, thumbtacked over the bookshelf. A ring of keys and an old windup alarm clock rested on a plank shelf on the left wall beside the bed, along with road atlases of Wisconsin, Minnesota, Michigan. Several jackets hung from nails just inside the door. Even through the deep cold and Darth's baseline sun-scorched opossum stink plugging her nose, the boathouse had just the right boy-smell, too: sharp deodorant, foot powder, Irish Spring.

Yet there were two other nose-crinkling odors. One was a camp-fire odor, or like chemistry class, when they'd ignited magnesium. The other was . . . Her mind flashed to chemo, and an oncology nurse feeling for a vein before hooking Alex up to a brown IV bag of cis-platin. *Hospital smell*, that was it. Alex hauled in more air, worrying the smells—and then forgot all about sulfur and flammable metals. Because *this* time . . .

Oh God. Her stomach tightened against a whiff of sweet summer.

She got a memory-pop, a flashbulb moment of her dad: *Relax, honey, she's wash and wear.*

"Oh please." Her voice came out squeaky. Her eyes snapped back to the bed, and then she was dropping onto her stomach and batting blankets out of her way, reaching beneath the bed. "Oh please, please, please," she chanted, sweeping her glove over bare floorboards, catching wooly dust kittens, a pencil, an old sock—before slapping metal. Scrambling to a cross-legged sit, she dragged out a dented red toolbox. She was shaking so badly she had to use her teeth to tug off her gloves before fumbling open the toolbox's icy chrome latch and throwing back the double lid.

Instead of tools, there was a small landfill of discarded candy wrappers and—no mistake—the dizzying aroma of chocolate and petrified coconut.

"Oh." She said it in that breathless, astonished way she did at a gorgeous sunset or a gift too beautiful to believed. Plunging her hands into the wrappers, she came up with a humongous, *giant* candy bar that she would've recognized even without the helpful blue and white wrapper and big black letters: ALMOND JOY KING SIZE.

"Sometimes you feel like a nut," she sang. Her grip kept slipping on the slick paper, and she finally ripped the wrapper with her teeth. A luscious perfume of sugar and butter and chocolate ballooned. The butter solids had separated, giving the milky chocolate a dusty, sickly cast. "And ask me if I care," she said. Teasing out a bar, she stuck the candy into her mouth and bit. There was a hollow *chuck*, a jab of pain in her jaw. The candy was frozen solid and, literally, rock hard. All she managed was to scrape off a few chocolate shards.

Probably best. Closing her eyes, she luxuriated in sweet chocolate melting over her tongue. *Might bring it up if I eat too—*

A fizz-fizz, pop-pop boiled into her nose, and she knew, a second before he gave her shoulder a warning nudge: Darth was getting impatient.

"Sit on it and spin, Darth." Yet when she reached for her knife, she did it slowly. No reason to give Darth an excuse. Placing the bar on the wood floor, she jockeyed the blade's tip into the chocolate, right behind that first almond, then rocked the knife back and forth, applying steady pressure until the bar broke in a small shower of chocolate-covered coconut.

"Oooh, you don't know what you are missing, Darth. On the other hand, more for me." Wetting a finger, she dabbed up all the shards, then popped the finger into her mouth. "Oh, thank you, God," she moaned. She was *definitely* taking all the wrappers for later. Give 'em a nice, long lick. Popping the bit of broken bar into her mouth, she tucked it into her cheek like a chipmunk. The rest she carefully wrapped and then slipped into an inside pocket, where her body warmth would thaw out the treat. She was still starving, but even that little bit of chocolate made her blood surge.

Yeah, well, don't get giddy, honey. The candy might be the extent of her luck. She didn't see any fishing gear, and her nose hadn't sussed out anything else other than that strange campfire odor and that hospital smell. Where were they coming from? There didn't seem to be much else here but the bureau and another bookshelf, made of sagging two-by-fours propped on cinderblocks, filled with hardcovers and paperbacks. A lot of novels, all stuff she'd either read or been meaning to but never got the chance: Tolkien, Asimov, Bradbury, Matheson. A broken-spined, scotch-taped copy of *Childhood's End*. *Lord of the Flies*. *Dune*, a book she'd read while getting chemo, that mantra about fear as the mind-killer ringing true as she watched the drip-drip of yellow poison flow into her veins. A good collection of Stephen King, too: *The Dead Zone*. *Desperation* and *The Stand*. *Duma Key*. *A Wrinkle in Time* was falling apart, and the spine of *Watership Down* was so creased she could barely make out the title.

But there were also a ton of newer textbooks: *Lupine Biology*. *Mammalian Speciation*. *The Ecology of Genetic Rescue*. *A Head of the*

Pack: The Wolves of Michigan's Isle Royale. A larger clutch on population genetics and evolution. A third of one shelf was devoted only to history: *Where the Buffalo Roam: Roosevelt and the Embattled Wilderness. When Darkness Reigned: Civilizational Collapse in the Middle Ages.*

"Whoa," she muttered. A voracious reader who also had been a history buff and hard-core mammologist was the last thing she'd expected. On the other hand, Peter was a problem-solver, a guy who'd obviously thought about allocation of resources. Someone who would've recognized that feeding the Changed garnered additional benefits, like a tidy buffer between Rule and the rest of the world. Fitting, somehow, that he'd read up on the Dark Ages.

She wouldn't mind crashing here awhile. *Childhood's End* looked awfully tempting. So did all that Stephen King. Rereading *Wrinkle* would be like picking up where you and your best friend left off. Chris would love this, too. A boy who'd dismantle and move an entire bookmobile's collection would want a crack at these. If she got out of this, she ought to bring him here.

Don't get ahead of yourself. She had to be practical. *You can dream, but food comes first.*

Searching each jacket, turning out pockets got her nothing but a crumpled handful of dollar bills liberated from a denim jacket, which she crammed into a parka pocket. Tinder was tinder. She was putting the jacket back when she paused. The garment was big, just as the boathouse had an older-boy feel to it. Its aroma was stark wintergreen and icy iron. While in Rule, she'd never paid that much attention, but now she inhaled deeply, wondering how scents *this* bold could hide so much.

So, was the house a gift? The chocolate of that Almond Joy chunk was gone, her tongue pebbly with coconut. Flipping the almond from the pouch of her cheek, she chewed, mulling this over. Her curiosity was stoked, which was somehow better than focusing only on that beaky gnaw in her stomach. *Or was this just a really old family vacation house where Peter went when he needed to think things over?* That felt right. Yesterday, when she swept the woods to set her snares, she'd also discovered an ancient, weathered tree house about thirty feet up a towering oak around back. Judging from the lake house's unfinished porch, Peter had been busy. The house had also been recently winterized, with double-paned windows redolent with the reek of putty and caulk. She scented relatively fresh insulation behind the drywall downstairs, the lingering tang of paint. A woodstove, so new the house smelled of scorched cast-iron, gave off heat in spades. (A lucky thing, too. There were two fireplaces, one upstairs and one down, but both were very old, the hearths blackened and cracked. The sting of creosote on her tongue was so strong, she bet you could take a chisel to the coal-black residue caking that flue and still not chip it all away. A wonder no one had started a chimney fire and burned the house down.)

He went to college, studied genetics and evolution, history. So maybe that was the point of the house. Peter had had a whole other life. From the looks of the house, he might have imagined eventually living here year-round.

At her back, she heard Darth suddenly hitch as his reek went from fizzy rot to grouchy stink. Despite everything, a grin crept over her lips. She knew what was bugging him. Darth might be an ox, but he had a bladder the size of a walnut. This might explain why Darth got to babysit. A guy who needed a potty break every couple of miles could be a real drag. For her, Darth's frequent need to go wee-wee wasn't a problem, although he had this habit of doing his business, like, practically *right* on top of her, which not only was TMI but ticked her off. Want rabbits to stay far away? Pee on the snare. Jerk.

She was tempted to hurry this up but then thought, *Oh, screw it. Don't rush this. There's something here, something important.*

As she stepped up to the bureau, a second flashbulb of memory popped: of Tom, eyes bright with fever, thigh shiny and taut with infection. But why? Chemistry lab and Tom . . .

Because I had to sterilize the knife before I cut him. That was it: that smell like burnt match heads, like flint against a striker. So, were there matches in the drawers? No, the odor was too strong for that. Gunpowder?

Or a gun. Swallowing against the knot in her throat, she leaned in a little closer, opened her mouth, and tasted the air. *Don't get your hopes up. It's probably not.* But the smell was stronger here and coming from the bottom drawer of this bureau.

So. If it *was* a gun, what then? She couldn't sneak that past Darth. *Unless I shoot him. But it would have to be loaded, and there'd be no way to check. Might even blow up in my hand if it's old and dirty or the mechanism's frozen.*

But Darth *did* need to take a whiz. She slid her eyes in a sidelong glance. The boy was doing the dying-to-pee two-step. *Wear him down. When he goes potty, that'll be your chance.*

As slowly as she could, she tugged the top drawer. The wood was swollen and yielded in grudging squalls. From the weight and hollow *thock* of wood against wood, she could tell it was empty. The second drawer held two pairs of boy's underwear and three pairs of balled socks.

As she pushed the second drawer shut, Darth broke, bolting from the boathouse. A moment later, she saw him hustling for the dock. *Well, that's one way to melt a fishing hole.* Wasting not a second more, she dropped to a crouch and pried that bottom drawer free. The balky wood jammed on its metal runner. *Come on, don't blow this.* Risking a fast peek around the bureau, she saw Darth stripping his gloves with his teeth. *Minute and a half, max.* Squelching her impatience, she wrestled the drawer shut then slowly pulled straight back.

This time, the drawer cooperated. *Hell.* Two pairs of jeans, two cargo pants. While that burnt magnesium scent was still strong, she had no hope of going through each and every pocket before Darth made it back.

"Come on." She slipped a hand beneath the jeans. "Please, God, just cut me a—" She gasped as her fingers curled around smooth metal. "No way," she said. "It can't be."

But it was.

A pistol.

60

"Penny *killed* someone?" Chris felt his jaw drop. "When? *Who?*"

"Well, more like *got* her killed. About two and a half years ago." With a weary sigh, Hannah dropped back into her chair. "It's a long story."

Two and a half years ago, he was a sophomore in high school. Simon would've been sixteen. Isaac Hunter had said that Penny was a year younger than Simon. "Give me the short version. Did you grow up in Rule, or are you Amish or . . ."

"Was. I left years back." She shrugged. "I wanted more. School, an education beyond the eighth grade. Peter and I met in Houghton when I was a freshman at Michigan Tech. He was already a senior."

"Peter went to college?" He blinked in surprise. "I always assumed he'd been a deputy since high school or something."

"Hardly. He was the TA for my freshman seminar in comparative zoology, managed the lab. Nice guy." Her mouth moved in an almost wistful grin. "Very *forceful*, a million opinions. There was this coffee place a block or two up from the river—Cyberia Cafe? Peter treated a couple times after lab. We'd grab coffee, hang outside the library along the Keweenaw Waterway."

Keweenaw. He had a vague notion that this was way north and east. "I'd never been much outside of Merton until I got to Rule."

"Oh, the Keweenaw's really beautiful. There's this bridge between Houghton and Hancock, which is a much smaller town on Copper

Island right across the waterway. Once you get past Hancock, there's virtually nothing on the island all the way out to Lake Superior except farms and golf courses, and then Copper Harbor at the very tip. I think about it sometimes, maybe settling up there?" Her expression turned dreamy. "Raid the university library, then go on past Hancock, find a nice, isolated farm just off Superior. Fish, grow crops, read books. That would be all right."

That sounded like something he would enjoy. "Maybe you should make it happen."

"Well, I couldn't do it alone, for one thing, and you have to get there, for another. Oh, and hope all the people-eaters have moved out of town." She gave another wry shrug. "Anyway, Peter really loved school. His big thing was Isle Royale. We'd go back and forth on what they should do about the wolves."

"Wolves? Isle Royale?" It was like listening to someone tell him a bedtime story in a foreign language. "Where's that?"

"In Lake Superior. It's a national park, but hardly anyone goes. It's tough to get there. It's where they were doing this fifty-year study on the wolf and moose populations?"

"They were?" He felt incredibly dense. "Why?"

She gave him a look. "Isle Royale's an *island*, but it's got wolves and moose. So how'd they get there?"

"Swim?"

"Only the moose. Wolves can't swim that far. The lead scientists were all in Houghton at Michigan Tech. They figured the wolves came across on ice bridges way back, but because of climate change, there hasn't been a stable bridge since the mid-eighties. So the wolves are stuck. Their population's been tanking for the last ten years. Before the world went dark, there were about nine wolves left. Only about half were females. So there was a lot of debate about how or whether to save them. Over the summers, Peter did fieldwork.

Tranquilizing wolves, collecting samples, fitting them with collars, hunting down moose carcasses. He was very passionate, thought it was our fault for wrecking the environment. I think if he could've figured out a way to sneak wolves onto the island, he'd have done it. You have to admire that."

"I guess." Chris felt a nasty ping of envy. If things hadn't fallen apart, that might have been *him* going to classes and arguing ethics over coffee. "How does all that relate to Penny?"

"Because of one really bad decision Peter made. The island's all backcountry and very remote. You either go five to seven hours by ferry, fly in on floatplane, or pilot your own boat. Peter had this vintage thing he'd refitted with a fiberglass hull. It was like Quint's boat in *Jaws*: pilothouse, engine room, galley. He turned the forepeak into sleepers. Over spring break of his senior year, he offered to take a bunch of us over to the island. The catch is, the park officially opens in mid-April, and this was mid-March. You can get into huge trouble if you're caught, but Peter knew a cove to slip into on the north end, closer to Canada. I figured, a little winter camping, a little hiking, a nice boat ride, it'd be fun. Twelve of us crowded onto this old boat, including Penny"—she paused—"and Simon. He and Peter were close, even then. I think the grandparents hoped Simon and Penny would hook up."

That was exactly what Isaac described, too. "They weren't like that?"

"I never got that vibe. From what Simon said, he always thought he should look after her the way Peter did for him."

Interesting. Just how close had Hannah and Simon been? "How did Penny feel?"

"Well, she and I never"—she inserted air-quotes—"*bonded*. She was nearly fifteen and still pretty young in a lot of ways. Peter had this real blind spot for her, just adored her. But she was already very troubled. You could see it, the way she hung on some of Peter's college friends. And it was"—her gray eyes slid up in a sidelong glance—"spring break."

Meaning lots of alcohol. "What happened?"

"Everyone got drunk," she said, simply. "That is, everyone but Simon. Even then, he was a very careful, very private kid. Being a freshman, I didn't know Peter's friends very well, so Simon and I hung. Talked about college, his interests, what I was doing. Anyway, there we are, in the middle of Lake Superior. No one's wearing a life jacket. It's March, and *freezing*. The water's forty degrees. Peter's completely wrecked, a beer in one hand or a shot, and knocking them back. People are goofing around. A bunch are below, some making out in the bunks and . . ." She punctuated the sentence with the arch of one eyebrow—"Penny, too, with a guy. I think Simon lost track of her. If he'd known, he'd have gotten her out, but I guess he was a little distracted, talking to me and keeping an eye on Peter."

He still didn't see where this was leading or how Penny got a girl killed. "So what happened?"

"Penny set the boat on fire," she said.

61

This wasn't just any pistol. Alex knew it as soon as she saw that hinged steel barrel, and a plastic baggy with a cartridge the size of a twelve-gauge shell.

A flare gun. She'd seen only one in her life, the time she and her parents had taken a coal-fired ferry boat that chugged between Ludington, Michigan, and Manitowoc, Wisconsin. The captain had shown her his flare pistol when he gave them a tour of the pilothouse. His flare gun had been orange plastic. This pistol was metal and looked old and worn.

She thumbed the release and broke the weapon open the way she would a single-shot shotgun. The barrel housed a removable metal insert. Opening the baggy, she shook out the shell. The cap was brass; the cartridge red, with BAM-PM 1-060-062 stamped in black. Below that was the word KALIBER and then numbers: 12/70. On the back was the word SIGNALPATRONEN, also in black.

No way she was leaving this behind. "And where are you, Darth?" Her heart gave an unpleasant lurch as she did a peek around the bureau just in time to see her guard zipping his fly. *Hell.* Her pants weren't exactly skinnies, but someone might notice a pocket bulge. Slipping the shell into the barrel, she quickly shoved the flare pistol beneath her sweatshirt and flannel into the small of her back, then fluffed out her parka.

You're crazy; you're nuts. One good whiff of that pistol and you're dead.

She was about to push up from the still-open drawer, but hesitated, her attention still pinned by that bizarre *hospital* smell. *Something still there.* Peering into the very back of the drawer, her eye ticked to a fluffy, feathery red splotch. She made a swiping grab and her hand closed around a very slim plastic tube that she instantly knew was both too narrow and too long to be a spare cartridge for the flare gun.

In the eight seconds before Darth clumped to the door, she had enough time to think how strange it was to find a flare pistol beneath a stack of jeans. Although she could wrap her head around it. This was a boathouse. When you were out on a boat and needed help, you got off a flare. The fact that there *was* no boat was a little strange. Didn't the gun belong where you might conceivably need and use it? Why *hide* it?

And now here was another puzzle squirreled away and under wraps, just like the signal gun: a common hospital item in an uncommon place.

All she could think as she stared was, *Peter. What the hell?*

Because what she held in her hand was a fluid-filled syringe.

62

The way Hannah told the story, it was a wonder anyone made it off that boat alive. The watertight fiberglass hull meant the wood beneath was dry as kindling, a fire waiting to happen.

Hannah was on deck at the time, propped against the pilothouse, her eyes closed against the wooziness in her head and the heave of her stomach: "It was so cold, I was turning blue." She lay there, shivering, until Simon peeled out of his jacket and draped that around her shoulders. *Wouldn't want you to catch your death* was what she remembered him saying. She'd just opened her mouth to thank him when there was a huge *bang* and something hot and white suddenly blasted through the hull not five feet from her face.

After that, Hannah's memories were a chaotic blur: screaming kids stampeding from below; flames shooting first out of the forepeak and then the hatch; the boat taking on water; the electrical failing a second after Peter, sobering fast, got off a Mayday. There was a life raft, but it was designed for eight, not twelve. Once Simon and Peter got the raft into the water, keeping people calm enough not to swamp it was another nightmare, especially when Peter's boat began to sink.

"It wasn't dark yet, but the water was so black Peter used a flashlight. That boat filled and rolled pretty fast. Once you were in the water, you really couldn't see, had no idea which way was up. I don't think he or Simon realized Penny and another kid *weren't* there until they did a head count," Hannah said. By then, the fire was out, but the boat had disappeared.

Both frantic, Peter and Simon jumped out of the raft and swam back to the spot where the boat had gone down. What happened next was . . . *a little hazy* was how Hannah put it. As Peter later told it to the Coast Guard, he and Simon dove a good fifteen or twenty feet, grappled their way through what was left of the hatch, and surfaced in the skeletal remains of the engine room. The remaining air pocket was tiny, no more than a ten-inch gap. Numb with cold and nearly exhausted, Penny was treading water that was up to her chin. The other girl, a townie no one really knew except for the boy who'd brought her aboard, was already dead.

"Peter told them the other girl must've gotten snagged on something that held her underwater," Hannah said. "Simon said the same."

"Who was she? The girl who died?"

"Amanda . . . Peterson? No, Pederson." She paused. "You know, I remember that at the time, there was one thing I thought was . . . weird. As soon as the boys got Penny to the surface? Peter screamed at Simon to take care of her and not follow, and then Peter dove back under, on his own, and he was gone a *long* time. I thought he'd drowned."

"Why would that be weird?" he asked. "He probably tried to get that girl's body out."

"I guess." Smoothing back her hair with one hand, Hannah rose to go. "Maybe you had to be there, but I know something happened down there, in that boat. I just don't know what."

"Why do you think that?"

"Because Peter never came back to school," she said. "And about six months later, Simon tried to kill himself."

63

Plopping down on the last step up from the boathouse, Alex decided to steal a few minutes to spaz in private. Chugga-chugging ahead like the little asthmatic engine that could, Darth was already halfway to the house. Or maybe he was daring her to run so he could shoot first, eat second, and ask questions later.

You have lost your mind, honey. She propped her back against a knotty red pine. The pistol knuckled her spine. She'd slipped the capped syringe into a right cargo pant pocket. What was she thinking? Wolf always slept close. If he sniffed or felt that pistol? She was sunk.

So far, all her grand schemes had been pipe dreams of an oh-so-daring getaway. But *now*, she had a real weapon. Two, if she counted the tanto. (That funky syringe she wasn't sure about. The more she mulled over that feathery thing, the more she thought: *fletchings*. Was this some kind of dart?) But no kidding around this time. Execute this just right—blind someone, set a few Changed on fire—she could swipe a couple rifles, have herself some real *gun*-guns. For that matter, she *could've* shot Darth right then and there. Of course, a twelve-gauge shell in a tiny little gun had to be loud. Still, she could've grabbed his rifle and skedaddled before anyone knew what was going on. If she *really* wanted to throw a monkey wrench into things? Set the house on fire. Those propane canisters she'd found, combined with popcorn-dry, resin-rich pine certain to throw off a ton of sparks—what's not to like?

So what's wrong with me? Wolf's not here. So it wasn't a question that she might hurt or kill him. But whoever was left standing might take it *out* on Wolf. That would be on her. *And so what?*

Tired of this endless, mental rat race, she reached into her parka, withdrew the candy bar, inhaled memories. *Jump, sweetheart.* "I agree, Dad." She slid another nibble of candy onto her tongue. "Live a little."

Why care about Wolf? How long was she supposed to be grateful? Wolf was not Chris. She was starting to think like those kidnap victims . . . what was it? Stockholm syndrome? *Sympathy with the devil's more like it.* She worried coconut between her teeth. *What is this,* I kissed a zombie and liked it? *He ate part of your shoulder, for God's sake. So what if he protects you now? He* put *you in this position—*

She suddenly stiffened. *Hello.* That familiar and yet very weird scent—wolf and not-wolf—was very close, much more so than ever before. Dead ahead, in fact, and practically in her lap. *Oh shit.* Did it sense easy prey? Here she was, alone, in the open. What help she might count on—*hah!*—was too distant to do her any good, if Darth even bothered.

Just be calm. The scent hadn't deepened to *And, oh, what big teeth you have,* but she felt her heart giddyap in a spastic gallop. She inched her eyes, sweeping up from untrammeled snow to the denser green of the woods and a screen of low cedar—and it was right there, so perfectly still that were it not for its scent, she'd never have known where to look.

What, she thought, *are you?*

64

A flare gun? Sighing, Chris massaged his aching temples and let himself sink more deeply into the bed. *What the hell had Penny been thinking?*

He was alone again, Hannah having locked him in almost a half hour ago, according to the old clock. He could hear her moving around in the kitchen downstairs, caught the chatter of plates and chinks of glass as she put together food to take out to Isaac in the lambing barn. His own lunch still waited. He should probably eat, but the prospect of dragging himself off the bed made him groan and pull a pillow over his eyes to blot out the bright afternoon light. After two weeks spent dreaming, he'd have thought he would never want to lie down again. Yet the creep of a deep weariness was too powerful to ignore, the bed very inviting—and he needed some time to digest all this.

Having burned so bright and hot, Peter's boat sank fast in water over five hundred feet deep. Neither it nor the dead girl were ever recovered, and so they joined the litter of wrecks at the bottom of the largest and deepest of the Great Lakes. Which meant that Peter's story—an engine room fire ignited by an electrical short—never could be investigated. According to Hannah, the Coast Guard and then the police questioned them but got nowhere. Simon was the only eyewitness who hadn't been drinking, and he backed up Peter.

"I knew what I'd seen," Hannah had said. "But it all happened so fast, I kept thinking I might be wrong. I didn't know it was even a flare until Simon finally told me. Can you believe Penny still had the gun? After she shot it off, she crammed everything into her pockets."

From below came the muted thump of a door: Hannah, leaving for the barn. The silence settled. His clock ticked off the seconds.

Why Hannah kept in touch with Simon was a mystery. All she said was, *We got close.* Even so, Simon's suicide attempt was a shock. But Chris could see it. He understood the impulse.

Your father kills his girlfriend. Chris hugged the pillow to his eyes. *You—the little kid—help him hide the evidence. You lie to the police because your dad says it's the only way.*

He remembered that, too. His father, reeking of booze, the smell of blood wreathing him like a fog: *They'll split us up, boy. Put you in a home where there won't be no one to give a shit about you. You want to be safe? You don't want boys and old men doing filthy things to you? You want a roof over your head? Then this is what you're gonna say. This is what you're gonna do.*

"Shut up, Dad," Chris muttered. "It was never about me. It was always about protecting you." And keeping secrets until you wake up one day to find you live with two monsters, the one with your dad's face and the thing rotting inside—

"Chris."

The sound of his name felt unreal, like the slash of an exclamation point at the end of a sentence you hadn't realized you'd written. The sound was short and sharp, like knuckles on a door, and knocked him from his thoughts. Before he could reply, he heard the doorknob rattle.

"Come in," he said, not moving from the bed. Probably Hannah, back from the barn, wanting his dishes. When he didn't hear the hinges complain, he waited a moment. "Hannah?"

The knock came again. This time, he tossed the pillow with a groan. "Hang on," he said, swinging his feet to the floor. That was when he remembered. "I can't unlock it from my side."

Hannah said something he didn't catch. "What?" he called. She said something else, but her voice was muffled. There was another rattle, followed this time by the scrape of the bolt. Without thinking much about it, he turned the knob and pulled open the door. "Sorry, I was—"

Everything in him—his brain, his breath and blood, the thump of his heart—stopped.

There, her lime-green scarf still twined around her neck, was Lena.

65

Alex had been right. It was a wolf—and it wasn't. *Some kind of hybrid.* This animal was much larger than even a malamute, but without the curlicue tail. Its fur was virtually white, with only streaks of gray. The shape of the head, snout, and ears reminded her of Jet, Chris's black German shepherd, but the facial markings and light black mask resembled a husky.

Why show itself now? Was that because of the candy? What it thought was an offer of food? Possibly, but the scent wasn't right. Like the alpha wolf, this animal's scent didn't scream *hunger* or *danger.* Over the lingering sweetness of chocolate and coconut, she could *taste* the emptiness here, all cold dust and gray ash. This wolfdog was both alone and lonely.

But where did you come from? For that matter, why had it risked following her? Maybe it was like the dogs before: how they *always* clamored to be near and protect her, if need be.

They stared at one another. Unlike Jet, the wolfdog's eyes were an intense, stunning gold. Only after they'd locked gazes did she remember that it was dangerous to stare down a wild animal. Yet as their eyes held, that *lonely* taste again washed over her tongue; her chest ached. It had been a long time since she'd seen a dog. Even a wolfdog was somehow more normal. It made her feel . . . human.

Moving slowly, she swiveled her head to the right. Head jutting like a Neanderthal's, Darth was clomping past the wraparound porch, heading for Bert and Penny, who were just emerging from the woods. From the crinkly nip in the air, she knew they'd hauled back mostly desert-dry pine, which she, oh joy, would then sort through, because these kids just didn't learn: *pine + fire = big trouble.* But this meant she had a few more minutes.

She turned back to the animal. "Hey, boy, whatcha doing?" she said, softly, knowing better. This was something poor, cranky, sweet little Ellie would've done: *Hey, strange animal, come give me rabies.* The thought pushed a lump into her throat. If Ellie magically reappeared, she could make nice to every animal in the forest, and Alex wouldn't bat an eye. *She* should know better, too. Given Wolf's interesting fetish, encouraging this animal to stick around was a death warrant. But she suddenly longed to touch it. Just ruffle her fingers behind its ears. Selfish, she knew, but she really, really needed this.

"Hey, boy, whatcha doing? You stealing my food? Huh? That's okay," she soothed, and saw the tip of its tail twitch back and forth. *Relax, breathe out; let go, so it can.* "But next time, you think you might leave me some—"

There was a sudden urgent push in her head, a kind of mental shove in the center of her brain. A split second later, she felt a heaving sensation that was like the unfolding of arms and legs, the swiveling of a gigantic head, the baring of needle-teeth. The opening of yellow eyes. *What the hell?* Her mind shimmied as if the ground were shifting under her feet, the snow ready to let go and carom down a rise and sweep her away. Gasping, she flinched away, nearly tumbling down the steps, barely aware of the wolfdog's small, queer yip of alarm.

The monster? Why was it waking up now? *Not because of Wolf.* There was no way to get used to a monster, but she *was* beginning to sense a difference in what the monster did. Never fully asleep now, the monster always poked its nose up for a sniff whenever Wolf was near. *That* feeling was close to her dream: fire and need. Desire. The monster reaching out in a lover's embrace because it wanted Wolf.

But this was different. *It's like that night Spider killed Jack, when I got yanked behind her eyes. Like when Leopard wanted me in the mine.* And just days ago, when Acne tried to kill her. This was bloodlust, a killing frenzy. There was something—someone—pulling at the monster, reaching in with clawed hands, dragging it along and into . . .

. . . into a mind that isn't hers, behind alien eyes—push-push, go-go—in a body she doesn't recognize—push-push-push—and isn't sure belongs to a girl. Go-go, push-push, she/he/it is moving with four others, just as fast and silent and gogogo: a red storm, pushpush over the snow, through trees, pushpushpush, a swirl she/he/it sees through many eyes. To its left, there are bright flashes of sun dazzle shining through breaks in the forest. That portion of the forest curves, following a broad swath, rimming a bowl of unbroken snow. Behind, not very far, there is the pushpushgogo. And there is another, almost a brother but still an enemy, and that one is screaming: GOGOGO, LET ME—

Very far ahead, there are six more, and the red storm drives pushpushpush them on, gogogo—and then what she sees and where she is collapses. There is another shimmy, a shift. Now, suddenly, she's jumped again to slip behind the eyes of someone else, who is chasing after three others. One has a head of wild, untamed hair; another is small and his pain is a ripe, bright scent. And there is a third, but he . . . it? . . . is hard to read; there is nothing to roll around the mouth—but pushpushpush her head is a red storm full of gogogopushpushPUSH—

66

Chris felt his mind try to push back, run away. But he could only stare, frozen. Petrified.

Lena was skeletal, all sharp angles and tented skin. Sunken in their sockets, her dull eyes were smudged with hollows the color of old coffee. Except for the scarf, her clothes were torn, filthy. Matted with forest rubbish, her thick hair was a tangle of dead leaves and broken twigs.

"Lena." Her name came in a wild, strangled choke. His heart suddenly kick-started in a chest that felt too narrow, his lungs squeezed between iron walls. "Wh-where . . . H-how . . ."

She said nothing, and for a split second, he thought, *She's not real. This is a trick. You feel guilty, that's—*

Then his eyes—the only working parts of him, it seemed—hooked on the bright lime-green scarf. *Oh God.* His head ballooned with horror. *The last time I saw that was the night we stayed in that school, when the Changed came.* Chris had stolen Lena's scarf and deliberately placed it in a pile of bodies. *Because I wasn't sure what was happening to her.* He remembered how his stomach had bottomed out when that boy, a Changed, wrapped Lena's scarf around his neck. But now Lena *had* her scarf and that meant . . .

"W-w-wait." He tried to step back, but his feet wouldn't budge. "L-Lena . . ."

With no sound at all, she came at him, a blur of clawed hands and tee—

"No!" Flailing, he scrambled bolt upright, thrashing his way off the bed, thumping to the floor hard enough to rattle the windows. Gasping, he sprawled on his back. His chest was drenched; his hair clung to his scalp.

"Relax, it was a dream," he said to the ceiling. He armed clammy sweat from his forehead. "Just a dream."

God, but so real, like the nightmares. His eyes crawled to the nightstand clock. Only five minutes had passed. Except for the clock, the house was dead quiet.

Dozed off. Pushing to a sit, he propped himself on his hands. "Why do I keep dreaming about you, Lena?" he whispered. This was going to eat him alive if he wasn't careful. Groaning, he rolled to hands and knees, then got a leg under, pushed to his feet, and staggered to the south window. The frozen pond was a golden oval. A long rectangle of blue-black shadow cast by the house stretched toward the far barn. The corral was empty, all the cows probably inside for the afternoon milking.

"Stop feeling sorry for yourself, Chris. Take a chance like you did with Alex. Stop hiding," he said to the room. He palmed chill glass. "For God's sake, you're not eight years old anymore. Tell Hannah or Isaac about Lena and Alex, but tell *someone*. Just do it. If they understand, they understand. If they don't . . ." Well, they wouldn't kill him to protect themselves, would they? His forehead crinkled with sudden disquiet. No, that was crazy. Would *he*, if the situations were reversed?

"No," he said. He'd give a person like him some supplies, then blindfold and lead him far away, point him in the right direction, and wish him luck. If Hannah and Jayden were smart, they'd move and never give him the chance to retrace his steps. Leaving all they'd built up would be hard, but they were strong, tight. They'd manage.

First chance he got, he should leave. There was nothing more he could do here, or discover. No army of willing children either. If that was Jess's plan, then she was insane. These were only kids, trying to survive. He couldn't force them to come back, wouldn't even ask.

As for the rest—all those secrets—okay, now he knew. Yay. And so what? The only unanswered question was whether the people in Rule suspected what Peter and the Council were up to and just kept their mouths shut. Did he really *care* enough to risk going back to dismantle the Zone, take on the Council?

"Maybe so." But not for them. *The kids Peter and I brought back; they didn't have a say. You can't let them grow up in the shadow of that. What kind of people will they be in the end?* Of all people, he should understand what it was like to grow up with ghosts and blood that never washed away.

His stomach picked that moment to grumble, an incongruous sound that made him laugh. He ought to eat up. This might be his last good meal for a long time. Just as he turned from the window, his eyes hooked on a very slight shift in the light, some dark slink out of the corner of his eye. He shot a quick but offhand glance, more from habit than anything else.

Two boys—Jayden and Connor, he thought—hurried over the snow toward the barn. *Oh* was all the thought he gave them, because he was preoccupied, focused on food and how to break the news about Lena and Alex before heading back to Rule. South was best, a straight shot that wouldn't take him but four days on foot. Three, if he hustled. Hunter said they had Nathan's gear. A lucky break. He could listen in with the radio, figure the best way to slip into the village without getting his head blown off.

The stew was stone-cold, the glutinous sauce clinging to chunks of potato and carrot and venison. He shoveled in a mouthful. The meat tasted a bit musty, gamy, and it was tough. Probably an older buck, or Jayden might not have dropped it right away. Peter once said that the longer a deer ran after it was shot, the gamier it tasted because of the acid buildup in—

"Muscle," he said out loud, around stew. *Wait a minute. What did I just see?* Leaning back, he carefully replaced his spoon in the bowl, replayed the view from his window. Two boys, heading for the barn. And this was a problem because?

"Because"—he swallowed—"they were hunting." *So if Jayden and Connor were hunting and checking traplines* . . . "Where's the game?" he said to his room. "Well, they might not have bagged anything, right? Everyone has bad days."

But hadn't Hannah said that Jayden *never* came back until he'd gotten something; that he always pushed the envelope and this scared the hell out of her?

Then Chris realized what he hadn't seen.

"Oh shit." His chair toppled as he darted back for the window. "It's not only that they don't have game. They don't have *guns.*"

The boys were much closer to that far barn now. No guns. No horses. No game—but that was because they were still *on* the hunt.

And instead of only two Changed, now . . . there were ten.

67

"Go, go, go." Alex could hear herself now, but the sound was tiny in her mouth, the red storm still huge in her mind. "Push, push," she said, unseeing, the words falling off her tongue. "Push push push. Go, go after them, go faster, go—"

A jolt of pain raced up her right thigh. Grunting, she hissed out a breath as she felt whatever had grabbed the monster in her head suddenly let go. She looked up to see Darth, who was just winding up for another kick.

"Stop, Darth, stop," she said, laboring to her feet. "I'm getting up, okay?" Yet, for once, she was almost glad to see him. *God, what the hell* was *all that?* She put an absent hand to an itch on her upper lip, then felt her thoughts stutter as her eyes fell first to her glove and then jumped to the step. Red spiders spattered the snow. *Oh no.* A clot of fear wedged in her chest. The last time she'd had nosebleeds, the monster had chewed up enough real estate to double in size. Maybe the red storm, that *pushpushpush*, was nothing other than the monster, now stronger and bigger, ripping up her brain.

So maybe that's what happened just now. The monster's developed to the point where it can do this . . . this . . . Well, whatever had just happened. She didn't even know what she could call it.

Darth nudged her again, this time with the business end of the rifle. "Yeah, yeah," she said, snuffling back blood. As she began trudging across the cut to the driveway, however, Darth moved on ahead again and she was able to flick a quick look toward the clutch of low cedar. At first, she thought the wolfdog was gone, but then spotted it well back, mostly hidden in the dense shadows beneath a blue spruce. *And how weird is that?* Darth didn't seem to notice or care about this animal. With those carcasses standing as ritual sentinels here and Wolf's cowl, Darth must have known the animal was there. Unless this was only Wolf's peculiar little fetish, his spirit guide or whatever, that Darth and the others put up with.

She turned her thoughts back over what she'd just experienced. What would she call that? A mind-jump? Or someone else dropping in? Both? *Think, Alex, how did it start?* She'd been with the wolfdog . . . but no, that wasn't *quite* right. The mind-jump had happened when she *relaxed* to coax the animal closer. She'd let down her guard, and then either her monster got out, or something—someone—grabbed it. Which meant what, exactly?

Her monster always woke up when Wolf was around. So Wolf could be on his way back, and she'd gotten a kind of subliminal whiff of him, one she hadn't really noticed or paid attention to because she was so used to the Changed. That was possible. She had no idea what the range of her spidey-sense might be, and it was probably dependent on the wind, which was relatively still at the moment. *But Wolf might be nearby.* One eye on Darth, she slowed and sampled the air, letting it whisk over her tongue. All she got, however, was the copper of her blood, pine, snow, the evanescent coil of the wolfdog. No Wolf.

Okay, scratch that idea. *Unless Wolf's on his way back and the monster knows this somehow.* Yeah, but how would that work? *Maybe the same way you got a premonition about someone and then your cell would ring.* Which would mean that her monster was syncing up in some funky way with Wolf?

"Well, honey, I hope that's not it." Her breath rose in a tangle of mist that the breeze picked apart. *But what did I see? What was that?*

Turning away from the house, she stared back down the hill at the lake. Just couldn't put her finger on—

"Wait a minute." She squinted against the yellow glare bouncing up from unbroken snow over icy water. *I saw this.* A feeling of unreality swept through her. *It's not the* same *perspective, but if that* was *the lake* . . . "During the mind-jump, I saw the lake on my left. So that means I was coming from the west." Her eyes widened. *And I saw three kids, way ahead, running away* . . .

"No, that's not quite right. Push-push-push," she whispered, her eyes watering against the light. "Go-go-go." What did that mean? "Think it through, Alex, come on."

First, she and the monster had jumped—no, no, been *pulled*—into someone, a boy. A Changed, brimming with the single-minded urgency and intensity of a pursuit. He'd been with that red storm, the *push-push go-go.* There'd been someone else, too, screaming: *Let me go-go-go.*

But then her perspective had shifted. *I jumped* ahead *and into someone else, another boy.* The feeling she'd gotten *then* was also different: not only the *push-push go-go* but a sense of being *driven* and *pushed* after two . . . no, three other Changed the way old-style cowboys might herd cattle. Two she'd seen pretty clearly: that lanky kid with the wild hair and a shorter, smaller . . .

"Oh my God," she breathed. *Alex, you idiot. That was* Marley, *which means the smaller kid has to be Ernie.* "And that means those other Changed are *all* chasing—"

The afternoon cracked open with a shot.

68

"Hannah!" Chris beat the window with his fist. Below, on the snow and now much closer to the barn, the Changed were splitting up, five right, five left. *Coming at them from both sides.* He slammed the thick, double-paned glass again. "Hannah, *Hannah!*"

Stupid, useless, what are you doing? He had to get out of the room. His fingers fumbled with the window latch, but it wouldn't budge, and a second later, when he saw the slot for a key, he understood why. "A lock?" Whoever had built this room *really* didn't want anyone getting out. So, either break the window and clamber down that trellis, or kick open his door. Neither was great, but the window would be faster.

Scraping up his chair, Chris grabbed the legs, wound up, and swung. He felt the impact in his wrists as the high split-rail back banged glass before bouncing back. The panes were seamed with a sudden silver tracery of cracks, like a psychotic spider's web. Roaring in frustration, he swung again. This time the panes shattered with a tremendous *crash*, the chair's ears and top rail smashing through. Whipping up cloth napkins Hannah had used to cover his food, he wrapped his fists, knocked hanging daggers out of the way, and bellowed: "*Hannah!* Hannah, look out, look out! Isaac, *Isaac!*"

Across the snow, he saw that steady, deadly stream of Changed suddenly come to a dead stop. They were too far away for him to make out faces, but he could see when they twisted to look back at the house. Good, *good*! He'd slowed them down, at least for a second. Cupping his hands, he screamed: "Hannah, *Hann*—"

The barn's west door suddenly swung open. A head appeared, a froth of white above broad shoulders. "*Isaac!*" Chris bawled. "Barricade the doors! There are ten, there are *ten*!"

The old man's head jerked back as the barn door snapped shut hard enough for Chris to hear the faint clap and then its echo. *Okay.* He'd warned them. Now to help them. Crossing to the door, he hesitated, studying the jamb, that lock. *God, a dead bolt?* Whatever. *Just do it.* Backing up, he aimed his right shoulder, grabbed his right arm with his left, then charged. He hit the door hard enough to feel the impact in his teeth. His shoulder let out a bark of pain. The door, solid oak and stout, shivered, but there was no splinter or scream of wood. He hammered the door again, and a third time, a grunt jumping past his teeth. By the fourth time, the bark in his shoulder was a roar, and still the door held tight.

"*Damn* it." Cold air gushed through the shattered window. His puffing breaths plumed as he planted his fists on his hips and tried thinking past the ache in his shoulder. *Maybe have to climb out the window after all.* That was when he noticed what he should have seen at the very beginning. This door locked from the outside but swung *in*.

"Hinges." He spun back to the table. Hannah hadn't given him a knife or fork, but . . . "There is no spoon," he said, giddily, sweeping that up along with one of Hannah's books. The spoon was heavy stainless steel and would break before it would bend. Wedging the handle under the hinge pin's flattop, he beat it with the book's spine. To his surprise, the pin let out a metallic *screak* after only a few blows and jumped a half inch from the knuckle. "Come on," he grunted, beating the spoon. The pin hitched another half inch. "Come on, come—"

The unmistakable crackle of gunfire came through the broken window. He froze, heart thumping. Another shot. The distant bawl of cattle and bray of horses.

Shit. "Got to get out," he said, using his fingers to pry the pin the rest of the way. The hinge uncoupled, and now he could see a gap between the top rail and frame. *One more, then I can just tear it down.* Dropping to a crouch, he braced his shoulder against the jamb, rocked the now nicked handle beneath the head of the middle pin. This time, there was more resistance from the weight of the door. His left hand ached from his death grip around the spoon; his right wrist was throbbing. The spoon had punched and then cut a crescent moon through the book's clothbound cover and a quarter inch of pages. *Thank God it wasn't a paperback*—and then he wondered if he wasn't getting just a little hysterical. More spackles and muted pops of gunfire, and now he was talking to the pin: "Let go, let go, let—"

Shooting straight up from the middle hinge, the pin popped free to clatter to the floor. Shoving the spoon into a back pocket, Chris flung the book aside, then wrapped his hands around the edge of the door and put his weight into it. The butt hinge cried in a long, high squall before giving way all at once. Raking the door aside, he bulled into the hall.

His room was at one end. Two doors on his right, one on his left, and, a little beyond that, a short banister marking the head of the stairs. Wheeling around the newel post, he pounded downstairs. Through pebbled glass sidelights on either side of the front door, he could see a huge porch he hadn't known was there because his room was at the back of the house. To his left was an enormous front room with several long benches that looked like some kind of meeting room. He spotted a swinging door at the far end. Jess's house had a door just like that, between the kitchen and parlor.

Grab a knife. Sprinting across the front room, he straight-armed the push plate, banging the door aside. *Maybe a poker from the woodstove.*

The kitchen was on the southeast corner of the house, same as Chris's room, and already going thick with shadows. Directly ahead were eight chairs ranged around the long oval of a butcher block pedestal table, draped with a light blue tablecloth and set for a meal, probably a late dinner for Jayden and Connor. An ornate, old-fashioned kerosene wick lantern with a frosted shade and green glass base stood in the center. To the right was a black cast-iron cookstove on a square of raised red block, with a box of oak splits, a pail for ash, a brush, and shovel. On the stove, a saucepan steamed. Three iron pots and two large skillets dangled from a potrack. Beyond the kitchen table were oak cupboards; a butcher block bristled with knives. The way out was a door with floral chintz to the left of an old-fashioned refrigerator.

Then he registered what he hadn't a split second before. The room wasn't toasty warm and it wasn't freezing. But there was a lingering raft of cold air, as if someone had just gone out—

Or come in.

That also was when he noticed how the flowery curtains over that kitchen door . . . still swayed. Not a lot, but enough.

It dawned on him then. The kitchen was right below his room. Whenever Hannah worked in here, he heard her. So when he'd shouted his warning, he'd shown the Changed exactly where, in which corner of the house, they should start looking.

A small shuffle.

Right behind him.

69

Rifle. Alex knew from that distinctive whipcrack. *Close, coming from the west.* Before the first echoes had died, she was pelting up the hill. "Penny, get in the house, get in the house!"

The smell was rolling from the woods, too: not only that familiar scent of cool shadows but a rancid fug of desperation. *It's Wolf, close enough to smell now.* Wolf was in trouble, maybe hurt. She felt herself reaching out to him before she even realized what she was doing—and deep in her brain, the monster again shuddered to life, her thoughts slipping sideways. In an instant, she was both in her body and elsewhere, seeing through Wolf's eyes: tangy fear in her mouth, sour sweat on her chest. Ahead, the house was coming together out of the trees, light winking off windows like beacons. Something heavy, the sack, tried to slip off her shoulder—

Only it's not me. Her head was huge. Yet everything that *was* her felt very far away, like Alice shooting up after nibbling that *Eat Me* cake. Alex was in here and out there, *with* Wolf.

The air crackled with more gunfire. The sound socked her back into her own head. *They're heading straight for us.* Her stomach double-clutched with dread. *Move, move, move!*

She sprinted for the house. Ahead, Penny and Bert were just scuttling inside, though Penny was awkward, slow. Darth grabbed the girl's arm and reeled her in. As Alex tore up the last few steps, the big boy clamped a hand the size of a ham on her shoulder and heaved her the final ten feet. She gave a startled yelp as she hurtled past the threshold to crash onto hardwood.

"Wait!" Scrambling up, Alex wedged herself between the door and jamb before Darth could slam it shut. He might not understand, but speech was all she had. Even Darth would get her meaning. "They're almost here! Those shots are close. Give Wolf a chance!" She could tell he didn't want to do it, smell it fuming through his pores, but his arm relaxed.

A minute, maybe more like thirty seconds. She tossed a wild glance around the room, trying to figure out the best cover. This great room was sparsely furnished: fireplace and woodstove on a brick pedestal to the left, leather couch and two upholstered armchairs on an oval rug in the center to catch the view from that big picture window. Not enough to really barricade the door, and trying to take cover in this great room would be suicidal. That sofa wouldn't stop a spitball. With that picture window, they'd be like fish in an aquarium.

Her eyes flitted past Penny, who'd retreated behind a long breakfast bar on which Alex had stashed the camp stove, Coleman lantern, and spare fuel canisters. The girl had the right idea. The kitchen was further back, and that window over the sink gave them a way out. Topple the refrigerator, and she could take cover there.

Second best would be up those stairs at the extreme right, which emptied into an open loft and then a short hall, down which was a bathroom and two bedrooms, one right, one left. Easier to defend, but just as easy to get themselves trapped.

Kitchen, then. It was closer and she liked the look of that back window more and more. Without a weapon, she couldn't help defend the house anyway. She had a brief moment to wonder why she would help them altogether and then thought, *Got a better chance* with *Wolf than the guys after him.*

Steaming past Bert, who clutched a twelve-gauge but was otherwise rooted to the spot, she dashed into the kitchen. There was a freestanding refrigerator on the left, an old retro model, aqua and white with a chrome handle. She'd already searched inside and found only four toxic eggs and a gray-green jungle fuzz that the jar claimed once was mayonnaise. Now, squirming into the gap between the wall and fridge, she braced her back, tucked her knees, planted her feet, and gave the fridge a hard shove. The refrigerator lurched and then toppled, slamming down with a thunderous crash. From deep in its metal guts came the smash of glass and clang of shelves; a second later, the gassy, fecal gag of fungus and gooey dead chick.

"Penny, over here!" Springing for the breakfast bar, she grabbed the girl's wrist. With a startled *eep*, Penny tried twisting away. "Stop it!" Alex panted, hauling the thrashing Penny the way she would a stubborn toddler. "You want to get shot? Get behind the refrigerator! Get—"

From across the room came the shriek of hinges. Marley blew through the front door on a blast of wintry air and a swirl of dreads. Swiveling, he socked his rifle home and got off another shot as Darth also opened up against the *spak* and crackle of more weapons' fire.

Wolf, where's Wolf? "Get down!" Shoving Penny behind the refrigerator, she ducked back into the great room. She heard the *pock* as a slug drilled into the heavy oak door and showered splinters. "Marley! Where's—"

A second later and to her horror, she had her answer as the boys blundered up the steps. A lumpy sack hung over Wolf's left shoulder. His right arm was wrapped around Ernie. As the two staggered inside on a fresh fusillade of snaps, the drone of bullets whirring overhead, she got a good look. Wolf's face was whiter than bleached linen.

And covered in blood.

70

Chris didn't turn. He barely thought. Maybe his mind had already ticked through the math and realized that facing whatever lay behind would only waste time—or make him freeze.

Chris dodged right. Out of his left ear, he heard a quick inhale, the sudden stomp of a boot; sensed something rushing in from the side. A hand whisked through his hair. Ducking, Chris raked the first chair he came to, flinging it without turning around. He heard the clatter of wood on the floor and then the stutter of boots as whatever was back there bumbled into the chair. But whoever—whatever—it was didn't fall. A second later, a huge hand snatched at his neck, got a fistful of shirt collar and the tight silk thermal underneath, and twisted.

Suddenly, his breath was gone. His heart began to pound as his vision reddened, first with panic and then lack of air. Flailing like a fish hopelessly snagged on a line it could not break, he got his hands up, but the silk thermal was so tight, he couldn't hook his fingers. His flannel shirt ripped; buttons popped free, pattering to the floor like jumping beans. Yet the strong silk weave only grew tauter and tighter. Whatever held him was shaking him now, like a puppet. Chris heard, but only dimly, the thump and thud of his boots skating over the floor. His knees buckled; Chris felt himself falling; felt the impact of the table against his forehead as he pitched forward. Something, a lot of somethings, bounced to the floor and smashed. Plates, a glass . . . Chris didn't know. Although his hips and legs were on the floor, his chest wasn't flat. The hardwood was still a half foot from his nose because the Changed was holding him up by that noose of silk, suspending his head and chest to allow gravity to do its thing. The Changed would let Chris's own weight kill him, bit by bit.

What happened next was an accident.

Chris's right hand closed over something. He registered that it was sharp, and his last chance.

Chris's fingers clutched that dagger of glass, and struck.

71

"No!" Squirting past Bert, Alex made a diving grab for Wolf as Darth and Marley muscled the door closed. Splashes of blood painted Wolf's face and hands and the wolf skin knotted around his neck. That lumpy sack he'd slung over his shoulder was sodden.

No. For one second—a single terrified moment—her stupid, stupid heart turned over. *No, you can't die, Wolf, you can't die!*

Then she realized that the blood wasn't his.

Ernie's face was gray, his lips dusky. To either side of his piggy little nose, his small pellet-gray eyes rolled. His hands clutched his soupy middle. From the strong stink of iron and the liquid slop as Wolf tore open the boy's jacket, she already had a pretty good idea of just how bad this was.

Ernie's abdomen was awash in gore. Some had already clotted into grape-jelly goo. Most of it was only tacky and a lot of it fresh. That was because the rips in his abdomen were ragged, wicked, and very deep: gaping wounds that began just beneath his left rib cage to slash through skin and belly fat and muscle. Bluing bags of wormy intestines bulged from three of the tears. The smell was gagging, round and thick and fecal. Eyeing the slow eel of a length of intestine, Alex saw how it was already beginning to bloat. She felt the knot in the pit of her gut try to *urp* its way into her throat.

Probably hooked him first, then ripped. Teeth and nails, she guessed, which meant that Wolf's group had gotten into it with that pack on their heels. She watched as a bubbler of blood surged in a bright fresh fountain. Tagged an artery, for sure. Well, this kid wouldn't have to worry about getting an infection from all that torn bowel. The bowl of his belly was overflowing, his lips paling as his arteries emptied. A clammy sweat filmed his face and neck, and the boy was starting to shudder with shock.

Her eyes tracked to that lumpy, blood-soaked sack. From the smell, the body inside was a man's this time, and there was a lot of blood. But no guts. Which was wrong. From experience, she knew that Wolf and his crew liked liver, loved the heart, tolerated kidneys, didn't much care for tripe. Much more to the point, though, Wolf *never* butchered or sank his teeth into a kill until he and his crew made it to safety. She understood why. Once upon a time and in a different life, her dad always hung their food well off the ground in a bear bag, same as Wolf and his crew secured their supplies in that stuff sack. When you were on the trail, you didn't want unwelcome visitors making off with your stash. (Why more Changed *didn't* flock to Wolf's little hideaway, like ants to spilled sugar, she didn't know. They had to smell the meat. She sure did.)

But the body in that sack, this man, was in pieces. He was *missing* several more, and here was Ernie, ripped to shreds, and other Changed out for Wolf's blood.

"You *stole* it from them? They caught you *stealing*?" And she'd been *worried* he was hurt? Wolf was tight-lipped, ashen, but his dark eyes—*Chris's* eyes—blazed. Bert, Ernie's brother, was hustling across the great room with his shotgun in one hand and her medic's pack swinging from the other. From the corner of her eye, she saw Darth lurch from the door, heading past the window for the far side of the room in an awkward crouch. For a fraction of a second, she almost bawled, *Get down, you idiot!* Darth would be as tempting a target as a metal duck in a midway: *Three hits, and the little lady gets a stuffed pig.*

Instead, she snatched her medic's pack from Bert and shouted, "Wolf, what do you expect me to do? I can't fix—"

The picture window imploded in an enormous, glassy splash. Darth's head was there one instant and red mist the next. Gasping, Alex ducked as fléchettes of razor glass whizzed overhead. An instant later, someone let out a choking screech. She jerked her head around and saw Bert's hands flying for his face. A splinter of glass, as long as her pinky, juddered from the ruin of his right socket. Another jagged dagger had driven into the soft underbelly of his jaw.

"Bert!" Horrified, she was pushing Wolf aside even as her last snippet of common sense clamored: *Get down, stay down!* She started for the boy. "Bert, Bert, don't touch it, don't—"

Bert let go of another blubbering shriek—and his shotgun.

She saw the disaster unfold in slo-mo: the jets of Bert's blood dividing into individual drops, the flash and shiver of glass, even the shotgun spiraling in a strange arabesque. Then time sped up; the eye of the barrel was looking at her, and her brain was shrieking, *Down, get down!*

A fraction of a second too late.

The shotgun hit just as something crashed into her and knocked her flat. Wolf covered her up as the shotgun roared a thunderous *ba-ROOM!* The slug *brrred* over Wolf's head, trailing hot brass and burnt powder before smashing into drywall with a heavy *thunk*. More shots jetted through the shattered window. Craning past Wolf's shoulder, she saw Bert's body jitter in a spastic little dance, then drop, face-first. Even with the cottony buzz in her ears, she heard the crunch as the glass dagger punched bone and then brain. Bert's arms and legs shot straight out, like those of a little kid yelling *surprise*, then went limp.

At the window, Marley was springing up and down, firing wild over the sill. From the *pock-pock* of return fire and *spangs* as bullets ricocheted off the cast-iron woodstove, she didn't think he hit much.

Got to hope those sparks don't ignite all that pine. Fire's the last thing we need. Ernie was a waxen doll in a blood lake. In the kitchen, Penny was screaming.

"You have to get her out." She was still pinned under Wolf, their faces only inches apart, his wolf skin so close she smelled the musty tang of the animal that had once worn it. She read his panic, smelled the sizzle of fear on his skin. If she could only get across her meaning! For a moment, she thought, *Alex, relax; let the monster out; let it help you.* She roped back the impulse. That *would* be insane. Instead, she put her hands on Wolf's shoulders and grabbed his eyes with her own. "Give me a gun, Wolf. Let me help—"

There was another huge *ka-BANG*, a flash of orange light as something exploded outside. A second later, a cyclone of pulverized earth and superheated air blasted through the ruined window, knocking Marley off his feet. The room was suddenly so hot, *scorching,* Alex felt the burn in her throat and lungs. Above her, Wolf's body went rigid, his face tightening in a pained grimace. The air inside and out dripped with sounds and smells and sensations: the peppery sting of spent explosives, an isolated scream from beyond the window, the mucky rain of smoking globs of quivering flesh, the stutter of weapons fire.

Then there was a silence, as if time had decided to take a very deep breath . . . and that was when Alex remembered what she had forgotten, because, now, she felt the sudden flare in the center of her brain: *Go-go. Push-push.*

The red storm—that strange mind—was here.

72

For three seconds, all Chris knew was he was facedown, on the floor, hacking and trying to breathe through a throat that felt as if a boot had planted itself on his windpipe and ground it to pulp. Blood from the rip on his forehead was dripping into his eyes and coursing down his cheeks. His mouth was coppery from where he'd bitten himself, and his right hand was slick, too, the fingers beginning to burn. Over the thin, airy shrieks whistling in and out of his throat, he could hear a guttural *awww, awww.* Not coming from him, though. Blinking against blood, he managed to turn his head—and felt his heart try to fail.

Propped against a far wall was a boy, glittery-eyed, shaggy. A giant. Chris was tall, just an inch shy of six feet, but this kid had him beat by at least four. The kid was big as a barrel, and most of that was muscle. Someone or something had gotten to the kid, though. Huge gashes scored most of the Changed's face and oozed pus. His lower lip was ripped in two, the flaps drooping to expose dusky blue gums and stained teeth.

The boy's hands were clapped to his right thigh. A triangle of smeary glass glimmered weakly in the thinning light, and blood was dripping to the floor. As Chris watched, the boy opened his ruined mouth and bawled again: *"Awwww."*

Got to move. Chest shuddering with every tortured breath, he struggled out of his ruined flannel, then tugged off the thermal.

He'd cut his right hand on that glass dagger, but the fingers worked. Staggering to his feet, he tried a step, slipped, clutched the table for balance. Over the drum of his heart, he heard the stomp of a boot as the boy pushed from the wall.

Oh God. Chris turned, his hands convulsing as he swayed. If not for the table propping him up, his knees might have given way again. For a split second, Chris's mind blanked. He forgot that he wanted to fight. He was trapped, weaponless, already hurt. Less than a minute ago, he'd been as close to death as when Hannah's poison oiled over his brain. Everything he might be able to use as a weapon—pots, pans, those knives—was behind him, miles away. So he could only watch the boy, this monster, totter toward him. This was the nightmare from his memory and fever dreams of Peter and Lena, and a lifetime spent awakening to find a father reeking of booze and staring down at Chris with hate. Of reading what was behind his father's red-rimmed eyes: *I'll be safe only when you're dead.*

Fight. Groping, Chris's hand closed over a plate. He whipped it, fast, in a Frisbee throw. The boy saw it coming and batted the dish away, but Chris had already scraped up a glass, another dish, a saucer, tossing everything he could get his hands on, listening to the crash, hearing the crunch, trying to work his way around the table. The Changed just kept coming, as inexorable as fate. Despite the boy's obvious pain, Chris also thought the kid was actually enjoying this. Maybe the kid was looking forward to some payback. Tear out a chunk with his teeth, hurt Chris pretty bad, but then set him loose: *Go on, little Chris. Run. Bleed. See how far you get.*

As if finally tiring of the game—maybe he was fed up with swatting away dishes, and that thigh *had* to hurt—the Changed boy grabbed the tablecloth and yanked. With a yelp of surprise, Chris danced out of the way as dishes and cutlery slithered to the floor in a splintery smash. The lamp's green glass fuel base burst, releasing a gagging stink of kerosene that made Chris's battered throat double-clutch.

Sweeping up a chair, the boy hurled it the way a basketball player pops that fast bullet of a pass. The kid's aim was perfect, the chair growing huge in his face. Startled, Chris had no time to duck. The boy's chair whacked his chest. Stunned, Chris stumbled and then came down on his back in a puddle of kerosene.

Get up, get up! Retching against fumes, he kicked free of the chair. Twisting, he tried to roll, get his feet under him, scramble out of the way. From the corner of his eye, he saw the boy's knee cock and then the kick coming. Dropping flat, Chris heard the boot whiz over his head. As he rolled to his right to get under the table, Chris felt the boy clamp onto his left ankle. Frantic, Chris wrapped his hands around the butcher block's heavy center pedestal for leverage, then kicked back with his right. His boot connected with a satisfying *thunk*, followed a second later by a heavy grunt. As the boy's grip slackened, Chris scrambled under the rest of the way, set his feet, and squirted out the opposite side. The woodstove was in front of him and now just to his right—and he spotted the weapon he needed. If he only had time . . .

Whirling, Chris got his hands under the heavy table, pulled straight up, and then pushed as hard as he could. The table toppled with a gigantic bang. The Changed only dodged to his right, but that was all Chris wanted: just to slow the kid down for another few seconds. As the boy barreled around the table, Chris's hands shot for the woodstove and the handle of that steaming saucepan. He let out a harsh bawl of pain as hot metal scorched his palms, but he willed himself not to let go; this was the only play he had. Still screaming, Chris loosed the pot in a savage backhand.

Both a gush of water just the near side of boiling and the heavy pan hit the Changed in the face. There was a hollow *chunk* as iron bounced against bone. A starburst of blood erupted on the boy's forehead. For a half second, the Changed boy went absolutely rigid—and then instead of a guttural *awww*, he let go of a long, high, girlish screech. Lurching backward in a clumsy wobble, the boy wallowed in a swirl of blue tablecloth and slick kerosene.

Bellowing, his hands shrieking with pain, Chris charged—not for the butcher block and its temptation of fine-edged steel, but for the hanging rack. Seizing a skillet, he wrenched it from its hook. Two feet away, the Changed was kneeling, fingers quaking over flesh that blazed a hot, boiled purple where it wasn't red with blood. Skillet in hand, Chris drove forward, already certain what needed doing, knowing nothing on earth would stop him. At the last second the Changed lifted his head, and Chris saw the left eye had gone as milky as boiled egg white.

From far away, another planet, came a shout, the clap of a door.

His name: "Chris! Chris, *wait!*"

73

"Get up, come on!" Shouldering Wolf aside, Alex squirmed out from under. A *hooshing* hum reverberated in her ears. The stink of cooking meat and burning hair was so heavy it was like sucking the char from a barbecue grill. Gobs of singed meat clung to Wolf's back and her hair.

Marley had been flattened. His nose, eyelids, and lips were gone. Fire had chewed his dreads to the scalp; his parka was melted to his chest. Where his face wasn't parboiled, the skin was black as briquettes. His teeth, insanely white, showed in a ghastly rictus.

"Easy!" A shout, muffled by the *hoosh* in her ears: the voice older, angry. Male. "You want to kill everyone in—"

Men? Were they the red storm, or working with it? *And what is that?* She felt her mind shuttle, the monster unsure what to do. *Even the monster doesn't know what this is.* At the same time, she could feel the pull, the temptation to let go and get lost in that thrumming surge that seemed to pulse with every beat of her heart: *push-push-push go-go-go.*

Dropping to a crouch, she scuttled toward the front of the house and risked a quick peep through the blasted rectangle of the ruined window. What had been a snow-mantled hill before was now a smoking crater: a sore of blackened earth and smoking remains. *Used some kind of grenade or bomb.* It was hard to tell how many bodies, because everything was in pieces: the stub of what looked like an elbow; a foot, minus four toes and half the sole; three-quarters of a blasted head teetering on the lip of the crater like a smashed Halloween pumpkin. Another Changed—lucky or unlucky, depending on your point of view—sprawled in a twisted tangle and a halo of blood spray.

What the hell? Whatever was going on here—and especially in light of the fact that there were *men* out here—this fight was over a whole lot more than who had dibs on what. Her eyes caught a flicker to the extreme left, the same direction from which Wolf and these dead Changed had come only five minutes before. Something white was darting through deep green cedar and hemlock. She saw the oval of a face, but there was something wrong with it, and the smell . . .

Weird. They were Changed, no doubt about it, but beneath the characteristic boiled sewage reek was another odor: harshly chemical, completely artificial. It reminded her of the metallic odor of the chemo the doctors had used on the monster, especially cisplatin, a drug that had made her puke her guts out. But why would any Changed smell that way?

Behind these weird Changed and in the trees, she spotted other figures hanging back, got a snootful of fusty old people and horses. *Men . . . with the Changed? How can that be—*

Her monster suddenly quivered, straight-arming her mind with that strange shove—*go-go-go push-push-push*—as either it, or what was out there, tried snagging hold. *Oh no, you don't.* Reeling back, she snatched up a splinter of glass. Not understanding, Wolf reached for her wrist, but she whirled away. "No, let me just—" Grimacing, she jabbed the glass into her thigh, a quick in-out. She let out a yelp of pain, but there was an abrupt snap in the dark center of her brain as the monster recoiled. *Good enough.* Her mind cleared and she looked up into Wolf's eyes, which were wide with shock.

"Come on, Wolf," she panted, tossing aside the bloodied glass, "before we all die." Scooping up Bert's fallen shotgun and Ernie's rifle, Alex bounded into the kitchen, wheeling right to drop behind the granite counter. Racking the pump, she thought about shucking rounds to count how many shots she had left and decided against it. The last thing she needed was to crawl after fumbled slugs. Figure one already gone, four left. The bolt-action should have five, maybe six, depending on if Ernie had gotten off a couple rounds.

None of this makes sense. What do they want? First, one group chases down Wolf and his gang because they've stolen food. Then those guys get slammed by these weird Changed. Now they're storming the place, but why? Can't be just over food.

To her right, she saw Penny's terrified eyes over the lip of the refrigerator. All of a sudden, a lightbulb went off, illuminating a nasty thought she couldn't ignore. *My God.* "Don't tell me this is about you," she said to the girl.

There was a gigantic bang from the great room, followed by a squeal of stressed wood against metal as something hit the front door. The heavy oak shuddered but held. Given the sound, she thought whoever was out there had a sledgehammer or log.

The air again erupted with gunfire, but this time it was close, coming from inside. Wheeling back, she saw Wolf, still in the great room but behind the overturned leather sofa. Springing up, Wolf popped off another shot, then dropped as bullets whined in. Another *boom* at the door; beyond the blown-out window, she saw those weird Changed dart past. Dancing from cover, Wolf sidestepped left, trying to get a shot at whoever was breaking down the door, then threw himself flat as the air rattled with another burring round of gunfire. Bullets clanked the woodstove's flue. Miniature geysers of stone and white dust erupted from the walls and hearth as the bullets came, very fast and in bursts.

Automatic weapons? Wolf was still on the floor, facedown, and for a fraction of a second, her heart seized. "Wolf!" She saw the white flicker of his face as he looked her way. "Wolf, come on, you can't do—" Another stutter of gunfire at the same instant the door let out a huge *CRACK*. The wood blistered inward, like a boil about to rupture, and she was so busy looking at that, she only half-registered something moving into view at the broken picture window. Looking back, she saw Wolf, still on the floor, and a pair of gloved hands hooked over the ruined sill.

Trying to get inside. "Wolf!" Coming out from cover, Alex sprang past the counter, the shotgun already coming up. "Stay down, stay down!" She fired once, muzzle flash sheeting, the slug too high, but she saw those hands let go. More bullets came ripping through to clank the woodstove. One drilled into the hearth just over her head, sending a jet of stone splinters pecking at her hair and neck. Dropping, she scrambled forward on hands and knees over jags and debris, feeling the bite of glass and tear of stone and the wash of heat from the woodstove less than twenty feet away, the icy waterfall of air spilling over the blasted sill.

She swarmed over to Wolf. "Either upstairs or out the back," she said, "but we can't stay here." Neither option was great. If they blew out the kitchen window for an escape, they might as well take out an ad. So that left going upstairs: get to the bathroom, put Penny in the tub, and then she and Wolf could pick off whoever tried coming up.

We'll run out of ammunition first. She jumped her eyes from the stairs to the kitchen, skimming past the counter cluttered with the loot she'd found in the basement: camp stove, the lantern, propane. *Still, higher's bet—*

"Wait a minute." Her gaze zeroed in again on the camp stove. The propane. "Fire," she said out loud. Yes, it really might work. There was all this fresh pine. The chimney was heavy with char and creosote. This close to the hearth, the air tasted like a lump of coal. *Yes, but it's also crazy; we'll be barbecued.* But it was the only thing she could think of. Scurrying back to the counter, she shoveled the three propane canisters into her arms and darted back to dump them into the hearth along with the sticky pine Penny and Bert had brought in less than half an hour before.

Behind and from the kitchen came another glassy explosion, followed by a girl's shriek. "Penny!" Barreling into the kitchen, Alex waded over a river of broken glass from the shattered window above the sink. Bits of glass glinted from the girl's hair; blood dribbled from her scalp and down her cheeks. "Come on," Alex said, trying to tug the panicked girl to her feet. "Penny, come on, don't fight me, we're going—"

There was the whipcrack of a rifle shot, the drone of a slug over her head, followed by a loud, sharp scream. Gasping, she looked up, saw the business end of Wolf's rifle pointing her way, then jerked around just in time to see an old man in a hunter's winter camouflage clap a hand to his spurting face and tumble back from the window.

Storming the place back and front. A moment later, the air tingled with that resin pop and then Penny stopped struggling and broke from behind the refrigerator as Wolf dashed up from the great room to meet her. Clattering out of the kitchen, Alex pointed at the stairs: "Bathroom, bathroom!" Behind, she heard the squall of hinges and fatiguing wood and thought they had maybe ten seconds left.

As she turned to follow Wolf and Penny, she spotted her green canvas medic pack resting on the floor near the door where it had been blown in that first explosion. She gave it exactly a millisecond's thought, then bulleted across the room, snagged the pack in a one-handed grab, and wheeled back to blast up the stairs. Peeling right, she saw Wolf kick open the bathroom door, whip aside a shower curtain, and cram Penny into the tub.

Downstairs, Alex heard another smash of metal against wood, more shots. And voices. It took every ounce of willpower *not* to scurry after Wolf and Penny. *Just a few more seconds.* She felt Wolf moving up behind her, and then his hand on her arm as he tried to pull her out of his way. But his shot would have to be dead-on, and there wouldn't be time for another.

She looked at him. "I have something better than the rifle," she said, and then she was pulling the flare gun from the small of her back. She read in his face and smelled in his scent the shock of recognition, and understood: Wolf *knew* this gun.

Below, she heard the door burst open. Peering around the corner, she spied three of those weird Changed, in camo-whites and armed with what she thought were Mac-10s, fanning out in the great room. In the center of her head, she felt the muted thump: *go-go push-push.* Then she heard murmurs—voices—and spotted four old men moving in from the kitchen to meet them.

Okay, Dad. Crouching, poking the pistol between the banister rails, steadying the flare gun in both hands, she picked her spot. *Just like the target range.*

She pulled the trigger.

74

"Chris!" someone shouted. "Chris, wait, let me—"

But Chris didn't stop to look, didn't stop to think, didn't stop, couldn't stop, wouldn't. Roaring, he brought the skillet around like a batter, so hard and with so much force he felt his shoulders try to pop from their sockets. The Changed boy was still gawping up at Chris when the skillet connected—and the sound, already so deep in Chris's memory and his nightmares, became real again: a solid slam, the *clunk* of an ax biting into a tree trunk. Of a hammer cratering bone and brain. Of the flat of a cast-iron skillet smashing skull.

The boy's head whipped to the side. Over the clamor in his head, Chris heard the sharp crackle as the neck snapped.

Panting, blood painting his cheeks, Chris stood over the body as a voice boomed: *Go on, boy, hit him again, hit him, go on . . .* "Go on," he said in a voice not his own. "Go on, boy, hit him bloody, make him pay, you know you w-want . . . you kn-know . . ."

Then his knees buckled as the ground opened and Chris swooned into the dark and—

"Chris." A voice in his ear, and then a shake. "Wake up. Open your eyes."

"*Nooo.*" He was on the snow again, under the tiger-trap, in a pool of blood, and slowly dying, freezing to death. Everything hurt. He tried turning from the voice, but a hand hooked his chin. "I can't," he said. "It's too hard; it hurts too much to see."

"Stop this," the voice said. "Open your eyes."

"Why?" he asked, even as his lids creaked open. Of course, it was Jess, with her Medusa hair and black-mirror eyes: Chris in the right, Chris in the left. Or Simon and Simon, depending on how you looked at it. "Why is this up to me? What do you want? What good does it do me to see anything? I can't *change* what's already happened. I couldn't help Alex. I didn't help Lena. Peter wouldn't let me because he never told me."

"You refused to see."

"*Fine.*" Another bolt of pain grabbed his throat. "Leave me alone," he wheezed, thinly. "Please, Jess, why can't you let me alone? Why won't you let me die?"

"Someone will die. Someone must. Without blood, there is no forgiveness."

"*You're* dead. This is the Land of the Dead, and I'm having a dream, but I don't understand. I want to know what this means."

"Tell me your dream, and I will tell you the truth."

"And what is *that*?" A weak laugh dribbled out of his mouth with a trickle of blood. "What's truth?"

"What lives here"—she drew her fingers, cool and dry, over his forehead—"is not the same as what resides here." She placed a hand over his heart, and he cried out because her touch was electric, bright and awful. "Let go of the hammer, Chris. Forgive yourself. Forgive Peter."

"Why does that matter?" He licked blood from his lips. "I already said I understand."

"And that is why"—another electric finger to his chest, prodding a scream—"this hurts so much. The truth of the heart is the more fearsome to bear, because from love springs grief. Truth is in your mouth, on your tongue, in your blood. Let go of your anger, Chris. Let Peter, as you remember him, speak to you."

"He can't," Chris said. "He's dead."

"Call him back." Jess pressed a palm over his eyes, and now he was truly in the dark again. "Quickly, Chris. In your blindness and from grief, call in love and do it now before it's too late, before Peter is lost, before the light goes—"

"—out?"

"No, I think he's coming around. Chris?" A tap on his cheek. "Chris, wake up."

Chris faded back, aware first of the sharp nibs of broken plates under his legs, and then the wall against his back, and finally a hand cupping the back of his head.

"Chris." Jayden patted his cheek again. "Are you all right? Is this the only one? Where's everyone else? Where's—"

"*Hannah.*" His eyes snapped open. Everything rushed back, like water into an empty glass. "Isaac," he wheezed again, clutching Jayden's arm. "*Barn.*"

"What?" Jayden shot a glance at Connor, who was also crouched alongside. "What are you talking about? What about the barn?"

"*Guns.*" Shots carried, especially now that there was nothing—no cars, no planes, no machinery—to mask them. How long had he been out? "Didn't you *hear?*"

"We heard gunfire," Connor said. "But we were north. We couldn't tell where it was coming from. As we got closer, I actually thought it was coming from the east."

East. There was something important about that. "No. Hannah and Isaac are in the barn, and there were Changed headed that way."

"What?" Connor was genuinely skeptical. "They can't find us. They've never found us."

"No? Then what do you call *that?*" Chris said, jerking his head toward the dead giant with the misshapen skull lying in a puddle of kerosene and water dyed purple with blood. Gripping Jayden's forearms for balance, he struggled to his feet. "I counted ten. I broke out the window in my room. I know Isaac heard me and saw them. But we have to go. I heard shots, but if there aren't any *now* . . ."

"All right." Jayden's skin was glassy with dread, but his mouth set as he ripped off his parka. "Take this. I'm smaller than you, but . . ."

"This works." The cuffs of Jayden's parka ended well above his wrists, and his shoulders felt like he'd slipped on a straitjacket. He jockeyed the zipper and managed to yank it halfway. "This is fine."

"Okay." Jayden looked doubtful. "You're pretty messed up. Can you fight?"

"Yes." Swiping up a cloth napkin, Chris smeared blood from his forehead, then wrapped his bleeding palm. "But I need a gun." When Jayden hesitated, Chris snapped, "Damn it, Jayden, let me help."

"All right, all right. Outside, in my scabbard, I've got a spare rifle." Jayden jerked his head toward the door. "Come on."

"How do you want to do this?" Chris asked as they banged out of the kitchen and down the back steps. Three horses, one loaded with four bulky game bags, had been hastily tethered to the wrought iron railing. The kitchen faced east, and the sun was well behind them now. Overhead, thin clouds scudded across blue sky on a northerly breeze. To his right, all Chris saw of the farm's southern end was the mica gleam of the frozen pond. There was also a strange whooshing, like wind gushing through a tunnel, but he couldn't tell from which direction the sound came.

"I'm open to suggestion. It's not like we've had to fight these things the way you have." Jayden yanked a well-used, scoped Remington 798 from its scabbard. "Loaded. Didn't fire it once today. Here." He dipped a hand into a saddlebag and came out with a handful of bullets. "No one's shooting now, but—"

"Shh." Frowning, Chris cocked his head, then darted a look around. The whooshing was still there, but he could've sworn there was a tinkling sound that reminded him of the fight with the Changed boy. *Glass.* "Did you hear that? It sounded like something—"

"Breaking." Jayden nodded. "Yeah. I did." He craned to look back at the house. "Are you *sure* no one else is—"

"Hey. Jayden?" Connor had drifted to the house's southeast corner. "I think you . . . I think you guys better come here."

Jayden shot Chris a look, and then they were both running toward the younger boy. "What is it?" Jayden's voice was so tight, it cracked. "Is Han—"

Now that Chris was closer, he could see what he hadn't before, both because of his angle and the wind. If they'd gone out the front, or Jayden and Connor had returned even a little more to the west, they'd all have seen—and smelled it—right away. The mystery of why they'd both heard shattering glass was obvious, too.

The barn was on fire.

75

There was a very loud *kerack*, followed by an intensely bright burst of red muzzle flash, a pillow of acrid gray smoke as the flare streaked out of the pistol. The fusee smashed into the pile of pine and propane canisters with a *kebang*.

And nothing really amazing happened. No explosions or fireballs. An orange-yellow rose blossomed. But that was it, for a split second, enough time for Alex to think, *Shi—*

Then there was a pop, a gasping *hoosh* as if some giant had just been sucker punched. The propane ignited with a roar. The blast, an intense neon orange, ballooned; pine logs exploded in a shower of yellow sparks. Below, the three Changed and the four men stopped dead, then turned as if mesmerized by the fire, the flames washing their features of definition, their shadows like dancing spiders on the opposite wall. Alex heard a high howl, felt the sudden rush of cold air being sucked into the now-surging fire, and thought, *Oh jeez—*

"*Go!*" she screamed, just as a massive gout of orange flame jetted from the mouth of the hearth. The sound of the bathroom window breaking was lost in a massive explosion, like the concussion of a cannon. The chimney ruptured. A streaming pillar of fire blew out, instantly igniting the three Changed in white and the old men into shrieking, writhing human torches. There was a stuttering sparkle of bullets as their weapons and ammunition exploded. Chunks of stone and masonry flew in a shower of shrapnel. The air churned hot and bright. Flares swam up the walls and spilled over the floor. A blast of hot wind whipped her hair and she thought she might be screaming. She felt Wolf seize her by the scruff of the neck, and then he was hauling her down the hall and into the bathroom.

One end of a flimsy plastic shower curtain was tied to the shower head, while the tongue fluttered from the gaping window over which he'd draped his parka. Already out, Penny was braced on her hands, feet planted wide, inching over the shingles like a pregnant fiddler crab.

"I'm okay," Alex said, breathlessly. Her eardrums felt broken. "You go. Help her down. I'm right behind you." Now that she was up here, she wasn't sure, all of a sudden, whether this was such a hot idea. The ground still looked really far away, and this northwest patch of the porch was glittery with ice crystals. *Slip and I'll break my neck.* Standing in the tub, she watched Wolf spider down to Penny, then coax her to the edge of the porch. At her back, she could feel the heat build; heard a high, eerie howl over the locomotive churn of the fire. Above the sink, a mirrored medicine chest suddenly gave way with a watery *kersplash* into the porcelain basin. Beneath her feet, the tub shifted and shivered, and she realized then that the house was coming down.

Get out, get out of the house! Hooking the medic pack onto both shoulders, she grabbed onto the shower curtain and levered herself over the sill. Glass teeth bit her rump through Wolf's parka, but then she was out, right hand still fisted around the shower curtain, the heel of the left jammed onto shingles. Now that she was on the porch, she could feel the jitter and sway. Something was bellowing, roaring like a blast furnace. Craning over her left shoulder, she caught a glimpse of an orange-yellow sword of flame knifing from the chimney into the sky. To her right, flames curled through the shattered picture window to lick at the roof. For a horrible second, she was frozen in place, hypnotized by the dance and sputter. Any moment now, the house would collapse and she'd still be here, clinging to the shower curtain only to be yanked back like a yo-yo and buried under a fiery avalanche.

Another tinkling smash. *Let go of the curtain.* An orange geyser spumed from a bedroom window. *Alex, let go.* On the porch, she saw Wolf and Penny nearly at the edge, but jouncing as the house shook. *Let go, Alex. Move!* Her mind knew what to do, but her body was locked, paralyzed. *Come on, go, let go, let—*

There was another belching eruption, a guttering *ker-POW*. She saw Penny suddenly bounce, Wolf's hand flash for a grab. Something very big, a chunk of blackened cast iron, cannoned from the side of the house to shoot straight into the trees. An evergreen disintegrated into splinters. Beneath her, the house was tilting, the walls beginning to collapse, the porch crumbling. A second later, an enormous shock wave gushed up the stairs. A gigantic fist of heat smacked her shoulders and blew her out of the window. The torn shower curtain fluttering in her fist, she flew in a dizzying tumble, banging over the shingles, pinballing out of control. Screaming, she caught a glimpse of bright sky, black shingles, orange flames, and then lost all that as she smashed into Wolf—

And hurtled from the roof.

76

Chris, Jayden, and Connor raced over the snow. Belching like a coal-fired train, the barn exhaled great chuffs of gray and black smoke. As they neared, Chris heard the bellows of cows and shrieks of horses. The sheep were bawling, high and shrill, over the pop and crackle of the fire. All the snow piled on the roof and layered on the sills had melted, and he could hear the fire complain in hissing sizzles as orange tongues licked from shattered windows on the barn's north face. The hex signs were blistering, the colorful paint flaring blood-red with firelight.

"Which end are the lambing pens?" he shouted at Jayden.

"W-west!" Jayden panted. "Why?"

"Look at the windows!" Chris sucked air, then shouted, punching out the words through pants: "They're . . . they're all broken on the north and . . . and west! Safest way to get in . . ."

"East!" Connor's face glistened with sweat. "The cows . . . and horses . . ."

But Hannah and Isaac were with the lambs. Which was exactly where the fire must've started. All he knew about fire was what they'd practiced in school: get down where the good air was, keep your eyes on the kid in front of you, and crawl like hell. Fighting a fire was a whole other problem. This wouldn't spread because of the snow and cold, but it might be a while before the fire ran out of fuel.

"Look!" Jayden shouted, and pointed. But this time, he sounded joyous. "Look, *look!*"

The east door popped open, releasing a roiling pillar of black smoke. A second later, cows surged through, with a clot of bawling sheep on their heels. Two figures lurched out next, one broader, man-sized: Isaac, one hand wrapped around Hannah's upper arm. Hannah had something clutched in her arms, and as Chris dodged around milling animals, he saw that it was a still-glistening, newborn lamb, its skin streaked with soot and ash.

"You have to get the lambs, we need to get the lambs!" She was trying to shout, but her voice was a strangled croak. Her face was smudgy, and there was soot around her mouth.

"Are they still in the pens?" Jayden asked. A horse's braying shriek cut the air. "Where's Rob?"

"With the horses. They're still . . ."

"I'm on it." Having unwound his scarf, Connor balled the wool and dunked the garment into the cattle trough. "There are only three to get out."

"You have to get to the lambs," Hannah insisted.

"Do the best I can." Connor said, but Chris read the look he gave Jayden. Connor knotted his dripping scarf over his nose and mouth. "Give me your scarf, Hannah. I can use it for a horse."

"Yes." Dazed, Hannah tugged sooty wool from her neck. "But the lambs—"

"What about the Changed?" Chris asked.

She turned him a distracted look. "Dead. They came in so fast." She dragged a quivering hand over her streaming eyes. "If you hadn't warned us . . . I still don't understand how they found—" Her eyes flicked past Jayden and Chris, and widened. "Isaac . . . Isaac!"

Chris whirled just in time to see Isaac, who'd staggered to the far end of the corral, begin to sag. "I'm all right," the old man gasped as Chris and Jayden sprinted to his side. Isaac's lips were purple. He pressed a hand to his chest. "Just need to . . ." Isaac hacked out a foamy gobbet of thick mucus and black spit. "Have to get the . . . the horses . . . the *lambs* . . ."

"We'll take care of that. What we have to do is get you out of the cold and the smoke," Hannah said. Still cradling the lamb, she nevertheless looked calmer, as if taking care of Isaac gave her something else to focus on.

"The . . . the *lambs* . . . ," Isaac spat again as Jayden and Chris got him to his feet. "Should go . . . go in the house until . . . until we can . . ."

There was another shriek that could have been a faraway scream of a hawk but sounded much more like a horse, in trouble. But the direction was all wrong, not coming from the barn.

"You hear that?" Jayden asked.

"Yeah." Frowning, Chris scanned the farm. From this angle, he couldn't see Jayden and Connor's horses behind the house. Over his shoulder, he saw Rob appear with two horses. A few seconds later, Connor melted from the smoke with the third. "Jayden, you said you thought you heard shots coming from the east."

"But only after we heard a larger cluster from the north," Jayden said. "Two sets of shots."

"Me, too. That's what I—" Chris broke off at a series of short, sharp claps of sound. Not shots, though.

"Dogs?" Hannah asked.

"Yeah. Coming from the east. The lake." Chris looked at Jayden. "Ellie."

77

The ground rushed for her face. Twisting, Alex thudded in an awkward heap on her right side, a blow that drove the air from her lungs in a sickening grunt. She lay there a second, stunned, right shoulder a bellow of pain, the heavy medic pack like an anvil on her back. The air was alive with the crackle of flames and that chugging roar, a sound like the thunder of a runaway train. Rolling onto her left, she thrashed to hands and knees. The snow here was already melting to pools of icy slush. A short distance away, Wolf was on his stomach, pushing himself out of the water, coughing and spitting. Still gasping for breath, she swept her eyes right. A dazed Penny was there, her hair falling down around her face.

But it was what Alex saw down the hill that set a hook of new fear in her chest.

They'd landed next to the house, on the hill, but far enough out that she had a view of the lake and, especially, that dead-end road. Wolf and the others had come in from the west and so had their pursuers. She'd spotted horses before, ones that must belong to the men they'd just crisped. Those animals were still there, churning in a restless knot, struggling to snap their tethers and escape the fire.

Yet what stilled her heart was what was even now emerging from the trees: more men on horses. There were two kids as well. One was younger than the other, but both wore the same camo-whites and were wreathed in that weird chemotherapy stink. Of the two, the smell coming from the younger kid—a boy—was stronger.

Last of all, another old man slipped out of the woods. In contrast to the others, he wore black instead of hunter's winter camo, and rode a glossy jet-black gelding. As soon as he appeared, that red storm—*push-push go-go*—intensified.

She flattened, tried to think. They had to get moving. *Make a run for the trees. If we can get far enough back before they see us* . . . Where was Wolf's rifle? Her gaze strafed the snow, saw nothing, and she knew there was no time to search. Running probably wouldn't help. All their pursuers had to do was follow their tracks, but she was damned if she'd wait to be taken.

She could see the men making their way down the road. A few had dismounted, including the younger kid. The older kid was moving very awkwardly, though, and as she watched one of the men reach to steady the kid's horse, she saw why: the Changed's hands were tied. Also, unlike the smaller boy, this Changed's head was bare. His hair, golden as the sun, fell past his shoulders. Something familiar about him, too.

But what really rocked her back was the moment that golden Changed looked their way and let out a shout: "Penny! Simon! Don't run, don't *run!*"

Oh God. She felt the ice leak into her veins.

Peter.

78

"Stop it, *stop it!*" Ellie screamed a split second before her horse shrieked. The far shore was bright with late afternoon sun. So she had no trouble seeing the jet of blood jump from Bella's flank. The mare reared, pedaling air with her front hooves. "Leave Bella alone!"

"Ellie, no!" Still clutching the auger with one hand, Eli yanked her back. Both dogs were barking, and as Roc gathered himself to bolt for shore, Eli let go of her to make a snatching grab for his dog's collar. "They're trying to get us to come to them . . . Roc, no, *sit!*"

"But they're hurting Bella!" Her mare's screams were drilling into her brain. The horses were easy pickings: tethered to the trees and unable to do much but kick whenever the people-eaters got too close. As bad as it was that the people-eaters had showed up altogether, Ellie thought they'd leave the animals alone. Waste of energy when you could be going after nice juicy little girls and boys. But then, after she and Eli retreated even farther from shore, the people-eaters started in on the horses, hitting them with clubs and now *this*. . . . She watched in horror as her mare suddenly crashed to the snow. One people-eater cocked his arm again. Whatever they were using—a machete, she thought—flashed down in a gleaming blur. This time, Bella's screech turned suddenly watery. "We have to *do* something!"

"We can't." Eli swabbed sweat from his forehead. The boy's face was the color of a boiled beet. "We have to keep going."

"But they're going to *kill* her." Ellie couldn't stop the tears streaming over her cheeks: grief for her stupid, stubborn Bella. And terror, for them.

"There's nothing we can do. They'll probably go for my horse next." Eli's voice choked with rage. "Come on, Ellie. This was your idea. Hurry!"

"Okay, okay." Ellie brought her hand ax down in another fast, hard, two-fisted chop. The edge bit slush ice in a dull *chuck*. The snow beneath her feet turned gray as water welled up through the seam. "I'm almost done here. What about you?"

"Going fast as I can." The auger was a red blur, the blades spinning, Eli cranking furiously. He was sweating so much, steam curled from his hair. "Soon as I finish this one . . ."

Then we break the ice and hope like heck Hannah gets here soon. She chopped again, heard the splintery crack of ice shearing apart. Across the snow, from the too-distant shore, she heard Bella give another bawling shriek that sent her heart cramming up behind her teeth. She tossed another grim look. Bella was kicking but more feebly. The people-eaters milled around, maybe trying to decide what to do now that she and Eli *hadn't* come dashing to the rescue.

Hate you. She whacked the ice again. There were nine people-eaters—ten, if you counted the girl she'd seen at the death house. The people-eaters didn't have guns, a plus. On the other hand, Eli only had two shots left in his rifle, and her Savage was in its saddle scabbard. At first she thought a people-eater might grab it, but the rifle wasn't scoped. Or they might not know how to work it. Or maybe shooting at her and Eli didn't seem to be nearly as much people-eater doo-dah fun as killing a poor defenseless horse. She was furious and scared right down to her bones and thought, really, if she didn't end up getting eaten today, it would be a miracle.

Behind her, the whir of the auger changed to a gurgle of steel churning water. The steeply curved line of fresh holes were spaced so close they looked like a string of black pearls. She'd told Eli to bunch the holes on purpose so the water would bleed between the gaps. All it would take for her to break through completely was one or two good hard chops.

"Got it." Eli straightened, breathing hard, then cast a nervous glance at the jigsaw of float ice and the larger, wider crescent of black water beyond the end of the ice shelf. "That's five. Think that's—" His voice faded as he looked back toward shore. "Ellie."

She knew before she turned. Evidently tired of waiting, the people-eaters were spilling onto the ice. "Come on." Dipping into her pail, she fished out a stringer, looped the steel chain around her waist, and snapped the keeper to a clip. "Okay, hang onto me. I'll chop us away."

"Is this going to hold if you fall in?"

"Sure," she lied, giving Eli a strained, teary smile that she knew was all teeth. "I was going to try for walleye, and they're real big. But maybe we don't want to find out?"

"Yeah." Putting aside the auger, Eli spread his legs, bent his knees, looped the chain twice around his gloved fists, then nodded. "Go."

Leaning over the break, Ellie swung. This time, instead of a *sploosh*, there was a *crack*. She felt the difference immediately as the ice bobbed. "I got it, here we go, hang on!" Ellie sang.

Then she planted her foot against the far edge and shoved.

Bad move.

79

They had to move, fast.

"Wolf." Alex whirled away from Penny; from the man in black and his red storm; from Peter, who was neither wholly human nor Changed. "Come on, we have to—"

She stopped when she saw the tears. Face white as chalk, Wolf was sitting up, but she saw the way he grabbed that left ankle, and knew. "No. No no no." She floundered through slush to grab his arm. He was shivering with rage and pain. "Listen to me," she said. "It may not be as bad as you think. Come on, Wolf, you can do this. I'll help you. Once we get clear, I'll wrap or splint it. I've got plenty of supplies. But you have to get up, you have to—"

Wolf shook his head. They were close enough that when his scent became Chris's—not only cool mist but bittersweet—the shift and the meaning were unmistakable.

"Don't do this." Her eyes suddenly burned with furious tears. "Wolf, they'll kill you. They'll take Penny. But if we can fight . . ."

This time, when he shook his head, he also reached a tentative hand. For a split second, Alex almost pulled away, but then Wolf had cupped her wet cheek and there was no going back. The touch was seismic, not desire or want or even need now but something inexpressibly sad. His touch was the morning a week after her parents died, when her aunt stroked her hair: *I would give anything to bring them back for you.* In that instant, Alex had understood what it was to have a piece of you gutter, an inner fire go cold.

This, she had not expected. Wolf had touched her before, almost as a master comforts a pet. Yet every thinking being dreams. The one thing she'd never considered was that despite their transformation, some Changed—or maybe only the very few like Wolf—might truly understand what it was they'd lost. Some might even be just as desperate to get it back.

"What are you doing, Wolf, what are you *doing?*" she whispered, as his hand roamed, his fingers tracing an eyebrow, feathering over her forehead, pausing over her mouth. Over the roar of the fire, she heard the men coming; felt the fist of the red storm trying to batter its way into her brain; knew Peter had led those men here—*did they see me? did Peter recognize me?*—and that they would be up the hill in no time flat.

But she let all that ride. That could wait. Instead, she gave Wolf the luxury of a few seconds to remember who Simon was and what that boy had been.

Then, she ran.

80

What Ellie hadn't considered was the weight, or that there were now two people and two dogs crowded into a jagged, icy ellipse thinner in some spots than others, and slick, too.

All of a sudden, the ice floe tilted, dipping far enough for a watery tongue to tease her left knee. She swayed, visions of sliding right off their ice island—and into the lake—of the ice closing above her head and her drowning—swarming to the front of her horrified mind. Behind, she heard Eli gasp, and then the scrabbling scritch of dogs' nails over ice. A gasping *aaahhh* ballooned from her mouth as her center of gravity shifted, and their jagged ice island—a twelve-foot shard of unstable slush ice, thick in the middle, razor-thin at the margins—canted and rocked.

"Don't move, don't move," Eli chanted. He was crouched low, his legs visibly quivering with the strain of holding himself stable. "Give it a chance to settle down."

"Oh boy," Ellie said, not moving a muscle. "I don't know if this was a really good idea."

"Now you tell me." But the banter was gone from his voice, and she could hear the slight quake. The stringer chain around her middle tightened as Eli fetched up another coil. "Okay, Ellie, we're still tipping. You have to slide toward the center on your butt, okay? Don't even try to turn, and do it *really* slow. Think like a daddy longlegs."

"I hate spiders," she breathed. Crabbing as slowly as she could, she moved first one arm and then the opposite leg—a delicate, mincing one-two—then switched, always keeping three points of contact. Their raft bobbed and tilted, the ice listing first left and then right.

"You're doing great." Eli's voice was breathless. "Almost here . . . okay, stop. Stop moving. I'm right behind you. See?" He eased a hand on her shoulder.

"Yeah. Thanks." As she tried tucking her feet under so she could stand, the raft suddenly pitched right.

"Whoa, whoa, whoa!" Eli's fingers hooked her collar. The chain clattered as he cinched up. "Ellie, listen, you can't move—"

"So fast," she wheezed. "I know. Sorry." This might be the very *last* dumb idea she'd have in her whole stupid life. Rolling away from the people-eaters as slowly as she could, she got herself on hands and knees. Still crouching, Eli wrapped his hands around her forearms, and together, they pulled themselves upright as the raft pitched and yawed an inch to the left then to the right.

"If we stay in the center, we ought to be okay." Eli hadn't released his grip. They were so close together she could see his lips shiver as he tried on a lopsided grin. "Now what?"

"We wait for help. You got off those shots. Hannah had to hear." She injected a confidence she didn't feel. Those shots drifting from the direction of the farm had been their first indication that anything was wrong, and that had been a while ago. Someone should've remembered them by now. Unless they couldn't. *No, Ellie, stop it. They're okay; Hannah and Jayden and Chris are fine.* The alternative was too awful to think about. "They'll chase them away, or kill them. Then all we have to do is either wait for the water to refreeze or . . . you know, Jayden will get a rope and toss it and pull us back. We'll be fine." *As long as we don't drift very far.* Water could take a very long time to refreeze, if ever, or might not refreeze into a bridge thick enough to hold them. *Oh, stop worrying, Ellie; Jayden will think of something. He's smart.* A rope, that's what he'd do: weight down a rope, toss it to them, then get a horse to pull them close until they could step onto better ice. Just like a floating raft in this lake her dad once took her to . . . Palm Brooks, that was it. Same principle.

"I hope so." Eli hadn't stopped hugging her. Sure, it was safer this way, but she didn't mind his arms around her one bit. "God," he said, "they're creeping me out."

She could see why. The people-eaters were still advancing in a wedge, the girl with the lime-green scarf drifting along at the rear. With the sun behind them, their spidery black shadows stretched like grasping fingers. At the sight, even the dogs had gone virtually silent, just the barest rumbles rolling from their mouths.

What do the people-eaters think they're going to do? Jump it?

"What if they jump?" Eli said. "It's like . . . only a couple, two, three feet."

It completely freaked her out that she'd been thinking the same thing. The gap of water between their raft and the more solid ice *was* growing just a little wider, but not fast enough; not by the leaps and bounds and feet they needed, but in a slow, lazy drift of inches.

"We got to make sure they don't," Ellie said.

"How? I can shoot two, but that's it," Eli said. "That's all the bullets I have left."

Leaving eight, and that was only *if* Eli actually hit anyone. "We should save the bullets," she said, not knowing why or for whom . . . unless she planned on asking Eli to shoot her. She didn't think she was that brave. Besides, what would happen to Mina if she was dead?

"Then how?"

"The auger. Extend the handle, and it'll be plenty long. If you hold my legs, I can stretch and use it to push us away."

"Oh boy, I hate this," Eli said, but he was starting to ease down to a crouch. Ellie followed him move for move, her heart kicking at her teeth every time the raft bobbled. When she was flat on her tummy and turned around, he worked out the handle and passed her the auger. "You know what this reminds me of?" he said. *"National Treasure.* You know, where Nicolas Cage and everybody else is trapped on this big square thing?"

"I never saw it." She worked her way toward the edge. One of the dogs must've moved, because she heard a frantic scrambling sound at the same time the raft dipped and water leaked onto the ice in front of her face. *Oh boy, I hate this, too.* She felt the water under their block of ice heave as the raft bobbed. A nasty vision floated through her mind: of the block tilting so far that she slid, face-first, into the water. She'd pull Eli along with her. Then, one of two things would happen: either the raft flipped like a pancake, trapping all of them, or only she'd be hooked, unable to turn around and grab an edge. Most lakes, no matter how still, had a current. The one here was stronger than most because of the spring to their right. So she'd drift left, under the raft, and drown with her back jammed up against the ice.

She wanted to wait for that water to retreat, but those people-eaters were still coming. So she wormed forward, then passed the auger through her hands and stretched, trying to hold the heavy blades steady. Squirming a few more inches, she sucked in between her teeth as the raft tipped another inch. Water was beginning to creep toward her arms. Maybe she should've let Eli do this; he was taller, only she wasn't strong enough to hold him if he slipped . . .

Shadows leaked over her hands. Her eyes clicked up, and her pulse stuttered. Nine of the people-eaters were nearly there. In the lead, that boy with the machete leered and hacked the air with a blade coppery with Bella's blood. Not far behind the main pack, that girl followed, the snake of her lime-green scarf trailing. This time around Ellie didn't think the girl looked so scared. In fact, that kid looked like she was really, really *dying* to get closer.

They'll cut us up. Paralyzed, she stared at her death storming over the ice. *It'll hurt . . .*

"Don't stop," Eli said, and gave the chain a yank. "Come on, Ellie. *Hurry.*"

"Okay." She snapped back. "I'm going."

"I *mean* it."

"I know." Her biceps were shuddering from the effort. As strong as she had grown, hanging on to almost nine pounds of steel at the very end of a slim aluminum pole was nearly too much. Tucking her elbows, she braced the auger against her chest. "Do they get off?"

"What? Who?"

"The guys in the movie." The people-eaters were very close now, their finger-shadows brushing her hair and arms in crawly spiders.

"Oh yeah." She felt the chain bite again as Eli redoubled his grip. "The good guys always make it. We'll do it, too. We're Jayden's *Killer Es*, remember? Good guys? So . . ."

She waited a beat, the steady thump of the people-eaters' march over the ice keeping pace with the race of her pulse. "Eli?" When he didn't respond, she risked a look. "E—"

His expression was one she knew. Her Grandpa Jack had worn the same mix of sorrow and shock and rage the day the Army people came to tell them that her daddy was dead.

"Eli," she said, heart going so fast her chest was about to explode. "What is it?"

"Lena," Eli whispered, aghast. Then, louder: *"Lena?"*

What happened next happened fast.

81

Bolting over the snow, Alex barreled into the trees. That burst of strength during the gunfight and then their escape was tailing off, the tang of adrenaline going stale on her tongue. She was huffing, her lungs laboring both from the cold and a smoky haze steaming through the trees in a thickening fog. Snatching a look back, she got a fix on the burning house. The roof was ablaze, a gigantic fiery tongue licking the sky. *A little further left, southeast, until I'm even with where the chimney used to be.*

Finding what she was looking for again—that was the problem. She'd come from a different angle the first time around. Back here, the snow was all torn up, not only from the frequent passage of game but her own meanderings. *Yeah, but all these tracks might be good.* Stopping a quick second, she eyed the path she'd taken so far. *They'll have a hard time figuring out which way I went—*

"Oh hell," she breathed. Against the snow, her prints were stark potholes etched in gray-black smears. *Must've been that last fireball, all that ash.* All anyone had to do was follow the yellow brick road right to that old oak—

A distant, shrill shriek. *Penny.* Those men must be up the hill. *Please, Peter, don't let them hurt Wolf.* She tensed, waiting for the shot that didn't come and didn't come. Which didn't mean a thing. She thought about those weird Changed, that red storm. What if they tried the same on Wolf? And Peter, something was very wrong with Peter; she could smell it . . .

You can't worry about that. Come on, think of something, a plan B. Except she didn't have one, and with those sooty tracks, she was leading them right to her. When they caught up, she wouldn't be able to fight for long. She was tiring fast. Snow sucked and grabbed her calves. Her thighs were lead, and she was battling not only snow and gnarled overgrowth that snatched at her pants and parka but days without proper food.

Keep going, don't stop. Plowing through a whippy tangle of branches, she heard the crackle and pop, felt them pluck and tear at her hair. To her right, she saw a snare flash past. *Crossing a trapline.* One look, and that would clinch it, too. *They'll know the Changed didn't set them.* Might even give the man in black ideas. He would be curious: *why* hadn't the Changed eaten her yet? That would make him all the more interested in Wolf: a Changed boy who protects a pregnant girl and keeps another, not Changed, for . . . a pet? *No, a friend.* Maybe, in Wolf's mind, she was even more.

A faint aroma of human skin, horse sweat, and toe fungus drifted in with the smoke. Men, on their way. How many? Couldn't tell. The Changed boy was big trouble, too, but her nose hadn't found him yet.

In fifty feet, she saw the slight break in the trees, felt her heart give a mighty thump of relief. Almost there. A few seconds later, she spotted four ratty boards nailed to the trunk of a towering oak. To the left and behind the oak was the corkscrew of a red pine. Not an option. But to the right grew a bristle of small, immature hemlock, and just beyond reared a huge, bedraggled white spruce, with low-hanging boughs still heavy with snow. Eyeing the spruce, the glimmer of an idea forming, she thought, *Wait a second.*

Her original plan had been simple. Thirty feet above, seated in its V, was the old tree house. Other than a slight warp in the boards and slivers of daylight, the platform was solid. So, get up there, try not to get shot, maybe even go higher or shimmy out on a long stout branch, drop to the snow well away from the tree, and keep running while they tried to figure out where she'd got to. Now, though, there was that *spruce* . . .

At the oak, she wrapped both hands around the lowest board and tugged. Black with mildew, the swollen board might have broken in summer, but the winter had iced it in place. Clambering up, she found the same in the second and third boards. She might be able to sell this without it, but a broken board added that extra touch that made her look like easy pickings, a scared little girl out of options.

And never mind that I am. Jumping to the snow, she backed up, eyed the trunk, then figured screw it. If it didn't work the first time, she wouldn't try again. Cranking up her right leg, she turned her hip, and pistoned up and out in a swift, hard kick. She felt the *bam* of the impact against the sole of her boot. To her amazement, neither her foot nor ankle broke. It didn't even hurt that much. With a crisp snap, the board sheared in a ragged split at the nailhead.

Excellent. Fishing the splintered fragment from the snow, she positioned it close to the trunk. Then she dropped to the snow and churned her arms and legs. *There.* Shaking snow from her hair, she picked herself up. If *that* didn't look as if she'd tried climbing up into the tree house but then fallen to the snow when the board broke, she didn't know what would.

Okay, now show them panic. Thrashing through unbroken snow, she attacked that densely packed hemlock, breaking branches, sending a shower of green growth to the snow. Anyone looking would see that this was one scared little bunny rabbit of a girl, so freaked out she tried running straight through the trees before turning back. A moron could figure this out.

Floundering for the drooping, heavy-limbed spruce, she swam beneath the boughs and through mounded snow into a fragrant cave.

Most of the light was blocked by the low-slung bell of limbs. The air was a little warmer here, the ground matted with dead brown needles. Dropping to her rump, she shucked the pack and pushed it far back, close to the trunk. Stripping off her soot-stained boots, she thought about it a second and then peeled and stuffed her socks inside. Socks would protect her feet from spruce needles and the cold but slow her down, and she sensed she would have only one chance to make this work. Squaring the boots beneath a dense, snow-matted bough, she wiggled out of the cave. Dancing back, bare feet already yammering that they *really* didn't appreciate this, she eyed the gap between the boughs and the snow line. The toes of her boots were just visible.

Okay, this would have to do. If she was lucky, it would look to the guys on her tail as if she'd first tried the tree house, panicked when the board broke, and then tried running through the hemlocks before giving up and ducking to hide like an ostrich under the spruce.

Diving back into her cave, she squirmed out of her grimy but still mostly white parka, draped the jacket over her head, eased down, and tucked herself into a crouch. Her calves would complain soon. That might be a relief since her feet were really nagging, the toes singing with the cold. Yet pain was good, pain kept her sharp. A passing glance, and her parka should look like heaped snow. The boots were what she wanted them to see. As for what happened after *that* . . . she hadn't quite worked that out. The flare gun was too loud. The tanto? Long blade, better reach, but what good was a knife in a gunfight?

The crackle of a breaking branch made her heart skip. To her left, the human stink was much stronger and . . .

Oh no no no. The hairs along her neck bristled at another aroma drifting in from her right. This was much more distant, but the chemotherapy tang, cisplatin wreathed in rot, was unmistakable.

A Changed, probably that boy. They're coming at me from both directions.

She wet her lips. She couldn't get out of this. But if she could get a gun, give them a fight . . . *Can't let them take me.* Using her fingers, she eased her parka up until she got a small sliver of daylight. *They'll turn me into Peter.* Or worse. If the red storm was any indication, the man in black would feel how she was different, and then there was just no telling. With her luck, he'd hack open her skull and try to figure out what made the monster tick. If he was *really* good and knew what he was doing, that wouldn't kill her either. The brain felt no pain. Once through the skull and dura, that red storm could flay and probe every cranny, every crevice, right down to the monster.

A thump, the squeal of snow to her left. Boots. Big guy. Spokes of hazy late-afternoon sun jabbed thick forest canopy. Through that narrow sliver, she saw white snow, a screen of hemlock, and the tall oak beyond that. Another thump—

A man passed in and then out of a shaft of sunlight. His white and gray hooded snowsuit was fringed, a fancy 3-D jacket with strips of fabric designed to look and flutter like leaves. When he stood absolutely still, she almost lost him in the trees. Light winked from his scoped rifle. His head bowed to study her trail. When he looked up, she saw him train a long look at the oak tree.

Go on, go on. Check it out. She stifled a moan of disappointment as the man, no fool, faded behind a neighboring pine. Easing his rifle to his shoulder, he sighted and then squeezed off a quick shot. There was the hornet's sting of a ricochet. From somewhere came the startled rasp of a crow. A second later, her ears perked to an odd series of cicada-like clicks.

Radio. She recognized the sound from her days in Rule. *Someone heard the shot, wants to know what's going on.* Probably that red storm. There was a pause, then a series of *break-break-breaks* as the hunter sent off his own code. *Thought I was up in the tree.* But she hadn't returned fire or screamed or died. So what was he waiting for?

Suddenly sprinting away from cover, the hunter made a mad,

weaving run for the oak. Fast for an old guy. If she *had* been up there, he'd be tough to hit. Crowding up to the trunk, the hunter shot straight up, threw his bolt, squeezed off another shot and then another and another: *crack-crack-crack-crack!* Probably some big holes in that tree house now, plenty of daylight. Enough to show him there was no one there.

More radio clicks. More returns from the hunter. Probably something like *roger-dodger, A-OK*.

Okay, now, please. She gnawed her cheek. *Look down. See the broken step.*

Socking his radio onto his hip, the hunter stepped away from the tree and tipped his head back as his eyes climbed branches, searching for a person huddled even higher. Then, *finally*, he dropped his gaze to the snow. His exaggerated, almost stupefied double take and then slow crane as his eyes followed her blundering progress made a boil of hysteria push against her lips. That quickly died as he threw his bolt, racked in another bullet, and started her way, the fake leaves of his fancy 3-D camo jacket fluttering.

She knew he was looking at her boots, which was good. She also knew something else that wasn't so good. That was a six-shot rifle, and he'd used five. It hit her then that she couldn't afford him getting off even one more shot. Every time that rifle cracked, the radio clicked.

All of a sudden, from her left, came a new scent, but one she recognized. *No, no!* A jab of terror spiked her gut. She should have thought of this. After all, this had happened in Rule, that very first night. *Go away; don't do it, you nut. Stay away, stay—*

"Come on out." Now that the hunter was close, all she saw were legs in sturdy, thick-soled winter boots. Ten feet away, no more. "I know you're there."

Make the play before he starts blasting. "I'm hurt." She pitched her voice into a high, small, shaky whimper. It actually helped that she was freaked. "I fell . . . when I t-tried . . ."

"Come out." His tone was flinty. "There's nowhere left to run."

"You've g-got a g-gun," she said. "Don't sh-shoot me."

"I will if you don't come out."

Maybe this was a guy who hated being a grandpa. "They were going to eat me. Don't let them get me."

"No one's going to hurt you," he said. Had that been gentler? She couldn't tell. His boots shifted a bit and then she saw one shuffle forward as he dropped to a crouch. That was bad. Any lower, and he'd realize those boots were empty. "Come—"

The scent she'd recognized suddenly bloomed peppery and hot. *No, no, no, he'll shoot, you nut.* Her stomach bottomed out. *Stay back!*

But the wolfdog didn't stay back. It charged because she was in trouble and it was part-dog, and dogs had done this for her once before, that first, awful night in Rule.

She saw the hunter pivot fast. "Jesus—"

"No, over here!" Shoving the parka aside, she surged from her cave. *"Here!"*

82

An inky shadow flickered over Ellie's head as the boy with the machete leapt the gap and landed behind her. A split second later, Eli was shrieking, his hands clapped over his middle, blood already pouring as the dogs surged.

The raft should've tipped right then. But at that moment, Ellie felt something give her arms a great *yank*. Instinctively countering the pull, Ellie looked back and nearly screamed.

It was the girl with the green scarf, the one Eli called Lena, stretched full-length on the ice. Two people-eaters had Lena's legs, tacking her in place. Wrapping her other hand around the auger's screw, Lena tugged again. Water slopped over the ice floe as it lurched closer.

"No!" Ellie gave the auger a furious shove, ramming it toward the girl's face. Startled, Lena let go, dodging as the auger's razor-sharp blades buzzed past. For a split second, Ellie saw not only hunger but bewilderment in Lena's expression. In that moment, Lena looked almost like a girl who just couldn't understand what she'd become.

That was where the good news ended, though. The instant was past in a flash. Now, with no one to anchor her and the raft over-stressed and unbalanced—poor Eli still screaming, the dogs snarling, the people-eater yowling and thrashing—the entire ice shelf tipped. Releasing the useless auger, Ellie tried swinging around to snag ice with her fingernails, but she might as well have tried climbing a vertical sheet of perfectly smooth glass. She felt the slide begin, her body pick up speed. *No, no, no, no!* Something cracked and then cracked twice more, and she thought she heard shrieks, but *she* was screaming, too, and wasn't sure if those cracks were ice, or something else.

Then she was out of time. Everyone and everything behind Ellie—the snapping dogs, Eli, the boy with the machete—whacked her broadside.

Shrieking, Ellie shot off the ice.

83

Alex shot from her hiding place. Out of the corner of her left eye, her vision blurred gray and white, and she sure as hell hoped the wolfdog would stop its charge. Then she had no more time to worry. All she cared about now was that this old man's rifle not go off.

At her shout, the hunter spun, his long gun swinging around. Right arm already cocked, she got in under the rifle but not fast enough. The muzzle flash and *crack* were virtually instantaneous. She never heard the shriek that crashed out of her mouth. The bullet burned a groove over her left temple. Something shattered in that ear, and by the time she registered the shot and that he was out of ammo, his seamed face filled her vision.

She stabbed.

She'd had time to think and mull over the *hospital* smell of that syringe, and why Peter might have it. She remembered his books. Mammalogy. Evolution. Genetics. Wolves.

Whether it was Penny Peter had first brought to the lake house or Wolf, the problem remained: how? How do you put down a foaming, frothing, feral Changed? How do you bring something like that under control?

If you had majored in mammalogy and studied animals in the wild, or were only a sheriff's deputy, you'd done it before: to frightened dogs, wolves that had to be relocated, coyotes you didn't want to kill. Even a bear or two. Or maybe you'd seen someone else do it. Whatever. You knew the theory: trank the hell out of those suckers. Put them to sleep—with a pressurized tranquilizer dart.

She stabbed with the needle: a quick, lunging jab.

She was aiming for the hunter's throat.

She got his eye.

84

As soon as the frigid water hit her face, most of Ellie's air gushed out in a shimmering, bubbling cascade. Her heart *whammed* her ribs like the steel toe of a boot. For a startling moment that seemed to last forever, her brain blanked out.

Then someone—Eli or a dog or the people-eater with the machete—landed on top and drove her deeper. A gout of icy water shot up her nose, the pain like red-hot pokers jammed into her brain. The cold punched at her eyes. The stringer chain was still around her middle, and for a weird second, she thought the lake might actually grab it and pull her down. With precious little air left, she struggled free of a tangle of arms and legs and looked up in time to see something coming straight down like a guided missile. Letting out a bubbling little cry—and the last smidgeon of her air—she jerked aside as the machete skimmed past.

Above, the churning water was murky with billowing curls of blood stirred by pedaling legs and paws. It was like being caught at the very bottom of a giant washing machine. Kicking, lungs imploding with the burn, she grabbed water and swept her arms in a mighty heave.

Shattering the surface, she gulped air so cold it torched her throat. Eli was nowhere in sight. Neither were the dogs. *No. They were just here.* "M-Mina?" she coughed. "Eli?"

To her right, Mina's head suddenly popped up like a float freed from the monster of a fish that had swallowed the hook. Chuffing, Mina turned frantic circles, looking for a place to go.

The raft. Furiously treading water, Ellie twisted, trying to get a fix on where she was. *Got to find the raft, something to hang onto, and Eli, where's—*

To her left came a watery crash and then the sound of someone hacking and spitting. A surge of relief: *Eli.* He'd know what to do. He was stronger than her. *But he's hurt, he's hurt, he was bleeding . . .* No, Eli was fine, he couldn't die, he'd be okay; they'd get out of this and she'd never, ever make fun of him again! "Eli!" Gasping, she croaked, "Eli, are you—"

A punch of panic stole her breath. Instead of Eli, it was the people-eater, hair streaming, face going white with cold, and only feet away. *No!* Stifling a scream, she stroked awkwardly, laying down distance, hoping that not even a hungry people-eater would be crazy enough to go after her now. For the moment, he only seemed confused and in shock like her, and that might give her time. Directly ahead, she spotted the ice raft rocking in the turbulence. To her dismay, the floe was moving away, dragged by the current, propelled by the chop and churn.

Maybe the ice shelf? No, no good. The people-eaters were there. So what was her choice? To tread water and hope help would come? How long would it take her to freeze to death, or drown? *I'm small, I don't weigh very much.* Maybe not long at all then. Ellie turned a wild half-circle, looking for something to grab, keep herself afloat. *And where's Roc, where's Eli?* They must be trapped under the ice; Eli might be drowning right now! *No, no!* She squeezed her eyes tight against the image of poor Eli, pounding ice with his fist, big shivery bubbles boiling from his mouth. Or worse yet, Eli, too weak to swim, sinking as blood smoked from his belly, with Roc locked in his arms. *I should get them, I should dive, I should try!* He would do it for her.

"I can't, I *can't.*" Her voice was squeaky and thin as a little mouse's.

She knew how to swim okay—dead man's float, sidestroke, a floppy kind of crawl where she always got water up her nose—but she wasn't great in the water. The cold blasted her face, leeched away what little warmth she had left. Her arms and legs were so heavy. Her boots had instantly filled with water, and her parka was bloated. Treading water now was like trying to run in concrete. *Eli, Eli, I'm sorry, I'm sorry.*

Turning again, she spotted the ice shelf, a jagged white margin that seemed very far away. She'd expected to see the girl in the green scarf, but Lena was gone. She had to try. If she could battle her way to the stable shelf, she might be able to hold on and help her dog, too. For how long she could do either, she didn't know, but anything was better than just drowning.

She flopped in an awkward, spastic splash that only sucked more energy and got her no closer to safety. The lake's fingers, inky and long, wrapped around her ankles and tugged, trying to pull her under, kill her. Everything hurt. Her hands, her feet, her face were throbbing. The cold hacked her skin, and she was shuddering all over. Without meaning to or even an awareness that it was happening, her head simply slid below the surface.

For a long, long second, she kept on sinking. Her body didn't seem to understand she was underwater. Then, it was as if something deep inside, what was left of her, woke up. Frantic, she clawed to the surface, spluttered, coughed out more water, looked for her dog.

Mina was gone.

No. Not even a brain yelp, though. No energy. And where was the people-eater? Everything was starting to get black . . . "N-nuh. Muh-muh . . ." Her mouth wasn't working. She dog-paddled, her head cranked so far back she stared at blue sky blushing orange and red, the end coming on. There was a small *huh* as Mina resurfaced, but barely, only her snout showing and two terrified eyes.

A slap of water swamped her chin. A wave broke around her head and rolled past. Another hard splash, closer. *Behind.* Twisting, she saw the people-eater crashing across the lake, heading for her.

"N-n-nuh." Dredging up a last burst of strength, she swept with both arms, pulling for open water, her thoughts as tiny and shivery as soap bubbles: *What's he doing, is he crazy?* The people-eater's splashing was closer, harder, wilder. Risking a peek, she let out a gaspy, gargly scream. Puffing like a bull, mad with hunger, the boy was gaining. A sudden, horrible thought blasted her brain: he would drown her. Drown her, tow her body back, and then *eat*—

"N-n-noooo!" she shrieked as he covered the last five feet in a giant surge. His hands battened on her head. She flailed, but it was like trying to fight an octopus. She went completely under. A glubby, strangled cry tried to boil past her lips, and she clamped hard, gulping it back. *Can't hold it, can't hold it, can't*—and then she really couldn't hang on any longer. Air bolted from her mouth, and with it, the last of her voice in a despairing wail.

Above, the boy gave a great, spastic jolt. His grip broke. With no thought other than getting her face into air, Ellie plowed to the surface. Snatching one precious breath, she saw the boy rearing, his hands shooting for her once more. Thought, *He's got me.*

"Ellie!" She was so disoriented, she thought the people-eater had spoken. *No, from the left.* Her eyes jerked toward the ice shelf.

There, a figure stood, starkly silhouetted against blue sky. And he had a rifle.

"Ellie!" Chris shouted. "Don't move!"

85

The needle punctured the globe of the hunter's left eye with a small but audible *pop*. Alex had so much momentum going, she couldn't put on the brakes. They fell, locked together, the hunter toppling, Alex still clutching that dart and riding him all the way down. When they hit, Alex felt the needle scrape and then punch through the delicate bone at the back of the socket. If her left ear hadn't been screeching, she might have heard the *pfffl* as the tranquilizer, under pressure, flooded the hunter's brain.

The hunter went instantly rigid. His remaining eye, filmy with age, bulged. His mouth jammed open. *No screams, no screams!* Letting go of the syringe, Alex clapped both hands over the old man's lips. His cheeks puffed in and out. Balls of muted sound pushed against her palms. The hunter's good eye pinned her with a disbelieving glare. How much he really saw, she didn't know, and she hoped this was all reflex. His body was starting to quiver and jitter; his hands flapped; the dart, with its merry red tail, danced; his boots drummed snow.

To her left, she felt the wolfdog hovering nearby and craned a look. Its ears were up, the tail nearly horizontal, and its snout wrinkled to show teeth. What she got from the smell was only *threat*. If it had wanted her, she'd be bleeding by now. *You, big boy, are a nut.*

Under her hands, the hunter's frantic puffing had ceased. The lone eye glared a glassy accusation. A moment later, through her good ear, she heard clicks from the dead man's radio.

Got to get out of here. Staggering back to the spruce, she got into her parka and pawed out her boots. Shadowing her, its alarm a red foam in her nose, the wolf dog took two soundless dancing steps, its meaning clear: *Let's go.*

"Don't I know it." But go where? In several more yards, she'd be in virgin snow, her trail obvious, and they had weapons. Her eyes fell on the dead hunter—and that Springfield. There was one shot left, but she smelled more bullets in the left front pocket of that camo-jacket. *Yeah, but take the rifle, and they know you're armed.* They might call for reinforcements, and then she was cooked. She might be cooked either way unless she killed that Changed boy. For that matter, they might not need the boy. That *push-push go-go* would wear her down, eventually. If the monster jumped again or, worse, the red storm got behind her eyes . . .

Oh, screw it. She snatched up the rifle. Her left temple throbbed from where the bullet had grazed her scalp, and her hair was already tacky with drying blood. *Not going down without a fight.*

But it might not come to that. If she could hide . . . But how? *How do you hide from the Changed?* From the minute the hunter first shot at the tree house to now, she thought five minutes had passed. The chemotherapy tang was closer, not charging but swooping in, making a beeline for that last shot. Keep up that clicking on the radio, and they'd find the body even faster.

What scared her more—now that she was paying attention—was the steadily increasing drumbeat of the *push-push go-go.* Maybe that was what the red storm wanted. If she lost control, she might be easier *to* control, or at least find. Every logical scrap of her shouted that she had to run. Yet the lizard part of her brain, everything that was instinct, yammered that hiding was better. Sometimes bunnies had the right idea. Be small, don't move, don't attract attention.

Don't attract attention. She looked at the wolfdog watching her. *Darth didn't see you. Maybe he didn't notice you. Or maybe couldn't? No time to figure this out.* The metal stink of cisplatin frothed through the trees. The red storm was a throb in the middle of her forehead, like a hidden third eye struggling to open. *Decide.*

Instead of shoving on her boots, she laced them together before draping them around her neck. Her feet were passing from burn to numb, but footprints weren't as noticeable as boots. Hooking the Springfield's carry strap across her shoulders like a samurai sword, she crouched over the body. The only blood was a gooey, meandering trickle from the ruined left eye. *Can't leave the syringe. That makes me both dangerous and a curiosity.* Gritting her teeth, she wrapped her hand around the plastic tube and pulled. She felt the scrape of bone again, and when she'd gotten the needle out, the socket puddled red. Shuddering, she recapped the needle with shaking fingers before sliding the syringe back into a cargo pocket. Then, working fast, she stripped the hunter of his fancy, 3-D camo-jacket.

"Come on," she whispered to the wolfdog, wincing at the throb of the red storm, that continual *push push.* Her lip squirmed under a slow, snaky dribble. Cupping a hand to her bleeding nose, she scurried for a screen of dense brambles maybe fifty yards back, cringing at every crackle under her increasingly clumsy feet. She heard the wolfdog's breaths as it followed. *Good.* The animal's prints would erase hers.

The woods here were wild, crowded with nearly impenetrable briars and underbrush. Diving into the snow, she shucked in the rifle, then swam through a narrow gap between two ragged, brambly clumps growing so close together their branches twined. She grimaced as briars forked her hair, tugged her wounded scalp—and, *oh hell,* the medic pack was still under the spruce. *No time, no time.* When she judged she was far enough, she wormed around on her stomach, figuring she'd have to coax the animal, but the wolfdog was already squirting in. *Smart boy.* It *knew* something wicked was coming this way.

Casting one anxious glance back, she saw no bright red gumdrop trail of blood marking the way. *Okay, this has to do, because, honey, we are out of time.* Heaping snow into the gap, she put an arm around the animal's neck, tucked her feet under her bottom, and hunkered down. The wiry growth was so thick, she thought they might be invisible—if they stayed absolutely still. This really could work. Hunters sat in blinds all the time; they perched in trees for hours. And fifty yards was half a football field. A lot of distance in which to get herself lost. Many people overlooked the obvious and what lay in plain sight every day. Smell . . . she couldn't do anything about that. There was no real wind here, not even a breeze. But she kept thinking of Darth, and then the wolf totems hanging next to that stuff sack. Something important there . . .

There was a heavy thud, and then another. A snap then crack of branches and brush, the crunch of snow. Not being very subtle, but maybe they thought they didn't need to be. The chemotherapy fug of that Changed boy was everywhere now. Yet the scent from that man in black, the eye in that red storm, was distinctive, too. Her nose balked, tripping over his odor: definitely old, that same fustiness of wet wool socks, but also saturated with a stench of polluted gray-green water reeking of burned urine and foamy detergent that was the stink of the Chicago River after a storm.

As much information as her nose gave her, she couldn't see more than a foot or two beyond her sheltering bramble canopy. Somehow that made it all the more frightening, because she couldn't assign a face to that dreadful odor, knock it down to size, make it human. It was like groping in the dark of a haunted house where what you imagined was always so much worse than what was real. *Stop, stop.* Clenching her jaws, she bore down, trying to force back the fear threatening to swamp her mind. She was shuddering, every muscle trying to get free of her body and run run run. *Calm down, you have to try to stay in control. It wants you to bolt, show yourself.*

She closed her eyes. On the screen of her lids, the *go-go push-push* was like blood pounding through arteries: the red storm working fingers through her eyes, in her mind, down her throat, and then into her heart, fisting the muscle, forcing it to a different beat: *push-push push-push go-go go*—

"Where are you?"

The sound was so sudden she nearly vaulted out of her skin. She pressed her lips together so tightly they tingled. Under her arm, the wolfdog was still as death. *Don't move, don't freak out.* Wondering which of them she was coaching, she hugged the animal a little closer. Her teeth were chattering *clickity-clickity-click.* Ramming her tongue between her jaw, she bit down to stop the noise and focus. *Don't bolt, little bunny; that's when the hunters get you, when they see the flash of your little white cotton tail.*

"I know you're close. I can just feel your edges." Even shouting across half a football field's worth of woods, the voice carried a certain mellow, authoritative reassurance that made her think of that actor who played Lucius Fox in the Batman movies. "My name's Finn. What's yours?"

That answered a question. This wasn't read-your-mind telepathy, which would've been just too voodoo for her anyway. *However he's doing this, he can't find me, doesn't see me.* Wait, that wasn't quite right. She remembered those bizarre shifts in perspective, that sense of distance collapsing—and that had happened to her before, hadn't it? When she was on Blackrocks, about to jump: an out-of-body experience the doctors said was a temporal lobe hiccup provoked by fear and fueled, maybe, by her baby chick of a monster.

So . . . Finn was an epileptic? Or took medicine? She thought so. That polluted smell was very strong but artificial, like those Changed with their chemo stink. Maybe taking the same drug—because it had to be a drug. She just knew. So how did this work for him?

The important thing: the voice was no closer, and the red storm couldn't get a fix. Which meant he was only guessing, calculating the probabilities.

Just as important: that chemotherapy, cisplatin fug wasn't getting stronger. So that altered, engineered Changed couldn't smell her either. Could be a couple different reasons for that.

Or maybe only you. She hugged the wolfdog tighter. The animal's ears swiveled like a bat's, but that was the only movement it showed at all. *Or it's the two of us, together.*

"Why are you still alive?" Finn's *push-push* amped up. "There's something different about you, isn't there? And about that boy . . . Simon? Maybe I'll pick him apart and find out."

If that polluted red storm thought she was going to go all girly, Finn had another thing coming. But how to fight him? Cancer, she knew. One thing the shrinks tried to teach you was how to wall off the monster, put it in a box, lock the door.

"Come on," the red storm said. "I know you're there."

Oh bullshit. Then you'd stop talking and your bloodhound boy would've already found me. The thought was angry, a kind of mental shove—

And then she caught herself. What had he said? *I feel your edges.*

Okay, there was something in that. The only way you could *feel* an edge was when you hit something solid. *It's like closing your eyes and trying to find your way around a wall. You only know where it ends when your fingers hit thin air.* Maybe the red storm found her by the obstacles she threw up to protect herself.

"What's your name?" Another strong red *push-push*, like the sweep of radar, trying to get a fix. "Come on, I can help you." *Push-push.* "We have a lot in common, can't you see that?"

She didn't see it, and now she couldn't let him see her. *Don't give him an edge. When he pushes, don't push back.* The idea of doing nothing scared the living daylights out of her. It would mean letting this wash through her without leaving a stain. She remembered Peter's bookshelf, and *Dune*: that mantra about fear and mind-killers.

Walk away. Let it go through me, over me. She knew how to walk away. She'd done that the day she'd left for the Waucamaw and a fight she knew she couldn't win. *So walk away from this. Don't give the red storm edges to feel.*

But would that work? Wouldn't the monster, deep in the lockbox of her mind, get out? Even if it didn't, the lockbox was like a drop of black ink on white paper. If the red storm saw it, she was done.

Unless I go just as dark. Closing her eyes again, she stilled her mind just as the wolfdog had frozen to a statue by her side. *There's only night, and no stars.*

Go dark.

Don't move.

86

"Take the shot," Jayden chanted. "Come on, Chris, take the shot!"

"One more second," Chris said. "If she surfaces too close . . ." He and Jayden were standing a good thirty feet from the edge, worried that the jagged shelf was too unstable and might crumble. In the water, at least fifty feet further out, the Changed boy was still there, but Ellie was not. His first shot was meant to startle. Ellie had been too close, and he'd been afraid to try for a kill shot. So he'd fired high; saw the boy flinch away at the rifle's whipcrack and his hold on the little girl break.

Wait until she clears, wait until you see her. He took up as much slack on the trigger as he dared. *Ellie, Ellie, come on, you were just there, you were just . . .*

"There!" Jayden cried as the little girl's head ruptured through the surface not six feet from the Changed. "Take it, Chris, take it!"

"Ellie!" Chris shouted, hoping she heard and understood. "Don't move!"

The crack of the shot. The kick against his shoulder. A sudden red mist ballooned above the Changed's shoulders, and then the headless body listed left and floated, buoyed by a bubble of air trapped under the dead kid's parka.

"Ellie!" Jayden was clutching a coil of rope he'd knotted to his packhorse's saddle. "Swim this way! Can you swim?"

"I don't think she can do it," Chris said. At the sound of her name, Ellie had turned an almost listless circle. She wore the shocked expression of the lone survivor of a car crash. Ten feet beyond her was Mina, who looked just as spent. *She won't make it.* Stripping out of Jayden's parka, he sucked air against a slap of cold on his bare chest, then dropped to the ice and began working the laces of his boots. "I'm going after her."

"Are you *crazy?*" Jayden clutched his shoulder. "You'll drown, too."

"No, I won't," he said, stripping off his boots. But people his age did die; he'd read about a fifteen-year-old kid who'd fallen through ice and had a heart attack from the shock. "Even in freezing water, it takes a little while, and I won't be in that long. You've got the rope, you've got the horse." Peeling off his socks, he scooped up the rope and threw in a quick bowline knot. Ellie would be too frightened and probably too weak to hold on, but if he could get the rope under her arms . . . He stood, screwing up his face against the sting on his bare feet. "All I have to do is get to her. Then you pull her in." He would try to grab the dog, too, or at least coax it to follow.

"All right." Jayden's jaw set. "Go. Hurry, Chris. Go go go!"

Blowing out two quick breaths, Chris inhaled deep and long, then plunged off the ice. The cold was much worse than he'd expected, but he kept focused, kept moving. Surfacing, he blew out, sucked in another breath, and started pulling for the girl.

"Ellie," he panted. He was trying not to hyperventilate, reminding himself that he would use up less energy if he stayed calm, took slow breaths. *But, oh my God, the* burn . . . His bare chest was already numb. Lightning shocks of pain lanced from his feet to his hips. "Ellie, I'm right here," he said. Those fifty feet never seemed so long, and he suddenly wondered just how much rope they had. *God, we never checked.* Too late to think about that now. He watched water slop around her chin and then her nose; saw how she didn't flinch. *Losing it.*

"Listen to me, Ellie," he called. "Are you listening? Put your head all the way back. Look at the sky, Ellie, look at the sky."

Her staring eyes rolled. They were glazed, and he wasn't sure she knew who he was. Then her head lolled back, but in slow motion, as if she were truly at the end of her strength.

Almost there. "Good, good." Turning to face the way he'd come, he paid out rope, praying that he didn't run out. Jayden, he saw, had guided his horse a little closer. *Can't drop the rope either.* The rope would sink, and once it was gone, it was gone. He could probably swim with her, but the cold was starting to get to him, too. To his left, the dog was paddling toward him now. *Get the rope around Ellie, grab the dog, and then we all—*

Then, suddenly, he was out of rope, and still short.

Shit. "Ellie." Grabbing the loop with one hand, he swam until the rope was taut and actually out of the water, then stretched his dripping, freezing free hand. Six lousy inches . . . "Ellie, you have to come toward me. E-Ellie, honey, take my hand. C-come on, you can do it!"

He watched her arms move but only feebly. One limp hand broke the surface, flopping like a fish. "E-Ellie, t-try again," he said, his teeth stuttering, his breath starting to come up short, the cold like iron cinching down around his ribs. *So close.* Thinking he really was going to have to let go of the rope, grab her, then swim for it. *Do something and do it now.*

Her hand came up in that same dreamy slow motion. This time, he lunged, hoping the sudden lurch wouldn't send the packhorse into a panic. He felt the slap of her hand, icy and wooden. His own fingers, numbing fast, cramped around her wrist and reeled her in.

"Okay, good, you're doing great," he said. She was shivering so hard the water danced. He worked the rope over her head and under her shoulders. The dog was there now, too, nudging at his shoulder with its snout. "I see you, girl, hang on, hang on," he said, unsure which *girl* he was talking to now. "Ellie," he said, getting his face in hers, grabbing her hands and trying to bend her fingers to curve around the rope. "You have to hang on. I'll help you, but I've got to help Mina, too. . . ."

That did something. He saw a tremor shiver over Ellie's face, her head slowly turn, her shock-trauma eyes crawling past him. "Muh-muh-muh," she stuttered.

"Right, it's Mina. You have to help Mina." Puffing now, treading more from memory, his feet numb and legs leaden. How long had he been in the water? Five minutes? He could only imagine how well her brain probably *wasn't* working right now. *But she recognizes the dog.* Still holding her hands around the rope, he got his free arm under the dog's chest. *Please, Mina, don't panic, don't bite me.* Chuffing, the dog let out a piteous whine and then stretched for Ellie, its tongue flicking out to try and lick her face.

"Muh-huh-huh," Ellie gasped. He could see the white crescents as her eyes began to roll back into her skull. Her fingers were chalk. "Cuh-Cuh-Chrisss . . ."

"I'm h-here," he stammered. *Won't let you go.* He sucked in a breath and pushed it out in a shout: "Juh-Jayden, pull! Pull!"

87

"It should be me," Ellie said, cradling Bella's head in her lap. Despite the dance of orange light from a fire Jayden and Connor had started two hours ago, her face was drawn and ashen. Her eyes crawled from Jayden, who looked uncertain, to a tight-lipped Hannah, who only looked more furious by the second. "She's my horse."

"But there's no need. Jayden can do this, or Connor," Hannah said, and Chris thought she really was trying to keep a lid on it. Jayden had refused to go anywhere without warming Ellie first. Chilled to his marrow, Chris hadn't argued. Stripping the girl out of her sodden clothes, they wrapped her in a saddle blanket and Jayden's parka. Chris had accepted Jayden's sweater and then waited, next to the fire, with Ellie cradled in his arms and the dog practically in his lap, too, while Jayden rode for help. He'd returned with clothing, thermoses of hot soup and tea—and a fuming Hannah.

"What you need is to stop fighting me, Ellie," Hannah pressed. "You need to come home."

"I'm not fighting. I'm just *saying*." Ellie's lower lip quivered. Bundled in a watch cap, two sweaters, snow pants, two pairs of socks, and a parka, she reminded Chris of the shrunken old women, swathed beneath reams of blankets, to whom he'd used to read back at Rule's hospice. At Ellie's tone, Bella let out another moan through a froth of scarlet foam. Gulping back a sob, Ellie stroked the horse's poll. "I should be the one to do it. I had to leave Eli and Roc. Don't make me leave Bella, too."

"It's not the same. Eli and Roc were not *your* fault." Hannah said it to Ellie but aimed daggers at *him*.

Chris knew she was right. This whole mess—the barn; Bella; Eli and Roc, trapped under the ice or at the bottom of the lake—was all on him. No one wanted to say it, but Chris thought they might not find the boy and his dog until spring, if then.

"Yes, it is. Cutting the ice was my idea, and now E-Eli . . ." Ellie looked up at Jayden. "Is my gun big enough? For Bella?"

Jayden shook his head. "You'd need to use one of our rifles."

"Which would be much too heavy," Hannah put in. "It's not your job, Ellie. You're not old enough. If you love Bella, you'll let us end her suffering."

"Hannah's right." Jayden bent, reached a tentative hand. "We have to go, Ellie. It's getting late. Hannah has to check Isaac, and the animals need us. Wouldn't you like to help?"

"Yes, but . . ." Ellie's brimming eyes overflowed. Bella groaned again. "Shh, girl." Ellie impatiently backhanded tears from her cheeks. "It's okay." To Jayden: "Of *course*, I'll help. But I want to help my horse, too."

"Then you'll let us—" Hannah began.

"I'll help you, Ellie," Chris said.

Hannah turned him a frosty glare. "Thanks, Chris." She said it like he was a bug. "But this has nothing to do with you."

No, it's got everything to do with me. Ignoring Hannah, he squatted until he and Ellie were eye to eye. "We can use my gun."

"Chris," Hannah said.

The distress on Ellie's face eased for a second before clenching again. "But it's too heavy for me."

"*Chris,*" Hannah said again.

"Leave him alone, Hannah," Jayden said.

"What?" Hannah goggled up at the other boy, who only returned her look with a resolute expression. "What did you say?"

"You heard me," he said. "I have a say in this, too, remember?"

"Jayden, this isn't the time to—"

"Here's what we'll do," Chris said to Ellie. "We'll hold the rifle together. I'll keep it steady and you pull the trigger. You'll have to use both trigger fingers, but you can do it."

"Really?" Ellie's chin quivered. "You'd do that?"

"*Chris,*" Hannah rasped, clearly having abandoned her argument with Jayden. To his ears, she sounded as if she were clamping back an impulse either to scream or blow his head off. Possibly both. "Ellie is too *young* to—"

"It's her choice, Hannah." Chris thought there was no irony in his tone. "Isn't choice what you're all about?"

"What?" Hannah blinked as if he'd slapped her, and then all her frustration—and her grief, Chris thought—poured out in a poisonous rush. "Don't twist this around. This is your fault, *your* responsibility. You brought this on us. You think helping her with something like this makes up for what you've done? For what you *didn't* do today?"

"Hannah," Jayden said. "That's not fair. We killed three. You weren't there."

Her eyes blazed in the firelight. "I didn't need to be. Chris had Lena. You said so. But he didn't take the shot. I don't know if I *care* to understand why—"

"For the same reason I'm not sure I could shoot you," Chris said, roughly. He kept reliving the moment: Lena in his sights, her face huge in the scope and so . . . *Changed*; that terrible sweep of mingled pity and dismay that stole his breath and robbed him of the chance to end this. Well, end *her*. He'd shot, finally, but pulled it at the last second. Then, it was all about Ellie. "I'd feel the same about Jayden, or *anyone* I know or care about."

Hannah gave a brittle laugh. "*This* is caring? You led them to us. You should've recognized what was happening to Lena, but you were blind, Chris; you were willfully blind. If you'd been honest from the beginning, we could've taken precautions. We could've *left*."

"We'll still have to leave," Jayden said. His face had paled.

"Yes, but on our terms, not after losing animals, a *child*. After Lena killed her own *brother*."

"Hannah." Ellie's face knotted. "*Don't*. Don't yell at Chris."

"You think you can wash away that kind of blood, Chris? There's no way you can make this right!" She actually balled her fist and shook it in his face. "Isaac's old. That fire did him no favors. If he lives, *he* might forgive you. You and Jayden may be best friends all of a sudden—"

"Hannah," Jayden said.

"And maybe Jayden understands, but I don't. I wish you *had* died."

"Hannah!" Jayden snatched her wrist. "*Stop* this!"

"Let me go, let me—" The *crack* her palm made on Jayden's cheek was brisk as a rifle shot. Seething, she wrenched free and screamed at Chris, "I wished we'd never *met* you! I wished you'd *stayed* dead! Why couldn't you have *died*, why didn't you *die*?"

"Hannah!" Ellie said. "Stop! Jayden, make her—"

"I don't know, Hannah." Every word was another twist of the knife, and Chris thought he deserved it all. What could he say? *I was afraid?* "I don't know why I'm alive, and I'm sorry I didn't die. You want me to leave and I will, first thing."

"No," Ellie began.

"Oh yes, of *course*." Hannah started for him. "Leave now, leave us to deal with *your* mess—"

Jayden put himself between Chris and Hannah. "What are you doing?" When she looked like she was going to swing again, Jayden put up his hands to ward her off. "What *are* you?"

"What *am* I?" That stole the wind from her sails for a second. She turned him an incredulous look. "What do you mean? I'm who I always was. I'm trying to keep us *alive*."

"Not this way," Jayden said quietly. "Yours is not the only voice, Hannah. It can't be."

"If you won't listen to me, listen to Jayden," Chris said. "You need to get control of yourself. This is Ellie's right, and I'm going to help her. If you really cared, if this was about *her* and not you, you'd see that."

Hannah opened her mouth, but Jayden said, "Please, shut the hell up, Hannah."

"Jayden." Her face crumpled with shock. "You're taking *his* side?"

"Chris was scared, and I would never hit you. Think about that. And, no, I'm taking Ellie's side." Showing her his back before she could reply, Jayden nodded at Chris.

He didn't need any more permission and paid Hannah no more mind. Chris cupped Ellie's hands. "Let me help you with Bella, okay? And tell Mina to lie down."

Together, they eased the horse's head to the snow. He waited, ignoring Hannah, who still fumed, but silently now, as Ellie tended to the dog and then bent to whisper into her mare's ear and kiss the horse's nose.

"Okay, this has a big kick, so be ready." Standing behind the little girl, he positioned her hands on the .30-06, then held the rifle's muzzle an inch from Bella's ear. "I've got it. Pull the trigger when you're ready."

"Okay." Ellie craned a look. "Thank you, Chris."

Her face shimmered, and he thought it was a good thing he didn't have to aim much, because he'd have to wipe his eyes. He had never felt more ashamed. This little girl was thanking him for getting her friend killed, and her horse, too. In a few more hours, he would also have to tell her about Alex and break her heart all over again. Jayden would hate him then, too.

But no more lies, Dad. You and I are done.

And was this Jess now, this sigh that might be wind or spirit: *That's right, Chris. Let go of the hammer.*

"I'm so sorry, Ellie," he said.

"I know." She looked back at her horse. "Love you, girl," she said to Bella, and pulled the trigger.

88

"Oh, boy-o, it's not that tough," Finn said, as if he really didn't care, like they were two buddies hanging out in the old man's tent, having a couple of cold brews after a hard day. Wielding his parang, Finn carefully shaved skin from a raw rump roast, squared on a cutting board, that might have been beef with excellent marbling. In a saner world, that is. Because that smudge of blue ink? Odds were high it didn't say USDA Select. "Just tell me: who's the girl?"

"I . . . I d-don't . . . *uhhh.*" Pete's neck rocked as another sudden spasm bolted through his head. His jaws locked to corral a hiss. "Don't . . . *know.*"

"Now why don't I believe that?" Finn sliced a thick, two-inch steak, probably against the grain. "I may not be a mind reader, but I saw your face. Why won't you give me a name?"

"Because I . . ." Another shuddering brain bomb. They'd been at this brutal game for the last five hours, ever since leaving the smoldering ruin of the lake house. Peter had read stories about people with brain aneurysms. The very few who survived said it was having nails pounded through their skulls. This was like that: intense pain, a pulse in the center of Peter's head and right behind his eyes, like the winged thing was scooping out more real estate with its claws. Not as awful as the brain storm that seized him that day on the snow with Davey, though. So why not? *Think, Peter; this is important.*

And yet . . . he didn't want Finn's fingers completely out of his head. As much as the brain bomb hurt, Peter craved that electric red swoon more. When Finn sent Davey and his altered Changed after Simon and Penny, the rush had been so intense, so *good*, the moan of pleasure escaped before Peter could trap it. Every muscle ached to join in the hunt. The *blood*. Finn knew it, too: *Like that, don't you, boy-o? I can give and take, you know. Give . . . and take.*

Finn was working himself and the Changed up to something, like predators ascending the food chain. First, Changed out for "training." Now, larger teams, like today. Peter sensed there was one more prize Finn wanted, one more test to run, and then they would head for Rule.

"How many times do I have to say it?" Peter managed through clenched teeth. "I don't know who she is. Why is it so important?"

"Oh, boy-o. You disappoint me." Sighing, Finn used the parang to push stew-sized chunks onto an aluminum camp plate. The tent was warm, the air rich with copper musk. "All right, let's take a break. *Phew-wee*." Finn flicked mock sweat from his broad brow. "I've worked myself into a lather. How about we try something easier, all right?"

"Whatever." Peter backhanded real sweat from his forehead. The cuffs around his wrists clinked. A guard had cinched them so tight there was blood where the steel had rubbed his skin raw. He swallowed, but with difficulty. The control collar not only chafed, but the chain looped through the metal D-ring was secured so high on the bars that Peter had no choice but to sit upright. Lucky for him, he hadn't needed sleep in weeks, or he'd strangle on his own weight.

Through the wire mesh dividing this stainless-steel transport cage, he saw Penny cringing against Simon. At least they weren't in restraints, and Finn had gotten his camp doc to wrap Simon's sprain, so that was something.

"Tell you what," Finn said, taking the filled plate and sidling close to Penny and Simon's half of the cage. "Let's talk about little Penny . . . well, *not* so little Penny."

"What do you want to know?" Peter said, his tone flat. Simon's eyes narrowed at Finn's approach. Suddenly rapt, however, Penny straightened, nostrils flaring.

"I'm curious." Finn moved the plate from side to side, smiling as Penny tracked it like a spectator at a tennis match. "Yes, smells *good*, doesn't it, Penny? Want some?" Finn brought the plate to within arm's reach. "Go ahead, dear. You know you want it. Take it."

Don't do it, Penny. A stupid thought. Illogical. Watching his sister's face rearrange itself—raw animal hunger replacing fear and suspicion—hurt so much Peter would've taken a brain bomb instead.

"Whoa, easy now," Finn chuckled as Penny's hand darted to grab a meaty fistful. "Wouldn't want you to choke, sweetheart. How many months is she, Peter?"

"Seven, more or less." *More, probably.*

"Oh." Finn's bushy white eyebrows arched as he ticked off the months on his fingers and then mugged fake astonishment. "Well, we *did* wait until the last second, didn't we?"

Penny had. He still remembered his shock when she told him: *I thought I was late.* He'd had to bite back the scream: *You thought you were late for three* months? But she was only sixteen. Too late, he discovered she'd already confided in a girlfriend and things had mushroomed from there, the rumor spreading through town. *Which is probably how Finn found out in the first place. Weller, maybe, or Lang.* Or given the depth of Finn's hatred for Rule, the old man might've had a spy there all along.

"How did you get her to the lake house?" Finn asked, proffering the plate again. Penny's cheeks were round as a chipmunk's, but she still grabbed a double handful. "Must've been difficult."

He tried to shake his head, but the collar brought him up short. "I took her on Friday, the day before . . . you know."

"Ah, the day before the world went away. You were going to come back?"

"Sunday night." The lake house was never meant as anything other than a place for Penny to hang for a single weekend while he scraped together the money and set up the appointment in Illinois. Messing up Penny's life more by forcing her to go through with the pregnancy would do no one any good. Beg forgiveness later. "Didn't quite make that."

"When *did* you go back?"

"Thursday night." It had taken that long to track down Simon and ride like hell.

"And she was still there? Poor girl must've been starving."

"Not really." When Finn leveled a look, he continued in a dead monotone, "She was with a . . . friend. Of mine." He paused. "From college."

"The father? That's interesting. Does put a new spin on the female praying mantis." Finn gestured at Simon, who hadn't made a move for the food. "I'd have thought he—"

"Never in a million years. Not Simon. We're family."

"Why do you think she stayed at the house?"

"Beats me." In part, he suspected that his having procured . . . well, just call them *supplies* . . . helped. There were a lot of very fresh corpses lying around in those early days. Really, he tried to think of it as taking clothes from owners who were past caring. Yes, it was crazy. But she was his sister. Whoever said that once you cross a line, it gets easier to do it again and again . . . they had something there. It was lucky he'd thought to bring food, too, because his college buddy was, literally, a gnawed pile of bones by then. But he also had the notion that the idea had been lodged in her brain from the very beginning. Safe because it was remote, the lake house was also familiar territory, too.

"What about Simon?"

He explained about the tranquilizer dart. Carting Simon to Penny was the only way Peter could think of to keep his friend alive and also get the message across: *Take care of her.* Not so complicated.

Even dogs understood simple commands. From the looks of the lake house and that stuff sack with its stockpile of goodies, that message had obviously stuck, although he knew Simon had wandered far. In all the time since the world died, Peter had caught only a few glimpses of Simon and his pack near Rule—always at a distance, and well upwind—but never Penny.

That feeding ground was ghastly but fascinating with its array of wolf carcasses and that skull pyramid. Peter couldn't begin to guess why Simon chose to wear a wolf skin either. *Peter* was interested in wolves. They'd been going to Isle Royale when the accident happened. So, for Simon, did the wolves represent a link to *him*? Possible, but Peter always sensed he was missing something.

"Well, you are the resourceful one, aren't you, boy-o?" Finn leveled a look at Simon. "What about you? Aren't you hungry, son?"

The only change in Simon was his eyes, which hardened to diamonds. This was something Peter never had seen in any Changed, not even Davey. Hunger was one thing. But hate was *personal*. So this was also interesting.

"Well," Finn said again, although his tone carried a measure of bemusement and . . . irritation? "You really *are* different. What I wouldn't give to get inside your head."

"That wasn't the deal. You promised not to hurt them," Peter said, thinking how empty that sounded. Look at *him*. Finn had carved Lang into kebabs.

"I haven't forgotten," Finn said, his voice stony, the avuncular grandpa gone. When Penny tried another snatch, Finn pulled the plate out of reach. "That's enough for now. You thirsty, Penny?" He tugged a water bottle from his hip. "Want something to wash that down?"

The drug. Peter's heart lurched. "Finn!" He tried a lunge, but the collar noosed down. Choking, he strained, throwing his head from side to side. "P-Penny . . . d-don't drink . . ."

"Relax, boy-o." Finn tossed the bottle through the bars. "You think I want to risk this baby? Not on your life. I am *very* interested in that little monster."

"Why?" Peter's throat felt as if he'd swallowed a blowtorch.

"For one thing, I'm curious to see if she eats her young. I'm completely serious about that. For another, that fetus was exposed. Interesting to see what pops out and what it becomes." Folding his arms, Finn nodded at the girl, who was guzzling water. "Look at that. Do you realize that she hasn't *once* offered anything to Simon? It's almost as if he's not there."

Peter *had* noticed. It was so strange, too, given how close they'd all been before. *It's like Penny's been erased.* His eyes shifted to Simon, and he was startled to find Simon's eyes on him. No hatred there, but Peter read plenty of hurt and confusion. Betrayal.

He saw Simon suddenly tense, then wedge himself between Penny and the bars. A moment later, a tent flap rustled as Davey, in his camo-whites, appeared with a guard who seemed to be mostly an ornament.

"Davey." Finn tossed a chunk. Snagging the meat with an expert, one-handed grab, Davey crammed the food into his mouth. His alert eyes never left Finn. "Good boy." Finn patted his leg the way an owner called an attentive puppy. "Let's talk to Peter, all right?"

"What more do you want to talk about?" But he knew. The red winged thing was shifting, needle claws pricking, digging in. Getting ready for . . . well, whatever round this was. "I told you about Penny and Simon—"

"Ah." Finn lifted a finger like a medical receptionist on an important call. "But not the girl."

"I don't know her," Peter said, wondering why he was working so hard at this. Perhaps this was something to hold on to, a little like dignity. But he also had a deeper reason. Finn was pissed he hadn't captured her. Peter liked that someone had actually beaten the asshole at his own game. Or, perhaps, never played to begin with. "Why do you care who she was?"

"Isn't it obvious?" Finn snapped Davey another hunk of meat in a backhanded Frisbee throw. "Whoever she is, she is *not* a Chucky. I saw that girl *speak*. She called to Penny, she was *talking* to Simon, and then she tore out of there, killed one of my best shooters . . . no, no, Davey." Finn held the plate out of reach as the boy made a grab. "Wait now, that's a good boy."

"Even if I knew who she was, which I don't, why is a name so important?"

"And you call yourself a good Christian? In the beginning was the Name, Peter." Finn's eyes were as colorless as a dead snake's. "What did Adam do soon as he opened those baby blues? He *named* everything. Put the world under his thumb. Then he got lonely, God made woman; Adam got to name *her*, assert his dominion, and everything was downhill from there. To *name* is to recognize. It is to gain access and *control*. Things are much scarier in the dark, where they are formless, than in broad daylight. I just want to bring her into the light, that's all."

Access? It was like Finn was talking about hacking a computer's hard drive. Not such a stretch, maybe. Say *carrot*, and the image, the taste, maybe the smell, popped into your head. So did memories. *So a name would be like . . . a password? Into the brain?*

This was begging for a brain bomb, but he couldn't resist. "You scared of her, Finn?"

"I'm interested."

Yeah, I'll bet you are. The way dogs reacted to her always bothered him. Now Peter wondered if she *had* been Changing into something very odd all along. Perhaps Chris made the same choice Peter and the Council had for all the other kids: chased her out before she could be killed. Or she might've only run. But what finally helped him understand just how unique she was came when he saw what Finn had: she talked . . . and Simon had *listened*. At some level, Simon *understood*; Peter saw it in his posture. Then, Simon touched her face—and she let it happen. She *gave* Simon that moment. So there was something there, all right. They were working together, helping each other. There was a bond, and what the hell was *that* about? Because, God, did this mean that Simon might come back? Or was Simon what Finn said he was: *very* different, a one-in-a-million fluke, a Changed with a foot in both worlds?

And she hid, somehow. There was no way she could've killed the hunter and still run fast enough to get away. *She was nearby and Finn still couldn't get his fingernails under her. Davey couldn't track her. So how did she do it?*

"Sorry," he said, although his throat was balky. "Can't help you. Don't know her."

"Mmm-hmm. Thought you might say that." Placing the dish of meat on the camp table, Finn reached into a breast pocket. "I keep forgetting that *you* are a much more effective weapon against yourself than I or anyone could ever be," Finn said, carefully cleaning blood from each finger with a linen kerchief. "Remember: I can give and take, Peter." Folding the kerchief into thirds, Finn tucked the cloth back into his pocket. "Give"—Finn's eyes slid from Peter—"and . . ."

"No!" Peter flailed, struggling against the collar. "No, Finn, leave him alone, *don't*—"

But Simon was already screaming.

89

Fading back from wherever she'd been, with her mind dark and eyes closed and body as motionless as a pillar of salt, and into the silence of those woods and bluing shadows was like reentering the world after a long, dreamless sleep. The wolfdog was still by her side. The only smells drifting through the woods were charred timber, scorched stone, crisped bone. Broiled wolf, and melted nylon. But no Changed, no Finn. No Wolf or Penny. No men.

Her bare feet were white and so cold tears sprang when she tried worming her toes into socks and then her boots before tottering to a stand. Using the hunter's .30-06 Springfield as a crutch, she'd picked her way from the screen of brambles, hobbling like an old woman.

The hunter's body lay where it had fallen. Only his radio was gone. Interesting. The body could be Finn's way of saying just how deeply he didn't care. Perhaps Finn would return to see if other Changed took the bait, but that felt wrong.

Which left a third possibility. The man in black had set out the equivalent of kibbles for a hungry stray: *Here, kitty, kitty. Don't be afraid*. If true, that would suggest he thought she *was* Changed. So, had Finn been bluffing with all his talk, just tossing out lines? Maybe.

All Finn could know for sure: Changed or not, she was the one that got away.

*   *   *

Picking over the hunter's body wasn't her favorite activity, but this guy was loaded for bear. Besides the ammo in his fancy camo, the hunter had a brick of 165-grain super shock tip bullets in his cargo pants and a small headlamp, as well as a flint and striker, an Altoids tin of char, an emergency blanket, a small wad of jute, and a plastic bag of Vaseline-smeared cotton balls. A seven-inch sheathed Buck knife was looped through his belt. She crammed everything into her medic's pack. Feeling more like a grave robber than ever, she unwound his scarf and peeled his watch cap. They smelled like old dead guy, but she needed the clothes.

The house was a smoldering ruin in a crater of rubble and melted snow already on its way to refreezing. Of the wolf totems, only the one hanging beside the stuff sack remained. The fire had burned hot and long enough to barbecue the corpse and partially melt the stuff sack. The body parts it once contained—a rack of ribs, an entire pelvis from waist to just above the thighs, one leg—were now in a heap on the snow. The charred wolf smelled like old cooked tires. The people parts smelled of overdone pork tenderloin. All the bodies, Changed and not, were crumbling, crisped stick figures with impossibly white teeth bared in the lipless grins of blackened skulls.

Skirting the crater, she went around to the porch side. No Wolf or Penny, but plenty of prints. No blood. *They didn't hurt Wolf; they took him alive.* The blast of relief made her knees wobble. That she *was* relieved . . . she didn't want to look at that just yet.

"But Finn must've come because of the baby," she said to the wolf-dog. "He's experimented on the Changed already. I think he's tried the same thing with poor Peter." So, should she *do* anything about that?

No, better question: Did she *need* to do anything at all?

She could act, if she wanted. She had an advantage, a bit of knowledge Finn didn't.

She'd first thought the whole wolf shtick was some weird religion, and it still might be. But Wolf *was* an exception. It was a leap, but she thought she was right. Somehow, Wolf figured it out, too.

The Changed couldn't smell wolves.

What she'd taken to be mystical mumbo jumbo, a way of marking territory, was wrong. Wolf had used wolf skins and carcasses to hide the feeding grounds outside Rule and his kills from other Changed. This was probably the same reason why Wolf had hung totems here, to shield the house *and* protect their food supply. She remembered that brief leap behind the eyes of the Changed who'd been chasing Wolf, Marley, and Ernie. The Changed had no trouble tracking the last two boys. *But they couldn't quite get a fix on Wolf.* He'd been a blank, camouflaged and invisible.

"That's why Darth didn't see you," she said to the wolfdog. "He couldn't smell you, so he never knew you were there." How would that work? Dogs were related to wolves. They always smelled each other's bums, and she bet wolves did, too. Come to think of it, whenever her aunt's cat got spooked, that little stinker let go of some really nasty-smelling goo from its butt. So maybe it wasn't such a stretch to imagine that the same secretions that might *lure* one species would either repel or not register with another.

The wolfdog was the key. So long as it stayed close, the Changed couldn't smell her. Sure, if they *spotted* her, she was cooked. But otherwise?

She was invisible.

"A week ago, I chowed down on ants, and now I catch two rabbits in one day. Wouldn't you know I'd hit the jackpot now? Here." Peeling skin from front paws and head, Alex tossed the carcass to the waiting wolfdog. "Make it last," she said, as the animal began bolting rabbit.

Wherever you came from and for whatever reason you picked me, I'm sure glad you showed up when you did. Picking up the second rabbit, she grabbed a back leg, punched through the thin skin with a thumb, and then began peeling the rabbit out of its skin, working fascia away from red muscle and finishing off by tugging the skin over the carcass's head like an inside-out bodysuit. This one, she'd gut and roast. No need for raw heart this time around.

She and the wolfdog spent the night in Peter's boathouse. The weird thing: she couldn't get comfortable. It had been months since she'd slept on a mattress and with a pillow, and she was uncomfortable, anxious. After a few hours of tossing, she gave up, wrapped herself in a blanket, strapped on the headlamp, and spread the atlases from Peter's bookshelf on the floor.

Once she hiked out to a main road and got her bearings, she could go anywhere. Her earlier ideas about warning Chris seemed naïve now, so much wasted energy. If Peter was with Finn, Rule was in much bigger trouble than she'd realized. She also had no way of tracking Tom. So, if she stayed in Michigan, only two destinations made sense: Rule or Oren. The dead boy from Oren had her whistle, which meant Ellie had been there. While she still might be, the chances of stumbling on one little girl were ten trillion to one.

Which left Rule, a place that felt radioactive.

But Finn has Wolf. He has Penny and Peter. I can't just let that go.

"Oh, don't be crazy, Alex. You're not Batman." On the floor, snugged against her left leg, the wolfdog's ears pricked. "Seriously?" she asked the animal. "Rescue them so they starve, or I have to shoot them to protect myself or, say, Ellie? Tom? Chris? If it came down to a choice between Wolf and Tom, I'd pick Tom. I'm not saying it would be easy, and it feels wrong because Wolf is . . . in-between, just like me," she finished in a whisper, definitely *not* understanding why her eyes stung.

Oh, stop feeling sorry for yourself. She rested a cheek on her knees. Yet Wolf *was* different now. In the beginning, she'd been only food; he'd chowed down on a slice of her shoulder, for God's sake. But then

Wolf saved her from Spider, kept her off-menu; rescued her from the mine and then Acne. They'd worked together to fight Finn's men before he'd made her leave him behind and save herself. Wolf *cared* about her. It was in what he did, and his scent.

"And I care what happens to him," she said, feeling the ooze of a tear and a weird hollowness in her chest. So, fine, all right, she was evil and maybe brainwashed, and this definitely wasn't *love* . . . was it? No, of course not, but she *cared*, okay? Shoot her.

But Wolf still has to eat. It wasn't as if Wolf was suddenly going to go vegan. Yes, he cared for her and she was pretty sure he would never hurt her now. That kind of amnesty might also extend to the people she cared about. For Wolf to live, though, he had to eat.

"I don't know what's right," she said to the wolfdog. "Maybe it's smarter to kill Wolf, but it would be like putting a gun to Tom's head, or Chris's." Wasn't that exactly what Tom *wanted* her to do if he Changed? Tom had killed Jim, his friend, to save her and Ellie. Could *she* do something like that? At the last second, if there was no other choice, she probably would. "But maybe we're not there yet. And what if Wolf *can* come back? Then I have to do something. I can't just *leave* him with Finn. It wouldn't be right." Penny . . . she wasn't sure what to do with her. But there was Peter, too, caught in between like her and Wolf. Whatever Finn had done to him might also be undone, eventually.

So, go to Rule? See if she picked up Wolf's scent? It was insane, but with the wolfdog, she might pull it off. As long as she didn't succumb to the *push-push go-go* . . .

"You know what I can't figure out?" she asked the wolfdog. "What that whole thing was. Like the monster either grabbed on *to* or got grabbed *by* Finn, then jerked me along for the ride. I hopped. First I land behind one set of eyes and then a whole bunch of other eyes, and then I jump to someone else, further ahead." She thought about that. "Know what it reminds me of?" At the wolfdog's look—*no, really, tell me*—she said, "High school bio."

Really? The wolfdog cocked its head. *Which part?*

"How the brain works and cells talk to each other." By that point in bio, the monster had shown itself, too, and she became somewhat of an expert. "The brain's an electrical system mediated by chemicals. But here's the thing," she said to the wolfdog. She was starting to get a little excited now; felt she was onto something. "The brain has *tons* of synapses, like more than the stars in the Milky Way. Even an electrical impulse would be too slow on its own for everything to work together the way it should. So the impulse has to *hop*. It jumps like a bunny from node to node along an axon, and that speeds everything up."

So what *if* Finn was doing that? "Like an out-of-body thing. A signal leapfrogging from mind to mind. Only it can't be a straight line. Too inefficient." And wouldn't the signal decay? She thought that was right; depending on the frequency, a radio signal could peter out fast, and hadn't cell towers worked the same way? *Unless you boost the signals somehow.* So how did Finn work around that? She thought about how the *push-push go-go* got stronger when Finn was closer. *Like roaming, or Wi-Fi. The monster got part of it, like a cell phone getting only a bar or two instead of four or five.* And then what had happened? The monster tried looping her in, on its own?

"Or maybe the monster couldn't help it." She said this slowly, testing each word. "Unless you disabled a computer's Wi-Fi, it would automatically search for a connection, a network, something to grab." With the exception of Wolf, for whom the monster seemed to have a special affinity, every time she'd leapfrogged into a Changed's mind was on the basis of both proximity and the strength of an emotion: lust, hunger. Rage. "But the monster can't *always* be receptive, because it doesn't happen all the time. I never *really* know what's going on; it's like being in a French class when all you speak is Russian. You *hear* sounds, but that's not the same as *knowing* what they mean—and I don't *hear* anything anyway. Whatever I figure out is from the scent."

Because it's not the right kind of signal, nothing to snag the monster's interest? Like lunch in the cafeteria . . . there's always the buzz of conversation, but unless you make an effort you don't pay attention, because you're either not interested or you're focused on something else: finding your friends, for example, or someone's called your name from across the room. The rest of the time, you don't hear anything, really, even though you register the noise.

So, a regular conversation between Changed wasn't *strong* or *interesting* enough to goose the monster? Even when she *did* hop—that time she'd dropped behind Spider's eyes, for example, way back at the lake house after Spider had killed poor little Jack—it wasn't like eavesdropping. She was never pulled into a wider conversation. *Because I really don't understand the language? Or maybe . . .*

"There's some other piece I'm not seeing." She also had this really crummy feeling that she had to experience the mind-jump a couple more times before she figured it out. If she followed Finn, she'd be asking for trouble, because if she *was* right about proximity and the monster *was* receptive, getting closer to Finn and his weird, altered Changed would increase the chances of her being detected or pulled in, or losing herself in the red storm.

"And Finn sensed the monster. He felt my edges." Which was also different. Wolf and Spider, Leopard, Acne . . . none showed any awareness of her or the monster at all. But Finn had. How could he do that?

"Hell if I know, and I'm not going to figure it out tonight." Her head ached, and she needed sleep. Clicking off the headlamp, she settled down next to the wolfdog, which groaned and put its chin on her belly. "I like you, too. If we ever see my dog again, you can't eat him, okay?" She stroked the animal's ears. "Should give you a name."

A name. She thought about that. *Finn wanted my name. He asked twice. Why?*

"Something important about a name . . ." She scrubbed the wolf-dog's chin. "So how do you feel about Buck? Great book, and you fit. Me, too. We're both half wild now, aren't we, boy?" That made her think of Peter's paperbacks. She should take a few. Long walk ahead, but that was all right. She needed time to think about what to do.

Still fidgety, she rolled onto her side and heard the crinkle of that Almond Joy wrapper in the pocket where she'd stowed the candy. So tempting to eat the other half. But she should hold off, maybe wait for a real celebration.

She let go of a very long sigh. "Because, sometimes," she said to Buck, "you just feel like a nut."

PART FIVE: MONSTERS

90

"Tom!" Weller, far behind on his grullo and barely audible over the thunder of hooves. "Wait, Tom, wait up!"

No, he couldn't wait, wouldn't stop, not just yet, maybe not ever. *Go go go.* His head was the size of the sky, the panic in his chest a claw. *Get out, get out, cut the wire, go!* Tom kicked his horse again. Felt the mare dig even deeper. The world streamed: snow and choking red funnel clouds from rotor wash; evergreens and the *thump-thump-thump* of helos; fingers of oaks scratching blue sky; body parts falling to earth in a ghastly rain; and that dead dog, careful, careful, they put bombs in everything, in dogs, in trash, in dead kids, and *go go go.*

If he'd stayed one more second, he might've put a bullet through Mellie's head. That he imagined what her head would look and sound like if he did frightened him even more.

Can't let it get me. He swept past a stack of burning tires; bloated dogs bobbing in sewage; a pile of rubbish, and that bottle that might not hold water at all; rubble where, five seconds ago, there'd been a house with children and laundry snapping on a line. *Can't let it take over.* Past a phalanx of screeching, wailing women, *shut up, shut up, shut up*—and Jim: Jim, in the Waucamaw; Jim, bellowing, charging . . .

"Tom!" Weller bawled. "Hold up before you lame or kill that poor horse, goddamn it!"

Of course, Weller was right. This was a bad move, stupid. A single, powerful jab through the diminished hard pack into a tangle

453

of branches or rocks would cripple the mare. He'd have to put it down—*shoot it like Jim*—over something he could've prevented.

"Ho, girl, ease down, ease down." Hearing his own voice helped. He pulled left, enough to turn the mare's head and break that gallop. Beneath him, he felt the horse's chest strain for breath. Gobs of thick foam lathered its face to the poll. "Sorry, girl," he said, patting the animal's shuddering neck, feeling the thrum of blood under his own, still-healing flesh. He was panting, too, and couldn't tell if that was only sweat on his cheeks. To his right, a Humvee wallowed at a near-ninety-degree angle, the driver's arm only just visible in yellow canal water because body armor was that heavy. He looked away. "Ease up, girl. We'll be okay."

But only if you get control of yourself. Turning the mare, he watched as Weller slowed his own horse to a trot. *Get it together, Tom, or you won't be able to help anyone.*

"Jesus." Reining in his blowing animal, Weller armed his forehead, then shrugged his bum right shoulder. "I won't ask what the hell you think you're doing."

There was brown blood caked on Weller's neck below the jaw he didn't have anymore, and Tom could see the useless worm of a blue tongue. *Not real.* Averting his eyes, Tom pulled in a breath that reeked of diesel fuel and burning oil. "I had to get out. I couldn't think . . ." He gathered himself. *Come on, Tom; look at him; Weller is fine; the rest is a damned flashback.* He forced his eyes back and thought, to his immense relief, that Weller could use a shave. "What Mellie wants makes no sense. You *have* to know that."

"I do." Weller threw him an irritated look. "But there are better ways to get your point across than challenging her in front of the kids. Only puts her back up."

"I know. I left because I didn't want to completely lose it in front of them."

"Oh no, it was so much better for the kids to see you tear out of camp like a crazy person." Screwing up his mouth, Weller spat, sighed, then prodded his silvery-white gelding north. "Come on, might as well walk the horses the rest of the way to the church and pick up Cindi and Chad. We can talk this out. You and me, Tom, we'll figure a way."

"How? Mellie won't listen. She thinks you're better off without me. Maybe she's right."

"Don't be stupid, Tom. Those kids need you, and I think you need them just as much."

"Then we have to stop her." After five seconds, he realized that the smell of fuel and oil had vanished, and he no longer heard the ululating wails of women. "She'll push those kids until there's an accident, Weller, or worse. Mellie will keep going until those kids are dead."

"Tom, take a breath." Mellie's tone was that of a playground monitor heading off an eight-year-old's tantrum at being forced off the jungle gym. "I hear you, but aren't you supposed to be heading for the church? We'll talk when you come back, all right? Now is not the time for this discussion."

"No, Mellie, you *don't* hear me and this *is* the time." Tom tossed a glance at a clutch of some two dozen kids. Only Luke stood apart, throwing worried looks, clearly wanting Tom to put on the brakes. The rest excitedly milled around the concrete cap of a cistern behind an all-metal equipment shed where Tom had set up shop several weeks before.

He'd been afraid this would happen. Kids loved a *ka-boom*. It was why he hadn't allowed anyone to watch him put together the penetrators they'd used in the mine. Gathering what was left—the det cord, the C4, caps, detonators, *everything*—he'd divvied it up, stashing most where no one would think to look. He only wished he'd remembered the aluminum powder and magnesium ribbon. And that bottle of glycerin. Stupid.

"Yes, it's great that Jasper's motivated. I agree he's smart. But Mellie . . . seriously? A ten-year-old monkeying around with thermite? Trying to slow the reaction?"

"Are you saying it can't be done? It was your idea, wasn't it?"

"Yes, for the time delays at the mine, when I thought we might need it." Thermite was a great primary incendiary. The problem was the reaction was very fast. He'd hit on the goofy idea of using fire retardants to stretch the reaction time, and it had worked. The last time he tried, he got nearly ten minutes, but the ratios had to be just right and he was still uncomfortable with an unpredictable incendiary whose temp topped over three thousand degrees. "Unless you're planning to rob a bank, I can't think why you need something that can melt steel. Mellie, these are *children*. *I* know what I'm doing."

"You do? Have you taken a good look in the mirror?" She flipped a dismissive hand at the Uzi, on a retention strap so his hand was on the pistol grip at all times. Jed's Bravo was slotted in a back scabbard. The Glock 19 rode in a cross-draw on his left hip, and he carried two knives: the KA-BAR in its leg sheath and a boot knife as a last resort. "Armed to the teeth. Riding out to the church every day as an escort? You look ready for Armageddon."

"I . . . what I do is . . ." Was *what*? Only common sense? That was a lie. Never far away to begin with, all the old horrors—flashbacks, nightmares, that awful crushing panic—had roared back after the fight on the snow to fuel the black monster growing in his chest. Whenever he walked into the farmhouse or barn now, he immediately scanned all the exits, tried to work out the fastest way to egress. *Get out, move, go, evade.* Two days ago, when a group of kids got between him and the door, a flood of adrenaline drowned his mind and then he was in a cold sweat, heart pounding, thinking, *Thirty-two rounds in the Uzi, nineteen in the Glock, five in the Bravo*, as he methodically devised an escape route, which children to shoot and in what order he should kill them. That scared him so badly he'd bolted, shoving Luke aside and banging out into the snow where he'd run, fast, air ripping his lungs until the razor panic dulled.

To Mellie, he said, "Don't twist this around to be about me, all right?"

"But this *is* about you. *You* want us to move. *You* want us to find a more secure location. You hide *our* det cord, *our* C4, everything, and all of a sudden, *you* have decided we don't need to go to Rule. These are not your decisions, Tom. *I'm* in charge, not you."

"Last time I looked, I was in charge, too." Weller had been so quiet, Tom forgot he was there. "Tom's right. Maybe there are better things we should be teaching those kids."

"Oh, how perfect." The frost in Mellie's tone was unmistakable. "A convert."

"Those things were *out* there," Tom said. "I *fought* one. I *saw* more. We need to *move.*"

"That was two weeks ago, Tom, and where are these monsters? Don't you think that if there were something to be worried about we'd have seen it by now? Now, I'm sorry about the mine. I'm sorry about Alex. But you need to get over that already."

"Mellie," Weller said sharply.

"If I had a nickel every time someone suggested I should just get over Afghanistan already, I'd be a millionaire five times over," Tom said. How could you get past a splinter that had worked into your eye and scratched deeper every time you blinked? "Hear me out, all right? Let's leave"—his throat tried to knot—"let's leave Alex out of it. Let's talk reality. Luke is fourteen, Cindi is twelve, Chad's thirteen. That leaves, what . . . three other twelve-year-olds?"

"Yes." Mellie's eyes were as testy as her voice. "And?"

"Do I need to spell this out? For God's sake, Mellie, *napalm*? These are *children*. They can't fight, and they certainly shouldn't march off to war. There's no reason to go to Rule."

"Oh? I know you said to leave Alex out of this, but tell me, Tom, would you have had this sudden change of heart if Alex hadn't been in the mine?"

"Yes. Wait . . . let me finish." He was honest enough to know this would come, but it still sent a knife through his heart. "Of course, I'd go to Rule. Nothing would stop me."

"So now that there's nothing you stand to *gain* . . ."

"I said *I* would go. Getting Alex out would be *my* fight."

"Really. You were happy enough for Luke to go with you, and Weller."

Tom opened his mouth, then closed it. *Happy* was the wrong word. But she was right.

"Uh-huh." Mellie nodded when he remained silent. "Don't pretend you're more noble or any better. Think about how you used Luke, risked his life for your gain—and then tell me I'm so much worse. There is only *one* person you truly care about, Tom, and she's *dead*. So get over it, Tom, or get out."

"*Mellie!*" Weller said. "Let's all just calm down, all right?"

"Oh, shut up, Weller." She rounded on him. "I'm tired of you taking his side. *Look* at him. He's unpredictable and dangerous. He's not fit to be around these children."

"I . . . I know I've had a few . . ." Tom stopped again. What was he going to say?

"Yes, a *few.* Go." She made a shooing motion. "Get out of here. Take your little ride to the church, escort Chad and Cindi, go play soldier, do *something* useful, but both of you, get out of my sight. Oh, and Tom? I'll thank you to return my explosives."

That was the moment his forefinger twitched and he imagined his bullet drilling her eye and fragging her skull—red mist, pink brain—and for him, how sweet the sound.

"Under the horse trough," he heard himself say. "Take it all. I never want to see or make another bomb as long as I live."

Then he got out of there, fast, afraid that he might just prove how dangerous he could be.

"She's right." Tom gave Weller a weary look. "Who am I to tell these kids anything?"

"You're human. But she did rip you a new one. Don't understand what got into her." Weller shook his head. "Stressed out like the rest of us, I guess. So what'd you have in mind?"

"I've said it: forget about Rule." To his left, the Lutheran church's bell tower rose from a far knoll hemmed by evergreens. Through gaps in the trees, Tom thought he saw Chad and Cindi's horses tethered to a bicycle rack. But were they lying down? He wished he hadn't left his binos back at camp. In another few feet, the trees closed in again. He looked at Weller. "This isn't a novel or movie where they can move from town to town and scavenge. Eventually, everything will run out. Take Jasper: he's smart enough to make thermite, but he's got no idea how to farm, hunt, keep himself warm, build a house that won't fall down. We have to help these kids create a life."

Wouldn't that also mean giving up on Alex? If he meant what he said, he would have to let go of the idea of searching for her. He didn't want to. Caring for these kids didn't come close to easing the ache. But Luke had come to *him*. Cindi had skied out to this church every day to be with *him*. He couldn't let them down. And, yes, he *was* still afraid of going to Rule. Of what he might do if he ever met Chris Prentiss face-to-face.

"Can't argue that," Weller said. "You have an idea where?"

"Yes." Jed's cabin, a stone's throw from Michipicoten Island, was a place Tom always imagined taking Alex. Thirty kids made that a nonstarter. Forget an island's limited resources; simply *getting* them all there would be a feat. He liked the *idea* of a large island, though.

"We go west or north, and stay far away from Rule."

"Not much north, except the Waucamaw," Weller said, still staring straight ahead.

"There's Oren and an Amish settlement west of that. They're farmers, right? Arable land is exactly what we need."

"Finding seed will be tough," Weller said. "Trying to grow enough to feed all those kids, figuring out how to preserve it for winter—"

"Will be hard," Tom said. "I understand that. But we have to do it sometime, and that might as well be now. The growing season up here is short. The longer we wait, the more difficult this will become, and before we know it, it'll be winter again. For all we know, there's still livestock to be found, and horses. We have to get to those animals before they die, too, or get so wild we'll never chase them down."

Weller's hand snuck to his mouth, a gesture Tom always associated with a man mentally rehearsing what to say next. "Maybe," Weller said. "But Amish . . . if there are any left alive, they tend to keep to themselves. Don't want outsiders—" Frowning, the old man abruptly straightened in his saddle and craned. "Tom . . . you get a good look at that horse? Up there by the church?"

Tom switched his gaze from Weller to the near bend in the road and the church, on its bald knob, just now coming into view. They were still a quarter mile away, but from this approach he could see a wedge of snow to the rear beneath which must lie a parking lot. In front, the snow was broken from horses, skis, and boots. The bike rack, where he'd seen the horses, was to the right of stone steps, and only just visible.

As was the single horse, on its side, in a bowl of shadow. Even then, it was on the tip of his tongue to observe that horses could lie so still it was easy to think they were dead.

But then, Tom saw the blood.

91

"So what'd you think?" Already a total spaz, Jasper was practically vibrating. Jiggling free an aluminum bowl from clamps suspended above a bucket of sand, he put the bowl to his eye. "Pretty cool, huh?"

"Mmm." Luke spared a glance at the blue button of Jasper's eye peering through the bottom. Never having seen thermite in action, he was startled at how high that shower of sparks leapt, a good five feet. The pillar of fire was even higher and so bright he'd shielded his eyes.

But where was Tom? Earlier, there'd been no mistaking Tom's dark look, or his anger. What surprised Luke was when, instead of staying and *stopping* this craziness, Tom wheeled away, really fast, then streaked off on his horse in the general direction of the church, with Weller a few minutes behind. Now, an hour later, still no Tom, no Weller.

Not good.

"Yeah, it was all right," he said to Jasper, who was dancing from foot to foot like he had to pee. "But unless you can slow it way down"—he wanted to add, *without blowing your head off,* but thought that would be lost on a nut like Jasper—"what do we need it for?"

"This is already fifteen seconds slower than the last batch." Jasper sounded offended. "I ground the aluminum coarser and that slows the reaction. But I saw a TV show where this arsonist used stuff from fire extinguishers to slow down the reaction, and so I was thinking, you know, why not? Tom kind of said something about that, and I *know* he was working on it, only he did it in secret and he won't show me what he did. But I think he figured out how to use . . . uhm . . ." Jasper screwed his lips to a rosebud in thought. "Ammonium phosphate. I think."

"Great," Luke said, with no enthusiasm at all. He pulled the bucket of sand from the concrete cistern cap. In the center was a large, gray, cow patty-like splotch of molten iron and aluminum slag still shimmering with heat. "Gas us all with ammonia. That'll be just swell."

"No, just phosphoric acid when the phosphorus combines with water. It won't *kill* you, not right away. Anyway, it *could* work," Jasper said. "It did on the show."

What had his parents let this kid watch? "This is reality, Jasper," Luke said, and turned to trudge toward the equipment shed. The going was much easier these days, what with the snowpack diminished, no more than six inches now, and a good foot less than it had been when they blew the mine. Now that they were into the middle of March, the first hints of spring sometimes came in sudden whiffs of sun-warmed air. The roofs of the buildings were showing. Breaking the ice over the horse troughs took only a hard kick.

After the demonstration, Mellie had stayed to enthuse before shooing the other kids back to their various chores: taking care of the horses, gathering wood for fires, slopping MREs into a pot for a communal supper. He looked for her now, sweeping his gaze left from the equipment shed, which sat at the base of the north slope and was the furthest of the outbuildings, to the cow barn where Mellie and Weller had set up their command post. They stockpiled their weapons there, too, Mellie or Weller doling out rifles from a locker to those kids on lookout or guard duty. Beyond the red rectangle of the barn was a hog shed where half the kids bunked. A little further on was a horse barn with a staved-in roof, though half the space was still serviceable. He could see people moving around, the fire flaring up in the center of the cow corral as kids fed it. A handful of yapping dogs raced and rolled on a near fan of land rising east to a knoll and then to pasture. As far as he could tell, Mellie wasn't down with the kids.

Probably at the house. Up to me to talk to her, I guess. After Tom, he was the oldest. Just work up the nerve, that was all. Tell Mellie what a crummy idea this all was and how they ought to be thinking about spring coming, finding a home. What was the worst she could say?

At the shed, he set the bucket of sand down next to the roller door, then ducked in via the side door, with Jasper on his heels. Emptied of farm equipment, the shed instead was divided into workstations, long planks supported by sawhorses. Tom's area was completely clear, all his equipment squirreled away somewhere only he knew. Jasper's work area was littered with rolls of magnesium ribbon, bottles of aluminum powder, sulfur, potassium nitrate, glycerin, a large plastic tub of plaster of Paris. Nearby, another of Jasper's buddies was experimenting with chunks of Styrofoam, gasoline, various soaps, sugar, and lighter fluid, trying to figure a way to make a suitably sticky version of napalm. Still another team was scoring old soda bottles with glass cutters for Molotov cocktails. The air smelled of chemical welds, gasoline, and old eggs.

What are we doing? They were developing weapons just to do it, Mellie setting them to various tasks like a guidance counselor slotting them into career paths. In a couple months, it would be spring. Would they still be living out of tents? Broken-down barns? How long did disasters go on?

"We need to find a home," he said.

"Huh?" Jasper glanced up from his perusal of a slender red fire extinguisher. "What?"

"Nothing." Tasting *home* hurt his mouth. His vision wavered, and he stood up suddenly, barking a knee against a sawhorse.

"You okay?" Jasper asked.

"Yeah." Knee throbbing, he gimped to the door. "Don't crack any of those fire extinguishers until I get back, okay?"

"I *wouldn't*," Jasper said, with the injured dignity of a kid eyeing a cookie jar. "What about potassium chloride? You know, Super-K extinguishers?"

"Wouldn't the chloride turn into chlorine gas? Won't that kill you pretty fast?"

He watched Jasper think about it. "Oh. Maybe." Jasper made a face. "Shoot."

"Yeah," Luke said, turning to go. "Reality blows."

He took his time slogging to the farmhouse, rehearsing what to say. Giving out grief had been his older sister's specialty. By the time his parents got around to him, either she'd worn them out, or they didn't much care. His mom once said that getting all worked up about kids was like worrying about dropped pacifiers: the first kid, you sterilized that sucker; the second kid, you wiped the Binky on your jeans. *And by the third, you let the dog lick it.*

That brought a grin. His mom always cracked him up. He should tell Cindi. She'd appreciate it. One thing Cindi was good at was telling stories, most of them about her mom. He liked listening, too, because she made it sound like a once-upon-a-time.

That's what we should be doing. We should be swapping stories and toasting marshmallows. Like home. The thought pushed a lump into his throat. At the farmhouse steps, he tipped a look back. Three of the dogs were still roughhousing, although a fourth was pointed east, nosing the knoll, and *yark-yark-yarking*. Now that he was up higher, Luke could easily eyeball the fields beyond the horse barn and the lookouts, black specks on a distant knoll.

We need a home. He studied their tent city and the kids at their chores, the orange candle of that bonfire. *A place to call our own.*

* * *

The farmhouse, a two-story with dormers, was quiet. The kitchen was empty, although a mug with the black and red tag of a teabag draped over the lip sat on the table, and a chair was pushed back. The air smelled of warm oranges. Maybe Mellie was sleeping? Uncertain now, he stood a moment, eyes on the ceiling, listening for footsteps. Nothing moved overhead. He knew that Weller slept on the ground level, but he had no idea if Mellie used the other back bedrooms.

He opened his mouth to call, then hesitated. Listened. The dog's *yark-yark-yark* was muffled, though he thought there might be two barking now. This seriously creepy vibe suddenly tickled his neck, like the day he snuck into his parents' bedroom and started opening drawers to discover, well . . . *things.* Like, *my dad reads these? They* do *things like that?* He kept expecting his dad to pop out of a closet. For weeks, whenever his dad put an arm around his mom, Luke broke into a sweat.

This was like that. He was someplace he didn't belong, about to see something he had no business seeing, not if he knew what was good—

From down the hall came a muted mechanical *click.* And then two more.

He went rigid. After a moment, the sounds came again: *click.* Pause. *Click-click-click.* Pause. *Click-click-click.*

Luke's heart skipped. He might not know the meaning, but he understood what this was.

Code.

92

When he spotted the blood, Tom made them peel off the road, get under cover, and wait. This went against every impulse that screamed he needed to get to Cindi and Chad, *right now*. But it was the same as it had been in Jed's shed when the bounty hunters came: panic, and everyone died. So, instead, he and Weller crept in gradually, ducking behind and under what scant cover they had.

The church's front doors were ajar, an open invitation they took, Weller sweeping low as he angled high because everyone forgot to look up. The church's interior was deeply shadowed, with dark corners from which anything might spring. Tom's eyes scoured the stone floor and along the pews for trip wires, a curl of det cord. But there was nothing.

The tower had seven landings accessible by wrought iron ladders fixed to limestone walls. Weller covered as he led the way, scrutinizing each rung and rail for wires, pressure switches. More nothing, and no one blasted down from above. A defunct carillon console was still just as thick with dust and cobwebs as it had been when Tom climbed down two weeks ago.

Which left only the trap at the top of the seventh ladder. Tom stood there a good minute, listening for the tread of a boot, a squeal of wood. He felt cold air seeping from the open belfry, and thin slivers of daylight glimmered through gaps in the wood. But there were no dead spaces, nothing blacked out. He used the tip of his Uzi to ease open the trap. Nothing went *ka-boom*, and there was no muzzle flash.

The first thing he saw in the belfry was that the stool, on which he'd perched for hours, lay on its side. Beside it, on the floor, was the rumpled mound of a sleeping bag. A book splayed, facedown, next to the stool and Cindi's binos, a pair of Nikon 8X42s that she liked for when the light started to go. Wrappers were scattered over the floor. A small litter of crumpled lunch bags and balled waxed paper half-covered Cindi's Nikons. A water bottle and thermos were overturned. The air smelled of cold chicken broth and wet noodles.

From the looks of it, the kids put up a fight. Yet as they headed down from the belfry and out of the church, Tom worried the tableau. Something was off, but damned if he knew precisely what.

"I don't know about this." Weller crouched over the mutilated body of Chad's dog. The animal had been decapitated, its severed head lying at the bottom of the steps like a discarded basketball. "That's a clean cut, and I'll bet it was the first one, too. Look at the blood spray. But"—he reached to turn the dog over—"if you look at these cuts here . . ."

"*Don't!*" Tom snatched Weller's wrist. "It could be booby-trapped; they plant *bombs* in dead dogs."

"Ease down, Tom. We're not in Afghanistan." Weller gave his hand a pointed glance. "Mind?"

"No. Just . . . be careful." Exhaling, Tom forced his hand to relax. He did not like this at all. The back of his neck was jumping. Being out in the open, on this bald knob, made him nervous. He and Weller were static targets, just *begging* to be picked off. "First time for everything."

"No arguments from me there." Weller rolled the dog's stiffening body, then grunted. "Look at the blood."

The vermillion pool was small, a few tablespoons. "Not enough." Tom turned back and eyed the spray-painted stone of the church's front. "So those had to come first, when the heart was still pumping. You're saying they cut the head off first and then mutilated the body after the dog was dead?"

"Be my guess." Weller held a hand over a slop of the dog's colon. "Cold. Blood's real thick. Whatever happened here happened a while back. Hours, probably. Same thing with Chad's horse." Like the dog, the mare's belly was ripped. Pulverized organs splattered the snow. The stink was terrible, a rancid, fecal odor that made a pulse of bile boil to the back of Tom's throat. The horse's skull had been hacked straight down through the poll, leaving an ax-shaped divot that neatly split the skull in two. "Hatchet or a big machete for the killing blow, and then they could take their time tearing up the animal once it was down. But Tom . . ." Weller aimed a forefinger at the stump of the dog's neck. "That is a *clean* cut."

Tom stared at Weller for a full ten seconds before he got it. "The dog was standing still. It recognized whoever did this."

"Or responded to commands, yeah. *Or* it could've been helped along."

"What are you talking about?"

"Look at the head. What's missing, something Chad's dog always wore?"

Tom's gaze raked over the dog's glazed eyes, the sagging half-shuttered lids, that lolling blue tongue. "The muzzle. Chad always muzzled his dog when he went on lookout."

"Right. I think someone removed the muzzle and fed the dog something. Put it to sleep and then you can chop off the head pretty easy. So, one thing's for sure, it couldn't have been a Chucky. That dog would *never* stand still or let it get close, *and* they only killed the one horse. Why do that unless you need the other? Chuckies don't ride."

"Unless, now, some do or can." Tom thought about that. "You know what else is wrong? There's nothing covert about this. It's like they're trying to spook or impress us. This all feels"—he waved a hand—"*arranged*." That jogged something else loose. "You remember upstairs? It looks like there was a struggle, right? But what *wasn't* there, Weller?"

"I don't follow."

"No brass. No smell of gunpowder."

"Maybe Chad never got off a shot."

"Come on, the place was a mess. Cindi dropped her book, the binos, kicked over her stool and the thermos, but Chad never fired a shot?" There was *still* something else wrong with that scene, too, a nag in his mind like a loose tooth begging to be nudged from its socket.

"You're saying it's the same as the dog? That they knew him?"

"Or had no reason to be scared until too late, yeah. But how many people, who could do something like this, do the kids know? There are only three: you, me—and Mellie."

"I hear you, but . . ." Weller shook his head. "I don't see it. Besides, she's been at camp all day. Couldn't have been Mellie, and I know it wasn't me."

Had he seen Weller earlier in the day? "She could've arranged for it to happen."

"What? She'd never do that. What are you saying?"

"You heard me," Tom said. "I think there's another player."

93

"Another player?" Weller echoed.

Tom nodded. "Has to be, unless it really was Mellie. But I'm thinking that it's someone she knows and who could convince the kids he wasn't a threat."

"I . . ." Weller's gaze danced to the snow as he drew a careful hand over his mouth. "I'm not seeing it, Tom. Why would she do that?"

Tom's stomach went leaden. He knew Weller's mannerisms and tells, and now he had to be careful. More compact, the arc of swing required to bring his Uzi to bear was much shorter than for Weller's rifle. This was a contest he could win. But they weren't there yet, and he had no wish to nudge them any closer to the brink. If this old man wanted Tom dead, he'd already had plenty of opportunities. "I guess that's what I'm asking you," he said.

For a long, tense moment, Weller only looked at him. He must've read something in Tom's face he didn't like, because the old man suddenly raised both hands in surrender. No way Weller would win in a draw down now. "Take it easy, Tom."

"Two kids are missing, this horse and the dog are hamburger, and I should take it easy?" When Weller said nothing, he said, "Do you know what's going on?"

"No," the old man rasped, then sighed. "Not entirely, and not anything about *this*."

"You want to tell me what you *do* know?" At Weller's silence, he said, "Am I *not* supposed to make it back alive?"

The utter astonishment on Weller's face was real. "What? Tom, that's crazy."

"According to Mellie, I'm the resident expert on crazy." Now he felt a simmer of anger, the sneak of a finger on his trigger guard. *Take it easy. Don't make a move you can't take back.* "What's going on?"

"I don't *know* what's going on here," Weller snapped. "Whatever game Mellie's playing, *if* she even is, I don't have a clue. Now I'm putting my hands down."

Sentimentality aside, he wasn't stupid. Tom took another step back. "You could put the rifle down, too."

"Not a chance in hell. I'd like to live to see tomorrow, thank you very much, and there is no way you're taking my weapon. So either shoot me and go save those kids, or we get out of here now, together, because I do . . . not . . . *like* this, Tom. There is something going down, and we are in the *wrong* place to stop it." When he didn't move, Weller grated, "Jesus Christ on a crutch, Tom, I do *not* want you dead. I don't want *any* more dead kids if I can help it. I will tell you what I know, but right now, all we got is each other, and *we* got to get to our kids. You're going to have to trust me that far. You have my word on it, Tom, soldier to soldier."

That, he believed. "All right," Tom said, breaking his elbow, hoping it wasn't the last thing he ever did. "But I'm not sure we should race back. We need to think this through because it might be that what's going down is going down now. We still need to find Cindi and Chad."

"I'm with you on all that." Weller's shoulders drooped with relief. "For what it's worth, I don't think Mellie would hurt the kids, not intentionally anyway."

"You don't sound very certain."

"Because I'm not," Weller said. "So let's go figure out what to do next."

* * *

They were halfway to the horses, Tom a step or two behind Weller because, soldier to soldier notwithstanding, it paid to be careful. All of a sudden, Weller came to a dead stop and tipped a look at the sky. "Where the hell's my head?"

Tom narrowly missed plowing into the older man's back. "What?"

"We're going to need to scout things out, work some sort of angle, right? Well, I don't have my binos. Do you?"

"They're back at camp. We can take Cindi's. I'll go back up—"

"No, you go on, get the horses. It's further, and I'm a lazy cuss." Cracking a grin, Weller was already trotting back up the steps. "Won't be but a minute."

It was when Tom was leading the horses back to the church that he realized what else it was that bothered him about that mess in the belfry.

An overturned stool. A dropped book. The tipped thermos. And garbage.

Cindi's a neatnik. Whenever she visited him, she carefully refolded paper bags, waxed paper. Yet now there was trash, and not just anywhere, but—

You're startled enough to drop a book and your binoculars. You kick over the stool. There's chicken soup on the floor, and litter. His eyes widened. *But that one mound of trash is piled on the binoculars, and that can't be, not if she dropped—*

"Weller!" Tom charged for the church. "Weller, *no, NO!*"

94

Click-click-click. Click. Click. And now a sputter, like a snake.

Static. The hairs stood on Luke's scalp. *Mellie's got a radio, and she's talking to someone, in code.*

Against every particle of good sense, he eased down the hall. The clicks sounded at erratic intervals. His pulse banged in his ears. This was dumb; what could he tell Tom? *Well, there was this funky clicking?* But if there *was* a radio and someone *spoke*—

From beneath his left boot came a loud, high squeal of a fatigued board: a real horror-show *CREEEEE* that made his brain freeze. A second later, he heard the telltale squall of bedsprings, and . . . "Hello?" The tone was sharp, the volume growing as Mellie moved for the bedroom door. "Who's—"

Get out, get out! Whirling for the front door, he stumbled onto the porch at the same moment a door slammed drywall and Mellie shouted, "*Who*—"

Still running, he took the front steps in three leaping strides and plunged down the slope. What to do, what to do? *Tom, Tom, where are you?* Tom would know; Tom, he could trust. But Luke was on his own, and all he could think of was to run. He'd automatically headed toward the equipment shed, but now he thought, *Wait, I'm safer around other people.* He veered toward the cow barn and corral, steaming through the snow. Ahead, there were knots of kids, the bonfire. All the dogs had trotted halfway up the knoll past the far horse barn and were barking their communal *yark-yark-yark*. In the back of his mind, in that very last second before things fell apart for good, he thought, *Wait, what's got them all . . .*

There was an immense explosion: not a boom but a *ker-POW* that was so violent, he felt the sound rebound and bounce and barrel its way around and over him. The blast echoed and caromed off the buildings. Gasping, his heart fluttering into his throat, he spun and looked north.

A pillar of smoke, a massive gray-black mushroom cloud, swelled and pillowed above the trees. Downslope, he could hear the other kids' chatter suddenly cease. For a second, even the dogs fell silent, and he forget all about Mellie and her strange coded clicks.

Because the only thing out there worth blowing was the church.

95

The church. Luke's blood slushed. Cindi was on lookout, and Chad—
and Weller had gone that way an hour ago; he'd taken off after . . .
after . . .

"No." It was a broken sound, hardly a word at all, and then he
was stumbling into an awkward, spastic run, aware that Mellie was
shouting after him. He heard the bang of a door, and saw Jasper,
face chalk-white, stumbling out of the equipment shed. Other kids
were rushing for and after him because he *was* the oldest and if *he*
thought there was something out there worth seeing . . . "No, no.
Cindi, Cindi! *Tom!*"

"What happened?" Jasper's shout was a needle of sound. "What
happened, what—"

All at once, the dogs started up again, but that steady *yark-yark-
yark* was now a yammer: a frenzied, rapid-fire staccato, as clear as
any alarm. The sound pierced the bright balloon of his panic—of
Cindi Cindi Cindi TOM—and he skidded to a stop so quickly he almost
tripped and fell to his knees. He turned, wondering what could possibly be more upsetting to the dogs than the bomb that had just
destroyed the church and killed his friends.

From the east, still well beyond the staved-in barn, two horses
bolted over the rise, scattering all the dogs but one, a blundering
chocolate lab that just wasn't quick enough. There was a high shriek
as one horse plowed it under and then a second, longer scream as

the horse's legs tangled. Crashing to its knees, the horse turned a complete flip. Screaming, the boy—Luke thought from the cap of sandy hair that it might be a twelve-year-old named Colin—blasted over the horse's head. The boy landed in a heap beyond his horse, which had already struggled up. Veering a sharp cut to the left, the other rider and horse only just missed the boy as they continued in their headlong crash down the hill.

What the hell? Colin was still on the snow, trying to wallow to his feet, but his horse was losing its head, panicking, rearing and plunging down. "Colin, get up! Look out!" Luke screamed as the boy only raised an arm. "Get up, run, *ruh*—"

The horse stabbed down, and Colin's yell abruptly cut out.

No. Luke clapped both hands to his mouth to hold back the scream. Both Colin and the dog were ruby splotches, like what was left after you swatted bloated mosquitoes. He scrambled to higher ground, not much caring anymore if Mellie snagged him or not, wallowing uphill until he had a good view to the east, the way the lookouts had come, wondering what in hell had scared them.

And then he saw them, in the distance.

Monsters, heading their way.

96

"Get in the barn!" Spinning on his heels, Luke waved the kids back. "Get in the barn! Jasper, everybody, get in the barn, barricade the doors, go, *go!*"

He saw Jasper suddenly whirl in an about-face and streak for the corral. Other children, who'd been surging for him, abruptly changed course, only to pile into those just behind. The air prickled with panicky screams, and Luke could hear the horses in their stalls braying in alarm. Kids shot right and left, like a rack of billiard balls on the first break. Some—the littlest ones—fell, and Luke watched, horrified, as two other kids stampeded over a fallen boy until a third scooped the kid up on the fly. Some headed for the barn, while a ragged cluster scurried north, streaming past the equipment shed and on down the road toward the trees. This wasn't a bad idea, but the forest was a good quarter mile distant and the kids would be caught out in the open, with no protection at all.

He dropped his arms, stopped shouting. Useless to try and herd or head them off, and no way to gather them all together. This was something they'd never practiced or prepared for.

But I can fight. Turning, he saw Mellie standing not thirty feet away. She faced east, watching that oncoming tide, her arms akimbo. Her .44 Mag gleamed in its holster. "Mellie, we have to unlock the guns! I need a gun!"

"Can't. Weller's got the keys." After a pause. "Church made a hell of a bang."

"You don't have *keys?*" That couldn't be right. He tried to think. Would she have them on her, or would she have left them back at the house? On her, he decided, somewhere. A pocket, in her coat, *somewhere.* But he couldn't just *take* them. What was he supposed to do, knock her down? "Well . . . ," he fumbled. The guns were in an old olive-drab trunk, secured with a padlock. "Then . . . then *shoot* the lock off!"

She didn't look at him. "That only works in movies, Luke. You need bolt cutters."

"Mellie, you have to have keys. Open the trunk." When she didn't turn, he snatched at her arm. "We have to *fight.*"

"No, we don't. We can't. Not against that many Chuckies. Go on, Luke. Get down to the barn. Keep everyone inside. I don't want more kids to get hurt than absolutely necessary. Any who manage to get to the trees, we'll gather later. They won't get far."

"Are you—" He would've said *crazy*, but the word evaporated in his mouth as her words finally registered. "Later." He let her arm go. "What do you mean, gather them later?"

She didn't answer but only stared at the advancing Chuckies. Given the shallowness of the snow, they were coming on pretty fast, but he had an idea of their numbers now. Maybe . . . thirty? Forty? Ten would've been too many. But what scared him more was how *quiet* they were. No shouts, no jungle screams. For an eerie second, he thought he might actually be looking at some kind of formation: armed Chuckies in front and beyond—

Oh no. He felt himself back up a step, away from Mellie. Beyond these Chuckies were at least twenty horses a half mile back of the advance force, and they were gaining fast, blasting over the snow in a wedge. Without binoculars he couldn't be sure, but he thought there were two distinct groups: men in gray and white winter camouflage—

And kids. Kids in white, still too distant to see faces, but he thought some were girls and all were old enough to be Chuckies. *No, that's crazy.* Horses didn't like Chuckies, although some didn't go as wild as others. *Or maybe there's something different about these Chuckies. There has to be.* Because these Chuckies *were* riding, and they were with people. Men.

He tried again. "Mellie, we still have time. Please, help us. Give me the keys."

"The best help I can give you is some advice," Mellie said, with that eerie calm. "Get in the barn. Run, Luke."

For a split second, he almost did what she said, because she *was* the adult. But then, he did the unthinkable, what he'd never have dared with any adult, because good kids like him didn't do things like this.

He hit her.

The move—a sudden punch to her chest—surprised him almost as much as her. Mellie was smaller but compact as concrete and no lightweight. Off-balance, Mellie only backpedaled. Now that he was committed, Luke stayed with her, grabbing her parka to keep her from falling, afraid that if she landed on her butt, he wouldn't get the gun in time. The flash of shock in her eyes hardened to anger, and then her right hand was reaching for that huge, wicked .44 Mag. No choice now. Luke's free hand jumped for the weapon. His fingers found the grip and yanked at the same moment that he gave her a shove that dumped her on her ass.

I've gone nuts. Panting, he held the massive revolver in both trembling hands. The gun wavered in his grip. The thing was a cannon. He could empty this sucker and never once hit a target. It occurred to him then that if she hadn't worn a cross-draw, he'd probably have a new hole in his head. No, two: front and back, and most of his skull gone, too.

"Give me the keys, Mellie." His stomach tightened as he cocked the revolver. "Please. I don't want to hurt you, but . . ."

"You're going to shoot me, Luke?" She stared up with eyes so colorless and cold, he felt the chill wrap its fingers around his heart. "You won't do it. You're not a killer."

"But why are you doing this? Why won't you *fight?*"

"This isn't a fight we're going to win—"

"But it's better than just *dying.*"

"No," she said. "You won't die, Luke."

Her certainty, that dead calm, scared him even more. "What are you doing, Mellie, what are you *doing?* Give me the keys, please, give me . . ."

Over the raging of his heart, he heard a new sound: a steady, inexorable *shush-shush-shush*, the sound a hundred snakes might make over sand. His eyes jerked toward the rise. The Chuckies, that first wave, were just spilling downhill. Some carried clubs or bats, and sun winked off a few machetes. Most, however, had no weapons at all. *Just their teeth, their hands.* He could see it, too: Chuckies swooping down and tearing little kids apart, plucking off arms and legs as easily as the wings and drumsticks of tender young chickens.

Something blurred to his left, a silent rush as Mellie shot up from the snow. Startled, Luke gave an abortive shout: *"Mel—"*

He had no memory of squeezing the trigger. More than likely, it was a simple flinch. The Magnum bucked. The shot was a thunderclap. The recoil jammed his wrists. Even in the midafternoon sun, the flash was very bright.

And he missed. Of course, he would. The gun was much too big, and he wasn't prepared. In another second, Mellie's fist drove into his stomach. Gagging and retching, he doubled over as the gun tumbled from his hands.

"You're lucky your brains are still inside your skull." Mellie reholstered her Magnum. "Don't try that again, Luke."

"Meh-*Mellie* . . ." His breath wheezed. "Wh-why are you—"

A ferocious clamor rose from the dogs. Sprinting uphill, the three remaining animals bulleted past Colin and the trampled lab. At the point of the spear was a fast, lean border collie named Tess. Sick with horror, he watched as she launched herself at a girl with a whip of blond hair—and a bat. The Chucky sliced hard and fast. He doubted the poor dog ever really saw it. They had to be at least three football fields away, and still he heard the *thunk* as the bat connected while Tess was in midair. A spurt of blood jumped straight up in a startling exclamation point, and Tess's head blew apart.

At that, the other dogs broke. One, a flop-eared red and white pit bull, squirted left and then shrieked as a Chucky brought a machete down in a two-handed ax swing. The third, a square and sturdy elk-hound, got the message. Whirling in mid-stride, the dog zoomed back down the hill, careering past the barn and the corral, heading north for the road and, beyond, the cover of forest. That dog always struck Luke as pretty darned smart.

Luke looked beyond the advancing Chuckies. From this vantage point, he could also see, much more clearly than before, the men on horseback—and one in the center, all in black, astride a gleaming horse the color of a raven's wing.

"No," he said, brokenly. The clicks he'd heard, the explosion, and now this . . . "No, no, no. What have you done, Mellie? What have you *done*?"

"What needed to be done," Mellie said, "to set us on the path for Rule."

97

"Where's Penny?" Peter tossed a wild look around the raft. "Where is she, where's—"

"I . . . I . . ." Chris was shivering. Icy water streamed from his dripping hair and down his neck. He was so numb with cold, he couldn't feel his feet. He looked left and somehow wasn't surprised to find Jess, regal as a queen, with her black-mirror eyes and Medusa hair.

"What is this?" he asked her. "Why am I here? This isn't my nightmare. It isn't even my memory. This is Peter and Simon's . . ."

"I have to go back." Peter ripped off his life vest. Beneath, he wore a pair of dripping camo over-whites, but there was something strange around his neck, a wide black . . . collar? "Penny's still in the boat, she's still—" Yanking an underwater flashlight from his belt, Peter threw himself into the water.

"Go with him," Jess said. "It's dark down there, and cold. Even with the light, he'll lose his way."

"No." Chris cringed. His arms were pebbly with gooseflesh. "And don't touch me again. This isn't my nightmare. It's his."

"It is also Simon's."

"Then let them keep it. I have problems of my own. Please, Jess." He closed his eyes, but he could still hear the cries of the gulls overhead and the slap of water on rubber. "I told Ellie the truth about Alex. I'm on my way to Rule. If I'm right, Lena's following. So

Hannah and Isaac are safe, at least from her. What more do you want from me? When will it be enough?"

"Truth comes from water and blood," Jess said. "If you truly care for Peter, then this is the only way, Chris."

"What does that mean, Jess?" He kept his eyes squeezed shut. He couldn't bear to see what he looked like in those black mirrors: spidery and strange, both himself and something alien. *How is this happening? Why?* "Is Peter alive? Is that it?"

"Do you want him to be?"

"God, yes."

"Then follow him into his darkness, Chris." He felt her hands on his back. "But don't forget to hold your breath."

"This is a dream, Jess." Opening his eyes, he stared down at his watery twin. "You can't die in your dreams."

"This is Peter's nightmare, and I don't think you want to test that," she said, and gave him a push.

The water was so cold it was fire. Chris sank, the water like chains, drawing him down. Below was the feeble bob of Peter's light and a sinking, gutted husk of a boat. Most of the aft deck was gone; the pilothouse was a ruin; the hole the fire made gaped like a wound. No choice now. He was committed. His lungs strained, the pressure building inside and out. The water was so oily, he was afraid to look away from Peter and the boat. As he neared, he saw Peter's light angle up. By some miracle, the deck aft of the engine room was intact. Using a metal ladder as a guide, Peter wormed through a square hatch.

Chris followed. Inside the wreck, the churning water was even blacker, curling with what looked like smoke. As he broke through into a very slim wedge of air and screams, he realized that what he was looking at—swimming through—was blood.

"Calm down, you have to calm down!" Peter was shouting. Both girls had their hands hooked around a pipe. Chris had no trouble recognizing Penny; the shrieking girl had Peter's jaw and eyes. The other girl, who looked much older, was no less frightened. Blood pumped from a large gash in her scalp. "Just follow me, Penny," Peter said. "We'll all get out, I promise."

"I can't!" Penny's lips pulled apart in a terrified grimace. "I can't hold my breath that long! I'll drown, I'll die!"

"*Penny.*" Peter was trying to pry his sister's hands free. "Let *go*—"

"I *can't!*" Thrashing, Penny lost it. "*I don't want to die, I don't want to*—"

"Help me." The other girl was pale as marble, her blood almost black in Peter's light. Water slopped over her chin. "I don't know how to swim, I can't—"

"We can't take them both at the same time." Peter's eyes shone with panic and tears. "It'll take two of us to handle Penny, and we *can't*—"

"N-no." One hand slipped, and the girl flailed. The air pocket had squeezed to a slim six inches. "No, don't leave me alone, d-don't—"

"Hang on." Lunging, Chris slapped her hands back onto the pipe. The air pocket was shrinking very fast, and he was freezing, getting tired out. He was horribly aware that the longer they stayed, the deeper the boat sank. As it was, he'd barely made it. "Can't you swim at all?"

"Nuh-no," the girl moaned. "Nuh . . ."

"We have to *go*." Peter had managed to loosen one of Penny's hands, but the other clung so fiercely to the pipe, he couldn't both hold her and work her free. "*Help* me."

"*No,*" the girl cried. "Wait!"

But Chris was already wrapping both hands around Penny's wrist, pulling with all his might, fighting her terror, and then her hands were free and he was shouting, "Peter! Go now, go *now!*"

"Penny!" Peter grabbed the still-screaming girl's face. "Penny, hold your breath, stop screaming, hold your—"

"No!" the other girl shrieked. "No, don't leave me here, don't—"

"Come on!" Peter bellowed, and then they were under the water, kicking out of the engine room, the three of them stroking their way through the hatch. Penny was still thrashing; Peter had one arm and Chris the other. Peter's light stabbed up, but Chris was no longer sure if that truly was the way. He could hear Penny: the boil of her breath and a thin mmm-mmm-mmm!

Stop screaming, stop screaming! Slapping his hand over her nose and mouth, Chris kicked hard. Too far above, the faint glimmer of a distant sky spread itself over the water, but his air was nearly gone; his lungs was blazing. I was wrong. I'm going to die down here in the dark; I'm going to drown in Peter's nightmare . . .

"No," Peter said—and because this was a dream, they were, suddenly, in the bobbing raft again, side by side. No Penny. No Jess. No wrecked boat, of course; that was lost to the dark, and the girl with it. "You can't stay here, Chris." Peter stared out over endless inky water. "I won't let you."

"A-are you d-dead?" He was shuddering so hard, his mouth balked. "Partly."

"Wh-what does th-that mean?"

"I'm not sure myself." Face still averted, Peter shook his head. "I think part of me died right here. You really should go, Chris. I don't know how long it's safe for you to stay."

"I'm n-not leaving you, Peter. Let me h-help you."

"I don't think you can." And then Peter turned. His eyes were no longer blue but as red as that drowned girl's blood might've been in light. "Still love me, Chris?" Peter said. Then: "Easy. Watch out you don't shoot—"

"Hunh!" Chris started awake, his hand stretching for his rifle even before he was fully upright.

"Whoa, watch it!" Ellie jumped, and as her armload of wood clattered to the ground, Jayden bolted to a sit, simultaneously trying to struggle out of a sleeping bag and free his gun hand.

"What?" Jayden said, wildly. *"What?"*

"Nothing," he said, feeling the sudden tension drain. When they made the decision to stop a few hours ago, the eastern horizon had been only a silver smudge. Now bright sun stabbed through trees. He scrubbed his face with his hands. "Sorry. I was having a bad dream and—"

"You have a lot of bad dreams," Ellie said, curtly. She gave the dog a hip-butt and began picking up scattered branches and twigs. "I thought we could have tea before we leave."

"Here." Chris made a move to get up. "Let me help."

"I can do it." Ellie snatched a branch out of reach. "I'm fine."

"Okay. Sure." When Ellie didn't reply, he looked over at Jayden. "Sorry about that."

"She's right. You do have a lot of bad dreams." Yawning, Jayden kicked out of his bag, stood, then grabbed his back. "Man, I knew there was a reason God invented the bed . . . Nope, sorry." He held up a hand. "I didn't say that. Don't tell me you didn't ask me to come—"

"Well, I didn't," Chris said.

"Because I'll tell you where to shove it," Jayden said.

"Where the sun doesn't shine," Ellie said, still not smiling, although Mina grinned.

"Right." Turning, Jayden stumbled off into the woods. "Be back."

Chris watched as Ellie first broke large twigs into smaller kindling and then pulled out her knife and began carefully fuzzing bark. "You're good at that."

"Alex taught me," Ellie said, eyes fixed to her task. Ever since they'd left, the little girl spoke to him only when necessary. He hadn't pressed. He was stunned enough she and Jayden had insisted on coming, although Jayden's rationale he half-understood and even agreed with: *It's not just you. I knew Lena before you did, and I don't know if I can stay with Hannah now, anyway.* Ellie, on the other hand, had simply refused to budge: *It's my choice.* No other explanation. At that, Hannah had been ready to spit nails. But what could she—or Chris—say? "How many more days until Rule?" Ellie asked.

"If we keep pushing? Two. No more than three, especially if the weather holds."

"Are you going to kill her?"

He knew who she meant. "If we see her. That was the idea behind leaving."

"I don't know if you should. Shoot Lena, I mean. She still feels . . . different."

"Why do you say that?"

"Because I was really close, twice, and got a good look at her face. You know how the people-eaters get that *hungry* stare? Like they're totally starving and you're a hot dog? She wasn't *all* the way like that. Her eyes also seemed . . ." He watched her think of the right word. "*Sorry.* Like my dad when he went back to Iraq? It was his job. He had no choice. I think Lena's the same way. She's *stuck.*"

"If she can't help herself, it doesn't matter. It's not like she's sick and we can wait for her to snap out of it. We don't know if that will ever happen. It wouldn't be right to let her go and keep hurting . . . killing other people." Or being miserable either, although that was wishful thinking. The Lena he'd seen was wild, and she never came in his dreams as anything else.

But what is Peter?

"What if she can?" Ellie said. "Stop herself?"

"That's an experiment we can't run, Ellie."

"Okay." The little girl's face closed. Reaching into a parka pocket, Ellie pulled out a small plastic container and unscrewed the cap. The contents, gooey and thick, reeked of turpentine.

This was the most she'd spoken to him in days. Hoping to get her going again, Chris asked, "Did Alex teach you that, too?"

"Yeah. I found a good tree not too far away." She used a stick to scoop out a nickel-sized dollop of pine resin. "Don't try to make nice. I'm not talking to you."

"Okay." Standing, he worked cramps from his legs. "How long did you sleep?"

"Enough." She scraped a flint over a tangle of cedar fuzz and pine needles. A shower of sparks jumped. Cupping the tinder, Ellie blew until a yellow flower blossomed, then slid the bundle beneath loosely laid twigs. "Is Peter, like, a best friend or something?"

"Yes." There was something hypnotic about watching a fire spread. "Best friend I ever had."

"You know him a long time?"

"No, but it feels like it."

"Are you worried that he's dead?"

It was a strange question. "How come you're asking?"

Still not looking at him, she moved a single shoulder. "Because I don't think you're sure. You asked him just now, in your sleep."

"It was a dream."

"Maybe. But when you were sick? I sat with you sometimes. You talked to Peter a lot, but you were more scared of him then. Now, you're . . ." She paused. "Sad."

"Oh." All of a sudden, his eyes itched. "I guess I am."

"Are you still mad at him?" Before he could answer, she turned her brimming eyes to his. "Because the last time my daddy went to Iraq? I was mad, and he came home in a box. I was pissed at Grandpa Jack, and then he died. The last morning I saw Tom and Alex, I'd gotten mad at them, too, the night before. We made up, but . . ." A tear dribbled down one cheek.

"You didn't make any of that happen," he said, part of him wishing that if evil thoughts could kill, his father would've keeled over five years before the Night of the Hammer. On the other hand, he couldn't have wished *that* hard, because he'd also lied for the bastard when the chips were down. "Were you angry at Eli?" When she shook her head, he said, "See?"

"But I'm afraid." Her lower lip shuddered. "I'm still mad at you. I understand *why* . . . but don't lie to me again, Chris. It hurts too much, and I don't want you to die, too."

The right thing to do would be to give her a hug, or touch her. But he didn't want to make a mistake. "I'm not going to die," he said, though he probably shouldn't make promises he mightn't keep. "I only want to try and do what's right. I'm not into this to get myself killed."

"Well, *that's* a relief," Jayden said, stomping from the woods. He looked as Ellie stifled a watery laugh. "What? What'd I say?" But his mouth was turned in a grin. *"Oohhh,"* he said, reeling the little girl in for a knuckle rub. "You thought I meant *that.*"

"Nooo," Ellie squealed, cracking up all over again.

"It is, however, an excellent question." Jayden gave Ellie's head a final tousle. "Lena or no Lena, what *is* the game plan once we get to Rule? People there you can trust?"

"A few." Crouching over a sparse patch of unbroken snow, he made an X. "If Rule's at the center of a clock, we're coming in from up here." He poked a finger at ten o'clock. "We have two choices: either loop clockwise to the hospice here"—he traced an arc to two o'clock—"or keep on this route and drop down to the southwest corner here." An X at seven o'clock.

"Which is faster?" Ellie asked.

"Six of one, half dozen of the other. We can trust Kincaid, the doctor, I think, and some girls I know who lived with Alex: Sarah and Tori. Greg and Pru, from my squad, are good guys, but they're all the way on the other side of town." He pointed to four o'clock. "The only catch is Jess's house, where Alex was? It's not that far from the Zone."

"Where the people-eaters are." When Chris nodded, Ellie continued, "Can't we go straight down and still end up where Alex lived?"

"Well, there are more houses and people, but . . . yeah, if we're careful."

"Sounds like those girls are the first stop then." Jayden went to his horse, pulled open a saddlebag, and withdrew a camp pot and three enameled mugs as well as a Ziploc of tea and another of fish jerky. "What then?"

"I don't know. I've been gone two months," Chris said, as Jayden carefully scooped handfuls of untrammeled snow into the pot. "It's the middle of March now. A lot could've happened." Given his many dreams, he was willing to bet on it.

"Okay." Nesting the pot over flames, Jayden doled out cups. "So, we go to Sarah and Tori and . . . what? You make like Moses—*let my people go*—or are we just going to bust everyone out?"

"I honestly haven't thought that far. Guess it depends on if I end up in the prison house."

"We won't let that happen," Ellie said, promptly.

Jayden only filled a tea ball with loose leaves. "How likely is that?"

"I'd be lying if I said it wasn't a real strong possibility. What I'm hoping is that the Council will listen. I can't believe that they'll just shoot me," he lied.

"They won't," Ellie said, fishing out a piece of jerky.

"Oh?" Jayden raised both eyebrows. "And *you* know this because—"

"Because," she said, gnawing jerky that was the color of an old loafer, "they'd have to shoot through me first."

He and Jayden looked at each other, and then Chris said, "Come again?"

"I saved your life, Chris. So . . . I'm responsible for you from now on."

"I think it goes the other way around," Jayden said. "He owes you."

"Yeah, but then he saved me from the lake."

"So we're even," Chris said. "I'm not letting you do anything dumb, Ellie."

"Too late. I'm here," she said. "Seriously, guys, you think they'll shoot a cute kid and her little dog, Toto, too?"

"I—" Chris started, then shut his mouth. He and Jayden traded another long look, and then they both began to laugh.

"See?" Ellie said, looking very pleased. She offered Chris the bag. "Jerky?"

98

Between Jed's maps and a thumbnail of the village's layout, Zone, patrols, and approach routes Weller once drew, Tom would've found what he was looking for easily enough. As with the lake, however, the crows pointed the way, sketching lazy pinwheels above the woods southwest of Rule. Now that they were into March and the daytime temps were inching past freezing most days, the faintly gassy smell helped, too. So did his horse, who finally balked a half mile shy and refused to budge. That was all right. On foot, he had a better chance of slipping in unnoticed. So he offloaded his gear, then unharnessed and gave the horse a healthy slap to send it on its way.

If you didn't know better, Tom thought you could almost imagine that you'd dropped into some horror story where the village appeases the local gods by sending out the occasional sacrifice. He knew better. Rule's story was written in the haphazard scatter of browning bones, scored by teeth and knives; the remnants of clothes and discarded backpacks; a hoary scraggle of wig so picked over there was nothing left but ripped lace and a few strands of too-red hair.

What almost troubled him more, however, was a wrecked pyramid of decaying human heads that lay at the end of a kind of processional way. This was marked by the skeletonized remains of animals heaped on thinning snow beneath gently swaying rib cages still dangling from paraline. From the shapes of the skulls and teeth, he thought these had been wolves. The whole setup was ritualistic, with a weird Blair Witch vibe. He wondered if this spot had been claimed by the Wolf Tribe, those Chuckies Cindi saw with Alex. If true, then Tom was now standing close to or in the same spot Alex once had. He didn't know if that was an omen, good or bad.

Either way, no Chuckies have been here for a while. Tom studied the crows hopscotching over that jumble of human skulls and disarticulated lower jaws. Only the barest remnants of leathery skin and desiccated muscle dangled from bone. Something had happened at that pyramid, too. The skulls hadn't simply fallen to the snow but been knocked off, some by several feet. One lay far to the right. From its position, he could almost imagine that someone had tried lobbing the skull like a stone. Nearby were two shredded, bloodstained bits of cloth: part of a parka and a flannel shirt. Torn off in a fight, maybe, but the edges weren't as frayed as he would've expected from a rip. Probably one honking sharp knife.

But where was the flood of Chuckies that was supposed to have born down on Rule? In the last four days, Tom had seen only a few and at a distance—and twice during the midafternoon, which was also very bad news.

Tom held his breath and listened. So still. This close, he ought to hear something: the *thock* of an ax, the distant clatter of wagons or horses. Perhaps, even the occasional voice. In the dead silence of the Hindu Kush, he'd once patrolled a mountainside and caught snatches of evening prayers ten thousand feet above a Pashtun village he never saw. But here? Nothing.

Where is everyone? He was certain he wasn't too late. With all those men and their wagons, the horses—and now, the kids—he had to have beaten Mellie and that old commander in black. Probably by no more than half a day, but even a few hours was better than nothing.

Something really wrong here. A slight movement to his right, and his gaze dropped in time to see a small field mouse squirm from an empty socket of that lone skull. The animal froze, only its whiskers trembling before it wheeled and scurried away. *Something rotten in Denmark, Yorick.*

Time to find out what. Time, Tom hoped, to save his kids.

It must've been an old mercury switch from a defunct thermostat connected to a battery. Move the garbage, disturb the switch, the leads spark, and *boom*. An easy bomb.

One second, he was shouting for Weller and dashing toward the church. The next, he was very cold and crumpled on his side, a lucky thing because there was old copper in his mouth, more blood drying under his nose and along his neck. If he'd been on his back, he might have choked to death on his own blood. His chest felt like someone had dropped a boulder on him. His ears hurt, and they *whooshed*: a good indicator that he still had eardrums to hear with. At first, he thought the sound was only from the blast wave, but when he rolled onto his back, gasping at jags of pain, he saw clots of black smoke chuffing over blue sky and realized that what he heard was the muted chugs of a fire that had yet to burn itself out.

Sitting up was an exercise in slow torture. Everything hurt. He wasn't coughing up any more of the red stuff, so his lungs might be okay. A blast could kill you a lot of different ways. Some—being vaporized or skewered by shrapnel or bleeding out because your leg was gone—were a lot faster than others. Have the bad luck of being too close to a blast wave, and the hollow organs—lungs, heart, guts— could burst, sometimes fast, sometimes slow. When he was finally up, he propped himself on his elbows, concentrated on moving air in and out of his aching lungs, studied what was left of the church—and realized just how lucky he'd been.

The church looked like something out of a travel brochure advertising tours of castle ruins. The tower had ruptured in a halo of stone and splintered wood. Mangled brass bells and sprays of shattered stained glass glittered on the snow. The blast had been powerful enough to fling the smallest bells toward the forest edging what had been the church's parking lot. The crowns of several nearby trees, principally heavier evergreens, had snapped while other, thinner hardwoods were bowled over by the blast wind. Three walls still stood, but the rest of the church was a gutted shell surrounded by blasted pews and the fluttering remnants of tattered hymnals.

He ought to be dead. They'd tethered the animals about an eighth of a mile away. He thought he'd covered half the distance back before he'd dropped the reins and sprinted for the church. So, tack on another fifty yards before the explosion? Either way, give or take, he was still too darned close. The fact that he'd been blown back so far, knocked unconscious, and bled from his nose and ears proved that. If the explosion had happened, say, in a town or a narrow alley, the blast overpressure would've ruptured his heart and blown his lungs apart. What saved his ass was that the church stood alone, with no nearby structures or even trees to capture and amplify the blast wave.

He was alive because of dumb luck, and that was all.

By some miracle, he still had his weapons: the Uzi on its retention strap, Jed's Bravo snugged in that back scabbard, and the Glock— Alex's Glock, as he thought of it—in its cross-draw. He had extra ammo stashed in his over-vest, too, also lucky because the horses had scattered. From their tracks, he knew at least one had not headed back to camp. That, he hoped, would be his ride, but hunting it down now would be a mistake. Instead, he kicked snow to hide his blood, then shucked his vest and used that to scour away the Tom-sized divot where he'd lain and the stumbling tracks he made as he headed into the trees.

They came a few hours later. By then, he'd moved downwind and well into the woods, hauling himself by painful degrees high into the deep recesses of a thick, sturdy cedar. There were three, and he recognized them all. Mellie's square, compact frame was easy. With his white hair cut high and tight and that black uniform, the way he carried himself, Tom thought the old guy was used to command.

But my God, I know you. His mind flashed to his battle with that blood-eyed girl on the snow. *You're one of the guys I saw watching from the woods.*

The third person was a kid, a boy in over-whites. The boy's head was up, sampling the air. Looking for *him*. Tom was too far away to see the boy's eyes, but he knew they were the same maddened red of that Chucky he'd fought to the death. Given the guy in black, Tom thought this must be the same boy he'd spotted in the trees two weeks ago.

But now this kid was riding a horse. *And he's working* with *people.* Tom's skin dewed with fresh sweat. *How is this possible?*

He watched as the three made a slow perambulation around the church in an ever-widening spiral. *Looking for tracks, trying to figure out if anyone got away.* The oldsters bent their heads to the snow, but the kid kept his head up like a bloodhound. The Uzi was silenced, chambered and ready to go, and now he inched a finger over the selector switch. *Kill them now? No way anyone will hear the shots.* But he wasn't a sniper, and he might miss. Worse, he was only one person, and he was willing to bet the old commander had a fair number of men. Try to rescue the kids on his own, he'd probably end up dead. *Wait for a better time. Think of a plan.*

Heart pounding, he watched as they continued their search pattern until the debris field petered out. Mellie and the commander conferred about something; the Chucky only scanned, turning his horse in a slow three-sixty. And then they left, returning to camp the way they'd come.

For the rest of that day and through the night, Tom stayed put, using his retention straps to anchor himself in case he dozed. The orange of the fire eventually diminished. What light there was splashed gray and dim from the waxing moon. The hissing in his ears diminished enough that he heard the flame's dying crackles and, at some point, a jangle of hardware. That made his pulse ratchet up a notch until he reconsidered that a solitary rider, at night, made no sense. Probably his horse, or Weller's. He thought about it for a few seconds, then decided he was much better off with a ride than without one. So he called to it as softly as he could, coaxing the animal into the woods, wincing at every crackle and snap of brush and brambles. In the moonlight, he saw the horse slip close to the tree in which he hid, and then stop.

That was the only good in an otherwise very long and terrible night. He still ached, his gimpy right leg complained, and now he was both hungry and thirsty. Scooping snow from nearby limbs, he let it melt down his throat to take the edge off. He even managed a fitful doze.

Mostly, he worried about the kids, and his next move. The one thing he didn't believe Mellie would do was kill the children outright. It just didn't fit. True, that commander had Chuckies. They would need food. But why waste kids? More than enough oldsters around to keep the Chuckies happy for a while.

What he kept coming back to was that boy. The old commander was messing around with the Chuckies. But how? *And why does he need my kids?* There had to be a reason why Mellie had gathered children for her buddy in black. Tom suspected she and the commander wanted the Rule children for the same reason.

Whatever that was.

Except for two dead dogs, a bigger blood splotch that looked as if it might have been a person, and a riderless horse nervously wandering around the horse barn, the farmstead was deserted. The horse trough had been moved, and the stockpile of explosives gear was gone. That, he'd counted on. First principles: all warfare is based on deception.

Every tent had been broken down and taken away—except his,

set apart, close to the trees. He stared for a very long time, first from across the corral and on his horse, and then on foot as he worked a careful perimeter, thinking, *Fool me once* . . . He bet Finn read Sun Tzu, too.

It took him a while. The snow was all broken up, deeply incised with horse hooves, boots, and—this was a surprise—the cut of at least seven or eight wagons. But he finally spotted what did not belong: a thin curl of det cord coiled around a corner guy and grommet of his tent. Following that took him to a trip-release hooked to the front zipper. Peering through a seam, he saw a half block of plastique, with a Vietnam-era M28 detonator stuck in one end, molded to the tent's center pole. The trip-release meant that he'd use more force on the zipper. One quick tug would arm the fuse and then *boom*.

Not good. He cut the cord with his KA-BAR, then broke down the rest of the bomb. *Either they think one or both of us got out, or they're being cautious.* Each scenario was bad news and meant he would have to be doubly careful when he searched the rest of the farmstead.

None of the barns were booby-trapped. He took his time with the equipment shed, studying the roof and where the walls met concrete and then snow. Nothing. Now that he had his gear and binos, he peered in through the one window. Bare sawhorses, empty shelves. Using paracord, he carefully tied one end to the doorknob and strung it out behind. Then he wound the other end around the saddle horn, boosted himself onto the saddle, and spurred the horse into a sudden gallop. Startled, the horse bolted, and the door caromed off its hinges. But nothing blew up.

Save for a single half-roll of magnesium tape and a bottle of aluminum powder that had rolled under a sawhorse, the equipment shed was a metal and concrete shell. Pocketing the magnesium and ground aluminum, he walked out to the cistern. The cap was still in place, but once bitten, twice shy. When he was satisfied it wasn't rigged, he shoved the heavy concrete to one side and peered in. His breath huffed out in relief. Still attached to an iron bolt on the cap's under-belly, the black paracord was taut, exactly as he'd left it. Reaching in, he hauled up the heavy pack in which he'd stowed the lion's share of his bomb-making materials.

Under Mellie's nose, the whole time.

Clearing a house of potential booby-traps takes time. All the rooms were clear and empty, except Weller's. *Interesting.* Both hands on his Uzi, Tom turned a slow look. With its tight hospital corners, Weller's rack could've passed any drill instructor's muster. From his few changes of clothing in a duffel to his cracked leather dopp kit, everything was squared and ordered. *Why not empty the room, or booby-trap it?* Two reasons: either the contents held no value . . . *or, on the off-chance Weller survived, they're telling him to kiss off.*

Every soldier carries keepsakes and charms, usually on them or in their over-vests: letters, pictures, Bibles, rosaries, scapulars. His own—a St. George medal from his grandmother and a picture of his little sisters—were tucked in the same sock drawer with his dog tags back home, and so much dust. The tags he wore now were Jed's. As far as he knew, Weller had no tags, but he was an old soldier and habits die hard.

They were in the dopp kit, the first place Tom looked, and pro-tected by a Ziploc baggy: a newspaper clipping and an old Polaroid. The clipping, almost three years old, read:

HOUGHTON VICTIM REMEMBERED AS "DETERMINED" AND "GOOD FRIEND"

Friends of Amanda L. Pederson recalled a vivacious, gener-ous, and hardworking young woman ready to offer a helping hand and determined to return to school and pursue a college degree.

"Totally devastated," was how Claire Mason characterized

her reaction to the news of Pederson's disappearance after a freak boating accident in Lake Superior. "I can't even imagine what she was doing out there with a bunch of college kids in the first place. She couldn't swim, and can you imagine her poor parents? How they'll never have a body? It's just terrible."

The boat on which Pederson was a passenger went down in the still-frigid waters of Superior after a fire broke out in the vessel's engine room. Repeated efforts by fellow passengers to free Pederson, trapped below deck, failed, and the vessel sank before a Coast Guard helicopter arrived on scene. Recovery efforts were suspended due to poor visibility and the depth of the lake, which has been recorded at over five hundred feet in that area. No further searches for the missing boat or Houghton resident are planned.

"Amanda was just the nicest girl," Jack Laparma, a close friend, said. "She'd had some hard times, but she was completely determined, ready to move on."

Pederson is reported to have enjoyed snowmobiling as well as time spent with family and friends.

The names of Pederson's fellow passengers as well as the boat's owner are currently being withheld until a preliminary investigation is completed and a cause of the engine fire can be established. Given the loss of the boat, however, and the reported lack of eyewitness accounts, a source close to the current investigation suggested that the death will be classified as accidental. No criminal charges are currently pending or anticipated.

Pederson is survived by her parents, Claire and Benjamin; a brother, Theodore; and grandparents Ron and Esther Pederson of Houghton, and William and Rosemary Weller of Marenisco.

The picture accompanying the article showed Weller's grand-daughter in jeans and a tee, sitting atop a picnic table. In the background was a river, boats, and a lift bridge.

The Polaroid was so aged most of the color had bled. The ghostly image of two men posed before a Quonset. Each held an M16. Both wore camo battle dress, but only Weller, just as grizzled then as now, sported three tabs on his left sleeve—special forces, rangers, and air-borne—and a smoke tucked behind one ear.

The man Tom zeroed in on stood to Weller's right: grim and blocky, with a barrel chest and thighs like tree trunks. His skull was so large, his dark hair, cut high and tight, looked like the bristles of a broom.

On the back, in faded ballpoint: *Finn '68 Ben Tre.* The name of the town or village meant nothing to Tom. He squinted at Finn's uni-form, trying to make out his rank. Major or lieutenant colonel—and was that a medical corps insignia? He thought it might be. Weller's three chevrons put his rank as a sergeant. *A commander and his sarge.*

Now, Tom had two names: Chris Prentiss and Finn.

Which monster to take on first . . . that was the question.

Weller had marked the most likely spots where Rule might post archers, but Tom spotted none, and no arrows came whizzing from the trees. While he was happy not to end up with an arrow through his neck or in his back, Tom began to suspect that something was seri-ously wrong. By the third block in from the woods, he was positive.

The doors of every house stood open. From the splintered jambs and screens hanging at cockeyed angles, these were forced entries. Each home had been stormed, searched, and then—his eyes drifted to a drippy, red, spray-painted X right of a jamb—ticked off the to-do list. Raids for food and other supplies would be his first guess.

But what if they were looking for Chuckies? If Rule's children and grandchildren and all their friends *had* returned, going door-to-door to hunt them down made sense. The timing was about right. Judging from blown snow in front halls, whatever happened was a couple weeks back. But you wouldn't stop there, would you? There was no timetable, no way of knowing when more kids might show up. You'd mount patrols and guards. So where was everyone?

He turned a slow, careful circle. Long icicles fanged eaves and gutters on those homes with southern and western exposures. Most of the houses facing north were mantled with thick snow. Anyone still around would need to stay warm. He sniffed and got a light scent of wood smoke: drifting down from the northeast and the center of town. He still didn't hear anything other than the faint sough of a light breeze. But people would be conserving energy, not moving around much.

Something orange and large suddenly slunk around the corner of a two-story to his left. Startled, he spun, Uzi up before he realized what he was looking at. The instant the cat spotted Tom, it froze, one paw poised above the snow. Something furry dangled from its jaws. They regarded one another for a beat. He couldn't speak for the cat, but his heart was hammering. Evidently unimpressed, the cat trotted up snowy steps, then eeled through an open front door.

Tom lowered his weapon. *A cat?* This made no sense. You break down doors; you look for supplies. In a starvation situation, pets were fair game. Dogs, he could see sparing; they sensed Chuckies. You needed horses, too. But no one really *needed*—

If he hadn't been staring after the cat, he never would have seen them. As it was, what his eye snagged on was a distant olive-green blur—a parka—and a quick spark of sun in the far woods to the left behind the house.

Theoretically, you could get into Rule any number of ways. Those two boys angling through the trees must have dropped down from the north. Both had rifles and were moving slowly, cautiously, their heads tilted to the snow. They hadn't spotted him yet, but they would.

Darting up the steps, he bolted into the house after the cat. As soon as he was inside, he noticed two things at the same time: a long-dried bloodstain on the floor and the stink of decay. That cat had a nice stash of rotting mice somewhere. Trotting past a narrow understairs closet to his left, he moved into the kitchen, which was a shambles. Cupboards stood open, drawers had been pulled and dumped. The pantry door was open by a hair. Several floorboards had been pried up, too, both in the pantry and out here, leaving dark rectangular slots wide enough for a person to drop through. The aroma of decay was stronger here, as was the smell of cold dirt from the crawl space under the house. The cat was nowhere in sight.

Sidestepping a gap, he peered over a window sill above the sink. The two boys were just clearing a woodpile alongside a detached garage. Both simultaneously looked over their shoulders at something further back. One boy—smaller, a mop of brown hair—made a warding-off gesture, waving someone back. *Bad news, if there's more than just these two.* Craning, he took his eyes away a split second to see if he could make out who else was there, and how many.

It was a split second too long. When he jumped his gaze back, the other boy—older, taller, dark-eyed—was looking right at him.

"Shit!" he hissed. He ducked, already knowing it was too late. But he still might be able to avoid a fight. Pivoting, he started out of the kitchen, intending to head for the second story because it was always easier to defend high and he might be able to make his way out a window. Something flickered to his left, and he saw a boy dashing around to the front and the second, taller boy, down low, wheeling around the kitchen side steps.

No time for the stairs. Dropping to a sit, Tom threw his legs over the edge of the gap in the kitchen floor, then slid all the way through. No more than two feet high, the crawl space was virtually pitch black except for thin stringers of light dashing through chinks in the floor. The air reeked of mildew and the eye-watering stench of dead mice.

Tongue cringing from the clog of decay, he took small sips through his teeth as he slithered, on his belly, over cold earth and deeper into the crawl space. The smell of rot and, now, a septic system desperately in need of emptying. The people who'd lived here must've kept on crapping until their toilets overflowed.

Far enough. Turning onto his side, he faced the way he'd come. Light glimmered through the gap. If they looked, they wouldn't see him so long as he remained still. Then he remembered that Chuckies saw very well in the dark. Either way, if it came down to a fight, he thought he had a chance. Even with Jed's Bravo in its scabbard, there was a foot of clearance between his Uzi and the underbelly of the house, plenty of room to roll.

Take out anything that comes through the gap. He tucked the silenced Uzi to his chest, business end trained on that wedge of silver light. After that, he would have to be fast. The remaining kid could shoot down, but both boys were carrying bolt-actions. He fingered the Uzi's selector to full auto. *Shoot up, really spray it, and then—*

Directly over his head, the floorboards creaked. A soft *screeee.* More steps, the gauzy light rippling as the boy moved across the kitchen. He heard more thumps as the second boy came down the front hall. Cringing back, Tom tried making himself as small as possible—

And felt a hand on his shoulder.

99

A scream surged up Tom's throat, crashed over his tongue, then flattened against the wall of his teeth. Tucking, he rolled away, once, twice, then brought the silenced Uzi to bear. Just before it was too late, in the split second before his finger tightened on the trigger and sprayed gunfire he could not take back, he saw what he'd missed before, because his eyes hadn't adjusted and he'd been focused on the gap, not what waited at his back, in the dark.

The Chucky who'd decided on the crawl space as his personal meat locker had been a busy, busy boy. In the gray gloaming, Tom thought there might be as many as four bodies, but certainly two, because of the heads. (Pro forma for an accurate count at any bomb scene: forget heads. Heads pop like corks from champagne. Count left feet.) The soft, fleshy parts—eyes, noses, lips, tongues—were gone. The heads stared with wide, black-eyed wonder. One body was being systematically consumed from the waist up, the Chucky probably reaching in and scooping out all the good stuff before setting to work on the leaner rib meat. Alongside a half-gnawed thigh was a spool of colon in a neat cobra's coil.

Jesus. Fear spidered down his neck. Either those boys were living here, or had dropped by to grab a quick snack. *And here, I've saved them the trouble of hunting me down.*

But they hadn't figured out where he was yet. Sweat oozing over his temples, he rolled away from the grisly sight and readied the Uzi.

He could still take them. If these Chuckies weren't the only ones, or they lived nearby, he would have to make tracks pretty fast. Maybe this was why the village had pulled back: because there were too many Chuckies and no way to defend against them all. *But then I should've spotted more, not just these two . . .*

Then, he heard one of the boys: "Did you—"

"—hear that?" Jayden whispered.

From his place in the middle of the kitchen, Chris gave Jayden a slow nod, then put a finger to his lips. The sound had been brief, a kind of scurry like a rat or opossum. *Or a raccoon.* He tipped a look at the hole in the floor. From the smell, it seemed as if something had taken up residence. Maybe the cat, whose prints he'd spotted in back. His gaze inched from the hole to the hall beyond Jayden. In the weak light, he saw watery tread marks. Too late to ask Jayden if there'd been water before.

They'd stopped at Jess's first. The house was empty, the girls' bedrooms cleaned out. Yet the floors in Jess's house were intact. This was not the case with two other houses on the same block that he knew had been occupied the last time he was in Rule. The only difference between those houses and Jess's was that Jess had a root cellar and basement. Every house without one or the other showed similar damage: floorboards pried up or simply splintered with sledges and axes, open drawers, crap on the floor, broken dishes, the backs of cupboards staved in with hammers.

Now he swept his eyes over the wreckage that had been the Landrys' kitchen. He thought he understood what had happened here. Whoever was left in Rule had gone around ripping up houses on footings to look in crawl spaces and behind walls for supplies that had been squirreled away. Then each house had been X'ed from the list.

Which means they're pretty desperate. His gaze lingered on the pantry door, open just a crack. Things certainly had gone downhill here in a—

A faint *squee* and then a shuffle from directly overhead. At the sound, his eyes darted to the ceiling. He *knew* it. That ghostly flash of a face hadn't been his imagination. Now, he was very glad he'd made Ellie wait behind the woodpile with Mina when the dog started getting antsy. Looking up at Jayden, he aimed a finger at the ceiling, then lifted his chin in the direction of the front hall. Nodding, Jayden turned a quiet about-face, hugged the left wall, and padded for the front door, with Chris only steps behind. Pausing at the bottom of the staircase, Jayden leaned in for a quick peek, then darted across to take up position in a doorway that led to a formal dining room. Moving past the understairs closet, Chris paused at the newel post, tapped his chest with a forefinger, then turned to aim at the stairs. He had a brief moment when he wondered just why he was bothering to clear this house, then considered that something had gotten under the dog's skin and that the only good Changed was a dead one.

Unless it's Lena, a small inner voice whispered. *This is what you wanted, right? For her to follow? So what if she got here first?*

No way, he thought right back. *Lena knows Jess, not the Landrys. She has no reason to be in* this *house.*

Unless she's running an end around, the voice said. *You drop north, so she circles, tracks you by scent, and meets you head-on.*

Yes, but accomplishing what? He was overthinking this. Lena hadn't shown herself at all in the last four days. He wondered now if she'd followed. Maybe he and Jayden weren't enough of a draw.

Can't worry about Lena now. He just hoped that whatever was up there wasn't armed. Socking his rifle against his shoulder, he followed his weapon in a slow creep up the stairs, keeping to the right, away from any squeaky centers. The hall above opened right and left, and he jumped his eyes to the right corner and then the left, bringing his rifle around, clearing each slice of the pie. To his relief, he had wall to his back the whole way. *Make it to the corner, clear left, then pivot, move to the right, clear that corner, then get the hell out of the stairway.* What they did next depended on how many doors were open—

Something vaulted from a side table snugged against the far wall. Jerking right, he brought his rifle around, but he was off-balance. The cat barreled into his chest, dug in with its claws, spat, and then launched itself, using him as a springboard, to catapult itself the rest of the way down the steps. With a yelp, he jerked off a wild shot, then staggered as his heel snagged. He fell backward, his head cracking a step hard enough to bring on a shower of shooting stars, and then he was watching his boots whip past as he turned a somersault and caromed down the steps.

"Are you okay?" Jayden's face, chalky with alarm, swam into view. "You could've broken your neck. Cat scared the hell out of me."

"Uh," Chris croaked. He could only lie a moment, listening to the bawl of his battered head. His right shoulder hurt where he'd collided with hardwood, but he thought it could've been worse. Propping himself up on his elbows, he gulped back against a swirl of vertigo, then made a face, worked his jaws, and spat out a gob of red foam. "Bit myself. Stupid cat."

"Just be glad that's all it was." Propping his own gun against the wall, Jayden helped him to his feet. "Can we get out of here? This place gives me the creeps, and it stinks. That cat's probably dragged in all sorts of crap. It's probably *crapping* all over the place."

"Sure." Shaking his head clear, he looked around and found his rifle, which had jumped from his hands to slide a few feet from the understairs closet. With a groan, he bent. "We should anyway," he said, flicking the safety. "Even though we're inside, someone might've heard the shot and come to check—"

At his back, the door to the understairs closet slammed open with a loud bang, and then Jayden was screaming, "Chris! Look out look out *look*—"

100

"This is dumb," Ellie muttered, darkly, one hand hooked under Mina's collar and the other clutching her Savage. Huddled by her side, Mina only shuffled but didn't break her stance. Any sound she might have made—and she *wouldn't*, no matter what Chris said, because Mina was *trained* to be quiet—was stifled by the loop of a leash cinched down around her snout. Ellie crept forward, aimed a peek around the corner of the woodpile three yards over, but saw only the garage nestled in the woods and the far corner of the house into which Jayden and Chris had gone what seemed *hours* ago.

Pulling back, she gnawed her lower lip, tried to think of what to do, how long to wait. She could feel the dog vibrating under her hand. Mina wanted to go, get in the fight . . . if there was one. Ellie still wasn't sure. Oh, she wasn't stupid. That gunshot had been very muffled, a tiny pop at this distance but distinct enough that she understood what it was. Yet there was only the one: no return fire at all. No shouts or screams either, which, even with *miles* between her and the house, she'd probably hear because it was so creepy-quiet.

Anyway, it wasn't as if she would go *running* to see what happened. Only little kids did that. But she should do something, because, right now, she figured one of two things was happening: either Chris or Jayden was picking himself off the floor because one of them had tripped, or they'd both been jumped and were now being torn up by a swarm of people-eaters—in which case, what were she and Mina doing sitting on their *butts*?

She snicked the safety of her Savage, on, off, on, off. On. Off. Made a decision.

"I'm going to count to ten," she said to Mina. "Then we're going." Which route to take? She ought to stay under cover, out of sight. Scooching forward, she gave Mina a little tug to move her out of the way, then hitched around for a better view of that yard *waaay* out there. Honestly, she needed binoculars. Her eyes roamed over gray trees and clean white snow blushing here and there with shafts of the setting sun; settled on the garage set well back in the woods. A straight shot from here, and then she could—

A twinkle of light. A second later, the garage door cracked open. A hand appeared, and then an arm, following by the hump of a shoulder . . . and Ellie watched as the girl, a spidery, slinky thing, emerged—with a *big* honking knife.

Oh! Ellie's heart jumped a jig. She crowded herself and Mina back fast. *Don't see me, don't see me!* In the brief glimpse she'd had of the girl—and oh boy, she was a people-eater, all right—Ellie registered only long hair clotted with dirt and something wrong with the girl's face. Like another people-eater had taken a big chunk? Ellie wasn't sure. She waited, her heart *boing-a-boing-a-boinging* in her chest, ears alert for the *shush* of snow or crack of a branch. Nothing came, and Mina didn't budge.

Okay, so the people-eater doesn't know I'm here. Lucked out. But now Ellie really had to do something. Maybe that shot she'd heard was a signal: *Come and get it; we got juicy boys.*

Easing just far enough to clear the woodpile, Ellie saw the girl, low to the ground, scuttling like a tarantula. Blocky and square, that knife looked more like a cleaver.

Ellie's hand squeezed her rifle, but who was she kidding? If she sent Mina after the people-eater, her dog might get chopped. Fire off a warning shot, though, that might help Jayden and Chris, but that people-eater would find her pretty quick, too. *But I have to do something . . .*

From deep in the house came a wild but very muffled shout, a sound swaddled in cotton, and then a soft *bam*. Something breaking, or a door slamming?

At the same moment the girl reached the corner, wormed her way beneath a long, whippy piece of metal where the house met the ground, and went *under* the house.

That did it. There was something inside with Chris and Jayden, something very bad, and now this equally awful people-eater was coming at them from behind.

"Go, Mina!" Jumping to her feet, Ellie whipped the leash off Mina's muzzle. The dog took off like a rocket, and Ellie was right behind, screaming, "Go, Mina, go, Mina, go, go, go!"

101

Chris only had time to register Jayden's shout and the crash of the door. In the next second, something launched itself into his back, spinning him completely around. He got a brief glimpse of the kitchen before the Changed—girl or boy, he didn't know—bowled him over, slamming him face-first to the floor. His forehead connected with wood, and he felt the tender skin, which was only just knitting up from the fight with that Changed in Hannah's kitchen, tear as he bounced. Face roaring with pain, blinking away a sudden wash of warm blood, he got one knee under him and tried bucking the Changed from his back. Behind him, near the stairs, Jayden was still screaming, and then he heard, dimly, what sounded like heavy boots clumping down steps. Another yelp from Jayden, this time one of panic, quickly choked off, and Chris realized that there *had* been something besides a cat upstairs after all.

Chris heard a whickering over his head; felt something slip around his neck. An instant later, he had no air. Dropping his useless rifle, he clawed, trying to work his fingers under the rope as the Changed put a knee in the middle of his back and pushed at the same time that it pulled. Chris felt his nails score his skin; his pulse thundered; black spiders scurried over his vision. His chest felt as if someone had dropped a huge weight, caving in ribs, smashing his lungs. He reached back to swat at his attacker with both hands but managed only increasingly feeble slaps. He felt the Changed grope then fist his hair, crank his head to expose his neck as the rope crushed his throat. Chris was losing control of his body now, beginning to jitter. The pain in his chest was ferocious, a hard boil that would blow him apart. Everything was going black, inside and out. He couldn't fight anymore. His legs were juddering uncontrollably now, and so were his hands. He only just registered the slap of wood, the drum of his boots.

All at once, his strength evaporated. He felt himself go limp, the rope saw through the tender flesh of his neck. What should have been a surge of bright pain was only the tiniest blister of a faraway firecracker, sputtering fast. His mind slipped, his hold on consciousness slewing as it had when Hannah's poison streamed through his veins. An insidious blackness oozed over his vision as the edges of his world collapsed.

Just before he lost his sight completely, he saw something—someone?—suddenly rear, seeming to emerge from the guts of the earth. A voice, very distant, as wispy as smoke: "Over *here!*"

But then, that was it. All at once, Chris was falling, all thought disintegrating, and where there should have been a floor or the ground or the earth to hold him, there was nothing except Jess pulling together in a swarm of shadows. He thought she might be saying something, but he was moving so fast, he shot past and never—

102

Rolling, Tom surged through the gap. The nearest Chucky, a beefy kid in stained jeans and a too-large camo-jacket, had a knee in the dark-eyed boy's back and a rope in one hand. Tom could tell the dark-eyed boy was nearly gone; the kid's body quivered, his face was black, and his eyes rolled to show the whites going crimson with hemorrhage. Beyond them, Tom glimpsed the smaller boy thrashing and kicking at another Chucky, a very large girl raining punches.

"Over *here!*" he shouted. Flinching, the beefy Chucky relaxed his hold on the boy, who collapsed in a heap and didn't move. Tom fired, a quick three-shot burst, a soft *pfft-pfft-pfft*. The Chucky's chest ruptured in a crimson starburst, and he was falling back even as Tom was clambering out of the crawl space and advancing, moving fast. The girl was still whaling away on the smaller boy, but now seemed to realize the danger, and she was rearing back, beginning to turn.

"*Stay down!*" Tom roared at the smaller boy. The girl flung herself to one side as Tom squeezed off another burst, stitching shots in the front and storm doors. Jags of glass splashed to the floor, and then the smaller boy was singing, "Gun, gun, she's got my gun!" Tom saw it at the same moment as the girl pivoted; heard the bolt being thrown as the barrel of a long gun swung around. Dropping to one knee, he ducked under her line of fire and aimed up. One second, the girl's head was there, and the next—

"Who . . ." The second boy was panting, trying to roll, get to his feet. Blood streaked his face. Tom couldn't tell if it was all his, but at least this kid was breathing. "Who are . . ."

Tom didn't reply. Turning, he raced back to the dark-eyed boy. The kid—seventeen, eighteen, he thought—was still down, not moving at all, sightless eyes staring, tongue purple and bulging, blood on his throat, that rope cinched tight. *God, no.* Tom dropped to his knees, stripped away the rope, then drew a hissing breath through his teeth at how deeply the kid's neck was cut.

"No." It was the smaller kid, his voice breaking. He knelt by the body. "No, no, he can't be dead, he can't—"

"Quiet." Turning his head, Tom listened for a breath. Nothing. No whisper of air against his cheek. *Kid, come on.* Closing his eyes, he put his head on the boy's chest. Silence. *Don't do this, kid, don't . . .*

Beyond Tom, from the kitchen, came the enormous *bang* of a door smashing drywall. Startled, still on his knees, he jerked up. Hurtling out of the pantry, swarming up from the gap in the floor through which he'd slithered only moments before, was a girl: a silent, deadly horror with a monstrous rip in one cheek through which he could see teeth and pink gums and tongue. In her hand was the largest, sharpest corn knife Tom had ever seen.

"Get back!" Sweeping the smaller boy aside with his right hand, Tom lunged for his Uzi with his left. She was so fast, all he had time for was a one-handed snatch, his left fist closing around the barrel of his Uzi, and then he was swinging up, aiming for her knife hand. She saw it coming and dropped in a lunge, like a fencer coming in under a blade, as the Uzi whizzed past. Pulled off-balance by his own momentum, Tom caught the glint, heard the corn knife whistling in a fast, sidelong chop for his exposed left flank, and thought that might just be the last mistake he ever made.

A brown blur rocketed into the girl from behind. There was a clash of teeth, and then the Chucky was screeching, surging to her feet as the dog clamped down on her left arm and dug in. Spinning free, the corn knife whirred past Tom's chest, missing by a fraction of an inch, to bury itself in the opposite wall. Out of the corner of his left eye, he saw the smaller boy scrambling for his rifle. Not three feet away, the Chucky whirled like a dervish, and the dog, jaws snapped tight, sailed round and round like a shot put.

And when he saw the dog, Tom thought, *Wait . . .*

To his right, the kitchen door suddenly crashed wide open. Flipping the Uzi to the ready, Tom jammed the stock into his shoulder and whipped his weapon around just as a corn-tassel blonde—much too young to be a Chucky; Tom still had the presence of mind to see that—bolted through the door.

"Mina!" the girl screamed, socking a Savage to her shoulder. *"Release!"*

At that, Tom felt his heart burst with a shock of disbelief and a swift, sweet, stunning joy. For him, and only for a split second, the world simply stopped, fell away, and there was nothing he wanted more than to sweep her up, hold her close, but then he was breaking his stance, pivoting back for the Chucky, trigger finger taking up the slack.

"Shoot her!" the brown-haired boy screamed as he charged to Tom's side. "Shoot her, Ellie, shoot her!"

They all fired, together, his Uzi still quiet but the boy's rifle roaring and even the Savage making a very large noise for such a puny gun.

Then, still on his knees—because, all of a sudden, he couldn't find his feet; he would fall for sure—Tom was shouting, throwing his arms wide. "Ellie! Honey! Ellie, *Ellie!*"

She'd been so focused on the dog and the Chucky, he doubted she'd registered anything else. At the sound of his voice, she turned, her eyes going huge and incredulous and so very blue, and then she was flying across the room as Mina, *wuffing* hysterically, darted for him, too.

"Tom!" she shrieked. "Tom! Tom! Tom!"

She'd have bowled him over; he was sure of it, because she was running so fast and his heart was so full; but he could take that, he wanted that—and she might have, too.

If not for Mina, beside herself with joy, who got there first.

103

"I like fires." Threading on another marshmallow, Chris held his stick well above the flame's reach. "Actually, I just like s'mores . . . hey, you're burning."

"Way I love them." Licking his fingers to avoid the scorch, Peter pinched blackened, molten marshmallows onto squares of Hershey's chocolate atop a graham cracker, sandwiched this with another cracker, and pressed until the white lava of marshmallows overflowed. Peter crammed the treat into his mouth. "And faster," he said around gooey s'more. "You going to let me get sick all by myself?"

"No," Chris said, but he brought his marshmallows no closer to the fire. He tipped a look at the night sky, milky with stars. The eye of the moon, whiter than a marshmallow, stared.

That's not right. Grimacing, he put a hand to a sudden ache in his chest: a weird pressure. *I'm dreaming again.*

"I'm not in any rush." The flames pulsed. Chris's breath fogged, although neither he nor Peter wore jackets or even hiking boots, just jeans, tees, sneakers. "I like it here."

"Me, too," Peter said, his voice gluey. His hair spilled around his shoulders like spun gold. His eyes were blue diamonds. "One of my favorite places on earth."

"But we can't *be* there, can we?" Chris thought they were on top of a mountain, high above a valley. Yet there was only the fire crackling on a table of flat rock and nothing beyond Peter but a dark blank. Considering the stars, maybe this was outer space. Or heaven.

"No. The fire's not allowed for real, but it's my space, my rules. My marshmallows." Swallowing, Peter skimmed his tongue over a molten dribble and groaned. "And chocolate. Oh my God, I forgot how good that tastes."

"So, we're in your head?"

"Pretty much. More like a . . . daydream. My safe place. Kind of where the last part of me hangs." Peter speared marshmallows with his stick. "Better get a move on with that s'more before they yank you back."

Yank me back? "How long do we have? I miss talking." This was not what he'd wanted to say, but the truth was embarrassing. He winced at another jab of pain. "What *is* that? Feels like someone's banging on my chest."

"Because he is. Trying to save your ass."

"What?" His brain caught up to what Peter had just said, and he recalled Jess's warning or, perhaps, her prophesy: *Someone will die. Someone must.* "Saving my ass. You mean, I'm—"

"*This* close." Peter pinched an inch of air between two fingers. "Heart stopped, and you're not breathing. I think Tom might've cracked a rib. Guy from the Red Cross who did ACLS for the deputies said it happens sometimes."

"Tom." He blinked. "*Alex's* Tom?"

"Yeah, Al—" Peter seemed to catch himself. "Her," he said, nibbling on a marshmallow. "You know these are good raw? I forgot that, too. That's the hell of this. I can come here, but I'll forget you and this. It's the only way I can keep this all safe from *him*. It's like I'm behind this one-way mirror, only I can't mike in and nobody outside knows I'm here."

This was so different from his previous experiences. Chris felt . . . safer. "Why am I not seeing you in a nightmare? That's all I've had until now," Chris said, thinking that he also hadn't tried dying quite so many times before either. He stared at his stick with its marshmallows that refused to brown—and what was up with that? On an impulse, he thrust the marshmallows into the flames. Nothing happened. The marshmallows didn't bubble or turn black. Withdrawing the stick, he broke off the tip and tossed it into the fire and watched as the flames refused to claim it. A log popped, releasing a swarm of sparks, but the wood itself remained unchanged. Extending his hand, he let his palm drift close and then into the flames. No heat. No pain.

"Like I said, we're in my special place. I guess all this"—Peter plucked up a marshmallow and stared as if studying a lab specimen—"probably can't work for you."

"Why?" Breaking a wedge of chocolate, Chris touched the dark wafer to his tongue. For an instant, he thought of Meg Murry sitting down to a meal that tasted of sand while her brother, lost and already under IT's control, ate quite happily. The chocolate had no smell and less taste than air. "Why haven't I been able to come here from the very beginning?"

"Maybe because you were still figuring things out. Digging for the truth, putting together the pieces." Blowing out his blazing marshmallows, Peter gestured with the stick, chalking streamers of white smoke. "Letting go enough to find a piece of the *real* me, I guess."

Truth comes from blood and water. "Letting go of the hammer."

"Yeah, but we don't need to get all biblical. This has way more to do with biology and the brain. I'm talking temporal lobe, out-of-body experiences. Isaac was right about that."

"And you? Are you really dead, or have you Changed or . . ."

"I think, for me, they're all related." Peter let go of a heavy sigh. "There is so much to tell you, and we don't have time for it all. I'm not sure we can even do this again."

"How are we doing it at all?"

"Dunno. I built the space a couple weeks ago, when you told me to."

"Me? How could I—"

"We're different. All Spared are. Some are really unique, like you and the way your brain's reacted to that drug Hannah gave you. Me . . . I was Changing before the Change. The boat? Lying?" Peter looked away. "Leaving that girl to drown."

He'd thought a lot about this. "Peter, there was no time. You couldn't save them both." He almost said, *Someone had to die*, but didn't. "Peter, she was your sister."

"But then I made it worse. I said that girl was already dead." Peter pulled in a shuddering breath. "The good guys don't lie. They don't choose. They save everybody."

That only happens in books. "Hannah said you tried."

"Yeah." Peter gave a bleak laugh. "For all the good *that* did. That one choice ruined Simon's life, probably Penny's, too, and then I set up the Zone, I *fed* . . ." Tossing his stick into the fire, his voice thickened with disgust. "Everything I build, everyone I love, I destroy."

"*I'm* still here," Chris said, quietly. He watched Peter's marshmallows turn to ash. The throbbing ache in his chest had sharpened and grown much stronger in the last few seconds. "We're not in a nightmare. No one is here but us, and your eyes are blue, Peter."

"That's because you're seeing the piece that's"—he tapped the back of his head—"tucked away and still, you know . . . *me*. The part you were meant to reach."

And the part I want to save, if I can. The thought popped into his head completely unbidden. "Maybe because you want to reach me, too. You said you were afraid, but I'm here. I found this place, and you. Let me help, Peter."

"You said that once before. I think you saved me then, a little. You told me to forgive myself." Peter shook his head. "But I can't. You shouldn't forgive me either."

"But I do, Peter," he said, then stiffened as his chest flared. *No, please, not yet.* "You're not lost, not while I can still find you."

"But I'm almost gone. I can feel that, too. This space?" Peter cast his eyes around their bubble of light holding off the dark. "I don't know how much longer I can hang on to it. Yeah, it's a part he can't control. I'm not sure he even knows about it. But he's getting stronger, and my space is shrinking. This fire, the marshmallows? They're all that's left."

"He?"

"Yes. F-F . . ." Peter's head suddenly snapped back. An arrow of pain shot across his face.

"Peter." Alarmed, Chris reached for his friend. "Peter, what's—"

"*N-no!*" Peter cringed. "D-don't touch me. M-my fault. To n-name is to control, to ac-access . . ."

"Access? Control? What are you talking about?"

"H-him. He wants to kn-know, but I haven't t-told . . ." Gasping, Peter pressed the heel of a hand to either temple. "Can't say names. Goes both ways. N-naming him lets him in."

"Who? How?"

"F-Finn . . . oh *God*, that hurts." Arching against a fresh tide of pain, Peter hissed, "Using a *d-drug*, not the same as what Hannah g-gave you but cl-close . . ."

"On whom? You?"

"*Y-yes*, and . . ." Peter snatched a gasp. "And *Ch-Changed*. Too much to ex-explain. No time. Ask T-Tom. He's guessed part . . . *aahh!*"

"Peter!" It took all Chris's willpower not to touch his friend. "Peter, tell me what to *do*."

"N-nothing you can do." Another wave of pain shuddered through Peter and shook loose a moan. "F-Finn is c-c-*coming*."

"Coming." Fresh sweat glistened on Peter's forehead and neck but in the light of a fire not as bright as before. Chris tossed a glance at the dimming flames just as that sharp pain grabbed his chest again.

No time. Either Finn had found Peter, or *he* was being pulled away, or maybe both. "Where? To Rule?"

Eyes still closed, Peter managed a nod. "He's got wuh-weapons. Men and *Changed* . . ."

"What—" A powerful talon of pain raked his chest. Chris couldn't hold back the groan. That familiar falling sensation was beginning, his vision fading, but he had to know this, he had to hang on! *Don't call me back, just a few more seconds!* "Wh-what does he want?"

"K-kids. M-more experi . . . *aaahhhh!*" Rolling to his knees, Peter clapped his hands to his head. "Get out, Chris. Pl-please. Before he s-sees, before he really *nuh-knows* you. Let th-them take you b-back . . . s-save yourself, save . . ."

"No." Maybe it was because of his pain, or Peter's terror and his certainty that when and if they met again, things would be very different—or perhaps it was because Jess had sent him from Rule to find his way—that now Chris chose a different path. Clasping the back of Peter's neck, he pulled his friend close and held him fast. "No, Peter, I won't."

"Ch-Chris, *don't!*" Peter's eyes brimmed, and Chris saw their true color beginning to bleed. Peter's hands clung to Chris's forearms. "Don't touch me. You have to—"

"Don't tell me what to do." Chris heard his voice break, felt the tears on his cheeks. "I'm going to save us, Peter. I'm going to save us both."

Then the black tide swept through and carried him away.

104

"Listen to me. I've seen this man. I've seen those Chuckies . . . the Changed? The ones he's altered. I know what they have and what they can do." Tom pointed to the Uzi as well as the contents of the pack he'd spilled onto the table of the hospice conference room. "Finn's well armed, well supplied, and he's got troops you don't. I guarantee you won't last an hour, much less a day. He'll wipe you out, then take the kids and call it even."

"So you're saying we just give up, let him run over us, and go down without a fight?" Scowling, Jarvis tossed a dark look at the two men—equally old and just as skeptical—who sat to either side of him. "What the hell kind of soldier are you?"

"Hey, hey," Kincaid rapped from his place to Chris's left. "Are you deaf, Jarvis? This boy's trying to help us *save* what we can."

"It's okay," Tom said, but Chris saw the splash of angry red seep over Tom's jaw. "You're scared, you're starving, things have fallen apart here. I get that. You don't know me and you certainly don't trust me, especially when I show up with your Public Enemy Number One." Tom tilted his head toward Chris. "I get that, too. But you won't win this fight."

"We have the right to defend ourselves," Jarvis said.

"No one's questioning that. But you have to decide what you're truly defending."

"Hell's that mean?"

"It means that we're not talking about fighting for *Rule*," Chris rasped, and winced. After four hours, all he could manage was a harsh whisper through a throat that felt as if he'd swallowed razor blades. What freaked him out was when he'd glanced in a mirror. A blood-encrusted, blue-black bruise circled his throat like a dog collar. The whites of his eyes were awash in red hemorrhage from broken capillaries, and nearly as bloodred as what he'd seen in his dream of Peter. Breathing hurt, the muscles grabbing with every inhale, and two cracked ribs complained, although Kincaid said busted ribs would've hurt ten times worse: *You're just damned lucky that boy knows battlefield medicine.* Lucky for him, Tom was very strong, too. After Chris's heart started up and he was breathing again, Tom had simply scooped Chris up, hustled them all to the perimeter guards, and promptly surrendered.

Although Jayden said there'd been a moment after they'd killed the girl with the corn knife when Tom had . . . hesitated: *When I said your name, you could see it in Tom's face, how surprised he was to find out who you were, and . . . it was so weird. Tom was angry. Like he already knew something about you, and hated your guts. If Ellie hadn't asked him what was wrong . . .*

Jayden hadn't said the rest, but his meaning was clear. Which made Chris wonder just what the hell Weller had said to Tom. He hadn't had the time to find out. For the moment at least, Tom seemed to have swallowed his rage at Chris in favor of working together and getting these old men to listen to reason.

"We're talking about defending the kids." At his tone, his black shepherd, Jet, pushed his snout into Chris's thigh and chuffed. Chris had been so happy to see that dog, he'd nearly bawled. "That's the only fight left," Chris said, scratching the big dog's ruff.

"We know that," Jarvis said. "Keep those bastards out of here."

"No." From his seat on Chris's right, Jayden spoke up for the first time. "That's not what Tom is saying. You're not listening. If Tom is right, you might as well throw the bullets. No, better yet . . . lob spitballs and shoot *yourselves* in the foot. Better use of the bullets."

"Yeah? Well, I don't recall asking for your opinion," Jarvis said.

"You want to yell, yell at me," Tom said patiently. "I know you have no reason to trust me, but please *listen*. This all makes sense, especially when you take into consideration what Weller's motives might've been, and that picture of him and Finn. Blowing the mine ought to have sent the Changed your way because so many are from Rule. They're your grandchildren, and their friends. But they haven't showed."

"That doesn't mean they've been rounded up. A few *have* returned." Smoothing a hand over a rumpled gray checked shirt, Yeager pulled himself a little straighter, but his chest had caved in; his sallow cheeks were sunken; the canny, once bird-bright eyes were now dull and hollow. "After that business with Ben Stiemke, we discovered and killed four more, but that's all."

"All that we found." Thin, bloody fluid dribbled onto Jarvis's chin from ugly scores on either side of his mouth. Smearing the mess away with the heel of a hand, he peeked and then ran his hand over a pant leg. "But now there's the two you shot, and that girl with the corn knife and the . . ." He tapped his cheek. "I might've seen her around town before."

"Claire Krueger." Once so bluff and round, Ernst looked like the Michelin tire guy with all the air let out. "She wasn't from Rule, but in the same year of high school as Ben."

"So who the hell knows how long they've been hunkered down there?" Jarvis said. "We pulled at least five bodies from that crawl space, and we've got about a dozen missing in the past couple weeks, not counting the Landrys themselves. They disappeared day after that . . ." Jarvis shot a sidelong glance at the Council, then quickly looked away, the small muscles in his jaw clenching. "That *thing* with Ben Stiemke. Honestly, we thought people were sneaking out. Can't blame them. Tell the truth, we haven't been working real hard to keep people who want to leave. So if that's all that's come out of the mine collapse, it's nothing we can't handle."

"But it's *not* all," Chris said in his husky, rough voice. He sounded like a chain smoker. "That's what Tom is *saying*."

"There were a *lot* of kids in that mine, a couple hundred at least, and more moving in and out," Tom said. "What Weller didn't know was that Finn *needed* me to blow the mine to make it easier for his people to hunt them down, like herding cattle or buffalo. If only a couple have shown their faces here, I bet he's rounded up quite a few, and if he's doing to *them* what I've seen in those altered Changed? You don't stand a chance, and neither do the children."

"You saying he'd kill kids?" Jarvis asked. "Shoot 'em, or feed 'em to his Changed?"

"No. The kids are valuable, but for different reasons." Chris had kept the details of his . . . dream? vision? out-of-body experience? . . . to himself. "He'd experiment on them."

Tom nodded. "I think that's why Mellie was gathering kids. This was never about raising an army to march on Rule. It was about finding guinea pigs, experimental subjects. Finn probably wants to see what happens to normal kids, or those he can catch in the process of Changing. The more I've thought about it, the more I think Finn's camp was always relatively close by, too. It's the only thing that explains why Mellie fought so hard to keep us there *and* why the Changed never attacked. Finn protected the camp. He probably deployed men to guard our perimeter, especially once the mine was gone."

"Okay. Let's say you're right. But . . . run?" Jarvis was shaking his head. "We're barely holding on now. There aren't enough supplies to go around for everybody."

"Who said anything about everybody?" Chris said, hoarsely. His words hung there, and Chris was content to let them. Of all the assembled men, Chris thought that, from the sudden narrowing of his eyes, only his grandfather had any inkling of what they were proposing.

"But . . ." Jarvis turned a blank stare around the room. "But if we can't fight and win . . ."

"He means the children." Yeager's gaze seemed to have regained some of its peculiar clarity. "And *only* the children."

"What are you talking about?"

"You can leave Rule, or you can stay. But *we* take the kids, not you. You can't come with us," Chris said. "You can't follow or try to find us either."

"*What?*" Jarvis spluttered. "That . . . that's crazy! You'd leave us here to *die?*"

"No. If most of you want to leave, go," Chris said. "I think you should get out of here."

"Get out?" Blue veins swelled on Jarvis's temples. "*Most?*"

"Some *have* to stay behind," Tom said, quietly. "If you don't put on a show, Finn will know you've been warned. You have to buy the kids time to get out."

"Wait a minute, wait a minute. You just said we shouldn't fight."

"What I meant is it has to be the right fight for the right reason and at the right time," Tom said. "You've gathered children, some by force and others not. You've told yourselves that it's for their benefit. But a prison is not a home. Hanging on to these children serves no other purpose now but yours. They have the right to their lives. Please." Tom looked at Jarvis and then the other men in turn. "Let Jayden and Chris take them someplace safer."

"No place is truly safe," Yeager said.

"But it will be better than here," Chris said. "We're asking for enough supplies and wagons to get the kids north, that's all. Say, four days, five."

"That'll clean us out," Jarvis said. "All we'll have will be a couple sticks of Juicy Fruit."

"If that's true, then you're already done," Tom said. "You've got too many mouths and not enough resources. If you can even find seed to plant, it'll be months before a harvest. Read some history. This is the Starving Time in Jamestown. The only thing you haven't done yet is eat your dead."

Jarvis was stony. "It would never come to that."

"No one thought the world would end either," Kincaid said. "Jarvis, for God's sake . . ."

"Kincaid, I can't just *decide*. We got to put this to a vote. Get the village together . . ."

"You can't," Tom said. "You don't have that kind of time, and people will discuss this to death. They'll panic, and you don't have the manpower to control a mob scene. Once it's done and comes down to a very simple choice—leave or stay—you'll have a much better chance of keeping people calm and maybe saving a few more lives. If I'm right, Finn is a half day behind me, but maybe a lot less. He's got the full moon working for him, too, which means he can move in and be ready to storm this place by dawn."

"Lenten Moon," Yeager put in. "The last full moon of winter. Appropriate, given our situation. *The sun will be turned to darkness, and the moon to blood.*" He lifted his hands in apology. "Joel. Also apt, considering the earthquake. The boy is right, Jarvis. You wanted a seat on the Council? Well, you *are* the Council now. Make a decision and beg for forgiveness later, but for our Lord's sake, make the right one."

"My God." Jarvis stared down at the table for a long moment, then nodded at something he saw there and looked up at Chris. "I heard what you said about the adults, but take Kincaid."

The doctor stirred. "Jarvis, I'm not asking for—"

"The kids will need him. He's probably the only adult here you can really trust." Jarvis's eyes shifted to Jayden. "He's taken good care of your sick before, and he's damned stubborn when it counts."

Privately, Chris had hoped they might convince Kincaid. Now he and Jayden looked at each other, and then Jayden turned to Kincaid. "Would you come?" Jayden asked. "We'd like that."

"I—" Kincaid's throat clicked in a dry swallow, and then he nodded. "Got to take care of a couple things, but . . . okay."

"Then you need to get moving," Tom said. "Pack up the children, get your supplies together, and get out now. There's barely enough time as it is."

"And what do we do once you're gone?" Jarvis asked.

"I'm not leaving," Tom said. "Not yet."

"What?" Chris heard the word drop out of his mouth. Beside him, Jayden said, "Tom, you can't—"

"Yes, I can," Tom said, still looking at Jarvis. "You have your kids, and Finn's got mine. I can't leave, not while there's still a chance I can do something to help them."

"Finn wouldn't *bring* them," Chris said.

"Not in the front lines. Chances are they're in the rear, three, four miles back. There won't be another or better opportunity to get them. Just have to keep Finn focused on Rule."

"So how do we do that?" Jarvis asked. "Scream and run around like chickens?"

"No. Finn's coming from the south. You have to mount a defense or put up a barricade . . . maybe an abatis . . ."

"What?"

"Trees. Cut them down so all the limbs face the enemy. Not only will your people have cover, but it will be much harder for Finn's men to get through. They'll have to go around. An obstacle like that will also keep him looking at Rule, not his rear."

Jarvis glanced at the other men, who nodded. "We can do that for you," Jarvis said.

"Good. Then pick your men, Jarvis, the ones you can count on not to run at the first shot," Tom said, "and buy me some time to get my kids."

105

The secret about what they were doing and who was coming Rule's way kept until about three a.m., just long enough for Chris and his people to retrieve the needed supplies and start packing up the kids, who were now gathered at the hospice. To Tom's surprise, only fifty or so oldsters, most of them refugees in Rule to begin with, elected to take a share of what supplies remained and get out of town. Of the roughly one hundred and fifty elderly remaining, Jarvis had chosen ten to man an abatis from trees they'd felled and then hastily arranged to guard the southern road, the most direct approach from the mine, which cut through rolling, sparsely forested countryside.

"I got a couple other men working on trees to barricade the north road out of town once the children are gone. Everyone else wants to wait in the church," Jarvis said to Tom, who'd visited the defunct school for a few, very special items before heading into the church's bell tower. "At least until Finn's in the village."

"Wait? What for? You can't be serious." Tom was horrified. "Jarvis, you need to make people leave. They'll be sitting ducks. They should get out of Rule. This isn't Judgment Day. This isn't Jonestown. For God's sake, no one's asking you to drink Kool-Aid. They'll kill you."

"But the Rev's right: no place is truly safe." Jarvis's eyes were so far back in his skull, you needed a flashlight to see them. "It comforts us to gather; I can't take that away. Besides, our grandchildren are finally coming home and . . ." His voice thickened. "They're our responsibility, always were. If my grandson's with Finn, I need to know he's at peace." No amount of argument changed the old man's mind, or anyone else's, and Tom finally gave up.

Later, crossing the square to the village hall, Tom spotted people trickling into the church. The stained-glass windows shimmered with color, something he'd have found calming on any other night. As he mounted the village hall steps, the faint strains of a hymn wound through the open church doors: *I fear no foe, with Thee at hand to bless.*

Bum leg nagging a touch from all the up-and-down—not to mention wrestling plastic primer buckets and bags of high-grade fertilizer into a back storage room just above the jail before humping back for cans of diesel and fuel oil and hoping he really *did* have the proportions down—he headed downstairs to check out the building's air-conditioning ducts. He'd already found they were just large enough for him to worm through. (Thank God he wasn't claustrophobic.) Now, to figure out how far he could stretch that det cord and if the math worked. All he needed to buy were fifteen, twenty lousy minutes on the outside.

And then the darkness will deepen, Tom thought. *Whether we like it or not.*

Two hours later, he heard the clump of boots.

"Tom?"

"Up here, Chris. To your left. Hold on." He was flat on his back, on a high shelf, a partially dismantled alarm clock in his hands, the jail's ceiling a foot from his face. Wedging a finger on the clock's escape wheel, he carefully seated a sliver of whittled matchstick between one tooth and the lever's entry pallet before slowly easing pressure on the wheel. The pallet bit into the wood but didn't break it. The clock's gears were still, the hands frozen. "So," Tom said, gently laying the clock aside and picking up a pair of crimpers, "guys at the barricade set?"

"About as ready as they can be. Kids should be away in another hour."

"Cutting it close. Going to be dawn soon."

"Can't be helped." Chris was taking in the tanks of propane, cans of gasoline, premix. "I knew all this stuff was here, but what you're planning? Gives me a whole different perspective."

"Yup. Just got to hope it's enough of a bang." Coring a hole in the end of a grayish-white block, he slipped in a slim length of tarnished pipe—yes, close enough to pass for an M18, a lucky break—then used his teeth to tear strips of black electrical tape. "You got your guys?"

"What's left. There weren't many of us Spared to begin with, and even fewer now. Pru and Greg are the oldest. I'd send both, but I held Greg back to go with us. There are some guys, Aidan and Lucian and Sam . . . after I left, they went over to the dark side. You know, locking up Pru and Greg? I don't trust Aidan and his guys but can't leave them. Wouldn't be right."

"Your people, your call. But you really want them for the long haul? Eventually, you'll have to choose."

"I know." Chris shrugged. "We're all Spared. If we make it, that might be the time to give them a share and cut them loose. Anyway, Pru and three other guys'll go after your kids when we say."

"Excellent." Tom gestured at a thermos on the floor. "Coffee, if you want. I've been mainlining for hours. I'm so jacked, I'm vibrating."

"Thanks." Uncapping the thermos, Chris poured out a cup, sipped, then blinked. "Wow, that's strong. I think my teeth just curled."

"Enjoy it while it lasts. Found it in Weller's stuff." Tom returned his attention to his work. That sea of red hemorrhage in Chris's eyes, so like Finn's altered Changed, unsettled him. "You sound better."

"Yeah. Kincaid said I was lucky my larynx didn't fracture." He heard Chris take another halting swallow. "How's this going to work exactly?"

"Going to wire the block to an alarm clock the way I already have four others. Once I pull the matchstick, clock's ticking. But this way, I can control exactly when we start instead of setting it now and then hoping we get lucky."

"Won't they hear it from the door? The ticking?" Chris gestured with a finger at a finished bomb attached to a bottom shelf. "That one's in plain view."

"Something interesting for Finn to look at. I'm betting they won't have time to yank them all before one blows," he said, amazed at how smoothly the lie flowed from his tongue.

"Wow, they really teach you guys a lot." Chris ran a forefinger over the cup's rim. "I saw this movie about this bomb disposal squad. You did stuff like that?"

"Yeah." Tom used his knife to flay electrical cord. The more jury-rigged this looked, all the better to fool Finn. "I know the movie."

"Did they get it right?"

"Some. Most of the time we sent in robots and built water charges or used a hunk of C4 to blow IEDs. The suit's a last resort." He paused. "I'm not trying to be an asshole, but I really don't want to talk about it right now. I have to stay focused. Going back there in my head . . . it's nowhere good."

"Okay." He felt Chris's eyes. "What did Weller say?"

He knew what Chris meant. "Nothing very nice," he said, ripping another long piece of electrical tape. Thank goodness, there was plenty. He'd worried he might not have enough for the real thing. "This isn't how I imagined we would meet."

"Oh?" Chris's voice grew cautious. "How was that?"

"I was going to kill you." He smoothed tape with the flat of his thumb. "For what Weller said you did to Alex. After the mine went, killing you was all I could think about. It was a . . . poison?" He felt his tongue test that, then shook his head. "That's not right. It was the only thing I had to hang on to, that hate. Hate makes you feel more powerful, like you can keep yourself pumped, so you put one foot in front of the other, thinking that you're going somewhere even if all you're doing is looping the same movie over and over in your head."

"Of how you were going to kill me."

"Technicolor." He nodded. "This afternoon . . . well, yesterday now . . . when Jayden called you by name, I thought, Jesus, it's *him*; this is the guy I've come to kill." Sighing, Tom folded his hands over his chest. When he was a kid, he used to lie like this in sweet-smelling grass and study clouds. "There was a second there when I thought, fine, let him die."

There was a long pause. "What changed your mind?"

"Ellie." He rolled his head to look down. "She was frantic. It finally dawned on me that Weller told so many lies, what he said about you might be just one more."

A brief smile flickered over Chris's lips. "Thanks for giving me the benefit of the doubt."

"You're welcome." Despite the weeks nurturing the monstrous blight in his soul, Tom liked this boy. In another time and place, they might be good friends. He felt a brush of sadness that, now, the chances were nil. He had so many questions, and no time. He wanted to ask about Alex: each memory, how she looked, what she said. He even thought he could take it if Chris and Alex . . . but did that matter now? Nothing could change how he felt about Alex, nothing, and he still had the miracle of Ellie, too: so sweet, a final gift.

Hang on to that. Everything that happened next would hinge on Chris, a boy he'd dreamt about so often and barely knew. *Hold on to Ellie and Alex until the very last second.*

"Kids are about ready," Chris said. "We should go."

"Yeah." Showing the other boy a tight smile, Tom tore off a few strips of electrical tape and began strapping the alarm clock to the gray-white block he'd fashioned. Not a bad looker, if he did say so himself. Ought to kick-start a couple hearts. "Few more seconds."

"Okay." Chris was quiet a moment. "You ever wonder who did it?"

"Did what? The EMPs?" He shook his head. "If this was a book or movie, there'd be some guy who'd explain it, give you all the answers. Tidy everything up, wrap it with a bow. We'll never know, and it doesn't matter. This is like war, Chris. When the soldiers come marching in, all you care about is protecting your family. When you're boots on the ground, all you think about is the mission and your buddies, your brothers. It's not political. There's no big picture. You don't agonize over the morality. Everything narrows down to the essentials. Yeah, some days—the impossible days when no matter how careful you are, someone will die—you wonder what it's all for. But in the end, there are your brothers, your people, and only that. You're not looking to die, but you'll sacrifice it all for them. I lost that for a while, too. When I went on leave, got stateside?" He paused, wondering if he really wanted to admit this, out loud, and then thought that, hell, in a few more hours, nothing he said now would matter. "I was on the fence, maybe a step away from never going back. Deserting. Had it all mapped out, too, how I would lay tracks in Michigan but then work my way over on the sly into Minnesota and then Canada. Big country, easy to get lost. But my best friend, Jim—we were on the same EOD team—I bet he knew something was up when I mentioned the Waucamaw. My family was in Maryland; there are plenty of nice places to camp there. So why was I going to the U.P.? I think that's why Jim invited himself along: to remind me of my brothers, my people. But then . . . the world died and it just wasn't an issue anymore."

"Would you have gone back if nothing had happened?"

"I'll never know, will I? I'd like to think that I would have. But then I found"—he swallowed back the lump—"found my people anyway. Found Alex and Ellie. For a little while, I got back what I'd lost. So, to hell with the rest, Chris. How this happened, who did it . . . all I care about, all that matters, is that Alex and Ellie helped me find myself again."

Chris was silent a long moment. "It was the whistle, Tom," he said, quietly.

"What?" For just a second, he'd been back in the Waucamaw: striding in with an armload of wood as Alex looked up with a smile that found its way into his chest. "What are you talking about?"

"Alex," Chris said, shaking out the dregs before carefully twisting the cup back onto the thermos. "She ran because of the whistle."

He remembered the high, impossible note that pierced his heart. "How do you know?"

Screwing on that cup seemed to take all Chris's concentration. "Ellie told me. She gave the whistle to a boy we brought back from Oren. I think her idea was that if Alex and you were in Rule, Alex would put it together that Ellie was somewhere up there, and you guys would go get her. So if Alex had a whistle at the mine, she must've found hers on that boy. Too much of a coincidence otherwise, isn't it? Alex left to go after Ellie. I got here too late, and the rest was just"—Chris tightened the cap—"lousy timing. Or good timing for Jess, I guess. If I'd gotten back sooner, I might've saved Alex. Knowing Jess, though, probably not. One way or the other, Jess was bound and determined that Alex should go, and then me, too."

He didn't know how he was supposed to feel. "Why are you telling me this?"

Chris's violent red eyes met his. "It's the end of the world, Tom. Rule is done. I don't know if we have a tomorrow. So there's one thing you need to get clear in your head. You found your people, and you *never* lost them. Alex left because she wasn't sure she could count on me to help her. Knowing how I was back then, she'd have been right. But I don't think she would've felt the same way about you, Tom," Chris said. "Not then—or ever."

Dawn was an hour away, more or less, as Chris walked the now empty hospice halls. All the terminal patients with whom he'd spent time were long dead. Illuminated only by moonlight, the halls were sultry with shadows. He slowed as he approached the only occupied room left. Through the open door came a light floral perfume, but the rest was silence. Hesitating a moment, he quietly rounded the corner and saw first the woman on the bed and then, belatedly, a figure huddled in a large bedside chair.

"Oh. I'm sorry," he said, already beginning to back out. "I didn't know—"

"No, no." Between the soft upholstery and a blanket, his grandfather looked gnomish. His bald scalp gleamed in a splash of silver-green moonlight that cut his face into deep black wedges and taut skin over stark ridges of bone. "You're not disturbing me. Leaving soon?"

"Yes. Sarah and Jayden are still settling the kids, but . . . soon," Chris said.

"What about you?"

"I'm staying a while longer with Tom. We'll leave together." Although Chris had a very bad premonition he couldn't put into words or quite shake: leaving wouldn't be quite so simple.

"Well, come in," Yeager said, beckoning. "You don't need my permission."

Chris crossed to stand over the bed. The silence was eerie. Jess lay on her back, hands curled over her stomach because the small muscles had atrophied with disuse. Someone had brushed her hair, which spilled over the pillow and her shoulders. Kincaid, probably. In the moonlight, the whites showed through her lashes in thumbnail slivers. Chris kept expecting her to say something, or those lids to snap open, and to see himself captured in those black-mirror eyes. The prolonged bout of REM sleep that had seized Jess for weeks had ended abruptly only a half hour ago, Kincaid said. Chris had felt only a mild shock when the doctor showed him the book from which he'd gleaned the drug's formula: *Ghost-Walkers: The Ethnobotanical Encyclopedia of Medicinal and Psychoactive Mushrooms*. In another half hour—and probably less, because Kincaid hadn't stinted on the dose this time—Jess would be past dreams.

"Would you like to sit?" Yeager indicated a chair with a bony hand that jutted from an arm as thin as a chopstick. His clothing puddled. "We haven't talked."

It was on the tip of his tongue to point out that he'd been in cardiac arrest part of the time and busy the rest, but he let that fizzle. The last time he'd seen this old man, his grandfather had smacked him around. Taking a seat also made him uneasy, as if he'd be conceding something, maybe getting himself under this old man's thumb. "What for? I don't have anything to say. I don't forgive you, if that's what you want. You and the Council let terrible things happen. I don't even care about whose idea it was first, because if it was Peter's, you should've said no. If it was yours, then you took advantage of Peter and that's even worse. You had every chance to stop this, but you didn't. You didn't even save Kincaid, a friend. You let Aidan take his *eye*, for God's sake. What could you say that will make any of that better, or even justify it?"

"Nothing," Yeager said, his tone void of emotion but not indifferent or cold. "But I thought you might have questions."

"Like I said—"

"Then I have one. How is my brother?"

"Last time I saw him, he was pretty sick from smoke inhalation." *Which was totally my fault.*

"I'm sorry for that. We haven't always seen eye to eye, but I admire him for setting up a place for children who wanted a different life from their parents. He always did want to help."

"He helped me when I was hurt. It's a long story." Coming back from the dead wasn't a subject he wanted to broach with this old man.

"How much did he tell you?"

"Pretty much everything. Some stuff, I figured out on my own."

"Ah. Do you have questions?"

Oh, about a million. Although he'd resolved that it didn't matter, that it was water under the bridge, he couldn't help being curious. "Yes. How did you decide? Between me and Simon, I mean."

"Mmm." Yeager knit his skeletal hands together. If he'd had a sickle, he could've passed as the Grim Reaper. "To be honest, I chose the infant on the right."

"What do you mean?"

"I could only take one. Your mother was holding you both at the time, and she cradled you on the left."

"What does that have to do with anything?" The mention of his mother stung. He heard the sharpness, his simmering anger, and decided, *Screw it.* "What difference did the *side* make?"

"Oh . . ." Yeager drew a slow hand over his bald scalp, the gesture of a man who'd once had hair to smooth. "Because Christ sits on God's right hand, I suppose. If you want something scriptural. But it's mystical, really. Goes back to the Jews. For them, the body's two sides mirror the divided nature of our soul. There is the power to give and hold back. The right hand is stronger; you give with your right, whether it's justice or kindness. With your left, you hold back. The left hand is discipline and restraint. The left hand keeps its secrets."

And lives in the shadows. His grandfather had just described him and his life to a T. "So you went for strength."

"I chose the sword." Yeager paused. "But in my arrogance I forgot that it takes just as much strength to refrain, be slow to anger and rash action. It's easy to trick yourself into thinking that in the righteousness of your anger, cruelty is justified. But you are strong, Chris, much stronger than I've given you credit for."

"I'm not strong," Chris said. Yet of all the things he remembered about Rule, a place where he thought he might finally find a home, the mornings after a fight were the most vivid: kneeling next to Peter in church, as everyone—including Alex, *especially* Alex—looked on, and feeling his grandfather's hands on his head in blessing. It was hokey and stupid and incredibly sexist, and yet he *had* felt pride: *This is what it's like not to be afraid. This is what it feels like to belong.* He was like Tom, wasn't he? *Looking for my people* . . . Except Alex was gone, and if his dreams held true, Peter was worse than dead. A strange lump forced its way into his throat. He should go. No way he'd break down now. He didn't forgive Yeager, he couldn't. Chris could let go of the hammer for Peter but never for this old man. "Sometimes I wait too long and then it's too late."

"But you never broke, Chris. You're following your path and still finding your way. Take it from an old man: sometimes, you get a second chance."

Not with Alex. What he said next surprised him. "What do I do about Simon? If he's alive . . . we're enemies. Did he even know about me?"

Yeager shook his head. "What you do depends on what you find."

"He eats people." *He's my brother; we're identical twins. He's me and I'm him.*

"If that is *all* he is, then you have your answer, don't you?"

"How can he be *more* than that?"

"I love him, Chris." Too dark to see his grandfather's expression, Chris heard the catch in his voice. "That makes him more."

That Yeager could not say the same about him hurt more than Chris would've imagined. Well, what did he expect? He'd shown up in town a virtual stranger, only a copy, a faded Xerox.

"Try not to be bitter for too long," Yeager said. "Life is hard enough."

"Whose fault is that? I was a *kid.* I saw you, what, five times before the world blew up? It was Peter who really cared, who went out of his way—" He swallowed back the rest. "How else am I supposed to feel?"

"You're entitled to your anger."

"I don't need your permission."

"But you're not stupid, Chris. Of all people, you should know what anger does to the soul. You have only to remember your father."

Chris stared. "You're going to lecture me about anger and my dad? You knew what he was like. It's why you agreed to take Simon in the first place. You were rich. You could have fixed things, done *something* to get me out of there. But you left me alone with him. So don't give me any bullshit about what anger does. I *don't* forgive you. That's what you're really asking for, so you can die and believe everything's all right. What you did and let happen—to me, to Peter, Alex—those are your mistakes, your sins to bear. Know what? Take it up with God, if you see him."

"*It is the time of the Lord's vengeance, and he will pay her what she deserves.* Jeremiah was referring to Babylon, not Rule, but I take your point. You asked about Simon. There really is only one choice you'll need to make: life or death."

Someone will die. Chris looked back at Jess. *Someone must.*

"I need to go," he said. "Kids are moving out soon."

"All right." Yeager peered up at him. "Why did you come? You've made it abundantly clear it wasn't to see me."

"I've been thinking a lot about Jess, I guess." Now it was his turn to pause. "Why did you think it was okay? She was married. So were you. You're a *reverend.*"

"Oh . . ." His grandfather brushed an errant strand of hair from Jess's forehead. "The heart wants what it wants, and only I was married. I was selfish, and she was vulnerable: beautiful, a widow. . . . At least, we thought so. Her husband had been declared legally dead."

"A mistake, or did he really disappear?"

"Perhaps a bit of both? Even before Vietnam, he was involved in some very . . . questionable projects." Yeager's hand lingered on Jess's cheek. "When did you figure it out?"

Technically, he'd known ever since Peter mentioned the name in a dream. But that wasn't something you could say, even to a guy who believed in the two halves of the soul.

"When Tom showed us the picture. Isaac said he was a business partner and then I remembered that it's the only mine shaft that was never finished," Chris said. "That's when I knew that Jess had been Finn's wife."

"Nooo." Clutching her Savage in one tight fist, Ellie stamped a foot, then pushed Mina's snout away when the dog turned a worried look. "Please don't make me. I want to stay with you. Why can't I?"

"Ellie, honey." While very bright, the moon kept ducking in and out of scudding high clouds, and he was having a hard time seeing her face. Crouching, Tom ducked his head, trying to catch her eyes. *Go easy; she's grown up a lot, but she's still only eight.* "Look at me. You have to listen. It won't be safe here."

"But I don't want to go with *them*." She waved an arm in the general direction of the wagons parked in the hospice's lot. From here, the wagons would head north on an old logging road that could be easily blocked once they were gone. The air was filled with the clatter of hooves on icy asphalt, the anxious whimpers and yips of the remaining dogs, and the piping exclamations and questions from the children. Most were under twelve and being hustled to one of two waiting wagons. To Tom's left, a bald kid with more piercings than a pincushion was boosting an egg-headed boy onto a flatbed where Sarah, a slender girl with a touch of a limp, waited.

"You know Jayden," he said.

"That's not what I mean. I should stay. I can help," Ellie said. "So can Mina." At the sound of her name, the dog's tail whisked. "We shouldn't split up, Tom. We only just . . ."

"I know, honey." He leaned forward a little to make himself heard over the axes biting trees and handsaws buzzing through trunks. Once the children were away, the trees would be felled to prevent Finn's men from using the road. A large force would have to bushwhack miles out of its way to follow. If Finn was up to chasing anyone. Tom was betting against it. "But I have to stay. If you're still here, I'll worry about you, and then I won't be able to do my job."

"But why does it have to be you? Why can't somebody else stay?"

"Chris *is* staying." He wasn't wild about that, but Chris wouldn't back down: *Your plan, my town, and you'll need help.* Best not to fight it, though. The first chance he got, he'd send Chris packing. "I'm the only one who can do this, Ellie. This is the way I can keep you safe." At the growing thunder in her expression, he cupped her face in his hands. "You and Alex were the best things to ever happen to me. I thought I'd lost you, and then there you were, like this miracle. I was so happy I thought I was going to burst. I would do anything for you. I know this is hard, but please do this for me."

"*Tom.*" Ellie blinked furiously. "I don't have anything to give you to keep you safe. Chris has my good-luck charm. I don't have anything else."

"Oh honey." He kissed first her right palm and then her left before pressing her small hands to his chest. "You're right here. That's all I need."

"But what about Alex?"

He worked around the tightness in his throat. "She's there, too. She'll always be."

"But I want her for real, Tom. Promise we'll look for her, together?" She raised her streaming face. "Please. Cross your heart and hope to die?"

For the second time in less than five minutes, he lied. "Cross my heart and—" He saw Chris, downslope, running their way. The boy's body language was enough.

This is it. "You have to go, honey." Scooping Ellie into his arms, he jogged to Sarah's wagon and boosted her in. "I'll be there as soon as I can."

"Tom!" Ellie grabbed Mina, who'd hopped in after, by the neck. "Tom, wait!"

"I'll be there," he repeated, then ran to the lead wagon, crowded with kids and dogs. Jayden was slinging a backpack to Kincaid, who was settling a teary girl and admonishing a silky golden retriever that kept trying to wash the girl's face. "You guys got to roll," Tom said.

"I hear that." Kincaid leaned down and grasped Tom's hand. "Luck. Stay safe, son."

"Right back atcha." Tom offered a hand to Jayden. "Be careful. Watch out for Ellie."

"Watch her yourself." Jayden surprised him by pulling Tom into an embrace. "I never thanked you," the boy said, roughly. "For, you know . . ."

"It's okay." Tom gave the boy a squeeze. "Good luck."

"Don't be long?" Jayden clung to Tom's forearms. "Stick with Chris. He's got a radio. I'll keep mine on so you two know where to find us. Don't get any dumb, stupid ideas, Tom."

Had Jayden read something in his face? "Don't worry. Now go." Turning, he saw Chris, at Ellie's wagon, reaching up to give the girl a hug. Chris's big black shepherd leapt nimbly alongside Mina and a sleek Weimaraner Chris said had belonged to Alex. Seeing them all together like that, knowing Ellie would be cared for and loved, made Tom feel . . . a little easier.

Beyond, a large dray hitched to a third supply wagon was snorting, picking up on the sudden urgency and eager to be off. Three other boys—Aidan, Sam, and Greg—were already on their horses. Aidan and Sam, who smelled like bad news, moved to take point, while Greg waited to bring up the rear.

Please, God. As Ellie's wagon rumbled past, he raised a hand. He thought Ellie shouted something, but her words were drowned by the clop of horses' hooves and the creak of wagons and the few excited *huffs* of dogs. *Please, keep her safe.*

In another moment, the moon hid its face, thick shadows swallowed the wagon, and Ellie was gone from him, again, lost to the dark.

106

"How long are we going to stay here?" Cindi asked the guard. She curled against Luke the way he remembered his cat used to: *warmth-seeking behavior*, his mom called it. Luke used to hate how much that cat shed, but now he really missed the dumb thing, not to mention his parents. Slipping an arm around Cindi's shoulders, he pulled her a little closer. A half hour after Finn's men and their Chuckies had streamed into camp, two more men had trotted up, leading a mare. When Luke spotted her and an ashen Chad astride the horse, he'd made an idiot of himself, twisting away from Mellie and capturing Cindi in a bear hug: *I thought you were dead, I thought you were dead!*

"S'up to the boss," the guard said, tipping coffee into a camp mug. Half a smoke was glued to the guard's lower lip. Exhaling a gray jet, he sipped, sighed, pulled in another drag, and said, in a strangled voice, "Wouldn't mind some decent sleep when this is done, though."

"So we're at Rule?" Luke waved away fumes. The way these guys smoked, they should chew burnt logs and get over it already. This particular old guard sported a ratty moustache so saturated with nicotine it was dirty orange. "Are we staying here? What about the kids in Rule?"

"You ask too many questions, you know that?" Turning away with a lazy shrug, the mustachioed guard hooked a thumb under the carry strap of his Uzi. "If I was you kids," he said, sauntering toward a much larger fire and the other three guards, all of them sucking cancer sticks, "I'd get some sleep instead of freezing your asses. Gonna be light in about an hour."

From his place opposite Luke, Chad muttered, "Yeah, well, it's my ass to freeze, butt-face." Sighing, he stirred a steaming MRE, listlessly chewed a mouthful of macaroni and cheese, then dropped the spoon into the pouch. "Stomach's too jumpy."

To Chad's left, Jasper piped up. "You going to finish that?"

"How can you *eat*?" Cindi asked.

"I'm hungry." Jasper shoveled in a huge mouthful. "Too wired to sleep," he said, his voice clogged by cheesy noodles. "This has to be it. I mean, he took all the Chuckies." He gestured with the spoon to a large stainless-steel animal cage, standing empty on a flatbed slotted in with the other wagons. "Even those guys."

"So if this is Rule," Cindi said, "and those kids are still there, what will they do with *us* now? Do you think they'll . . . that they might . . ."

"No," Luke said, and put both arms around her. He wanted to say something movie-tough, like Finn's guys would have to get through him first, but the words just wouldn't come.

"But we should make a move." Chad tossed a look over his shoulder to check for the guards, then leaned closer. "We're the three oldest. There's four of them, three of us."

"Hey," Jasper said around a mouthful of macaroni. "I'm here."

"You're ten. Keep eating." Chad rolled his eyes. "If we can get guns . . ."

"Yeah, well, *if* is a pretty big word right now," Luke said.

"But we're just sitting here."

"I don't see that we can do anything else."

"I agree with Chad." When Luke looked down at her, Cindi continued in a whisper, "Except for those guards, everyone else is gone. We'll probably never have a better shot."

"And go where, Cindi?" Luke asked.

"Anywhere. Luke, we could raid the supply wagons, grab some guns and food, and go."

"Cindi, we have thirty kids. Us three and a couple other guys can handle a gun, and that's it. How would we move everyone and all the stuff we need? We can't outrun Finn."

"But I don't like waiting around for Finn to decide what happens next." Chad jerked his head at the transport cage. "You want to end up in one of those?"

"No, I don't," Luke said to Chad. "But staying alive beats dying."

"Not if we end up like Peter," Jasper said.

After five days with Finn and his weird Chuckies, who were exactly like the girl Tom had fought weeks ago, Luke had a queasy sense of what was in store.

Peter was too old to be a Chucky, older than Tom for sure, by a couple years. But his eyes were raving red, and God, he ate what the Chuckies did: thawed slabs of frozen oldsters stacked like cordwood in a special Chucky chuck wagon. Which meant that Finn had probably given Peter the same crap Tom figured someone fed those Chuckies in white. Only it hadn't worked on Peter, who spent half his time in his cage screaming—*let me go, let me go, let me go go go*—and the other half trying to get at Finn. Sometimes Finn hurt him pretty bad. Never laid a hand on Peter, but wow, a couple seconds with Finn and that creepy Davey, who followed Finn everywhere like a dog, and Peter was moaning, howling, clutching his head.

"It's like he hears something." When Luke turned his gaze away from the transport cage, Cindi said, "You know? When Peter starts up with the *let me go* stuff? But how? He's only . . . *half* a Chucky, you know?"

"But crazy," Chad said.

"Not all the time," Luke said. "All this stuff, the *go go go*, that usually starts up whenever Finn moves out."

"Telepathy?" Cindi asked.

"Can't be straight telepathy." Swallowing the last of the mac and cheese, Jasper licked the plastic spoon. "At least, not like the movies or what you're thinking."

"What else could it be? You were at the barn." What had happened when Finn's Chuckies descended on their camp scared Luke silly: how they broke formation, half going left and the rest like a marching band at halftime, streaming to the right. Then, the Chuckies had done . . . nothing. Only waited, staring, their concentration utterly complete. It was so quiet that Luke could hear the crackle of the fire and the jangle of hardware as horses tossed their heads. It was the weirdest thing, but Luke sensed that the Chuckies were being . . . held back? Yes, they'd wanted him. They'd wanted Mellie. What they'd most hungered after was all those juicy kids huddled in the barn.

But they weren't allowed. They were like . . . puppets? That wasn't quite right. It was as if something or someone held them back on invisible leashes: *this far and no farther.*

"Yeah, but have you ever tried following your own thoughts? Real complicated." Smoothing the empty MRE pouch on his thighs, Jasper began rolling the plastic into a tight tube. "Plus, you have the problem of signal strength and complexity."

Luke and Cindi looked at each other. "What are you talking about?" Luke asked.

"Thoughts are, you know, jumbly," Jasper said.

"Okay. So?"

Jasper gave him a *duh-hello* look. "What does Peter do? Does he talk about a *gazillion* things? No. He keeps saying the same thing over and over again: *go, go, go, let me go.*"

"Yeah, but he's crazy," Chad said.

"Not all the time." Jasper peered through the tube he'd made like a pirate with a spyglass. "He's worse when the Chuckies are on the move. Other times, he's normal."

"He eats people," Cindi said. "His eyes are weird."

"Okay, not *normal*-normal, but not all Chucky either. Whenever Finn *does* take him along, Peter's either tied up or with a couple guards."

"Probably because Finn can't control him very well?" Luke said.

"Or all the way, yeah. And the times Finn's left him here? Peter's not as loud and crazy. He gets better the longer Finn's gone. I think it's a cumulative exposure and distance thing, like, you know, Wi-Fi."

Wuh? "So?" Luke asked, and then as Jasper swiveled, still with the tube to his eye, added, "Would you quit that? It's annoying."

"*Fine.*" Jasper heaved a long-suffering sigh. "I don't think Peter's saying *let me go*, like get me out of this cage so I can go home. He might mean, *let me go go go after them. Go go go* is the command. Maybe all Finn does are simple commands piggybacked on other signals."

"I don't even know what that means," Cindi said.

"Yeah, the Chuckies aren't radios," Chad said.

Radios. Luke turned that over. *Wi-Fi. Something important there . . . something Jasper said about signal strength, not just distance but something else.*

"*Guys.* What do you think a thought is?" Jasper said. "Electrical impulses, that's all. The body's full of electricity. You've got gradients across your skin and ion flow in cells."

"What?" Cindi said. "So how does that work in this situation?"

"Well, thoughts are chemical and electrical . . . I don't know." Jasper's shoulders rose and fell. "Look, I can't tell you *how* Finn's doing it, but he can't be slinging real complicated stuff around, or if he is, only a couple Chuckies get the whole thing. Maybe even just one Chucky."

"Whoa. Wait a sec." Cindi sat up. "He's right. Two groups of Chuckies, the ones in white . . ."

"And everybody else," Chad said. "Like, maybe it doesn't work with every Chucky?"

"Or he doesn't need a ton to get the job done," Luke said. "But he's limited by distance, like when your Wi-Fi drops out when you're too far from a network." He kept thinking: *signal strength; signal strength and a network . . .*

"Okay, I buy that. But . . ." Chad threw up his hands. "So what? We're still stuck."

Luke didn't see how this helped either, but his head felt like he'd spent all night cramming for a test he was sure to bomb. Sometimes when he walked away from a problem, the answer popped into his head. "I'm going for water." As he stood, all four guards perked up. "Water," he said, holding up his canteen and giving it a shake.

"Hold on." Heaving to his feet, the mustachioed guard lumbered over. A lit cigarette jutted from his mouth. "All right, let's go," he said, handing over a flashlight.

"It's not like I'm going to run anywhere," Luke complained, but the guard only grunted and made a *get going* gesture with the Uzi.

The stream was beyond the kids' tents and a short distance into the woods. Following his flashlight, Luke ducked into the trees, where the light was worse and the shadows thicker. Ahead, he heard the churn of water over stones. The final twenty feet to the stream took a sharp drop. "I ain't going down there. Bad for my knees. Make it quick," the guard said, as the orange coal of his smoke danced. "Freezing my ass."

Oh, bite me. Carefully picking his way over stones and scrims of ice, Luke fanned the light over the sparse snow along the stream's edge, looking for a safe spot where he wouldn't wind up wet. As the beam flickered past a splotch of slush, he spotted something that only registered when his light had already skimmed past. Puzzled, he turned the beam back and saw two things: snow heaped around a rock where all the rest nearby were still covered, and a trio of animal prints. Probably an animal had disturbed the snow as it stepped past. From the prints, at first glance, he thought: *wolf.* Huge, too. That print was bigger than his hand, and fresh. As in, not long ago.

Considering *that,* all of a sudden, he was glad for the guard and his gun. *Make this quick is right.* The last thing he needed to run into was a hungry wolf. He had enough problems. Heart pounding, he swiveled right, dragging his light over a curving meander—and froze when two green coins flared alongside the silver oval of a face.

The green eyes belonged to a honking *huge* gray-white wolf.

But the face belonged to a girl.

107

Luke was so freaked, a scream fizzed into his throat that he just as quickly bottled behind clamped teeth. The impulse to turn and run was so strong the flashlight jittered from a sudden fit of the shakes.

The wolf didn't move. But the girl did, raising a warning finger to her lips and then crooking her hand the way Morpheus had to Neo: not *bring it on* but *come here.*

For a split second, he thought, *Oh, you got to be kidding.* This was like the wolf in *Little Red Riding Hood.* Get near a strange kid who was *just* the right age to be a Chucky? Hell no. Then he considered that this girl was a) hiding and b) with an animal, and that except for Finn's weirdo Chuckies, all the ones he knew were the kind who snacked first and asked questions later.

"Kid, what the . . ." The mustached guard's voice was lost as the guy hacked, then hawked up something from deep in his chest. He spit and then croaked, "Damn coffin nails." Louder: "What's the holdup?"

"Uh . . ." Luke dragged up his voice from his toenails. The girl was shaking her head. "There's a lot of ice. Be up in a couple seconds."

The guard muttered something, and Luke thought the guy might come down after all. But then a flame leapt as the guard lit up a fresh smoke. Turning, he saw that the girl was now only a foot away, her wolf—or maybe a really big husky or something—at attention by her side.

"Who are you?" he whispered.

"How many guards?" she murmured. Now that she was closer, he thought she must be around seventeen, eighteen, and decked out in a funky, fluttery camo-jacket, the hood cinched down tight, accentuating high cheekbones, a narrow nose, and strong jaw. The sharp dash of a widow's peak was just visible high on her forehead, but he couldn't tell what color her hair was. Her eyes, though, were an intense, deep emerald green, as bright as the wolf's. From her clothing and roughed hands—not to mention that Springfield she was packing and the sheathed knives strapped to either leg—he thought she'd been in the woods, on her own, for a long time. She looked like a wild wolf-girl.

"Four. One here, three back at the tents." He paused. "Are you from Rule?"

She shook her head. "Weapons?"

"Uzis, and they all have pistols."

A deep wrinkle formed between her eyebrows. "Can you handle a gun?" When he nodded, she said, "Get the guard to come down."

It was on the tip of his tongue to ask what she was going to do, then he considered how that was just dumb. Nodding, he stood and called, "Hey, I need some help down here? I . . . I . . ."

"What the hell," the guard said, bored, no question in his tone at all. "What happened."

Luke injected a note of misery. "I fell in," he said, then plunged his hand into ice water and splashed around. "And my boot came off. I can't find it and . . ."

"Aw, Jesus." An exasperated sigh, followed by the clop of heavy feet. "Hang on."

"Thanks." Luke managed a pathetic note. He risked a quick peek with the light, but the girl and her humongous wolf or dog or whatever had vanished. Swiveling, he pegged his flashlight beam to the guard, who was working his way down in a crabbing sidestep. Too late, he remembered: *Shit, I'm supposed to have lost my boot.* "Hey," he said, then dropped to his knees, angling his light until the beam splashed directly into the guard's face. "Over here."

"Jesus, kid." Squinting, the guard put up both hands to shield his eyes. A fresh cigarette was screwed into his mouth. "Move the light, you're gonna—"

Luke saw the girl, who must've scrambled higher until she was well above the guard, suddenly rear into view like an actor caught in the flare of a full spot. Her elbows were cocked, and then she was jabbing fast. The butt of her Springfield hit the guard's skull with a loud *thock.* The old man grunted, a short *huh*; his cigarette shot away from his mouth, the orange eye streaking like a comet. The guard's feet tangled, but he was already unconscious, completely limp, only his momentum tumbling him face-first to a skidding stop just short of the water.

Whoa. For a stunned second, Luke could only stare as the girl swiftly stripped the guard of his Uzi and passed over the handgun to him. Standing, she let out a loud cough at the same moment she cranked back the Uzi's bolt, the metallic *crick-crack* lost in the noise. "I really don't want to risk shots," she whispered, then suddenly winced. A hand snuck to her temple, and she swayed as if from a sudden shove. "The sound will . . ." She broke off with a harsh grunt.

"Are you okay?" He reached an automatic hand but reconsidered when the wolf, obviously sensing the girl's discomfort, whined and then nosed the girl's thigh. She looked like someone had just clocked her, but her expression was eerie, something he'd seen before. Then he had it: she looked a little like Peter when Finn lobbed one of his brain-bomb things. Luke let his hand drift back to his side, suddenly unsure she wouldn't go just as ape-shit. Maybe she was a Finn experiment who'd escaped.

"I'm fine." A tight smile died midway to her mouth. Sprawled at their feet, the felled guard snored. Kneeling, she turned the old man's head until his breathing quieted.

"Who are you? Where'd you come from?"

"Been following you the last two days," she said. Her wolf was, he thought, some kind of half-breed, a cross between a wolf and a malamute or huge husky. "Had to wait until they moved out. Buck." Turning, she patted her leg and the wolfdog eeled to her side. "All right," she said, jerking her head toward the slope. "Get as many down here as you can."

"How do I do that?"

Now, a true smile, as fleeting as a swift high cloud, touched her lips. "Panic."

"Help, *help!*" And then while Cindi was still digesting that, Luke followed the cry with a screech that raised the hairs on her arms and neck.

"Oh!" Heart cramming into her mouth, she jumped up and cast a wild look in the direction from which Luke's screams had come. "Luke?" she called. "Luke, what—"

"What's going on?" Chad cried. He and Jasper had bolted to their feet. Weapons drawn, the three guards were hurrying over just as Luke clawed his way out of the grainy half-light. His eyes were shiny as headlamps.

"What is it, kid?" one of the guards demanded as Luke stumbled over. "Where's—"

"By the stream. I think he . . . he had a heart attack or something. He just kind of grabbed his chest and—" Luke's face crumpled. "I don't know CPR!"

"Aw, shit. He ain't breathing? Shit. All right, come on, come on, quit bawling and show us, kid." Slinging his weapon onto his shoulder, the guard gave Luke a push. "We're going to have to carry him," he said to the others as they hurried off, all talking at once: "Where the hell is the flashlight?" "What do you mean, you dropped it, kid?" "Jesus, I *told* him to knock off those damn smokes after he run out of pills for his ticker—"

Cindi waited until the guards had disappeared into the trees, then looked at Chad and Jasper. "Luke knows CPR," she said, quietly. "Tom taught us, remember?"

"He didn't teach me," Jasper said.

"You're too little." Cindi saw that Chad now had the still hissing coffeepot in one hand. "Something's going down. Cindi, Jasper," Chad said, "grab a couple rocks from around the fire. Don't burn yourselves."

"They have guns," Cindi protested as she grabbed a sharp-edged stone as big as her hand.

"Maybe not for long," Chad said, interposing his body and squaring off so Cindi and Jasper were behind him. "Anything really bad happens, you just run."

From the trees came muffled cries, a sharp *What—* " Then a deep, throaty growl and the *bap* of a handgun that made Cindi jump.

"Oh shit." Chad was breathing hard. "I can't tell if . . ."

If those are animals or Chuckies. Cindi pulled in a squeaky inhale that she stifled with a hand. More sounds now: the clatter of rocks, a strange yipping cry, a *crack.*

"Jeez, that was an Uzi. Maybe you guys better get out of here," Chad said.

"We stay together." Cindi's heart was fluttering like the wings of a trapped parakeet. "I'm not leaving you to get eaten."

"Can't be Chuckies or animals. Luke's still alive . . . Hey!" Jasper pointed to where the guards and Luke had disappeared. "Look!"

What first emerged from the trees was a gigantic gray-white wolf, as big as a Warg in that battle from the second *Lord of the Rings* movie, only not as ugly and with no snarling, sword-wielding Orc either.

Still, Cindi gasped, took a step back. *No way I can run fast enough.*

"Oh man, that thing's *huge*," Chad said, his voice shaky. "Where—"

Two figures trotted out next. The first to pull together was Luke, weighted down with rifles. "Luke!" Cindi started forward, relief singing in her veins. She'd had visions of Luke with his throat torn out and blood splashed over his chest. "What's—" She skidded to a stop as a second person came into view: an older girl, in a queer camo getup, with an Uzi in her hands and a bolt-action rifle over her shoulder.

Hey, haven't I seen her somewhere before? "Who are you?" she asked.

"My name's Alex," the girl said. "Who are you guys? How come you're with Finn?"

At that, all four of them—Cindi, Luke, Jasper, and Chad—looked at one another before turning to the girl. Cindi opened her mouth, but Luke beat her to it. "Alex?" Luke said. "*Tom's* Alex?"

The girl halted in mid-stride, astonishment leaking over her face. "You . . . you know Tom?" One hand went to her throat. "You've seen Tom? You've *seen* him?"

"Sure, we all did," Jasper said, and Cindi could have strangled the stupid kid. "Tom was our friend. He helped us."

"Did?" Alex paled. Her green eyes went suddenly glittery and wet. "*Was?*"

"Yes." Luke tossed Cindi an unhappy glance before turning back. She knew just how he felt.

"I'm sorry, Alex," Luke said, helplessly. "But Tom's dead."

108

"I don't see them," Tom said. He and Chris had taken it fast, urging their horses down the shimmering cut of a trail that wound through a dense grill of hardwood and evergreen to the lookout that perched southeast on a broad basalt plateau a hundred yards up from the hastily erected abatis. Now, standing in the lookout's cab some seventy-five feet aboveground, he lowered his binoculars. Overhead, the brightest stars shone from deep, dark cobalt, but to the east, a smear of silver smudged the horizon. To his right, clouds smoked over a light green basketball of a moon balanced on the rim of trees. With the diminished snowpack and large swatches of bare ground, they no longer had the advantage of reflected moonlight. Shadows wavered over this southern approach. Bad luck for them, good for Finn.

"Gonna be daylight soon. It's the damn clouds. Glass it south and wait for it," Jarvis said. "They're already over the rise. Can't make out if they got weapons. . . . There. Dead ahead. You see them?"

"Yeah." The shadows rolled aside as if someone had peeled away a blanket, and then, through his binoculars, Tom saw something that reminded him of columns of black ants swarming over a checked tablecloth. With the fitful light, it was impossible to tell just how many they were talking about here, but he guessed there must be at least a couple hundred Changed. The sizes seemed right. These were kids, moving nimbly and swiftly in a relentless tide, coming on fast, spilling down the hill. At that pace, they'd be here in less than thirty minutes, just in time for the first glimmerings of sun.

Smart. His men will be able to see what they're shooting at. The light would work to *Tom's* advantage later, however. The trick would be keeping Finn's men in the square just long enough. *Ten, fifteen minutes, that's all.*

"Hey," Chris said, standing at Tom's right elbow. "Top of the hill? See those horses?"

"I see them." Impossible to miss, the horses were just moving over the crest. He'd known some would ride: Mellie, Finn, a few of Finn's men. What he had not expected was the gleam of over-whites. "That's them. The altered Changed I told you about."

"The ones in white? On horseback?" Jarvis sounded startled. "I know horses don't react quite as bad, but . . . my God . . . there have to be at least twenty or thirty of them."

"If they're so good at fighting, why aren't they leading the charge?" Chris asked. "Wouldn't you want your best guys on point?"

"Well, not if you want them to *stay* your best guys. This is like the Mongol hordes." Tom could see men now, too, to the extreme right and left, broader in the chest and clad in what looked like soft gray and white winter camouflage. From the occasional wink of metal, he knew the men were armed, and some, he thought, might be carrying bulkier munitions; he just couldn't tell what yet. "Let the grunts take the bullets."

"Our grandkids as cannon fodder." Jarvis was silent a moment. "Spooky, the way they move, how quiet they are." Another brief silence. "How's he controlling them?"

"Don't have a clue," Tom said, still straining to pick up Finn and failing. Until sunrise or the riders were closer, Finn—probably all in black on that gelding—would be virtually invisible. Instead, he trained his binoculars beyond, sweeping the distant knolls and flatlands.

"Maybe he gets into their heads." Chris's ragged voice was hushed. "You said he has to be giving them something because of their eyes. What if they can hear his thoughts?"

"I can sort of buy that with the altered ones." Tom slowly panned right to left. The night was starting to unravel and gray, and he shifted his gaze slightly off-center the way he might if trying to glimpse a distant galaxy. *God, please, make them be there.* "But that doesn't explain the others . . ." He stopped as he spied an orange flicker in the middle distance. "Got 'em. West, near the tree line. There's a stream there, still iced up in parts, but flowing pretty good now. That's where I would put my camp." He looked over at Chris. "Good a time as any to send Pru and your guys. They can be there pretty fast."

Nodding, Chris tugged out his radio just as Jarvis said, "Tom, you see those guys breaking off from the main body?"

"Yeah, I do." Four men on horseback were storming past the advance line of Changed. Still too dim for him to make out well, but he was getting a very bad vibe.

"What," Jarvis asked, "are they doing?"

109

Over the past few minutes, that *push-push go-go* had surged back with a vengeance, knocking the breath from Alex's lungs. From its deep cave, the monster seethed the way a worm eeled under the thin skin of a too-ripe fruit.

Running out of time. Her aunt always said that time healed. Yet time had only brought *her* more people to care about, and lose. The sobs she kept swallowing back tried climbing her throat. All she wanted was to howl, break something. Maybe shoot someone. *Stop, Alex. You are no different from these kids. Focus. There's still Wolf and Peter. Chris might be in Rule, too. You have to help them. Tom wouldn't want to see you like this. Be strong for him.*

"Take this." Leaning down from the saddle, Alex handed the Springfield to Luke. Without a rifle scabbard, the more compact Uzi would be easier to handle. Tucking the guard's pistol, a blued Colt Gold Cup .45, into the small of her back, she slotted an extra magazine for both weapons into her cargo pants. She felt a mild ping of unease that she didn't have time to search for a Glock, then pushed that aside. The Colt would do just as much damage. *Just remember to flip the safety.* Still, not having a Glock felt like a bad omen. "Between this and what's in the wagons, you have plenty of food and firepower."

"For a fight?" Luke said, his voice tight.

"If it comes down to that." The day was coming on fast. In the first wash of silver spreading over the eastern horizon, there was enough light to see how pinched and white Luke's face was. "It doesn't have to. Take the tents, a couple wagons, and get out of here."

"Alex, there are thirty of us. We'll be easy to follow, easy to catch again."

There was no sugarcoating this. "You'd rather wait for Finn?"

"But why can't *you* stay?" Cindi's glasses blazed with reflected firelight. "They're *Chuckies*. What do you care? We're *normal*. We need you *more*. Tom would *never* leave. We're supposed to believe that there are *good* Chuckies? And Peter, so he's only half a Chucky—so *what*? Why are you taking his side?"

"Whoa," Luke said. "Cindi, calm down."

"What if I don't want to be calm? This is like helping terrorists! Just because Wolf didn't kill you, Alex, doesn't mean he's *good*. It's like you've been brainwashed or something."

"And you might be right," Alex said. "But Peter *is* a friend. I have other friends in Rule. Wolf saved my life when he didn't have to. That counts for something, and I have to deal with it right *now*. I have to go to Rule and *try* to do something, anything, or a lot more people are going to die, including kids like you. If I can take Finn by surprise, if I can stop or kill him"—and where was *that* coming from?—"then he won't come after you again. Everyone wins." She paused. "Pretty much."

"And what about all those other Chuckies?" Cindi asked.

"They're at least four miles away. Most are on foot. Plenty of time."

"Well, the white Chuckies have horses," Jasper said, and then, as if in afterthought: "Of course, if you kill Finn, the network kind of falls apart and they might not work so well. The signal intensity will degrade for sure."

"What? What do you—" Alex began, but then Cindi interrupted, "So we keep running is what you're saying." The younger girl's lips were quivering now. "You're just *leaving* us."

Alex felt a twang of impatience. "Oh, for God's sake, yes, you *run*. You're not three years old. Step up to take care of yourselves, because, right now, there's no one else. Even if I stayed, I am *one* person. I'm not that much older than you and I've got . . ." She bit back the possible words—*cancer, a monster*—before any could jump out of her mouth. *God, Alex, calm down; she's just a kid.* Closing her eyes, she took a steadying breath, then looked down at the teary-eyed girl. "I'm sorry, Cindi. Maybe Tom *would* stay. That doesn't make him right and me wrong. It makes us different. I wish . . ." She pushed back the sudden choke. "I wish he was alive so we could argue about it. But don't think this is easy, or that I'm not scared to death."

No one said anything for a long moment. Then Luke stepped closer. "What if we wait for you? Tom would want us to.We pack up and move, say, a mile or so west, into the woods."

This was the mountain again, the day of the Zap, when she was saddled with Ellie and terrified out of her mind. She didn't want all this on her. Yet if Ellie hadn't been there, would she have tried so hard? Ever left the Waucamaw? Every step she'd taken since the Zap had been because of someone else. She might still be lost if not for Ellie and Tom and Chris. Even Wolf. All those connections led her out of those woods, from a very black place, and pulled her from the brink of a leap where there was nothing and no one waiting but death.

Tom said we saved each other. She ran her eyes over the upturned faces. *Maybe* he *was saving me for this.*

"If I can," she said to Luke, "I'll be back. We'll figure this out. But don't wait too—"

A quick kick of pain, a fireball behind her eyes. Deep in her mind, the monster flexed, teased awake, and she could feel it stretching, trying to muscle open that box. She blinked, and it was as if the shutter of a camera suddenly opened, a third eye—

—*and she is behind those eyes again, in that body she is beginning to think might be a boy's and in the heart of the pushpush gogo. High on a horse, dressed in white, the red storm on the left, and the other screaming: GOGOGO LET ME GO. Silently streaming over patchy snow, flowing with the pushpush gogo of the red storm, breathing in the ripe meat smell it wants, he wants, she craves. In the distance is a high hill and the stark outlines of a tower—*

—then a shift—

—into and through many eyes—

—a shimmer—

—and now, closer still— pushpush gogogogo—she is looking through a tangled curtain of matted hair. This body is another boy, and he is wild at the aroma of salt and meat, of prey dead ahead and just up that hill, in the tower—gogo pushpush—I want I want I want I need—pushpush gogo—

Two rumbling *booms* suddenly cannoned like distant thunder. Some of the kids let out startled cries. Snapping back behind her own eyes, Alex saw two faint yellow-orange candles shoot into a pewter sky due north. The flares faded fast, swallowed by distance, the coming day to her left, and the gleam of the moon, low on the western horizon.

That tower. That's where the Changed boy was focused: the tower, and men. Meat.

"Go, Alex. Good luck," Luke said. "We'll watch for you. Come back."

She wanted to say she would, but all those words hung in her throat. "Stay safe."

Then she spurred her horse as Buck sprang after, and galloped for Rule.

110

Tom wasted ten minutes piecing it together. By then, Jarvis was on the ground and Chris was trotting down the last flight. On the final landing twenty feet above the ground, Tom turned a troubled look back. Those men should've been on them, or very close. A fast horse can cover a lot of ground in no time flat. And yet . . . Glassing the plain through breaks in the trees, he saw they'd dismounted. Maybe—he chewed his lower lip—a half mile? Working on . . .

"Tom?" Chris, just below. "What is it? You see something?"

"Yeah, but their backs are to me. Can't tell what . . ." As a cloud finally drifted aside to bathe the plain with moonlight, he raised his binoculars. "Why send only four—"

"Tom?" Chris's voice was sharp. "What . . ."

"Oh Jesus." Alarm ripped through Tom's gut as he finally understood. Two men were kneeling, and now he could see what they balanced on their shoulders.

"RPGs!" Whirling, Tom planted his hands on the metal guardrail. "RPGs, *RP*—"

111

"Jesus Christ, kid," the bald boy snarled. With dawn filtering through low-slung evergreens, Ellie saw the creep's hair was growing back around spidery scabs. "Give me the damn gun."

"*No.*" Ellie hugged the Savage to her chest. This was so embarrassing. All around, kids, most older and a few younger, were all big eyes and sniggery mouths. To her right, a tiny girl with a froth of fine, nearly white hair was cringing, like Ellie had sneezed and gotten her all boogery. "It's my gun. Jayden lets me."

"This isn't Jayden's wagon, and I don't care." Creep totally freaked her out. All those eyebrow hoops, and that safety pin, crusted with old blood, through his right earlobe, not to mention the tongue stud . . . it was just plain sick, like the kid got off on deciding what part to stab next. As if life wasn't bad enough already. "Now hand it over," the boy said.

"Lucian, leave her alone." It was the thin, tired-looking girl, Sarah, who was driving the swaying wagon as they jounced over humped ice and sparse snow. "She's not hurting anybody."

"Yet," Lucian said. "You want that gun to go off?"

"It's safetied," Ellie said. Sensing her distress, Mina clambered to her feet and pushed her snout into Ellie's stomach while Jet and Ghost also struggled up to see what was the matter. That started a general heaving and jostling of the other dogs, which staggered and bumped

kids, who started up with the complaints, and blah, blah, blah. . . .
Maybe they'd let her walk. That would certainly solve the whole gun
thing. Exasperated, she pushed Mina to a sit. "My finger's not even in
the guard. What do you think, it's going to go off on its own?"

"All right, listen," Sarah said, *hoing* the horse to a halt. Sarah's
expression reminded Ellie of teachers she'd like to forget: sympathetic about her dad but always saying stuff like *we can't have that kind
of behavior in class.* "Give Lucian the gun, please? I can't drive with you
guys arguing and a loaded gun pointed at my back."

"It's aimed at the *sky,*" Ellie said. Well, trees: dense forest hemmed
this snaky curlicue of a road. Limbs jutted like fingers trying to lace.
They were making lousy time; she bet they weren't more than three,
four miles out. If they needed to turn around or move fast? They
were sunk. Jayden was having a heart attack; Ellie saw him in the
driver's box of that first wagon, his head going every which way, trying to watch everywhere at once. "Even if it went off, which it *won't,*"
she said, "it wouldn't hurt anybody."

"I don't give a fuck. Don't make me come back there, kid," Lucian
warned.

The other kids' eyes were saucers; a bunch of boys started in
with the elbow-jabs: *Whoa, F-bomb.* Oh, why had Tom put her in this
wagon? She should've hopped right out and run over to Jayden's. "But
I know what I'm *doing,*" she said as one of the boys on horseback
eased to their wagon, ducking beneath branches as he did so.

"Problem here?" The boy, about Jayden's age, had dark curly hair,
kind of like Tom's, which was wavy and thick. Ellie thought he even
looked a bit like Tom, and then saw why in this boy's eyes, which
were smudged with purple and . . . sad. Like Tom's, even when he
said he was happy to see her. Ellie knew why, too: Tom hurt, all the
time, because of Alex. Ellie only wished she knew how to make that
better. *Maybe if I love him enough, hug him enough . . .*

"We're fine, Greg," Lucian said, his tone like a boy with one eye on the playground monitor and the other on the kid whose butt he wanted to kick.

"Yeah, I guess that's why the wagon's stopped," Greg said in an unimpressed *uh-huh* way that made Ellie bite her cheek to keep back the snicker. He cut the girl a look. "Sarah?"

"I *said* we got this." Heaving to his feet, Lucian stepped onto the flatbed, brushing past feathery branches to wade through dogs and kids. Towering over Ellie like a giant-killer, Lucian jabbed a finger into Greg's chest. "This is *my* wagon. This kid's got a gun, *I* want it, and *you're* not in charge here, *Greg-guh*."

"Calm down, Lucian." Sarah looked like a whipped puppy. "Guys, look, let's just settle this and get going, okay?"

"But it's safetied, right? So what's the harm?" Greg said.

"Yeah," Ellie said. This Greg kid was okay. "If we get into trouble, we'll need every gun we've got."

"Oh, bullshit." Lucian snorted. "We get into trouble, ain't no little girl .22 gonna save our butts."

"Fine," Ellie shot back. "So if I'm not going to save your butt, you mind if I save mine?" *That* got everyone nudging elbows and whispering again. *I don't care; you're not my friends.* She glowered up at Lucian. "What's your *problem*?"

"A very good question," Greg said.

"Greg," Lucian growled. "Don't push me, man."

"Or what? You going to kill me now? You had your shot," Greg said.

"She should give it," the white-haired girl suddenly piped in that lisping singsong every kid knew: *Okay, but don't blame me.* She had to be, what, *six*? The girl clutched a Lalaloopsy doll with a spray of fuchsia curls. "My mommy said guns kill people."

About half the kids gave solemn nods, but a trio of boys shrugged and one elfish, older kid with big ears said, "I don't see what's the big deal. I wish *I* had a gun."

"Greg," Sarah said, still with that nervous, whipped-puppy look. "This isn't going to change what's happened."

"You weren't locked in a cell, Sarah," Greg said, but he was looking at Lucian. "You weren't spit on and punched. You didn't clean chunks of dead kid from a church floor, or shovel horse shit with your bare hands."

Whoa. No wonder Chris left Rule. The way Greg and Lucian were eyeing each other, she had a terrible feeling that neither needed much of an excuse.

Her closet-voice: *Don't make trouble, Ellie.*

"Fine. Look, I'm giving it." Fuming, she watched Lucian shuck the round in the chamber, then work the bolt and empty the Savage's magazine.

"There you go." Lucian had this big nasty smirk all over his stupid face. Slipping her bullets into a pocket, he handed back the rifle. "We get where we're going, you can have the bullets back. And Greg?" Lucian stomped for the driver's box. "Thanks for your concern, man. Now fuck off."

"Lucian," Sarah said.

We are so not living on the same farm. Probably wouldn't give back her bullets either. Turning, she reached out to touch Greg's leg. "He's kind of a jerk, huh?"

"Fucking heard that," Lucian said.

"Yeah. Like . . . *seriously*," Greg said, with a perfectly straight face. She almost cracked up. "I didn't mean to get you in trouble."

"You didn't. Don't worry about it," Greg said, but didn't smile. As Sarah snapped the reins and their wagon started up, he let them pull ahead. "See you later."

Okay, so Greg seemed all right. *But I still wish Tom was here, and Chris. I want to go home.* Dragging an arm across her eyes, she slouched into her parka, digging her chin under the zipper until the collar was up around her nose, and glared down at her boots. *I want my daddy and Grandpa Jack and Tom and Alex.* The dogs had settled down, although Mina kept dropping her chin on Ellie's lap. "Quit it," she said, shoving the animal away. "I'm fine."

"It's really safer," the white-haired girl said. "My mommy—"

"Yeah, well, your mom's dead, and so is mine, so shut up." As soon as the words dropped out, she cringed, and her closet-voice shouted, *ELLIE!*

"That wasn't nice," said the elfish boy.

"I know." Pulling in a deep breath, she turned to the little girl. "Sorry. That was really mean."

"Mmm-hmm." The girl's eyes were moist blue pools. Her lips, delicate as rose petals, quivered as she dropped her face into her doll's crazy, silly hair.

Would she ever learn to keep her big mouth shut? Laying down the Savage, Ellie put an arm around the little kid's heaving shoulders. To her astonishment, the tears she'd held back streamed over her cheeks, too. "Don't cry. I just get mad sometimes."

"*I* get mad *all* the time," the elfish boy said.

"I miss my mommy." The white-haired girl used her doll's hair to wipe her eyes. "I keep waiting for things to get better, only they never do."

"They will," Ellie said, trying to jam in a whole bunch of *oh-wow* she really didn't feel. Grandpa Jack always said to look on the bright side, only everywhere Ellie turned, it was still dark, even in the middle of the day. *Engage brain before tongue,* her dad always said. "Remember how awful it was in the beginning, when everything went crazy?"

"It's still bad now," said one of the elbow-jab boys. His buddies nodded.

"Not where we're going. We have cows and sheep, and there are lakes. Hannah knows about plants, and I catch lots of fish."

"You fish?" The elfish boy looked impressed. "Can I come?"

Too late, she remembered Eli and Roc, still down there somewhere. *Never fishing* there *again*. But she said, "Sure." All the kids were looking now, and smiling, like she'd brought in this great show-and-tell. She gave the little girl a squeeze. "Really, things will be great—"

From somewhere far behind came two thundery rumbles. Every hair rose on Ellie's arms. Gasping, she sat straight up and turned to look the way they'd come, as did all the children and the dogs, too. The wagons stopped rolling; the horses ceased clopping. While the forest was still gloomy with dissolving shadows, slashes of bright light showed through the trees to the east. Due south, Ellie caught brief, bright pillows of pulsing orange light.

"Oh." Sarah's hand was over her mouth. Beside her, Lucian had gone so pale his stubble looked like dirt. "Oh God," Sarah said.

The dogs began to bark. All around, kids were jabbering: "Wow." "What was that?" "Did you *see* that?" "Is it a fire?" At her elbow, the white-haired girl had her hands clapped to her ears and squeaked over and over again, "What was that? What was that? What was that?"

"Explosions!" The elfish boy's voice rose above the general gabble. "Like *bombs*."

Tom does bombs. She was trembling. So much fear and dread coiled through her body that when Mina suddenly let out a frenzied, furious volley of barks, she almost sprang out of the wagon. "Mina, stop!" Twisting, she buried her face in the dog's neck, not really registering right away that the dog was wildly trying to pull away. *Please, God, please, not Tom, not Tom, not—*

"Hey. Hey, look." It was the white-haired girl, her voice now a wavering whisper no more substantial than a faint breeze and so soft Ellie was the only one who heard. "Everybody."

I don't want to look anymore. She kept her head down. *It never gets better. Everyone dies.* When Mina suddenly growled, Ellie looked up and said, "No, Mi—"

And stopped.

Everyone else—everyone, that is, except for the now growling dogs and the white-haired girl—still stared back the way they'd come, and they were all talking at once. Many kids had begun to cry, although above the din, she thought she heard the old doctor's voice drifting back from Jayden's wagon: "What is it, Daisy? Where? Jayden, son, I think we got trouble. I think—"

Oh boy, I think he's right. Their dogs and the little girl were riveted to the trees on their left. The little girl was so terrified she'd stopped crying. Barely daring to breathe, Ellie inched her eyes west, away from a new day—

And saw stark silhouettes slip from behind tree trunks that, in such bad light, you might mistake for fence posts. Or dead trees.

Except posts didn't move. Trees didn't have arms or legs.

Or teeth.

112

In the instant after Tom's warning shout, the world hiccupped. Something kicked Chris in the back. There was a brief sensation of hurtling through air. Then, there was nothing: no impact, no dreams this time around, or nightmares either, quite possibly because he was living one. But time lurched, like a really old movie missing the middle reel, the story dropping out.

The next thing he knew, he was facedown, hands clawing for purchase, blindly worming his way over a still-hissing debris field of splintered wood, twisted metal, molten glass. In the distance, he heard the *dong-bong* of the church bell, sounding the alarm. When had that started up? The air boiled with screams and wails. Someone was bellowing, *"What what what what!"* Much closer, someone was moaning. After another second, he understood the moans were his. He tasted blood at the back of his throat. His stinging face was wet with melted ice and snow, but his hand came away red, and he thought, *I can see this; I can see color.*

Because there was light.

Time, *time* . . . how much had passed, how much? The world was both bright and murky. Intermittent black clouds smoked over sky that was denim overhead and a lighter turquoise to the east from the first spokes of sunlight. The air stank of spent fuel, burning wood, scorched metal, and overdone Sunday roast. *Those clouds . . . smoke . . .* The sparse pines on this plateau were torches. Behind and off to his right came the crackle and sputter of another, larger fire.

Got to get out of here. Rolling, he looked toward the tower a hundred feet away. All that remained was a gnarled ruin of skeletal struts and one remaining flight of steps leading nowhere. One horse, Jarvis's, was down, its belly a ragged blast crater of mangled entrails. Night, his blood bay, was still on his feet. Tom's dun mare was in the trees. One hand pressed to his head, the other clutched around a rifle, a man tottered and screamed, *"What what what . . ."*

"Jarvis?" Staggering to his feet, Chris coughed, moaned again as his cracked ribs sent knifing jabs through his chest. "Jarvis, where's Tom, wh—"

"Here." To his right, a tangle of wire mesh moved. Chris saw first the bore of the Bravo, still in its scabbard, and then Tom, on hands and knees, struggling against a pile of debris.

Uh-oh. Wobbling over, Chris dragged away mesh and smashed wood. His heart turned over when he saw the spike of metal sticking out of a star of blood and ripped cloth from a spot high on Tom's left thigh, just beneath his hip. "How bad?" Chris dropped to his knees. He reached a hand, then snatched it back, afraid he'd make something worse.

"Dunno. Don't think it's that deep. Doesn't feel broken, and it's not pumping. Help me up." Tom suppressed a groan as Chris got a shoulder under and boosted him up. "Hurts like hell," Tom said, his face screwed against pain.

"Can you walk? Can you ride?"

"Yeah." Hissing, Tom took a limping experimental step and then another. "I'll make it. We're both lucky we're not dead from the pressure—" Tom stopped, sniffed, then said, "Oh shit."

"What?" Chris said, but Tom was already lurching for the edge of the basalt plateau. Smoke jetted, like the exhalations of a subterranean dragon, from somewhere just below. Wincing with every jarring step, Chris caught up and squinted down. In science, they'd studied Mt. St. Helen's, and Chris remembered the way the blast flattened all those trees. This wasn't quite as bad, but it was close. The blazing abatis looked as if it had been smashed by a giant's boot. Nearby trees had toppled. He could see where snow had either been vaporized instantly by the heat or melted.

Four men, two RPGs. Chris's eyes roamed the wreckage. The legs were easy to identify, as were the half-torsos and . . . and . . . "H-heads." He hadn't meant to say anything. It just came out. The heads were very distinct. A few looked like eight balls, without the white: no skin, no hair. Others had cracked open like walnuts to release red and pink sludge. "Tom, I see—"

"Yeah. Come on." Turning, Tom started in a fast hobble for the trees. "We've lost a lot of time. Going to be full daylight soon. We need to get to town before the Changed get here. Jarvis!" Tom called to the old man, still turning his circles. "Come on! We have to—"

"What?" Jarvis whirled so fast a foamy line of spit flew. His eyes, crimson with broken capillaries, started from their sockets. Blood trickled from his nose, and one ear. He shot the bolt of his rifle. "Stay away from me, stay away!"

"Whoa, whoa, whoa!" Tom held up both hands. "Jarvis, calm down, man. We got to go, the Changed—"

"Who? What?" Jarvis screamed. *"What what—"*

"What's wrong with him?" Chris asked.

"Probably the pressure wave. Scrambles some people up. Jarvis," Tom tried again, "listen to me, man. It's okay, but we have to *go*, we have to—" Suddenly, Tom stiffened and turned back toward the plateau and the smoking tower.

"What?" Chris asked. "What do you—" Then, over the crackle of flames, Chris heard it, too: the sharp snap of brush, the stomp of boots on rock.

Deep in the smoke, something moved. Something . . . dark *blue.* For a disorienting moment, Chris thought the *smoke* was pulling together, changing color, becoming parkas and then jeans—and then he realized that what he saw were Changed, a lot of them, surging up the rise only a hundred feet away, materializing like invaders teleported from a distant planet.

"Chris." Tom clamped a hand on his arm and tugged. "Come on. Don't look, just go."

Oh my God. Chris was paralyzed, rooted to the spot. Jarvis was screaming again—*"What what what"*—and Chris was thinking, *I don't know, I don't know, I don't . . .*

"Chris!" Tom snapped him around so quickly Chris had to clutch Tom's arms to keep his feet. "I said, don't *look* at them. Get on your *horse*, Chris! Get on your horse, *now!*"

"O-okay," Chris gasped. He took off in a stumbling run, Tom crowding behind, urging him on. Snatching his bay's reins, Chris tried to boost to his saddle, but his feet wouldn't work. "Come on," he heard himself plead, "come on, come on, come—"

He heard them: boots stirring debris, kicking wood, crunching glass. *Getting louder.* His back prickled. *Coming closer, don't look, don't look, don't!* But then, he did snatch a glance—*stupid*—and a nail of terror jabbed his heart. The Changed, so many, *too* many, were fanning out, spilling over the plateau, charging right for them.

"Chris, *no!*" Tom was already whipping his horse around. "Don't look! Come on! You've got time, just don't panic!"

Too late. Socking his boot in a stirrup, he grabbed leather and swam to an awkward half-sit on his saddle. Tried not to look. Couldn't help it. The Changed, these children of Rule, were less than fifty feet away. In the coming day he could see their mouths open in silent snarls and their eyes, their eyes, so wide, so wild. No weapons, only teeth and clawed fingers and—

Don't look, Chris. No voice but his own, one that wanted him to live. *Move, or you're dead.*

But it was fascinating, appalling, awful: every nightmare come to

life and why deer froze in headlights and people died at train cross-
ings and Moses covered his eyes. No one can help but stare at the
monster, because horror is a cousin to awe.

"Chris, no, what are you doing? *Chris!*" Tom shouted as the same
moment that Jarvis bellowed, *"Whaaaat! Whaaat whaaa—"*

Braying, Night finally shied, Chris's panic communicating itself
to a shocked animal that understood death was a hair's breadth away.
The bay reared. Not yet fully seated, Chris let out a strangled cry as
the slide started. He felt himself peeling backward; he was falling, he
was going to fall into the Changed and their arms, and they would get
him, they were there, they were—

"Ho!" Bullying his prancing mare alongside, Tom snatched at
Night's bridle. "Chris, set your damn knees, grab his mane or withers, and get on, *get on!"*

Sobbing out a breath, Chris scrambled for a handhold. Night's terrified eyes rolled; his head snapped back and slammed Chris's face.
The blow was terrific, so hard that Chris's vision blacked. Stunned,
he lost his grip, began to slump . . .

And then there were hands, everywhere: skittering over his left leg
and thigh, fingers clutching to pull him off—and he thought, *I'm done.*

An enormous bang came from someplace over his head. The
questing hands suddenly fell away. Another bang. To Chris's left, a
Changed boy slapped both hands to the crater where his nose had
been, and tumbled back. Still dazed, Chris felt Tom's fingers claw his
shoulder.

"Don't lose it, man!" Tom shouted, manhandling Chris onto the
saddle. "You can't lose it, Chris, come on!" Despite his injury, keeping
to his mare with only his knees, Tom had a big black Glock in one
hand and Chris's shoulder in the other. Another girl with very long,
filthy hair made a lunging grab. Cursing, Tom swung down, stuck the
pistol in the girl's face. The Changed was so intent on *him* she never
saw Tom, much less the gun, and—*bang!* Her head shattered, skull

and scalp and brains and blood and wild hair flaring in a wet spray.

"Sit *up*!" Tom roared. "Get *up*, Chris, sit—"

The crack of a shot, not from Tom but to their right. The high *zing* of a bullet ricocheting off a tree. Bellowing, Jarvis fired again. This time, a Changed boy staggered as a red sunburst suddenly flared over his right breast. The line didn't exactly falter, but some Changed peeled off, heading for Jarvis, and that gave Chris the precious two seconds he needed to slot his foot into his stirrup.

"All right, come on!" Tom shouted. Wheeling, they kicked their horses to a run and bulleted into the trees, heading back for Rule's center three miles in their future.

It wasn't a mistake, but Chris snagged one last look. Two Changed had their arms around the still-bellowing Jarvis. The three danced a drunken pirouette. Then another Changed joined in, and then more and more, and then Jarvis wasn't bellowing but screeching, the Changed boiling over him the way ants devoured prey, and there was blood, so much of it.

And more to come because it's the end of the world. Chris faced forward. His eyes stung. His cheeks were wet, and he didn't think that was only blood. *It's the end, it's the end, it's the end.*

113

"Get away from the edge! Get away from the edge of the wagon!" Ellie shouted, but no one was listening; everyone was shrieking, kids twisting this way and that to see. It was like a disaster movie where the Martians suddenly busted up and everyone turned to scared rabbits, all big eyes and open mouths, right before the Martians blasted them from their clothes.

"Move, get up!" Snatching her Savage by the barrel, she sprang to her feet, cocking the weapon like a T-ball bat just as a hand hooked onto the wagon behind the elfish boy who wanted to fish. "Get out of the way!" she screamed, and brought the stock hammering down.

The people-eater bawled as its knuckles split wide open. As the boy—*was* that a boy under all that hair?—gawped up in surprise and pain, she punched his face with the butt. Toppling, the people-eater tumbled into two others, the three going down like bowling pins.

Oh boy, we are in so much trouble. Around her legs, the growling dogs were jostling, trying to wedge together in a wall of balled muscles and bared teeth. In front on the driver's box, Lucian was on his feet. Racking his shotgun's pump, Lucian *boomed* out a shot, and suddenly, a girl was missing her head, twin ropes of blood still pulsing because the heart hadn't yet got the message. Banging out shots with an enormous, bucking black pistol, Sarah was hitting absolutely nothing, only driving the swarm back with the sheer volume of fire. How long could she keep it up, though? Ellie knew they didn't have a lot of ammo. The way Sarah was running through that clip, unless she had a couple spare magazines . . .

Maybe Lucian figured out the same thing at the exact same instant: that Sarah was only wasting bullets. That if he wanted to hang on to his creepy scalp, he better book. All of a sudden, Lucian bent, scooped up a pack, hitched it over his shoulder, butted away one people-eater, booted another in the face, and leapt from the box.

"Wait! You have my bullets!" Ellie shouted as Lucian hit the ground and sprinted for the far trees. In the thick tangle of brush and low-hanging boughs, she lost sight of him almost immediately. Not one people-eater followed, probably because there were all these tasty kids.

Now what? All around, kids were still screaming and only sitting as the dogs tried surging to her left where the majority of the people-eaters were. If the kids would just let the dogs through! Grabbing the elfish boy by the shoulder, Ellie tugged. "Get behind me, get behind the dogs!" she shouted.

The kid threw her a wild, open-mouthed stare. For a second, she thought she'd gotten through, but then he scrambled in the exact *wrong* direction, for the driver's box. A flat-faced people-eater with only half a nose suddenly reared up. Shrieking, the elfish boy got an arm up. Half-Nose latched a hand and yanked. Jackknifing, the elfish boy managed to butt his free hand against the wagon. For an instant, he swayed, facedown, like a poorly balanced teeter-totter.

"Sarah!" Ellie shouted as Half-Nose drew back for a strike. "Sarah, behind you!" Pivoting, Sarah jabbed that enormous pistol at Half-Nose, squeezed the trigger—and nothing, out of ammo, completely dry. The elfish boy bawled a blood-curdling scream as Half-Nose locked his jaws on the back of the boy's neck, right around his spine. A moment later, the elfish boy, still kicking, flipped out of sight.

"*Noooo!*" Blinking back tears, Ellie turned, started swinging blindly, cutting an arc, miserably aware that it was only a matter of time before a people-eater wrested away the Savage or another got in under a swing. *Slow down, slow down; pick a target; you'll get tired and then they'll get you.* She forced herself to wait, let the dogs protect her. Jet and Ghost, the largest, stood hip to hip, snapping whenever a people-eater got close. Crowding to the front, Mina was pressing her rump against Ellie to herd her back, except the little white-haired girl was cowering behind Ellie's legs. Caught in a sandwich of dog and little girl, Ellie felt her balance start to go. *No, no!* If she fell, she might not be able to get back up in time.

"Mina, *hold!*" She could barely hear herself over the din: screaming kids and barking dogs and braying horses. Shots spackled and popped as the very few kids with guns fired. But they had no room to maneuver, and their aim was wild.

In Jayden's wagon, a people-eater, bat in hand, vaulted onto the driver's box. Jayden ducked as the bat whizzed. Long gun socked to his shoulder, the doctor with the eye patch bellowed something—maybe *stay down* or *don't move*—and then a spume of bright yellow muzzle flash leapt. The people-eater's arms shot out in a surprised way, like Wile E. Coyote, and tumbled off. At the rear, two more people-eaters, all arms and legs and clubs, scrambled onto the flatbed. One launched itself into shrieking children like a diver from a high platform. As the golden retriever, Daisy, and three other dogs converged, kids spilled over the sides of the wagon: their only move, and a terrible one, like buffalo being driven from a cliff.

Where are the guys on the horses, Aidan and Sam, where are they?

A scream, far back. Ellie whipped around. Greg's horse was trying to spin free from the four people-eaters grabbing at Greg's legs and the reins. Three more swarmed onto the driver's box of the third wagon. The driver, a girl with a long brown braid down to her waist, shrieked again as a lanky boy, with a duster like Neo's in *The Matrix*, whipped the braid around the girl's neck. Bucking, eyes buggy, the girl heaved and flopped like a fish slowly suffocating in the bottom of a boat. Balling a fist, the Neo Kid smashed the girl's face as a second people-eater, a ratty boy in fire-engine-red snow pants, leapt onto the thrashing girl. His head darted for her neck like a scorpion stabbing its stinger. Blood spewed; Rat Boy came up with a chunk of meat in his mouth. Bawling, the wagon's horse reared in a clash of hooves and spurted forward.

The wagon did Greg a favor, and them none. As the wagon hurtled on, the people-eaters clinging to Greg's horse scattered; one scrawny kid slipped with a shriek that cut out as a wheel sliced his gut. Greg's horse danced away onto a narrow ribbon of road along the tree line. Hunkered low on the animal's withers, Greg ducked as low-lying branches whirred over his head. Still on the driver's box, Neo Kid and Rat Boy staggered, then turned as the distance between them and Ellie's wagon dwindled.

Watching the horse charge and the wagon swell, Ellie had six seconds: one to be paralyzed; two to understand that a collision was inevitable and that either the horse would stampede its way onto their flatbed or come to a sudden screeching stop, catapulting Neo Kid and Rat Boy into their wagon, where the two would find not only dogs to fight but lots of new things to eat. In the last three seconds, Ellie knew she'd better do something, or she was a goner.

"Mina, *release*! Out of the wagon!" Snatching the white-haired girl's hand, Ellie took the width of the flatbed in two huge strides. "Get out get out *get out*!"

114

The village square was completely empty. Racing past the gazebo, Tom and Chris pulled up at the northwest corner between the village hall and church. Dismounting before the dun mare had come to a complete stop, Tom snatched Night's reins before Chris could swing down.

"No." Tom's face was pinched. Clutching his wounded, still-oozing thigh just above the protruding bit of metal, he said, hoarsely, "Not you."

"What? No, I'm fine now." From the open doors of the church came the rise and fall of a hymn, but the bell was silent. "You shouldn't climb with that leg. I'll take the bell tower, you do the jail, and—"

"No." Tom backhanded sweat from a glassy upper lip. "You can't be part of this."

"What?" Despite Tom's admonition, Chris dismounted. "Tom, what are you doing?"

"Someone has to stay behind," Tom said. "We both know that."

"No, I don't *know* that." He grabbed Tom's shoulders. "Are you *crazy*? They'll *be* here. The bombs are on *timers*, for God's sake. So *why*?"

"Because if something goes wrong, I'm the only one who knows what to do."

"*Tom.* If you stay, you'll die. They'll catch you."

"They won't. I'll stay out of sight. Babysit those honeys until the last second." Tom laid a hand over one of his. "Chris, please, there's no time. Don't make this harder for both of us. If the bombs don't blow, all this will be wasted. Those people in that church will die for nothing."

"They'll die anyway." His eyes were starting to sting. "They made their choice."

"And this is mine. Chris, I *have* to. This way, I buy you time. We stop Finn's Changed. We stop Finn. Then the children, yours and mine, will be safe."

"We don't know if we got yours yet. If we didn't—"

"Then we tried. If you can, you find them. Look, we both know the threat doesn't end here. There are way more Changed than us. But this way, you guys have a chance."

"Please, Tom." His eyes brimmed. "You saved my life, *twice*. Please, *please*, don't stay here. Set the bombs and come with me."

"I can't, Chris." Tom cupped the back of Chris's neck. "Come on, man, please. This is hard enough. Believe me, I don't want to die. There's Ellie, and Alex is still out there, I feel it; I should never have lost faith, because she's strong; she won't quit. But I *have* to do this for my people—"

From the north, and not far away at all, in fact, there came the faint but unmistakable sputter and spackle of gunfire.

"Oh God." Chris felt his heart seize. "Tom, that's got to be the wagons."

"*More* Changed? But how?" Tom's skin was whiter than bone. "Finn's south."

"I don't know, but we got to go. Come on!" When Tom didn't move, Chris clutched his arm. "Tom, they *need* us!"

"Chris, I . . . I can't. Damn it, I . . ." Shrugging off the Uzi's carry strap, Tom threw the bolt, then clicked the safety and thrust out the weapon. "Selector switch," Tom said, pointing. "One- or three-shot bursts. For God's sake, don't go full auto or you'll be dry in four seconds."

"Tom, no, I can't—"

"Yes, Chris, you can. You have to, just like I have to stay. There's no other way. You can do this." Tom was slapping two spare mags into Chris's hands. "Keep count, pick your shots, be careful, don't lose your head. You got forty rounds in each clip and there are thirty-one left in the mag you got, one in the chamber already. You have plenty of firepower, and you're silenced. Huge advantage. They won't know you're there until you're on top of them. The kids are close, Chris. You can be there in minutes if you move fast, but you have to leave right now."

"But Tom, the kids, they need help—"

"Don't you think I *know* that?" Tom grabbed Chris and shook him. His strange and smoky blue eyes blazed with fury and frustration. The cords, taut as steel, stood in his neck. "Don't you know this is *killing* me? *Ellie* is out there, but Finn is going to *be* here, and there is no choice and we are out of *time*! Now, stop arguing and *go* before it's too *late*!"

He knew he had to do it. "Goddamn you," Chris said. Instead of batting Tom's hand away, he pulled Tom into a fast and ferocious hug. Then, without another word, he broke away and charged for Night, flinging himself up onto the saddle. He cut one last look: not at Rule but Tom, so strong and ready to sacrifice it all because, when there was no other way, that's what you did to keep your people safe.

"Go, Chris," Tom said.

Kicking Night to a gallop, Chris spun his horse and thundered away.

115

The charging wagon was three seconds away . . . and now the people-eaters milling around theirs saw the danger, broke, fell back . . . and then there were two seconds and the animals were spilling out . . .

Not pausing to see if anyone followed, Ellie planted her right boot, then flung herself and the white-haired girl in a high and long arc. The little girl was shrieking, the sound sharp as a nail. Ellie landed with a solid thump. The little girl barreled into her a second later, driving Ellie's chin into the ground. Her mouth fired with a dart of red pain.

There was a huge, splintering crash as the out-of-control horse slammed into the back end of their flatbed. Gasping, blood on her tongue, Ellie craned back. Braying, the horse clattered sideways, trying to work its way around the stalled wagon. Shrieking children foamed over the sides. Something shifted in the supply wagon, or perhaps an axle snagged, because all of a sudden the wagon tipped, dragging down the thrashing horse. Cardboard boxes and packs tumbled out. Many burst, and then people-eaters, who'd scattered just before the collision, closed ranks. As Mina bolted to her side, Jet, Ghost, and four other dogs boiled around the other kids, snarling and snapping, trying to keep the people-eaters at bay. Only Sarah remained on the now-empty wagon, still clinging to the driver's box, a curtain of hair over her face, empty pistol in one hand.

"Sarah!" Sweeping up her Savage, Ellie scrambled to her feet. "Sarah, get off the wagon, come *on!*"

Dazed, the older girl pulled her head around as if swimming through a sticky dream and then half jumped, half fell from the driver's box. A gangly, bucktoothed people-eater swooped in from the left and closed fast. Sarah saw it coming and froze.

"No, Sarah, don't stop! Keep running!" Ellie screamed. "Keep—"

From her right came the crack of a shot. A scarlet blossom flowered over Bucktooth's back. The people-eater crashed to the road in a spectacular belly flop a foot shy of where Sarah still cringed. Greg dashed from the trees, on foot, three kids in tow: "Sarah, grab the kids, grab the kids! Get behind the dogs!"

Part of Ellie wanted to go back to the older kids, to Greg and Jayden. But right now, she and the white-haired girl hadn't been noticed, and that would change. Even with Mina, they were too exposed. But she remembered how quickly Lucian had been lost from sight. *Get far enough, fast enough, and hide until Tom and Chris get here.* The wagons hadn't made great time, and that meant they weren't *that* far from Rule. So Tom would hear the shots, and he'd come *really* fast. She wouldn't have to hide for very long.

"Come on," she said to the white-haired girl, still sprawled on the ground.

"But my dolly!" The little white-haired girl was bawling. From the ruby smear on her lower lip, she must've bitten her tongue, too. "My dolly, I lost my doll!"

"Forget the stupid doll! Mina!" Slinging the Savage's carry strap on her shoulder, Ellie wheeled and tugged the little girl along in a stumbling run through spare snow. There was no clear path; she was bushwhacking through dense undergrowth that snagged and grabbed at her legs. The little girl was stumbling and gasping, "Wait, wait, wait," but Ellie didn't slow down, didn't reply, just kept on going. Spiky branches whipped her cheeks and stung her forehead, snarled in her hair. Mina had pulled ahead by several paces, and Ellie followed her dog, thrashing through briary brush still crinkly with ice. She didn't like that she was making so much noise. If they could get somewhere safe and hide . . . Behind were shouts and gunshots and braying horses, but the sounds were fast diminishing, as noise always died in dense forest. She would have to be careful not to lose the road entirely, because Tom and Chris would eventually come. If they could. If those explosions didn't mean that they—

Stop it, Ellie, stop it. Putting up one arm to protect her eyes, Ellie put her head down and plowed through, forcing a way where none existed. *Tom will come. So will Chris. Jayden is already here, and so is Greg. All you have to do is hide.*

"Ah!" The little girl let out a pained cry. "Stop, *stop!* I'm stuck, I'm *stuck!*"

"Quiet!" Ellie hissed. *Only* people *talk, you dummy; you want someone to hear?* Impatient and scared out of her wits, Ellie saw that the twisted fingers of thorny brambles clutched the little girl's hair at the crown in a dense tangle. "Okay, hang on," Ellie muttered, unlimbering the Savage. "Just hold still."

"Owow*ow!*" the white-haired girl complained as Ellie fussed with the snarl. Squinting, the girl bared her teeth. "That *hurts!*"

"Well, it's really *tangled,*" Ellie said, so beside herself with fear, she thought about just *going* already. Wincing against the sting of thorns, she fumbled over the ratty tangle. She glanced at her dog. Ears perked, mouth closed, nostrils flared—but no real alert. That was good. But this stupid tangle just wouldn't *come.* Tugging her Leek from her pocket, she snicked the silver-gray serrated blade in place with her thumb.

The little girl's eyes were saucers. "What are you *doing?*"

"I'm cutting it."

"Why? *No.*"

Ellie opened her mouth to yell, then said, "I'm Ellie. What's your name?"

"Debbie?" The girl's chin was quivering again. "My daddy called me Dee."

"Dee, I can't get your hair untangled." Another crackle of brush from somewhere behind, but the sound was fleeting and she was focused on Dee, besides. "I have to cut it, or we rip it. Ripping will hurt. Cutting won't."

"*Nooo,*" Dee said, blue eyes pooling again. "It's my *hair.*"

Just do it. Slipping the Leek's serrated edge under a gnarled clot of the girl's hair, she sawed. "It'll grow back."

"But, but . . ." Dee kept squirming. "Can't you just chop the branches?"

"*No,* I can't." She was going to stab this kid if she didn't quit it. "Stop moving. Just this last little—"

At that moment, Mina let out a single, hard *huff.*

Oh boy. Ellie's insides went as still as she'd wanted Dee to be. She saw that Mina wasn't looking the way they'd come either, but the way *ahead,* where they wanted to go. Behind her. At her back.

"What?" Dee said when Ellie froze. "What is—"

"Shh!" Nerves clanging, Ellie bent, got her Savage, and slowly straightened. When she shifted, a spiky pine bough broke with a crispy crinkle. Mina's ears only twitched. Her dog didn't break stance to look at her at all.

"Oh." It was Dee, and Ellie recognized the tone from when the girl had warned them in the wagon: *Hey. Hey. Everybody.*

Ellie turned—and what wove through the trees turned her guts to shivery Jell-O.

There was only one, but gosh, that was enough. The girl had a dinged-up, rusty-looking aluminum bat, which meant she'd had practice.

And the girl also had something else quite distinctive. As soon as

Ellie saw it, she understood, instantly, how all these people-eaters had found them to begin with.

In her terror, it was the one thing she'd actually thought about. How come the people-eaters were here, waiting for them? Finn was sweeping up from the south. That didn't mean the way north was *clear*, but she and Jayden and Chris had come into Rule from roughly this direction a little more than twelve hours ago. Yeah, true: they'd come down a little west of here. But they'd run into no people-eaters. Mina hadn't alerted once. So why were the people-eaters here now?

Everyone knew: people-eaters return to the familiar. Chris was familiar. So was Jayden. Chris's idea was to use himself as bait to draw them away so Hannah and Isaac and the others would be safe, and then kill the people-eaters when they attacked. Only nothing and no one ever did.

Once they'd made it to Rule, everything had happened so fast, become such an emergency. Chris getting hurt bad and almost dying, and then Tom, and now Finn coming and the big rush to get out of the village . . . well, in the end, they just forgot. It slipped their minds.

And look, Chris's plan *had* worked. Just at the wrong time.

Because here was the girl, and Ellie knew only one people-eater with a lime-green scarf.

Lena.

116

"Stay behind me," Ellie said, snicking the Leek shut and dropping it in a front pocket. Not bothering to see if Dee minded, she hefted the Savage. Growling her *don't even think about it* rumble, Mina had put herself between them and Lena.

Lena stopped short, about thirty feet away. She wasn't as hollow-eyed as before. Except for the scarf, her clothes were different. From the stains on that bat, Ellie thought Lena had picked up a couple snacks on the road the way Ellie's daddy used to stop at a Kwik-Mart for Krispy Kremes and Slim Jims. Already lean, the girl looked wolfish, like all that walking and fresh air and time in the woods had coaxed the animal out of hiding. Or maybe *Lena* was finally gone, the beast eating up her insides until all that remained was the glove of her skin.

But she still has the scarf. Ellie had no idea why, but then her thoughts jumped to Dee and her doll, the whistle Alex had always worn until she gave it to Ellie. The whistle was a . . . souvenir? That wasn't right. For *her*, the whistle was Alex. For Alex, the whistle was her dad. Maybe the scarf was what Lena had been before everything fell apart.

From behind Ellie, back toward the road, came a faint crack of gunfire. Another. Two more. She couldn't say if the gunfire had ever ceased. Whoever was doing the shooting was in the wrong place to help them anyway. The idea flitted through Ellie's brain that she could shout, or have Dee scream. If it was the good guys, they might find them in time.

Unless it's not. Perhaps Finn had blown through Rule and steamed north to grab them. If so, shouting would only land her and Dee in an equally terrible fix.

"Leave us alone, Lena." Don't ask Ellie why; it just popped out.

"You *know* her?" Dee's voice was a mousy shrill.

"Sort of." Lena's head tilted like a dog's, and then the older girl took a step. "Don't," Ellie said, choking up on the Savage. Swinging first would be a bad idea. Lena was taller and her reach was longer. All Lena had to do was wait for her to miss. Then, one crack of that bat upside the head and Ellie's skull would break like an egg. Mina would try to protect her, but she didn't want Lena to kill her dog.

Lena took another step, then halted when Mina's rumble intensified. "Please, Lena," Ellie said, "go away, just go away, just—"

Lena came at them, so swift and silent, Ellie never had time to say anything, much less give a command. At the same moment, Mina broke, not waiting for Ellie to tell her what to do but racing to close the gap. Two feet from Lena, Mina readied herself for the leap, and that was when Ellie finally snapped to; saw the danger, because she'd read the angle of that bat; knew exactly what Lena was going to do, because, as Jayden once explained: *If you're ever attacked by a dog or coyote, remember that they never come straight on. Dogs and coyotes and wolves always jump.*

"Mina, *no!*" Ellie screamed, way too late, way too slow, because Mina was so fast, so brave, and *she* was stupid, stupid, *stupid* . . .

Lena swung. Ellie heard the cut of the bat, a whickering *whir;* saw the dull twinkle of aluminum in the light of this new day. The bat caught Mina under her jaw, smashing with a wicked brute force that snapped the dog's head back with a loud and sickening *crack!* Mina never cried out or made a sound. There was no leap of blood. The blow sent the dog sailing off-target to crash into a hummock of dirty snow and forest litter.

"*Mina!*" Ellie shrieked, and darted forward. Behind her, Dee was screaming again, a sound Ellie barely heard over the thunder in her head. Ahead, through a furious red haze, she saw Lena stride to her fallen dog, her Mina, and bring that bat high over her head like a sledgehammer. Ellie had a moment's hope when she wondered if Mina might still be alive—or if Lena only wanted to make sure.

Then Ellie was beyond caring, barely thinking, only moving, charging with murder on her mind and her heart already breaking. Roaring, she brought the Savage around in a vicious slice just as Lena began to turn. Speeding through air, the rifle axed Lena's middle, knocking the girl away from her dog, her *dog*! Ellie barely registered the blow, wasn't really aware she connected until Lena stumbled onto her heels. Off-balance, Lena backpedaled a few steps before her feet skidded on a patch of slick snow. As she fell, Lena lost her grip on the bat, which turned a drunken cartwheel before thumping to the ground a few feet to Lena's right. That put the aluminum bat on Ellie's left, and she had one second, one *second* . . . and hesitated, unsure if she should try for the bat or not.

One second was all the animal-Lena needed. In a flash, she was rolling, hand shooting for the bat, fingers outstretched.

"No!" Ellie brought the Savage down like that huge hammer her daddy once used to ring the bell on a county fair midway and win her a stuffed monkey. The rifle caught Lena's left arm at the elbow with a tremendous *whack*. Lena let out a screech. Breaking apart from the force of the blow, the Savage splintered, the entire wooden stock assembly shearing from the barrel. Staggering from her own momentum, Ellie felt her boots skitter over snow humped atop old leaves and then her feet cut out from under. The Savage's barrel spun off like a discarded baton. Crashing down hard on first her left ankle and then her hip, the blow knocked out her breath and sent an electric shock into the small of her back. A wheezy scream winged off her tongue. Retching, Ellie rolled onto her stomach. The forest wavered and she had a brief second when she wondered if this was what happened before you passed out.

There came the rustle of leaves as the monster gathered herself. Ellie looked up. On her feet, only ten feet away, Lena swayed, her face a clench of fury and pain. Her scarf dragged like the long, lime-green tongue of a sick lizard. From that nasty kink, her left arm seemed to suddenly have grown a second elbow.

With her good right hand, Lena picked up the bat.

"I hate you," Ellie choked. Tears streamed over her cheeks. "You killed my *dog*." Her closet-voice was shrieking, *Get up, Ellie, get up, get up!* So why wasn't she listening? Because she was on her belly. Getting up meant pushing to hands and knees, setting her feet, and she was too furious and frightened to take her eyes from this girl. What you couldn't see and only imagined was always scarier than what was real. Lena was already bad enough.

But Ellie did one thing. Her hand snuck into her pocket—and found her Leek. The knife was slim and, with the blade folded away, only just filled her hand.

Lena came for her, and Ellie watched her come and thought, *You have to wind up. Even for a swing like this, you'll have to batter up.*

"I used to feel sorry for you." She had no idea where Dee was. Since she wasn't screaming, maybe Dee had run off or fainted. It didn't matter. The only thing that did was this murderer who'd led the people-eaters to Eli and Roc; whose friends had burned Isaac's barn and baby lambs. Who'd just killed her dog, her sweet Mina, who'd been nothing but good, and who was the very last tie to her daddy, the very last. "I thought you were different. But I hope Chris finds you," she said as she lost sight of Lena's face because the girl was so very close. What swam before Ellie's eyes were boots and legs . . . and that dinged-up bat, still dangling from Lena's right hand. "I hope he kills you," she said to the bat. "I hope Chris—"

The bat swung out of sight.

Batter up. Snapping the Leek's blade home, Ellie threw her fist around and stabbed. Very sharp and with that wonderful point so good for picking out fishing line, the blade drove into Lena's calf just above her left boot, slicing fabric, then skin and meat. Ellie rammed so hard and fast she felt the scrape of metal on bone.

Lena *screamed*. Not a screech or shriek, but a shrill, undulating *wail*. Ellie just had the presence of mind to hang on and yank her knife free as Lena lurched back. Not three inches from Ellie's nose, the bat thudded to the earth. Ellie made a snatching grab and clambered upright. Her hip and ankle didn't like that, but tough. Bawling, Lena was cramped over her bleeding leg, trying to grab it with her right hand because her left arm was broken.

Can't run away now, can you? Ellie choked up on the bat. *Kill you. One good swing.*

At that moment, Lena's head snapped up. An expression of both recognition and astonishment and . . . was that fear? longing? . . . spread over her face as she peered at something behind Ellie. For a second, Ellie thought this girl looked almost human again.

"Ellie." The voice was close. "Don't do it."

"Why not?" Her voice sounded very strange. Her gaze did not waver, but Lena did shimmy as if a pane of flawed glass suddenly separated them. "She killed my dog. She took away my daddy. I'm not such a little kid anymore, Chris."

"I know, Ellie," Chris said, "and I'm sorry about that."

"But I *want* to kill her."

"That's why you shouldn't."

Now she did look. Chris had Tom's gun, the small one, and she wondered—a very fleeting glimmer of a thought, barely conscious—why Tom wasn't there. But Jayden was, a short distance away, rifle to his shoulder. A white tousle and one blue eye peeped from behind Jayden's legs. *She'd* done that with Grandpa Jack at the funeral. As if not looking all the way made saying good-bye to her dad hurt any less.

And beyond, on the ground, was Mina, her Mina, lying oh-so-still.

"I let her go once." Chris's dark eyes, still so red, ticked her way, then back. The radio on his hip chirped like a mad cricket, but he paid no attention. "She's my responsibility."

Lena looked small and sad again with her broken arm and bloody leg. If this were a movie, Ellie bet this was when, all of a sudden, the wild-girl got it together and called, *Chris!* So then everybody could go *aawww* because—see?—even monsters have feelings. Then Lena would run off into the forest—*tra-la*—in a stupid fairy-tale happily-ever-after because people want happy endings and, you know, maybe monsters get better.

But this was Ellie's real life, and that was the enemy, and there were no do-overs.

"It's not your fault, Chris. You didn't make her into a monster." She paused, thinking there was something to that: like when you made crummy choices, then had to own up to a mistake and live with whatever happened next. "You didn't kill anybody."

"Not when I should have," Chris said, and pulled the trigger.

117

The red storm kept her company the whole way: a constant mutter, like the throb of a toothache. Her monster was very interested, too. She felt it elbowing its way around, pressing its nose right up to the limits of her skull, like a kid yearning to go out and play. *Oh, I don't think so.* Bearing down, she sawed her teeth into her lower lip and felt the monster give a sharp, angry kick. *Suck on it, you poor baby.*

She cut northwest, keeping a good distance and some forest between her and Finn. The eastern sky brightened, going silver and then white before bluing to a light turquoise overhead. Over the thump of her horse's hooves she heard someone shouting: not screaming so much as bellowing, a wild and incoherent note that Alex thought was a single word, repeated over and over again. *Coming from that plateau. Someone still alive up there.* She threw a glance, but there were too many trees, and she was much too far away to catch the scent. If she'd been closer, she might not have managed anyway because of the fire and all the Changed. The air was saturated with their stink.

She came in south of the feeding ground and that terrible pyramid. She had no desire to see either again, and no time besides, but she smelled them. So did the horse, which balked.

"Fine," she said, swinging a leg around to dismount. "I'm not really sure I blame—" Alex gasped at a sudden shimmy, the shift, as the monster steamed to life, working its way out in fingers, and she felt herself start to fall—

—into someone else, behind its eyes, his eyes. Ahead, there is black smoke and the GOGOGO as the others work their way toward distant flames and the scream of meat. It—he—looks left, to the red storm in black on a black horse and the pushpush of the gogo—and the one who only screams LET ME GO LET ME GOGOGO. Further away, there are others streaming uphill and now many eyes full of the GOGOGO—

And then there is the jump she knows, a shimmy and shift, and then she's there in another body, a girl's. She can feel the difference. She's in the middle of a jostle of bodies, a tangle of arms and legs, and GOGOGO—

Dead ahead, there is a boy, not like her at all. He is a scream of meat. He is food, and she smells his desperation and panic as he tries to get onto his horse. But he won't be able to manage it, because this boy's fear is strong and she is close now; his full, rich, raw scent fills her mouth, and— PUSHPUSH—she will have him. She rushes for the boy, pushing her way through the others—GOGO—she lunges, feels the rake of her nails on his leg, and he turns a terrified look, and she sees—

"No"—but she could barely hear herself. "Chris, run, get away, run—"

There was a sudden *snap*, either the monster letting go, or her finally recalling it, she couldn't be sure. Her vision cleared and fixed on Buck, hovering over her, a paw on her chest. Her gaze shifted to jagged chinks of sky showing through branches. *Fell off my horse.* Struggling to a sit, she wiped a trickle of blood from the corner of her mouth and listened to her pulse thunder.

That was Chris. She was almost positive. The horse, a blood bay, was right, and she'd gotten a fleeting look at his face . . . Right hair, the face was the same, but bruised, and there was something wrong with his eyes. "Red," she breathed. Buck nudged her neck, and she let herself sag against the wolfdog. Chris's eyes were red. The same as Peter's? No, the more she thought about it, the surer she was that

Chris was hurt. From that girl's perspective, Chris was food: blood and salt, fear and sweat. Meat.

Strong, too, that red storm. Every time that *push-push go-go* amped up, her monster leaked through. Throttling it back when there were only Finn and a few altered Changed around wasn't as hard. But an increase in numbers meant more intensity, a wider spread. She wasn't sure she could maintain control.

Scraping up the Uzi from where she'd dropped it, she clawed to her feet. For a moment, she thought about leaving the green canvas medic pack, now stuffed to capacity not only with medical supplies but several books and odds and ends she'd picked up along the way. The pack would only add weight, slow her down.

But Chris looked hurt. Hefting the pack onto her shoulders, she broke into a staggering, wobbly run, with Buck trotting alongside. *Chris is here, and he's in trouble. I've got to do* something *to help, somehow.*

If she only could figure out what.

Passing through Rule—its deserted streets, those wrecked houses— was like wandering through the defunct set of a disaster movie. The windows of many houses were shattered. Some had no doors. She paused only once: at Jess's house, its door hanging askew like a rotten tooth ready to fall from its socket. Part of her wanted to go inside. She'd left her parents behind, squared on the desk in her room. But the chances of their ashes still being there were about as good as her stopping Finn.

Need to keep going. She eyed a red, spray-painted *X* that wept from the lintel over the ruined door. *It's like that old Bible story, the one about the Angel of Death.* Except all these houses hadn't been passed over. There were still bodies inside a few, and dead Changed, too.

But Chris was among the living, and the living needed help. *And Peter, Wolf, Penny . . . what do I do, what should I do?* She was still turning that over as she neared the square, dodging from house to house, slinking through backyards. As she remembered the square's layout, the church was on the northwest corner. Jess's house was west of the square, which meant she was coming up behind the village hall. What she'd do once she got there, she didn't know. Was there a back entrance, a way into the building? If so . . . what then? Make her way to the roof? Could she even do that? How would that help?

You'd better figure this out, honey. The fug of all those Changed, altered and otherwise, bled through the air, growing stronger the closer she got. Finn's people must be nearly to the square. Their stink made the hackles rise in a Mohawk along Buck's spine. She felt her monster suddenly perk right up, too—and, a split second later, understood why as she teased out an odor of shadows and cool mist and rot.

Wolf. She parsed more smells, got denim and wintergreen, hard steel and desperation mingling with the stench of chemo: *Peter's there, too.*

So tempting to give the monster a little leash, see if it might slip behind Wolf's eyes. *What if I could control it?* Send it out to very specific targets? That was . . . a little creepy, and crazy, too. Let the red storm set its hook, and she'd be as helpless as a swimmer in a rip current. Yet the idea of actually letting the monster go, making it work *for* her . . . *Can I do that?* Her hand snuck to caress the wolfdog's neck. God, this would be like naming her monster, which her cancer docs encouraged: fighting back by thinking of the monster as something separate and apart. One guy even gave his cancer a Twitter account. She had wanted no part of her tumor: not to name it, draw it, visualize it. She'd only fought until she couldn't fight anymore, and left for the Waucamaw, where her tumor became a monster with slitty eyes and needle-teeth—and had saved her life, a couple of times over now.

Face it, Alex, the monster is a part of you, whether you like it or not.

"So what are you saying, you nut?" she murmured. "You want to jump off Blackrocks? Gonna send out the monster with a message?"

It was crazy sci-*fry*. *But Finn does it, somehow.* Look at those weird Changed and poor Peter. But what if she got snagged by the red storm and couldn't get free? What if who *she* was drowned in it? Somehow, she thought that could happen.

People, all old, gathering in the square. Her schnoz was full of fusty stained underwear and doughy skin. She heard them, too, a low buzz. *But no kids.* Where could they be? She didn't smell Chris either, and her stomach tightened with dread. *Take it easy. He was on a horse.* If he was smart, he was already long gone. With enough warning, *all* the kids might be, too. Could be why she smelled none. *Except Finn made his move while it was still dark.* So how would Rule have known Finn was on his way?

A distant crackle, like a string of firecrackers. She glanced north. Someone shooting out there, but far away, easily several miles. The kids? Maybe, and probably not fighting Finn's people. She'd followed him long enough to know that no one had split off from the main group.

Oh God. What if those were Rule's kids, and there were *Changed* out there? Would Finn's, well . . . *signal* bleed that far? That wide? How much range did this guy have?

Range, there's something about that; that kid, Jasper, mentioned Peter, and how Peter got better whenever Finn was further away. He said if Finn died, the network would fall apart.

She'd thought of the same thing when trying to figure out how Finn managed all those Changed. *I know the signal hops because the monster does, and I go along for the ride.* And look what had happened to her when Finn's Changed attacked that plateau: big surge, huge signal, and she woke up on the snow. *But what does that mean? How can I use this? What does it mean?*

Dead ahead, she spied a short alley, lined with detached garages, that trickled into the village hall's parking lot. Nosed to the back wall alongside a large green Dumpster were three sheriffs' cruisers, minus their tires and doors, resting on their rims. To the right was a single driveway that led to the square. The long, stained-glass breezeway connecting the school to the church was on her left. Tall trees marched up to the rectory and school, and, as she recalled, a side door into the church off a courtyard.

Pulling Buck close, she crouched in a drift of old snow behind the last detached garage on the left and at the very edge of the alley. Two choices: the village hall or the church. Keep to the woods, and she and the wolfdog had a much better chance of slipping inside the church. *They were ringing the bell, too.* Which meant the tower was open. *Get up high, scope things out, see where Peter and Wolf and Penny are in relationship to Finn.* She might even spot Chris. The Uzi had a scope. Wait, could she shoot Finn? *Oh, get real, honey.* She wasn't a sniper. She didn't know if the Uzi even had the range. Besides—she felt her chest squeeze down—what would happen if Finn died? With all those Changed, she bet: nothing very good.

"They'll be off the leash. They'll go out of control." When the wolfdog let out a soft whimper, she stroked his ears. "I know. I smell them, too." The Changed's rank fog was getting stronger by the second. "I hear you, boy, we're going."

As she scurried past the village hall, she caught a strange odor: just the slightest curl, like a finger of spiced smoke dissipating on a strong breeze. The *spice* made her falter. *No.* She battened down on the association before the grief could wind itself up and undo her. *Enough, Alex.* She centered herself, focused on the beat of her heart. *You're upset; it's your imagination. You* want *it to be Tom.* "Get through this, and you can cry later," she muttered.

She took another, deliberate inhale. This time, there was no spice, no phantom of Tom. What she got was diesel fuel and scorched . . . metal? Like a blackened can of beans set to heat in a campfire. Yet the smell was also oddly chemical: gunpowder and . . . She flashed to a summer's afternoon: her dad, cursing, aiming a fire extinguisher.

The chalky chemical gush, and her mother fretting about how they'd have to wear masks to clean up the mess: *There's the phosphoric acid to worry about.*

Then the village hall was behind her, and she and the wolfdog were darting into the woods around the rectory. After slipping in the side door, she and Buck cowered on the landing, sniffing and listening. Something awful had gone down in the sanctuary and the basement, too. Her mouth puckered at the tang of cold blood and spent gunpowder. The black maw of the basement door exhaled mangled flesh and sweat and fear and a Changed, for sure, an eye-watering reek of stewed, smooshed raccoon.

Dusty bolts of colored light streamed through the stained rosette window at the east end of the church. The pews were empty, although the smell of people and a few spent candles lingered. . . . *Wait a minute.* Gathering more air into her mouth, she tongued the aroma, then gasped. "Oh God. Acne . . . *Ben?*" He'd come back to Rule after all. *And died here, in the church.* The aroma was . . . violent. Wreathed in a mélange of bleach and pine tar, Ben's smell was *everywhere*, as if they'd scrubbed and scrubbed, knowing that nothing could erase the stink of this horrific death. The altar cloth was gone, as was the platform's carpet. Someone had tried scrubbing Ben's blood from the wall where the cross still hung, but too late. The sight of those ghostly, purple splashes drew a cold finger down her neck. How anyone could still *worship* here, she couldn't imagine.

More blood in the vestibule, worked into stony crevices. She couldn't tell whose, and she had no time to worry the smells. The bell tower door was open. No one up there she could suss out, although the reek of Finn's Changed cascaded in a waterfall of cold air. The church doors were also slightly ajar, and through the crack, she saw them, as well as Finn's men and horses, streaming into the square.

Sprinting up the tower's circular steps with Buck on her heels, his nails clicking on stone, Alex vaulted into a short, stone passageway.

Light streamed in through rectangular slots in the wall that reminded her of a castle's arrow loops, only much wider. From the square, she caught the clop of horses, a low muttering from people, but no screams. Which was strange: with all those Changed, she'd expected hysteria and a fight. Yet there was no gunfire at all, here or north now either. Ahead, she spotted ropes and a wood console, the kind bell chimers used to play melodies. One rope dangled, probably attached to that working bell.

She was so intent on getting a look at the square that she'd already turned aside before her brain processed what she'd seen: a bulky rectangle, in shadow, fixed to the lower left corner of that carillon console.

Oh. Her eyes ticked back. *Shit.*

A bomb.

118

"What?" Greg heard Chris snap into his walkie-talkie. His voice was very loud in the hush; most kids had stopped crying. Sarah had gathered the youngest into a solemn knot to wait until they were ready to move out. On the bed of Jayden's wagon, a blood-spattered Kincaid was tending to a boy whose arm had been broken by a bat. They'd been lucky, though. The survivors mostly had bumps, scrapes, cuts, bruises. Except for Ghost, whose right ear was ripped off by a Changed, the dogs had made out just fine.

Well. Greg tossed a look toward the back of the wagon train. *Almost all the dogs.* Sitting cross-legged on the ground, Ellie looked like a kid whose parents were just killed in a hit-and-run. Not far from the truth, what with Tom staying behind. Forefinger corking her mouth, the little girl—Dee?—leaned against Ellie while Ghost, a blotchy bandage wound around his ruined ear in a lopsided turban, sprawled by Ellie's side. Jet and Daisy sat nearby.

"What's that?" Chris said. Normally, they used coded breaks, but Pru had come through in an excited sputter of static. So either the message was complicated or Pru was in a big hurry. Plugging an ear with a pinky, Chris walked a short distance away from Ellie and the dogs and held the walkie up to the other ear. "Say again, Pru."

Can you hear me now? And then Greg thought, *That's not even remotely funny.* Clamping a bloodstained parka with an elbow, he bent, hooked the girl who'd been driving the supply wagon under the arms, then glanced up at Jayden, who had the legs. When Jayden nodded, they hefted the body, sidestepped a dead Changed boy with only a nubbin of a nose, and laid the girl out alongside the others. Counting Aidan, Sam, and Lucian—all of whom had booked—they'd lost nine kids total. Not a disaster, but one kid was too many. They were also down the two horses Aidan and Sam used to get away.

Oh, but you guys had better keep away from us, because I will shoot you. Greg really meant that, too. Shaking out the parka, he draped it over the girl's head and shoulders. There, that was the last. Once they rearranged the supplies, they'd load the dead, including Mina, and move out. The idea of traveling a full day with the dead sent shivers up his spine. They couldn't waste time burning the bodies here, though. The smell would give away their position. *If the gunfire hasn't already.* But no one other than Chris had come storming up the road, and he'd said Finn was close but not yet in Rule.

"Think they found them?" Jayden had come to stand next to him. The other boy had a new collection of bruises to add to the ones he'd gotten earlier. His right eye, crusted with blood, was already swelling shut. "Tom's kids?"

"Either that or—" He read the sudden stiffening of Chris's back, heard him bark something into the radio. *Crap.* As sorry as he was about Lena, he was glad Chris shot her. *Sure would be nice for something to break our way for a change.*

"Oh brother," Jayden said. Chris had spun on his heel, but not to head back to them. He was running toward Night and rapping out orders into the walkie.

"Chris, wait!" Greg jogged over, Jayden on his heels. "Where are you going? Did they—"

"I have to go back." Chris's bruised and battered face was tight. He swung up onto Night's saddle. "You guys get out of here. Leave your radio on. I'll catch up when I can."

"Why? But you're here. What—"

"They found the kids about a half mile from where Tom thought they were." Chris gathered Night's reins. "But listen to this: Finn also has Peter."

"Peter?" Greg felt his lips numb. "Chris, we can't leave Peter—"

"I know that." Chris's voice was grim. "But it gets worse. Finn's done something to Peter, made him like the Changed. Not all the way, but the kids said he's pretty far gone."

Greg's stomach worked itself into a cold knot. "If he's still Peter, we need to get to him. You and me, we'll go back."

"And maybe get yourselves killed?" Jayden put a hand on Greg's arm. "Think about this a minute. Tom set bombs. How long do you two really have before they blow? Finn's there by now, or pretty close. Tom will wait until they're in the square, but that's all."

"Look, I just killed a girl I knew pretty damn well. I can't abandon Peter, not if there's a chance he can come back to us. You and Hannah and Isaac have your way, and I have mine. Maybe, if I'm really lucky, I grab Tom, too." Chris took a deep breath. "And I'm not letting Alex go, not again."

"What?" Greg wasn't sure he'd heard right. "*Alex?* What does she—"

"The guards were already down when Pru got there. Tom's kids said Alex helped them." He wheeled Night around. "And she's headed to Rule."

119

A bomb.

A red swoop of terror nearly knocked Alex's feet out from under. About the size of a small shoebox, the bomb consisted of an oversize alarm clock wrapped to a putty-like block, probably C4, with black electrical tape. Wires snaked from some lead-colored tube to attach to the alarm's bell and hammer. The bomb was fixed to the console with more electrical tape.

Got to get out of here. Sweat suddenly pearled in the hollow of her throat. *Got to get out of the church.* Who knew when this thing was going to blow?

But that was when she noticed two things she hadn't because of her fear. One, the clock wasn't ticking. Two, the bomb didn't smell right.

Now, she didn't know squat about bombs. That Rule even *had* crap like this was amazing. That they'd thought to rig a bomb to the church was equally astonishing. But shouldn't a time bomb be ticking? This was an old-fashioned alarm. Her aunt had one, and those suckers were *loud*. Swallowing back the flutter in her throat, she crept close enough to study the clock face. The smaller alarm hand pointed to the twelve. The minute and hour hands showed that the clock had been primed for a thirty-minute delay before the ka-boom. This particular clock had a very thin, spindly second hand, too, but that was still.

They never had a chance to set it. She let out a long, relieved breath. Still, might not be safe here. What if the bomb got jarred loose, or some vibration started the countdown?

But then, there was the smell. She worried it. Of all the scents C4 *might* have . . . "Bread?" Still on hands and knees, she dropped to her stomach, wormed closer, got her nose to within an inch. She pulled in air. Plastic, from the electrical tape; the steel of the alarm clock; a gunpowder aroma from that lead-colored thing, so a detonator or blasting cap or whatever—and something else, something vital that tugged at memory. But what she got most was flour and oil and *lots* of salt, an odor that took her back to first grade.

"My God," she whispered. "It's homemade Play-Doh. It's a *fake.*"

Why would anyone plant this? Just to scare the bejesus out of someone? Got to be another reason. "Maybe they wanted to buy time," she told Buck. "Make someone think they've found a bomb when they haven't. But buy time for what?" To keep them, Finn's guys, busy? Or *maybe* . . . "You reassure them that you've got nothing. Cry wolf often enough, everyone relaxes. They think you're an idiot."

She could feel the questions piling up in her brain: How did they know to set the decoys? Who could've done it? But the only question she could afford time to consider was whether to get out of the tower. *Yeah, but go where?* If someone came up, she'd be in trouble, but she *was* here, Finn was down there, and this was as good a place to hide as—

From beyond the tower came a loud *bang.* Not a gunshot, but more like the slam of a door. Scuttling to a slot in the stone, she lifted up on her toes until the square below slid into view.

And felt the bottom drop out of her world.

It was like a mob scene from *The Lord of the Rings*: a crowd of old people, in puffy parkas and wool caps, gathered before the village hall steps. Surrounding them, like a parade guard, were ranks of boys and girls, about two hundred, in tattered clothing. The Changed were weaponless because they had no need. From the hollow, clawing scent mingling with roadkill, these kids were hungry. Many of the old people were weeping; a smell of water and salt laced the air. That made sense, too. If Ben Stiemke came back, and these Changed had been around the mine, then many of these elderly were looking into the faces of their grandchildren.

Beyond the moat of Changed were horses and the twenty some-odd, white-clad kids who made up Finn's altered Changed. And were they wearing collars? Surrounding them in a rough, U-shaped fan were armed men in standard winter camouflage.

At the bottom of the village hall steps, she spotted Yeager's bald head, Ernst's girth. Two others, Born and Prigge, looking withered. No robes. Considering Ben Stiemke and all that old blood in the church, it was a good bet the Council hadn't been calling the shots for a while.

Flanked by armed guards on the landing were three others she recognized. Collared and in white, gold mane loose around his shoulders, Peter was rigid. She was surprised to see that his hands weren't tied. On the other hand, the guns, one jammed to Wolf's temple and a second to Penny's, were probably control enough. At the scent of Wolf's fuming rage, her monster gave her a nudge, wanting to get out, make contact.

Tall and broad and black, Finn was on the landing, too. A square woman, with a very large gun, stood on his left. A boy with dark hair—an altered Changed, clad all in white—hovered to his right, like a pet dog. But it was what and who she saw next that made her heart try to break apart in her chest.

The slam had come from the village hall doors. Two of Finn's men were bulling their way out with someone else—bloody and bat-tered—who still put up a real fight, kicking and bucking so much that two more men bounded up the steps to help. One jackham-mered a very hard, fast, and brutal punch to their prisoner's gut, bad enough to double him over. Bad enough that Alex, for all the distance between them, heard the gasping cry jump from his mouth as he crumpled and sagged to his knees.

At the sound, she fell to her own. Everything came together, all the pieces: the early warning; why the children were gone; that fleeting scent at the village hall and on this decoy bomb she hadn't dwelled on, something so minute, barely there at all—and she'd had to hold her grief at bay because there were so many more important things to worry about, like keeping the monster in check and her head from being blown off.

Of course, he'd handled it, fashioned this, labored to make it as flawless and perfect as he could: something that would fool the eye for just long enough. There was no one else capable. She should've understood that from the very beginning because of his scent, musk and smoke and spice so rich and sweet and strong, what she'd told herself was only wishful thinking.

But it was real. He's *real. He's alive, he's* . . . If she hadn't clapped both trembling hands to her mouth, she surely would have screamed his name.

Tom.

My God.

They had Tom.

120

He hadn't lied to Chris. When he cooked up this cockamamy plan, he had one very healthy leg and one that was plenty strong, only slightly gimpy. The timing had worked fine. After the RPGs, that changed. So he miscalculated, didn't factor in distance, how far and fast he could hobble on a bloody leg with a hunk of metal in it that kept wanting to give out. A lot of time got chewed up while he got the ball rolling, lurched his way to the huge compressor on the roof and then around back, making doubly sure all the outside vents were sealed. The last thing he needed was for the smell of burning thermite and live det cord to leak. He went as fast as he could, but by the time he was gimping back around the building and up the village steps to head for the jail, Finn's men were halfway across the square—and he just . . . froze. Like Chris on the plateau: he looked, and the sight of all those Changed stopped him dead a good five seconds. Three seconds too long, as it turned out.

Which was *not* the plan. First principles, again: hold out bait, entice the enemy, lull them into believing they were safe. The *idea* was to arm the decoys, set off his incendiary, then hustle back to the real deal—that back room filled with propane tanks, C4, cans of fuel oil, and his homemade ANFO—and keep tabs on Finn while he waited for the thermite three stories above to eat through the floor and into an air conditioning duct where it would set off a long snake of det cord. If something failed along the way—say, the thermite didn't work or the det cord didn't ignite—or if it looked like Finn was delayed or ready to leave, all Tom had to do was wait for the right moment and then touch off the explosives himself. So, let Finn discover the fakes. Even if they suspected he'd survived the church, Mellie already thought she had all his bomb-making materials. That was the whole point of putting that small stash under the horse trough back at their old camp to begin with. The decoys here would reassure them they were right. Buy the kids a little more time, and then *boom!*

Great plan. Sucked about the leg. Anyway, it was bad. Frightened men are brutal. Storming the building, they crowded into the jail where he was desperately monkeying up metal shelves. It took four to pry him off, and they did it with enough violence that the back of his head cracked stone. He still felt the warm wet slither of blood down his neck. The rain of punches and blows was worse. One particularly well-aimed kick nearly buried that metal dagger in his left thigh, and his right flank, the recipient of a steel-toed boot, was screaming. Be lucky not to have busted a kidney. The only consolation? Tom's eyes brushed Jed's Timex. Assuming he got the right proportions of ABC to ground aluminum and plaster of Paris, and his math was correct—having experimented with those fire extinguishers enough, he was pretty sure it was—he had about, oh, fourteen minutes left to worry about that.

"Found him in the jail," the steel-toed kidney kicker was saying, "with the fuel stores. Trying to start these up, but they're fakes. Just, I don't know, bread dough or something."

"There's nothing?" Finn was much bigger than Tom had guessed from that picture: a wide, imposing giant, all in obsidian-black, with a head that looked chiseled out of stone. On the other hand, Finn might seem huge because Tom was on his knees. Standing slightly off Finn's right shoulder was that dark-haired boy in white, the one with Finn at the ruined church. Now that he was close, Tom saw how the kid's savage, red eyes watched Finn with this eerie, quivering attentiveness reminiscent of a really well-trained dog waiting for a command.

"Not a single live bomb?" Finn asked Kidney Kicker.

"What about smoke?" This came from the woman next to Finn. "Cigarettes? Anything burning? It's how he did it the last time."

Kidney Kicker pulled a frown. "Nothing like that. We'd have smelled det cord or smokes. No C4 either. Just these fakes. Probably thought he could get us going, running around, looking for the real deal, to buy those kids more time. Even if he tried the cigarette trick, we've been here long enough that if there *was* a bomb, it'd have gone off by now."

"And we'd all be in hell before we knew we were dead," Finn said, without a trace of irony. He tossed a look over his shoulder. "Which I'm sure you'd approve of, Yeager."

"You need my approval?" Yeager's face was calm, though his hungry eyes raked the face of a boy to Tom's right. Tom nearly had a heart attack when he first spotted the kid. For a second, he thought, *Oh my God, they got him before he could get away.* But this boy's hair was longer, almost to his shoulders. No fresh blood on his face or in his hair, no necklace of blue-black bruises, no cuts or raw flesh. This boy's eyes were dark brown, almost black, no hemorrhage at all. Chris was lean, but this Changed was gaunt, his sunken cheeks like axheads. Then, of course, there was the very pregnant girl hanging onto the boy's left arm.

Simon? Which meant the girl was Penny. His eyes ticked to the big blond with the mad red eyes, and he saw the sister's ghost in the brother's jaw, the shape of his nose. *Has to be Peter.*

At the sound of Yeager's voice, Simon stirred, although without much energy. Tom knew the look. Throw a burlap bag over that kid's head, slap on plasticuffs, squat him next to a mud-baked wall, and Simon could've doubled as a captured Taliban. Finn had broken

Simon—and you were talking about breaking a monster.

Yeager saw it, too. To Tom, the old man looked like a weary scarecrow with no straw. "I won't beg, Finn." Yeager gestured to the waiting crowd. "We made our choice."

"In a hurry to die? You'd be amazed how stubborn the body is, Yeager." Finn turned back to Kidney Kicker. "Anything else?"

"Only his weapons." The man held up Jed's Bravo and the Glock 19. "Lucky he was so busy trying to fake us out, he didn't take a shot. Coupla knives, too."

"That's not right." Mellie gave him a narrow look, her gray eyes careful and suspicious. Other than the blocky square of her head, she didn't look like her brother. "He had an Uzi."

"Yeah, and you would know. I saw where you got all my other stuff from under the damn trough," Tom said, knowing the dismay showed. He tried pulling himself a little straighter, but his stomach grabbed and the words came on a grunt. He braced his middle with one arm. He kept the other hand propped on his right thigh, over that divot of scar from Harlan's bullet, to keep from falling over. A crazy thought sparrowed: now he had a matched set—scar on the right, scar on the left. "I lost the gun in the explosion at the church."

"But not your head." Finn's right hand rested on the revolver's pearled handle, his index finger keeping time in a slow, thoughtful *tap-tap-tap*. Like the tick of a countdown. A sheathed parang hung from his left hip. "Mellie said you were smart. I wondered if you'd made it."

"Yeah, I noticed you wired my tent. What'd you do?" His lips skinned back in a grimace against a jab of pain. "Count left feet?"

"Would've, if there'd been any to count." One of Finn's bushy white eyebrows arched. "I suppose we have you to thank for all this? No children? Well, but those *shots*. Does give you the willies, doesn't it? All those poor kids, so much shish kebab."

This guy really was an asshole. "No shots now," he said, and noticed that Simon's gaze had drifted from his grandfather to the bell tower. The tiniest crinkle had appeared between the boy's brows, almost as if he'd spotted something. Was one of Finn's men up there? Well, no big deal. There was only another decoy to find.

"I hope not. But, well, I've got *your* kids." Finn eyed him. "What tipped it?"

"The trash." Bracing his side helped as long as he didn't take too deep a breath. At least he was no longer gasping. The ache in his back was down to a dull roar. Not much longer he'd have to deal with either, though, or Finn. *First principles: keep him busy, keep him relaxed, looking at me. All warfare is based on deception.* "Cindi always picked up. Not like I've never seen IEDs hidden under garbage. I just wish it hadn't taken me so long."

"I'm impressed. I mean that, sincerely." Finn gave him a speculative look with eyes that were colorless and cobra-flat. "That's twice now you've survived. First on the snow, now this. And here I thought you were just another dumb grunt. That'll teach me. How old are you?"

"Why does that matter?"

"Well." Finn hooked a thumb at Peter, who only glared mutely. "Let's just say *he's* from the bad section of the Petri dish. If I'm not mistaken, you're younger."

"Never." Tom knew where this was going. The fact that none of them had much longer to argue this didn't stop the chill from shivering down his spine. "Not in a million years."

"That's what I said." Peter suddenly let go of a broken, brittle laugh. "I fought, I—"

"Peter." Ernst's flaccid jowls were streaked with tears. He lumbered a half-step before two of Finn's men moved in to block him. "Don't. You're not to blame."

"Then who is?" Peter looked at Tom with brimming, vermillion eyes. "You won't be able to hold out forever. Best thing is to die fast. Cut your throat first chance you—"

"Please be quiet, Peter. We've had so many interesting talks, I'd be sorry to lose you now." Finn's hand hovered over that Colt, although his eyes never left Tom. "But Peter *does* have a point. Everyone has a price, an Achilles heel. We just need to find yours."

"You have my kids. I don't have anything left for you to take." He was afraid to glance at Jed's Timex. Funny how subjective time was, dragging when you most wanted it to fly. He hadn't lied to Chris. He didn't want to die. There *were* the kids and Ellie to live for, and Alex, out there, somewhere. *Stay alive, Alex, stay safe. Please understand this was the only way.*

"Don't wish your life away, Tom"—and then there was a rasp of metal against leather, a blur of motion as Finn brought his parang around in a slashing cut that cleaved air with a whistle. A laser burned across Tom's chest as blood spilled down his front. Crying out, Tom began to fall before Finn got a fist in his hair and that newly blooded blade to Tom's throat. Tom heard gasps and alarmed cries from the old people. Yeager and Ernst were shouting, trying to work their way up the steps, but it was Peter who broke from his guards and started forward. "Finn, *no!*"

"Be *quiet*, Peter," Finn said. Through a sudden, wavering sheen of tears, Tom saw the big boy's head snap. A shriek bulleted from Peter's mouth as he crumpled.

"D-don't," Tom managed. His heart hammered. Warm streamers of blood were drizzling to cold stone. A millimeter deeper and Finn would've flayed bone. *Hold on, Tom, you can stand this. Just a few more minutes.* On the other hand, if Finn cut his throat, this would end for him a lot sooner. Six of one, half dozen of the other. "Leave him alone. Your fight's with me, Finn."

"We're fighting? I don't think so. Look at what you've done, the lengths you've gone and what you've suffered, and then tell me that your fight is with *me*. Isn't it with yourself, Tom?"

"*Finn!*" Yeager strained against men no less old but much stronger. "In the name of God—"

"God left Rule a long time ago. You know the real question, Yeager? How can your god allow for someone like me? Because make no *mistake*, Tom." Finn loomed in his sight, huge and terrible. "You may *think* you're used up, ready to die. I promise you're not. The body endures even if the spirit does not. I know where the arteries are, what you *really* need to survive, how to make you last a *very* long time. You *think* you need this?" Finn angled the blade until that keen, silvered edge grazed the underside of Tom's nose. "Or your eyelids or lips or fingers? Those hands? Believe me, you don't—"

"Stop!" A sudden, very clear voice, from Tom's left: "Don't!"

What? Over the boom in his ears, Tom felt his mind trying to battle its way from this fog of new pain. Above him, he saw Finn's head snap up, those colorless cobra's eyes suddenly huge with shock—and was that recognition? *Who?*

"Wait!" Quick as lightning, Finn let Tom go, whipping around to the sound of weapons being readied. Mellie's huge Magnum was already in her fist as all of Finn's men drew down; the guard next to Penny had clambered atop the brownstone balustrade, the better to aim . . .

"No!" Finn shouted. Half-turning, he spotted the guard on the balustrade and sprang, moving surprisingly fast for an old man, that bloody parang already sweeping up. "Hold your fire, don't—"

There came a *crack*, the man jerking off a shot at the precise moment that Finn's blade caught the barrel of the weapon. Crying out, the man staggered as his shot went wild, and then let out a loud screech as Finn cut the parang in a broad sweep across his middle. A gush of bright red blood spattered stone as the guard clutched at his spurting stomach and crumpled, tumbling from the balustrade.

"No, God!" the guard shrieked. He got a hand up. *"Don't—"* Whatever else had been on his tongue died as Finn brought the parang down in a hard chop.

"I *said*," Finn roared, as he booted a mighty soccer kick at the guard's head that sent it rocketing down the village hall steps, "no one *fires!*"

"Elias?" Still straight-arming her Magnum, Mellie craned a faltering look back, paling at the sight of gouts of thick blood still pumping from the raw stump of the guard's headless corpse. "What are you—"

"Do what I say!" Finn bellowed, brandishing the dripping parang. "No one fires! Let her through!"

My God, Finn knows *her.* The realization blazed like a pillar of orange fire from an IED. Still reeling, Tom now saw that Simon—that boy with Chris's face who had looked so beaten just a few moments ago—was staring with a look of disbelief that was quickly shifting to dismay and dread. On the ground, not far from him, Peter was moaning: "No no no, don't, this is what he wants, this is what Finn *wants.*"

They *all* knew her: Finn and Peter. Simon. But how? *No, God.* Tom's heart beat even faster, this time with fresh horror. A terrible cold was creeping through his veins to seep into his brain and bones, and he heard himself moan, felt himself die just a little bit more. *No, please, God, don't do this. Aren't I enough? What more can I give you? Please, don't take her, please.*

Struggling to his feet, he watched her come: hands up, rifle held high. She was tauter than he remembered. Her expression was tight, steely with resolve. Her eyes were very bright, a brilliant green; her long hair as deeply rich and red as his blood.

She was his breath, and he would give all he had to save her. He could; there was still time to get clear. There was nothing Finn could do about the hidden thermite eating metal, the buckets of home-made ANFO, the redundant coils of det cord that would, in a very few seconds, spark to life. The bombs would blow. Rule would die, but *she* didn't have to. Life with Finn wouldn't be much of one, but without life, there was no hope—and she was hope, for him, most of all.

But he couldn't let Finn get away either. There were the kids to think about—and Ellie, only eight, just getting started.

This was Afghanistan again, that day in the blare of sun and on the rocks, with that little boy and girl: an impossible choice.

God, what good is a choice when it isn't one? When it truly is between two evils, and neither less evil than the other? If I save Alex, Finn gets the kids. If I say nothing and the bombs go . . .

Choose, Tom. He felt that steady pressure, that hand in his mind, trying to knock him down, make him bend and break. *Alex or the children: choose—and do it fast.*

Because he and Alex had less than eight minutes left.

121

After they'd taken her weapons, she'd come to stand on his right. As she passed, her hand brushed his, the touch so potent he nearly gasped at the scorch and sudden burn in his heart. When she turned to face Finn, her eyes skimmed his for only a moment, but long enough for Tom to see that minute shake of her head. He wasn't exactly sure what she was warning him about, but he kept his mouth shut. He wasn't certain he could trust himself to speak anyway.

"You wanted to find me," she said to Finn. "Well, here I am."

"You *know* this girl?" Mellie asked. Her gray eyes shot to Tom, then to Finn. "How? Where?"

"Oh, here and there." Wiping his gored parang on the trousers of the headless guard, Finn sheathed the weapon. His cobra-eyes ticked from her to Tom, then back. Finn looked both fascinated—and wary. "You killed one of my best hunters," he said to her.

"It was an accident." If there was any fear there, Tom didn't hear it. But he sensed she was waiting for something, and thought, from the tense line of her jaw, she was working hard, too. But working hard at what? *Or is she holding back?* "You must not have cared about him too much, or else you wouldn't have left the body and all his nice gear," she said. "Thanks for that, by the way."

"You're welcome." His snake's eyes raked her up and down. "How did you do it? Not even Davey could find you."

"Davey?" Maybe it was Tom's imagination, but he thought there was the very slightest difference in her tone. Her laser-green gaze slid to the boy—Davey—then back.

"Yes. You're *very* different." Finn turned to consider Simon, whose face was a study in anguish, before regarding her again with genuine curiosity. "Is Simon . . . *fond* of you? Is that why they let you live?"

What? Tom felt his stomach lurch into his throat. *What?*

"What do you want, Finn?" she asked.

"You're able to block me," Finn said. "How? What is it about you that's so different?"

She looked at Finn for a long moment. "I have cancer."

The words hit Tom so hard he almost lost it. Probably would've—collapsed, screamed, grabbed her, wrapped her up, because *no one* was touching her, no one would hurt her ever again, and he would fight for her, he would *fight*—if she hadn't warned him to keep his mouth shut. *No, Jesus, please.* His right leg was already shuddering, and now he thought he might actually fall. A red mist crept over his vision. Really, this couldn't get any worse. There was no hell in the hereafter to worry about. They were living it.

"A brain tumor." Her voice trembled, just a little. A scarlet flush stained her cheeks.

"Really?" Finn only looked intrigued. "Terminal?"

"That's what they said." She moved a shoulder in a shrug. "I'm still here."

"Fascinating. Are you epileptic? From the tumor?"

"No, are you?"

"No." The corner of Finn's mouth twitched. "So you *felt* it. How are you controlling it? Or are you? You look tense. Barely holding on, is that it? I'll bet it's worse when I *drive* them, isn't it?" When she didn't reply, Finn said, "What's your name?"

"*Don't!*" Peter strained against the three guards wrestling him back. "Don't do it, don't tell him! It's how he gets access!"

Access? Tom stared at Peter. *To what?*

"Peter, it's all right," she said.

"But then he'll control—"

"Quiet, boy-o." Finn's revolver was in his hand in the same flash of speed with which he'd wielded that parang. "Don't push it—"

"Stop, Finn. Don't hurt him," she said—and looked at Davey. "Alex. My name is Alex."

Alex. Tom saw Davey's eyelids flutter, and his nostrils flare. *What are you doing?*

"*Noooo,*" Peter moaned. "Alex, no, you don't understand—"

"No, Peter," Alex said. "I think I do."

"Do you, *Alex?*" Finn said, in the gentle, almost wheedling tone of a kindly grandfather. "I doubt that. So let me . . . *show* you."

Flinching, Alex sucked in a quick, pained breath, her head suddenly snapping the way Peter's had when Finn hurt him—and Tom couldn't take it anymore.

"Stop, Finn. *Please,*" he said, hoarsely. Peter was grimacing, his head moving in a spastic jerk as his fists clenched. All around, the air seemed to hum as the Changed, including Davey, shifted, the way runners take their marks. He felt the guards grab his arms as he tried to get between Finn and Alex. "Stop what you're doing, don't hurt her, don't—"

"N-no, Finn," Alex stammered. Her eyes rolled to the whites. A thin trickle of blood oozed from a nostril. "L-let me—"

In the tower:

Tom. She had to save him. She had to let the monster out and do *something*, and she had to do it now, right now, before it was too late. And if she couldn't get back to herself?

It won't matter. Can't let Tom die. Stop being such a scared bunny and do this; this is for Tom, for Chris, for Wolf and Peter, for everybody. No one she cared about would be safe if she didn't try. She had to trust herself, stop fighting who she was, let the monster go, let it touch Wolf.

It wanted to anyway, and Wolf would be easiest to reach, because the monster's interest was selective.

Steeling herself, she gave the monster substance: built it a gargoyle of a body; went the whole hog, the way the doctors always wanted. Sketch that boogeyman some slit eyes, needle-teeth, scales and wings, claws long as scimitars, a forked tail. Then she imagined the monster reaching out with one scaly arm; felt it unspool from her mind to *tap-tap* with a single talon. Wolf reacted and turned a look, actually *knew* she was there—and for a second, she saw Tom with much more clarity through eyes that were not hers. No *exchange* of thoughts, no insights, but she was *in* Wolf's head for a split second.

She kept the message very simple, stupid: *Look.* And Wolf did.

Davey was harder, different, worse—like jumping from Blackrocks, only at night into black goo. His was a dark language that she only caught when it was very strong in the sweep of the *go-go, push-push.* She went fast, too. A quick dart, in and out, no message. Finn would be there, holding the boy back; otherwise, Davey and all the Changed would have been tearing these people apart. She didn't want Finn to feel her, not yet.

Again, that dizzying sidestep, doubling, dropping behind the windows of Davey's eyes—

And there was Tom, again, but through Davey this time. Davey's *focus*, though—so taut and mica-bright it was like riding a laser—was Finn: Finn's smell, his eyes, even the voice.

The old man—his signal?—*was* there, too, in the background: a thin red river coursing through an intricate landscape. Not the roaring fury of the *push-push go-go*, though, because there was no killing to be done at the moment.

She let the monster drift on the current, very briefly; flow from Davey's perspective to the others, all the altered Changed: Tom and Finn and the square seen from different perspectives and varying points on the same river, like a glimpse of the world through the myriad facets of the eye of a giant fly.

Because Davey and the altered Changed were Finn's network, his cell towers, and the unaltered Changed were networked to one another. She knew *that* because none of the Changed, not even Davey, reacted when Finn hurt Peter. Finn didn't need to use Davey or the altered Changed to get to Peter in that way. But when Finn wanted to reach those Changed he hadn't altered, he *had* to go through Davey. Finn was limited the same way *she* was: the Changed were all on a different circuit, speaking to one another on a frequency that neither Finn nor she could directly access without a kind of gateway.

Simple commands piggybacking on a more generalized signal. That had to be how Finn was doing it. For Finn, Davey was the way into the conversation. When Finn urged on the Changed, all Peter got was the bleed, the leakage, same as she. The further away Finn was, the less she and Peter were affected by the *push-push go go.*

One signal, repeated and boosted through one conduit and then into many, just as Jasper said.

Now, as Finn amped it up; as he *showed* himself in a surge of the red storm; as she felt the hammer and the thrum and the sweeping *power* of the *push-push go-go*, Alex let herself go. Let everything fall, all those barriers and walls, no holding back, because this *was* the leap her father tried to prepare her for all those years ago at Blackrocks, whether he had known it or not: *Jump to me, sweetheart. Take a chance and jump.* This was the end and it was for keeps, it was forever, and *do it, Alex, do it, do it for love, do it for Tom,* save *him,* because it was the very last and only play left.

She could feel it, that same ballooning in her mind, the sidestep and shimmy, the shift.

Gathering herself, marshaling as much of the monster's frenzied energy as she could, she dropped all the barriers, each and every mental firewall. Alex leapt; felt herself and the monster falling and then crashing into the roaring red tide of the *go-go-go-go*, swamping Davey, swamping the Changed, as the monster—all yellow eyes and needle-teeth and scaled arms—exploded from its deep dark well and unfurled in a sudden bloody flower to seep into Davey, into the altered Changed, and all the others, even into Peter: *gogogogoGOGOGO*—

"N-no, Finn," Alex said, working to get the words out, and through it, Tom heard the deep venom in her voice, almost a growl. "L-let *me* . . . sh-show *you!*"

Her back arched; her eyes gleamed; her features twisted into a naked kind of raw fury he knew from battle, when the enemy was swarming over the rocks and you had no ammo and all that was left, everything that separated life and death, was the razor-thin margin of what the body knew and what it would do to cling to every last moment. Alex seemed to *grow* in front of his eyes into something new, breaking from a cocoon and revealing something not quite human living behind the eyes of a girl whose face was etched with a diamond on his memory and yet never truly known or seen until now. Until the moment she let herself break, let the mask slip, dared to make herself known, dared it all.

For a split second, time gathered itself, swelled like a trembling teardrop ready to fall—and then the time splintered and broke apart.

And Alex *wailed*. The sound was a keening, as clear and piercing as the note of her father's whistle that called to him from the endless night of a dark and desperate place where the monsters lived. But this was also a roar, a call to battle: a swooping crescendo that went on and on and on, one that raised the hair on his head and sent Tom's heart crowding into his mouth.

"Alex!" He had to do something; he had to break this, get her out, get them both *out*! The guards had fallen back; everyone seemed frozen. Without realizing, *he'd* actually recoiled a step, but Tom now started forward, no clear idea of what he meant to do, only knowing that he *must* take her away from here—

But then, to his left and just beyond Finn, Davey's head whipped, those mad vermillion eyes going wide as he shrieked, his cry twining around Alex's, becoming one. To his right, Peter was howling a ululating note, and Simon and Penny were screeching, and then all the Changed, altered and not, wailed. It was a cry that rose to an insane bellow and in voices that were many and voices that were one, resolving to a single note, and that voice was Alex, it was Alex, and it said—

Minutes out of Rule, still in forest but running up the hospice road, Chris abruptly reined in Night. Ahead, a shuddering *roar* billowed from the trees. It was like something from television, on Saturdays in fall when his father mainlined beer and cursed the Wolverines: that peculiar kind of whooping bellow a college crowd made in a packed football stadium. Yet *this* cry was also unearthly, a shriek that was one voice made of many, and Chris couldn't tell if he was listening to pain or ecstasy—or a little bit of both.

"My God," he said as the horse pranced and snorted, "do you *hear* that?"

"Yeah. And screams, too, not just that . . . that *sound*." Greg's eyes were bright with urgency and early morning light. "Are we too late? Do you think the bombs . . ."

"No. If we can hear that, we'd have heard the explosion." *Or explosions.* The idea was that there would be no one left *to* scream, or at least not for very long. "I think . . . God, I think those are the *Changed*."

"Chris." Greg was staring. "The Changed don't speak."

They do now. Something's given them a voice. The sound was so eerie he was shivering. "I think they're *saying* something. You hear it? Actual words?"

"Yeah. I do," Greg said. "It sounds like—"

* * *

"GO GO GO!" Eyes blazing, crackling with sudden energy, Alex wailed: *"KILL FINN KILL FINN KILL HIS MEN KILL FINN KILL—"*

"What's happening?" Mellie shrieked. Turning a wild circle, she clapped her hands to her ears as the Changed bellowed. "Elias, Elias, what are they *doing*, what's—"

"No!" Finn shouted, but his was a voice in the wilderness, a tiny speck, like listening to a scream lost to the thunder of a whirlpool.

And then, for Tom, everything snapped, the world cracking wide in a furious maelstrom of sound and movement just as it had the day the world died, and the night they blew the mine and the ground had shuddered under his feet. Only now, instead of a black tornado of birds and a rampaging of deer and bewildered animals and his brain trying to tear itself apart and the mouth of the earth yawning wide to swallow him for good—this time, the end belonged to the Changed.

As one, all the Changed began to move, storming and rampaging through the square. The Rule people were screaming, slipping, tangling with one another in their rush to escape, but there was nowhere to go. They were hemmed in by the Changed and Finn's men and a chaos of horses wheeling and rearing, their hooves clashing down on ice and earth to break bodies, crush heads. The Changed wheeled on Finn's men, most of whom were still trying to raise their weapons two seconds too late. The Changed charged, the weird, altered Changed leaping from braying horses, the others like puppets suddenly cut free of their strings to fall on Finn's men, swirling and seething and boiling in a mad, chaotic frenzy. The square erupted as Finn's men fired wild, bullets buzzing in high hornet-like whines. It was like watching a scene from a movie where an army overruns a village; where, soon, there will be no one left.

On the landing, Alex *keened*: hands by her head, fingers spread wide, eyes bulging, blood on her mouth from the red river leaking from her nose, as if the something that had burst *from* her was blowing her apart. To Tom's left, Mellie screamed again as a girl raced up the steps to throw herself on the woman in a fast, flat dive. Crashing back against a balustrade, Mellie rebounded from the stone, rolled, and tried scuttling away. Swarming over Mellie's back, the girl latched onto the old woman's neck with her teeth. Howling, Mellie reared like a horse trying to throw its rider, hands wildly scrabbling for purchase.

To Tom's right, Peter suddenly launched himself, a fury of golden hair and mad eyes, with Simon—that boy who might have been Chris in a different life—only a step behind: *"Kill him kill him kill him—"*

But Davey, Finn's pet, his very special boy, was closer and already turning, lips skinning from his teeth, manic red eyes wild with rage.

"No, Davey!" Finn shrieked, one arm upraised, a hand going for his Colt as Davey uncoiled like a caged panther finally breaking from its prison. *"NO NO N—"*

Finn, as fast as he was, never had a chance. Davey barreled into the old man, bearing them both, thrashing, to the stone. Finn's pistol spun away. Pistoning his legs in the frantic way of a man desperate to keep a rabid dog from ripping out of his throat, Finn hammered Davey's chin with his right boot. A spume of blood splashed Davey's white uniform; Davey's eyes rolled in their sockets, and the boy began to slide. Finn wound up for another kick that never connected as Peter and Simon, still roaring, converged. Peter was screaming: *"He's mine, he's mine!"* Grabbing the old man by the throat, he hammered Finn's head into the brownstone landing, a hard percussive blow. Blood spurted from Finn's burst scalp, but the old man was still fighting, screeching now like his sister. Planting a boot in Peter's chest, he pounded Peter back. Tom saw a flash of metal as Finn whipped the parang from its sheath, heard the whicker of a vicious backhanded slice that sizzled like a snake. Peter shrieked and there was a wash of bright red blood, and then Peter was clutching his middle, blundering back as the Changed boiled through the square, heading right for them, coming for Finn.

All this happened in less than ten seconds, and it finally got him moving. *Five minutes, less than five minutes, got to get to a horse, get us the hell out of here!* And break Alex, break her free of this! As Tom turned for her, he caught a blur from the corner of his eye. Maddened to a killing fury, Penny was spinning for her guard. Breaking from his paralysis, the guard swung his weapon, a Mossberg 500 shotgun. As that big black bore started coming around in a wide sweeping arc, Tom knew that not only would this man die trying—he would miss.

"Alex!" Pivoting, Tom lunged first one awkward step on his hurt leg, then two. Incredibly, he saw *her* whirl in a fan of bloodred hair. For a moment, he thought she was running for him. But she wasn't. She charged Finn, and the change he saw in her face—that same killing fury he read in Peter and Davey and Simon and all the Changed—stilled his heart. Tom understood, at once, that if he did not break this now, before she reached Finn, she was lost and he might as well let the Mossberg's slug find its mark. Hell, he would stand and hold her fast and make sure it killed them both.

He threw himself in a desperate dive, smashing into her a nanosecond before the shotgun *boomed*. The slug *brrred* a hot trail over his head. There was a splash of imploding glass as a window exploded somewhere beyond. He wrapped her up, getting up one arm to protect her head and neck, throwing the other around her waist. They fell in a heap. Tom tried rolling onto his back at the last second so he could take the brunt of it, but he was awkward, in pain, off-balance, and only managed half a turn. They smacked stone that was going wet and red now with all this blood from the Changed and men alike. When they hit, Alex's shriek cut out. Tom felt his breath blast from his lungs, but he hung on and then he was hugging her close as she thrashed and kicked and snarled to get away. He felt the bite of glass and stone on his back and the wild beat of her heart against his, and he was screaming, too, *screaming* into her raving, bloody face: "Alex, Alex, it's me, it's me, it's *Tom!*"

For an instant—and just an instant—that feral glint in her green eyes sharpened on *him*. He really did think that if she went for his throat, he would let it happen. In another five minutes and change, Alex wouldn't be there anyway. For him, letting her go, again, was not an option. If he *had* to die, better this way, with and by her. But then her head rocked; he had the sense of something snapping either away or back into place, or maybe both. Her eyes, still so green and bright, firmed to a different reality. Firmed to *him*.

"Tom." There was wonder there, a searching, and a whisper that he heard as a shout because he really did have her now, no-holds-barred; this moment was the beginning of forever. "Tom?"

He ached to skim her hair from her face and drink her in. Instead, the world slammed back in with a vengeance, time restarting itself, and he became aware of shots and screams and the riot of Changed and men, of the violence seething all around.

"Alex, we have to get out of here, *right now*. This place is going to blow in five minutes, maybe less." Rolling, he helped her set her feet, grabbed her arm. In the square, there were horses, and all they needed was one. "Come on, come on!"

"Wait!" Tossing a wild look around, she let out a gasping cry: "No, no, Peter, *Peter*!"

When the screams and the guns started, it never occurred to Chris, for a second, to turn back. If anything, he urged Night on even faster. This was a collision he would not avoid, a fight from which he wouldn't back down. If there ever was a *right* time to pick up the hammer, that time was now.

They were coming in fast from the northeast corner, a hundred yards from the far end of the church. He could see the chaos now, the tide of Changed sweeping over Finn's men. Off-leash, the Changed were tearing people apart in chunks, plunging their hands into bloody craters to reel out double handfuls of guts. The square was awash in bodies and pieces of bodies and gore—and old people, still standing, as the past embraced its blighted future. He saw a woman, her gray hair a storm cloud, dart for a brute of a boy: "Lee, Lee, *Lee!*" Lee's huge arms whipped the old woman—*Travers,* Chris thought, *her name's Travers; she likes to garden*—from her feet. The boy spun his grandmother around in what might almost be joy. When Lee sunk his teeth into that woman's throat, the look on her face was a species of an awful, final ecstasy.

"Look!" Greg was pointing toward the village hall. "On the landing!"

Chris looked—and felt his heart fail. The steps were heaving with Changed scrambling and fighting and tearing at bodies. From its bulk, one of the dead was Ernst. And his own grandfather? He didn't see Yeager. But what he did spot on the landing, surging like some behemoth breaking the surface of the sea, was Tom.

Tom was saturated with blood, so much that he looked as if he'd plunged into a deep pool of red paint. He was staggering, too; there was a body draped over his neck and shoulders in a fireman's carry. Tom had a pistol in his free hand, and he was banging out shots, trying to clear a path. Black shotgun in hand, Alex was by his side; Chris recognized her at once and there was . . . my God, was that a *dog*? Where had it come from? Huge, its white coat flecked with gore, the animal was snarling and spinning at any Changed that tried getting close. Tom's rifle scabbard dangled from Alex's right shoulder. Grabbing up an enormous green canvas pack, she slung it over her left shoulder and then she was shouting something to Tom, wheeling toward the Changed boy swooping in, coming for Tom's blind spot. The shotgun bucked in her hand with an enormous *boom.* The Changed toppled back in a loose-limbed splay. Alex turned a brief look to her right, and Chris saw her lips move, understood what she was screaming: *Come on!* But he couldn't see to whom she was speaking and, suddenly, didn't care, because it caught up to him then that the body over Tom's shoulders wore white going crimson. Where that fall of hair wasn't gold, it was a deep rust-red.

Peter. "No! Alex! *Tom!*" Spurring Night, Chris plunged into the crowd, beating a path. He snatched the reins of a stamping, riderless roan, thinking, furiously, *Get him on a horse, get Peter to Kincaid, get out get out get out!* Trying to cover the distance between them was like battling a stormy sea in a rowboat with a soupspoon. The roan was shying and squealing, and he could feel Night tensing, struggling to find a safe place to set his hooves. Hands tore at his legs. The square was a sea of teeth and snarling faces. This was the nightmare of the plateau again, only this time he was trying to control two horses. Greg had pulled beside him, and Chris heard the crack of shots as they battled their way the last fifty feet.

"Chris, no! Stay on your horse!" Tom's face was tense, pinched with pain, wet with sweat and gore. There was an enormous bloody slash across his chest, and he was breathing hard. Alex's back was pressed to his, the Mossberg in her hands, that big dog still whirling and snapping. "Greg, help me! Chris," he said, as Greg hurried around, "pass down the Uzi!"

"Here!" Chris stripped the weapon from his shoulders, turned it butt-first. "How bad is he, how bad?"

"Bad. Alex!" Tom shouted over his shoulder. "Take the Uzi!"

Instantly, she broke her elbows so the Mossberg aimed at the sky, and wheeled, one hand stretching for the new weapon. As soon as her fingers wrapped around the butt of the Uzi and he felt her connect, Chris let go. But she *did* look up. Their eyes met, and he said, *"Alex . . ."*

"I know, Chris. Me, too. Help Peter." Limbering the Mossberg, she turned back to cover and buy them time.

"Chris!" Tom called. "You'll have to hang on to him until we can get clear!"

"How much time left?" he cried, steadying Night with his knees.

"Not enough! All right, let's go, let's go!" Tom shifted his weight, came down on a knee, and then Peter was swooning into Greg's arms as Tom hefted Peter's legs.

"*Hurry!*" Alex shouted. She was backing up, the Uzi in both hands, trying to cover all sides at once. One of Finn's men—old, but with only a few streamers of white hair—swam at her in a panic, arms cranking in a herky-jerky crawl. Before she could get off a shot, the wolfdog surged. Screaming, the old man reeled as blood spurted from a rip above his elbow.

"Down, Buck!" As the wolfdog jumped back, Alex darted in with the Uzi, slamming the butt into the man's jaw, one quick and vicious jab. There was a jet of crimson as the old man's skin split, and he went down. In the next second, the Changed had him, and he disappeared, shrieking, one grasping bloody hand reaching straight up as if trying to claw his way from a grave.

"Lift him, Greg, easy, easy!" Tom said. Peter's face was white as salt, the blood like bright spray paint. As Greg and Tom wrestled Peter onto his saddle, Chris saw the cramp of pain in Peter's face and heard his moan.

"God, oh God, Peter, hang on, hang on!" Chris said as Peter fell into him, his back spooning against Chris's chest. "I've got you, it'll be okay."

"C-c-cold." Peter was gasping. There was so much blood, Chris could taste the iron in his mouth. Peter's head lolled. "S-so c-c-cold . . . C-Chris, s-sorry, s-so sorry, I t-t-tried . . ."

"Shh, you did fine," Chris said, tremulously, sobs welling in his throat. "You're going to be okay. I've got you, Peter." Peter was shuddering, struggling for breath. *I'm going to save you; I'm going to save us both.* Wrapping his arms around Peter, Chris took his friend's weight and held him tight. "I won't let you fall, Peter; I've got you, I've got you, you won't fall."

"All right, Greg, on your horse, let's go!" Grabbing the roan's reins from Chris, Tom turned to shout, "Alex, you ride with me—" He stopped, sudden panic blooming on his face. "Alex, where's Alex?"

"What?" Confused, Chris threw a look down to where she'd been, then up, toward the hall. He spotted her, that red scream of hair, as she and the dog pushed past Changed and fighting men, and exploded for the steps—and a body. "There!" Chris shouted.

"Alex, *no!*" Aghast, Tom was already surging, whipping the pistol like a club, trying to beat a path. "Alex, there's no time—less than ninety seconds! What are you doing, what are you *doing?*"

But she kept going, didn't falter, and in that last second—before the shot—Chris understood why.

Laid out like a sacrifice, his grandfather was crumpled on the steps. The only reason Chris recognized him at all was because Yeager was bald. His face was ripped, but the head was still attached. The rest was a loose-limbed heap of gore and torn flesh.

Crouched alongside Yeager's body was a boy, bloodied and bruised. A girl, very pregnant, hovered nearby, uncertain, clearly terrified. As Alex banged through, only the boy looked up.

My God. The jolt of surprise was like a crack of lightning splintering his brain. There was an instant where the engine of time hitched, jumped its tracks, and then simply ceased.

"Chris?" Greg said, the confusion clear. "Who—"

"Wolf, *please!*" Above all that clamor, he still heard her shout. "You have to leave, you have to go, Wolf! You have to run, you have to—"

And then they all saw, at the same terrible moment, what Alex did not: a monster, suddenly risen; a ruin of flesh and bone, virtually naked, clothed only in tatters and red rivers of blood streaming from rips and slashes and bites. A long flap of scalp hung in a limp flag of maroon flesh and gray hair. Pink skull showed from forehead to crown as if this monster was in the process of unzipping and shrugging from its skin to be born.

"YOU!"—and that was the only clue Chris had that this thing once had been a woman. Her arm, dripping blood and gleaming with bone, swung up, fist jabbing toward Alex, the chrome of a huge Magnum revolver winking in the day's new light. *"YOU!"*

"MELLIE, *NO!"* Tom shrieked, his pistol drawing down, at the same instant that Chris screamed, "Alex, *Alex*, look out, *look out, look—"*

It was, she thought, the strangest feeling, like waking from the dark chaos of a long fever-dream with her mind burning bright and clear: coming back to herself not within her parents' embrace but the shelter of Tom's arms.

Now, here they were, fighting for every remaining second, in the middle of the end of the world, and no time left, in this growing garden of the dead. Yet there was nowhere on earth she *should* be other than with Tom and Chris and her people, waiting to welcome her back, take her away.

Although the monster still searched. She felt it reach because she *did* want Wolf gone and safe. So when she spotted Wolf with Yeager, all she could think was that he *had* to leave and take this one last leap away from Rule to whatever future waited. Maybe it was wrong to feel that way about a boy that was half monster, but so the hell what.

"Wolf!" Frantic, she grabbed his arm. She kept an eye on Penny, but the girl only seemed petrified, which was fine because they had problems enough. "You need to go, you need to get out!"

Wolf was weeping. Big tears burned in ruby trails through blood. For a second, she knew what he felt. For this, she needed no monster. This was a boy who'd just lost everything, not only Yeager but Peter, too. For him, there was no home left, no place to go. It was like looking down at herself at her parents' funeral. Or on the day of her diagnosis: huddling in a chair in a too-cold office and seeing for the first time what a monster, living in the dark and eating you alive, really looked like.

"Wolf, *please*." She could feel her lips trembling, the tears burning her eyes. "It'll get better, I promise it will, but you have to try, you have to go, Wolf, you have to run, you have to—"

There was no transition at all. Despite how much had happened, less than three minutes had passed since the moment she let her monster go. So there was a lot of gunfire and people were still shrieking. The crack of one gun was nothing new, although . . . was that *Tom*, scream—

Something clubbed her, very hard, in the back. She saw Wolf flinch. Fire licked her chest. For that dead space between heartbeats, she and Wolf only stared at each other. She still heard gunfire, but it was so different. No cracks or heavy *bangs*. Only a muted, distant crackle like tired cellophane.

Then her legs folded. There was the dark, waiting below, but only that. It was Blackrocks again.

Except this time, it was the water—cold and deep—that jumped for her.

Alex probably never heard. There was so much noise. The Magnum's boom was lost in the twin roar of Tom's pistol and Greg's rifle. What was left of Mellie tumbled back, and then Tom and Greg were stumbling forward as Chris forced Night to follow.

Awkwardly cradling Alex in his arms, the boy—Simon, his brother—was staggering to a stand as that huge dog snarled but dared not strike. Alex was tall, a handful for anyone, and limp now: dead weight, eyes closed, the long white swan of her neck dropping back. From Night's saddle, Chris could see where the shot plowed into her back because of the red starburst halfway down her right chest where the bullet cored through. When her chest struggled up, Chris heard a horrible, sudden cawing sound, like the croak of a dying crow.

Penny was already trying to back away. When Simon saw them coming, he took a half step back as if to turn and try to run. But then his eyes ticked up to Chris, and Simon's face—*my face*, Chris thought—bleached white.

"Please," Tom said, his voice breaking. He held out his arms. "Wolf . . . Simon, please give her to me. Let us help her."

"Tom. *Chris*, what the hell . . ." Greg had dismounted and already come up with Chris's Uzi, which he trained on Simon. "Guys," Greg said, shakily, "we have to go, we have to *go*."

"I know." For that second, Chris saw, in Simon's anguish and the tears streaming over his cheeks, not a Changed but a boy struggling with what he wished for versus what he could have. "Simon . . . please," he said, tightening his arms around Peter, who was now unconscious. Although his friend was very heavy, his was a weight Chris could bear. "She belongs with us."

At that, Simon took a clumsy, hesitant step. Tom met him halfway, scooping Alex into his arms and then turning for his roan, limping fast as the dog broke from Simon and bounded after. "Give him the gun," Tom tossed over his shoulder to Greg. "Give it to him, get on your horse, and let's go, now, *now*."

"*What?*" Greg's head jerked to Chris. "Chris, I know he's got to be your brother, but this is like Lena. He's still—"

"Do it." Chris looked down at Simon as Greg held out the Uzi the way you'd offer a python a snack. As soon as Simon got a hand on the barrel, Greg dropped the weapon and sprinted back to his horse. "Run, Simon," Chris said to his brother. "Do you understand? Go, get out, take Penny, and *run*—"

"Come on!" Tom bellowed. He held Alex to his saddle as Chris did Peter: against his chest, in his arms. She was still as death, and Chris couldn't tell if she was breathing anymore. Wheeling his roan, Tom kicked the animal to a gallop. "Forty seconds, go, *go!*"

"Run, Simon!" Chris shouted, and then he was pulling the blood bay around, spurring Night to a dead run, giving the horse his head. "Go, Night, go, Night, go!"

Forty seconds. They blasted past a knot of feeding Changed, the newly dead, and those who would join them soon enough. Rushing from the square, counting in his head: *thirty-nine-one-thousand, thirty-eight-one-thousand, thirty-seven—*

He made it to thirty.

The end came when he was five blocks away. It was how he'd always thought the end of the world should have been: not the silence of the EMPs and the scream of birds but a huge blistering roar, like the detonation of a neutron bomb; a *clap* and then a blaring, pillowing, swelling *BAH-BAH-BAH-ROOOM.* Captured by buildings and reflected off stone, the sound was enormous. Chris felt the air blow past in an enormous, gushing *whoosh.* The windows of the houses on this block suddenly shattered as the pressure wave barreled past and tried scooping him from his saddle. The ground shuddered so violently he felt the shiver in his spine, saw it in the cascading showers of residual snow shaken loose from roofs.

Gasping, he turned a look back. Intensely bright, insanely brilliant gouts of bloody light burst from the hall's ruptured windows, like the fiery breaths exhaled from the many mouths of monsters rising from the deep. He could feel the gush of heat, and more surging after. The entire village hall didn't just fall away; it blew apart in a rocketing hail of stone and steel and surging fireballs that rolled in orange-red waves to crash over the Changed and braying horses and every living soul still in that square. That light was so bright it cut him a long, fleeing shadow. His eyes shouted with pain as if he'd tried staring into the heart of the sun. If there were shrieks and screams, he couldn't hear them.

But closer, in his arms, he felt Peter stir, and heard him moan.

Things were now falling, in a shower, from the sky: a rain of stone and flaming wood. Limbs blown from trees stabbed down in jagged, flaming spears. And there were bodies, in pieces: legs and arms, the scorched blackened balls of skulls. The haunches of horses and stumps of bone and more flesh too blasted even to guess at. A block and a half away, a horse's head, mane ablaze, blistered a burning arc to slam the roof of a house before tumbling off.

"Chris!" It was Tom. Still dazed, he turned and saw Tom and Greg and that enormous wolfdog waiting at the mouth of the road that would take them to the hospice and away from Rule.

When he reached them, Chris said, stupidly, "It was so . . so *big*."

"I know," Tom said. In his arms, Alex cawed a breath. Gathering her, Tom swung his horse and pointed them north.

"Let it go, Chris," Tom said. "Don't look back."

THE LONG WALK

IT FELT LIKE EARLY SUMMER, ALTHOUGH HE COULDN'T BE EXACTLY sure. Chris sat cross-legged on a flat table of greenstone-speckled basalt in a drench of sun. The day was cloudless, the sky a hazy white where it edged the indigo of the lake but a deeper, stonewashed denim directly overhead. Smelling of cool iron and tangy spruce, a northerly breeze feathered his hair. Drifting up from the valley some thousand feet below came the solitary grunt of a wood frog. Directly north, off the far coast, he counted at least five thin and rocky tree-studded slivers and a larger green splash spread over the water like an outstretched hand.

Teasing out the blade of a pocketknife, he sliced a wedge of cheese, tore off a hunk of flaky baguette, and laid the cheese on top. Holding the food under his nose, he inhaled a buttery aroma of warm cheddar and fresh-baked bread, then took a bite. He moaned.

From just off his right shoulder came a low laugh. "Good, isn't it?" Peter said.

"Oh my God," he mumbled around bread and cheese. "I've got to learn how to make this."

Peter's laugh was light as a breath of air. "Well, first you got to have a couple cows. And, oh, some flour. Yeast. Sugar. Rennin and—"

"A guy can dream." He tore off more bread. "Don't be such a dweeb."

"*Moi?* Never." A gurgle, then Peter's swallow and contented sigh. "Want some?"

"Gee." He pretended to think. "I don't know . . . I'm not legal."

"As a duly appointed officer of the law and your guide, I insist. Promise not to fall off the ridge and no one will know," Peter said. "Besides, the old rules don't apply anymore, especially here."

"Well, when you put it that way." Chris took the bottle that Peter passed over his shoulder. Cool condensation beaded the glass. When he put the lip to his mouth, what flowed over his tongue was crisp and cold and tasted a little like . . . grapefruit? Closing his eyes, Chris drank, concentrating on the wine's flavor.

Thinking: *I have to remember this, all of it, every second. This may never come again.*

"So." He could feel the warmth already flooding into his head and thought he really might have to be careful on the way down. If that was an issue here. If Peter ever *came* down. "Tell me what I'm looking at."

"Thunder Bay to your left," Peter said, pointing northwest to a distant, hazy ribbon of purple mountains. "From where we are on the Greenstone Ridge, Amygdaloid Island is the furthest barrier island, that really long, thin one due north. That big splotch to the right"— from the corner of Chris's right eye, a hand pointed the way—"is the western edge of Five Finger Bay. I've portaged all through there. Talk about a killer. All I carried was a kayak and a pack. Think about a *canoe.* My shoulders ached for days."

"Sounds terrible."

"Hence, the need for medicinal wine. But it really is . . . heaven."

"No," Chris said, a little giddy with the wine. "It's Michigan."

"Smart-ass. I could hike this whole ridge, all forty-plus miles from one end of Isle Royale to the other, take my time, make this walk as long as I wanted—and still not see a single person or hear anything other than birds and frogs. In spring there are more butterflies than you can imagine. A few times, I've even heard the wolves."

"Weren't you lonely?"

"Back then? Not really. Maybe because it wasn't forever. You always went back to your life."

"What about now?" Dangling the bottle between his fingers, Chris gave the wine a swirl, then took another swallow. *Grapefruit and apples and . . . vanilla?* No, that wasn't right.

"Lonely?" Peter let go of a long breath, and then Chris felt his friend's hand giving his right shoulder a squeeze. "A little. You get used to it. This is my space, Chris. I can't go or be anywhere else. But you can." A small silence. "Are you going to?"

"I don't know." He sipped wine. "I'm not sure."

"No?" When he didn't reply, Peter gave his shoulder another squeeze. "Hey. Talk to me. What's going on? This isn't about Alex, is it?"

"Oh . . . no, I'm okay with that. This isn't a dumb love triangle from a book or something. She's had to deal with enough. Bothers me that she pitches her tent away from us, though. She's been doing that ever since we walked into the Waucamaw."

"Maybe because she started this walk, on her own, a long time ago. Besides, she nearly died. You know what that's like."

This was true. Thank Tom and what every soldier knew to save a buddy's life, or his own. Otherwise, Alex never would've survived the ride back to Kincaid. Chris still remembered the *hiss* of escaping air when Tom slid that IV needle high up between two right ribs to help her breathe. How Tom had then tried, so hard, to give Peter a chance, too. For Alex, the only saving grace was that the bullet came in low enough to miss the big arteries and high enough not to take out her liver. That still left that collapsed lung, macerated muscle and tissue, and two smashed ribs. Kincaid had made very good use of that combat pack. Someone—Ellie, Tom, or Chris—stayed by her side the entire journey to Isaac's new location. Once she could get up, Tom spent hours making her walk even when she didn't want to, carrying her outside, and, in general, hovering like a hawk.

Since then, Alex had done . . . okay. Splitting off from Jayden, Greg, Pru, Sarah, and all the children—the Rule kids, and Tom's—a week ago had tipped some mental scale. Passing that ruined ranger's booth, the wreckage of her car still in the lot, it seemed to Chris that Alex had retreated a little more into herself with each passing mile.

"Tom and I are just giving her space to figure it out," Chris said. "Can't make her want to be with us, although it's hard on Ellie. We haven't told her everything, and she doesn't understand."

"Do you?"

"A little. Alex is . . . she's not all here. You can see the distance in her eyes." Sometimes, he wondered if memories were all she saw. Given what lived in her head, there was always another possibility, too upsetting to want to think about for long. "Tom spends every evening with her. She'll talk to him. He understands way better than I ever will." The ping of hurt was small but still stung. Everything he said to Tom in the jail at Rule, he'd meant. Tom and Alex were just . . . *right* for each other. "Tom says it's like Alex has come back from a long war. That makes sense. She was with the Changed for months. She actually *cared* about Simon."

"But Simon does have your face. She never would've let herself care or risked her life for him if she didn't feel the same way about you."

"I know that. We're family, I guess. Tom said that once you found your people, you found yourself. Except . . . I'm still not sure."

"I thought you liked Jayden."

"Oh no, he's great. I'm relieved he came up with this. Forget everything that happened: I'd *never* have fit with Hannah. She's too territorial. I want to live someplace *I* make, try and do it right this time, find a balance. And, you know, avoid Changing or getting eaten."

"Both are going to be problems for a long time, but not forever. The Change is a dead end, Chris. It's not a disease. It was an event. The only children who will Change from here on out will be like Ellie—too young to Change right away—or like you, kids who still might Change down the line."

"Thanks. That's just so reassuring."

"But it's the truth. Then there are the ones like Penny's baby. Maybe it'll pop out just like the Changed, and maybe it won't. Finn talked about this once; said that those babies who weren't Changed might not live, because their parents would eat them."

"Come on. They're not gerbils."

"Most mammals will destroy defective babies. But say they survive. They won't be anything like their parents. They might not be able to communicate with them at all. All they'll have in common is eating people. But that's a behavior, Chris. It's not destiny. The Changed *could* eat other meat, plants; their digestive systems haven't changed. It's only their brains that have been altered. For *them*, it's permanent."

Well . . . maybe. There was Simon, but that might be only a pipe dream. How would you check up on something like that anyway?

"One way or the other," Peter said, "the Changed are doomed. Either you kill them, their children kill them, or they kill their unaffected children to save themselves. Without children, they're done for as a species. So, what I'm saying is, yeah, worry about getting eaten, but don't base your whole future around it." Peter's grip on his shoulder tightened. "Chris. You should go to Copper Island with them. Hannah won't be there. This is your time. Forget the farmland and how hard surviving the first few years will be for a second. Think about the university, the library, the *books*. Tenured professors hang around until they drop. If some survived, they can help you. You need this just as much as the kids, and maybe more, because you and Tom and Alex and Kincaid and Pru, everyone who's older . . . you guys are the teachers now. Not just practical stuff like farming and building a house . . ."

"All of which I don't know how to do." He slid a bit of baguette onto his tongue and let it dissolve. "Or how to bake bread."

"But you can learn. I'm totally serious about this. The Dark Ages were dark for a lot of reasons, but mainly because the Church controlled everything and burnt books. People stopped learning and forgot how to dream. Yes, Chris, you might Change. But you also know how to dream in a very particular way."

"That's from the drug." And how should he understand all that: coming back from the dead twice over, what he was able to do now in his dreams—crossing into this place, finding Peter? Were these visions? Hallucinations? Was this really heaven, or only one island in the Land of the Dead?

"No, this is all you now, Chris," Peter said. "Yes, the drug triggered your ability, but you're in control."

"Of what? Do you know what this is, Peter? Do you understand why I was"—he almost said *chosen*—". . . *how* I'm doing this? What it means?"

"No, but that's what the future's about, Chris: for you to become and discover who you are. What's important is that you found me. You brought yourself here, and no one *but* you can do this. You are truly unique. Now, become more. *Dare* more. Dream differently, and then teach the kids. Give them the gift of knowledge. Help them learn how to try, because from that springs hope. You may not do it, Chris, but one of these children or *their* kids *will* figure out how to turn on the lights again." Peter's hand suddenly slid away. "Oh hell. Sorry, but . . ."

"It's time? Already?" Sudden tears pooled. It didn't seem right that all this—the mountain and that valley, this lake—could be so perfect when he could feel this sad. "What if I can't find you again?"

"You will." Peter's voice was even and very calm, as if their roles had reversed. "You can come back anytime you want. All you have to do, Chris, is remember how to dream."

"But I'm afraid." He closed his eyes. "I'm afraid I'll make a mistake again, a big one, like I did with Lena. And what about Simon?"

"Simon will be what he will be. You will make mistakes. Count on it. You're only human. But you've found your people, Chris. Go back now. Help them, and let them heal you." Peter's hand cupped his neck. "Finish the wine. Wouldn't want it to go to waste."

He tipped the last sweet swallow over his tongue. *Apples*, he decided. *Apples and honey.*

Then Chris turned to face his friend. "Peter, I—" But he lost what he wanted to say, his voice suddenly stoppering in his throat as Chris finally saw Peter as he was now.

Peter was in the sun. All Chris's dazzled eyes made out was a stark silhouette: the form of a head and those broad shoulders and strong chest, and that glistening fall of golden hair. The glow around Peter was so very bright, Chris had to close his eyes.

"Shh. I know. I love you, too. It'll be all right, I promise." Peter placed a cool hand over Chris's eyes. "Wake up now, Chris, and give them back the light."

Peter's touch bled away. When Chris woke, it was to Ellie, staring down.

"Hi. Sorry, but Tom said we better go while we still have daylight." She cradled a cloth sack about the size of a softball in both hands. Ghost was behind her. When the dog saw Chris's eyes open, his right ear perked while the nubbin of his left only twitched.

"Okay." He lay swaddled in a sleeping bag on fragrant hemlock. He didn't want to move, not just yet, afraid he would tear the frail web of that vision. Worried he might never get it back.

"Chris." The girl's eyes studied his face, her brows puckering in a frown. "Are you going to be okay? Did you have a bad dream again?"

"No," Chris said, sitting up and swiping away wet from his cheeks. To the west, the sun was just beginning to melt into the lake. The wind had kicked up and now cut a chill down his spine. Clouds were gathering, too, their underbellies glowing a lush peach with the sunset. From high in the trees came the staccato *rata-toc-toc-toc-toc* of a woodpecker. A scent of wood smoke hung in the air. He looked to the crackling fire, where Alex and Tom perched on low stones. They weren't speaking, but Chris saw Tom take her hand and their fingers lace. It didn't hurt, maybe because he was used to it now and this really *wasn't* one of those books. It was late April, almost May, and spring was coming, and these were his people.

"You sure you're okay?" Ellie asked.

"Yes. I'll be fine." He reached to cup her cheek. "For once, sweetie, it was a really good dream."

Space. That was all Tom said when she asked. *Give her some time, honey.*

Time, space: Ellie just didn't get that. She had this terrible feeling about Alex that she couldn't put into words because they were so tangled up in memories of her dad and how weird he was whenever he came back from Iraq. Sleeping on the floor instead of a bed. Just . . . not all there. Like Alex.

And time was almost up. Cupping her cloth bag in both hands, Ellie walked between Chris and Tom as Ghost, Jet, and Buck followed. Tomorrow, they'd leave Mirror Point to make their way from the Waucamaw to Houghton and then across the bridge onto Copper Island. She worried about that, too. Houghton had been this *major* town. Big towns were trouble, even if they were going to cross the bridge and, maybe, blow it if they had to.

Chris and Tom said they couldn't hide in the woods forever. All the books and equipment and, maybe, professors as old as Isaac and Kincaid were too valuable to just let die. Tom said someone had to be the first to come out of hiding—*leave the wire* was what he called it—and make a stand. So, might as well be them.

Yeah, just so I don't get eaten. She arrowed a quick glance toward Alex, but she was on Tom's right. All Ellie really got was a glimpse of her hair. *Just so Alex comes back all the way.* If she could. No . . . that was wrong: if Alex would *let* herself.

We have to help her stay. Ellie wasn't sure if she knew how. They had walked for such a long time already. Maybe this was as far as Alex wanted to go. She hadn't *said* anything . . . but Ellie just had this feeling.

She even kind of got why. The first night they made camp in the Waucamaw, she'd screwed up her courage and asked Tom about hiking back up to Moss Knob: *It's where me and Alex left Grandpa Jack.* It was a long shot; she wasn't dumb. October happened six months ago and it was the end of April now. Almost spring, which also meant that Ellie wouldn't have to wear a parka, like, *every single second*. Although Alex said spring always came late to the Upper Peninsula—it was why all the trees were still bare and it got cold at night—and they still might get snow. Heck, Alex once saw snow in *June* when she and her folks went to Marquette and Alex's dad dared her to jump off Blackrocks because, sometimes, you just feel like a nut.

Mostly, what Ellie liked? That Alex told a story about her parents. It made for a really good time, even if Alex went off to her own tent and away from them after that. Ellie didn't know why Alex giving them that story was important, but she had a feeling that stories were a kind of remembering. (Like reading to them around the fire at night, another good thing Alex was doing: *A Wrinkle in Time*, one of Peter's books. A pretty terrific story Alex said her mom read to her.) And look, Alex gave her the whistle back, said Ellie should keep it safe. Alex still wore Mickey. So if Alex trusted them with all these memories—books and stories and a whistle—that was good, right? You didn't give memories to just anybody, right?

Anyway, Tom had listened about Moss Knob and then said, "Ellie, if that's what you want, of course, I'll help you. But honey, I honestly don't think he'll be there. It's been a long time."

She wasn't a stupid little kid anymore. Tom didn't have to say the rest. Dumb idea. So they didn't go. But that didn't mean Grandpa Jack's ghost wasn't still hanging around on Moss Knob. That made her sad and a little guilty, too. Like when they walked out of here, his ghost would be lonely. If she could just figure a way to fix that . . .

"Oh, guys," Alex suddenly said, and Ellie heard the wonder in her voice. "Look."

Ellie looked up. Just a few feet away, the trail petered out. What she first spied were the gold underbellies of clouds above and a huge expanse of blue-black water below, spread as far as the eye could see: away into forever. The trees simply ended. In four more steps, Ellie found herself on the narrow crescent of a towering sandstone bluff heavy with moss. To her right, a waterfall cascaded over red and brown and yellow rocks in a silver-white ribbon. She could hear the tick of the dogs' nails over stone, and hoped like crazy they didn't slip, because it was a *long* way down. This being Mirror Point, she wondered if you really could see yourself from way up here. From the clouds in the water, she thought you just might. (The clouds, which had been with them ever since they'd come to the Waucamaw, totally blew. Because Ellie had kept an eye on that moon. Hadn't said anything to anyone. But she kept turning it over: *what if*.)

Yet there was still enough sun to spray the bluffs. The sight made her chest go tight, but in a good way. The light turned what you'd only think were regular old rock-rocks into bands of deep rust-red and gold and, best of all, neon orange, as bright as Iraqi sand. On the water itself, the fall's ripples shimmered like molten lava.

When she saw this, Ellie realized: Alex's parents were right. This was where Alex's mom and dad had fallen in love, and Mirror Point was all so bright and beautiful and there were so many colors, even as clouds threatened, it really was the perfect place to begin—and to end. To sleep forever. This didn't make everything suddenly okay. But the ache in Ellie's chest wasn't quite as sharp. It felt like her insides were the lid on a jar of strawberry jam, capped too tight, and now someone strong enough had finally twisted to release all that pressure with a little *pop*.

Tom must've sensed something. He was really good at that. Without her even asking, he bent and picked her up so she could wrap her legs around his middle and thread her arms around his neck and let him carry her to the edge, just the way her daddy used to when she was only a little kid.

Please, God. Gripping her cloth sack by the neck, Ellie buried her face in Tom's shoulder. *Please make it all right. Please make it better so we can be us again.*

Chris went first. His cloth sack was heavier, and more than enough for each of them. Holding his fist over the water, Chris said, "I'm not sure what's the right thing to say. It's weird that I lived in Rule, but I don't know the Bible much. Maybe because we were always reading the wrong parts, I don't know. But I keep having this dream about . . ." Pausing, Chris cleared his throat. When he started up again, his voice quavered and Ellie saw the first tears rolling down his cheeks. "I keep dreaming about this mountain and a valley, and it's beautiful, the most beautiful place I've ever seen. But I think it's beautiful in my dream only because you're there, Peter. You did a lot . . . a lot that was wrong, *really* wrong, but I think you . . . you did it out of love. That doesn't make it right . . . but I understand, a little better, about . . . about love. Because you did save me. You c-cared what happened to m-me. Nobody . . . nobody ever d-did that before. So I wish I could've s-saved you. Because I n-never got a ch-chance to tell you, I never s-said it . . ." Chris stopped again and used his arm to wipe his eyes. "I love you, Peter," he said, lips trembling and the tears still coming—and his weren't the only ones. "And I forgive you . . . and I hope you let me find you again, because I miss you . . . I m-miss . . ."

And then Chris couldn't talk anymore. He was crying that hard. His fist relaxed and he let part of Peter go in a rain of gray dust and ashes that the breeze snatched and whirled and spun down to golden water. Then they all released Peter to the wind and the lake until he was gone.

For a little while, maybe just a few moments, Chris stood alone, with only an empty sack. It was Alex who went to Chris first, and all of a sudden, he was crying into her shoulder. For a second, it was just the two of them, swaying together, until Alex looked to her and Tom. Alex's face was wet. In the sunset, her hair was red as the rocks. When Alex held out her hand, Ellie's heart flopped in her chest.

This is good. She clung to Tom's neck as he carried her over, limping a bit because his leg was still on the mend. The dogs bounced after, not only because they didn't want to be left out, but whenever Alex went, they followed unless you made them mind. When they were close, Alex pulled Tom and her into the hug, too.

And this—Ellie slipped an arm around Chris's neck, so she held them all—*is better. This is Meg Murry, in the garden.*

They stood in that embrace for a long time. No one pulled back until Chris was ready. So it took a while and that was fine. What was the rush? Even crying with Chris, Ellie never felt so warm, not even with a really good parka. Eventually, though, she did have to take her turn. Her sack wasn't half so large, but that was all right. There was still plenty for everyone.

A week ago, the same night she asked Tom about Grandpa Jack, Ellie had said, "I don't know what to say. It doesn't have to be about God or anything, does it?"

"It can be whatever you want. You don't have to say anything, honey, if you don't want to." Crouching, Tom chaffed her arms with his hands as if trying to help her get warm. Which was when she noticed she was shivering, and what was with *that*? "There are no rules. If there are words, say them. If not, if your heart's too full, that's okay, too."

Now, with her right fist suspended over the water, and Tom's hand in her left, she stood on her own two feet. Alex was to her right, very close, and she felt Chris move behind her, which was the perfect spot.

You can do this. This is for Eli and Roc, too. This is for everybody.

"I didn't want you." Her teeth snuck out to grab her lower lip, which had started to quake, but she couldn't both chew her lip and talk, so she let go. Her eyes were blurry again, and she figured, *crap*, she was going to cry through this whole thing. "You weren't my idea . . . and I . . . I was really m-mean to you for a l-long t-time. I was m-mean to ev-everybody, es-especially Grandpa J-Jack." Her voice thinned and went squeaky high, and she kept having to snuffle. Behind, she heard Ghost whine and then felt his nose bump her butt. "And I'm really s-sorry about that. You turned out to be the b-best friend I ever . . . I ever h-had . . . and he was a good grandpa and you pro-protected me and made me feel better. M-mostly . . ."

She stopped. Her throat was all clogged up and she could barely see. It was like she was underwater. Oh boy, she just knew this was going to happen.

Just say it, Ellie. It was the closet-voice, the one that helped her save Chris; the one that might be made up of every person she had ever loved, and wasn't it good that some of those people were still here? *Say it fast, honey, and let this go.*

"Ellie?" It was Tom, his voice very low, so gentle, and he said the exact right thing. Not *you don't have to go on*, like she was a stupid little kid, but, "Whatever you say and however you say it will be the right thing."

Listen to Tom, the closet-voice said. *Smart guy.*

She sucked in a fast breath. "Mostly, I was mad at my daddy." Ellie said it quick, pushed it right out, and all of a sudden she wasn't crying anymore. For a split second, it felt the same as emerging from the trail to this space of open sky and gold lava-water: like she'd stepped out of her own way to find the right path to what was true. "He went back when I didn't want him to, and then he was dead, and I thought that meant he must not love me very much. But you were his, and *you* loved me. So that must mean he did, too."

She was crying again. "Good-bye, Mina," Ellie said, and let her dog go. "I love you, girl. Good-bye, Grandpa Jack." And then she managed the rest: "I l-love you, Daddy."

She tried to watch Mina go, see exactly where her dog ended up, but couldn't tell. Everything was wavery from the water below and in her eyes, and there were so many colors that it seemed Mina and her daddy and Grandpa Jack could be anywhere.

But that was, maybe, because heaven was, too.

"This is it." Stirring hot water into a enameled camp mug, Tom watched the dark granules dissolve, then sprinkled a white snow of creamer. "Enjoy every last drop."

"Believe me, I will." Accepting a mug of decaf, Alex sipped and sighed. "That tastes so good, I don't even care that it doesn't have bullets. Seriously, there's no more?"

"Last packet until we get to Houghton. Unless we get lucky at some Kwik-Mart that hasn't been picked over. Any Starbucks got hit a long time ago." Cupping his own mug in his left hand, Tom propped himself against a large boulder. Laying an arm across her shoulders—but gently, mindful of her still-tender ribs—he pulled her a little closer. "If they even *had* Starbucks up here."

"They did." She let her head rest against his chest. "But I think only Marquette and . . . Mackinac Island? Yeah, I remember because a ton of the hotels on the island weren't air-conditioned, and it was *so* hot when we went this one time, but there's my dad chugging a venti with sweat pouring down his face."

"My kind of guy. Had his priorities straight." The fire had burnt down to hot orange coals. Directly across, chin on paws, Buck was in a half-doze, eyes slitted against the glow. This was the time of day Tom liked best: sitting and talking for hours, or sometimes the two of them only staring into the guttering flames as she nestled and he stroked her hair. Leaving her out here, with only Buck for company, wasn't a highlight. Every night he hoped she would say, *Hang on a sec. I'll come with you.*

"Chris said Hannah mentioned a coffee place not far from the university where all the college kids hung." Blowing on his mug, he sucked back a steaming mouthful. A finger of heat drew a line down his chest to expand in his stomach, a warmth that matched the pulse of the fire against his face. "We might get lucky. I'd suck a used filter if I thought it would help."

She gave a small laugh. "How far?"

"Once we're out of the Waucamaw? About eighty, ninety miles as the crow flies."

"Long walk."

He couldn't quite decipher her tone. Maybe because, for him, *long walk* meant something very specific and so different. "Probably a good week." He sipped coffee. "Not like we haven't walked before. We've already mapped it out with Jayden. If something changes, we've worked out places along the way and easy landmarks where Jayden could leave messages. Like, in Houghton, the coffee place? And once you're across the bridge, Jayden said there's this old brownstone synagogue that—"

"It might be better," she said, quietly, "if I didn't."

For a second, he couldn't match the words to their meaning, and then he felt the coffee curdle in the pit of his gut. *No, come on, God, not when we're so close.* He set his mug down with the kind of concentration and care he might give a breaching charge. "What are you saying?"

Another pause. She straightened until they were no longer touching and said, into the fire, "I've thought about this, I really have."

Her voice had gone a little dead, a tone he knew well from her story of Daniel's slow slide into the Change and, at the last, his suicide. Tom's blood slushed. "You're staying. *Here.* In the Waucamaw, by yourself." *Take a breath, Tom. Go easy, don't push. Count to ten.* He made it to three. "Alex, what the hell are you thinking?"

Even in firelight, her eyes were too dark. "I'm thinking it's dangerous for you. Wolf's already found me once before. He can find me again."

"If he's still alive."

"I think he might be. I can't tell for sure, but this thing in my head . . . I've got control, but it's . . . lonely, too. You know? I feel it, sometimes, *searching.*"

"I thought you said you were getting better at keeping it under wraps." He heard the sharpness that was nearly an accusation. But he couldn't help it. A spike of panic darted up his spine. *No, she can't do this, she can't; I won't let her.* He said, more deliberately, "Even if it is, you haven't smelled any Changed. Neither have the dogs."

"Yet. Once we leave the Waucamaw, start to head to where the people *were* and maybe still are . . . I probably will."

"So what? The Changed are a fact of life. They're the enemy. Big deal."

"It's different for you. You don't have something living in your head."

"Oh bullshit. What the hell do you think a flashback is?" *TOM . . .* Folding his knees made that left leg yammer. For once, that nip of pain was good, because it crammed the rest back down his throat. Closing his eyes, he bowed his head and huffed out that quick jump of anger.

Out with the bad. "I'm sorry. That wasn't fair. I know it's not the same."

"It's okay. Maybe it is the same, in a way. I think what I'm saying is that, yes, I smell the Changed. Yes, the monster's pretty well-behaved . . . for a monster."

"Don't make a joke out of this." Now he threw her a sharp look. "Don't make a joke of how I feel."

"I'm not." Her eyes shimmered, but her voice was steady. "I'm trying to make you understand. Sometimes, I have dreams, and those are new. What I did with Finn . . . I think that opened up some kind of door in my head."

"You *dream* about the Changed?" He felt his anger giving way to a blast of shock. "You *see* them?"

"Sometimes." Her throat moved in a swallow. "I think it's because I'm seeing *through* someone, like I did in Rule, at the end. I'm not sure who or what it is. But it's when I'm asleep, Tom. I can't control that. I can't do anything about my dreams."

"Alex." He sat up straighter. "Why didn't you say anything? Why didn't you tell me?"

"I'm telling you now. Tom, back in Rule, if you hadn't tackled me on the landing, I'm not sure I wouldn't still be in that"—she made a vague gesture with her cupped hand near her head—"*frenzy.* It was *terrible* and wonderful at the same time. I know that sounds crazy. But I understand what Peter must've felt, that *rush,* how powerful it is, when nothing else matters but killing. So I know I can get lost."

"All the more reason why you should stay with us, stay anchored. Let us help." *Let me.*

"But, Tom, *think.* If I can see through them, what are the chances that, eventually, it might go the other way? What if I draw or lead Changed *to* us? Nobody will be safe."

"Those are a lot of ifs . . . no, be quiet. Let me finish," he said when she opened her mouth. "In the last month, nothing's happened. There have been no Changed. No one has followed us. We stayed with Isaac for weeks, near where Changed had been, and saw none. You're right; I'm not you. But I do know a little about scary dreams and how they take over. I also don't buy that your dreams are the only reason that you don't want to come. Because so what if the monsters come, Alex?" He wanted to touch her, grab her arms, pull her close. In all this time and during these many weeks, he'd never rushed her, hadn't kissed her, done *nothing* but try to help her come back. If she thought he was going to let her go without a fight . . . "Let them come, Alex. Let the monsters try to take you. They'll have to get through me, and that will never happen."

"That's not a promise you can make, Tom."

"I will kill them," he said, very distinctly. "No one is taking you from me. That's all there is to it."

"And if you die because of me?"

"That will be my choice, Alex, but it won't come to that."

"Are you going to choose for Ellie, too? For Chris and Kincaid? For Jayden? For all the other children?"

Closing his eyes, he tipped his head back and spoke to the night sky. "I . . . will *not* . . . leave you here." He lowered his gaze to hers. "I refuse. If you won't come, I'm staying, too. I'm not leaving you, Alex, never again."

"No." The shock rippled across her face. "No, Tom, I won't let you do that."

"I'm not leaving you," he repeated. "You're not the only one who gets to choose. Now, you either walk out of here with us, tomorrow, or we wave good-bye to Ellie and Chris. Period."

Her mouth turned into a thin gash over her chin. "Tom, *why* are you doing this? Why are you making this harder for me?"

"You don't think this is hard on me?"

"Of course, I know it is. But don't you see I'm trying to protect you?"

"And don't you see that I *love* you?" he shouted. *To hell with this.* He gathered her in his arms. If she pulled away, he would let her go. You couldn't hang on to someone bound and determined to get away. But she didn't, although she was crying, wide-eyed and silent, her tears streaming over cheeks that looked pale even in firelight.

"Alex." And then he did what he'd ached to do for weeks: skimmed hair from her face, the better to see and touch and memorize every inch, each feature, from the curve of her brow to the bow of her lips and the angle of that stubborn jaw. "Alex, I don't care that you have cancer. I don't care if all or part of that cancer is a monster. I care about *you*, and I have walked, alone, for a very long time. I did it in Afghanistan, and I did it in the Waucamaw. I might have walked until I couldn't anymore if we hadn't found each other. But we did, and I am so tired of walking alone. Please, Alex, please walk with me. Be brave enough to walk out of here *with* me. Leave this place. Only ghosts live here. Come with us. Come with *me*."

"Tom." She raised a trembling hand to her mouth. "I was dying when I got here."

"Me, too," he said. "Just in a different way."

"But what if I'm really still dying and don't know it? What if it gets stronger, and I get sick again? It's already bad enough to have a monster. What if the cancer's not *all* monster? What if it's also *cancer*? I don't know how much time we'll have."

"Join the rest of the human race," he said, which made her give a watery laugh—and that loosened a terrible knot in his chest. *Yes, God, yes, please do this for me. Just this once, please.* "All I know, the only thing about which I am absolutely certain, is that I love you. Walk with me, Alex. Walk with me today"—he kissed one cheek and then the other, tasting her skin and wet salt—"and tomorrow"—and then he brushed her lips with his and felt them part and her sigh in his mouth.

"Walk with me, Alex," he whispered. "Walk with me for as long as we have."

What happened next was for them, and them alone.

The monster tugged her awake.

For a second, she wondered if it had been a dream: a *nice* dream but still . . . wishful thinking. Then she inhaled musk and sweet smoke and spice and *Tom*—Tom, warm and solid and real—and heard his deep sleep-breathing. She eased her head until she could make him out in the dim light suffusing the tent. A hand on her stomach, he lay on his side, an arrow of light silvering his hair.

Her eyes drifted over his face. There'd been this science fiction show her dad loved, pretty old, not *Star Trek* but something about a space station, and there was a number in the title . . . six? No, five. Anyway, there were these funky aliens with their funky rituals. One was to watch a beloved as he slept, because that was when all the masks fell away and you saw a person for what he was. Sounded pretty silly. And yet . . . Tom, in sleep and maybe for once dreaming well, was as he always had been: steady and sure, brave and stubborn. Someone to walk with. Someone to love, and that was wonder enough. There was no difference, although—

Wait a second.

She resisted the urge to bolt upright. She closed her eyes, opened them. Nothing changed. There was Tom, sleeping, and there was—

You watch. Easing a hand from her sleeping bag, she extended a single finger. *It's a crazy hallucination or something. I'm not really seeing this.*

Heart pounding, she watched as the tip of her finger rolled out of the grainy darkness—and became visible. Jumped out from shadow to cross into that sliver of light seeping through a thin seam of a tent flap to glitter over Tom's hair.

Oh my God. She pulled her hand back, gave it a good hard stare as if expecting a smudge of luminous paint to show itself. Of course, there was none. Still careful not to wake him—no sense being a ninny, especially if she was wrong—she tipped her head all the way back until she could see through that seam. The thing was, though, she *couldn't* see through to the other side.

Because the glow through the seam was *that* bright.

She heard her breath leave in a sudden rush, taking a small *oh* with it. She lay still a moment longer, thinking it over before carefully oozing from the bag, feeling Tom's hand slip from her skin. Thank God, she had the side with the zip. It took her another few seconds to work into her parka. Grimacing at the touch of cold nylon against her feet, she minced her way to the tent flaps, holding her breath against the slight *sss* as she worked the zipper. Then she ducked out of the tent—and stopped dead.

Ahead, not fifty feet away, the forest was awash in shimmering silver blue shafts, bright enough to cut tall, inky shadows. She could make out the tree limbs on beds of needles; the individual stones around her banked fire, the coals dozing under a blanket of ashes; even the gleam of individual grommets on her tent. From his place close to the fire ring, Buck's head raised and cocked a question at her sudden appearance in the middle of the night, especially since she'd kicked him out of the tent.

"Holy shit," she whispered, and watched in a kind of awe as her breath smoked not sickly green-gray . . . but blue. She'd set her boots outside the tent, and now she fumbled them up, her fingers suddenly clumsy, mouth dry. *I should wake up Tom. He'll want to see this. We should get the others.* Yes, but she wanted to be certain first. She jammed her bare feet into her boots. Too late, she realized that in her rush, she'd forgotten to shake them out. To her relief, her toes discovered that no one had dropped in for a visit.

She'd made camp within a sheltering stand of hemlock and sugar maple, but there was a clearing to her left. Now, pushing to her feet, she darted that way with Buck galumphing after. In only a few seconds, she splashed into a pool of light so intense that what she first saw, to her right, was only the long fingerling of her shadow as it ran away. She could see Buck's shadow, too, and the double gleam in his eyes as he stared, wondering what in *hell* had her so worked up. Turning on her heels, she looked left and up through a break in the canopy . . .

And into a night sky where the thick web of clouds had, finally, pulled apart. Only the brightest stars showed. That was because the moon was high and full—and white.

"Oh my God." Her hand flew to her mouth. "You're there, you're really there, you're back, you're the *moon*, you're—"

At that moment, Buck grumbled a low warning. She heard a soft *shush* of a foot over earth.

Then, to her left, the smell rolled from the deep black of the forest.

She hadn't lied. She really did believe that her monster only worked one-way: a drop behind the eyes of someone else, and not vice versa.

The odor might have been there for a while, although not too long. Earlier, she'd been outside with Tom and smelled only the strong, keen, cold metal of Superior, the fresh resin of woods, the fire—and Tom, of course. She'd been very focused on him, his taste, the feel of his mouth and hands, and then the urgency of his body against hers. His scent saturated her skin and hair and every part of her. Tom was so strong, a hum in her blood, and what they made together was so sweet as to eclipse all else.

Now, though, she recalled the dream, brief but vivid, that had awakened her. The image was more like a crane shot from a faded video: a swooping pan that showed woods and a blur that might be a tent and then the lake, not black or sickly green, but steely blue and sparking with moonlight where small waves curled over rocks.

That was when the monster raised its head and took a whiff, and she woke.

"It's all right," she said to the wolfdog, not knowing if this was true. Yet she smelled no spike of danger here: only cool shadows and gray mist, a hint of apple.

And rot. That was there, too. Still.

She mightn't have spotted him if not for the moon. He was that far back in the trees. Just a suggestion of a person there, a stick figure cut out of black construction paper.

At the sight, everything in her that *was* human iced. Not the monster, though, with its scaly arms and needle teeth. Wolf was a buddy, someone with whom to play. For her, it was as though the monster decided to take her worst nightmare and make it real.

This would end in only one of two ways: with Wolf dead or— eeny-meeny-miny-mo—Tom, Chris, Ellie. Take your pick.

"You can't do this, Wolf," she said to that dark silhouette in the trees. "They'll kill you." *Or I will, to protect them.* "I want to walk with Tom. I'm sorry, Wolf. Go back to Penny. She needs you. I wish I could help you be Simon again, but I don't know how. I don't know if you can." *Or if I should try.*

Yet her right hand just happened to be in her parka pocket, and she felt two things, both of which crinkled. One she'd put there a while back. Hadn't forgotten it. She was saving it for a special occasion. Until this second, she thought she would share it with Tom and Chris and Ellie. A kind of celebration as they began their long walk, together, toward something new.

The other was her mother's letter, the one Ellie stole back from Harlan. Having read it enough times to memorize it, she didn't need the moon's strong light. The lines that jumped out of the black of her mind now, though, were ones her dad penned.

A word of advice, sweetheart: when you're at the brink; when it's a choice between what's safe and what might be better, even if what's best is also scary, take a chance, honey. Take a deep breath and—

She hadn't lied to Tom. She had . . . omitted? No, that was wrong, too. She hadn't quite understood, that was all. In retrospect, assuming the monster might jump behind alien eyes when it hadn't been properly introduced went against her experience.

In the last week, her dreams were crowded with images she recognized: the deserted ranger's station, her smashed Toyota, that sign pointing the way to Moss Knob and Luna Lake. All familiar places along this long walk back to her past.

For Wolf, though, they were all new.

So, now . . . Wolf saw what she did? By getting into her dreams? Or quietly slipping behind her eyes while she was awake yet unaware? There was no way to be certain which, but either would answer how he'd managed to track her down. With Buck, Wolf shouldn't have been able to smell her at all. Unless that, too, was Changing.

Something else to think about: If Wolf *could* see through her, even if only when she dreamt, what about . . . emotions? Thoughts? What if, somehow, she now could do what Finn couldn't? Not piggyback on a signal but truly receive one?

Take a chance.

Could she do this? She felt her impatient monster pressing its nose against the glassy backs of her eyes. *Should* she? This wouldn't be a *tap-tap*. This would be as it was on the snow while the lake house burned, but instead of Wolf trying to rediscover who he'd been in her face, it would be she who reached for *him*, like Meg Murry pushing past IT to find her brother.

When you're at the brink; when it's a choice between what's safe and what might be better—

Gathering herself, she closed her eyes and let a tendril, one monstrous and scaly little arm, go. Her mind shimmied with the sensation of a swoon that was a leap . . . and then she was behind Wolf's eyes and could see herself: hair loose and legs bare, in a silver-blue pearl of moon.

And then for a moment—and only that—she also let go of *herself*, trusting in love and her strength, allowing the door to open enough to brush his mind with tentative, ghostly fingers and truly *feel* for the boy beneath the monster. She gasped as her chest filled with a deep and bitter ache that was Wolf's grief and loneliness and longing.

She opened her eyes. Her monster wasn't pleased to come back— she could tell from that spastic little flutter—but it knew what it could do to itself. Anyway, she was busy. One more thing she really needed to try.

"I don't want you to die, Wolf, if you can be Simon again. If you think you might be close." She withdrew the half of that King Size Almond Joy she'd saved for a treat, a celebration of the possible. Stooping, eyes still on the boy wreathed in shadows, she prized out the cardboard insert. The wrapper crinkled in the hush. A perfume of rich chocolate and sweet coconut and spicy almond swelled. Moving carefully, she set the candy atop its wrapper on the ground between them.

Because what the hell: sometimes, you feel like a nut.

Take a chance, honey. Take a deep breath and—

"Jump, Wolf," she said.

And then Alex took a step back and waited with Buck, in fresh moonlight, to see what would happen next.

THE CAST OF CHARACTERS

Alex Adair: living with her aunt in Illinois after her mom, an ER doc, and dad, a cop, died in a helicopter crash three years ago. Suckier still, Alex carries a monster in her head: an inoperable brain tumor that's stolen her sense of smell and many of her memories, especially those of her parents. After two years of failed chemotherapy, radiation, and experimental regimens, Alex has decided to call the shots for a change. As the series opens, Alex has run off on what might well be a one-way backpacking trek through the Waucamaw Wilderness in Michigan's Upper Peninsula. She intends to honor her parents' last wishes and scatter their ashes from Mirror Point on Lake Superior. As it happens, she's also got her dad's service Glock, just in case she opts out of a return. After the Zap, Alex gets her sense of smell back in spades, a super-sense that also allows her to intuit emotions and, on one occasion, catch a glimmer of what goes on inside the mind of a wolf. Which is pretty funky. Much more to the point, like the dogs, she is able to detect the bloated roadkill stink of the Changed. Oh, and all of a sudden, every dog is her new best friend.

Ellie Cranford: sullen, uncooperative, a trifle whiny, a kid Alex has to keep herself from slapping silly. What can you say? The kid's eight. Her dad's KIA in Iraq, her mother split years back, and Ellie's now being cared for by her grandfather, Jack, who might have the patience of a saint, but cut the kid a break. She hates camping, and it's not like she hasn't got good reason to be a little pissy anyway. Initially rescued by Alex and then Tom, Ellie is kidnapped by some very nasty adults who see her as a meal ticket.

Mina: Ellie's dog, a Belgian Malinois, and formerly her dad's

MWD (military working dog). Mina also has the patience of a saint but packs a mean bite. The nasty adults take her, too.

Tom Eden: a young soldier and explosive ordnance specialist on leave from Afghanistan; a competent guy who complements Alex in a lot of ways. After Alex fends off a pack of wild dogs, Tom saves both Ellie and Alex by shooting his buddy, Jim, who's gone through a major lifestyle change. Steady and calm, someone to whom Alex is instantly attracted, Tom also has a few secrets of his own. The biggest is just why he's in the Waucamaw to begin with. After they leave the (relative) safety of the Waucamaw—we're talking wild dogs, booby traps, and kids who've suddenly decided that people make excellent Happy Meals—Tom is shot while trying to prevent the nasty adults from stealing Ellie.

Chris Prentiss: the grandson of Reverend Yeager and Rule's de facto second-in-command, though he grew up in another town. Dark and reserved, a bit of a brooder, Chris has an uncanny ability to find Spared, especially up north around Oren and its nearby Amish community. He falls for Alex in a big way after she comes to Rule. Despite her initial determination to escape, Alex eventually reciprocates his affection.

Peter Ernst: Rule's overall commander, although he takes his marching orders from the Council of Five, representatives from Rule's founding families who run the village. At twenty-four, Peter is the oldest Spared, and he's fiercely protective of Chris. Peter has a thing going with Sarah, one of Alex's housemates.

Sarah, Tori, and Lena: Alex's housemates; all refugees to whom Rule offered sanctuary. Of the three, Sarah's a tad bossy. Good-natured Tori alternately crushes on Greg (another Spared who is part of Chris's squad) and Chris, and still makes a mean apple crisp. Taciturn, irreverent, and originally from that Amish community near Oren, Lena's a girl with 'tude. Having manipulated Peter, Lena once tried to escape—only to be caught in the Zone, a no-man's-land buffer zone through which those who are Banned (i.e., kicked out of Rule for various offenses) must travel in order to leave Rule's sphere of influence.

Reverend Yeager: a descendant of one of Rule's five founding families. Filthy rich from having run a very profitable mining company, Yeager heads the Council of Five. (The other Council members are Ernst, Stiemke, Prigge, and Born.) Before the Zap, Yeager was quietly dementing away in the Alzheimer's wing of Rule's hospice. After the Zap, however, Yeager was Awakened. Like Alex, he possesses a super-sense and can determine emotions and truthfulness through touch.

Jess: a tough cookie with a penchant for spouting Bible verses. Jess seems to have her own agenda when it comes to who should be making the decisions for Rule. She's hot for Chris to stand up to his grandfather. For a variety of reasons—all of them very good—Chris is reluctant. Jess also makes no secret of encouraging Chris and Alex to become, well, a little closer.

Matt Kincaid (Doc): scruffy, pragmatic, sharper than a tack, and Rule's only doctor. He is also an Awakened, though he has no super-sense. He is the only one who knows about Alex's brain tumor as well as her super-sense of smell. Kincaid has suggested that the monster might be dead, dormant, or busy organizing into something entirely different.

Jed and Grace: an elderly couple from Wisconsin who've rescued and nursed Tom back to health. A vet, Jed suffered brain damage that left him blind in one eye and a tad addled. After the Zap, his vision returned as a super-sense. Stricken with Alzheimer's, Grace Awakened, recovering her extensive nursing knowledge as well as developing an uncanny facility with numbers.

Wolf: the nickname Alex has given to the leader of a band of Changed, who also just happens to be Chris's identical twin (and of whose existence Chris is unaware). Although Wolf seems by turns attached and attracted to Alex and protects her from ending up as a Happy Meal for the rest of his crew (Beretta, Acne, Slash, and Spider), Alex can't decide if Wolf is only saving her for dessert.

Leopard: the leader of a rival group of Changed and Spider's main squeeze.

Daniel: recruited along with his little brother, Jack, by Mellie. Daniel leads a doomed raid to rescue Alex. Spider murders Jack, who ends up as that evening's main course.

Weller: one of Peter's men, Weller is really working for Finn (see below). Why he's thrown in with the militia leader seems more to do with revenge against Peter for some past, unknown grievance than a beef with Rule.

Elias Finn: Vietnam vet and now leader of a secretive, long-established militia. Several of his men have infiltrated Rule and captured Peter, but Finn seems more interested in whether the Changed can be tamed and, by subjecting Peter to endless life-or-death bouts, how quickly they can learn. Yet his long-term goals, as well as the reasons for his intense hatred for Rule, are unclear.

Davey: a Changed boy Finn is taming—and training.

Mellie: a grandmotherly sort, who's gathering up and arming kids to march against Rule.

Luke and Cindi: part of Mellie's band. At fourteen, Luke is oldest and very attached to Tom. The daughter of a child psychiatrist and the band's lookout, Cindi major crushes on Tom.

WHO'S WHERE AND DOING WHAT AT THE END OF SHADOWS

Alex: is caught in the collapse of the old Rule mine and falling down an escape shaft that is rapidly flooding.

Tom: is heartbroken and blames himself for Alex's death. When Luke and Cindi tell him that Mellie and Weller (injured in the mission to destroy the mine) plan to march on Rule soon, Tom admits that he's afraid to go because his hatred for Chris, whom Weller said was responsible for turning Alex out of Rule, is so black and monstrous, he wants nothing more than to murder the other boy.

Chris: is unconscious, dying, and pinned beneath an iron-spiked tiger-trap outside Oren.

Peter: is still Finn's prisoner. Having killed numerous Changed in exchange for food and water—and, ironically, taught Changed like Davey the best way to fight—Peter is now faced with a choice: eat human flesh, or starve.

Lena: is fighting the urge to feed on Chris, whom she no longer truly recognizes. Startled by the sudden appearance of a dog, she takes off only to find herself surrounded by a band of Changed that's been shadowing her for days.

Wolf: had disappeared after being shot by Spider. Just before she's herded into the mine, however, Alex thinks she catches his scent with her super-sense.

Jess: is badly injured, comatose, and probably still in Rule under Kincaid's care.

The Body Count: Jed, Grace, Daniel, Jack, Leopard, Beretta, Slash. Spider and Acne were presumably caught in the mine collapse.

ACKNOWLEDGMENTS

To say that this trilogy's been a wild ride is an understatement. I don't think I've ever gone through so many boxes of Kleenex, and I suspect I'll think about these characters and what has become of them for quite awhile.

Offering my thanks to the many people who've made this journey possible seems so little for those who've given so much, but my gratitude for both their belief in me and hard work in helping these books see the light of day is nearly boundless. First and foremost, my editor, Greg Ferguson, deserves a medal for the hours he put into going through these manuscripts with a flea comb. I don't think I've laughed so hard either; Greg's a guy who's not above getting so wrapped up in the story that his comments practically scream off the page: *But I want to know what happens next, and I want to know right NOW!* (Heh-heh: gotcha.)

To my She-To-Whom-No-One-Else-Holds-A-Candle agent, Jennifer Laughran, a woman who continues to not only watch my back but has this uncanny knack of making the right call at exactly the right time . . . you know, when you're right, you're right. And, thanks: I needed that.

For all the wonderful folks, past and present, at Egmont USA with whom I've had the great good fortune to work, special thanks go yet again:

To Elizabeth Law, a woman who knows how to make lemonade from lemons: You. Me. Dinner.

To Ryan Sullivan, crackerjack copy editor and all-around fan: Great catches, man. Your love for this series really came through.

To Katie Halata, Mary Albi, and Alison Weiss for being ever-available, tweeting your fingers off, answering questions (even on weekends!), and taking care of business no matter what the hour: I owe each of you a dry martini, and probably three. (Although, yeah, I admit that when you volunteered to help during your honeymoon, Katie . . . well, gosh, I didn't know whether to be grateful or worried. Priorities, girlfriend.)

To Deb Shapiro: Thank you for organizing my life. It's a dirty job, but someone has to do it.

To all the Random House team members of sales and marketing out there in the trenches: Thank you for getting my work in front of readers and giving these books their best shot.

My deepest thanks also go to my publishers abroad, who took a chance on this trilogy and dedicated so much of their time and energy on its behalf. A very special shout-out to Niamh Mulvey, Roisin Heycock, Alice Hill, and the rest of the production team at Quercus UK: Tea was lovely, but those zombie cocktails were brilliant. I do believe I've recovered enough for a repeat.

To Dean Wesley Smith and Kristine Kathryn Rusch: You were right. I was ready.

To my husband, David: Come on, admit it. You'll miss my shaking you awake at 2 a.m. to discuss a plot point; you know you will. So . . . okay, then. Must be time for another series.

And, lastly, to all the bloggers, fans, Twitterati, and Facebook friends from around the world, who shared their love for the series with me and anyone who would listen: Thank you so much for having the courage to reach out and let me know how this trilogy has touched you. I have loved living and making the journey with you. Here's my world, and welcome to it.